OLI

GW00472371

DINAH MARIA MULOCK CRAIK born 20 April 1826 in ~~~~~
Trent, was the eldest child of Thomas Mulock, an Irish non-conformist preacher of fixed views and unstable temperament. Her mother was a well-to-do tanner's daughter, Dinah Mellard. Raised and educated at Newcastle under Lyme, Dinah Maria briefly helped her mother run a school there, but in 1839 the family moved to London. Her literary career began in earnest after her mother's death in 1845, when her father refused to support his three children further. Between 1846 and 1849 her poems and stories appeared in leading periodicals, among them *Chambers's Edinburgh Journal*, *Dublin University Magazine*, and *Frasers Magazine*. Five major novels between *The Ogilvies* (1849) and the internationally acclaimed *John Halifax, Gentleman* (1856), together with a steady flow of fiction, essays, poetry, and children's literature, established her as a prolific and well-respected writer. With the exception of *John Halifax, Gentleman*, which charted the development of modern England through the rise of its poor, virtuous, and industrious hero, her work found its most enduring and enthusiastic audience in the female common reader rather than among the arbiters of high culture. Deeply humane, didactic and pious, her writings cautiously and conservatively championed women's employment, artistic aspirations, emotional needs, and maternal rights. In 1865 she married George Lillie Craik, her junior by eleven years, and in 1869 adopted a daughter, Dorothy, from a parish work-house. Craik dramatized the contrast between physical weakness and moral strength through the recurrent theme of disability in her fiction, including *Olive* (1850), *John Halifax, Gentleman*, and her best-known children's book, *The Little Lame Prince and his Travelling Cloak* (1875). Her work was widely translated and constantly republished in both cheap paper and bound library editions, and Craik remained a best-selling author until well after her death in 1887.

CORA KAPLAN is Professor of English at Southampton University. The author of *Sea Changes: Essays on Culture and Feminism*, she is working on a book on the rise of racial thinking in Victorian Britain.

ANNE HARTMAN is researching into Victorian literature at Birkbeck College, University of London.

ANGÉLIQUE RICHARDSON is a lecturer in English at Exeter University.

OXFORD WORLD'S CLASSICS

*For almost 100 years Oxford World's Classics have brought
readers closer to the world's great literature. Now with over 700
titles—from the 4,000-year-old myths of Mesopotamia to the
twentieth century's greatest novels—the series makes available
lesser-known as well as celebrated writing.*

*The pocket-sized hardbacks of the early years contained
introductions by Virginia Woolf, T. S. Eliot, Graham Greene,
and other literary figures which enriched the experience of reading.
Today the series is recognized for its fine scholarship and
reliability in texts that span world literature, drama and poetry,
religion, philosophy and politics. Each edition includes perceptive
commentary and essential background information to meet the
changing needs of readers.*

OXFORD WORLD'S CLASSICS

DINAH MULOCK CRAIK

Olive
The Half-Caste

Edited with an Introduction by
CORA KAPLAN

Notes by CORA KAPLAN *with*
ANNE HARTMAN *and*
ANGÉLIQUE RICHARDSON

OXFORD
UNIVERSITY PRESS

OXFORD
UNIVERSITY PRESS

Great Clarendon Street, Oxford OX2 6DP

Oxford University Press is a department of the University of Oxford.
It furthers the University's objective of excellence in research, scholarship,
and education by publishing worldwide in

Oxford New York

Athens Auckland Bangkok Bogotá Buenos Aires Calcutta
Cape Town Chennai Dar es Salaam Delhi Florence Hong Kong Istanbul
Karachi Kuala Lumpur Madrid Melbourne Mexico City Mumbai
Nairobi Paris São Paulo Singapore Taipei Tokyo Toronto Warsaw

with associated companies in Berlin Ibadan

Oxford is a registered trade mark of Oxford University Press
in the UK and in certain other countries

Published in the United States
by Oxford University Press Inc., New York

British Library Cataloguing in Publication Data

Data available

Library of Congress Cataloging in Publication Data
Craik, Dinah Maria Mulock, 1826–1887.
Olive; and, The half-caste / Dinah Craik ; introduced by
Cora Kaplan
1. Physically handicapped women—England—Fiction. 2. Young
women—England—Fiction. 3. Family—England—Fiction. I. Craik,
Dinah Maria Mulock, 1826–1887. Half-caste. II. Title. III. Title:
Half-caste. IV. Series.
PR4516.O45   1996   823'.8—dc20   95–25866
ISBN 0–19–283326–X

1 3 5 7 9 10 8 6 4 2

Typeset by RefineCatch Limited, Bungay, Suffolk
Printed in Great Britain
Cox & Wyman Ltd., Reading, Berkshire

CONTENTS

INTRODUCTION

'THE modern novel is one of the most important moral agents of the community. The essayist may write for his hundreds; the preacher preach to his thousands; but the novelist counts his audience by the millions. His power is threefold—over heart, reason, and fancy.'[1]

This enthusiastic testament to the positive power of the popular novel, voiced by Dinah Maria Mulock[2] (later Dinah Mulock Craik), introduced an 1861 essay on George Eliot in *Macmillan's Magazine*. Its sweeping claims and its moral optimism were both inspired by Craik's own early success in the literary marketplace, but they were, as well, ethically grounded in her pious but progressive Christianity and her belief in the force of female influence. For while the generic masculine in Craik's tally of audiences and authorial sway—'his hundreds . . . his thousands . . . his power'—suggested at one level a continuity among writers and speakers in the context of an ever-expanding public for moral rhetoric, there were more unsettling implications in her commentary. Using the size of audiences alone as her gauge of moral influence we can see Craik setting the radically expanded authority of novelists of both sexes against the more modest and limited reach of the pulpit. Her comparison implied that the dominance of 'modern' popular narrative marked a recent and decisive shift in the relative power of sacred and secular discourse. Such an ascendance of the novel, a sign of modernity which Craik firmly endorsed, had as its unstated corollary a widening arena for women writers and thinkers. Novels and novelists were granted the status of moral agents in Craik's polemic, a status safe-guarded in her case by her pious Christian faith. Nevertheless, the contrast she makes between congregations and reading publics high-lighted the changes taking place in the character and disposition of the distinct communities they addressed.

Craik's readers would have known that she was actively contributing to the effect she was describing, for as one of the most prolific of the well-known women writers of her day—forty-five volumes published in her lifetime—she practised what she preached in the secular

---

[1] 'To Novelists—and a Novelist', *Macmillan's Magazine*, 3 (1861), 442.
[2] Mulock did not marry George Lillie Craik, nephew of her friend the historian and writer of the same name, until 1865, when she was 39. For simplicity I have called her by her married name, by which she is now better known, throughout this Introduction.

pulpits open to her sex.[3] Nor was her text as restricted as is sometimes imagined. Popular domestic fiction—in which the narrative
focus was private life and women's subjectivity—provided ambitious
young writers like Craik with an opportunity to enter and reshape much
wider debates about gender relations, public morals, religion, science,
community, and nationality in mid-nineteenth century Britain.

Craik's second novel, *Olive*, appeared in 1850 when the author, at just
24, was already something of a youthful phenomenon on the literary
scene, with stories and poems in a wide range of periodicals, and
children's books and a well-received novel, *The Ogilvies* (1849), behind
her. It was an ambitious work, whose themes included the struggle
between faith and science, the claims of women artists, and the troubling
effects of cross-ethnic and interracial alliances. *Olive* traces the history
from birth to marriage of its eponymous heroine, the diminutive
'deformed' daughter and only child of a *mésalliance* between a stern
Scottish laird, Captain Angus Rothesay, and an orphaned English
beauty, Sybilla Hyde. Olive, born with a slight spinal curvature, survives
and overcomes her parents' rejection, studies with an eccentric artist to
become a successful painter, supports and cares for her frail, blind
mother after her father's death, and lives to love, marry, and bring back
into the fold of Christianity and human love a sceptical young minister,
Harold Gwynne, whose interest in science, and passionate pursuit
of its 'truth' had led him towards a debilitating atheism. Olive's own
Bildungsroman becomes interwoven with that of another girl, an orphan,
Christal Manners, whose family and racial origins are, at first, unknown.
Through Christal, the novel takes on the potentially sensational issues
of miscegenation and illegitimacy. However, of all these interwoven
themes, defect and disability received, in Craik's hands, the most
original treatment. Physical disability of various kinds was to become a
recurring signature of her fiction; it figures prominently in her best
remembered books, *John Halifax, Gentleman* (1856) and her children's
tale, *The Little Lame Prince and his Travelling Cloak* (1875). Its first,
fresh deployment in *Olive* endowed the novel with an innovative pathos
that brought it to critical notice and orchestrated its wider concerns.

In these early entrepreneurial years of her working life, when she was
submitting material everywhere, Craik honed a precocious talent for
judging her potential public and correctly anticipating what topics
would remain current, sometimes by recapitulating in her own fiction

---

[3] Principally a novelist, Craik also published several books of poetry for adults, and one for
children. Of her social and cultural essays, *A Woman's Thoughts about Women* (1858) remains
the best known.

stories by other writers that seemed to hook and hold their readers. She took a calculated but successful risk with *Olive*, for example, in re-working some of the narrative elements of the much-noticed and controversially received *Jane Eyre* (1847). However, it was as part of her own rapidly growing *œuvre*, one that soon gathered a distinctive following, that *Olive* remained a steady seller throughout Craik's life-time, reprinted often in both quality and cheap editions. Craik's senti-mentality and didactic piety had its contemporary critics, yet her work commanded in her day a large and loyal audience. She was often mentioned alongside the Brontës and George Eliot, although Eliot, at least, tartly dismissed the comparison, relegating Craik as a writer who was 'read only by novel readers . . . never by people of high culture.'[4] Craik's books are rarely opened today by either class of reader, but, like most popular domestic fiction of the last century, *Olive*'s appeal faded not merely because its tone and style went out of fashion, but because the particular crises of gendered and familial relations it explored were superseded by other, more current, versions. Like the great mass of fiction that has failed to enter the select historical canon of literature, *Olive* remained largely forgotten and unmourned, until, once again, the tropes of gender, disability, and race which shaped and coloured its story found a resonating echo in our present cultural conversations.[5]

Now, as at the time of its publication, we might enter *Olive*'s imagi-native world by recognizing Craik's novel as both a companion and a countertext to *Jane Eyre*. Each novel provided a related but alternative blueprint for female subjectivity and survival—Olive's passive en-durance of both rejection and violence seems offered as a direct con-trast to Jane's self-styled 'heathen' resistance to personal, familial, and institutional tyrannies—a resistance judged by some of Brontë's con-temporary critics as profoundly 'unchristian.'[6] Both novels are set in the early nineteenth century, but their historical framing is only minimally relevant to their concerns, which unmistakably address volatile and unresolved issues from the troubled 1840s. Each initiated a detailed inquiry into the hybridity endemic to British identity and nationality; in fact the exploration of these questions was part of a narrative strategy which moved their respective heroines from the despised margins of the normal and the entitled to the centre of bourgeois safety. In *Olive* the

---

[4] *The George Eliot Letters*, ed. Gordon S. Haight (New Haven: Yale University Press, 1954–78), 9 vols., iii. 302.

[5] *Olive* was reprinted in facsimile in 1975 (New York: Garland) in response to its proto-feminist content and a new interest in women's writing.

[6] Elizabeth Rigby [later Lady Eastlake], *Quarterly Review*, 83 (Dec. 1848), 153–85.

issue of a racially freighted national identity is thematically introduced through the unhappy mixed marriage between Angus Rothesay and Sybilla Hyde, Olive's parents, and dramatized in the troubling, invasive presence of the quadroon and octoroon mother and daughter, Celia and Christal Manners. These women, who are clearly identified by the end of the novel as the offspring of generations of imperial miscegenation, are fictional relatives of a much more grotesque and racially ambiguous rendering of female alterity, *Jane Eyre*'s 'white creole', Rochester's mad wife Bertha Mason. Throughout *Jane Eyre* and *Olive*, the hierarchies of difference between men and women, between the classes, and between racial categories are both juxtaposed and intertwined. Craik's interest in the subject of race was by no means exhausted by her treatment of it in *Olive*, but immediately took another and very different narrative turn in the short story, 'The Half-Caste: An Old Governess's Tale' included in this edition, which appeared first as volume 12 of *Chambers's Papers for the People* in 1851 and was quickly reprinted in a collection of her short fiction, *Avillon and Other Tales* (1853).

Today Craik is known almost entirely through the one book least characteristic of her writing overall, *John Halifax, Gentleman*. This novel of 1856, an immediate international success, celebrated the creation of modern England between 1780 and 1834 by charting the exemplary rise of the gentleman in question from virtuous poor lad to virtuous wealthy industrialist. Although it contains some harrowing scenes of poverty and class unrest, articulating the economic crises and social fears of the 1840s and 1850s as much as those of the earlier decades in which it is set, the social fantasy that the novel helps to engender is essentially harmonious and optimistic. The combined qualities of its crippled male narrator, Phineas Fletcher, and its hero, John Halifax, embody Craik's projected vision of an idealized masculinity—sensitive, moral, socially responsible, and entrepreneurial—that both constructed and justified the thriving bourgeois nation. In contrast, a more complex and clouded vision of private and public emerged in Craik's other early fiction. By making both *Olive* and 'The Half-Caste' available together for a modern audience we are able to see with what considerable skill the prolific young writer engaged the issues of her day, piecing together the exemplary moral materials of her stories into designs both more radical for their time and more critical perhaps of its social fabric than they might at first appear.

Jane Eyre may have provided a popular and controversial fiction for Craik to play upon as she constructed her own female *Bildungsroman*, but *Olive*'s story appropriates and revises many other cultural narratives, among them the author's own biography. While exploring the dialogue that *Olive* attempts to initiate with *Jane Eyre*, we need also to attend to the variety of contemporary incidents and stories that become part of *Olive*'s revision of the trajectory and fate of the poor, plain heroine, that favoured protagonist of mid-nineteenth-century fiction. In Raymond Williams's classic consideration of the literature of the 1840s, she is said to stand in for the generic figure, 'man alone', the individual whose plight embodied the period's more encompassing anomie and anxiety.[7] Sally Mitchell's excellent study of Craik's career—the only full-length treatment extant—emphasizes throughout the importance of gender, and makes the deft observation that *Olive*'s 'emotional power' is that of *Jane Eyre* 'twisted one degree tighter.'[8] Yet in arguing that the intensified evocation of female abjection in the novel appeals to universal 'feelings of rejection and difference' (a view that echoes even as it dehistoricizes Williams's analysis), as well as 'everywoman's sense that her body is imperfect',[9] Mitchell blurs the historically specific ground of *Olive*'s inspiration and effects .

If we begin somewhat perversely, not with Olive herself, or her 'hopeless deformity' but with the men in her life, the rationale for some of Craik's narrative choices can be more clearly located in the topical issues of the late 1840s and in Craik's own interpretation of her personal history. In *Olive*, Craik's alternative types of the masculine, each flawed in its own way, are, in the order the heroine encounters them: Olive's father, Angus Rothesay, whose economic interests are based in Jamaica; Michael Vanbrugh, the dedicated type of the great artist who trains her; and the man Olive comes to love, the Reverend Harold Gwynne, an unhappy widower who has lost his religious faith. Vanbrugh alone has no corollary in Brontë's work, but his loveless proposal to Olive, a proposal motivated by his desire to make her a great artist, mirrors St John Rivers's equally instrumental but less altruistic proposal to Jane that she accompany him to India as a co-missionary. Olive's reply, that such a loveless match 'would be a heavy sin', recalls Jane's brusque rejection of Rivers. Angus Rothesay and Harold Gwynne are more direct translations of the two competing male figures in *Jane Eyre*, Edward Fairfax Rochester, the reformed Regency rake with a noble lineage and West Indian connections, and St John Rivers, the icy but charismatic minister torn between worldly desires and missionary zeal.

---

[7] Raymond Williams, *The Long Revolution* (Harmondsworth: Penguin, 1965), 85.
[8] Sally Mitchell, *Dinah Mulock Craik* (Boston: G. K. Hall, 1983), 30.
[9] Ibid. 30–1

In her creation of Harold Gwynne we can see Craik borrowing and reworking some of the elements that made St John Rivers such a compelling figure for Brontë and her audience, if not for modern readers. When Olive first encounters Gwynne in Harbury, where she and her now blind mother have moved, he appears cold, charismatic, and masterful, an honourable man but, rather like Rivers, with some crucial emotional component missing. His rationalist and scientific enquiries have led him to reject the 'simple truths' of the religion he must preach. His impossible position is illustrated by his determination to leave his child ignorant of Christian teaching until she reaches an age where she can assess it intellectually, and his penchant for making his sermons as secular as possible: common sense, popularized versions of the moral teachings of Locke and Bacon. That he is psychologically ill-fitted for his profession is made clear, when the death of a humble parishioner's child proves that he is wholly unable to comfort the bereaved parents with the traditional heartfelt words of 'revealed religion'. Like Rivers, Harold is a fool for a pretty face; his first marriage, which ended with the death of his wife, was motivated by physical attraction rather than mature love. However, in the disposition of Harold's problem, Craik offers an alternative solution to the contemporary problem of ministers without vocation, at once more radical and more conservative than Brontë's. St John Rivers is made to forgo the worldly public career he wished for but could not afford; instead his restlessness takes him from his safe parish to a sacrificial life and death as a missionary, a trajectory at once imperial and Christian, which Brontë is moved to celebrate at a healthy distance from both its distasteful intimacy with subaltern subjects and its fatal climate which makes early martyrs of Europeans. Harold Gwynne, on the other hand, once his faith is restored through Olive's love, is permitted to quit the Church and make his mark on the scientific world he hankers after, his 'fame', in the final pages, taking precedence, in a reversion to gender norms, over Olive's artistic career. Craik argues, if only obliquely through Olive's example, for a Christianity more local and less crusading, intellectual, or factional, siding 'with no party, high church or evangelical' as Mrs Gwynne puts it (p. 88), a Christianity based on the practice of inclusive sympathy for others. Craik deals with the challenge to faith seemingly posed by science in the 1840s and after, by securing it firmly inside the domain of a humanist and feminized Christianity. This solution may seem simplistic, foreclosing without exploring the deep tensions between a secular science and Christian tradition—in *Olive*, for example, Harold's particular scientific expertise and interests are kept deliberately vague.

However, Craik's strategy is not so distant from that taken by authors of popular and controversial books on science. Robert Chambers's anonymously published *Vestiges of the Natural History of Creation* (1844), to take a leading example, introduced evolutionary ideas to an eager general public, but was careful to do so within the explicit terms of expressly revealed faith.[10] Moreover, one can perhaps see an indirect influence on Craik of the hugely popular *Vestiges* itself, which argued for the progressive transmutation of forms from animal through human, both in the intermixture of ethnological and biblical language in the opening page of *Olive*, and in its general belief in what Chambers, in an earlier essay, had called, 'the improvability of our own species' based on the knowledge that 'even the lower animals are capable of being improved, through a succession of generations, by the constant presence of a meliorating agency.'[11] Indeed, in both physical and cultural terms, this improvement takes place both in Olive, whose deformity all but disappears as she grows up, and in Zillah, the protagonist of Craik's story 'The Half-Caste', who also sheds the supposed 'backward' traits of her Hindu mother so apparent in her child self. Such optimistic popular ethnological thinking can be read as analogous to Craik's general social views on tolerance and the human capacity for improvement; they act as a makeweight for the bleaker undercurrents of her use of deformity, race, and disability. In Craik's hands, science and intellectual life, like the novel itself in her essay quoted earlier, posed no threat to the perfectibility and peace of domestic or national order; they could act to enhance it, if placed within an ethical Christian context .

At a more familial level, *Olive* is much more concerned with literal and symbolic questions of paternity than *Jane Eyre*, as the recasting of Rochester as an absent, unstable, and duplicitous father instead of a Byronic lover suggests. This emphasis has its ideological roots in Craik's fairly traditional view of gender hierarchy, which defined the limits of her strong commitment to female independence and her encouragement of women's artistic endeavours. Her deep interest in a critique and revision of the role of fathers and the paternal function, a revision aimed not at taking away their power but rather ensuring that it was justly exercised, is in line with her belief, expressed in *A Woman's Thoughts about Women* (1858), in the subordination of women to men in marriage

---

[10] James Secord argues that Chambers had only a 'distant and abstract' belief in God, but believed that his middle-class readers needed such assurances. 'Behind the Veil: Robert Chambers and *Vestiges*', in James R. Moore (ed.), *History, Humanity and Evolution*. (Cambridge: Cambridge University Press, 1989), 171.

[11] Robert Chambers, 'Educability of Animals', *Chambers's Edinburgh Journal*, 22 (1842), 97–8.

and the family as well as in the arts and the public sphere. There is a biographical dimension too. Behind Craik's portrait of Angus, Olive's father—at his worst moments an unforgiving husband, an abusive drunk, and a secret adulterer whose rash speculations leave his heirs so reduced in fortune that young Olive first takes up a career as a painter in order to supplement the family income—is the even seedier and less domesticated figure of Thomas Mulock, Craik's father. Thomas Mulock was a nonconformist Irish preacher, an Evangelist of fiercely reactionary views who emigrated to England in 1812. His occasional incarceration in mental institutions, disastrous business ventures, and final abandonment of his three children after his wife's death was the traumatic catalyst that thrust his eldest child and only daughter—brought up as a lady and adequately educated in spite of her precarious childhood—into the literary marketplace before her twentieth birthday. *Olive* gave Craik the space to develop a narrative where she could both damn and forgive the type of the treacherous father, while weaving a kind of family romance around the more mundane facts of her background and youth. The role of nurse and nurturer that is so central to Olive's story in her relationship to her mother and to Harold Gwynne, was crucial to Craik's construction of moral heroics across her writing, giving fictional testimony to her own part in caring for her dying mother and her orphaned and abandoned younger brothers. Maternal and filial feeling are preeminent virtues in *Olive*. In Angus Rothesay and his relatives, however, Craik preserves her Celtic heritage—Thomas Mulock came from minor Irish gentry—upgrading it in terms of class and culture by making Angus part of a solid Scottish landowning family, although one no longer wealthy. Angus weds a child-bride, a beautiful and penniless English orphan; Thomas, less romantically, married the thirty-something daughter of a well-off tanner's widow from Newcastle under Lyme.

Indeed the omnipresence of the father, when set beside the dominance of the theme of good parenting in *Olive*, is one of its most striking differences from Brontë's novel, making visible the pivotal lack of direct paternal—and maternal—power in *Jane Eyre*. Jane Eyre's parents—carried off by typhus contracted from the poor in the urban parish where her father was a minister—have only a parenthetical significance—and bear almost no emotional weight in a novel where fathers in general are dead, undeclared, or absent, and where mothers, when brought to our attention, are bad or mad—sometimes both. The novel's celebration of the domestic and familial is saved for the closing vignette of Jane and Rochester with their first-born son. This final reparative family portrait captures at once the productive success of cross-class marriage and the creation, in spite of adversity, of a new kind of national identity. Their union, and its fertility, acknowledges and legitimates the ethnically mixed genealogy of the English evidenced earlier in the novel in the 'irregular features' shared by both Jane and Rochester. In their Ferndean retreat these two are defended against the contamination of European or colonial outsiders, whose narrative representatives are all women, Rochester's monstrous first wife and his sequence of degraded European mistresses. In vivid contrast, the first half of *Olive* dwells on what *Jane Eyre* seems happy to forget—the potential for disaster in the mixing of types *within* the British Isles—a disaster made incarnate, but ambiguously so, in Olive's deformity.

Through her narration of the troubled marriage of Sybilla and Angus and their initially horrified responses to the physical 'imperfection' of their only child, Craik joins an animated and divided dialogue about cultural and racial differences within Britain, a debate that had both direct social and political referents such as the causes and effects of the Irish famine of 1848, and the class conflict symbolized by Chartist agitation, but was more obliquely expressed through other social, political, and economic anxieties. Throughout what contemporaries dubbed the 'hungry forties', the attempted construction of a coherent ethnicity whose common denominator was whiteness appeared in the work of influential writers and thinkers—Dickens and Carlyle prominent among them—as a unifying bond through which the warring rich and poor might understand their common interest.

The search for a consoling fiction of national belonging was both supported and complicated by the popular expansion of the sciences of ethnology and ethnography in the 1840s and 1850s. Chambers's *Vestiges* contained an underlying optimism in human progress, but other dominant arguments on origin and difference offered a scientific imprimatur for racially driven biological arguments about human diversity, which could, when applied in their most extreme form to the mutual hostilities between classes, reduce these threatening antagonisms to innate, immutable psychological aversion between races. Established ethnologists such as the physician James Cowles Prichard, who held to the theory of single origin for mankind, with separate races developing in response to environment, found themselves pitted against aggressive new adversaries who argued for the multiple, unequal origins of human types, or at least the immutable difference of separate races from a moment lost in prehistory. By the 1840s both sides in these controversies were highlighting the instinctive repulsion of one race for another, but their respective arguments about its scientific and cultural significance were deeply at odds.[12] While most of the ethnological and ethnographic writers focused primarily on distinguishing darker skinned races from each other and, crucially, from European types, the most influential new voice in racial thinking in Britain, the Scottish anatomist Robert Knox, whose paradigm of racial antagonism, summarized in his slogan 'race is everything', sought to displace other causal theories of human conflict, triumphantly brought the debate home to the heterogeneous and warring populations of the British Isles, a topic which he reported made even his most jaded audiences sit up and listen.[13] In this period discussions about origins and difference proliferated in every quarter and genre—represented by the runaway success of Chambers's anonymous *Vestiges*, the theatrical staging of exhibitions of indigenous peoples in London, and provincial exhibitions, but were equally prominent in *The Lancet* and the general cultural journals directed at the educated middle class. These omnipresent issues had unavoidable implications for the way in which gender and sexual difference was being constructed across the cultural terrain. For, as historian of science Nancy Stepan has persuasively argued, these racial theories were being reciprocally and analogically constituted in the mid-nineteenth century alongside those of sexual difference.[14]

When, in *Olive*, Scottish Angus appears as the prototype of a certain extreme of masculinity—tall, craggy, proud, reserved, and emotionally cold and unsympathetic—and English Sybilla is described as 'very small in stature and proportions—quite a little fairy', as well as pleasure-loving, childlike, and childish—so hyper-feminine in fact that a viewer might not know whether she was a 'woman or a spirit' (p. 8)—we can see Craik mapping the cultural and racial divisions between Celt and Anglo-Saxon, and between the human and its others, on the most exaggerated versions of sexual differentiation. Little Olive, product of this marriage of opposites, is, apart from her 'deformity', a true amalgam of her parents' types, her miniature size reproducing her mother's 'fairy' genealogy but her features resembling those of the Rothesays. While Craik significantly offers neither current medical nor lay superstitious explanations for the child's physical flaw, its appearance in the offspring

---

[12] For accounts and analyses of these thinkers and debates see Nancy Leys Stepan, *The Idea of Race in Science* (London, Macmillan, 1982), and Robert J. C. Young, *Colonial Desire: Hybridity in Theory, Culture and Race* (London, New York: Routledge, 1995).

[13] Robert Knox, *The Races of Men: A Fragment* {Philadelphia: Lea & Blanchard, 1850; repr. Miami: Mnemosyne (1969)}, 7.

[14] Nancy Leys Stepan, 'Race and Gender: The Role of Analogy in Science', *Isis*, 77 (1986), 216–77, reprinted in David Theo Goldberg (ed.), *Anatomy of Racism* (Minneapolis: University of Minnesota Press, 1990), 38–57.

of such an ill-matched pair immediately draws the novel into the orbit of the highly charged ethnological debates about racial hybridity. Knox, like some other polygenetic thinkers, modelled racial difference on the distinctions between species; he maintained that the mulatto would be 'sterile, like mules' and insisted that no new races could be created by the interbreeding of the more closely allied white races, but that one dominant type of the contributing race would always prevail.[15] In this absolutist (and counterfactual) racial model the child of mixed parentage with a visible, distinguishing birth defect might seem at first glance very like the unfortunate mulatto, the aberrant and sterile issue of a union never meant to be. This callous eugenic conclusion is the very one that Craik's narrative works so hard to dispel by making Olive a consistent force for good in every sphere she enters, so much the saviour of her mismatched parents that she virtually takes over the parental role, and, after her father's death, becomes the single emotional and financial support to her increasingly dependent mother. To drive the point home Craik lifts 'the curse of hopeless deformity' (p. 14) pronounced on the infant child by the English doctor who attends her birth, allowing her eventually to be loved and to marry. Whatever the racial, cultural, and sexual dissonances in the Rothesays' troubled alliance, whatever visible imperfection in the hybrid issue of such unions, these children, the novel argues, must be cherished, for they can become the soul and even the backbone of the British nation.

Craik's use of physical disability in *Olive* cannot, therefore, be read solely as a sign of the abjection of women or the vicissitudes of femininity, but rather as the integration of these specifically gendered meanings with others more local and more universal. 'Deformity' in the mid-nineteenth century was a catch-all term for physical anomalies from Olive's slight spinal curvature which was, as the novel's narrative voice emphasizes, neither 'disgusting' nor 'painful' for the viewer, to the bearded women, midgets, and dwarves—the 'freaks' of the London exhibitions—where, an 1851 *Punch* cartoon suggested,' 'deformito-mania' pulled in crowds seeking the thrill of repulsion and the confirmation of their own normality.[16] These exhibitions were booked into the same venues and were frequently compared in the press to the shows of indigenous peoples—American Indians, Hottentots, and Kaffirs, as well as exotic children of unknown racial types whose

[15] *Races of Men*, 316.
[16] My discussion of the shows of London is drawn from Richard D. Altick, *The Shows of London* (Cambridge: Belknap Press of Harvard University Press, 1978) especially ch. 19, 'Freaks in the Age of Improvement'. For the *Punch* cartoon, see Altick, p. 254.

mysterious origins provided the draw. Deformity and racial otherness, perhaps even the threat of the former in a fusion with the latter, were closely related phenomena. Just as Charlotte Brontë adventitiously combined the *mis-en-scène* of the exhibitions and the madhouse to dramatize the moment when Bertha Mason is revealed in her 'goblin's cell', as a 'beast or human being, one could not, at first sight, tell' emitting the 'fiercest yells, and the most convulsive plunges'[17] to the astonishment of the stunned wedding party, so Craik, in her case inviting rather than deflecting her reader's sympathies, exploited the more sentimental side of the exhibitions' spectacular appeal in a critical scene in *Olive*. Angus, who had left for a five-year stay in Jamaica two months before Olive's birth, has been kept by his wife in entire ignorance of his child's condition. Now, at last, he must meet little Olive.

The door opened, and Elspie led in a little girl. By her stature she might have been two years old, but her face was like that of a child of ten or twelve—so thoughtful, so grave. Her limbs were small and wasted, but exquisitely delicate. The same might be said of her features; which, though thin, and wearing a look of premature age, together with that quiet, earnest, melancholy cast peculiar to deformity, were yet regular, almost pretty. Her head was well shaped and from it fell a quantity of amber-coloured hair—pale 'lint-white locks', which, with the almost colourless transparency of her complexion, gave a spectral air to her whole appearance. She looked less like a child than a woman dwarfed into child-hood; the sort of being renowned in elfin legends, as springing up on a lonely moor, or appearing by a cradle-side; supernatural, yet fraught with a nameless beauty. She was dressed with the utmost care, in white, with blue ribands; and her lovely hair was arranged so as to hide, as much as possible, the defect, which, alas! was even then only too perceptible. It was not a humpback, nor yet a twisted spine; it was an elevation of the shoulders, shortening the neck, and giving the appearance of a perpetual stoop. There was nothing disgusting or painful in it, but still it was an imperfection, causing an instinctive compassion—an involuntary 'Poor little creature, what a pity!' (p. 23)

'Instinctive compassion' and 'pity' will prove to be much less than the full recognition of her humanity that the adult Olive needs, but Craik was being bold enough at this historical moment in asserting that sympathy rather than disgust or revulsion were the innate and normal responses to bodily difference. We can glimpse how contested this view was becoming if we compare it to Brontë's brutally unpitying exposure of Bertha Mason's madness and physical degradation. As the above description of Olive indicates, in its artful combination of the pathetic and the grotesque, deformity remains in the novel an aesthetic

---

[17] Charlotte Brontë, *Jane Eyre* (1847), ed. Margaret Smith (Oxford World's Classics, 1980), 307–8.

aberration. Sybilla's perfect fairy proportions and ethereal aspect are wrenched out of scale in her daughter, where the dissonance between Olive's size, demeanour and age produces an effect eerily 'supernatural', 'spectral', and 'elfin', not simply, as in her mother, a woman retaining rather too much of the child, but a child who is 'less like child than a woman dwarfed into childhood'. Angus's 'instinctive' response when faced with the 'last daughter of the ever-beautiful Rothesay line' who has been 'led to claim the paternal embrace', is to recoil; recognizing paternity but refusing compassion he puts 'his hand before his eyes, as if to shut out the sight' (p. 23).

The description of Olive in this passage mines and condenses a rich range of related images from the period, allowing the author to symbolize to her nineteenth-century readers more than the misfortunes of middle-class femininity. A prematurely aged appearance was not only ascribed to birth defects like Olive's, but to the effects of severe childhood illness. The unease reflected in the narrator's uncertainty about Olive's age and status—child or woman—intersects with the related confusion of the social investigator and popular journalist Henry Mayhew when, in the same years as the writing and publication of *Olive*, he interviewed an 8-year-old watercress-seller who had 'lost all childish ways' and 'was indeed in thoughts and manner, a woman'.[18] We might speculate that the 'loss' of childhood as an imagined physical or psychological state, occasioned on the one hand by Olive's deformity and on the other by the watercress-seller's economic necessity made them both hard to place within the matrix of the normal. The uncanny reversal of development suggested by a 'woman dwarfed into childhood' articulated a commonplace observation about the demeanour of the girl-children of the most destitute of the English poor, but it had its necessary complement in the stereotype of women from the supposedly subordinate classes—and races—as ripening too early into a specifically sexualized maturity, a cliché to which *Olive* later turns in its depiction of the octoroon, Christal Manners.

While the images of childhood and femininity that *Olive* both called upon and called up widened the novel's social reference for its readers, they also complicated its Christian humanitarian message. Nevertheless, in its opening pages, *Olive* bravely tries out an inclusive humanism. The reader is asked to view 'the helpless lump of breathing flesh' that is the material form of every newborn child as a humbling image of the 'poor,

[18] Henry Mayhew, *London Labour and the London Poor* (London: George Woodfall and Sons, 1851), 4 vols., i. 151–2. See also Carolyn Steedman's discussion of this passage in *Landscape for a Good Woman: A Story of Two Lives* (London: Virago, 1986), 126–7.

mean, and degraded' (p. 3) of all nations. *Olive*'s particular story carries a clear denunciation of the psycho-politics of aversion that were becoming an increasingly common element in the social and political thinking of the 1840s. In Craik's novel any revulsion produced by Olive's deformity—as well as other forms of difference—is read either as socially conditioned prejudice, or an instinct that may be easily overcome on an hour's acquaintance with her.

The first part of *Olive* traces the effects of the heroine's deformity through her childhood and adolescence, as it throws into relief the troubled dynamics of difference in the Rothesays' 'mixed' marriage, and in their treatment of their daughter. In relation to deformity, Craik's humanism ran deep, but the novel is not nearly so even-handed in its distribution of its ethnic sympathies. Although Olive spends most of her life in different parts of England, her story begins and ends in an idealized Scotland. And while Celtic masculinity needs radical re-education—Angus is depicted as morally corrupted, and Harold Gwynne at first as stiff and cold—the novel's Scottish women—nurse Elspie, Olive's great-aunt Flora Rothesay, and Alison Balfour Gwynne, Harold's mother—embody an altogether sturdier, more muscular and moral femininity than the undeveloped, unreliable, and sickly English wives, Sybilla Rothesay and Sara Derwent, Harold Gwynne's first partner. Revising Victorian ideas of womanhood through the supposed attributes of race, Craik is able to combine in Olive the gentle and passive qualities of English femininity with the intelligence, stoicism, loyalty, and generosity ascribed by her to Scottish women. The Celtic turn in the story moves an eccentric, synthesized Britishness (with the Celtic in dominance) to the centre of its social history, and shifts Anglo-Saxon Englishness to the margins of the novel's ethical as well as its geographic narrative. This eccentricity masks and absorbs other ways in which the novel at critical points appears more socially radical as well as more compassionate than *Jane Eyre*. While Jane paints in her spare time, Olive acquires a public reputation and an income, though Craik suggests, in the last chapter, that as a wife 'it was a natural and a womanly thing that in her husband's fame, Olive should almost forget her own' (p. 325). The ideal of bourgeois marriage is therefore also written as the union of an established artist and a renowned scientist; perhaps a highland outpost of the nation-state was the safest place to locate such a wishful, progressive fantasy of love and work.

In *Olive*'s revision of *Jane Eyre* one can see Craik turning the disturbing ambiguities and productive ambivalence of Brontë's novel into a more straightforwardly improving story—for this, as she says in her essay on George Eliot—should be the aim of the novel. Nowhere is this straightening out of plot and purpose more apparent than in *Olive*'s reworking of Brontë's West Indian theme through the introduction of Celia and Christal Manners in Chapter XXI. In introducing the West Indies into their fictions, both Brontë and Craik were responding in part to the attention the former slave-holding colonies were commanding in England during the 1840s. A fall in sugar revenues earlier in the decade, and mixed reports of the progress of the newly freed black population whose independence became complete only in 1838 with the ending of the apprentice system, were partly responsible for the break-up of the temporary alliances and uneasy consensus that had led to the abolition of slavery. The supposedly well-fed but idle freedman were now unfavourably contrasted with the starving, deserving poor of England. By 1846 the young Disraeli was calling abolition a failure and recommending to parliament the reimposition of slavery, while in 1849 Carlyle, advocating a more coercive system of labour in the West Indies, caused a furore with his essay 'The Negro Question' published in *Fraser's Magazine* (a title he later changed to the more offensive 'The Nigger Question'), which deployed the most graphic racial epithets to dehumanize and emasculate African workers.[19] Sympathy towards people of African descent was increasingly targeted in the press (and in fictional figures like Dickens's Mrs Jellyby) as feminine sentimentality which neglected the fate of the deserving white poor at home.

Both *Jane Eyre* and *Olive* rewrite the debates about the economic interdependence of mother country and colony, and the relative status of Europeans and colonial subjects, from the perspective of the white women of Britain. Rochester and Angus make their fortunes in the West Indies, but at a social cost to the integrity of family life in the metropolitan nation, a cost summed up in their transgressive sexual commerce with West Indian women, who cannot be abandoned in the colonial setting when the men return home but by force (in Bertha's case) or through their own agency (in Celia Manners's) are made to invade the sacrosanct terrain of England. Here they act as hostages to the fortunes of the mother country, disturbing the creation of a peaceable kingdom not by threatening the direct survival of the English poor, but by their disruptive effect on economically and socially vulnerable middle-class

[19] Thomas Carlyle, 'The Negro Question', *Fraser's Magazine*, 40 (Dec. 1849), 670–9. For the rise of racial thinking in the 1840s see Philip Curtin, *The Image of Africa: British Ideas and Action, 1780–1850* (Madison: University of Wisconsin Press, 1964) and Catherine Hall, *White, Male and Middle Class: Explorations in Feminism and History* (Cambridge: Polity Press, 1992), especially 'Missionary Stories: Gender and Ethnicity in England in the 1830s and 1840s', 205–54.

women. This revision might seem at first a full-scale feminization of contemporary cultural narratives about race, a change in casting which substitutes gender relations and domestic politics for the class and imperial issues which dominated the public debates about the future of the West Indies and its newly freed subjects. Yet this transposition is not really so complete, because in both novels the heroines have also been emblematically associated with the poor and oppressed.

Jane Eyre plays a kind of hide-and-seek with its racial themes, for while Bertha comes of a white Creole family—Rochester describes her, at first meeting, as a woman in the style of his aristocratic English neighbour, Blanche Ingram—her 'savage face' and 'fearful blackened inflation of the lineaments' show her, in her Thornfield incarceration, as transformed into or revealed as racially other.[20]

Olive is much more direct. Celia Manners enters the story as an object of bourgeois charity, not as an 'ordinary poor person, but that strange foreign-looking woman', whose wrecked beauty is compared to that of an 'Eastern queen' (p. 129). But Celia herself dispels some of the mystery about her origins, angrily telling the adolescent Olive and her companion that she comes 'from a country where are thousands of young maidens, whose blood, half-Southern, half-European, is too pure for slavery, too tainted for freedom', and who 'have no higher future than to be the white man's passing toy' (p. 131). Her child Christal, 'a little, thin-limbed, cunning-eyed girl, of eight or ten' (p. 130) with discordant colouring— 'black eyes and fair hair' (p. 129)—has, with Celia's help, constructed a family romance about herself as the daughter of 'a rich lady' and 'a noble gentleman' who 'drowned together in the deep sea, years ago' (p. 130). These two, we learn later, are the mistress and illegitimate child of Angus Rothesay, for Celia, like the well-remembered poet-performer heroine of Mme de Staël's *Corinne* (cited elsewhere in *Olive*, and one of the most widely read novels of the first half of the nineteenth century), has followed Angus to England.[21] The child Christal is educated abroad after Celia's death with money provided by Angus, and returns to England from her French school a young woman, still ignorant of her status and race, to join the milieu of Olive and her mother. Both mother and child—ironically named Manners—have multiple roles to play in *Olive*'s plot, but it is useful first to see in them a critique of the handling not only of Bertha Mason but of Rochester's actress-mistress Céline Varens and her daughter Adèle, Jane's pupil in Brontë's novel. While

---

[20] Jane Eyre, 297.
[21] *Corinne* is cited in both *The Ogilvies* and *Olive*. See explanatory note to p. 126.

Celia and Christal are full of bitter pride and anger—vengeful, envious, and murderous anger in Christal's case, when she discovers the secret of her family origins—their fury, although excessive and frightening, and obliquely coded as a racial trait, also has its source in real injustices. In Bertha Mason, rage is the irrational effect of her degenerate heredity; it is never ascribed to any act of Rochester's, who is represented by himself and by the author as her victim. *Jane Eyre*, against its own narrative logic, stubbornly stops short of allowing little Adèle, Rochester's ward, to be identified as Rochester's bastard daughter. Craik's Angus, in contrast, through his economic provision for Celia and Christal, and his confession to Olive in a letter to be opened after Sybilla's death, acknowledges his sin, his mistress, and his child. Although Christal attacks and nearly kills Olive, as Bertha does Jane, Christal herself is not held responsible for her actions, although Craik has her 'choose' a retreat, perhaps temporary, perhaps permanent, in a Scottish nunnery. In one of the most poignant and polemical passages of the novel, Olive overcomes her own single moment of 'instinctive repugnance' (p. 277), at Christal's simultaneous difference and likeness, and, drawn by the ties of blood, determinedly tries to befriend her sister and claim their sororal relation. It is Christal, although she softens at the novel's end, who still cannot fully accept Olive's pity and friendship.

At this and other points, the racial politics of aversion, while never as violently framed as in *Jane Eyre*, do subtly but surely infect *Olive* through the history of Celia and Christal, for onto their psyches is projected all the bitterness and anger that Olive herself is never allowed to feel at the absence of full parental love, other cruel responses to her disability, or the supposed impossibility of her ever being desired or married. The narrative, borrowing again from *Jane Eyre*, punishes these parental lapses with inexorable physical retribution, Sybilla with blindness and Angus with an early accidental death. Yet Olive herself remains the prisoner of Craik's determination to make her at every moment the angel in the house, an impossible example of actively virtuous femininity exercised always in the passive tense. In this respect Jane Eyre's identifications with rebel slaves and heathens, identifications which must by the novel's end be disavowed, are both more feminist in their defence of women's right to resist and more troubling in the novel's final repudiation of that right for racially marked other women.

There remains the question of the racial and sexual politics that dictate the dynamic between Olive's physical and Christal's emotional deformity. Olive's visible imperfection, we are told, had already become much less noticeable in the adult than in the child. Yet the eruption of Christal's rage seems to be the narrative trigger that releases Olive from her 'curse' into Harold's love. In *Olive*, as in *Jane Eyre*, rage is necessary for the survival of poor, plain heroines but for them to become legitimate progenitors of their class and nation, surrogate and ultimately expendable women must enact it for them. Yet in *Olive* this solution leaves a pathological trace on the story, for the physical stigma that Olive bears cannot be wholly erased through the manipulation of plot or metaphor, and its stubborn persistence, which surfaces at the end of *Olive*, opens up another set of unanswered questions about the composition and future of normative national subjectivity. *Jane Eyre* closes with biological motherhood, but Craik does not risk the possibility of the reproduction of Olive's spinal curvature; she implicitly limits Olive's maternal opportunities to her role as 'new mamma' to Harold's daughter Ailie (p. 325).

If miscegenation and its consequences are a subplot in *Olive*, never entirely freed from its service to the development of its heroine, in 'The Half-Caste' Craik allows herself to address the question head on. This time it is through the heroine's story, that of the heiress Zillah Le Poer, legitimate daughter of an Englishman and an Indian princess, as told to the reader by Zillah's 'Old Governess'. In striking contrast to *Olive*, in this tale the mixed-race child is the would-be victim of English greed and prejudice. Her uncle's family treat her with a contempt grounded in their belief in her 'small capacity'. The uncle falsely tells the governess, Cassandra, that Zillah is illegitimate, the result of irregular 'ties between natives and Europeans' and that 'her modicum of intellect is not greater than generally belongs to her mother's race. She would make an excellent *ayah*' (p. 340). The first impression Zillah makes on her governess bears this out. Although she was 'almost a woman' with 'an olive complexion, full Hindoo lips, and eyes very black and bright . . . her dull, heavy face had the stupidity of an ultra-stupid child' (p. 337). Nor, in spite of Cassandra's consistent kindness to her, was she an immediately apt pupil, for as Cassandra explains, 'it is a great mistake to suppose that every victim of tyranny must of necessity be an angel . . . oppression . . . dulls the faculties, stupefies the instinctive sense of right, and makes the most awful havoc among the natural affections' (p. 341). Only a long period of steady affection and gentle instruction—and time away from her uncle—combats the laziness that Cassandra ascribes to 'the languor' of Zillah's 'native clime', or the 'demoniac' look in her black eyes (p. 341).

'The Half-Caste' is a liberal parable for its time, arguing for education, nurture, and environment as the most important factors in analysing and creating parity between races. While Craik recycles typical biologically based prejudices, she goes some way to argue against their deterministic implications. Zillah turns out to be eminently educable. Rescued by the governess from her scheming and abusive relatives, she grows into a beautiful, intelligent woman, who eventually marries Cassandra's family friend and employer, Mr Sutherland, and gives birth to a little 'Cassia', a child with 'her mother's smile, and her father's eyes and brow' (p. 372). Although Zillah wins the man whom the governess also loves, and does so with a beauty that is always described as surmounting as well as depending on her racial otherness, Craik explicitly refuses to make of the white narrator an abject female victim displaced by the encroachment of a dark-skinned seductress. In line with Craik's penchant for resolutions which are neither punitive or adversarial, Cassandra does not shrivel into bitter spinsterhood, but retains her affective relationship to the Sutherland household, and turns herself into a writer.

'The Half-Caste' refutes what it must partly reproduce, the xenophobic lesson usually attached to the period's paranoid fantasies of the invasion of England by women of other races. However, the story stoutly affirms the intellectual capacity of the supposedly inferior Hindoos, and, unlike *Olive*, sanctions legitimate union between races, or at least between Indian women and English men. More boldly, it affirms the full integration of mixed-race children into English bourgeois life, even though this is predicated on the 'whitening' of succeeding generations— little Cassia is predictably blonde. At a moment when scientific racial thinking was promoting the immutable difference in capacities between races, and decrying hybrid unions as a sign of the unnatural or perverse, 'The Half-Caste' carried, beneath its simple melodrama, an unmistakable political thrust. Nor had Craik finished with such topics, which had almost as much salience in her early work as the insistent trope of deformity and disability was to have in her wider *œuvre*. The heroine of *Agatha's Husband* (1853) is also the child of an Anglo-Indian father, a thoroughly English girl in manner and name, but with 'very dark . . . not over clear' skin and 'full, rich lips', whose colouring and features are admiringly likened by her very fair English suitor to that of the 'Pawnee Indian' among whom he has spent his youth.[22] Agatha's racial inheritance remains ambiguous and undeveloped in the novel as a whole, but its casual inclusion as a way of exoticizing sexual attraction between physical opposites, rather than as a potential social problem, has a

---

[22] *Agatha's Husband* (New York: Harper & Brothers, n.d.), 1, 2, and 16.

certain subversive power of its own. While the young writer clearly chose her themes in part for their sensation value, the British families and communities that she imagined in these fictions could hardly be defined as ethnic enclaves of whiteness. In both *Olive* and 'The Half-Caste' Craik was deliberately writing against the grain of the prejudice that informed the fiction of her more illustrious and better-remembered peers. For this reason as well as on its own terms and for its own pleasures, Craik's fiction deserves a new audience and a more historically informed analysis.

NOTE ON THE TEXT

THE edition of *Olive* reprinted here was first published in three volumes in 1850 by Chapman and Hall, London. A cheap edition, advertised as 'revised', appeared in 1854, although the changes to the text were not extensive. It remained a steady seller in this period, going through eight editions by 1865, now in a single rather cramped, small print volume. In 1875 there appeared an edition with illustrations by G. Bowers. The novel was still in print in 1895. Throughout Craik's lifetime the title-page usually read 'By the author of . . .' instead of printing her name. In the first edition she was only 'the author of "The Ogilvies"', but by 1865 '"John Halifax, Gentleman," "The Ogilvies," The Head of the Family," "Agatha's Husband," Etc. Etc.' suggested the order of popularity of her best-known novels, and her productivity. For this Oxford World's Classics edition punctuation has been standardized to current modern practice. 'The Half-Caste; An Old Governess's Tale, Founded on Fact' first appeared in *Chambers's Papers for the People* (Edinburgh: William and Robert Chambers, 1851) 12/94, and was afterwards reprinted in a collection of her short fiction, *Avillon and Other Tales*, in 1853.

SELECT BIBLIOGRAPHY

BIOGRAPHIES, MEMOIRS

Ellis, Stewart Marsh, 'Dinah Maria Mulock (Mrs. Craik)', *Bookman*, 70 (Apr. 1926), 1–5.

Oliphant, Margaret, 'Mrs Craik', *Macmillan's Magazine*, 57 (1887), 81–5.

Reade, Aleyn Lyell, *The Mellards and Their Descendants, Including the Bibbys of Liverpool with Memoirs of Dinah Maria Mulock and Thomas Mellard Reade* (London: Arden Press, 1915).

CRITICAL STUDIES

James, Henry, 'A Noble Life', in *Notes and Reviews* (1921; Freeport: Books for Libraries Press, 1968).

Kaplan, Cora, '"A Heterogeneous Thing": Childhood and the Rise of Racial Thinking in Victorian Britain', in Diana Fuss (ed.), *Human All Too Human* (New York: Routledge, 1995) 169–99.

Mitchell, Sally, Dinah Mulock Craik (Boston: G. K. Hall, 1983).

Perkin, Russell J., 'Narrative Voice and the "Feminine" Novelist: Dinah Mulock and George Eliot', *Victorian Review*, 18 (Summer 1992), 24–42.

Showalter, Elaine, 'Dinah Mulock Craik and the Tactics of Sentiment: A Case Study in Victorian Female Authorship', *Feminist Studies*, 2 (1975), 5–23.

GENERAL STUDIES

Altick, Richard D., *The Shows of London* (Cambridge: Belknap Press of Harvard University Press, 1978).

Armstrong, Nancy, *Desire and Domestic Fiction: A Political History of the Novel* (Oxford: Oxford University Press, 1987).

Beer, Gillian, *Darwin's Plots: Evolutionary Narrative in Darwin, George Eliot, and Nineteenth-Century Fiction* (London, Routledge, 1983).

Curtin, Philip, *The Image of Africa: British Ideas and Action, 1780–1850* (Madison: University of Wisconsin Press, 1964).

Colby, Robert A., *Fiction with a Purpose* (Bloomington: Indiana University Press, 1967).

Davidoff, Leonore, and Hall, Catherine, *Family Fortunes: Men and Women of the English Middle Class, 1780–1850* (London: Hutchinson, 1987).

Gilman, Sander, *Difference and Pathology: Stereotypes of Sexuality, Race and Madness* (Ithaca, NY: Cornell University Press, 1985).

Hall, Catherine, *White, Male and Middle Class: Explorations in Feminism and History* (Cambridge: Polity, 1992).

Meyer, Susan, *Imperialism at Home: Race and Victorian Women's Fiction* (Ithaca, NY: Cornell University Press, 1996).

Michie, Elsie B., *Outside the Pale: Cultural Exclusion, Gender Difference, and the Victorian Woman Writer* (Ithaca, NY: Cornell University Press, 1993).

Mitchell, Sally, *The Fallen Angel: Chastity, Class and Women's Reading, 1835–1880* (Bowling Green, Oh.: Bowling Green University Press, 1981).

Religion in Victorian Britain, vols. i, ii, iv (ed. Gerald Parsons, 1988); vol. iii (ed. James R. Moore, 1988); vol. v (ed. John Wolffe, 1997) (Manchester: Manchester University Press).

Sharpe, Jenny, *Allegories of Empire: The Figure of Woman in the Colonial Text*, (Minneapolis: Minnesota University Press, 1983).

Showalter, Elaine, *A Literature of Their Own: British Women Novelists from Brontë to Lessing* (Princeton: Princeton University Press, 1977).

Spivak, Gayatri Chakravorty, 'Three Women's Texts and a Critique of Imperialism', *Critical Inquiry*, 12 (1985), 243–61.

Steedman, Carolyn, *Strange Dislocations: Childhood and the Idea of Human Interiority* (London: Virago, 1995).

Stepan, Nancy, *The Idea of Race in Science: Great Britain, 1800–1960* (London: Macmillan, 1982).

Williams, Raymond, *The Long Revolution* (Harmondsworth: Penguin, 1965).

Young, Robert J. C., *Colonial Desire: Hybridity in Theory, Culture and Race* (London: Routledge, 1995).

FURTHER READING IN OXFORD WORLD'S CLASSICS

Brontë, Charlotte, *Jane Eyre*, ed. Margaret Smith.

—— *Villette*, ed. Margaret Smith and Herbert Rosengarten.

Lewis, Matthew, *Journal of a West India Proprietor*, ed. Judith Terry.

Staël, Mme de, *Corinne*, trans. and ed. Sylvia Raphael, with an introduction by John Isbell.

A CHRONOLOGY OF DINAH MULOCK CRAIK

1826   Born Dinah Maria, 20 April in Stoke-on-Trent, eldest child of Thomas Mulock, nonconformist preacher of Irish extraction, and Dinah Mellard, a tanner's daughter.

1831   Moves to Newcastle under Lyme where she is raised and educated. Her mother keeps a small school, where Dinah, aged 13, begins to teach Latin and other subjects.

1839   Family moves to London where Dinah studies languages and drawing.

1841   First publishes poems in *Staffordshire Advertiser*.

1845   Death of her mother. Her father ceases to support the family; beginning of her career as a writer.

1846–   From this date onwards stories and poems regularly appear in popular magazines, including *Chambers's Edinburgh Journal*, *Good Words*, *Sharpe's London Magazine*, and *Once a Week*.

1849   *Cola Monti; or the Story of Genius*, a children's book, and *The Ogilvies* her first novel, published.

1850   *Olive* published.

1851   'The Half-Caste: An Old Governess's Tale, Founded on Fact' appears in *Chambers's Papers for the People*.

1853   *Agatha's Husband* published. Short fiction collected in *Avillon and Other Tales*.

1856   *John Halifax, Gentleman* published to great acclaim.

1858   *A Woman's Thoughts About Women*, essays previously in *Chambers's*, published as a book.

1859   *Poems*, her first book of verse, published.

1864   Awarded a civil list pension of £60 per annum.

1861   Essays collected as *Studies from Life*.

1865   Marries George Lillie Craik, eleven years her junior and a partner in Macmillans which publishes some of her later work.

1869   Moves to Corner House at Shortlands, Kent, designed by Craik with architect Norman Shaw. Adopts a baby daughter,

Dorothy, from a parish workhouse. Death of Thomas Mulock.

1875 *The Little Lame Prince*, her best-known children's story, published.

1878 Edits *A Legacy*, a memorial of working–class teacher and poet John Martin.

1889 Dies at Shortlands, the author of forty-five volumes of poems, novels, children's stories, and essays, many translated into other languages.

Olive

CHAPTER I

'Puir wee lassie, ye hae a waesome welcome to a waesome* warld!'

Such was the first greeting ever received by my heroine, Olive Rothesay. However, she would be then entitled neither a heroine, nor even 'Olive Rothesay', being a small nameless concretion of humanity, in colour and consistency strongly resembling the 'red earth', whence was taken the father of all nations. No foreshadowing of the coming life brightened her purple, pinched-up, withered face, which, as in all new-born children, bore such a ridiculous likeness to extreme old age. No tone of the all-expressive human voice thrilled through the unconscious wail that was her first utterance, and in her wide-open meaningless eyes had never dawned the beautiful human soul. There she lay, as you and I, reader, with all our compeers, lay once—a helpless lump of breathing flesh, faintly stirred by animal life, and scarce at all by that inner life which we call spirit. And, if we, every one, were thus to look back, half in compassion, half in humiliation, at our infantile likeness—may it not be that in the world to come some who in this world bore an outward image, poor, mean, and degraded, will cast a glance of equal pity on their well-remembered olden selves, now transfigured into beautiful immortality.

I seem to be wandering from my Olive Rothesay; but the time to come will show the contrary.

Poor little spirit! newly come to earth, who knows whether that 'waesome welcome' may not be a prophecy? The old nurse seemed almost to dread this, even while she uttered it, for with the superstition from which not an 'auld wife' in Scotland is altogether free, she changed the dolorous croon into a 'God guide us!' and, pressing the babe to her aged breast, bestowed a hearty blessing on her nursling of the second generation—the child of him who was at once her master and her foster-son.

'An' wae's the day that he's sae far awa', and canna do't himsel, my bonnie bairn! It's ill coming into the warld without a father's blessing.'

Perhaps the good soul's clasp was the tenderer, and her warm heart throbbed the warmer to the new-born child, for a passing remembrance of her own two fatherless babes, who now slept—as close together, as when, 'twin-laddies', they had nestled in one mother's bosom—slept beneath the wide Atlantic which marks the sea-boy's grave.

Nevertheless, the memory was now grown so dim with years, that it vanished the moment the infant waked and began to cry. Rocking to and fro, the nurse tuned her cracked voice to a long-forgotten lullaby—

something about a 'boatie'.* It was stopped by a hand on her shoulder, followed by the approximation of a face which, in its bland gravity, bore 'MD' on every line.

'Well! My good—excuse me but I forget your name.'

'Elspeth, or mair commonly, Elspie Murray. A very gude name, doctor. The Murrays o' Perth* were——'

'No doubt—no doubt, Mrs Elsappy.'

'*Elspie*, sir. Ye maunna ca' me out o' my name, wi' your unceevil English tongue,' added the pertinacious old dame.

'Well, then, Elspie, or what the deuce you like,' said the doctor, vexed out of his proprieties. But his rosy face became rosier when he met the horrified and sternly reproachful stare of Elspie's keen blue eyes as she turned round—a whole volume of sermons expressed in her, 'Eh, sir?' Then she added, quietly,

'I'll thank ye no to speak ony mair sic words in the ears o' this puir innocent new-born lassie. It's no canny.'*

'Humph!—I suppose I must beg pardon again. I shall never get out what I wanted to say—which is, that you must be quiet, my good dame, and you must keep Mrs Rothesay quiet. She is a delicate young creature, you know, and must have every possible comfort that she needs.'

The doctor glanced round the room, as though there was scarce enough comfort for his notions of worldly necessity. Yet though not luxurious, the antechamber and the room half-revealed beyond it seemed to furnish all that could be needed by an individual of moderate fortune and desires. And an eye more romantic and poetic than that of the worthy medico might have found ample atonement for the want of rich furniture within, in the magnificent view without. The windows looked down on a lovely champaign, through which the many-winding Forth span its silver network, until, vanishing in the distance, a white sparkle here and there only showed whither the river wandered. In the distance, the blue mountains rose like dim clouds, marking the horizon. The foreground of this landscape was formed by the hill, castle-crowned—than which there is none in the world more beautiful or more renowned.

In short, Olive Rothesay shared with many a king and hero the honour of her place of nativity. She was born at Stirling.*

Perhaps this circumstance of birth has more influence over character than many matter-of-fact people would imagine. It is pleasant, in afterlife, to think that we first opened our eyes in a spot famous in the world's story, or remarkable for natural beauty. It is sweet to say, 'Those are *my* mountains', or 'This is *my* fair valley'; and there is a delight almost like that of a child who glories in his noble or beautiful parents, in the grand historical pride which links us to the place where we were born. So this little morsel of humanity, yet unnamed, whom by an allowable prescience we have called Olive, may perhaps be somewhat influenced in her nature by the fact that her cradle was rocked under the shadow of the hill of Stirling, and that the first breezes which fanned her baby brow came from the Highland mountains.

But the excellent presiding genius at this interesting advent 'cared for none of these things'. Dr Jacob Johnson stood at the window with his hands in his pockets—to him the wide beautiful world was merely a field for the exercise of the medical profession—a place where old women died, and children were born. He watched the shadows darkening over Ben Ledi*—calculating how much longer he ought in propriety to stay with his present patient, and whether he should have time to run home and take a cosy dinner and a bottle of port before he was again required.

'Our sweet young patient is taking a nice sleep, I think, nurse,' said he, at last, in his most benevolent tones.

'Ye may say that, doctor—ye ought to ken.'

'I might almost venture to leave her, except that she seems so lonely, without friends or attendance, save yourself.'

'And wha's the best nurse for Captain Angus Rothesay's wife and bairn, but the woman that nursed himsel?' said Elspie, lifting up her tall gaunt frame, and for the second time frowning the little doctor into confused silence. 'An' as for friends, ye suld just be unco' glad o' the chance that garr'd the leddy bide here, and no amang her ain folk. Else there wadna hae been sic a dowie welcome for her bonnie bairn. Maybe a waur, though, God forgie me'; added the woman to herself, with a sigh, as she once more half buried her little nursling in her capacious embrace.

'I have not the slightest doubt of Captain Rothesay's respectability,' answered Dr Johnson. *Respectability*! applied to the scions of a family which had had the honour of being nearly extirpated at Flodden-field, and again at Pinkie.* Had the trusty follower of the Rothesays heard the term, she certainly would have been inclined to annihilate the presumptuous Englishman. But she was fortunately engaged in stilling the cries of the poor infant, who, in return for the pains she took in undressing it, began to give full evidence that the weakness of its lungs was not at all proportionate to the smallness of its size.

'Crying will do it good. A fine child—a very fine child,' observed the doctor, as he made ready for his departure, while the nurse proceeded in her task, and the heap of white drapery was gradually removed, until from beneath it appeared the semblance of a very, very tiny specimen of babyhood.

'Ye needna trouble yoursel to say what's no true,' was the answer; 'it's just a bit bairnie—unco' sma'. An' that's nae wonder, considering the puir mither's trouble.'

'And the father is gone abroad?'

'Just twa months sin' syne. But eh! doctor, look ye here,' suddenly cried Elspie, as with her great, brown, but tender hand she was rubbing down the delicate little spine of the now quieted babe.

'Well—what's the matter now?' said Dr Johnson, rather sulkily, as he laid down his hat and gloves. 'The child is quite perfect, rather small perhaps, but as nice a little girl as ever was seen. It's all right.'

'It's no a' richt,' cried the nurse, in a tone trembling between anger and apprehension. 'Doctor, see!'

She pointed with her finger to a slight curve at the upper part of the spine, between the shoulder and neck. The doctor's professional anxiety was aroused—he came near and examined the little creature, with a countenance that grew graver each instant.

'Aweel?' said Elspie, enquiringly.

'I wish I had noticed this before; but it would have been no use,' he answered, his bland tones made earnest by real feeling.

'Eh, what?' said the nurse.

'I am sorry to say that the child is *deformed*—born so—and will remain so for life.'

At this terrible sentence Elspie sank back in her chair, overpowered with blank dismay. Then she started up, clasping the child convulsively, and faced the doctor.

'Ye lee, ye ugly creeping Englisher! How daur ye speak so of ane o' the Rothesays—frae whase blude cam the tallest men an' the bonniest leddies—ne'er a lamiter* amang them a'. How daur ye say that my master's bairn will be a——. Wae's me! I canna speak the word.'

'Poor woman!' mildly said the doctor, 'I am really concerned!' He looked so, and considerably frightened besides.

'Haud your tongue, ye fule!' muttered Elspie. While she again laid the child on her lap, and examined it earnestly for herself. The result confirmed all. She wrung her hands, and rocked to and fro, moaning aloud.

'Ochone, the wearie day! O, my dear master, my bairn, that I nursed on my knee! how will ye come back an' see your first-born, the last o' the Rothesays, a puir bit crippled lassie.'

A faint call from the inner room startled both doctor and nurse.

'Good Heavens!' exclaimed the former. 'We must think of the mother. Stay—I'll go. She does not, and she must not know of this. What a blessing that I told her the child was a fine and perfect child. Poor thing, poor thing!' he added, compassionately, as he hurried to his patient, leaving Elspie hushed into silence, still mournfully gazing on her charge.

It would have been curious to mark the changes in the nurse's face during that brief interval. At first it wore a look almost of repugnance as she regarded the unconscious child; and then that very unconsciousness seemed to awaken her womanly compassion.

'Puir hapless bairnie, ye little ken what ye're coming to! Lack o' kinsman's love, and lack o' siller,* and lack o' beauty. God forgie me—but why did He send ye into the waefu' warld at a'?'

It was a question, the nature of which has perplexed theologians, philosophers, and metaphysicians, in every age, and will perplex them all to the end of time. No wonder, therefore, that it could not be solved by the poor simple Scotswoman. But as she stood hushing the child to her breast, and looking vacantly out of the window at the far mountains which grew golden in the sunset, she was unconsciously soothed by the scene, and settled the matter in a way which wiser heads might often do with advantage.

'Aweel! He kens best wha's made the warld and a' that's in't; and maybe He will gie unto this puir wee thing a meek spirit to bear ill luck. Ane must wark, anither suffer. As the minister says, It'll a' come richt at last.'

Still the babe slept on, the sun sank, and night fell upon the earth. And so the morning and evening made the first day of the new existence, which was about to be developed, through all the various phases which compose that strange and touching mystery—a woman's life.

CHAPTER II

There is not a more hackneyed subject for poetic enthusiasm than that sight—perhaps the loveliest in nature—a young mother with her first-born child. And perhaps because it is so lovely, and is ever renewed in its beauty, the world never tires of dwelling thereupon.

Any poet, painter, or sculptor, would certainly have raved about Mrs Rothesay, had he seen her in the days of convalescence, sitting at the window with her baby on her knee. She furnished that rare sight—and one that is becoming rarer as the world grows older—an exquisitely beautiful woman. Would there were more of such!—that the ideal of physical beauty might pass into the heart through the eyes, and bring with it the ideal of the soul's perfection, which our senses can only thus receive. So great is this influence—so unconsciously do we associate the type of spiritual with material beauty, that perhaps the world might have been purer and better if its onward progress in what it calls civilization had not so nearly destroyed the fair mould of symmetry and loveliness which tradition celebrates.

It would have done any one's heart good only to look at Sybilla Rothesay. She was a creature to watch from a distance, and then to go away and dream of, scarce thinking whether she were a woman or a spirit. As for describing her, it is almost impossible—but let us try.

She was very small in stature and proportions—quite a little fairy. Her cheek had the soft peachy hue of girlhood; nay, of very childhood. You would never have thought her a mother. She lay back, half-buried in the great armchair; and then, suddenly springing up from amidst the cloud of white muslins and laces that enveloped her, she showed her young, blithe face.

'I will not have that cap, Elspie; I am not an invalid now, and I don't choose to be an old matron yet,' she said, in a pretty, wilful way, as she threw off the ugly ponderous production of her nurse's active fingers, and exhibited her beautiful head.

It was, indeed, a beautiful head! exquisite in shape, with masses of light brown hair folded round it. The little rosy ear peeped out, forming the commencement of that rare and dainty curve of chin and throat, so pleasant to an artist's eye. A beauty to be lingered over among all other beauties. Then the delicately outlined mouth, the lips folded over in a lovely gravity, that seemed ready each moment to melt away into smiles. Her nose—but who would destroy the romance of a beautiful woman by such an allusion? Of course, Mrs Rothesay had a nose; but it was so entirely in harmony with the rest of her face, that you never thought whether it were Roman, Grecian, or aquiline. Her eyes—

> She has two eyes, so soft and brown—
> She gives a side-glance and looks down.

But was there a soul in this exquisite frame? You never asked—you never cared! You took the thing for granted; and whether it were so or not, you felt that the world, and yourself especially, ought to be thankful for having looked at so lovely an image, if only to prove that earth still possessed such a thing as ideal beauty; and you forgave all the men, in every age, that have run mad for the same. Sometimes, perchance, you would pause a moment, to ask if this magic were real, and remember the calm, holy airs that breathed from the presence of some woman, beautiful only in her soul. But then you never would have looked upon Sybilla Rothesay as a women at all—only a flesh-and-blood fairy—a Venus de Medici* transmuted from the stone.

Perhaps this was the way in which Captain Angus Rothesay contrived to fall in love with Sybilla Hyde; until he woke from the dream to find his seraph of beauty—a baby–bride, pouting like a vexed child, because, in their sudden elopement, she had neither wedding-bonnet nor Brussels veil!*

And now she was a baby–mother; playing with her infant as, not so very long since, she had played with her doll; twisting its tiny fingers, and making them close tightly round her own, which were quite as elfin-like, comparatively. For Mrs Rothesay's surpassing beauty included beautiful hands and feet; a blessing which nature—often niggardly in her gifts—does not always extend to pretty women, but bestows it on those who have infinitely more reason to be thankful for the boon.

'See, nurse Elspie,' said Mrs Rothesay, laughing in her childish way; 'see how fast the little creature holds my finger! Really, I think a baby is a very pretty thing; and it will be so nice to play with until Angus comes home.'

Elspie turned round from the corner where she sat sewing, and looked with a half-suppressed sigh at her master's wife, whose delicate English beauty, and quick, ringing English voice, formed such a strong contrast to herself, and were so opposed to her own peculiar prejudices. But she had learned to love the young creature, nevertheless; and for the thousandth time she smothered the half-unconscious thought that Captain Angus might have chosen better.

'Children are a blessing frae the Lord, as maybe ye'll see, ane o' these days, Mrs Rothesay,' said Elspie, gravely; 'ye maun tak' them as they're sent, and mak' the best o' them.'

Mrs Rothesay laughed merrily. 'Thank you, Elspie, for giving me such a solemn speech, just like one of my husband's. To put me in mind of him, I suppose. As if there were any need for that! Dear Angus! I wonder what he will say to his little daughter when he sees her; the new Miss Rothesay, who has come in opposition to the old Miss Rothesay—ha! ha!'

'The auld Miss Rothesay! Ye speak a wee bit too lightly, seeing she's your husband's aunt,' observed Elspie, feeling it necessary to stand up for the honour of the family. 'Miss Flora was a braw,* braw leddy ance, as a' and Rothesays aye were.'

'And this Miss Rothesay will be too, I hope, though she is such a little brown thing now. But people say that the brownest babies grow the fairest in time, eh, nurse?'

'They do say that,' replied Elspie, with another and a heavier sigh; while she bent closer over her work, and her hard coarse features softened into a look of deepest compassion.

Mrs Rothesay went on in her blithe chatter. 'I half wished for a boy, as Captain Rothesay thought it would please his uncle; but that's of no consequence. He will be quite satisfied with a girl, and so am I. Of course she will be a beauty, my dear little baby!' And with a deeper shadowing of mother-love piercing through her childish pleasure, she bent over the infant; then took it up, awkwardly and comically enough, as though it were a toy she was afraid of breaking, and rocked it to and fro on her breast.

Elspie started up. 'Tak' care, tak' care! ye'll hurt it, maybe, the puir wee—— Oh, what was I gaun to say!' and she stopped hastily, with an expression of anguish which showed how hard was concealment to her honest nature.

'Don't trouble yourself,' said the young mother, with a charming assumption of matronly dignity; 'I shall hold the baby safe. I know all about it.'

And she really did succeed in lulling the child to sleep; which was no sooner accomplished than she recommenced her pleasant musical chatter, partly addressed to her nurse, but chiefly the unconscious overflow of a simple nature which could not conceal a single thought.

'I wonder what I shall call her—the darling! We must not wait until her papa comes home. She can't be "baby" for three years. I shall have to decide on her name myself. Oh, what a pity! I, who never could decide anything. Poor dear Angus! he does all—he had even to fix the wedding day!' And her musical laugh—another rare charm that she possessed—caused Elspie to look round with mingled pity and affection.

'Come, nurse; you can help me, I know. I am puzzling my poor head for a name to give this young lady here. It must be a very pretty one. I wonder what Angus would like? A family name, perhaps, after one of those old Rothesays that you and he make so much of.'

'Oh, Mrs Rothesay! And are ye no proud o' your husband's family?' said Elspie, reproachfully.

'Yes, very proud; especially as I have none of my own. He took me—an orphan, without a single tie in the wide world—he took me into his warm loving arms'—here her voice faltered, and a sweet womanly tenderness softened her eyes. 'God bless my noble husband! I *am* proud of him, and of his people, and of all his race.* So come,' she added, her childish manner reviving, 'tell me of the remarkable women in the Rothesay family for the last five hundred years—you know all about them, Elspie. Surely we'll find one to be a namesake for my baby.'

Elspie—pleased and important—began eagerly to relate long traditions about the Lady Christina Rothesay, who was a witch, and a great friend of 'Maister Michael Scott', and how, with spells, she caused her seven stepsons to pine away and die; also the Lady Isobel, who let her lover down from her bower window with the long strings of her golden hair; and how her brother found and slew him;—whence she laid a curse on all the line who had golden hair, and such never prospered, but died unmarried and young.

'I hope the curse has passed away now,' gaily said the young mother, 'and that the latest scion will not be a golden-tressed damsel. Yet look here'—and she touched the soft down beneath her infant's cap, which might, by a considerable exercise of imagination, be called hair—'it is yellow, you see, Elspie! But I'll not believe your tradition. My child shall be both beautiful and beloved.'

Smitten with a sudden pang, poor Elspie cried, 'Oh my leddy, dinna think o' the future. Dinna!——' and she stopped, confused.

'Really, how strange you are. But go on. We'll have no more Christinas nor Isobels.'

Hurriedly, Elspie continued to relate the histories: of noble Jean Rothesay, who died by an arrow aimed at her husband's heart; and Alison, her sister, the beauty of James the Fifth's reckless court,* who was 'no gude'; and Mistress Katharine Rothesay,* who hid two of 'the Prince's' soldiers after Culloden,* and stood with a pair of pistols before their bolted door.

'Nay, I'll have none of these—they frighten me,' cried Sybilla, hiding her pretty face with a pretended alarm; 'I wonder I ever had courage to marry the descendant of such awful women. No! my sweet innocent! you shall not be christened after them,' she continued, stroking the baby-cheek with her soft finger. 'You shall not be like them at all, except in their beauty. And they were all handsome—were they, Elspie?'

'Ne'er a ane o' the Rothesay line, man or woman, that wasna fair to see—the fairest in the land,' cried Elspie.

'Then so will my baby be!—like her father, I hope—or just a little like her mother, who is not so very ugly, either; at least, Augus says not.' And with a charming consciousness, Mrs Rothesay drew up her tiny figure, patted one dainty hand—the wedded one—with its fairy fellow; then— touched perhaps with a passing melancholy that he who most prized her beauty, and for whose sake she most prized it herself, was far away—she leaned back and sighed.

However, in a few minutes, she cried out, her words showing how light and wandering was the reverie, 'Elspie, I have a thought! The baby shall be christened Olive!'

'It's a strange, heathen name, Mrs Rothesay.'

'Not at all. Listen how I chanced to think of it. This very morning, just before you came to waken me, I had such a queer, delicious dream.'

'Dream! Are ye sure it was i' the morning-tide?' cried Elspie, aroused into interest.

'Yes; and so it certainly means something, you will say, Elspie? Well, it was about my baby. She was then lying fast asleep in my bosom, and her warm, soft breathing soon sent me to sleep too. I dreamt that somehow I had gradually let her go from me, so that I felt her in my arms no more, and I was very sad, and cried out how cruel it was for any one to steal my child, until I found I had let her go of my own accord. Then I looked up, after awhile, and saw standing at the foot of the bed a little angel—a child-angel—with a green olive-branch in its hand. It told me to follow; so I rose up, and followed it over a wide desert country, and across rivers and among wild beasts; but at every peril the child held out the olive-branch, and we passed on safely. And when I felt weary, and my feet were bleeding with the rough journey, the little angel touched them with the olive, and I was strong again. At last we reached a beautiful valley, and the child said, "You are quite safe now." I answered, "And who is my beautiful comforting angel?" Then the white wings fell off, and I only saw a sweet child's face, which bore something of Angus's likeness and something of my own, and the little one stretched out her hands and said, "Mother!"'

While Mrs Rothesay spoke, her thoughtless manner had once more softened into deep feeling. Elspie watched her with wondering eagerness.

'It was nae dream; it was a vision. God send it true,' said the old woman, solemnly.

'I know not. Augus always laughed at my dreams, but I have a strange feeling whenever I think of this. Oh, Elspie, you can't tell how sweet it was! And so I should like to call my baby Olive, for the sake of the beautiful angel. It may be foolish—but 'tis a fancy of mine. Olive Rothesay! It sounds well, and Olive Rothesay she shall be.'

'Amen; and may she be an angel to ye a' her days. And ye'll mind o' the blessed dream, and love her evermair. Oh, my sweet leddy, promise me that ye will!' cried the nurse, approaching her mistress's chair, while two great tears stole down her hard cheeks.

'Of course I shall love her dearly! What made you doubt it? Because I am so young? Nay, I have a mother's heart, though I am only eighteen. Come, Elspie, do let us be merry; send these drops away'; and she patted the old withered face with her little hand. 'Was it not you who told me the saying, "It's ill greeting ower a new-born wean." There! don't I succeed charmingly in your northern tongue?'

What a winning little creature she was, this young wife of Angus Rothesay! Probably the only person who did not think so was the old Highland uncle, Miss Flora's brother, who had disinherited his nephew and promised heir for bringing him a *Sassenach** niece.

'A charming scene of maternal felicity! I am quite sorry to intrude upon it,' said a bland voice at the door, as Dr Johnson put in his shining bald head.

Mrs Rothesay welcomed him in her graceful, cordial way. She was so ready to cling to every one who showed her kindness—and he had been very kind; so kind that, with her usual quick impulses, she had determined to stay and live at Stirling until her husband's return from Jamaica. She told Dr Johnson so now; and, moreover, as an earnest of the friendship which she, accustomed to be loved by every one, expected from him, she requested him to stand godfather to her little babe.

'She shall be christened after our English fashion, doctor, and her name shall be Olive. What do you think of her now? Is she growing prettier?'

The doctor bowed a smiling assent, and walked to the window. Thither Elspie followed him.

'Ye maun tell her the truth—I daurna. Ye will?' and she clutched his arm with eager anxiety. 'An' oh! for Godsake, say it saftly, kindly. Think o' the puir mither.'

He shook her off with an uneasy look. He had never felt in a more disagreeable position.

Mrs Rothesay called him back again. 'I think, doctor, her features are improving. She will certainly be a beauty. I should break my heart if she were not. And what would Angus say? Come—what are you and Elspie talking about so mysteriously?'

'My dear madam—hem!' began Dr Johnson. 'I do hope—indeed, I am sure—your child will be a good child, and a great comfort to both her parents——'

'Certainly—but how grave you are about it.'

'I have a painful duty—a very painful duty,' he replied. But Elspie pushed him aside.

'Ye're just a fule, man!—ye'll kill her. Say your say at ance!'

The young mother turned deadly pale. 'Say *what*, Elspie? What is he going to tell me? Angus——'

'No, no, my darlin' leddy! your husband's safe'; and Elspie flung herself on her knees beside the chair. 'But, the bairnie—(dinna fear, for it's the will o' God, and a' for gude, nae doubt)—the sweet wee bairnie is——'

'Is, I grieve to say it, deformed,' added Dr Johnson.

The poor mother gazed incredulously on him, on the nurse, and lastly on the sleeping child. Then, without a word, she fell back, and fainted in Elspie's arms.

CHAPTER III

It was many days before Mrs Rothesay recovered from the shock occasioned by the tidings—to her almost more fearful than her child's death—that it was doomed for life to suffer the curse of hopeless deformity. For a curse, a bitter curse, this seemed to the young and beautiful creature, who had learned since her birth to consider beauty as the greatest good. She was, so to speak, in love with loveliness; not merely in herself, but in every human creature. This feeling sprung more from enthusiasm than from personal vanity, the borders of which meanness she had just touched, but never crossed. Perhaps, also, she was too conscious of her own loveliness, and admired herself too ardently to care for attracting the petty admiration of others. She took it quite as a matter of course; and was no more surprised at being worshipped than if she had been the Goddess of Beauty herself.

But if Sybilla Rothesay gloried in her own perfections, she no less gloried in those of all she loved, and chiefly in her noble-looking husband. And they were so young and impassioned, so quickly wed and so soon parted, that this emotion had no time to deepen into that soul-united affection which is independent of outward semblance; or, rather, becomes so divine, that instead of beauty creating love, love has power to create beauty.

No marvel then, that not having attained to a higher experience, Sybilla considered beauty as all in all. And this child—her child and Angus's, would be a deformity on the face of the earth, a shame to its parents, a dishonour to its race. How should she ever bear to look upon it?

Still more, how should she ever dare to show the poor cripple to its father, and say, 'This is our child—our first-born.' Would he not turn away in disgust, and answer that it had better died?

Such exaggerated fancies as these haunted the miserable and erring mother, when she passed from her long swoon into a sort of fever; which, though scarce endangering her life, was yet for days a source of great anxiety to the devoted Elspie. To the unhappy infant this madness—for it was temporary madness—almost caused death. Mrs Rothesay positively refused to see or notice her child, scorning alike the tearful entreaties and the stern reproaches of the nurse. At last Elspie ceased to combat this passionate resolve, springing half from anger and half from delirium—

'God forgie ye, and save the innocent bairn—the dochter He gave, and the whilk ye're like to murder—unthankfu' woman as ye are,' muttered Elspie, under her breath, as she quitted the room and went to succour the almost dying babe. Over it her heart yearned as it had never yearned before.

'Your mither casts ye aff, ye puir wee thing. Maybe ye're no lang for this warld, but while ye're in it ye sall be my ain lassie, an' I'll be your ain mammie, evermair.'

So, like Naomi of old, Elspie Murray 'laid the child in her bosom and became nurse unto it'. But for her, the life of our Olive Rothesay—with all its influences, good or evil, small or great, as yet unknown—would have expired like a faint-flickering taper.

Perhaps, in her madness, the unhappy mother might almost have desired such an ending. As it was, the disappointed hope, which had at first resembled positive dislike, subsided into the most complete indifference. She endured her child's presence, but she took no notice of it; she seemed to have forgotten its very existence. Her shattered health supplied sufficient excuse for the utter abandonment of all a mother's duties, and the poor feeble spark of life was left to Elspie's cherishing. By night and by day the child knew no other resting-place than the old nurse's arms, the mother's seeming to be for ever closed to its helpless innocence. True, Sybilla kissed it once a day, when Elspie brought the little creature to her, and exacted, as a duty, the recognition which Mrs Rothesay, girlish and yielding as she was, dared not refuse. Her husband's faithful retainer had over her an influence which could never be gainsaid.

Elspie seemed to be the sole regent of the babe's destiny. It was she who took it to its baptism;—not the festal ceremony which had pleased Sybilla's childish fancy with visions of christening robes and cakes, but the beautiful and simple 'naming' of Elspie's own church.* She stood before the minister, holding the desolate babe in her protecting arms; and there her heart sealed the promise of her lips, to bring it up in the knowledge and fear of God. And with an earnest credulity, which contained the germs of purest and loftiest faith, she, remembering the mother's dream, called her nursling by the name of Olive.

She carried the babe home and laid it on Mrs Rothesay's lap. The young creature, who had so strangely renounced that dearest blessing of mother-love, would fain have put the child aside; but Elspie's stern eye controlled her.

'Ye maun kiss and bless your dochter. Nae tongue but her mither's suld ca' her by her new-christened name.'

'What name?'

'The name ye gied her yer ain sel.'

'No, no. Surely you have not called her so. Take her away; she is not my sweet angel-baby—the darling in my dream.' And Sybilla hid her face; not in anger, or disgust, but in bitter weeping.

'She's your ain dochter—Olive Rothesay,' answered Elspie, less harshly. 'She may be an angel to ye, yet.'

While she spoke, it so chanced that there flitted over the infant face one of those smiles that we see sometimes in young children—strange, causeless smiles, which seem the reflection of some invisible influence.

And so, while the babe smiled, there came to its face such an angel brightness, that it shone into the mother's careless heart. For the first time since that mournful day which had so changed her nature, Sybilla Rothesay sat down and kissed the child of her own accord. Elspie heard no maternal blessing—the name of 'Olive' was never breathed; but the nurse was satisfied when she saw that the babe's second baptism was its mother's repentant tears.

There was in Sybilla no hardness or cruelty, only the disappointment and vexation of a child deprived of an expected toy. She might have grown weary of her little daughter almost as soon, even if her pride and hope had not been crushed by the knowledge of Olive's deformity. Love to her seemed a treasure to be paid in requital, not a free gift bestowed without thought of return. That self-forgetting maternal devotion, lavished first on unconscious infancy, and then on unregarding youth, was a mystery to her utterly incomprehensible. At least it seemed so now, when, with the years and the character of a child, she was called to the highest duty of woman's life. This duty comes to some girlish mothers as an instinct, but it was not so with Mrs Rothesay. An orphan, and heiress to a competence, if not to wealth, she had been brought up like a plant in a hot-bed, with all natural impulses either warped and suppressed, or forced into undue luxuriance. And yet it was a sweet plant withal; one that might have grown, ay, and might yet grow, into perfect strength and beauty.

Mrs Rothesay's education—that education of heart, and mind, and temper, which is essential to a woman's happiness—had to begin when it ought to have been completed—at her marriage. Most unfortunate it was for her, that ere the first twelvemonth of their wedded life had passed, Captain Rothesay was forced to depart for Jamaica, whence was derived his wife's little fortune; their whole fortune now, for he had quitted the army on his marriage. Thus Sybilla was deprived of that wholesome influence which man has ever over a woman who loves him, and by which he may, if he so will, counteract many a fault and weakness in her disposition.

Time passed on, and Mrs Rothesay, a wife and mother, was at twenty-one years old just the same as she had been at seventeen—as girlish, as thoughtless, eager for any amusement, and often treading on the very verge of folly. She still lived at Stirling, enforced thereunto by the entreaties, almost the commands, of Elspie Murray, against whom she bitterly murmured sometimes, for shutting her up in such a dull Scotch town. When Elspie urged her unprotected situation, the necessity of living in retirement, for the 'honour of the family', while Captain Angus was away, Mrs Rothesay sometimes frowned, but more often put the matter off with a merry jest. Meanwhile she consoled herself by going as much into society as the limited circle of Dr and Mrs Johnson allowed; and therein, as usual, the lovely, gay, winning young creature was spoiled to her heart's content.

So she still lived the life of a wayward, petted child, whose natural instinct for all things good and beautiful kept her from ever doing what was positively wrong, though she did a great deal that was foolish enough in its way. She was, as she jestingly said, 'a widow bewitched'; but she rarely coquetted, and then only in that innocent way which comes natural to some women, from a universal desire to please. And she never ceased talking and thinking of her beautiful, noble Angus.

When his letters came, she always made a point of kissing them half-a-dozen times, and putting them under her pillow at night, just like a child! And she wrote to him regularly once a month—pretty, playful, loving letters. But there was in them one peculiarity,—they were utterly free from that delicious maternal egotism which chronicles all the little incidents of babyhood. She said, in answer to her husband's questions, that 'Olive was well'; 'Olive could just walk'; 'Olive had learned to say "*Papa* and *Elspie*".' Nothing more.

The fatal secret she had not dared to tell him.

Her first letters—full of joy about 'the loveliest baby that ever was seen'—had brought his in return echoing the rapture with truly paternal pride. They reached her in her misery, to which they added tenfold. Every sentence smote her with bitter regret, even with shame, as though it were her fault in having given to the world the wretched child. Captain Rothesay expressed his joy that his little daughter was not only healthy, but pretty; for, he said, 'He should be quite unhappy if she did not grow up as beautiful as her mother.' The words pierced Sybilla's heart; she could not—dared not tell him the truth; not yet, at least. And whenever Elspie's rough honesty urged her to do so, she fell into such agonies of grief and anger, that the nurse was obliged to desist.

Sometimes, when letter after letter came from the father, full of enquiries about his precious first-born,—Sybilla, whose fault was more in weakness than deceit, resolved that she would nerve herself for the terrible task. But it was vain—she had not strength to do it.

The three years extended into four, and still Captain Rothesay sent gift after gift, and message after message, to his daughter. Still he wrote to the conscience-stricken mother how many times he had kissed the 'little lock of golden hue', severed from the baby-head; picturing the sweet face and lithe, active form which he had never seen. And all the while there was stealing about the old house at Stirling, a pale, deformed child; small and attenuated in frame—quiet beyond its years, delicate, spiritless, with scarce one charm that would prove its lineage from the young beautiful mother, out of whose sight it instinctively crept.

Thus the years fled with Olive Rothesay and her parents; each month, each day, sowing seeds that would assuredly spring up, for good or for evil, in the destinies of all three.

CHAPTER IV

The fourth year of Captain Rothesay's absence passed—not without anxiety, for it was wartime, and his letters were frequently interrupted. At first, whenever this happened, his wife fretted extremely—*fretted* is the right word, for it was more a fitful chafing than a positive grief. Sybilla knew not the sense of deep sorrow. Her nature resembled one of those sunny climes where even the rains are dews. So, after a few disappointments, she composed herself to the certainty that nothing would happen amiss to her Angus; and she determined never to expect a letter until she received it, and not to look for *him* at all until he wrote her word that he was coming. He was sure to do what was right, and to return to his dearly loved wife as soon as ever he could. And, though scarce acknowledging the fact to herself, her husband's return involved such a humiliating explanation of truth concealed, if not of positive falsehood, that Sybilla dared not even think of it. Whenever the long-parted wife mused on the joy of meeting—of looking once more into the beloved face, and being lifted up like a child to cling round his neck with her fairy arms, for Angus was a very giant to her—then there seemed to rise between them the phantom of the pale, deformed child.

To drown these fancies, Sybilla rushed into every amusement which her secluded life afforded. At last she resolved on an exploit at which Elspie looked aghast, and which made the quiet Mrs Johnson shake her head—an evening party—nay, even a dance, at her own home.

'It will never do for the people here; they're "*unco gude*",' said the doctor's English wife, who had imbibed a few Scottish prejudices by a residence of thirty years. 'Nobody ever dances in Stirling.'

'Then I'll teach them,' cried the lively Mrs Rothesay; 'I long to show them a quadrille—even that new dance that all the world is shocked at. Oh! I should dearly like a waltz.'

Mrs Jacob Johnson was scandalized at first, but there was something in Sybilla to which she could not say nay—nobody ever could. The matter was decided by Mrs Rothesay's having her own way, except with regard to the waltz, which her friend stanchly resisted. Elspie, too, interfered as long as she could; but her heart was just now full of anxiety about her nursling, who seemed to grow more delicate every year. Day after day the faithful nurse might have been seen trudging across the country, carrying little Olive in her arms, to strengthen the child with the healing springs of Bridge of Allan,* and invigorate her weak frame with the fresh mountain air—the heather breath of beautiful Ben-Ledi. Among these influences did Olive's childhood dawn, so that in after-life they never faded from her.

Elspie scarce thought again about the gay party, until when she came in one evening, and was undressing the sleepy little girl in the dusk, a vision appeared at the nursery door. It quite startled the old Scotswoman at first, it looked so like a fairy apparition, all in white, with a green coronet. She hardly could believe that it was her young mistress.

'Eh! Mrs Rothesay, ye're no goin' to show yoursel in sic a dress,' she cried, regarding with horror the gleaming bare arms, the lovely neck, and the tiny white-sandalled feet, which the short and airy robe exhibited in all their perfection.

'Indeed, but I am! and 'tis quite a treat to wear a ball-dress. I, that have been smothered up in all sorts of ugly costume for nearly five years. And see my jewels! Why, Elspie, this pearl-set has only beheld the light once since I was married—so beautiful as it is—and Angus's gift too.'

'Dinna say that name,' cried Elspie, driven to a burst of not very respectful reproach. 'I marvel ye daur speak of Captain Angus—and ye, wi' your havers* and your jigs,* while yer husband's far awa', and your bairn sick! It's for nae gude I tell ye, Mrs Rothesay.'

Sybilla had looked a little subdued at the allusion to her husband, but the moment Elspie mentioned the little Olive, her manner changed. 'You are always blaming me about the child, and I will not bear it. She is quite well. Are you not, Baby?'—the mother never would call her *Olive.*

A feeble, trembling voice answered from the little bed, 'Yes, please, mamma!'

'There, you hear, Elspie! Now, don't torment me any more about her. But I must go downstairs.'

She danced across the room in a graceful waltzing step, held out her hand towards the child, and touched one so tiny, cold, and damp, that she felt half inclined to take and warm it in her own. But Elspie's hawk-eyes were watching her, and she was ashamed. So she only said, 'Good night, Baby!' and danced back again, out through the open door.

For hours Elspie sat in the dark room beside the bed of the little child, who lay murmuring, sometimes moaning, in her sleep. She never did moan but in her sleep, poor innocent! The sound of music and dancing rose up from below, and then Mrs Rothesay's clear, bird-like voice was heard in many a blithe ditty.

'Ye'd better be hushin' your puir wee bairnie here, ye heartless woman!' muttered Elspie, who grew daily more jealous over the forsaken child, now the very darling of her old age. She knew not that her love for Olive, and its open tokens shown by reproaches to Olive's mother, were sure to suppress any dawning tenderness that might be awakened in Mrs Rothesay's bosom.

It had not done so yet, for many a time during the dance and song did the touch of that little cold hand haunt the young mother, rousing a feeling akin to remorse. But she threw it off again and again, and entered with the gaiety of her nature into all the evening's pleasure. Her wild enjoyment was at its height, when an old acquaintance, just discovered— an English officer, quartered at the Castle—proposed a waltz. Before she had time to say 'Yes' or 'No', the music struck up one of those enchanting waltz-measures which, to all true lovers of dancing, are as irresistible as Maurice Connor's 'Wonderful Tune'. Sybilla felt again the same blithe young creature of sixteen, who had led the revels at her first ball, dancing into the heart of one old colonel, six ensigns, a doctor, a lawyer, and of Angus Rothesay. There was no resisting the impulse: in a moment she was whirling away.

In the midst of the dizzy round the door opened, and, like some evil spectre, in stalked Elspie Murray.

Never was there such an uncouth apparition seen in a ballroom. Her grey petticoat exhibited her bare feet; her short upper gown, that graceful and picturesque attire of the Scottish peasantry, was thrown carelessly over her shoulders; her *mutch** was put on awry, and from under its immense border her face appeared, as white almost as the cap itself. She walked right into the centre of the floor, laid her heavy hand on Sybilla's shoulder, and said,

'Mrs Rothesay, your husband's here!'

The young wife stood one moment transfixed; she turned pale, afterwards crimson, and then, uttering a cry of joy, sprang to the door—sprang into her husband's arms.

Dazzled with the light, the traveller resisted not, while Elspie half led, half dragged him—still clasping his wife—into a little room close by, when she shut the door and left them. Then she burst in once more among the astonished guests.

'Ye may gang your gate,* ye heathens! Awa wi' ye, for Captain Rothesay's come hame!'

Sybilla and her husband stood face to face in the little gloomy room, lighted only by a solitary candle. At first she clung about him so closely that he could not see her face, though he felt her tears falling, and her little heart beating against his own. He knew it was all for joy. But he was strangely bewildered by the scene which had flashed for a minute before his eyes, while standing at the door of the room.

After a while he drew his wife to the light, and held her out at arm's length to look at her. Then, for the first time, she remembered all. Trembling—blushing scarlet, over face and neck—she perceived her husband's eyes rest on her glittering dress. He regarded her fixedly, from head to foot. She felt his expression change from joy to uneasy wonder, from love to sternness, and then he wore a strange, cold look, such a one as she had never beheld in him before.

'So, the young lady I saw whirling madly in some man's arms—was you, Sybilla—was *my wife*.'

As Captain Rothesay spoke, Sybilla distinguished in his voice a new tone, echoing the strange coldness in his eyes. She sprang to his neck, weeping now for grief and alarm, as she had before wept for joy; she prayed him to forgive her, told him with a sincerity that none could doubt, how rejoiced she was at his coming, and how dearly she loved him—now and ever. He kissed her, at her passionate entreaty; said he had nothing to blame; suffered her caresses patiently; but the impression was given, the deed was done.

While he lived, Captain Rothesay never forgot that night. Nor did Sybilla; for then she had first seen that cold, stern look and heard that altered tone. How many times was it to haunt her afterwards!

CHAPTER V

Next morning Captain Rothesay and his wife sat together by the fireside, where she had so often sat alone. Sybilla seemed in high spirits—her love was ever exuberant in expression—and the moment her husband seemed serious she sprang on his knee and looked playfully in his face.

'Just as much a child as ever, I see,' said Angus Rothesay, with a rather wintry smile.

And then, looking in his face by daylight, Sybilla had opportunity to see how changed he was. He had become a grave, middle-aged man. She could not understand it. He had never told her of any cares, and he was little more than thirty. She felt almost vexed at him for growing so old; nay, she even said so, and began to pull out a few grey hairs that defaced the beauty of his black curls.

'You shall lecture me presently, my dear,' said Captain Rothesay. 'You forget that I had two welcomes to receive, and that I have not yet seen the little girl.'

He had not indeed. His eager enquiries after Olive overnight had been answered by a pretty pout, and several trembling, anxious speeches about 'a wife being dearer than a child'. 'Baby was asleep, and it was so very late—he might, surely, wait till morning.' To which, though rather surprised, he assented. A few more caresses, a few more excuses, had still further delayed the terrible moment; until at last the father's impatience would no longer be restrained.

'Come, Sybilla, let us go and see our little Olive.'

'Oh, Angus!' and the mother turned deadly white.

Captain Rothesay seemed alarmed. 'Don't trifle with me, Sybilla—there is nothing the matter? The child is not ill?'

'No; quite well.'

'Then, why cannot Elspie bring her?' and he pulled the bell violently. The nurse appeared. 'My good Elspie, you have kept me waiting quite long enough; do let me see my little girl.'

Elspie gave one glance at the mother, who stood mute and motionless, clinging to the chair for support. In that glance was less compassion than a sort of triumphant exultation. When she quitted the room Sybilla flung herself at her husband's feet.

'Angus, Angus, only say you forgive me, before——'

The door opened, and Elspie led in a little girl. By her stature she might have been two years old, but her face was like that of a child of ten or twelve—so thoughtful, so grave. Her limbs were small and wasted, but exquisitely delicate. The same might be said of her features; which, though thin, and wearing a look of premature age, together with that quiet, earnest, melancholy cast peculiar to deformity, were yet regular, almost pretty. Her head was well shaped, and from it fell a quantity of amber-coloured hair—pale 'lint-white locks', which, with the almost colourless transparency of her complexion, gave a spectral air to her whole appearance. She looked less like a child than a woman dwarfed into childhood; the sort of being renowned in elfin legends, as springing up on a lonely moor, or appearing by a cradle-side; supernatural, yet fraught with a nameless beauty. She was dressed with the utmost care, in white, with blue ribands; and her lovely hair was arranged so as to hide, as much as possible, the defect, which, alas! was even then only too perceptible. It was not a humpback, nor yet a twisted spine; it was an elevation of the shoulders, shortening the neck, and giving the appearance of a perpetual stoop. There was nothing disgusting or painful in it, but still it was an imperfection, causing an instinctive compassion—an involuntary 'Poor little creature, what a pity!'

Such was the child—the last daughter of the ever-beautiful Rothesay line*—which Elspie led to claim the paternal embrace. Olive looked up at her father with her wistful, pensive eyes, in which was no childish shyness—only wonder. He met them with a gaze of frenzied unbelief. Then his fingers clutched his wife's arm with the grasp of an iron vice.

'Tell me! for God's sake, deceive me no longer. Is that our daughter, Olive Rothesay?'

She answered, 'Yes.' He shook her off angrily, looked once more at the child, and then turned away, putting his hand before his eyes, as if to shut out the sight.

Olive saw the gesture. Young as she was, it went deep to her child's soul. Elspie saw it too, and without bestowing a second glance on her master or his wife, she snatched up the child and hurried from the room.

The father and mother were left alone—to meet that crisis most fatal to wedded happiness, the discovery of the first deceit. Captain Rothesay sat silent, with averted face; Sybilla was weeping—not that repentant shower which rains softness into a man's heart, but those fretful tears which chafe him beyond endurance.

'Sybilla, come to me!' The words were a fond husband's words; the tone was that of a master who took on himself his prerogative. Never had Angus spoken so before, and the wilful spirit of his wife rebelled.

'I cannot come. I dare not even look at you. You are so angry.'

His only answer was the reiterated command, 'Sybilla, come!' She crept from the far end of the room, where she was sobbing in a fear-stricken, childish way, and stood before him. For the first time she recognized her husband, whom she must 'obey'. Now, with all the power of his roused nature, he was teaching her the meaning of the word. 'Sybilla,' he said, looking sternly in her face, 'tell me why, all these years, you have put upon me this cheat—this lie!'

'Cheat!—lie! Oh, Angus! What cruel, wicked words!'

'I am sorry I used them, then. I will choose a lighter term—deceit. Why did you so *deceive* your husband?'

'I did not mean it,' sobbed the young wife. 'And this is very unkind of you, Angus! As if Heaven had not punished me enough in giving me that miserable child!'

'Silence! I am not speaking of the child, but of you; my wife, in whom I trusted; who for five long years has wilfully deceived me. Why did you so?'

'Because I was afraid—ashamed. But those feelings are past now,' said Sybilla, resolutely. 'If Heaven made me mother, it made you father to this unhappy child. You have no right to reproach me.'

'God forbid! No, it is not the misfortune—it is the falsehood which stings me. All these five years I have toiled and toiled—comforting myself with thoughts of you and our child, dreaming over your letters—oh, Heaven! what a dupe I have been!'

And his grave, mournful tone, rose into one of bitter anger. He paced the room, tossed by a passion such as his wife had never before seen.

'Sybilla!' he suddenly cried, pausing before her; 'you do not know what you have done. You little think what my love has been, nor against how much it has struggled these five years. I have been true to you—ay, to the depth of my heart. And you to me have been—not wholly true.'

Here he was answered by a burst of violent hysterical weeping. He longed to call for feminine assistance to this truly feminine ebullition, which he did not understand. But his pride forbade. So he tried to soothe his wife a little with softer words, though even these seemed somewhat foreign to his lips, after so many long-parted years.

'I did not mean to pain you thus deeply, Sybilla. I do not say that you have ceased to love me!'

Would that Sybilla had done as her first impulse taught her; have clung about him, crying 'Never! never!' murmuring penitent words, as a tender wife may well do, and in such humility be the more exalted! But she had still the wayward spirit of a petted child. Fancying she saw her husband once more at her feet, she determined to keep him there. She wept on, refusing to be pacified.

At last Angus rose from her side, dignified and cold, his new, not his old self; the lover no more, but the quiet, half-indifferent husband. 'I see we had better not talk of these things until you are more composed—perhaps, indeed, not at all. What is past—is past, and cannot be recalled.'

'Angus!' She looked up, frightened at his grave manner. She determined to conciliate him a little. 'What do you want me to do? To say I am sorry? That I will—but,' she added with an air of coquettish command, 'you must say so too.'

The jest was ill-timed; he was in too bitter a mood. 'I thank you, but you exact too much, Mrs Rothesay,'

'*Mrs Rothesay*! oh, call me Sybilla, or my heart will break!' cried the young creature, throwing herself into his arms. He did not repulse her; he even looked down upon her with a melting, half reproachful tenderness.

'How happy we might have been! How different had been this coming home if you had only trusted me, and told me all from the beginning.'

'Have you told *me*? Is there nothing you have kept back from me these five years?' said the young wife, in her pretty, wilful way.

He started a little, and then said resolutely, 'Nothing, Sybilla! I declare to Heaven—nothing! save, perhaps, some trifles that I would at any time tell you; now, if you will.'

'Oh no! some other time, I am too much exhausted now,' murmured Sybilla, with an air of languor, half real, half feigned, lest perchance she should lose what she had gained. In the sweetness of this reconciled 'lovers' quarrel', she had almost forgotten its hapless cause. But Angus, after a pause of deep and evidently conflicting thoughts, referred to the child.

'She is ours still. I must not forget that. Shall I send for her again?' he said, as if he wished to soothe the mother's wounded feelings.

Alas, in Sybilla's breast the fountain of mother's feeling was as yet all sealed. 'Send for Olive?' she said, 'oh no! Do not, I implore you. The very sight of her is a pain to me. Let us be happy together, and let the child be left to Elspie.'

Thus she said, thinking not only to save herself, but him, from what must be a constant pang. Little she knew him, or guessed the after-effect of her words.

Angus Rothesay looked at his wife, first with amazement, then with cold displeasure. 'My dear, you scarce speak like a mother. You forget, likewise, that you are speaking to a father. A father who, whatever affection may be wanting, will never forsake his duty. Come, let us go and see our child.'

'I cannot—I cannot!' and Sybilla hung back, weeping anew.

Angus Rothesay looked at his wife—the pretty, wayward idol of his bridegroom-memory—looked at her with the eyes of a world-tried, world-hardened man. She regarded him too, and noted the change which years had brought in her almost boyish lover of yore. His eye wore a fretful reproach—his brow, a proud sorrow.

He walked up to her and clasped her hand. 'Sybilla, take care! All these years I have been dreaming of the wife and mother I should find here at home; let not the dream prove sweeter than the reality.'

Sybilla was annoyed—she, the spoiled darling of every one, who knew not the meaning of a harsh word. She answered, 'Don't let us talk so foolishly.'

'You think it foolish? Well, then! we will not speak in this confidential way any more,' said Angus, shrinking back into his reserve. 'I promise, and you know I always keep my promises.'

'I am glad of it,' answered Sybilla. But she lived to rue the day when her husband made this one promise.

At present, she only felt that the bitter secret was disclosed, and Angus's anger overpast. She gladly let him quit the room, only pausing to ask him to kiss her, in token that all was right between them. He did so, kindly, though with a certain pride and gravity—and departed. She dared not ask him whether it was to see again their hapless child.

What passed between the father and mother whilst they remained shut up together there, Elspie thought not—cared not. She spent the time in passionate caresses of her darling, in half-muttered ejaculations, some of pity, some of wrath. All she desired was to obliterate the impression which she saw had gone deeply to the child's heart. Olive wept not—she rarely did; it seemed as though in her little spirit was a pensive repose, above either infant sorrow or infant fear. She sat on her nurse's knee, scarce speaking, but continually falling into those reveries which we see in quiet children even at that early age, and never without a mysterious wonder, approaching to awe. Of what can these infant musings be?

'Nurse Elspie,' said the child, suddenly fixing on Elspie's face her large eyes, to look into which seemed like looking into a spring, not knowing what secrets may lie—depth within depth—beneath the dark blue waters. 'Elspie, was that my papa I saw?'

'It was just himsel, my sweet wee pet,' cried Elspie, trying to stop the little girl's question with impassioned caresses; but Olive went on.

'He is not like mamma—he is great and tall, like you. But he did not take me up and kiss me, as you said he would.'

Elspie had no answer for these words—spoken in a tone of quiet pain—so unlike a child, in whom are the springs of anger and revenge, but rarely of wounded feeling. It is only after many years that we learn to suffer and be silent.

Was it that nature, ever merciful, had implanted in this poor girl, as an instinct, that meek endurance which usually comes as the painful experience of after-life?

A similar thought passed through Elspie's mind, while she sat with little Olive at the window, where, a few years ago, she had stood rocking the new-born babe in her arms, and pondering drearily on its future. That future seemed still as dark in all outward circumstances—but there was one ray of hope, which centred in the little one herself. There was something in Olive which passed Elspie's comprehension. At times she looked almost with an uneasy awe on the gentle, silent child, who rarely played; who wanted no amusing, but would sit for hours watching the sky from the window, or the grass and waving trees in the fields; who never was heard to laugh, but now and then smiled in her own peculiar way—a smile almost 'uncanny', as Elspie expressed it. At times the old Scots-woman—who, coming from the debatable ground between Highlands and Lowlands,* had united to the rigid piety of the latter much wild Gaelic superstition—was half inclined to believe that the little girl was possessed by some spirit. But she was certain it was a good spirit; such a darling as Olive was—so patient, and gentle, and good—more like an angel than a child.

If her misguided parents did but know this! Yet Elspie, in her secret heart, was almost glad they did not. Her passionate and selfish love could not have borne that any tie on earth, not even that of father or mother, should stand between her and the child of her adoption.

While she pondered, there came a light knock to the door, and Captain

Rothesay's voice was heard without—his own voice, soothed down to its soft, gentlemanlike tone; it was a rare emotion, indeed, that could deprive it of that peculiarity.

'Nurse, I wish to see Miss Olive Rothesay.'

It was the first time that formal appellation had ever been given to the little girl. Still, it was a recognition. Elspie heard it with joy, for her excited and indignant fancy had almost pictured the parents disowning their child. She answered the summons, and Captain Rothesay walked in.

We have never described Olive's father—there could not be a better opportunity than now. His appearance did not belie his race, which, though of late generations somewhat mingled with Lowland blood, had been originally pure Gaelic. His tall, active form—now subsiding into the muscular fulness of middle age—was that of a Hercules of the mountains. The face combined Scottish beauties and Scottish defects, which, perhaps, cease to be defects when they become national peculiarities. There was the eagle-eye; the large, but perfectly chiselled features—especially the mouth; and also there was the high cheekbone, the rugged squareness of the chin, which, while taking away beauty, gave character to the whole.

When he came nearer, one could easily discern that the features of the father were strangely reflected in those of the child. Altered the likeness was—from strength into feebleness—from manly beauty into almost puny delicacy; but it did exist, and, faint as it was, Elspie perceived it.

Olive was looking up at the clouds, her thin cheek resting against the embrasure of the window, gazing so intently that she never seemed to hear her father's voice or step. Elspie motioned him to walk softly, and they came behind the child.

'Do ye no see, Captain Angus,' she whispered, ''tis your ain bonnie face—aye, and your mither's, wha dee'd when ye were a bit laddie. Ye mind her weel?'

Captain Rothesay did not answer, but looked earnestly at his little daughter. She, turning round, met his eyes. There was something in their expression which touched her, for a rosy colour suffused her face; she smiled, stretched out her little hands, and said, 'Papa!'

How Elspie then prided herself for the continual tutoring which had made the image of the absent father an image of love!

Captain Rothesay started from his reverie at the sound of the child's voice. The tone, and especially the word, broke the spell. He felt once more that he was the father, not of the blooming little angel that he had pictured, but of this poor deformed girl. However, he was a man in whom a stern sense of right stood in the place of many softer virtues. He had resolved on his duty—he had come to fulfil it—and fulfil it he would. So he took the two little cold hands, and said—

'Papa is glad to see you, my dear.'

There was a silence, during which Elspie placed a chair for Captain Rothesay, and Olive, sliding quietly down from hers, came and stood beside him. He did not offer to take the two baby-hands again, but did not repulse them, when the little girl laid them on his knee, looking enquiringly, first at him, and then at Elspie.

'What does she mean?' said Captain Rothesay.

'Puir wee lassie! I tauld her, when her father was come hame, he wad be fain to tak' her in his arms and kiss her.'

Rothesay looked angrily round, but recollected himself. 'Your nurse was right, my dear.' Then pausing for a moment, as though arming himself for a duty—repugnant, indeed, but necessary—he took his daughter on his knee, and kissed her cheek—once, and no more. But she, remembering Elspie's instructions, and prompted by her loving nature, clung about him, and requited the kiss with many another. They melted him visibly. There is nothing sweeter in this world than a child's unasked, voluntary kiss!

He began to talk to her—uneasily and awkwardly—but still, he did it. 'There, that will do, little one! What is you name, my dear?' he said, absently.

She answered, 'Olive Rothesay.'

'Aye—I had forgotten! The name at least, was true.' And he spoke bitterly. The next moment, he set down the child—softly—but as though it was a relief.

'Is papa going?' said Olive, with a troubled look.

'Yes; but he will come back tomorrow. Once a day will do,' he added, to himself. Yet, when his little daughter lifted her mouth for another kiss, he could not help giving it.

'Be a good child, my dear, and say your prayers every night, and love nurse Elspie.'

'And papa too, may I?'

He seemed to struggle violently against some inward feeling, and then answered, with a strong effort, 'Yes.'

The door closed after him abruptly. Very soon Elspie saw him walking with hasty strides along the beautiful walk that winds round the foot of the castle rock. The nurse sat still for a long time thinking, and then ended her ponderings with her favourite phrase—

'God guide us! it'll a' come richt at last.'

Poor, honest, humble soul!

CHAPTER VI

The return of the husband and father produced a considerable change in the little family at Stirling. A household, long composed entirely of women, always feels to its very foundations the incursion of one of 'the nobler sex'. From the first morning when there resounded the multiplied ringing of bells, and the creaking of boots on the staircase, the glory of the feminine dynasty was departed. Its easy *laissez-aller*, its lax rule, and its indifference to regular forms, were at an end. Mrs Rothesay could no longer indulge her laziness—no breakfasting in bed, and coming down in curl-paper. The long gossiping visits of her thousand-and-one acquaintances subsided into frigid morning calls, at which the grim phantom of the husband frowned from a corner, and suppressed all idle chatter. Sybilla's favourite system of killing time by half-hours in various idle ways, at home and abroad, was terminated at once. She had now to learn how to be a duteous wife, always ready at the beck and call of her husband, and attentive to his innumerable wants.

She was quite horrified by these at first. The captain actually expected to dine well and punctually, every day, without being troubled beforehand with 'What he would like for dinner?' He listened once or twice, patiently too, to her histories of various small domestic grievances, and then requested politely that she would confine such details to the kitchen in future; at which poor Mrs Rothesay retired in tears. He liked her to stay at home in the evening, make his tea, and then read to him, or listen while he read to her. This was the most arduous task of the two, for, dearly as she loved to hear the sound of his voice, Sybilla never could feel interested in the prosy books he read, and often fell half asleep; then he always stopped suddenly, sometimes looked cross, sometimes sad; and in a few minutes he invariably lighted her candle, with the gentle hint that it was time to retire. But often she woke, hours after, and heard him still walking up and down below, or stirring the fire perpetually, as a man does who is obliged to make the fire his sole companion.

And then Sybilla's foolish, but yet loving heart, would feel itself growing sad and heavy; and her husband's image, once painted there in such glittering colours, began to fade. The real Angus was not the Angus to her fancy. Joyful as was his coming home, it had not been quite what she expected. Else, why was it that at times, amidst all her gladness, she thought of their olden past with regret, and of their future with doubt, almost fear?

But it was something new for Sybilla to think at all. It did her good in spite of herself.

While these restless elements of future pain were brooding in the parents, the little, neglected, unsightly blossom, which had sprung up at their feet, lived the same unregarded, monotonous life as heretofore. Olive Rothesay had attained to five years, growing much as a daisy in the field, how, none knew or cared, except Heaven. And that Heaven did both know and care, was evident from the daily sweetness that was stealing into this poor wayside flower, so that it would surely one day be discovered through the invisible perfume which it shed.

Captain Rothesay kept to his firm resolve of seeing his little daughter in her nursery, once a day at least. After a while, the visit of a few minutes lengthened to an hour, even two. He listened with interest to Elspie's delighted eulogiums on her beloved charge, which sometimes went so far as to point out the beauty of the child's wan face, with the assurance that Olive, in features, at least, was a true Rothesay. But the father always stopped her with a dignified, cold look.

'We will quit that subject, if you please.'

Nevertheless, guided by his rigid sense of a parent's duty, he showed all kindness to the child, and his omnipotent sway over his wife exacted the same consideration from the hitherto indifferent Sybilla. It might be, also, that in her wayward and informal nature, the chill which had unconsciously fallen on the heart of the wife, caused the mother's heart to awaken. Feelings unwonted began to dawn faintly in Mrs Rothesay's bosom; they were reflected in her eyes; and then the mother would be almost startled to see the response which this new, though scarcely defined, tenderness created in her child.

For some months after Captain Rothesay's return, the little family abode in the retired old-fashioned dwelling on the hill of Stirling. Their quiet round of uniformity was only broken by the occasional brief absence of the head of the household, as he said, 'on business'. *Business* was a word conveying such distaste, if not horror, to Sybilla's ears, that she asked no questions, and her husband volunteered no information. In fact, he rarely was in the habit of doing so—whether interrogated or not.

At last, one day when he was sitting after dinner with his wife and child—he always punctiliously commanded that 'Miss Rothesay' might be brought in with the dessert—Angus made the startling remark:

'My dear Sybilla, I wish to consult with you on a subject of some importance.'

She looked up with a pretty, childish surprise.

'Consult with me! Oh, Angus! pray don't tease me with any of your hard business matters; I never could understand them.'

'And I never for a moment imagined you could. In fact, you told me so, and therefore I have never troubled you with them, my dear,' was the reply, dignified, with just the slightest shade of satire. But its bitterness passed away the moment Sybilla jumped up and came to sit down on the hearth at his feet, in an attitude of comical attention. Thereupon he patted her on the head, gently and smilingly, for he was but a young husband still, and she was such a sweet plaything for an idle hour.

A plaything! Would that all women considered the full meaning of the term—a thing sighed for, snatched, caressed, wearied of, neglected, scorned! And would, also, that every wife knew that her fate depends less on what her husband makes of her, than what she makes herself to him!

'Now, Angus, begin—I am all attention.'

He looked one moment doubtfully at Olive, who sat in her little chair at the further end of the room, quiet, silent, and demure. She had beside her some purple plums, which she did not attempt to eat, but was playing with them, arranging them with green leaves in a thousand graceful ways, and smiling to herself when the afternoon sunlight, creeping through the dim window, rested upon them, and made their rich colour richer still.

'Shall we send Olive away?' said the mother.

'No, let her stay—she is of no importance.'

The parents both looked at the child's pale, spiritual face, felt the reproach it gave, and sighed. Perhaps both father and mother would have loved her, but for a sense of shame in the latter, and the painful memory of deceit in the former.

'Sybilla,' suddenly resumed Captain Rothesay, 'what I have to say is merely, how soon you can arrange to leave Stirling?'

'Leave Stirling?'

'Yes; I have taken a house.'

'Indeed! and you never told me anything about it,' said Sybilla, with a vexed look.

'Now, my little wife, do not be foolish; you know that you never wish to hear about business, and I have taken you at your word; you cannot object to that?'

But she could, and she had a thousand half-pouting, half-jesting complaints to urge. She put them forth rather incoherently; in fact, she talked for five minutes without giving her husband opportunity for a single word, and yet she loved him dearly, and had in her heart scarce any objection to being saved the trouble of thinking beforehand; only she thought it right to stand up a little for her conjugal prerogative.

He listened in perfect silence. When she had done, he merely said, 'Very well, Sybilla; then we will leave Stirling this day month. I have decided to live in England. Oldchurch* is a very convenient town, and I have no doubt you will find Merivale Hall an agreeable residence.

'Merivale Hall. Are we really going to live in a Hall?' cried Sybilla, clapping her hands with childish glee. But immediately her face changed. 'You must be jesting with me, Angus. I don't know much about money, but I know we are not rich enough to keep up a Hall.'

'We *were* not rich, but we are now, I am happy to say,' answered Captain Rothesay, with a look of dignified triumph.

'Rich! very rich! and you never told me!' Sybilla's hands fell on her knee, and it was doubtful which expression was dominant in her countenance—womanly pain, or womanly indignation.

Angus looked annoyed. 'My dear Sybilla, listen to me quietly—yes, quietly,' he added, in a resolute tone, seeing how her colour came and went, and her lips seemed ready to burst out into petulant reproach. 'When I left England, I was taunted with having run away with an heiress. That, I did not do, since you were far poorer than the world thought—and I loved little Sybilla Hyde for herself, and not for her fortune. But the taunt stung me, and, when I left you, I resolved never to return until I could return a rich man on my own account. I am such now. Are you not glad, Sybilla?'

'Glad—glad to have been kept in the dark like a baby—a fool! It was not proper treatment towards your wife, Angus,' was the petulant answer, as Sybilla drew herself from his arm, which came as a mute peace-maker to encircle her waist.

'Now you are a child, indeed. I did it from love—believe me or not, it was so—that you might not be pained with the knowledge of my struggles, toils, and cares. And was not the reward, the wealth, all for you?'

'No; for yourself.'

'Pray, hear reason, Sybilla!' her husband continued, in those quiet, unconcerned tones, which, to a woman of quick feelings, and equally quick resentments, were sure to add fuel to fire.

'I will not hear reason. When you have these four years been rolling in wealth, and your wife and child were—oh, Angus!' and she began to weep.

Captain Rothesay tried at first, by explanations and by soothings, to stop the small torrent—the 'continual dropping' of fretful tears and half-broken accusations. All his words were misconstrued or misapplied. Sybilla would not believe but that he had slighted, ill-used, *deceived* her.

At the term the husband rose up sternly.

'Mrs Rothesay, who was it that deceived me?'

He pointed to the child, and the glance of both rested on little Olive. She sat, her graceful playthings fallen from her hands, her large soft eyes dilated with such a terrified wonder, that both father and mother shrank before them. That fixed gaze of the unconscious child seemed like the reproachful look of some angel of innocence sent from a purer world.

There was a dead silence. In the midst of it the little child crept from her corner and stood between her parents, her little hands stretched out, and her eyes full of tears.

'Olive has done nothing wrong? Papa and mamma, you are not angry with poor little Olive?' said the faint, sweet voice, falling like oil on the troubled waters.

For the first time, as she looked into the poor child's face, there flashed across the mother's memory the likeness of the angel in her dream. She pressed the thought back, almost angrily, but it came again. Then Sybilla stooped down, and, for the only time since her babyhood, Olive found herself lifted to her mother's embrace.

'The child had better go away to bed,' said Captain Rothesay, restlessly, but yet gently.

Olive was carried out, nestling closely in her mother's arms.

When Sybilla came back the angry pout had passed from her beautiful face, though a grave, troubled shadow still remained there. She made tea for her husband, tried to talk on common topics once or twice, but he gave little encouragement. Before retiring to rest, she said to him, timidly—

'There is no quarrel between us, Angus?'

'Not in the least, my dear,' he answered, with that composed deprecation of any offence, given or received, which is the most painful check to an impulsive nature; 'only, we will not discuss matters of business together again. Women never can talk things over quietly. Good night, Sybilla.'

He lifted his head a little, a very little, for her accustomed kiss. She gave it, but with it there came a sigh. He scarcely noticed either one or the other, being apparently deep in a large folio 'Commentary on the Proverbs', for it was Sunday evening. He lingered for a whole hour over the last chapter, and chiefly the passages—

'Who can find a virtuous woman: for her price is far above rubies. The heart of her husband doth safely trust in her: so that he shall have no need of spoil. . . . She openeth her mouth with wisdom: and in her tongue is the law of kindness.'

At this, Captain Rothesay closed the book, laid his arms upon it; and sighed—oh, how heavily! He did not go to bed that night until his young wife had lain awake for hours, regretting and resolving; nor until, after many determinations of future penitence and love, she had at last wept herself to sleep for very sorrow.

CHAPTER VII

Looking back on a calm and uneventful childhood,—and by childhood we mean the seven years between the babyhood of five and the dignity of 'teens',—it always seems like a cloudy landscape, with a few points of view here and there, which stand out clearly from the rest. Therein the fields are larger and the sky brighter than any we now behold. Persons, places, and events assume a mystery and importance. We never think of them, or hear them named afterwards, but there clings to them something of the strange glamour of the time when 'we saw men as trees walking'.*

Olive's childhood was passed in the place mentioned by her father. Merivale! Oldchurch! In her future life the words, whenever heard, always sounded like an echo of that dreamy time, whose sole epochs are birthdays, Christmas days, the first snowdrop found in the garden, the first daisy in the field. Such formed the only chronicle of Olive's childhood.

Its earliest period was marked by events which she was too young to notice, troubles which she was too young to feel. They passed over her like storm-clouds over a safely sheltered flower—only perceived by the momentary shadow which they cast. Once—it was in the first summer at Merivale—the child noticed how pleased every one seemed, and how papa and mamma, now always together, used to speak more tenderly than usual to her. Elspie said it was because they were so happy, and that Olive ought to be happy too, because God would soon send her 'a wee wee brother'. She would find him some day in the pretty cradle, which Elspie showed her. So the little girl went to look there every morning, but in vain. At last her nurse said she need not look there any more, for God had taken away the baby brother as soon as it came. Olive was very much disappointed, and when she went down to her father that day she told him of her trouble. But he angrily sent her away to her nurse. She looked ever after with grief and childish awe on the empty cradle.

At last it was empty no longer. She, a thoughtful child of seven, could never forget the impression made, when one morning she was roused by the loud pealing of the Oldchurch bells, and the maids told her, laughing, it was in honour of her little brother, come at last. She was allowed to kiss him once, and then spent half her time, watching, with great joy and wonderment, the tiny face, and touching the tiny hands. After some days she missed him; and after some more Elspie showed her a little heap in the nearest churchyard, saying, that was her baby brother's cradle now. Poor little Olive!—her only knowledge of the sweet tie of brotherhood was these few days of silent watching, and the little green mound left behind in the churchyard.

From that time there came a gradual change over the household, and over Olive's life. No more long, quiet hours after dinner, her father reading, her mother occupied in some light work, or resting on the sofa in delicious idleness, while Olive herself, little noticed, but yet treated with uniform kindness by both, sat on the hearthrug fondling the sleepy cat, or gazing with vague childish reverie into the fire. No more of the proud pleasure, with which, on Sunday afternoons, exalted to her grave papa's knee, she created an intense delight, out of what was to him a somewhat formal duty, and said her letters from the large family Bible. These childish joys vanished gradually, she scarce knew how. Her papa she now rarely saw, he was so much from home, and the quiet, dreamy house wherein she loved to ramble, became a house of feasting, her beautiful mamma being the centre of its gaiety. Olive retreated to her nursery and to Elspie, and the rest of her childhood was one long, solitary, pensive dream.

In that dream was the clear transcript of all the scenes amidst which it passed. The old hall, seated on a rising ground, and commanding views which were really beautiful in their way, considering that Merivale was on the verge of a manufacturing district, bounded by pastoral and moorland country. Those strange furnace-fires,* which rose up at dusk from the earth, and gleamed all around the horizon, like red fiery eyes open all night long, how mysteriously did they haunt the imaginative child! Then the town, Oldchurch, how in her after-life it grew distinct from all other towns, like a place seen in a dream, so real and yet so unreal! There was its castle hill, a little island within a large pool, which had once been a real fortress and moat. Old Elspie condemned alike tradition and reality, until Olive read in her little 'History of England' the name of the place, and how John of Gaunt had built a castle there.* And then Elspie vowed it was unworthy to be named the same day with beautiful Stirling. Continually did she impress on the child the glories of her birthplace, so that Olive in after-life, while remembering her childhood's scenes as a pleasant land of earth, came to regard her native Scotland as a sort of dream paradise. The shadow of the mountains where she was born fell softly, solemnly, over her whole life; influencing her pursuits, her character, perhaps even her destiny.

Yet there was a curious fascination about Oldchurch. In the cloudy memories of her childhood it rose up, as she used to go there with Elspie, at far distant intervals. The two great wide streets, High-street and Broad-street, intersecting one another in the form of a cross: the two churches—the Old Church, gloomy, and Norman,* with its ghostly grave-yard; and the New Church, shining white amidst a pleasant garden cemetery, beneath one of whose flowerbeds her baby brother lay. The two shops, the only ones she ever visited, the confectioner's, where she stood to watch the yearly fair, and the bookseller's, whither she dragged her nurse on any excuse, that she might pore over its incalculable treasures.

Above all, there was fixed in her memory the strange aspect the town wore on one day—a Coronation day—the grandest gala of her childhood. One king had died and been buried. Olive saw the black-hung pulpit and heard the funeral sermon, awfully thundered forth at night. Another king had been proclaimed, and Olive had gloried in the sight of the bonfires and the roasted sheep. Now, the people talked of a Coronation day.* Simple child! She knew nothing of the world's events or the world's destinies, save that she rose early to the sound of carolling bells, was dressed in a new white frock, and taken to see the town—the beautiful town, smiling with triumphal flower arches, and winding processions. How she basked in the merry sunshine, and heard the shouts, and the band playing 'God save the King', and felt very loyal, until her enthusiasm vented itself in tears.

Such was one of the few links between Olive's early life and the world outside. Otherwise she dwelt, for those seven years of childhood, in a little Eden of her own, whose boundary was rarely crossed by the footsteps of either joy or pain. She was neither neglected nor ill-used, but she never knew that fullness of love, on which one looks back in after-life, saying deprecatingly, and yet sighing the while, 'Ah, I was indeed a spoiled child!' Her little heart was not positively checked in its overflowings; but it had a world of secret tenderness that, being never claimed, expended itself in all sorts of wild fancies. She loved every flower of the field and every bird in the air. She also—having a passionate fondness for study and reading—loved her pet authors and their characters, with a curious individuality. Mrs Hofland* stood in the place of some good aunt, and Sandford and Merton* were regarded just like real brothers.

She had no one to speak to about poetry; she did not know there was such a thing in the world. Yet she was conscious of strange and delicious sensations, when in the early days of spring she had at length conquered Elspie's fears about wet feet and muddy fields, and had gone with her nurse to take the first meadow ramble, she could not help bounding to pluck every daisy she saw; and when the violets came, and the primroses, she was out of her wits with joy. She had never even heard of Wordsworth; yet, as she listened to the first cuckoo note, she thought it no bird, but truly 'a wandering voice'. Of Shelley's glorious lyric ode she knew nothing; and yet she never heard the skylark's song without thinking it a spirit of the air, or one of the angels hymning at Heaven's gate. And many a time she looked up in the clouds at early morning, half expecting to see that gate open, and wondering whereabouts it was in the beautiful sky.

She had never heard of Art, yet there was something in the gorgeous sunset that made her bosom thrill; and out of the cloud ranges she tried to form mountains such as there were in Scotland, and palaces of crystal such as she read of in her fairy tales. No human being had ever told her of the mysterious links that reach from the finite to the Infinite, out of which, from the buried ashes of dead Superstition, great souls can evoke those two mighty spirits, Faith and Knowledge; yet she went to sleep every night believing that she felt, nay, could almost see, an angel standing at the foot of her little bed, watching her with holy eyes, guarding her with outspread wings.

O Childhood! beautiful dream of unconscious poetry; of purity so pure, that it knew neither the existence of sin nor of its own innocence; of happiness so complete, that the thought, 'I am now happy', came not to drive away the wayward sprite which never *is*, but always is to come! Blessed Childhood! spent in peace and loneliness and dreams! We would fain look back lovingly on our own, as Olive Rothesay may yet look on hers—feeling that hidden therein, lay the germs of a whole life.

CHAPTER VIII

Olive Rothesay was twelve years old, and she had never learnt the meaning of that word whose very sound seems a wail—sorrow. And that other word, which is the dirge of the whole earth—death—was still to her only a name. She knew there was such a thing; she read of it in her books; its shadow had passed her by when she missed her little brother from the cradle; but still it had never stood by her side and said, 'Lo, I am here!' Her circle of love was so small, that it seemed as though the dread spectre could not enter. She saw it afar off; she thought upon it sometimes in her poetical dreams, which clad the imaginary shape of grief with a strange beauty. It was sweet to be sad, sweet to weep. She even tried to make a few delicious sorrows for herself; and when a young girl—whose beautiful face she had watched in church—died, she felt pensive and mournful, and even took a pleasure in thinking that there was now one grave in the new churchyard which she would almost claim to weep over as her own.

Such were the strange tendencies of this child's mind—ever toward the melancholy and the beautiful united. Quietly pensive as her disposition was, she had no young companions to rouse her into mirth. But there was a serenity even in her sadness; and no one could have looked in her face without feeling that her nature was formed to suit her apparent fate, and that if less fitted to enjoy, she was the more fitted for the solemnity of that destiny, to endure.

She had lived twelve years without knowing sorrow, and it was time that the first lesson, bitter, yet afterwards sweet, should be learned by the child. The shaft came to her through Elspie's faithful bosom, where she had rested all her life, and did rest now, with the unconscious security of childhood, which believes all it loves to be immortal. That Elspie should grow old, seemed a thing of doubtful future; that she should be ill or die, was a thing that never crossed the child's imagination.

And when at last, one year in the fall of the leaf, the hearty and vigorous old woman sickened, and for two or three days did not quit her room, still Olive, though grieving for the moment, never dreamed of any serious affliction. She tended her nurse lovingly and cheerfully, made herself quite a little woman for her sake, and really half enjoyed the stillness of the sick-room. It was a gay time—the house was full of visitors—and Elspie and her charge, always much left to one another's society, were now alone in their nursery, night and day. No one thought the nurse was ailing, except with the natural infirmity of old age, and Elspie herself uttered no word of complaint. Once or twice, while Olive was doing her utmost to enliven the sick-chamber, she saw her nurse watch her with eager love, and then sink into a grave reverie, from which it took more than one embrace to rouse her.

One night, or rather morning, Olive was roused by the sight of a white figure standing at her bedside. She would have been startled, but that Elspie, sleeping in the same room, had many a time come to look on her darling, even in the middle of the night. She had apparently done so now.

'Go to your bed again, dear nurse,' anxiously cried Olive. 'You should not walk about. Nay, you are not worse?'

'Aye, aye, just a wee bit waur, maybe; but dinna fear, dearie, we'll bide till the morn,' said Elspie, faintly, as she tried to move away, supporting herself by the bed. But soon she sank back dizzily. 'It's nae use, I canna gang. My sweet lassie, will ye help your puir auld nurse.'

Olive sprang up, and guided her back to her bed. When she reached it, Elspie said, thoughtfully, 'It's strange, unco' strange, my strength is a' gane.'

'Never mind, Elspie dear, you are weak with being ill; but you will get better soon. Oh, yes, very soon!' answered the child, with the eager certainty of desire.

'It's no that'; and Elspie took her child's hands and looked wistfully in her face. 'Olive, what suld ye say gin ye were to tine your puir auld nurse, an' I were to gang far awa'?'

'Go where?'

'Unto God,' said Elspie, solemnly.—'Dearie, I wadna grieve ye, but I'm aye sure this sickness is unto death.'

It was strange that Olive did not begin to weep, as many a child would have done; but though a cold trembling crept through her young frame at these words, she remained quite calm. For Elspie must be kept calm likewise, and how could she be so if her child were seen to suffer. Olive remembered this, and showed no sign of grief or alarm. Besides, she could not—would not believe a thing so fearful as Elspie's death. It was impossible.

'You must not think thus—you must think of nothing but getting well. Lie down and go to sleep,' she said, in a tone of almost womanly firmness, which Elspie obeyed mechanically. Then she would have roused the household, but the nurse forbade. By her desire Olive again sought her pillow.

It had always been her custom to creep to Elspie's bed as soon as she awoke, but now she did so long before daylight, in answer to a faint summons.

'I want ye, my bairn. Ye'll come to your auld nurse's arms—maybe they'll no haud ye lang,' murmured Elspie. She clasped the child once, with an almost passionate tenderness, and then, turning away, dropped heavily asleep.

But Olive did not sleep. She lay until broad daylight, counting hour by hour, and thinking thoughts deep and strange in a child of her years— thoughts of death and eternity. She did not believe Elspie's words; but if they should be true—if her nurse should die—if this should be the last time she would ever creep to her living bosom!

And then there came across the child's mind awful thoughts of death and of the grave. She struggled with them, but they clung with fearful tenacity to her fancy. All she had heard or read of mortality, of the coffin and the mould, came back with a vivid horror. She thought—what if in a few weeks, a few days, the hand she held should be cold, lifeless; the form, whose faint breathings she listened to, should breathe no more, but be carried from her sight, and shut up in a grave—under a stone? And then where would be Elspie—the tender, the faithful—who seemed to live but in loving her? Olive had been told that when people died, it was their bodies only that lay in the grave, and their souls went up to heaven to be with God. But all her childish reasoning could not dissever the two.

It was a marvel, that, loving Elspie as she did, such thoughts should come at all—that her mind was not utterly numbed with grief and terror. But Olive was a strange child, there were in her little spirit depths of which no one dreamed.

Hour after hour she lay in these ponderings, so horrible, yet fraught with such a strange fascination, and starting with a shudder every time they were broken by the striking of the clock below. How awful a clock sounds in the night-time, and to such a watcher—a mere child too! Olive longed for morning, and yet when the dusk of daybreak came, the very curtains took ghastly shapes, and her own white dress, hanging behind the door, looked like a shroud, within which——. She shuddered—and yet, all the while, she could not help eagerly conjecturing what the visible form of death would be.

Utterly unable to endure her own thoughts, she tried to rouse her nurse. And then Elspie started up in bed, seized her with burning hands, and asked her who she was, and what she had done with little Olive.

'I am little Olive—indeed, I am,' cried the terrified child.

'Are ye sure? Aweel then, dearie, dinna greet,' murmured poor Elspie, striving vainly against the delirium that she felt fast coming on, 'My bairn, is it near morn? Oh, for a wee drappie o' milk or tea.'

'Shall I go and call the maids. But that dark, dark passage—I dare not,' cried Olive, whose wild imagination often exposed her to the terrors of a superstition far beyond mere childish fear of darkness.

'It's no matter, bide ye till the daylight,' said Elspie, as she sank again into heavy sleep.

But the child could not rest. Was it not cruel to let her poor nurse lie suffering burning thirst, rather than encounter a few vague terrors? and if Elspie should have a long illness, should die—what then would the remembrance be? Without another thought the child crept out of bed and groped her way to the door.

It is easy to laugh at children's fancies about 'ghosts' and 'bogy', but Dante's terrors in the haunted wood* were not greater or more real than poor little Olive's, when she stood at the entrance of the long gallery, dimly peopled with the fantastic shadows of dawn. None but those who remember the fearful imaginings of their childhood, can comprehend the self-martyrdom, the heroic daring, which dwelt in that little trembling bosom, as Olive groped across the gloom.

Half-way through, she touched the cold handle of a door, and could scarce repress a scream. Her fears took no positive shape, but she felt surrounding her Things before and Things behind. No human courage could give her strength to resist such terrors. She paused, closed her eyes, and said the Lord's Prayer all through. But '*Deliver us from evil*' she repeated many times, feeling each time stronger and bolder. Then first there entered into her heart that mighty faith 'which can remove mountains'; that fervent boldness of prayer with the very utterance of which an answer comes. And who dare say that the Angel of that child, 'always beholding the face of the Father in Heaven', did not stand beside her then, and teach her in faint shadowings the mysteries of her life to come.

Olive's awestruck fancy became a truth—she never crept to her nurse's bosom more. By noon that day, Elspie lay in the deathly torpor which marks the last stage of rapid inflammation. She did not even notice the child, who crept in and out of the thronged room, speaking to no one, neither weeping nor trembling, but struck with a strange awe, that made her countenance and mien almost unearthly in their quietness.

'Take her away to her parents,' whispered the physician. But her mother had left home the day before, and Captain Rothesay had been absent a week. There were only servants in the house, and they looked at her often, said, 'Poor child!' and left her to go where she would. Olive followed the physician downstairs.

'Will she die?'

He started at the touch of the soft hand—soft but cold, always cold. He looked at the little creature, whose face wore such an unchildlike expression. He never thought to pat her head, or treat her like a girl of twelve years old, but said gravely, as though he were speaking to a grown woman:

'I have done my best, but it is too late. In three hours, or perhaps four, all will be over.' He quitted the room, and Olive heard the rattle of his carriage-wheels. They died away down the gravel road, and all was silent. Silent, except the twitter of a few birds, heard through the stillness of a July evening. Olive stood at the window and mechanically looked out. It was so beautiful, so calm. At the west, the clouds were stretched out in pale folds of rose colour and grey. On the lawn slept the long shadows of the trees, for behind them was rising the round, red moon. And yet, within the house was—death.

She tried to realize the truth. She said to herself, time after time, 'Elspie will die!' But even yet she could not believe it. How could the little birds sing and the sunset shine, when Elspie was dying? At last the light faded, and then she believed it all. Night and death seemed to come upon the world together.

Suddenly she remembered the physician's words. 'Three hours—four hours.' Was that all? And Elspie had not spoken to her since the moment when she cried and was afraid to rise in the dark. Elspie was going away, for ever, without one kiss, one goodbye.

Weeping passionately, Olive flew back to the chamber, where several women stood round the bed. There lay the poor aged form, in a torpor which, save for the purple face and the loud, heavy breathing, had all the unconsciousness of death. Was that Elspie? The child saw, and her tears were frozen. The maids would have drawn her away.

'No—no,' Olive said, in a frightened whisper; 'let me look at her—let me touch her hand.'

It lay outside the bedclothes, helpless and rigid, the fingers falling together, as they always do in the hour of parting life. Olive touched them. They were cold—so cold! Then she knew what was death. The maids carried her fainting from the room, and she entered it no more.

Mrs Rothesay had returned, and frightened and grieved, now wept with all a woman's softness over the deathbed of the faithful old nurse. She took her little daughter to her own sitting-room, laid her on the sofa, and watched by her very tenderly. Olive, exhausted and half insensible, heard, as in a dream, her mother whispering to the maid:

'Come and tell me, when there is *any change*.'

Any change. What change? That from life to death—from earth to Heaven! And would it take place at once? Could they tell the instant when Elspie's soul departed, 'to be beyond the sun'?

Such and so strange were the thoughts that floated through the mind of this child of twelve years old. And from these precocious yearnings after the infinite, Olive's fancy turned to earthly, childish things. She pictured with curious minuteness how she would feel when she awoke next morning, and found that Elspie was dead;—how there would be a funeral; how strange the house would seem afterwards; even, what would be done with the black bonnet and shawl which two days since Elspie had hung up against the nursery door, never to put on again.

And then a long silent agony of weeping came upon the child. Her mother, thinking she slept, sat quietly by; but in any case, Olive would never have thought of going to her for consolation. Young as she was, Olive knew that her sorrow must be borne alone, for none could understand it. Until we feel that we are alone on earth, how rarely do we feel that we are *not* alone in heaven. For the second time this day, the child thought of God. Not merely as of Him to whom she offered her daily prayers, and those repeated after the clergyman in church on Sunday, but as One to whom, saying 'Our Father', she could ask for anything she desired.

And she did so, lying on the sofa, not even turning to kneel down, using her own simple words. She prayed that God would comfort her when Elspie died, and teach her not to grieve, but to be a good patient child, so that she might one day go to her dear nurse in heaven, and never be parted from her any more.

She heard the maid come in and whisper to her mamma. Then she knew that all was over—that Elspie was dead. But so deep was the peace which had fallen on her heart that the news gave no pang—caused no tears.

'Olive, dearest,' said Mrs Rothesay, herself subdued into weeping.

'I know all, mamma,' was the answer. 'Now I have no one to love me but you.'

The feeling was strange, perhaps even wrong; but as Mrs Rothesay clasped her child, it was not without a thrill of freedom and exultation that Olive was all her own now.

'Where shall Miss Rothesay sleep tonight,' was the whispered question of the maid. Olive burst into tears.

'She shall sleep with me. Darling, do not cry for your poor nurse; will not mamma do instead?'

And looking up, Olive saw, as though she had never seen it before, the face which, now shining with maternal love, seemed beautiful as an angel's. It became to her like an angel's evermore.

How often, in our human fate, does the very Hand that taketh, give!

CHAPTER IX

Mrs Rothesay, touched by an impulse of regretful tenderness, showed all due respect to the memory of the faithful woman who had nursed with such devotion her husband and her child. For a whole long week Olive wandered about the shut-up house, the formal solemnities of death, now known for the first time, falling heavily on her young heart. Alas! that there was no one to lift it beyond the terrors of the grave to the sublime mysteries of immortality.

But the child knew none of these, and therefore she crept, awestruck, about the silent house, and, when night fell, dared not even to pass near the chamber—once her own and Elspie's—now Death's. She saw the other members of the household enter with solemn faces through the perpetually locked door. What must there be within? Something on which she dared not think, and which nothing could induce her to behold. At times she forgot her sorrow; and, still keeping close to her mother's side, amused herself with her usual childish games, piecing disjointed maps, or drawing on a slate; but all was done with a quietness, sadder than even tears.

The evening before the funeral, Mrs Rothesay went to look for the last time on the remains of her faithful old servant. She tried to persuade little Olive to go with her; the child accompanied her to the door, and then weeping violently, fled back and hid herself in another chamber. From thence she heard her mother come away—also weeping, for the feeble nature of Sybilla Rothesay had lost none of its tender-hearted softness. Olive listened to the footsteps gliding downstairs, and there was silence. Then the passionate affection which she had felt for her old nurse rose up, driving away all childish fear, and strengthening her into a resolution which until then she had not dared to form. Tomorrow they would take away Elspie—*for ever*. On earth she would never again see the face which had been so beloved. Could she let Elspie go without one look, only one? She would enter the awful room now, and alone.

No tongue can tell the intensity of love that must have been in that young child's heart to nerve her thus!

It was about seven in the evening, still daylight, though in the darkened house dimmer than without. Olive drew the blind aside, took one long gaze into the cheerful sunset landscape to strengthen and calm her mind, and then walked with a firm step to the chamber door. It was not locked this time, but closed ajar. The child looked in, a little way only. There stood the well-remembered furniture, the room seemed the same, only pervaded with an atmosphere of silent, solemn repose. There would surely be no terror there.

Olive stole in, hearing in the stillness every beating of her heart. She stood by the bed. It was covered, not with its usual starry counterpane, the work of Elspie's diligent hand through many a long year, and on which her own baby fingers had been first taught to sew—but with a large white sheet. She stood, scarce knowing whether to fly or not, until she heard a footstep on the stairs. One minute, and it would be too late. With a resolute hand she lifted the sheet, and saw the white fixed countenance, not of sleep, but death.

With a shriek so wild and piercing that it rang through the house, Olive sprang to the door, fled through the passage, at the end of which she sank in convulsions.

That night the child was taken from the house, and never entered it until some weeks after, when the grass was already springing on poor Elspie's grave.

It is nature's blessed ordinance, that in the mind of childhood the remembrance of fear or sorrow fades so fast. Therefore, when Olive came back to Merivale, and saw the house now smiling within and without amidst the beauty of early autumn, the horrors of death passed from her mind, or were softened into a tender memory. Perhaps, in the end, it was well for her that she had looked on that poor dead face, to be certain that it was not Elspie. She never thought of Elspie in that awful chamber any more. She thought of her as in life, standing knitting by the nursery window, walking slowly and sedately along the green lanes, carrying the basket of flowers and roots, collected in their rambles, or sitting in calm Sunday afternoons with her Bible on her knee.

And then passing from the memory of Elspie once on earth, Olive thought of Elspie now in heaven. Her glowing imagination idealized all sorrow into poesy. She never watched the sunset, she never looked up into the starry sky at night, without picturing Elspie as there. All the foibles and peculiarities of her poor old Scottish nurse became transmuted into the image of a guardian invisible, incorporeal; which seemed to draw her own spirit nearer to heaven, with the thought that there was one she loved, and who loved her, in the glorious mansions there.

So do pure hearts ever feel when the first beloved goes; and oh, how ought we to feel when we have many beloveds passed thither, each following the other's holy footsteps, and heralding ours to the one home!

From the time of her nurse's death, the whole current of Olive's life changed. It cast no shadow over the memory of the deep affection lost, to say that the full tide of living love now flowed towards Mrs Rothesay as it had never done before, perhaps never would have done but for Elspie's death. And truly the mother's heart now thirsted for that flood.

For seven years the little cloud which appeared when Captain Rothesay returned, had risen up between husband and wife, increasing slowly but surely, and casting a shadow over their married home. Like many another pair who wed in the heat of passion, or the wilful caprice of youth, their natures, never very similar, had grown less so, day by day, until in mature age their two lives, instead of flowing onward in one bright loving current, had severed wider and wider. There was no open dissension that the wicked world could take hold of, to glut its eager eyes with the spectacle of an unhappy marriage; but the chasm was there, a gulf of coldness, indifference and distrust, which no foot of love would ever cross.

Angus Rothesay was a disappointed man. At five-and-twenty he had taken a beautiful, playful, half-educated child

His bride and his darling to be,

forgetting that at thirty-five he should need a sensible woman to be his trustworthy sympathizing wife, the careful and thoughtful mistress of his household. When hard experience had made him old and wise, even a little before his time, he came home expecting to find her old and wise too. The hope failed. He found Sybilla as he had left her—a very child. Ductile and loving as she was, he might even then have guided her mind, have formed her character, in fact, have made her anything he liked. But he would not do it; he was too proud. He brooded over his disappointed hope in silence and reserve; and though he reproached her not, and never ceased to love her in his own cold way, yet the respect, the sympathy were gone. Her ways were not his ways, and was it the place of a man and a husband to bend? After a few years of struggling, less with her than with himself, he decided that he would take his own separate course, and let her take hers.

He did so. At first she tried to win him back, not with a woman's sweet and placid dignity of love, never-failing, never-tiring, yet invisible as a rivulet that runs through deep green bushes, scarcely heard and never seen. Sybilla's arts—the only arts she knew, were the whole armoury of girlish coquetry, or childish wile, passionate tenderness and angry or sullen reproach, alternating each other. Her husband was equally unmoved by all. He seemed a very rock, indifferent to either sunshine or storm. And yet it was not so. He had in his nature deep, earnest, abiding tenderness; but he was one of those people who must be loved only in their own quiet, silent way. A hard lesson for one whose every feeling was less a principle than an impulse, Sybilla could not learn it. And thus the happiness of two lives were blighted, not from evil, or even lack of worth in either, but because they did not understand one another. Their current of existence flowed on coldly and evenly, in two parallel lines, which would never, never meet!

The world beheld Captain Rothesay in two phases—one as the grave, somewhat haughty but respected master of Merivale Hall; the other as the rash and daring speculator, who was continually doubling and trebling his fortune by all the thousand ways of legal gambling in which men of capital and merchandise can indulge. There was in this kind of life an interest and excitement. Captain Rothesay sprang to it as many another man would have sprung to far less sinless means of atoning for the dreary blank of home.

In Mrs Rothesay the world only saw one of its fairest adornments—one of those 'charming women' who make society so agreeable; beautiful, kind-hearted—at least as much so as her thoughtless life allowed; lively, fond of amusement—perhaps a little in the extreme, for it caused people to note the contrast between the master and the mistress of the Hall, and to say what no wife should ever give the world reason to say. 'Poor thing! I wonder if she is happy with her husband?'

But between these two stood the yet scarce recognized tie which bound them together—the little deformed child.

CHAPTER X

'Captain Rothesay?'

'My dear?'

Reader, did you ever notice the intense frigidity that can be expressed in a 'my dear'! The coldest, cruellest husband we ever knew once impressed this fact on our childish fancy, by our always hearing him call his wife thus—poor, pale, broken-hearted creature! He 'my-deared' her into her grave.

Captain Rothesay also used the epithet with that formality which was chilling enough in its way. He said it without lifting his eyes from the book, 'Smith's Wealth of Nations',* which had become his usual evening's study now, whenever he was at home. That circumstance, rare enough to have been welcome, and yet it was not welcome, now subdued his wife and daughter into silence and quietness. Alas! that ever a presence which ought to be the sunshine of a household should enter only to cast a perpetual shade.

The firelight shone on the same trio which had formed the little after-dinner circle years ago at Stirling. But there was a change in all. The father and mother sat—not side by side, in that propinquity which is so sweet, when every breath, every touch of the beloved's garment gives pleasure; they sat one at each corner of the table, engrossed in their several occupations of reading with an uncommunicative eagerness, and sewing in unbroken silence. Each was placed within a chilling circle of thoughts and interests in which the other never entered. And now the only point of meeting between them was the once-banished child.

Little Olive was growing almost a woman now, but she was called 'little Olive' still. She retained her diminutive stature, together with her girlish dress, but her face wore, as ever, its look of premature age. And as she sat between her father and mother, now helping the one in her delicate fancy-work, now arranging the lamp for the other's reading, continually in request by both, or when left quiet for a minute, watching both with anxious earnestness, there was quite enough in Olive's manner to show that she had entered on a woman's life of care, and had not learned a woman's wisdom one day too soon.

The captain's last 'my dear' found his wife in the intricacies of a Berlin wool pattern, so that she did not speak again for several minutes, when she again appealed to 'Captain Rothesay'. She rarely called him anything else now. Alas! the time of 'Angus' and 'Sybilla' was gone.

'Well, my dear, what have you to say?'

'I wish you would not be always reading, it makes the evening so dull.'

'Does it?' and he turned over another leaf of Adam Smith, and leisurely settled himself for its perusal.

'Papa is tired, and may like to be quiet. Suppose we talk to one another, mamma?' whispered Olive, as she put aside her own work—idle, but graceful designings with pencil and paper—and, drawing near to her mother, began to converse in a low tone. She discussed all questions as to whether the rose should be red or white, and what coloured wool would form the striped tulip, just as though they had been the most interesting topics in the world, Only once her eyes wandered wistfully to the deserted 'Sabrina', which, half sketched, lay within the leaves of her 'Comus'.* Mrs Rothesay observed this, and said, kindly—

'Let me look at what you are doing, love. Ah!—very pretty! What is it. Sabrina? Tell me all about her.' And she listened, with a pleased, maternal smile, while her gratified little daughter dilated on the beloved 'Comus', and read a passage or two in illustration. 'Very pretty, my love,' again repeated Mrs Rothesay, stroking Olive's hair. 'Ah! you are a clever child. But now come and tell me what sort of winter dresses you think we should have.'

If any observer could have seen a shade of disappointment on Olive's face, he would also have seen it instantly suppressed. The young girl closed 'Comus' with the drawing inside, and came to sit down again, looking up into the eyes of her 'beautiful mamma'. And even the commonplace question of dress soon became interesting to her, for her artistic predilection followed her even there, and no lover ever gloried in his mistress's charms, no painter ever delighted to deck his model, more than Olive loved to adorn and to admire the still exquisite beauty of her mother. It stood to her in the place of all attractions in herself—in fact, she rarely thought about herself at all. The consciousness of her personal defect had worn off through habit, and her almost total seclusion from strangers prevented its being painfully forced on her mind.

'I wish we could leave off this mourning,' said Mrs Rothesay. 'It is quite time, seeing Sir Andrew Rothesay has been dead six months. And, living or dying, he did not show kindness enough to make one remember him longer.'

'Yet he was kind to papa, when a child; and so was Auntie Flora,' softly said Olive, to whose enthusiastic memory there ever clung Elspie's tales about the Perthshire relatives—bachelor brother and maiden sister, living together in their lonely, gloomy home. But she rarely talked about them; and now, seeing her mamma look troubled, as she always did at any reference to Scotland and the old times, the little maiden ceased at once. Mrs Rothesay was soon again safely and contentedly plunged into the mysteries of winter costume.

'Yours must be handsomer and more womanly now, Olive; for I intend to take you out with me now and then. You are quite old enough; and I am tired of visiting alone. I intended to speak to your papa about it tonight; but he seems not in good humour.'

'Only tired with his journey,' put in the sweet little mediator. 'Is it not so, papa?'

Captain Rothesay started from a dull, anxious reverie, into which his reading had merged, and lifted his face, knitted and darkened with some inward care, heavy enough to make his tone sharp and angry, as he said,

'Well, child, what do you want?'

'Do not scold Olive; it was I who wished to speak to you.' And then, without pausing to consider how evidently ill timed the conversation was, Mrs Rothesay began to talk eagerly about Olive's 'coming out', and whether it should be at home or abroad; finally arguing that a ball at Merivale would be best, and entering at large on the question of ball costume. There was nothing wrong in anything she said, but she said it at the wrong time. Her husband listened first with indifference, then fidgeted restlessly in his chair, and at last subsided into an angry silence.

'Why don't you speak, Captain Rothesay?' He took up the poker and hammered the fire to small cinders. 'Of course, you will be reasonable. Say, shall it be as I have arranged?'

'No!' The word came thundering out—as Captain Rothesay rarely thundered; for he was calm and dignified even in his wrath. Immediately afterwards he rose up and left the room.

Sybilla grew pale, sorrowful, and then melted into tears. She tried not to let Olive see them. She was still too faithful a wife to seek in any way to turn the child against her father. But yet she wept; and drawing her young daughter closer to her arms, she felt the sweetness of having a child—and such a child—left to love her. In proportion as the wife's heart closed, the mother's opened.

Ere long, Captain Rothesay sent for little Olive, to read the evening newspaper to him in his study.

'Go, love,' said Mrs Rothesay; and she went. Without fear, too; for her father never said a harsh word to *her*. And as, each year of her life, the sterling truth and stern uprightness of his character dawned upon her, she could not fail to respect him, even while she worshipped her sweet-tempered, gentle mother.

Captain Rothesay made no remark, save upon the subject she was reading, and came in with Olive to tea, just as usual. But when he had finished, and was fast sinking back into that painful reverie which seemed to oppress him, his weak, ill-judging wife recommenced her attack. She talked gently when speaking of Olive, even affectionately—poor soul! She persuaded herself, all the time, that she was doing right, and that he was a hard-hearted father not to listen to her. He did listen, apparently; and she took his silence for consent, for she ended with—

'Well, then, it is quite settled; the ball shall be at Merivale, on the 20th of next month?'

Angus turned round, his blue eyes glittering, yet cold as steel—'Mrs Rothesay, if you will worm the truth out of me, you shall. By next month you may not have a roof over your head.'

He rose up and again quitted the room. Mrs Rothesay trembled—grew terrified—but tried to reassure herself. 'He only says this in anger, or else to frighten me. I will not believe it.' Then conscience whispered, that never in her whole life had she known Angus Rothesay to tell a falsehood; and she trembled more and more. Finally, she passed into a violent fit of nervous weeping—a circumstance by no means rare. Her health was weakened by the exciting gaieties of her outward life, and the inward sorrow which preyed upon her heart.

This night—and not for the first time either—the little maiden of fifteen might have been seen, acting with the energy and self-possession of a woman—soothing her mother's hysterical sufferings—smoothing her pillow, and finally watching by her until she fell asleep. Then Olive crept downstairs, and knocked at her father's study door. He said 'Come in' in a dull, subdued tone. She entered, and saw him sitting, his head on his hand, jaded and exhausted, leaning over the last embers of the fire, which had gone out without his noticing it. If there had been any anger in the child's heart, it must have vanished at once, when she looked upon her father thus.

'Oh! is that you, Olive?' was all he said, beginning to turn over his papers, as if to make a show of occupation. But he soon relapsed into that unknown thought which oppressed him so much. It was some minutes before he completely roused himself, and saw the little elfin-like figure standing beside him, silent and immovable, with the taper in her hand.

'Shall I bring your candle, dear papa? It is eleven o'clock and more.'

'Where is your mother, Olive?'

'She is gone to bed;' and Olive paused, uncertain whether she should tell him that her mamma was ill. Again there was a silence—during which, do what he would, Captain Rothesay could not keep his eyes from the earnest, wistful, entreating gaze of his 'little Olive'. At last, he lifted her on his knee, and took her face between his two hands, saying, in a smothered tone,

'You are not like your mother; you are like *mine*—aye, and seem more so as you grow to be a woman.'

'I wish I were a woman, that papa might talk to me and tell me anything which he has on his mind,' whispered Olive, scarcely daring to breathe that which she had nerved herself to say, during many minutes of silent pondering at the study door.

Captain Rothesay relapsed hastily into his cold manner. 'Child, how do you know?'

'I know nothing, and want to know nothing, that papa does not wish to tell me,' answered Olive, gently.

The father turned round again, and looked into his daughter's eyes. Perhaps he read there a spirit equal to, and not unlike, his own—a nature calm, resolute, clear-sighted; the strong will and decision of a man, united to the tenderness of a woman. From that hour father and daughter understood one another.

'Olive, how old are you?—I forget.'

'Fifteen, dear papa.'

'Ah! and you are a thoughtful girl. I can talk to you as to a woman— pah! I mean, a sensible woman. Put out your candle; you can sit up a while longer.'

She obeyed, and sat with him for two whole hours in his study, while he explained to her how sudden reverses had so damaged his fortune, that it was necessary to have a far smaller establishment than Merivale Hall.

'Not that we need fear poverty, my dear child; but the future must be considered and provided for. Your mother's jointure, should I die—nay, do not look sad, we will not talk of that—and then, too, your own portion, when you marry.'

Olive blushed, as any girl of fifteen will do, when talked to on such a topic, even in the most businesslike way. 'I shall not marry, papa,' said she, expressing the thought which had come to her, as it does to most young girls who love their parents very dearly, too dearly to imagine a parting.

Captain Rothesay started, as if suddenly recollecting himself. Then he regarded her earnestly, mournfully; and in the look was something which struck on Olive's memory as though she had seen it before.

'I had forgotten,' muttered Captain Rothesay to himself. 'Of course, she will never marry. Poor child!—poor child!'

He kissed her very tenderly, then lighted his candle, and went upstairs to bed, holding her hand all the way, until they parted at her room door, when he kissed her a second time. As he did so, she contrived to whisper—

'Mamma is sure to wake; she always does when you come in. Kiss mamma, too.'

Olive went to bed, happier than she could have believed possible, had any one told her in the morning that ere night she would hear the ill news of having to leave beautiful Merivale. But it was so sweet to feel herself a comfort to both parents—they who, alas! would receive no comfort from each other.

Only, just when she was falling asleep, the thought floated across Olive's mind—

'I wonder why papa said that of course I should never marry!'

CHAPTER XI

'Dear mamma! is not this a pretty house, even though it is in a town?— so pretty, one need hardly pine after Merivale!'

Thus said Olive when they had been established some time in their new abode, and sat together, one winter evening, listening to the sweet bells of Oldchurch—one of the few English parishes where lingers 'the curfew's solemn sound'.*

'A pretty house, if any one came to see us in it, my dear; but nobody does. And then we miss the close carriage so much. To think that I have been obliged to refuse the Stantons' ball, and the dinner-party at Everingham. How dull these long winter evenings will be, Olive!'

Olive answered neither *yes* nor *no*; but tried quietly, by her actions, to disprove the fact. She was but a child—scarcely would have been called a clever child; was neither talkative nor musical; and yet she had a thousand winning ways of killing time, so sweetly that each minute died, dolphin-like, shedding glorious hues.

A very romantic simile this—one that would never have crossed Olive's innocent brain. She only knew that she loved her mother; and therefore tried to amuse and make her happy, so that she might not feel the change of circumstances—a change so unimportant to Olive, so vital to Mrs Rothesay.

Olive, this night, was peculiarly successful in her little *ruse* of love. Her mother listened while she explained a whole sketchbook of designs, illustrative of half-a-dozen modern poets. Mrs Rothesay even asked her to read some of the said poets aloud; and though not of an imaginative temperament, was fain to shed a few womanly tears over Tennyson's delicious home lyrics, especially 'The Queen of the May', and 'The Miller's Daughter'.* Finally, she was coaxed into sitting to her daughter for her portrait, which Olive thought would make a design exactly suited to the heroine of the latter poem, and chiefly at the verse—

> Look through mine eyes with thine. True wife,
>> Round my true heart thine arms entwine;
> My other dearer life in life,
>> Look through my very soul with thine.

And, reading the verses over and over again, to bring the proper expression to her mother's face, the young girl marvelled that they brought likewise a look so sad, that she would fain have made some excuse, and terminated the sitting.

'No, no, my dear, it amuses me, and I can talk with you the while.'

But Mrs Rothesay did not talk much; she was continually falling into a reverie. Once she broke it, with the words—

'Olive, my child, I think, now we lead a quieter life, your papa will stay at home more. He seems to like this house, too—he never liked Merivale.'

'Dear old Merivale!' said Olive, with a sigh. It seemed ages since she had left the familiar place.

'Do not call it *dear*. It was a dreary home. I did not think so at first, but I did afterwards.'

'Why, mamma?' asked Olive. She was glad to lure her mother on to talk a little, if only to dispel the shadow which so ill became Mrs Rothesay's still fair face.

'You were too young to know anything then—indeed you are now, almost. But somehow, I have learned to talk with you as if you were quite a little woman, Olive, my dear.'

'Thank you, mamma. And what made you dislike sweet Merivale?'

'It was when your papa first began to take his long journeys—on business, you know. He was obliged to do it, I suppose; but, nevertheless, it was very dull for me. I never had such a dreary summer as that one. You could not remember it, though—you were only ten years old.'

Olive did remember it faintly, nevertheless—a time when her father's face was sterner, and her mother's more fretful, than now; when the shadow of many domestic storms passed over the pure spirit of their unconscious child. But she never spoke of these things; and, lest her mother should ponder painfully on them now, she began to talk of lighter matters. Yet though the sweet companionship of her only daughter was balm to Mrs Rothesay's heart, still there was a pain there which even Olive could not remove. Was it that the mother's love had sprung from the ruins of the wife's happiness; and that while smiling gaily with her child, Sybilla Rothesay's thoughts were with the husband who, year by year, was growing more estranged, and whom, as she found out too late, by a little more wisdom, patience, and womanly sympathy, she might perhaps have kept for ever at her side?

But none of these mysteries came to the knowledge of little Olive. She lived the dream-life of early girlhood—dwelling in an atmosphere still and pure as a grey spring morning, ere the sun has risen. All she learnt was from books; for though she had occasional teachers, she had never been sent to school. Sometimes she regretted this, thinking how pleasant it would be to have companions, or at least one friend of her own age, to whom she might talk on the various subjects of which she had of late begun to dream. These never passed the still sanctuary of her own thoughts; for some instinct told her that her mother would scarce sympathize with her wild imaginations in Art and Poetry. So she thought of them always by herself, when she was strolling about the small but pleasant garden that sloped down from the back of the house to the river; or when, extending her peregrinations, she went to sit in the summer-house of the garden adjoining, which belonged to a large mansion close by, long uninhabited. It was quite a punishment to Olive when a family came to live there, and she lost the use of the beautiful, deserted garden.

Still, it was something new to have neighbours. She felt quite a curiosity respecting them, which was not diminished when, looking out one day from the staircase window (a favourite seat, from which every night she watched the sun set), Olive caught a sight of the new occupants of her former haunts.

They were two little boys of about nine or ten, playing noisily enough—as boys will. Olive did not notice them much, except the youngest, who appeared much the quieter and gentler of the two; but her gaze rested a long time on a girl, who seemed to be their elder sister. She was walking by herself up and down an alley, with a shawl thrown over her head, and her thick, black hair blown about by the March winds. Olive thought she looked very picturesque—in fact, just like some of her own fantastic designs of 'Norna on the Fitful Head', 'Medora watching for Conrad', &c. &c. And when the young stranger drew nearer, her admiration was still further excited, by perceiving under the shawl a face that needed but a little romantic imagination to make it positively beautiful. Olive thought so, and accordingly sat the whole evening drawing it from memory, under various characters, from Scott, Byron, Moore, and Coleridge.

For several days after, she took a deep interest in watching the family party, and chiefly this young girl—partly because she was so pretty, and partly because she seemed nearly about her own age, or perhaps a year or two older. Olive often contrived to walk in her garden when her neighbours were in theirs—so that she could hear the boys' cheerful voices over the high hedge. By this means she learnt their Christian names, Robert and Lyle—the latter of which she admired very much, and thought it exactly suited the pretty, delicate younger brother. She wished much to find out that of their sister—but could not; for the elder girl took little notice of them, or they of her. So Olive, after thinking and talking of her for some time, as 'my beauty next door', to Mrs Rothesay's great amusement, at last christened her by the imaginary name of Maddalena.

After a few weeks, it seemed as though the interest between the young neighbours became mutual—for Olive, in her walks, sometimes fancied she saw faces watching *her*, too, from the staircase window. And once, peering over the wall, she perceived the mischievous eyes and pointed finger of the elder boy, and heard the younger one say, reproachfully—

'Don't—pray! You are very cruel, Bob.'

And Olive, deeply blushing—though at what she scarcely knew—

fled into the house, and did not take her usual garden walks for some days.

At last, when, one lovely spring evening, she stood leaning over the low wall at the garden's end, idly watching the river flow by beneath, she turned round, and saw fixed on her, with a curiosity not unmingled with interest, the dark eyes of 'Maddalena'. Somehow or other, the two girls smiled—and then the elder spoke.

'The evening was very fine,' she said; 'and it was rather dull, walking in the garden all alone.'

Olive had never found it so; but she was used to it. Her young neighbour was not; she had always lived in a large town, &c. &c.

A few more simple nothings spun out the conversation for ten minutes. The next day it was resumed, and extended to twenty; during which Olive learnt that her young beauty's name, so far from being anything so fine as Maddalena, was plain Sarah—or *Sara*, as its owner took care to explain. Olive was rather disappointed—but she thought of Coleridge's lady love; consoled herself, and tried to console the young lady, with repeating

My pensive Sara! thy soft cheek reclined, &c.*

At which Miss Sara Derwent laughed, and asked who wrote that very pretty poetry?

Olive was a little confounded. She fancied everybody read Coleridge, and her companion sank just one degree in her estimation. But as soon as she looked again on the charming face, with its large, languishing Asiatic eyes, and delicate mouth—just like that of the lotus-leaved 'Clytie', which she loved so much—Olive felt all her interest revive. Never was there any girl over whom every form of beauty exercised more fascination. By the week's end she was positively enchanted with her neighbour, and before a month had passed the two young girls had struck up that romantic friendship peculiar to sixteen.

There is a deep beauty—more so than the world will acknowledge—in this impassioned first friendship, most resembling first love, whose faint shadowing it truly is. Who does not, even while smiling at its apparent folly, remember the sweetness of such a dream? Many a mother with her children at her knee, may now and then call to mind some old playmate, for whom, when they were girls together, she felt such an intense love. How they used to pine for the daily greeting—the long walk, fraught with all sorts of innocent secrets. Or, in absence, the almost interminable letters—positive love-letters, full of 'dearest's and 'beloved's, and sealing-wax kisses.* Then the delicious meetings—sad partings, also quite lover-like in the multiplicity of tears and embraces—embraces sweeter than those of all the world beside—and tears, but our own are gathering while we write—Ah!

We also have been in Arcadia.*

Gracious reader! grave, staid mother of a family!—you are not quite right if you jest at the days of old, and at such feelings as these. They were real at the time—and most pure, true, and beautiful. What matter, if years, sweeping on, have swept them all away, or merged them into higher duties and closer ties? Perhaps, if you met your beautiful idol of fifteen, you would see a starched old maid of fifty, or a grandame presiding over the third generation; or, perchance, in seeking thus, you would find only a green hillock, or a stone inscribed with the well-known name. But what of that? To you the girlish image is still the same—it never can grow old, or change, or die, Think of it thus; and then you will think, not mockingly, but with an interest almost mournful, on the rapturous dream of first friendship which now came to visit Olive Rothesay.

Sara Derwent was the sort of girl of whom we meet some hundreds in a lifetime—the class from whence are taken the lauded 'mothers, wives, and daughters of England'. She was sincere, good-tempered, affectionate; not over-clever, being more gifted with heart than brains; rather vain, which fault her extreme prettiness half excused; always anxious to do right, yet, from a want of decision of character, often contriving to do wrong.

But she completely charmed the simple Olive with her beauty, her sparkling, winning cheerfulness, and her ready sympathy. So they became the most devoted friends. Not a day passed without their spending some portion of it together—Olive teaching the young Londoner the pleasures of the country; and Sara, in her turn, inducting the wondering Olive into all the delightful mysteries of life, as learnt in a large home circle, and a still larger circle of society. Olive, not taking aught from the passionate love with which she looked up to her mother, yet opened her warm heart to the sweetness of this affection—so fresh, so sudden, so full of sympathetic contact. It was like a new revelation in her girlhood—the satisfying of a thirst, just beginning to be felt. She thought of Sara continually; delighted in being with her; in admiring her beauty, and making interests out of every interest of hers. And to think that her friend loved her in return, brought a sensation of deep happiness, not unmixed with gratitude.

Sara's own feelings may be explained by one sentence of a letter which she wrote to an old schoolmate. Therein she told how she had found 'such a dear, loving, gentle thing; a girl, not pretty—even slightly deformed; but who was an amusing companion, and to whom she could confide everything. Such a blessing in that dull place, Oldchurch!'

Poor little Olive!—

CHAPTER XII

As the summer advanced, Olive Rothesay and her new friend, sanctioned by the elders of both families, took long walks together, read, and practised. Not that Olive practised, for she had no voice, and little knowledge of music; but she listened to Sara's performances for hours, with patience, if not with delight. And then they talked—oh, what talks those were!

Now, reader, be not alarmed lest we should indulge you with the same. Go back into your own repertoire of early friendships, and that will suit us quite as well. Still, we may just say, that these young friends flitted like bees over every subject under heaven, and at last alighted on the subject most interesting at their age—love.

It is curious to note how the heart first puts out its tendrils and stretches them forth toward the yet unknown good which is to be in after-life its happiness and its strength. What folly of parents to repress these blind seekings after such knowledge—this yearning which nature teaches, and which in itself involves nothing wrong. Girls *will* think of love, whether or no! How much better, then, that they should be taught to think of it rightly; as the one deep feeling of life. Not, on the one hand, to be repressed by ridicule; or, on the other, to be forced by romance into a precocious growth; but to be entered upon, when fate brings the time, rationally, earnestly, and sacredly.

Olive Rothesay found, with considerable pain, that Miss Derwent and she did not at all agree in their notions of love. Olive had always felt half-frightened at the subject, and never approached it save with great awe and timidity; but Sara did not seem to mind it in the least. She talked of a score of 'flirtations' at quadrille parties—showed her friend half-a-dozen complimentary billet-doux which she had received, and all with the greatest unconcern. By degrees this indifference vanished under the influence of Olive's more earnest nature; and at last, when they were sitting together one night, listening to the fierce howling of the wind, a little secret came out.

'I don't like that equinoctial gale,' said Sara, shyly. 'I used to hear so much of its horrors from—from a friend I have—at sea.'

'Indeed. Who was that?'

'Only Charles Geddes. Did I never speak of him? Very likely not—because I was so vexed at his leaving college and running off to sea. It was a foolish thing. But don't mention him to papa or the boys.' And Sara blushed—a real, good, honest blush.

Olive did the same—perhaps from sympathy. She continued very thoughtful for a long time; longer even than Sara. They were not many days in making out between them the charming secret for which in their hearts they had been longing. Both were thirsting to taste—or at least to see each other taste—of that enchanting love-stream, the stream of life or of death, at whose verge they had now arrived.

And so, it somehow chanced that however the conversation began, it usually glided into the subject of Charles Geddes. Sara acknowledged that he and she had always liked one another very much, though she allowed that he was fonder of her than she was of him; that, when they parted, he had seemed much agitated, and she had cried—but they were mere boy and girl then. It was nothing—nothing at all.

Olive did not think so; and, contrasting all this with similar circumstances in her pet poems and novels, she wove a very nice romance round Charles Geddes and her beloved Sara, whom she now began to look upon with greater interest and reverence than ever. This did not prevent her reading Sara a great many lectures on constancy, and giving her own opinions on what true love ought to be—opinions which were a little too ethereal for Miss Derwent's comprehension, but which she liked very much, nevertheless.

Olive took quite an affectionate interest in her friend's lover—for lover she had decided that he must be. Not a day passed that she did not eagerly consult the *Times*' 'shipping intelligence'; and when at last she saw the name of Charles Geddes' vessel, as 'arrived', her heart beat, and tears sprang to her eyes. When she showed it to Sara, Olive could hardly speak for joy. Little simpleton! she counted her friend's happiness as if it were her own. She kept the secret even from her mother; that is, in the only manner Olive would conceal aught from any one so beloved, by saying, 'Please, mamma, do not ask me anything.' And Mrs Rothesay, who, always guided by some one, was now in a fair way to be entirely guided by her daughter, made no enquiries, but depended entirely upon Olive's wisdom and tenderness.

Charles Geddes came to Oldchurch. It was quite a new life for Olive—a changed life, too; for now the daily rambles with her friend were less frequent. Instead of which, she used to sit at her window, and watch Sara and Charles taking long strolls in the garden, arm-in-arm, looking so happy, that it was beautiful to see them.

Who can describe the strange, half-defined thoughts which often brought tears to the young girl's eyes as she watched them thus! It was no jealousy of Sara's deserting her for Charles, still less was it envy; but it was a vague longing—a desiring of love for love's own sake. Not as regarded any individual object, for Olive had never seen any one in whom she felt or fancied the slightest interest. Yet, as she looked on these two young creatures, apparently so bound up in each other, she thought how sweet such a tie must be, and how dearly she herself could love some one. And her yearning was always *to love* rather than *to be loved*.

One morning, when Olive had not seen Sara for a day or two, she was hastily summoned to their usual trysting-place, a spot by the riverside, where the two gardens met, and where an overarching thorn-tree made a complete bower. Therein Sara stood, looking so pale and serious, that Olive remarked it.

'Has anything happened?'

'Nothing—that is, nothing amiss. But oh! Olive, what do you think? Charles put this letter into my hand last night. I have scarcely slept—I feel so agitated—so frightened.'

And in truth she looked so. Was there ever a very young girl who did not, on receiving her first love-letter?

It was an era in Olive's life, too. She even trembled, as by her friend's earnest desire she read the missive. It was boyish, indeed, and full of the ultra-romantic devotion of boyish love; but it was sincere, and it touched Olive deeply. She finished it, and leaned against the thorn-tree, pale and agitated as Sara herself.

'Well, Olive,' said the latter.

Olive threw her arms round her friend's neck and kissed her, feeling almost ready to cry.

'And now, dear, tell me what I must do,' said Sara, earnestly; for of late she had positively begun to look up to Olive, so great was the influence of the more thoughtful and higher nature.

'Do! Why, if you love him, you must tell him so, and give him your whole lifelong faith and affection.'

'Really, Olive, how grave you are! I had no idea of making it such a serious matter. But, poor Charles!—to think that he should love me so very much!'

'Oh, Sara—Sara!' murmured Olive, 'how happy you ought to be!'

The time that followed was a strange period in Olive's life. It was one of considerable excitement, too; she might as well have been in love herself, so deeply did she sympathize with Sara and with Charles. With the latter, even more than with her friend; for there was something in the sincere, reserved, and yet passionate nature of the young sailor, that answered to her own. If he had been her brother, she could not have felt more warmly interested in Charles Geddes and his wooing. And he liked her very much, for Sara's sake first, and then for her own, regarding her also with that gentle compassion which the strong and bold delight to show to the weak. He often called her 'his faithful little friend'; and truly she stood his friend in every conceivable way, by soothing Sara's only parent—a most irascible papa—to consent to the engagement, and also by lecturing the gay and coquettish Sara herself into as much good behaviour as could be expected from an affianced damsel of seventeen.

Charles Geddes went to sea again. Poor little Olive, in her warm sympathies, suffered almost as much as the young man's own betrothed, who, after looking doleful for a week, consoled herself by entering, heart and soul, into the gaieties of the gayest Christmas that ever was spent by the society of Oldchurch. Everywhere Miss Derwent was the belle, and continually did her friend need to remind her of the promise which Olive herself regarded as such a sacred, solemn thing.

The love adventure in which she had borne a part had stirred strange depths in the nature of the young girl. She was awakening slowly to the great mystery of woman's life. And when, by degrees, Sara's amusements somewhat alienated their continual intercourse, Olive was thrown back upon her own thoughts more and more. She felt a vague sadness—a something wanting in her heart, which not even her mother's love could supply.

Mrs Rothesay saw how dull and pensive she was at times, and with a tender unselfishness contrived that, by Sara Derwent's intervention, Olive should see a little more society; in a very quiet way, though; for her own now delicate health, and Captain Rothesay's will, prevented any regular introduction of their daughter into the world. And sometimes Mrs Rothesay, pondering on Olive's future, felt glad of this.

'Poor child! she is not made for the world, or the world for her. Better that she should lead her own quiet life, where she will suffer no pain, and he wounded by no neglect.'

Yet, nevertheless, it was with a vague pleasure that Mrs Rothesay dressed Olive for her first ball—a birthday treat—coaxed by Sara Derwent out of her formidable papa, and looked forward to by both young girls for many weeks.

No one would have believed that the young creature, on whom Mrs Rothesay gazed with a tenderness, not unmingled with admiration, had been the poor infant from which she once turned with a sensation of pain, almost amounting to disgust. But, learning to love, one learns also to admire. Besides, Olive's defect was less apparent as she grew up, and the extreme sweetness of her countenance almost atoned for her figure. Yet, as the mother fastened her white dress, and arranged the golden curls so as to fall in a shower on her neck and bosom, she sighed heavily.

Olive did not notice it; she was too much occupied in tying up a rare bouquet—a birthday gift for Sara.

'Well, are you quite satisfied with my dress, dearest mamma?'

'Not quite'; and Mrs Rothesay fetched a small mantle of white fur, which she laid round Olive's shoulders. 'Wear this, dear; you will look better then—see.' She led her to the mirror, and Olive saw the reflection of her own figure, so effectually disguised, that the head, with its delicate and spiritual beauty, seemed lifting itself out of a white cloud.

''Tis a pretty little mantle, but why must I wear it, mamma?—the night is not cold,' said Olive, unconsciously. So little did she think of herself, and so slight had been her intercourse with the world, that the defect in her shape rarely crossed her mind. But the mother, so beautiful herself, and to whom beauty was still of such importance, was struck with bitter pain. She would not even console herself by the reflection, with which many a one had lately comforted her, that Olive's slight deformity was becoming less perceptible, and that she might, in a great measure, outgrow it in time. Still it was there. As Mrs Rothesay looked at the swan-like curves of her own figure, and then at her daughter's, she would almost have resigned her own once-cherished, but now disregarded, beauty, could she have bestowed that gift upon her beloved child.

Without speaking, lest Olive should guess her thoughts, she laid the mantle aside, only, with a trembling affection, she whispered in bidding adieu, 'Dear, if you see other girls prettier, or more admired, more noticed than yourself, never mind! Olive is mamma's own pet—always.'

Oh, blessed adversity! oh, sweetness, taught by suffering! How marvellous was the change wrought in the mother's heart!

Olive had never in her life before been at an orthodox 'private ball', with chalked floors, rout seats, and a regular band. She was quite dazzled by the transformation thus effected in the Derwents' large, rarely used dining-room, where she had had many a merry game with little Robert and Lyle. It was perfect fairyland. The young damsels of Oldchurch—haughty boarding-school belles, whom she had always rather feared, when Sara's hospitality brought her in contact with them—were now grown into perfect court beauties. She was quite alarmed by their dignity, and they scarce noticed poor little Olive at all. Sara, sweeping across the room in all the blaze of her remarkable loveliness, to say nothing of her mother's long-hidden jewels, appeared to the eyes of her little friend a perfect queen of beauty. But the vision came and vanished. Never was there a belle so much in request as the lively Sara.

Only once, Olive looked at her, and remembered the sailor-boy, who was, perhaps, tossing in some awful night storm, or lying on the lonely deck, in the midst of the wide Atlantic. And she thought, that when her time came to love and be loved, she would not feel everything quite so lightly as Sara.

'How pleasant quadrilles must be!' said Olive, as she sat with her favourite Lyle, watching the dancers. Lyle had crept to her, sliding his hand in hers, and looking up to her with a most adoring gaze, as indeed he often did. He had even communicated his intention of marrying her when he grew a man—a determination which excited the great ridicule of his elder brother.

'I like far better to sit here quietly with you,' murmured the faithful little cavalier.

'Thank you, Lyle; still, they all look so merry, I almost wish some one had asked me to dance.'

'You dance, Miss Rothesay! What fun! Why nobody would ever dance with you,' cried rude Bob.

Lyle looked imploringly at his brother: 'Hush! you naughty boy! Please, Miss Rothesay, I will dance with you at any time, that is, if you think I am tall enough.'

'Oh, quite; I am so tiny myself,' answered Olive, laughing; for she took quite a pride in patronizing him, as girls of sixteen often affectionately patronize boys some five or six years their junior. 'You know, you are to grow up to be my little husband.'

'Your husband!' repeated Bob, mischievously. 'Don't be too sure of getting one at all. What do you think I overheard those girls there say? That you looked just like an old maid; and, indeed, no one would ever care to marry you, because you were——'

Here Lyle, blushing crimson, stopped his brother's mouth with his little hand; whereat Bob flew into such a passion, that he quite forgot Olive, and all he was about to say, in the excitement of a pugilistic combat with his unlucky *cadet*.* In the midst of which the two belligerents—poor, untaught, motherless lads—were hurried off to bed.

Their companionship lost, Olive was left very much to her own devices for amusement. Some few young people that she knew came and talked to her for a little while, but they all went back to their singing, dancing, or flirting; and Olive, who seemed to have no gift nor share in either, was left alone. She did not feel this much at first, being occupied in her thoughts and observations on the rest. She took great interest in noticing all around. Her warm heart throbbed in sympathy with many an idle, passing flirtation, which she in her simplicity mistook for a real 'attachment'. It seemed as if every one loved, or was loved, except herself. She thought this, blushing as if it were unmaidenliness, when it was only nature speaking in her heart.

Poor Olive! perhaps it was ill for her that Sara's 'love affair' had aroused prematurely these blind gropings after life's great mystery, so often.

Too early seen unknown, and known too late.*

'What! tired of dancing already?' cried Sara, flitting to the corner where Olive sat.

'I have not danced once yet,' Olive answered, rather piteously; for she was a blithe little lassie in the main, and began to long for a quadrille.

'Come—shall I get you a partner?' said Sara, carelessly.

'No, no; every one is strange to me here. If you please, and if it would not trouble you, Sara, I had much rather dance with you.'

Sara consented with a tolerably good grace; but there was a slight shadow on her face, which somewhat pained her friend.

'Is she ashamed of me, I wonder?' thought Olive. 'Perhaps, because I am not beautiful. Yet, no one ever told me I was *very* disagreeable to look at. I will see.'

As they danced, she watched in the tall mirror Sara's graceful, floating image, and the little pale figure that moved beside her. There *was* a contrast! Olive, who inherited all her mother's love of beauty, spiritualized by the refinement of a dawning artist soul, felt keenly the longing regret after physical perfection. She went through the dance with less spirit, and in her heart there rang the idle echoes of some old song she knew:

> I see the courtly ladies pass, with their dark and shining hair;
> And I coldly turn aside to weep—'Oh, would that I were fair!'

The quadrille ended, she hid herself in her old corner; and Sara, whose good nature led her to perform this sacrifice to friendship, seemed to smile more pleasantly and affectionately when it was over. At least Olive thought so. She did not see her beautiful idol again for some time; and feeling little interest in any other girl, and none at all in the awkward Oldchurch 'beaux', she took consolation in her own harmless fashion.

This was hiding herself under the thick curtains, and looking out of the window at the moon.

—Sara's voice, close by, talking to a young girl whom Olive knew. But Olive was too shy to join them. She greatly preferred her friend, the moon.

'I quite smiled to see you dancing with that little Olive Rothesay, Miss Derwent. For my part, I hate dancing with girls—and as for *her*—— But I suppose you wanted to show the contrast between you.'

'Nay, that's ill-natured,' answered Sara. 'She is a sweet little creature, and my very particular friend.'

Here Olive, blushing and happy, doubted whether she ought not to come out of the curtains. It was almost wrong to listen—only her beloved Sara often said she had no secret in the world that she had not told to Olive.

'Yes, I know she is your friend, and Mr Charles Geddes' great friend too; if I were you, I should be almost jealous.'

'Jealous of Olive—how very comical!' and the silver laugh was a little scornful. 'To think of Olive's stealing any girl's lover! She, who will probably never have one in all her life—poor thing!'

'Of course not; nobody would fall in love with her! But there is a waltz, I must run away. Will you come?'

'Presently—when I have looked in the other room for Olive.'

'Olive is here,' said a timid voice. 'Oh, Sara, forgive me if I have done wrong; but I can't keep anything from you. It would grieve me to think I heard what you were saying, and never told you of it.'

Sara appeared confused, and with a quick impulse kissed and fondled her little friend: 'You are not vexed, or pained, Olive?'

'Oh, no—that is, not much; it would be very silly if I were. But,' she added, doubtfully, 'I wish you would tell me one thing, Sara—not that I am proud, or vain; but still, I should like to know—why do I seem different from other girls? Why did you and Jane Ormond say just now that nobody would ever love me?'

'Don't talk so, my little pet,' said Sara, looking pained and puzzled. Yet, instinctively, her eye glanced to the mirror, where their two reflections stood. So did Olive's.

'Yes, I know,' she murmured, 'I am little, and plain, and in figure very awkward—not graceful, like you. Would that make people hate me, Sara?'

'Not hate you; but——'

'Well, go on—nay, I *will* know all!' said Olive, firmly; though, gradually, a thought—long subdued—began to dawn painfully in her mind.

'I assure you, dear,' began Sara, hesitatingly, 'it does not signify to me, or to any of those who care for you; you are such a gentle little creature, we forget it all in time. But perhaps with strangers, especially with men, who think so much about beauty, this defect——'

She paused, laying her arm round Olive's shoulders—even affectionately, as if she herself were much moved. But Olive, with a cheek that whitened and a lip that quivered more and more, looked resolutely at her own shape imaged in the glass.

'I see, as I never saw before—so little I thought of myself. Yes, it is quite true—quite true.'

She spoke beneath her breath, and her eyes seemed fascinated into a hard, cold gaze. Sara became almost frightened.

'Do not look so, my dear girl; I did not say that it was a positive *deformity*.'

Olive faintly shuddered: 'Ah, that is the word! I understand it all now.'

She paused a moment, covering her face. But very soon she sat down, so quiet and pale that Sara was deceived.

'You do not mind it, then, Olive—you are not angry with me?' she said, soothingly.

'Angry with you—how could I be?'

'Then you will come back with me, and we will have another dance.'

'Oh, no, no!' And the cheerful good-natured voice seemed to make Olive shrink with pain. 'Sara, dear Sara, let me go home!'

CHAPTER XIII

'Well, my love, was the ball as pleasant as you expected?' said Mrs Rothesay, when Olive drew the curtains, and roused her invalid mother to the usual early breakfast, received from no hands but hers.

Olive answered quietly, 'Every one said it was pleasant.'

'But you,' returned the mother, with an anxiety she could scarce disguise—'who talked to you?—who danced with you?'

'No one, except Sara.'

'Poor child!' was the half involuntary sigh; and Mrs Rothesay drew her daughter to her with deep tenderness.

It was a strange fate, that made the once slighted child almost the only thing in the world to which Sybilla Rothesay now clung. And yet, so rich, so full, had grown the springs of maternal love, long hidden in her nature, that she would not have exchanged their sweetness to be again the petted, willful, beautiful darling of society, as she was at Stirling. The neglected wife—the often ailing mother—dependent on her daughter's tenderness, was happier and nearer to heaven than she had ever been in her life.

Mrs Rothesay regarded Olive earnestly. 'You look as ill as if you had been up all night; and yet you came to rest tolerably early, and I thought you slept, you lay so quiet. Was it so, darling?'

'Not quite; I was thinking,' said Olive, truthfully, though her face flushed, for she would fain have kept her bitter thoughts from her mother. Just then, Mrs Rothesay started at the sound of the hall bell.

'Is that your father come home? He said he might, today or tomorrow.' And she positively trembled.

Olive went downstairs. it was only a letter, to say Captain Rothesay would return that day; and would bring—most rare circumstance!—some guests to visit them. Olive seemed to shrink painfully at this news.

'What, my child, are you not pleased?—It will make the house less dull for you.'

'No, no——I do not wish; O mamma! if I could only shut myself up, and never see any one but you——' And Olive turned very pale. At last, resolutely trying to speak without any show of trouble, she continued— 'I have found out something that I never knew—at least, never thought of before—that I am different to other girls. Oh, mother! am I then so painful to look upon? shall I, indeed, cause people to dislike me wherever I go?'

She spoke with much agitation. Mrs Rothesay burst into tears.

'Oh, Olive! how wretched you make me, to talk thus. Unhappy mother that I am! Why should Heaven have punished me thus?'

'Punished you, mother?'

'Nay, my child—my poor innocent child! I did not mean that,' cried Mrs Rothesay; embracing her with a passionate revulsion of feeling.

But the word was said—to linger, for ever after, on Olive's mind. It brought back the look once written on her childish memory—grown faint, but never quite erased—her father's first look. She understood it now.

Mrs Rothesay continued weeping, and Olive had to cast aside all other feelings in the care of soothing her mother. She succeeded at last; but she learnt at the same time that on this one subject there must be silence between them for ever. It seemed, also, to her sensitive nature, as if every tear and every complaining word were a reproach to the mother that bore her. Henceforth her bitter thoughts must be wrestled with alone.

She did so wrestle with them. She walked out into her favourite meadow—now lying in the silent, frost-bound mistiness of a January day. It was where she had often been in summer with Sara, and Charles Geddes, and the little boys. Now everything seemed so wintry and lonely. What if her own future life were so—one long winter day, wherein was neither beauty, gladness, nor love?

'I am "*deformed*". That was Sara's own word', murmured Olive to herself. 'If this is felt by one who loves me, what must I appear to the world? Will not all shrink from me—and even those who pity, turn away in pain? As for loving me——'

Thinking thus, Olive's fancy began to count, almost in despair, all those whose affection she had ever known. There was Elspie, there were her parents. Yet, the love of both father and mother—how sweet soever, now—had not blessed her always. She remembered the time when it was not there.

'Alas! that I should have been, even to them, a burden—a pang!' cried the girl, in the first outburst of suffering, which became ten times keener, because concealed. Her vivid fancy even exaggerated the truth. She saw in herself a poor deformed being, shut out from all natural ties—a woman, to whom friendship would be given but in kindly pity; to whom love—that blissful dream in which she had of late indulged—would be denied for evermore. How hard seemed her doom! If it were for months only, or even years; but, to bear for a whole life this withering ban—never to be freed from it, except through death! And her lips unconsciously repeated the bitter murmur, 'O God! why hast thou made me thus?'

It was scarcely uttered before her heart trembled at its impiety. And then the current of her thoughts changed. Those mysterious yearnings which had haunted her throughout childhood, until they had grown fainter under the influence of earthly ties and pleasures—returned to her now. God's immeasurable Infinite rose before her in glorious serenity. What was one brief lifetime to the ages of eternity? She felt it: she, in her weakness—her untaught childhood—her helplessness—felt that her poor deformed body enshrined a living soul. A soul that could look on Heaven, and on whom Heaven also looked—not like man, with scorn or loathing, but with a Divine tenderness that had power to lift the mortal into communion with the immortal.

Olive Rothesay seemed to have grown years older in that hour of solitary musing. She walked homewards through the silent fields, over which the early night was falling—night coming, as it were, in the midst of day, where the only light was given by the white, cold snow. To Olive this was a symbol, too—a token that the freezing sorrow which had fallen on her path, might palely light her on her earthly way. Strange things for a young girl to dream of! But they whom Heaven teaches are sometimes called—Samuel-like—while to them still pertains the childish ephod and the temple porch.

Passing on, with footsteps silent and solemn as her own heart, Olive came to the street, on the verge of the town, where was her own dwelling and Sara's. From habit she looked in at the Derwents' house. It had all that cheerful brightness given by a blazing fire, glimmering through windows not yet closed. Olive could plainly distinguish the light shining on the crimson wall; even the merry faces of the circle round the hearth. And, as if to chant the chorus of so sweet a scene, there broke out on the clear frosty air the distant carillon of Oldchurch bells—marriage-bells, too—signifying that not far off was dawning another scene of love and hope; that, somewhere in the parish, was celebrated the 'coming home' of a bride.*

The young creature, born with a woman's longings—longings neither unholy or impure, after the love which is the religion of a woman's heart—the sweetness of home, which is the heaven of a woman's life—felt that from both she was shut out for ever.

'Not for me—alas! not for me,' she murmured; and her head drooped, and it seemed as though a cold hand were laid on her breast, saying, 'Grow still, and throb no more!'

Then, lifting her eyes, she saw shining far up in the sky, beyond the mist and the frost and the gloom, one little star—the only one. With a long sigh, her soul seemed to pass upward in prayer.

'Oh God! since Thou hast willed it so—if in this world I must walk alone, do Thou walk with me! If I must know no human love, fill my soul with Thine! If earthly joy be far from me, give me that peace of Heaven which passeth all understanding!'

And so—mournful, yet serene—Olive Rothesay reached her home.

She found her friend there. Sara looked confused at seeing her, and appeared to try, with the unwonted warmth of her greeting, to efface from Olive's mind the remembrance of what had happened the previous evening. But Olive, for the first time, shrank from these tokens of affection.

'Even Sara's love may be only compassion,' she bitterly thought; and her calm endurance was again changed into grief and humiliation. She betrayed neither; for her father's nature was in the girl—his self-command—his proud reserve. Sara Derwent only thought her rather silent and cold. Little she wondered at this, though her regret rose at having been so foolish as to talk to her poor little friend in the way she did.

There was a constraint on both—so much so that Olive heard, without testifying much pain, news which a few days before would have grieved her to the heart. This visit was an adieu. Sara had been suddenly sent for by her grandfather, who lived in a distant county; and the summons entailed a parting of some weeks—perhaps, longer.

'But I shall not forget you, Olive. I shall write to you constantly. It will be my sole amusement in the dull place I am going to. Why, nobody ever used to enter my grandfather's house, except the parson, who lived some few miles off. Poor old soul! I used to set fire to his wig, and hide his spectacles. But he is dead now, I hear, and there has come in his place a young clergyman. Shall I strike up a little flirtation with *him*, eh—Olive?'

But Olive was in no jesting mood. She only shook her head.

Mrs Rothesay looked with admiration on Sara. 'What a blithe young creature you are, my dear. You win everybody's liking. I wish Olive were only half as merry as you.'

Another arrow in poor Olive's heart!

'Well—we must try to make her so when I come back,' said Sara, affectionately. 'I shall have tales enough to tell; perhaps, about that young curate. Nay, don't frown, Olive. My cousin says he is a Scotsman born—and you like Scotland. Only his father was Welsh, and he has a horrid Welsh name—Gwyrdyr, or Gwynne, or something like it. But I'll give you all information.'

And then she rose—still laughing—to bid adieu; which seemed so long a farewell, when the friends had never yet been parted but for one brief day. In saying it, Olive felt how dear to her had been this girl—this first idol of her warm heart. And then there came a thought almost like terror. Though fated to live unloved, she could not keep herself from loving. And if so, how would she bear the perpetual void—the yearning, never to be fulfilled?

She fell on Sara's neck and wept. 'You do care for me a little—only a little.'

'A great deal—as much as ever I can, seeing I have so many people to care for,' answered Sara, trying to laugh away the tears that—from sympathy, perhaps—sprang to her eyes.

'Ah, true! And everybody cares for you. No wonder,' answered Olive.

'Now, little Olive, why do you put on that grave face? Are you going to lecture me about not flirting with that stupid curate, and always remembering Charles. Oh! no fear of that.'

'I hope not,' said Olive, quietly. She could not talk more, and they bade each other goodbye; perhaps not quite so enthusiastically as they might have done a week ago, but still with much affection. Sara had reached the door, when with a sudden impulse she came back again.

'Olive, I am a foolish, thoughtless girl; but if ever I pained you in any way, don't think of it again. Kiss me—will you—once more?'

Olive did so, clinging to her passionately. When Sara went away, she felt as though the first flower had perished in her garden, the first star had melted from her sky. It seemed a foreshadowing of that lonely fate, the portion of some humble ones, unblessed with the power to inspire other hearts with their own warmth. Alas! for that love which ever sees its objects come and go, brighten and fade, while it alone endures, and its very constancy becomes its deepest woe. Yet, not so. Greater—far greater—than the rolling, changing planets, is the sun; that burns on in its eternal loneliness, an emblem of that One Love which, from its infinite solitude, guides and sustains the universe.

Sara gone, Olive went back to her old dreamy life. The romance of first friendship seemed to have been swept away like a morning cloud. From Sara there came no letters—save a brief one, during her first week at Waterton. Olive wrote once or twice, even thrice. But a sense of wounded feeling prevented her writing again. Some tidings she gained from Robert and Lyle, that their sister was quite well, and very merry. Then, over all the dream of sweet affection fell a cold silence.

It might have utterly frozen so young and sensitive a heart, but that in Olive's own home were arising many cares. A great change came over her father. His economical habits became those of the wildest extravagence—extravagance in which his wife and daughter were not likely to share. Little they saw of it either, save during his rare visits to his home. Then, he either spent his evenings out, or else dining, smoking, drinking—horrible orgies of dissipated men—disturbed the quiet house at Oldchurch.

Many a time, till long after midnight, the mother and child sat listening to the gay tumult of voices below; clinging to each other, pale and sad. Not that Captain Rothesay was unkind, or that either had any fear for him, for he had always been a strict and temperate man. But it pained them to think that any society seemed sweeter to him than that of his wife and daughter—that any place was become dearer to him than his home.

One night, when Mrs Rothesay appeared exhausted, either with weariness or sorrow of heart, Olive persuaded her mother to go to rest, while she herself sat up for her father.

'Nay, let some of the servants do that, not you, my child.'

But Olive, innocent as she was of all worldly guile, had accidentally seen the footman smile rudely when he spoke of 'master coming home last night'; and a vague thought struck her, that such late hours were discreditable in the head of a family. Her father should not be mocked in his servants' eyes.

She dismissed the household and waited up for him alone. Twelve—one—two. The hours went by like long years. Heavily at first drooped her poor drowsy eyes, and then all weariness was dispelled by a feeling of loneliness—an impression of coming sorrow. At last, when this sense was gradually merging into fear, she heard the sound of the swinging gate, and her father's knock at the door.

A loud, unsteady, angry knock—one that made her feet fly swifter even than by the impulse of affection.

'Why do you stay up for me? I don't want anybody to sit up,' grumbled Captain Rothesay, without looking at her.

'But I liked to wait for you, papa.'

'What! is that you, Olive?' and he stepped in with a lounging heavy gait—that of a person overpowered with fatigue, as his young daughter thought.

'Did you not see me before? It was I who opened the door.'

'Oh! yes—but—I was thinking of something else,' he said, throwing himself into the study chair, and trying with an effort to seem just as usual. 'You are—a very good girl—I'm much obliged to you. The pleasure is—I may truly say—on both sides.' And he energetically struck the table with his hand.

Olive thought this an odd form of speech; but her father's manner was grown so changed of late—sometimes he seemed quite in high spirits, even jocose—as he did now.

'I am glad to see you not much tired, papa. I thought you were—you walked so wearily when you first came in.'

'I tired? nonsense—child! I have had the merriest evening in the world. I'll have another tomorrow, for I've asked them all to dine here. We'll give dinner parties to all the county.'

'Papa,' said Olive timidly, 'will that be quite right, after what you told me of your being now so much poorer?'

'Did I? Pshaw! I don't remember. However, I am a rich man now; richer than I have ever been.'

'I am so glad; because then, dear papa, you know you need not be so much away from home, or weary yourself with the speculations you told me of; but come and live quietly with us.'

Her father laughed loudly. 'Foolish little girl! your notion of quietness would not suit a man like me. Take my word for it, Olive, home serves as a fantastic dream till five-and-twenty, and then means nothing at all. A man's home is the world.'

'Is it?'

'Ay, as I intend to show to you. By the by, I shall give up this stupid place, and enter into society. Your mother will like it, of course; and you, as my only child—eh—what did I say?' here he stopped hastily, with a blank, frightened look—then repeated, 'Yes—you, my only child, will be properly introduced to the world. Why, you'll be quite an heiress, my girl,' continued he, with an excited jocularity that frightened Olive. 'And the world always courts such; who knows but that you may marry in spite of——'

'Oh, no—never!' interrupted Olive, turning away with bitter pain.

'Come, don't mind it,' continued her father, with a reckless indifference to her feelings, quite unusual to him. 'Why—my little sensible girl—you are better than any beauty in England; beauties are all fools, or worse.'

And he laughed so loud, so long, that Olive was seized with a great horror, that absorbed even her own individual suffering. Was her father mad? Alas! there is a madness worse than disease, a voluntary madness, by which a man—longing at any price for excitement or oblivion—'puts an enemy into his mouth to steal away his brains'.* This was the foe—the stealthy footed demon, that had at last come to overmaster the brave and noble Angus Rothesay. As yet it ruled him not—he was no sot; but his daughter saw enough to know that the fiend was nigh upon him—that this night he was even in its grasp.

It is only the noblest kind of affection that can separate the sinner from the sin, and even while condemning, pity. Fallen as he was, Olive Rothesay looked on her father mournfully—entreatingly. She could not speak.

He seemed annoyed, and slightly confounded. 'Come, simpleton, why do you stare at me—there is nothing the matter. Go away to bed.'

Olive did not move.

'Make haste—what are you waiting for? Nay, stay; 'tis a cold night—just leave out the keys of the sideboard, will you, there's a good little housekeeper,' he said, coaxingly.

Olive turned away in disgust, but only for a moment. 'In case you should want anything, let me stay a little longer, papa; I am not tired, and I have some work to do—suppose I go and fetch it.'

She went into the inner room, slowly, quietly; and when safe out of sight, burst into tears of such shame and terror as she had never before known. Then she sat down to think. Her father thus; her mother feeble in mind and body; no one in the wide world to trust to but herself; no one to go to for comfort and counsel—none, save Heaven! She sank on her knees and prayed. As she rose, the angel in the daughter's soul was stronger than the demon in the father's.

Olive waited a little, and then walked softly into the other room. Some brandy, left on the sideboard, had attracted Captain Rothesay's sight. He had reached it with a noiseless hand, as if the act still conveyed to his dulled brain a consciousness of degradation. Once he looked round suspiciously; alas, the father dreaded his daughter's eye! Then stealthily standing with his face to the fire, he began to drink the tempting poison.

It was taken out of his hand! So noiseless was Olive's step, so gentle her movement, that he stood dumb, astonished, as though in the presence of some apparition. And, in truth, the girl looked like a spirit; for her face was very white, and her lips seemed as though they never had uttered, and never could utter, one living sound.

Father and daughter stood for some moments thus gazing at each other; and then Captain Rothesay threw himself into his chair, with a forced laugh.

'What's the matter, little fool? Cannot your father take care of himself? Give me the brandy again.'

But she held it fast, and made no answer.

'Olive, I say—do you insult me thus?' and his voice rose in anger. 'Go to bed, I command you! Will you not?'

'No!' The refusal was spoken softly—very softly—but it expressed indomitable firmness; and there was something in the girl's resolute spirit, before which that of the father quailed. With a sudden transition, which showed that the drink had already somewhat overpowered his brain, he melted into complaints.

'You are very rude to your poor father; you—almost the only comfort he has left!'

This touch even of maudlin sentiment went direct to Olive's heart. She clung to him, kissed him, begged his forgiveness, nay, even wept over him. He ceased to rage, and sat in a sullen silence for many minutes. Meanwhile Olive took away every temptation from his sight. Then she roused him gently.

'Now, papa, it is time to go to bed. Pray, come upstairs.'

He—the calm, gentlemanlike, Captain Rothesay—burst into a storm of passion that would have disgraced a boor. 'How dare you order me about in this manner! Cannot I do as I like, without being controlled by you—a mere chit of a girl—a very child.'

'I know I am only a child,' answered Olive, meekly. 'Do not be angry with me, papa; do not speak unkindly to your poor little daughter.'

'My daughter! how dare you call yourself so, you white-faced, mean-looking hunchback——'

At the word, Olive recoiled—a strong shudder ran through her frame; she moaned one long, sobbing sigh, and no more.

Her father, shocked, and a little sobered, paused in his cruel speech. For minutes, they remained—he leaning back with a stupefied air—she standing before him; her face drooped, and covered with her hands.

'Olive!' he muttered, in a repentant, humbled tone.

'Yes, papa.'

'I am quite ready. If you like, I'll go to bed now.'

Without speaking, she lighted him upstairs—nay *led* him; for, to his bitter shame, the guidance was not unneeded. When she left him, he had the grace to whisper—

'Child, you are not vexed about anything I said?'

She looked sorrowfully into his hot, fevered face, and stroked his arm with her pale hand. 'No—no—not vexed at all! You could not help it, poor father!'

She heard her mother's feeble, sleepless voice speaking to him as he entered, and saw his door close. Long she watched there, until beneath it she perceived not one glimmer of light. Then she crept away, only murmuring to herself—

'God! teach me to endure!'

CHAPTER XIV

'What is the matter with the child today?' said Captain Rothesay to his wife, with whom, oh, rare circumstance! he was sitting *tête-à-tête*. But this, and a few other alterations for the better, had taken place in consequence of his longer stay at home than usual, during which an unseen influence had been busily at work. Poor Olive! Was it not well for her, that, to temper the first shock of her bitter destiny, there should arise, in the dreary blank of the future, duties so holy, that they stood almost in the place of joys?

'How dull the girl seems!' again observed Captain Rothesay, looking after his daughter, with a tenderness of which he afterwards appeared rather ashamed.

'Dull, is she?' said the mother; 'oh, very likely, poor child! She is grieving to lose her chief friend and companion, Miss Derwent. News came to her this morning that Sara is about to be married.'

'Oh, indeed!' and Captain Rothesay made an attempt at departure. He hated gossiping, even of the most harmless kind. But his wife, pleased that he condescended to talk to her at all, tried to amuse him in her own easy way.

'Poor Sara! I am glad she is going to have a home of her own—though she is young enough to marry. But I believe it was a very sudden affair; and the gentleman fell so desperately in love with her.'

'More fool he!' muttered Captain Rothesay.

'Nay, he is not a fool at all; he is a very sensible, clever man, and a clergyman too; Miss Derwent said so in her brief note to Olive. But she did not mention where he lived; little indeed she told, but that his name was Gwynne—'

Captain Rothesay turned round quickly.

'—And Sara speaks of his mother being a stiff old Scotswoman. Ah, you are listening now, my dear. Let me see, I think Miss Derwent mentions her maiden name. The silly girl makes quite a boast of her lover's ancient family, on the maternal side.'

'There is no silliness in that, I hope, Mrs Rothesay?'

'Certainly not—was I not always proud of yours?' said the wife, with a meekness not newly learnt. She hunted in her reticule for Sara's letter, and read.

'Ah, here is the name—Alison Balfour: do you know it?'

'I did once, when I was a boy; but that is long ago,' said Captain Rothesay, in a suppressed tone.

'Stay! do not go away in that hasty manner. Pray, talk to me a little more, Angus; it is so dull to be confined to this sick-room. Tell me of this Alison Balfour; you know, I should like to hear about your friends.'

'Should you?—that is something new. If it had been always so—if you had indeed made my interests yours, Sybilla!' There was a touch of regret and old tenderness in his voice. She thought he was kind on account of her illness, and thanked him warmly. But the thanks sent him back to his usual cold self; he did not like to have his weakness noticed.

Mrs Rothesay understood neither one state of feeling nor the other, so she said, cheerfully, 'Come, now for the story of Alison Balfour.'

'There is no story to tell. She was merely a young companion of my aunt's, Flora. I knew her for some years—in fact, until she married Mr Gwynne. She was a noble woman.'

'Really, Angus, I shall grow jealous,' said Mrs Rothesay, half in jest, half in earnest. 'She must have been an old love of yours.'

Her husband frowned. 'Folly, Sybilla! She was a woman, and I a schoolboy!'

And yet the words galled him, for they were not far off the truth. True, Alison was old enough to have been his mother; but many a precocious lad of sixteen conceives a similar romantic passion, and Angus Rothesay had really been very much in love, as he thought, with Alison Balfour.

Even when he quitted the room, and walked out into the road, his thoughts went backward many years; picturing the old, dull mansion, whose only brightness had come with her presence. He remembered how he used to walk by her side, in lonely mountain rambles—he a little boy, and she a grown woman; and how proud he was, when she stooped her tall stature to lean upon his arm. Once, she kissed him; and he lay awake all night, and many a night after, dreaming of the remembered bliss. And, as he grew a youth, what delicious sweetness in these continued dreams! what pride to think himself 'in love'—and with such a woman! Folly it was—hopeless folly—for she had been long betrothed to one she loved. But that was not Owen Gwynne. Alas! Alison, like many another proud, passionate woman, had married in sudden anger, thereby wrecking her whole life! When she did so, Angus Rothesay lost his boyish dream. He had already begun to find out that it was only a dream; though his first fancy's idol never ceased to be to him a memory full of all that was noble and beautiful in womanhood.

For many years, this enchanted portion of Captain Rothesay's past life had rarely crossed his mind; but when it did, it was always with a half-unconscious thought, that he himself might have been a better and a happier man, had his own beautiful Sybilla been more like Alison Balfour.

This chance news of her awakened memories connected with other scenes and characters, which had gradually melted away from Angus Rothesay's life, or been enveloped in the mist of selfishness and worldliness which had gathered over it, and over him. He thought of the old uncle, Sir Andrew Rothesay, whose pride he had been; of the sweet aunt Flora, whose pale beauty had bent over his cradle with a love almost like a mother's, save that it was so very, very sad. One had died estranged; the other—— He would not let many weeks pass before he sought out Miss Flora Rothesay: that he was determined on! And, to do so, the best plan would be, first to go and see Alison—Mrs Gwynne.

Captain Rothesay always kept his intentions to himself, and transacted his matters alone. Therefore, without the aid of wife or daughter, he soon discovered in what region lay Mr Gwynne's curacy, and determined to hasten his customary journey to London, that he might visit the place on his way.

The night before his departure came. It was really a melancholy evening; for he had stayed at home so long, and been most of the time what his wife called 'so good', that she quite regretted his going. The more so, as he was about to travel by the awful railway—then newly established—which, in the opinion of poor Mrs Rothesay, with her delicate nerves and easily roused terrors, entailed on him the certainty of being killed. She pleaded so much and so anxiously—even to the last—that when, in order to start at daybreak, he bade 'goodbye' to her and Olive overnight, Captain Rothesay was softened even to tenderness.

'Do you really care so much about me, Sybilla?' said he, half mournfully.

She did not spring to his arms, like the young wife at Stirling, but she kissed his hand affectionately, and called him 'Angus!'

'Olive!' said the father, when, having embraced his wife, he now turned to his daughter, 'Olive, my child! take care of your mother! I shall be at home soon, and we will be very happy again—all three!'

As they ascended the staircase, they saw him watching them from below. Olive felt so content, even though her father was going away. She kissed her hand to him, with a blithe gesture, and then saw him go in and close the door. When the house sank into quietness, a curious feeling oppressed Captain Rothesay. It seemed to take rise in his wife's infectious fears.

'Women are always silly,' he argued to himself. 'Why should I dread any danger? The railway is safe as a coach—and yet, that affair of poor Huskisson!* Pooh! what a fool I am!'

But even while he mocked it, the vague presentiment appeared to take form in his mind; and sitting, the only person awake in the slumbering house, where no sound broke the stillness, except the falling of a few cinders, and the occasional noise of a mouse behind the wainscoat, somewhat of the superstitions of his northern youth came over him. His countenance became grave, and he sank into deep thought.

It is a trite saying, that every man has that in his heart, which, if known, would make all his fellow-creatures hate him. Was it this evil spirit which now struggled in Captain Rothesay's breast, and darkened his face with storms of passion, remorse, or woe? He gave no utterance to them in words. If any secret there were, he would not trust it even to the air. But, at times, his mute lips writhed; his cheeks burned, and grew ghastly. Sometimes, too, he wore a cowed and humbled look, as on the night when his daughter had stood like a pure angel to save him from the abyss, on the brink of which he trod.

She had saved him, apparently. That night's shame had never occurred again. Slowly, his habits were changing, and his tastes becoming home-like. But still his lonely hours betokened some secret hidden in his soul— a secret which, if known, might have accounted for his having plunged into uproarious excitement, or drunken oblivion.

At length, as by a violent effort, Angus Rothesay sat down and began to write. He wrote for several hours—though frequently his task was inter-rupted by long reveries, and by fits of vehement emotion. When he had finished, he carefully sealed up what he had written, and placed it in a secret drawer of his desk. Then he threw himself on a sofa, to sleep during the brief time that intervened before daybreak.

In the grey of the morning, when he stood dispatching a hasty break-fast, he was startled by a light touch on his arm.

'Little Olive!—why, I thought you were fast asleep.'

'I could not sleep when papa was going away; so I rose and dressed. You will not be angry?'

'Angry—no!' He stooped down and kissed her, more affectionately even than was his wont. But he was hasty and fidgety, as most men are when starting on a journey. They were both too busy for more words, until the few minutes during which he sat down to wait for the carriage. Then he took his daughter on his knee—an act of fatherly tenderness rather rare with him.

'I wish you were not going, or that I were going with you, papa,' Olive whispered, nestling to him, in a sweet, childish way, though she was almost a woman, now. 'How tired you look! You have not been in bed all night.'

'No; I had writing to do.' As he spoke, his countenance darkened. 'Olive,' he said, looking at her with sorrowful, questioning eyes.

'Well, dear papa.'

'Nothing—nothing. Is the carriage ready?'

'Not yet. You will have time just for one little thing—'twill take only a minute,' said Olive, persuasively.

'What is it, little one?'

'Mamma is asleep—she was tired and ill; but if you would run upstairs, and kiss her once again before you go, it would make her so much happier—I know it would.'

'Poor Sybilla!' he muttered, remorsefully, and quitted the room, slowly—not meeting his daughter's eyes; but when he came back, he took her in his arms, very tenderly.

'Olive, my child in whom I trust, always remember I did love you—you and your mother.'

These were the last words she heard him utter, ere he went away.

CHAPTER XV

Captain Rothesay had intended to make the business excursion wait on that of pleasure—if pleasure the visit could be called, which was entered on from duty, and would doubtless awaken many painful associations; but he changed his mind, and it was not until his return from London, that he stayed on the way, and sought out the village of Harbury.

Verbal landscape painting is rarely interesting to the general reader; and as Captain Rothesay was certainly not devoted to the picturesque, it seems idle to follow him during his ten-mile ride from the nearest railway station to the place which he discovered was that of Mrs Gwynne's abode, and where her son was 'perpetual curate'.*

Her son! It seemed very strange to imagine Alison a mother; and yet, while he thought, Angus Rothesay almost laughed at himself for his folly. His boyish fancy had, perforce, faded at seventeen, and he was now—pshaw—he was somewhere above forty. As for Mrs Gwynne, sixty would, probably, be nearer her age. Yet, not having seen her since she married, he never could think of her but as Alison Balfour.

As before observed, Captain Rothesay was by no means keenly suscep-tible to beauty of scenery; otherwise, he would often have been attracted from his meditations by that through which he passed. Lovely wood-lands, just bursting into the delicate green of spring; deep, still streams, flowing through meadows, studded with cattle; forest roads shadowed with stately trees, and so little frequented, that the green turf spread from hedge to hedge, and the primroses and bluebells sprang up almost in the pathway. All these composed a picture of rural loveliness, which is peculiar to England, and chiefly to that part of England where Harbury* is situated. Captain Rothesay scarcely noticed it, until, pausing to consider his track, he saw in the distance a church upon a hill. Beautiful and peaceful it looked—its ancient tower rising out against the sky, and the evening sun shining on its windows and gilded vane.

'That must surely be my landmark,' thought Captain Rothesay; and he made an enquiry to that effect of a man passing by.

'Aye, aye, measter,' was the answer, in rather unintelligible Doric; 'thot bees Harbury Church, as sure as moy name's John Dent; and thot red house—conna ye see't?—thot's our parson's.'

Prompted by curiosity, Rothesay observed—'Oh! Mr Gwynne's. He is quite a young man, I believe? Do you like him—you good folk hereabouts?'

'Some on us dun, and some on us dunna. He's not much of a parson, though; he wunna send yer to sleep wi' his long preachings. But oi say the mon's a good mon: he'll coom and see yer when you're bad, an' talk t' ye by th' hour; though he dunna talk oot o' th' Bible. But oi'm a lad o' t' forest, and 'll be a keeper some toime. That's better nor book-larning.'

Captain Rothesay had no will to listen to more personal revelations from honest John Dent; so he said, quickly—'Perhaps so, my good fellow.' Then he added, rather hesitatingly—'Mr Gwynne has a mother living with him, I believe. What sort of person is she?'

'Her's a good enough lady, oi reckon; only a bit too proud. Many's the blanket her's gen[1] to poor folk; and my owd mother sees her every week—but her's never shook hands wi' her yet. Eh, measter, won ye[2] go?'

This last remark was bellowed after Captain Rothesay, whose horse had commenced a sudden canter, which ceased not until its owner dismounted at the parsonage gate.

This gate formed the boundary of the garden—and a most lovely spot it was. It extended to the churchyard, with which it communicated by a little wicket door. You passed through beautiful parterres and alleys, formed of fragrant shrubs, to the spot

> Where grew the turf, in many a mouldering heap.*

It seemed as though the path of death were indeed through flowers. Garden and churchyard covered the hill's summit; and from both might be discerned a view such as is rarely seen in level England. It was a panorama—extending some twenty or thirty miles across the country—where, through woodlands and meadowlands, flowed the silver windings of a small river. Here and there was an old ruined castle—a manor house, rising among its ancestral trees—or the faint, misty smoke-cloud, that indicated some hamlet or small town. Save these, the landscape swept on unbroken, until it ended at the horizon in the high range of the D——shire hills.

Even to Captain Rothesay, this scene seemed strangely beautiful. He contemplated it for some time—his hand still on the unopened gate; and

---

[1] She has given.   [2] Will ye.

then he became aware that a lady, whose gardening dress and gardening implements showed she was occupied in her favourite evening employment, was looking at him with some curiosity.

The traces of life's downward path are easier to recognize than those of its ascent. Though the mature womanhood of Alison Balfour had glided into age, Rothesay had no difficulty in discovering that he was in the presence of his ancient friend. Not so with her. He advanced, addressed her by name, and even took her hand, before she had the slightest idea that her guest was Angus Rothesay.

'Have you, then, so entirely forgotten me—forgotten the days in our native Perthshire, when I was a bit laddie, and you, our guest, were Miss Alison Balfour?'

There came a trembling over her features—ay, aged woman as she was! But at her years, all the past, whether of joy or grief, becomes faint; else, how would age be borne? She extended both her hands, with a warm friendliness.

'Welcome, Angus Rothesay! No wonder I did not know you. These thirty years—is it not thus much?—have changed you from a boy into a middle-aged man, and made of me an old woman.'

She really was an elderly lady now. It seemed almost ridiculous to think of her as his youth's idol. Neither was she beautiful,—how could he ever have imagined her so? Her irregular features—unnoticed when the white and red tints of youth adorned them—were now, in age, positively plain. Her strong-built frame had, in losing elasticity, lost much of grace, though dignity remained. Looking on Mrs Gwynne for the first time, she appeared a large, rather plain woman. Looking again, it would be to observe the noble candour that dwelt in the eyes, and the sweetness—at times even playfulness—that hovered round the mouth. Regarding her for the third time, you would see a woman whom you felt sure you must perforce respect, and might, in time, love very much—if she would let you. Of that gracious permission you would long have considerable doubt; but once granted, you would never unlove her to the end of your days. As for her loving *you*, you would not be quite clear that it did not spring from the generous benevolence of her nature, rather than from any individual warmth toward yourself; and such was the reserve of her character, that were her affection ever so deep, she might possibly never let you know it until the day of your death.

Yet she was capable of attachments, strong as her own nature. All her feelings, passions, energies, were on a grand scale: in her, were no petty feminine follies—no weak, narrow illiberalities of judgement. She had the soul of a man, and the heart of a woman.

'You were gardening, I see?' said Captain Rothesay, making the first ordinary remark that came to his mind, to break the awkward pause.

'Yes; I do so every fine evening. Harold is very fond of flowers—and that reminds me I must call him to you at once, as it is Wednesday—service night, and he will be engaged in his duties soon.'

'Pray, let us enter the house; I should much like to see your son,' said Angus Rothesay. He gave her his arm; and they walked together, through the green alleys of holly, to the front door. Then Mrs Gwynne stopped, put her hand over her eyes for a moment, removed it, and looked earnestly at her guest.

'Angus Rothesay! how strange this seems!—like a dream—a dream of thirty years. Well, let us go in.'

Mechanically, and yet in a subdued, absent manner, she laid her bonnet and shawl on the hall table, and took off her gardening gloves, thereby discovering hands, which, though large, were white and well formed, and in their round, tapered delicacy exhibited no sign of age. Captain Rothesay, without pausing to think, took the right hand.

'Ah! you wear still the ring I used to play with when a boy. I thought ——' and, recollecting himself, he stopped, ashamed of his discourtesy in alluding to what must have been a painful past.

But she said, quietly, sadly, though without any agitation, 'You have a good memory. It was left to me, ten years since, on the death of Archibald Maclean.'

Strange that she could thus speak that name! But over how many a buried grief does the grass grow green in thirty years!

In the hall, they encountered a young man.

'Harold,' said Mrs Gwynne, 'give welcome to an old—a very old friend of mine—Captain Angus Rothesay. Angus, this is my son—my only son, Harold.'

And she looked upon him as a mother, widowed for twenty years, looks upon an only son; yet the pride was tempered with dignity, the affection was veiled under reserve. She, who doubtless would have sustained his life with her own heart's blood, had probably never since his boyhood suffered him to know a mother's passionate tenderness, or to behold a mother's tear.

Perhaps that was the reason that Harold's whole manner was the reflection of her own. Not that he was like her in person; for nature had to him been far more bountiful; and Harold Gwynne, though not above mediocre height, was considerably above mediocre beauty. But there was a certain rigidness and harshness in his mien, and a slightly repellant atmosphere around him. Probably, not one of the young lambs of his flock had ever dreamed of climbing the knee of the Reverend Harold Gwynne. Though he wore the clerical garb, he did not look at all apostle-like; he was neither a St Paul nor a St John. Yet a grand, noble head it was. It might have been sketched for that of a young philosopher—a Galileo or a Priestley, with the heavy, strongly marked brows. The eyes—hackneyed as the description is, no one can paint a man without mentioning his eyes: those of Harold Gwynne were not unlike his mother's, in their open, steadfast look; yet they were not soft, like hers, but of a steel grey, diamond clear. He carried his head very erect; and these eyes of his seemed as though unable to rest on the ground; they were always turned upwards, with a gaze—not reverent or dreamy—but eager, enquiring, and piercing as truth itself.

Such was the young man with whom Captain Rothesay shook hands, congratulating his old friend on having such a son.

'You are more fortunate than I,' he said; 'my marriage has only bestowed on me a daughter.'

'Daughters are a great comfort sometimes,' answered Mrs Gwynne; 'though, for my part, I never wished for one.'

The quick, reproachful glance of Harold sought his mother's face; and shortly afterwards, he re-entered his study.

'My son thinks I meant to include a daughter-in-law,' was Mrs Gwynne's remark, while the concealed playfulness about her mouth appeared. 'He is soon to bring me one.'

'I know it—and know her, too; by this means I found you out. I should scarcely have imagined Sara Derwent the girl for you to choose.'

'*He* chooses, not I. A mother, whose dutiful son has been her sole stay through life, has no right to interfere with what he deems his happiness,' said Alison, gravely. And, at that moment, the young curate reappeared, ready for the duties to which he was summoned by the sharp sound of the 'church-going bell'.*

'I will stay at home with Captain Rothesay,' observed Mrs Gwynne. Her guest made a courteous disclaimer, which ended in something about 'religious duties'.

'Hospitality is a duty too—at least we thought so in the north,' she answered. 'And old friendship is ever somewhat of a religion with me. Therefore I will stay, Harold.'

'You are right, mother,' said Harold. But he would not that his mother had seen the smile which curled his lip as he passed along the hall, and through the garden towards the churchyard. There it faded into a look, dark and yet mournful; which, as it turned from the dust beneath his feet to the stars overhead, and then back again to the graves, seemed to ask despairingly, at once of heaven and earth, for the solution of some inward mystery.

While Harold preached, his mother and Captain Rothesay sat in the parsonage and talked of their olden days, now faint as a dream. The rising wind, which, sweeping over the wide champaign, came to moan in the hillside trees, seemed to sing the dirge of that long-past life. Yet the heart of both, even of Angus Rothesay, throbbed to its memory; as a Scottish heart ever does to that of home and the mountain-land.

Among other long unspoken names came that of Miss Flora Rothesay. 'She is an old woman now—a few years older than I; Harold visits her not infrequently; and she and I correspond now and then, but we have not met for many years.'

'Yet you have not forgotten her?'

'Do I ever forget?' said Alison, as she turned her face towards him. And looking thereon, he felt that such a woman never could.

Their conversation, passing down the stream of time, touched on all that was memorable in the life of both. She mentioned her husband—but merely the two events, not long distant each from each, of their marriage and his death.

'Your son is not like yourself—does he resemble Mr Gwynne?' observed Rothesay.

'In person, yes, a little; in mind—no! a thousand times no!' Then recollecting herself, she added, 'It was not likely. Mr Gwynne has been dead so many years that my son'—it was always *my* son—'has no remembrance of his father.'

Alas! that there should be some whose memories are gladly suffered to perish, with the falling of the earth above them.

A thought like this passed through the mind of Angus Rothesay. 'I fancy,' said he, 'that I once met Mr Gwynne; he was—'

'My husband!' Mrs Gwynne's tone suppressed all further remark—even all recollection of the contemptible image that was intruding on her guest's mind—an image of a young, roistering, fox-hunting fool. Rothesay looked on the widow, and the remembrance passed away, or became sacred as memory itself. And then the conversation glided as a mother's heart would fain direct it—to her only son.

'He was a strange creature ever, was my Harold. In his childhood he always teased me with his "why and because"; he would come to the root of everything, and would not believe anything that he could not quite understand. Gradually I began to glory in this peculiarity, for I saw it argued a mind far above the common order. Angus, you are a father; you may be happy in your child, but you never can understand the intense pride of a mother in an only son.'

While she talked, her countenance and manner brightened, and Captain Rothesay saw again, not the serene, stern widow of Owen Gwynne, but the energetic, impassioned mountain-girl, Alison Balfour. He told her this.

'Is it so? Strange! And yet I do but talk to you as I often did when we were young together.'

He begged her to continue—his heart warmed as it had not done for many a day; and, to lead the way, he asked what chance had caused the descendant of the Balfours to become an English clergyman?

'From circumstances. When he was very young and we two lived together in the poor Highland cottage where he was born, my boy made acquaintance with an Englishman, one Lord Arundale, a great student. Harold longed to be a student, too.'

'A noble desire.'

'I shared it too. When the thought came to me that my boy would be a great man, I nursed it, cherished it, made it my whole life's aim. We were not rich—I had not married for money'—and there was a faint show of pride in her lip—'yet, Harold must go, as he desired, to an English university. I said in my heart, "He shall!" and he did,'

Angus looked at Mrs Gwynne, and thought that a woman's will might sometimes be as strong and daring as a man's.

Alison continued—'My son had only half finished his education when fortune made the poor poorer. But Scotland and Cambridge, thank Heaven! were far distant. I never told him one word—I lived—it matters little how—I cared not! Our fortune lasted, as I had calculated it would, till he had taken his degree, and left college rich in honours—and then ——'

She ceased, and the light in her countenance faded. Angus Rothesay gazed upon the aged mother as reverently as he had done upon the good angel of his boyish days.

'I said you were a noble woman, Alison Balfour.'

'I was a mother, and I had a noble son!' was her only answer.

They sat a long time silent, looking at the fire, and listening to the wind. There was a momentary interruption—a message from the young clergyman, to say that he was summoned some distance to visit a sick person.

'On such a stormy night as this!' said Angus Rothesay.

'Harold never fails in his duties,' replied the mother, with a smile.

Then turning abruptly to her guest—'You will let me talk, old friend, and about him. I cannot often talk *to* him, for he is so reserved—that is, so occupied with his clerical studies. But there never was a better son than my Harold.'

'I am sure of it,' said Captain Rothesay.

The mother continued—'Never shall I forget the triumph of his coming home from Cambridge. Yet it brought a pang, too; for then first he had to learn the whole truth. Poor Harold! it pained me to see him so shocked and overwhelmed at the sight of our lowly roof and mean fare; and to know that even these would not last us long. But I said to him—"my son, what signifies it, when you can soon bring your mother to your own home." For he, already a deacon, had had a curacy offered him, as soon as ever he chose to take priest's orders.'

'Then he had already decided on entering the church?'

'He had chosen that career in his youth. Towards it his whole education had tended. But,' she added, with a troubled look, 'my old friend, I may tell you one doubt, which I have never yet breathed to living soul— I think at this time there was a struggle in his mind. Perhaps his dreams of ambition rose higher than the simple destiny of a country clergyman. I hinted this to him, but he repelled my questionings. Alas! he knew, as well as I, that there was now no other path open for him.'

Mrs Gwynne paused, and then went on, as though speaking more to herself than to her listener.

'The time came for Harold to decide. I marvelled not at the trouble and restlessness which oppressed him, for I knew how strong ambition must be in a man like him. God knows I would have worked, begged, starved, rather than he should be thus tried. I told him so, the day before his ordination; but he entreated me to be silent, with a look such as I never saw on his face before—such as I trust in God I never may see again. I heard him all night walking about his chamber; and the next morning he was gone ere I rose. When he came back, he seemed quite excited with joy, embraced me, told me I should never know poverty more, for that he was in priest's orders, and we should go the next week to the curacy at Harbury.'

'And he has never repented?'

'I think not. He is not without the honours he desired; for his fame in science is extending far beyond his small parish. He fulfils his duties scrupulously; and the people respect him, though he sides with no party, high church or evangelical.* We abhor illiberality—my son and I.'

'That is clear, otherwise I had never seen Alison Balfour quitting the kirk for the church.'

'Angus Rothesay,' said Mrs Gwynne, with dignity, 'I have learned, throughout a long life, the lesson that trifling outward differences matter little—the spirit of religion is its true life. This lesson I have taught my son from his cradle; and where will you find a more sincere, moral, or pious man than Harold Gwynne?'

'Where indeed, mother?' echoed a voice, as Harold, opening the door, caught her last words. 'But come, "no more o' that, an thou lovest me!"'

'Harold!' She looked at him commandingly, and the light tone in which he had spoken was quelled. The coldness of reserve grew up between mother and son once more.

CHAPTER XVI

Captain Rothesay found himself at breakfast on the sixth morning of his stay at Harbury—so swiftly had the time flown. But he felt a purer and a happier man every hour that he spent with his ancient friend.

The breakfast room was Harold's study. It was more that of a man of science and learning* than that of a clergyman. Beside Leighton and Flavel, were placed Bacon and Descartes; dust lay upon John Newton's Sermons, while close by, rested in honoured well-thumbed tatters, his great namesake, who read God's scriptures in the stars. In one corner lay a large unopened packet—marked 'Religious Society's Tracts'; it served as a stand for a large telescope, whose clumsiness betrayed the ingenuity of home manufacture. The theological contents of the library was a vast mass of polemical literature, orthodox and heterodox, including all faiths, all variations of sect. Mahomet and Swedenborg, Calvin and the Talmud, lay side by side; and on the farthest shelf was the great original of all creeds—the Book of Books.

On this morning, as on most others, Harold Gwynne did not appear until after prayers were over. His mother read them, as indeed she always did morning and evening. A stranger might have said, that her doing so was the last lingering token of her sway as 'head of the household'.

Harold entered, his countenance bearing the pallid restless look of one who lies half-dreaming in bed, long after he is awake and ought to have risen. His mother saw it.

'You are not right, Harold. I had far rather that you rose at six and studied till nine, as formerly, than that you should dream away the morning hours, and come down looking as you do now. Forgive me, but it is not good for you, my son.'

She often called him *my son* with a beautiful simplicity, that reminded one of the holy Hebrew mothers—of Rebecca or of Hannah.*

Harold looked for a moment disconcerted—not angry. 'Do not mind me, mother; I shall go back to study in good time. Let me do as I judge best.'

'Certainly,' was all the mother's reply. She reproved—she never 'scolded'. Turning the conversation, she directed hers to Captain Rothesay, while Harold ate his breakfast in silence—a habit not unusual with him. Immediately afterwards he rose, and prepared to depart for the day.

'I need not apologize to Captain Rothesay,' he said, in his own straight-forward manner, which was only saved from the imputation of bluntness by a certain manly dignity—and contrasted strongly with the reserved and courtly grace of his guest. 'My pursuits can scarcely interest you, while I know, and *you* know, what pleasure my mother takes in your society.'

'You will not stay away all this day too, Harold. Surely that is a little too much to be required, even by Miss Derwent,' spoke the quick impulse of the mother's unconscious jealousy. But she repressed it at once—even before the sudden flush of anger awakened by her words had faded from Harold's brow. 'Go, my son—your mother never interferes either with your duties or your pleasures.'

Harold took her hand—though with scarce less formality than he did that of Captain Rothesay; and in a few minutes they saw him gallop down the hill and across the open country, with a speed beseeming well the age of five-and-twenty, and the season of a first love.

Mrs Gwynne looked after him with an intensity of feeling that in any other woman would have found vent in a tear—certainly a sigh. But neither was easily awakened in her nature; it was too deep.

'You are thinking of your son and his marriage,' said Angus.

'That is not strange. It is a life crisis with all men—and it has come so suddenly—I scarcely know my Harold of two months since in my Harold now.'

'To work such results, it must be an ardent love.'

'Say, rather, a vehement passion—love does not spring up and flower, like my hyacinths there, in six weeks,' answered Mrs Gwynne, smiling with that quiet humour which formed a curious and apparently contradictory trait in her character. 'But I murmur little. Reason, if not feeling, tells me that a mother advancing in years cannot be all in all to a young man.

Harold needs a wife—let him take one! They will be married soon; and if all Sara's qualities equal her beauty, this wild passion will soon mature into affection. He may be happy—I trust so!'

She folded her hands over her breast, less in meekness than to press down its swelling emotion. Well she knew that woman's deepest love, as mother, sister, wife, is often but another name for self-denying martyrdom.

'But does your son's affianced return his love?' asked Rothesay.

'Is there any girl who would not love my Harold?' spoke the quick-rising maternal pride. But she almost smiled at it herself, and added—'Really, you must excuse these speeches of mine. I talk to you as I never do to any one else; but it is all for the sake of olden times. This has been a happy week to me. You must pay us another visit soon.'

'I will. And you must take a journey to my home, and learn to know my wife and Olive,' said Rothesay. The pure influence of Alison Gwynne was unconsciously strengthening to all good; and though, from some inexplicable feeling, he had spoken but little of his wife and child, there were growing up in his mind many schemes, the chief of which were connected with Olive. But he now thought less of her appearing in the world as Captain Rothesay's heiress, than of her being placed within the shadow of the noble nature of Alison Gwynne, and so reflecting back upon her father's age that benign influence which had been the blessing of his youth.

He went on to tell Mrs Gwynne more of his affairs and of his plans than he had communicated to any one for many a long year. In the midst of their conversation came the visitation—always so important in remote country districts—the every-other-day's post.

'For you—not me. I have few correspondents. So I will go to my duties, while you attend to yours,' said Mrs Gwynne, and departed.

When she came in again, Captain Rothesay was pacing the room with a vexed and disordered aspect.

'No ill news, I hope,' said the voice, which, when it chose, could soften to all a woman's sympathy.

'No, my kind friend—not exactly ill news, though vexatious enough. But why should I trouble you with them?'

'Nothing ever troubles me that can be of use to my friends. I ask no unwelcome confidence. If it is any relief to you to speak, I will gladly hear. It is sometimes good for a man to have a woman to talk to.'

'It is—it is! Would that I had been blessed with common sense at home,' thought Rothesay in his heart. And that heart opening itself more and more, he told her his cause of annoyance. A most important mercantile venture would be lost to him for want of what he called 'a few paltry hundreds', to be forthcoming on the morrow.

'If it had been a fortnight—just till my next ship is due; or even one week, to give me time to make some arrangement! But where is the use of complaining? It is too late.'

'Not quite,' said Alison Gwynne, looking up after a few moments of deep thought; and, with a clearness which would have gained for her the repute of 'a thorough woman of business', she questioned Captain Rothesay, until she drew from him a possible way of obviating his difficulty.

'If, as you say, I were in London now, where my banker or some business friend would take up a bill for me; but that is impossible!'

'Nay—why say that you have friends alone in London?' replied Alison, with a gentle smile. 'That is rather too unjust, Angus Rothesay. Our Highland clanship is not so clean forgotten, I hope. Come, old friend, it will be hard if I cannot do something for you. And Harold, who loves Flora Rothesay almost as much as he loves me, would gladly aid her kinsman.'

'How—how! Nay, but I will never consent,' cried Angus, with a resoluteness through which his first eager sense of relief was clearly discernible. Truly, there was coming upon him, with this mania of speculation, the same desperation which causes the gambler to clutch money from the starving hands of those who even yet are passionately dear.

'You *shall* consent, friend,' answered Mrs Gwynne, composedly. 'Why should you not? It is a mere form—an obligation of a week, at most. You will accept that for the sake of Alison Balfour.'

He clasped her hand with as much emotion as was in his nature to show.

She continued—'Well, we will talk of this again when Harold comes in to dinner. But, positively, I see him returning. There he is, dashing up the hill. I hope nothing is the matter.'

Yet she did not quit the room to meet him, but sat apparently quiet, though her hands were slightly trembling, until her son came in. In answer to her question, he said—

'No, no; nothing amiss. Only Mr Fludyer would have me go to the Hall to see his new horses; and there I found——'

'Sara!' interrupted the mother. 'Well, perhaps she thought it would be a pleasant change from the dullness of Waterton during your absence; so never mind.'

He did mind. He restlessly paced the room, angry with his mother, himself—with the whole world. Mrs Gwynne might well notice how this sudden passion had changed his nature. A moralist looking on the knotted brow, which indicated the most majestic intellect, would have smiled to see—not for the first time—a great and wise man making of himself a slave, nay, a very fool, for the enchantments of a beautiful woman.

His mother took his arm and walked with him up and down the room, without talking to him at all. But her firm step and firm clasp seemed to soothe—almost force him into composure. She had over him at once a mother's influence and a father's control.

Meanwhile, Captain Rothesay busied, or seemed to busy himself, with his numerous letters, and very wisely kept nearly out of sight.

As soon as her son appeared a little recovered from his vexation, Mrs Gwynne said,

'Now, Harold, if you are quite willing, I want to talk to you for a few minutes. Shall it be now or this evening?'

'This evening I shall ride over to Waterton.'

'What not one evening to spare for your mother, or—' she corrected herself speedily, 'for your beloved books?'

He moved restlessly.

'Nay, I have had enough of study; I must have interest, amusement, excitement. I think I have drunk all the world's pleasures dry, except this one. Mother, don't keep it from me; I know no rest except I am beside Sara.'

He rarely spoke to her so freely, and, despite her pain, the mother was touched.

'Go, then, go to Sara; and the matter I wished to speak upon we will discuss now.'

He sat down and listened, though often only with his outward ears, to her plan, wherewith Captain Rothesay might be saved from his difficulty.

'It is a mere nominal thing; I would execute it myself, but a woman's name would scarcely do. Yours will. My son Harold will at once perform such a trifling act of kindness for his mother's friend.'

'Of course—of course. Come, tell me what to do; you understand all these business affairs—wise woman that you are, mother!' said Harold, as he rose up to seek his guest.

Captain Rothesay scrupled a while longer; but at length the dazzling vision of coming wealth absorbed both pride and reluctance. It would be so hard to miss the chance of thousands, by objecting to a mere form. 'Besides, Harold Gwynne shall share the success,' he thought; and he formed many schemes for changing the comparative poverty of the parsonage into comfort and luxury. It was only when the pen was in the young man's hand, ready to sign the paper, that the faintest misgiving crossed Rothesay's mind.

'Stay, it is but for a few days—yet life sometimes ends in an hour. What, if I should die, at once, before I can requite you? Mr Gwynne, you shall not do it.'

'He *shall*—I mean, he will,' answered the mother.

'But not until I have secured him in some way.'

'Nay, Angus; we "auld acquaintance" should not thus bargain away our friendship,' said Mrs Gwynne, with wounded pride—Highland pride. 'And besides, there is no time to lose. Here is the acceptance ready—so, Harold, sign!'

And Harold did sign. The instant after, glad to escape, he quitted the room.

Angus Rothesay sank on a chair with a heart-deep sigh of relief. It was done now. He eyed with thankfulness the paper which had secured him the golden prize.

'It is but a trifle—a sum not worth naming,' he muttered to himself; and so, indeed, it seemed to one who had 'turned over' thousands like mere heaps of dust. He never thought that it was an amount equal to Harold's yearly income for which the young man had thus become bound.

Yet he omitted not again and again to thank Mrs Gwynne, and with excited eagerness to point to all the prospects now before him.

'And, besides, you cannot think from what you have saved me—the annoyance—the shame of breaking my word. Oh! my friend, you know not in what a whirling, restless world of commerce I live! To fail in anything, or be thought to fail, would positively ruin me and drive me mad.'

'Angus—old companion!' answered Mrs Gwynne, regarding him earnestly, 'you must not blame me if I tell you this is wrong. In one week I have seen far into your heart—farther than you think. Be advised by me; change this life for one more calm. Home and its blessings never come too late.'

'You are right,' said Angus. 'I sometimes think that all is not well with me. I am growing old, and business racks my head sadly sometimes. Feel it now!'

He carried to his brow her hand—the hand which had led him when a boy, which in his fantastic dream of youth he had passionately kissed; even now, when the pulses were grown leaden with age, it felt cool, calm, like the touch of some pitying and protecting angel.

Alison Gwynne shook her head gently. 'My friend, you say truly all is not well with you. Let us put aside all business, and walk in the garden. Come!'

Captain Rothesay lingered at Harbury yet one day more. But he could not stay longer, for this important business venture made him restless. Besides, Harold's wedding was near at hand; in less than a week the mother would be sole regent of her son's home no more. No wonder that this made her grave and anxious—so that even her old friend's presence was a slight restraint. Yet she bade him adieu with her own cordial sincerity. He began to pour out thanks for all kindness—especially the one kindness of all, adding—

'But I will say no more. You shall see or hear from me in a few days at farthest.'

'Not until after the wedding—I can think of nothing till after the wedding,' answered Mrs Gwynne. 'Now, farewell, friend! but not for another thirty years, I trust!'

'No, no!' cried Angus, warmly. He looked at her as she sat in serene, subdued age, by the light of her own hearth—life's trials conquered—life's duties fulfilled—and she appeared not less divine a creature than the Alison Balfour who had trod the mountains full of joy, and hope, and energy. Holy and beautiful she had seemed to him in her youth; and though every shadow of that passionate idealization, once called love, was gone, still holy and beautiful she seemed to him in her age.

Angus Rothesay rode away from Harbury Parsonage, feeling that there he had gained a new interest to make life and life's duties more sacred. He thought with tenderness of his home—of his wife, and of his 'little Olive'; and then, travelling by a rather circuitous route, his thoughts rested on Harold Gwynne.

'The kind-hearted, generous fellow! I will take care he is requited double. And tomorrow, before ever I reach Oldchurch, I will go to my lawyer's and make all safe on his account.'

Tomorrow! He remembered not who sayeth, 'Boast not thyself of tomorrow.'*

CHAPTER XVII

Olive sat mournfully contemplating Sara Derwent's last letter—the last she knew it would be. It was written, not with the frank simplicity of their girlish confidence, but with the formal dignity of one who the next day would become a bride. It spoke of no regret, no remorse for her violated troth; it mentioned her former promise in a cold, businesslike manner, without inferring any changed love, but merely stating her friends' opinion on the 'evil of long engagements, and that she would be much better married at once to Harold Gwynne, than waiting some ten years for Charles Geddes'. How lightly won and lightly lost are hearts like that of Sara Derwent!

But to Olive this change seemed a positive sin. She shuddered to think of Sara's wicked faithlessness; she wept with pity, remembering poor Charles. The sense of wrong, as well as of misery, had entered her world at once; her idols were crumbling into dust. She mourned now, not only the hopelessness of being loved, but the hopelessness of finding aught to love with the adoration that requires nothing less than perfection to fulfil all its aspirings. To love—not to be loved—could now be her only blessing; was this, also, to be denied? Life grew painful to her, and a morbid bitterness was settling on her soul.

She read the account that Sara had somewhat boastfully written, of her prospects, her pretty home, and of Harold's devotion to her. 'This clever man—this noble man (as people call him, and most of all his mother)— I could wind him round my little finger. What think you, Olive? Is not that something to be married for? You ask if I am happy. Yes, certainly, happier than you can imagine.'

'That is true indeed,' murmured Olive; and there came upon her a bitter sense of the inequalities of life. It seemed that Heaven to some gave all things; to others, nothing! But she hushed the complainings, for they seemed impious. Her spirit grew calm beneath the faith she had been taught by Elspie, which, though carried by the old Scotswoman into all the mystic horrors of Calvinistic predestination,* yet had sweetness at its root. For it was a faith that taught the peace of resting childlike beneath the shadow of that Omnipotent Will, which holds every tangled thread of fate within one mighty Hand, which rules all things, and rules them continually for good.

While thinking thus, Olive was sitting in her 'bower', as she called her favourite place of solitude. It was a garden seat, placed under the thorn-tree, and shut out from sight of the house by an espalier of apple-trees. Not very romantic, certainly, but a most pleasant spot, with the sound of the 'shallow river' gliding by, and of many a bird that 'sang madrigals'* in the meadows opposite. And Olive herself, as she sat with her hands crossed on her knee, her bending head and pensive eyes out-gazing, added no unmeet picture to the still beauty of the scene. Many a lovely woman might have coveted the meek yet heavenly look which cast sweetness over the pale features of the deformed girl.

Olive, sitting with her eyes cast down, was some time before she became conscious that she was watched—long and earnestly; but by an innocent watcher—her 'little knight', as he had dubbed himself, Lyle Derwent. His face looked out from the ivy leaves at the top of the wall. Soon he had leaped down, and was kneeling at her feet, just like a young lover in a romance. Smiling, she told him so; for in truth she made a great pet of the child, whose delicate beauty pleased her artist's eye, while his gentleness won her affection.

'Well, and I will be your lover, Miss Olive,' said he, stoutly; 'for I love you very much indeed. I should so like to kiss you—may I?'

She stooped down; the little clinging arms, the sweet childish kiss, moved her almost to tears.

'Why are you always so sad, Miss Rothesay? why do you never laugh, like Sara, or the other young ladies we know?'

'Because I am not like Sara, or like any other girl. Ah! Lyle, all is very different with me,' said Olive, sighing softly. 'But, my little knight, this can scarcely be understood by one so young as you.'

'Though I am a little boy, I know thus much, that I love you, and think you more beautiful than anybody else in the world—even than Sara.'

And speaking rather loudly and energetically, he was answered by a burst of derisive laughter from behind the wall.

Olive crimsoned; it was one more of those passing wounds which her sensitive nature now continually received. Was even a child's love for her deemed so unnatural, and worthy to be mocked at thus cruelly? Lyle, with a quickness beyond his years, seemed to have divined her thoughts, and his gentle temper was roused into passion.

'I will kill Bob, I will! Never mind him, sweet, dear, beautiful Miss Rothesay; I love you, and I hate him.'

'Hush! Lyle, hush! that is wrong.' And then she was silent. Her heaving breast and white cheek alone revealed how deeply the arrow had entered. The little boy stood by her side, his face still burning with indignation.

Soon Olive's trouble subsided. She whispered to herself, 'It must be always thus—I will try to bear it,' and then she became composed. She bade her little friend adieu, telling him she was going back into the house.

'But you will forgive all, you will not think of anything that would tease you?' said Lyle, hesitatingly.

Olive promised, with a pale, patient smile.

'And to prove this, will you kiss your little knight once again?'

'If you desire it.'

Her soft drooping hair swept his cheek; her lips touched his. Afterwards, when, in his childish but most fanciful musings, Lyle Derwent used to dream of an angel's kiss, it always seemed to him like this of Olive Rothesay's—her last!

The young girl entered the house. Within it rested the slumberous quiet of a Sunday afternoon. Her mother had gone to a distant church, and there was none left 'to keep house', save one of the maids and the old grey cat, that dozed on the window-sill in the sunshine. The latter was a great pet of Olive's; and the moment it saw its young mistress, it was purring round her feet, following her from room to room, never resting until she took it up in her arms. The love even of a dumb animal touched her then. She sat down on her own little low chair, spread on her lap the smooth white apron which Miss Pussy loved—cats have delicate and refined tastes sometimes—and so she leaned back, soothed by the monotonous song of her purring favourite, and thinking that there was at least one living creature who loved her, and whom she could make happy.

She sat at the open window, seeing only the high, green privet hedge that enclosed the front-garden, the little wicket-gate, and the blue sky beyond. How still everything was! By degrees the footsteps of a few late churchgoers vanished along the road; the bells ceased—first the quick, sharp clang of the new church, and then the musical peal that rang out from the grey Norman tower. There never were such bells as those of Oldchurch! but they melted away in silence; and then the dreamy quietness of the hour stole over Olive's sense.

She thought of many things—things which might have been sad, but for the slumberous peace that took away all pain. It was just the hour when she had used to sit on the floor, leaning against Elspie's knees, generally reading aloud in the Book which alone the nurse permitted on Sundays. Now and then—once in particular she remembered—old Elspie fell asleep; and then Olive turned to her favourite study, the Book of Revelations. Childlike, she terrified herself over the mysterious prophecies of the latter days, until at last she forgot the gloom and horror, in reading of the 'beautiful city, New Jerusalem'.

She seemed to see it—its twelve gates, angel-guarded, its crystal river, its many-fruited tree—the Tree of Life. Her young but glowing fancy, unable to separate truth from allegory, created out of these marvels a paradise, material in itself. She knew not that heaven is only the continual presence of the Eternal. Yet she was happy; and in her dreams she never pictured the land beyond the grave, but there came back to her, as though the nearest foreshadowing of its deep, holy rest, the visions of that Sunday afternoon.

She sat a long time thinking of them, and of herself—how much older she felt since then, and how many troubles she had passed through. Troubles! Poor child!—how little knew she those of the world! But even her own small burthen seemed lightened now. She leaned her head against the window, listening to the bees humming in the garden— bees, the only Sunday workers, and even they seemed to toil with a kind of Sabbatic solemnity. And then, turning her face upwards, Olive watched many a fair white butterfly, that, having flitted a while among the flowers, spread its wings and rose far into the air, like a pure soul weary of earth, and floating heavenward. How she wished—girlish dreamer!—that she could do likewise; and leaving earth behind—its flowers as well as weeds, its sunshine as its storm—soar into another and a higher existence!

Not yet, Olive—not yet! None receives the guerdon, save he who has won the goal!

A pause in the girl's reverie—caused by a light sound that broke the perfect quietness around. She listened; it was the rumbling of carriage-wheels along the road—a rare circumstance; for the people of Old-church, if not personally devout, lived in a devout atmosphere, which forbade pleasure-drives on the day of rest.

A momentary hope struck Olive that it might be her father returning home, where he was now daily expected. But he was a strict man; he never travelled on Sundays. Nevertheless, Olive listened mechanically to the wheels: they dashed rapidly on—came near—stopped. Yes, it must be her father.

Full of joy, she flew to the hall door, to welcome him. There, stood, not her father, but a little hard-featured old man, Mr Wyld, the family lawyer. Olive drew back, sorely disappointed; for if in her gentle heart lingered one positive aversion, it was felt towards this man—partly on his own account, partly because his appearance seemed always the forewarning of evil in the little household. He never came, but, at his departure, Captain Rothesay wore a frowning brow, and indulged in a hasty temper for days and days. No marvel was there in Olive's dislike; yet she regretted having shown it, and said courteously—

'Pardon me, Mr Wyld, but I thought it was my father. I am sorry that he is not at home to receive you.'

'Nay, I—I did not come to see Captain Rothesay,' answered the law-yer, betraying some confusion and hesitation beneath his usual smooth manner. 'The fact is, my dear young lady, I bring a letter for your mother.'

'From papa?' cried Olive, eagerly.

'No, not exactly; that is——. But can I see Mrs Rothesay?'

'She is at church. She will be at home in half an hour, probably. Will you wait?'

He shook his head.

'Nay, there is nothing wrong—nothing about papa?' said Olive, growing frightened.

'Don't alarm yourself, my dear.'

Olive shrank from the touch of his hand, as he led her into the parlour.

'Your papa is at my house. But I think, Miss Rothesay, as your mother is not at home, you had better read the letter yourself.'

She took it with a hand that trembled despite her will. Slowly, silently, she read it through—twice; for the words seemed to dazzle and blaze before her eyes. Then she looked up helplessly. 'I—I cannot understand.'

'I thought the doctor wrote plainly enough, and broke the matter cautiously, too,' muttered Mr Wyld; adding aloud, 'Upon my honour, my dear, I assure you your father is alive. It is a painful task—a very painful task, to bring this news.'

'Tell me—I cannot read, I cannot see—Oh, my poor father!' And then she sank down slowly where she stood, as if pressed by some heavy, invisible hand. Mr Wyld thought she had fainted—but it was not so. In another moment she stood before him, quiet, cold, nerved by this great woe to a firmness which was awful in its rigid composure.

'I can listen now. Tell me everything!'

He told her in a few words how Captain Rothesay had come to his house the night before, and while waiting his return, had taken up the newspaper. 'Suddenly, my clerk said, he let it fall with a cry, and was immediately seized with the fit from which he has not yet recovered. There is hope, the doctor thinks; but, in case of the worst, you must come to him at once.'

'Yes, yes, at once!' She rose and walked to the door, guiding herself by the wall, and groping as if she were blind.

'Nay, Miss Rothesay, what are you doing? You forget we cannot go without your mother.'

'My mother! Oh, heaven! it will kill my mother!' And the thought brought tears, the first that had burst from her. It was well, or her bewildered brain might have reeled beneath the sudden blow.

She awoke to consciousness and strength. In this great crisis, there came to her the wisdom and forethought that lay dormant in her nature. She became a woman—one of those of whom the world contains few—at once gentle and strong, meek and fearless, patient to endure, heroic to act.

She sat down for a moment and considered. 'Fourteen miles it is to B——. If we start in an hour, we shall reach there by sunset.' Then she summoned the maid; and said, speaking steadily, that she might by no sign betray what might in turn be betrayed to her mother—

'You must go and meet mamma as she comes from church; or, if not, seek her there. Tell her there is a message come from my father, and ask her to hasten home on his account. Make haste yourself. I will keep house the while.—There, that is done—she will not guess anything,' added Olive, as the woman left the room, murmuring a little, but never thinking to disobey her young mistress—so sudden, so all-constraining, was the dignity which had come upon the girl. Even Mr Wyld felt it; and his manner changed from smooth, patronizing condolence, to a respect not unmingled with awe.

'What can I do, Miss Rothesay?' he said, humbly. 'You turn from me. No wonder, when I have had the misfortune to be the bearer of such evil tidings.'

'Hush!' she said; for there was tenfold bitterness in the sound of his harsh voice, croaking regret and sympathy. Mechanically she set wine before him—he eagerly swallowed it; even then prating, between the draughts, of his deep sorrow, and earnest hope that no serious evil would befall his good friend, Captain Rothesay.

Olive could endure no more. She fled away, shut herself up in her own room, and fell on her knees; but no words came, save the bitter cry 'O God, have pity on us!' And there was no time, not even to pray, except with the silent voice of her heart.

She pressed her hands on her brow, and once more thought what she had to do. At that moment, through the quietness of the lonely house, she heard the clock striking four. Never had time's passing seemed so awful. The day was fleeting on whose every moment perhaps hung a life.

Something she must do, or her senses would have failed. She thought of little things—aught that might be needed when they reached her father. Quietly she went into Mrs Rothesay's room, and put up some clothes and necessaries, in case they stayed more than one day at B——; her mother's large, warm shawl, too, for she might have to sit up all night. In these trifling arrangements what a horrible reality there was! And yet she scarce felt it—she was half stunned still.

It was past four, and her mother had not come. Every minute seemed an eternity. Olive walked to the window and looked out. There was the same cheerful sunshine—the bees humming, and the butterflies flitting about, in the sweet stillness of the Sabbath afternoon, as she had watched them an hour ago. One little hour, to have brought into her world such utter misery.

She thought of it all, dwelling vividly on every accompaniment of woe—even as she remembered to have done when she first learned that Elspie would die. She pictured her mother's coming home; and almost fancied she could see her now, walking across the fields. But no; it was someone in a white dress, strolling by the hedgerow's side; and Mrs Rothesay that day wore blue—her favourite pale blue muslin, in which she looked so lovely. She had gone out, laughing at her daughter for saying this. What if Olive should never see her in that pretty dress again!

All this, and more, clung to the girl's mind, with a horrible pertinacity. And then, through the silence, she heard the Oldchurch bells awaking again, in the dull minute-peal which told that service-time was ended, and the afternoon funerals were taking place. Olive, shuddering, closed her ears against the sound; and then, gazing out once more, she saw her mother stand at the gate. All unconscious still, Mrs Rothesay looked up at the window and smiled.

Olive had never thought of that worst pang of all—how she should break the news to her mother—her timid, delicate mother, whose feeble frame quivered beneath the lightest breath of suffering. Scarcely knowing what she did, the daughter flew downstairs.

'Not there, mamma—not there!' she cried, as Mrs Rothesay was about to enter the parlour. Olive drew her into another room, and made her sit down.

'What is all this, my dear?—why do you look so strange? Is not your papa come home? Let us go to him.'

'We will, we will! But, mamma'—One moment she looked speechlessly in Mrs Rothesay's face, and then fell on her neck, crying, 'I can't, I can't keep it from you any longer. Oh, mother, mother! there is great trouble come upon us; we must be patient; we must bear it together. God will help us.'

'Olive!' The shrill terror of Mrs Rothesay's voice rang through the room.

'Hush! we must be quiet, very quiet. Papa is dangerously ill at B——, and we must start at once. I have arranged all. Come, mamma, dearest!'

But her mother had fainted.

There was no time to lose. Olive snatched some restoratives, and then made ready to depart. Mrs Rothesay, still insensible, was lifted into the carriage. She lay there, for some time, quite motionless, supported in her daughter's arms—to which never had she owed support before. As Olive looked down upon her, strange, new feelings came into the girl's heart. The natural instinct of filial tenderness seemed transmuted into a devotion passing the love of child to mother, and mingled therewith was a sense of protection, of watchful guardianship.

She thought, 'What if my father should die, and we two should be left alone in the world! Then she will have none to look to save me, and I will be to her in the stead of all. Once, I think, she loved me little; but, oh! mother, dearly we love one another now.'

When Mrs Rothesay's senses returned, she lifted her head, with a bewildered air. 'Where are we going? What has happened? I can't think clearly of anything.'

'Dearest mamma, do not try—I will think for us both. Be content; you are quite safe with your own daughter.'

'My daughter—ah! I remember, I fainted, as I did long years ago, when they told me something about my daughter. Are you she—that little child whom I cast from my arms? and now I am lying in yours!' she cried, her mind seeming to wander, as if distraught by this sudden shock.

'Hush, mamma! don't talk; rest quiet here,' was the soothing answer.

Mrs Rothesay looked wistfully in her daughter's face, and there seemed to cross her mind some remembered sense of what had befallen. She clung helplessly to those affectionate arms—'Take care of me, Olive!—I do not deserve it, but take care of me!'

'I will, until death!' was Olive's inward vow.

And so, travelling fast, but in solemn silence, they came to B——. Alas! it was already too late! By Angus Rothesay's bed of death they stood—the widow and the fatherless!

CHAPTER XVIII

The tomb had scarcely closed over Captain Rothesay, when it was discovered that his affairs were in a state of irretrievable confusion. For months, he must have lived with ruin staring him in the face. His sudden death was then no mystery. The newspaper had startled him with tidings—partly false, as afterwards appeared—of a heavy disaster by sea, and the failure of his latest speculation at home. There seemed lifted against him at once the hand of Heaven and of man. His proud nature could not withstand the shock; shame smote him, and he died.

'Tell me only one thing!' cried Olive to Mr Wyld, with whom, after the funeral, she was holding conference—she only—for her mother was incapable of acting, and this girl of sixteen was the sole ruler of the household now. 'Tell me only that my father died unblemished in honour—that there are none to share misfortune with us, and to curse the memory of the ruined merchant.'

'I know of none,' answered Mr Wyld. 'One fear your father had was vain—the missing ship has come safe to land. True, there are still remaining many private debts, but they may be paid.' And he cast a meaning glance round the luxuriously furnished room.

'I understand. It shall be done,' said Olive. Misery had made her very wise—very quick to comprehend. Without shrinking, she talked over every matter connected with that saddest thing—a deceased bankrupt's sale.

The lawyer was a hard man, and Olive's prejudice against him was not unfounded. Still, the most stony heart has often a little softness buried deep at its core. Mr Wyld looked with curiosity, even with kindness, on the young creature who sat opposite to him, in the dim lamplight of the silent room, once Captain Rothesay's study. Her cheek, ever delicate, was now of a dull white; her pale gold hair fell neglected over her black, dress; her hand supported her care-marked brow, as she pored over dusty papers, pausing at times to speak, in a quiet, sensible, subdued manner, of things fit only for old heads and worn hearts. Mr Wyld thought of his own two daughters, whom he had left at home, blithe in their untried youth, and felt a vague thankfulness that they were not as Olive Rothesay. Tenderness was rare in his nature; but in all his intercourse with her, he could not help treating with a sort of reverence the dead merchant's forlorn child.

When they had finished their conversation, he said, 'There is one matter—painful, too—upon which I ought to speak to you. I should have done so before, but I did not know it myself until yesterday.'

'Know what? Alas! alas! is there more trouble to come upon us?' answered Olive, sighing bitterly. 'But tell me all.'

'*All*, is very little. You know, my dear Miss Rothesay, that your late lamented father——' he puckered his face into an expression of condolence, but seeing Olive's restless gesture, smoothed it out again—'your father was quite speechless and senseless, until his death—that is, almost. But my wife, who never quitted him—ah! I assure you she was a devoted nurse to him, was Mrs Wyld.'

'I thank her deeply, as she knows.'

'Well, she has just told me, that a few minutes before his death, your poor father's consciousness returned; that he seemed struggling in vain to speak; at last, she placed a pencil in his hand, and he wrote—one word only, in the act of writing which he died. Forgive me, my dear young lady, for thus agitating you, but——'

'The paper—give me the paper!' gasped Olive.

Mr Wyld pulled out his pocket-book, and produced a torn and blotted scrap, whereon was written, in characters scarcely legible, the name '*Harold.*'

Olive wept over the blurred letters, seeming almost to behold the quivering, death-struck hand which had formed them. She wearied herself in agonized conjecture over the mystery, now apparently for ever sealed.

'Do you know any one who bears that name?' asked the penetrating lawyer.

'No. Yes—one,' added she, suddenly remembering that the name of Sara's husband was Harold Gwynne. But between him and her father she knew of no single tie. It must be a mere chance coincidence. Nevertheless, she would have asked something concerning him, save that the whole Derwent family were gone to their sister's wedding, which took place, not at Oldchurch, but in a distant county.

'It is hopeless!' cried Olive. 'I know no clue, and I dare not tell this to my mother yet. We must let the matter rest.'

Mr Wyld, feeling his professional acuteness at stake, took up the paper, with an air of mysterious importance. 'If it were a woman's name, now— I executed a little commission once.'

'What did you say?' asked Olive, looking up at him with her innocent eyes. He could not meet them; his own fell confused, for he remembered that she was her father's child.

'What did I say, Miss Rothesay? Oh, nothing—nothing at all; only that if I had a commission—to—to hunt out this secret. We lawyers are acute sometimes, you know,' said Mr Wyld, ingeniously twisting his words to an opposite meaning.

Olive thought he was angling for more fees; and inwardly disgusted, she resolved to put a stop to his interference. 'I thank you, Mr Wyld; but a daughter would not willingly employ any third person to "hunt out" her father's secret. His papers will doubtless inform me of all needful things that he might wish executed; therefore we will speak no more of this subject.'

'As you will.' He gathered up his blue bag and its voluminous contents, and made his adieux, leaving to welcome solitude the young creature whom a hard fate had made his assistant in tasks so unsuited for her sex and years.

But Olive had scarcely sat down again, and, with her head leaning on her father's desk, had given vent to a sigh of relief, in that she was freed from Mr Wyld's presence—when the old lawyer again appeared.

'Miss Rothesay, I merely wished to say, if ever you find out anything— anything that you don't know now—or need any advice or information about that paper, or any other, I'm the man to give it. Good evening!'

Olive thanked him coldly, somewhat proudly, for what she deemed a piece of unnecessary impertinence. However, it quickly passed from her gentle mind; and then, as the best way to soothe all her troubles, she quitted the study, and sought her mother's side.

Of Mrs Rothesay's affliction we have as yet said little. Many and various are earth's griefs; but there must be an awful individuality in the stroke which severs the closest human tie, that between two whom marriage had made 'one flesh'.* And though some coldness had loosened this sacred tie, still no power could utterly divide it, while life endured. Angus Rothesay's widow remembered that she had once been the loved and loving bride of his youth. As such, she mourned him; nor was her grief without that keenest sting, the memory of unatoned wrong. From the dim shores of the past, arose ghosts that nothing could ever lay, because death's river ran eternally between.

Sybilla Rothesay was one of those women whom no force of circumstances can ever teach self-dependence or command. She had looked entirely to her husband for guidance and control, and now for both she looked to her child. From the moment of Captain Rothesay's death, Olive seemed to rule in his stead—or rather, the parent and child seemed to change places. Olive watched, guided, and guarded the passive, yielding sorrow-stricken woman, as it were, with a mother's care; while Mrs Rothesay trusted implicitly in all things to her daughter's stronger mind, and was never troubled by thinking or acting for herself in any one thing.

This may seem a new theory of maternal and filial bond, but in the world it is frequently so. If we look around on those daughters who have best fulfilled that holy duty, without which no life is or can be blest, are they not women of firm, steadfast nature—able to will and to act? Each of them could say, 'I am as a mother unto my mother. I, the strongest now, take her in her feeble age, like a child to my bosom—I shield her, and cherish her, and am to her all in all.'

And so, in her heart, resolved Olive Rothesay. She had made that vow when her mother lay insensible in her arms; she kept it faithfully; until eternity, closing between them, sealed it with that best of earth's blessings—the blessing that falls on a duteous daughter, whose mother is with God.

When Captain Rothesay's affairs were settled, the sole wreck of his wealth that remained to his widow and child was the small settlement from Mrs Rothesay's fortune, on which she had lived at Stirling. So they were not left in actual need; or even Olive's brave spirit might have quailed, and her sweet nature been stung into evil by the bitterness of want.

Still, she and her mother were poor—poor enough to make them desire to leave prying, gossiping Oldchurch, and settle in the solitude of some great town. 'There,' Olive said to herself, 'I shall surely find means to work for her—that she may have not merely necessaries, but comforts.' And many a night—during the few weeks that elapsed before their home was broken up—she lay awake by her sleeping mother's side, planning all sorts of schemes; arranging everything so that Mrs Rothesay's vacillating mind might not be annoyed with arguings or consultations. When all was matured, she had only to say, 'Dearest mother, should we not be very happy living together in London?' And scarcely had Mrs Rothesay assented, than she found everything arranged itself, as under an invisible fairy hand—so that she had but to ask, 'My child, when shall we go?'

The time of departure at last arrived. It was the night but one before the sale. Olive persuaded her mother to go to rest early; for she herself had a trying duty to perform—the examining of her father's private papers. As she sat in his study—solitude and darkness around her—the young girl might have been forgiven many a pang of grief, even of superstitious fear. But Heaven had given her a hero-soul, not the less heroic because in all things it was so entirely a woman's.

Her father's business papers she had already examined: these were only his private memoranda. But they were few; for, throughout his whole career, Captain Rothesay had lived within himself. His thoughts never found vent in words; there were no data of any kind to mark the history of a life, which was almost as unknown to his wife and daughter as to any stranger. Of letters, she found very few; he was not a man who loved correspondence. Only, among these few, she was touched deeply to see some, dated years back, at Stirling. Olive opened one of them. The delicate hand was that of her mother when she was young. Olive only glanced at the top of the page, where still smiled, from the worn, yellow paper, the words, 'My dearest, dearest Angus;' and then, too right-minded to penetrate further, folded it up again. Yet, she felt glad; she thought it would comfort her mother to know how carefully he had kept these letters. Soon after, she found a memento of herself—a little curl, wrapped in silver-paper, and marked with his own hand, 'Olive's hair'. Her father had loved her then—aye, and more deeply than she knew. It soothed her heart to remember the love once borne to her by the dead. She knew that no change could take *that* love from her now.

The chief thing which troubled Olive was the sight of the paper on which her father's dying hand had scrawled 'Harold'. No date of any kind had been found to explain the mystery. Once she had tried to talk with her mother on the subject, but it affected Mrs Rothesay to a degree so agonizing that Olive was obliged to cease. She determined to think of the matter no more, but to put the paper by in a secret drawer.

In doing so, she found a small packet, carefully tied and sealed. She was about to open it, when the superscription caught her eyes. Thereon she read her father's solemn desire—nay, entreaty—that it should after his death be burnt *unopened*.

His faithful daughter fulfilled his will. Instantly, without pausing to think, she threw the packet on the fire; even turning aside, lest the flames, while destroying, should reveal anything of the secret which seemed guarded by her dead father's prayer. Only once, forgetting herself, the crackling fire made her start and turn, and she caught a momentary glimpse of some curious foreign ornament; while near it, twisted in the flame into almost life-like motion, was what seemed a long lock of black hair. But she could be certain of nothing, she hated herself for even that involuntary glance. It seemed an insult to the dead.

Still more did these remorseful feelings awake, when, her task being almost done, she found one letter addressed thus:

'For my daughter, Olive; but I charge her not to open it until she is alone in the world.'

Alone in the world! His fatherly tenderness had looked forward, then, even to that bitter time which might come one day, when, her mother safely laid to rest, Olive would be alone—a woman no longer young, without husband, or child, or smiling home. She doubted not that her father had written this letter to counsel and comfort her at such a season of desolation, years after he was in the dust.

His daughter blessed him for it; and her tender tears fell upon words which he had written, as she saw by the date, on that night—the last he ever spent at home. She never thought of breaking his injunction, or of opening the letter before the time; and after considering deeply, she decided that it was a mystery too sacred even for the ear of her mother, to whom it would only give pain. Therefore she placed it in the private drawer of her father's desk—now her own—to wait until time should bring about the revealing of this solemn secret between her and the dead.

Then she went to bed, wearied and worn; and, creeping close to her slumbering mother, thanked God that there was one warm living bosom to which she could cling, and which would never cast her out.

O mother! O daughter! who, when time has blended into an almost sisterly bond the difference of years, grow together, united, as it were, in one heart and one soul by that intense love which is beyond even 'honour' and 'obedience', because including both—how happy are ye! How blessed she, who, looking on her daughter—woman grown—can say, 'Child, thou art bone of my bone, and flesh of my flesh, as when I brought thee into the world!'* And thrice blessed is she who can answer, 'Mother, I am all thine own—I desire no love but thine—I bring to thee my every joy; and my every grief finds rest on thy bosom.'

Let those who know this happiness rejoice! Let those who only know its memory pray always, that God would make that memory live, until the eternal meeting at the resurrection of the just!

CHAPTER XIX

In one of the western environs of London is a region which, lying between two great omnibus outlets, is yet as retired and old-fashioned as though it had been miles and miles distant from the metropolis. Fields there are few or none, certainly; but there are quiet, green lanes (where in springtime you may pluck many a fragrant hawthorn branch), and market-gardens, and grand old trees; while on summer mornings you may continually hear a loud chorus of birds—especially larks—though these latter 'blithe spirits' seem to live perpetually in the air, and one marvels how they ever contrived to make their nests in the potato-grounds below. Perhaps they do so in emulation of their human neighbours—authors, actors, artists, who in this place 'most do congregate', many of them, poor souls! singing their daily songs of life out in the world, as the larks in the air; none knowing what a mean, lowly—sometimes even desolate—home is the nest whence such music springs.

Well, in this region there is a lane (a crooked, unpaved, winding, quaint, dear old lane!); and in that lane there is a house; and in that house there are two especially odd rooms—where dwelt Olive Rothesay and her mother.

Chance had led them hither; but they both—Olive especially—thanked chance, every day of their lives, for having brought them to such a delicious old place. It was the queerest of all queer abodes, was Woodford Cottage. The entrance door and the stable door stood side by side; and the cellar staircase led out of the drawing-room. The direct way from the kitchen to the dining-room was through a suite of sleeping apartments; and the staircase, apparently cut out of the wall, had a beautiful little breakneck corner, which seemed made to prevent any one who once ascended from ever descending alive. Certainly, the contriver of Woodford Cottage must have had some slight twist of the brain, which caused the building to partake of the same unpleasant convolution.

Yet, save this slight peculiarity, it was a charming house to live in. It stood in a garden, whose high walls shut out all view, save of the trees belonging to an old dilapidated, uninhabited lodge, where an illustrious statesman had once dwelt, and which was now creeping to decay and oblivion, like the great man's own memory. The trees waved, and the birds sang therein, for the especial benefit of Woodford Cottage, and of Olive Rothesay. She, who so dearly loved a garden, perfectly exulted in this one. Most delightful was its desolate, untrimmed luxuriance—where the peaches grew almost wild upon the wall, and one gigantic mulberry-tree looked beautiful all the year through. Moreover, climbing over the picturesque, bay-windowed house, was such a clematis as never was seen! Its blossoms glistened like a snow-shower throughout the day; and in the night-time, its perfume was a very breath of Eden. Altogether, the house was a grand old house—just suited for a dreamer, a poet, or an artist. An artist did really live therein; which had been no small attraction to draw Olive thither. But of him, more anon.

At present let us look at the mother and daughter, as they sit in the one parlour to which all the glories of Merivale Hall and Oldchurch had dwindled. But they did not murmur at that, for they were together; and now that the first bitterness of their loss had passed away, they began to feel cheerful—even happy.

Olive was flitting in and out of the low windows which opened into the garden, and bringing thence her apronful of flowers, to dispose about the large, somewhat gloomy, and scantily furnished room. Mrs Rothesay was sitting in the sunshine, engaged in some delicate needlework. In the midst of it she stopped, and her hands fell with a heavy sigh.

'It is of no use, Olive.'

'What is of no use, mamma?'

'I cannot see to thread my needle. I really must be growing old.'

'Nonsense, darling'—Olive often said 'darling,' quite in a protecting way—'Why, you are not near forty yet. Don't talk about growing old, my own beautiful mamma—for you are beautiful; I heard Mr Vanbrugh saying so to his sister, the other day; and of course he, an artist, must know,' added Olive, with a sweet flattery, as she took her mother's hands, and looked at her with the deep admiration which love alone creates.

And truly the admiration was not uncalled for. Over the delicate beauty of Sybilla Rothesay had crept a spiritual charm, that increased with life's decline—for her life *was* declining, early maturity having caused early decay. Not that her health was broken, or that she looked withered and aged; but still there was a gradual change, as of the tree which from its richest green melts into hues that, though still lovely, indicate the time, distant but certain, of autumn days, and of leaves softly falling earthwards. So, doubtless, her life's leaf would fall.

Mrs Rothesay smiled; sweeter than any of the flatteries of her youth, now fell her daughter's tender praise. 'You are a silly little maiden; but never mind!—Only, I wish my eyes did not trouble me so much. Olive, suppose I should come to be a blind old woman, for you to take care of.'

Olive snatched away the work, and closed the strained, aching eyes with two sweet kisses. It was a subject she could not bear to talk upon; perhaps, because it rested often on Mrs Rothesay's mind; and she herself had an instinctive apprehension that there was, after all, some truth in these fears concerning her mother's sight. She began quickly to talk of other matters.

'Hark, mamma, there is Mr Vanbrugh walking in his painting-room overhead. He always does so when he is dissatisfied about his picture; and I am sure he need not be, for, oh! how beautiful it is! Miss Meliora took me in yesterday to see it, when he was out.'

'She seems to make quite a pet of you, my child.'

'Her kitten ran away last week, which accounts for it, mamma,' said Olive, wickedly. 'But indeed I ought not to laugh at her, for one must have something to love, and she has nothing but her dumb pets.'

'And her brother.'

'I wonder if anybody ever loved him, or if he ever loved anybody,' said Olive, musingly. 'But, mamma, if he is not handsome himself, he admires beauty in others. What do you think?—he is longing to paint somebody's face, and put it in this picture; and I promised to ask. Oh, darling, do sit to him! it would not be much trouble, and I should be so proud to see my beautiful mamma on the Academy exhibition next year.'

Mrs Rothesay shook her head.

'Nay, mamma—here he comes to ask you for himself,' cried Olive, as a tall, a very tall shadow darkened the window, and its corporeality entered the room.

He was a most extraordinary-looking man, was Mr Vanbrugh. Olive had, indeed, delicately called him 'not handsome', for you probably would not see an uglier man twice in a lifetime. Gigantic and ungainly in height, and coarse in feature, he certainly was the very antipodes of his own exquisite creations. And for that reason he created them. In his troubled youth, tortured with a keen, passionate sense of that blessing which was denied him, he had said, 'Providence has created me hideous—I will out-do Providence; I, with my hand, will continually create beauty.' And so he did—ay, and where he created, he loved. He took his art for his mistress, and, like the Rhodian sculptor,* he clasped it to his soul night and day, until it grew warm and lifelike, and became to him in the stead of every human tie. Thus Michael Vanbrugh had lived, for fifty years, a life solitary even to moroseness; emulating the great Florentine master,* whose christian name it was his glory to bear. He painted grand pictures, which nobody bought, but which he and his faithful little sister Meliora thought the greater for that. The world did not understand him, nor did he understand the world; so he shut himself out from it altogether, until his small and rapidly decreasing income caused him to admit into his house the widow and daughter. He might not have done so, had not Miss Meliora hinted how lovely the former was, and how useful she might be as a model, when they grew sociable together.

He came to make his request now, and he made it with the greatest unconcern. In his opinion, everything in life tended toward one great end—Art! He looked on all beautiful forms of nature as only made to be painted. Accordingly, he stepped up to his inmate, with the following succinct address:

'Madam, I want a Grecian head. Yours just suits me; will you oblige me by sitting?' And then adding, as a soothing and flattering encouragement: 'It is for my great work—my "Alcestis!"*—one of a series of six pictures, which I hope to finish one day.'

He tossed back his long iron-grey hair, and his eyes, lighted with wild genius, scanned curiously the gentle creature, whom he had hitherto noticed only with the usual civilities of an acquaintanceship consequent on some months' residence in the same house.

'Really, Mr Vanbrugh, you are very flattering. If it will oblige you in any way,' began the widow, faintly colouring, and appealing to Olive, who looked delighted; for she regarded the old artist with as much reverence as if he had been Michelangelo himself.

He interrupted them both—'Ay, that will just do'; and his long, gaunt fingers drew in the air some magic circles over Mrs Rothesay's head. 'Good line of brow—Greek mouth. If, madam, you would favour me with taking off your cap. Thank you, Miss Olive. *You* understand me, I see. That will do—the white drapery over the hair—ah, divine! My "Alcestis" to the life! Madam—Mrs Rothesay, your head is glorious; it shall go down to posterity in my picture.'

And he walked up and down the room, rubbing his hands with a

delighted pride, which, in its perfect simplicity, could never be confounded with paltry vanity or self-adulation. '*My* work, *my* picture,' in
which he so gloried, was utterly different from—'I, the man who painted
it.' He worshipped—not himself at all; and scarce so much his real work,
as the ideal which ever flitted before him, and which it was the one great
misery of his life never to have sufficiently attained.

'When shall I sit?' timidly enquired Mrs Rothesay, still too much of a
woman not to be flattered by a painter's praise.

'At once, madam, at once, while the mood is on me. Miss Rothesay,
you will lead the way; you are not unacquainted with the arcana of my
studio.' As, indeed, she was not, having before stood some three hours in
the painful attitude of a 'Cassandra raving',* while he painted from her
outstretched and very beautiful hands.

Happy she was the very moment her foot crossed the threshold of a
painter's studio, for Olive's love of Art had grown with her growth, and
strengthened with her strength. Moreover, the artistic atmosphere in
which she now lived had increased this passion tenfold; and while her
hand secretly laboured to attain perfection, her mind was expanding, so
that the deeper things of Art were opening unto her.

'Truly, Miss Rothesay, you seem to know all about it,' said Michael
Vanbrugh, when, in great pride and delight, she was helping him to
arrange her mother's attitude, and at last became absorbed in admiration
of the graceful 'Alcestis'. 'You might have been an artist's daughter or
sister.'

'I wish I had,' said Olive, softly.

'My daughter is somewhat of an artist herself, Mr Vanbrugh,' observed
Mrs Rothesay, with a due maternal pride; which Olive, deeply blushing,
soon quelled by an entreating motion of silence.

But the painter went on painting; he saw nothing, thought of nothing,
save his 'Alcestis'. He was indeed an enthusiast. Olive watched how,
beneath the coarse, ill-formed hand, grew images of perfect beauty; how,
within the mortal frame, almost repulsive in its ugliness, dwelt a mind
which had power to produce the grandest ideal loveliness; and there
dawned in the girl's spirit a stronger conviction than ever of the majesty
of that genius which is superior to all human accident.

It was a comforting thought to one like her, who, as she deemed, had
been deprived by Nature of so many of life's sweetnesses. For the sense
of personal deformity, aroused by Sara's words, and increased by her
father's cruel epithet, had now taken such strong hold on her mind, that
it might perhaps never be obliterated.

The sitting had lasted some hours, during which it took all poor Mrs

Rothesay's gentle patience to humour Olive's enthusiasm, by maintaining that very arduous position in life, an artist's model. 'Alcestis' was getting thoroughly weary of her duties, when they were broken by an advent rather rare at Woodford Cottage—that of the daily post. Vanbrugh grumblingly betook himself to the substitute of a lay figure and drapery, while Mrs Rothesay read her letter, or rather looked at it, and gave it to Olive to read—glad, as usual, to escape from the trouble of correspondence.

Olive examined the superscription, as one sometimes does, uselessly enough—when breaking the seal would explain everything. It was a singularly bold, upright hand, distinct as print, free from all caligraphic flourishes, indicating, as most writing does indicate in some degree, the character of the writer. Slightly eccentric it might be, quick, restless, in its turned-up Gs and Ys, but still it was a good hand—an honest hand. Olive thought so, and liked it. Wondering who the writer could be, she opened it, and read thus:

MADAM,

From respect to your recent affliction I have kept silence for some months—a silence which, you will allow, was more than could have been expected from a wronged man. Perhaps I should not break it now, save for the claim of a wife and mother, who are suffering, and must suffer, from the results of an act which sprung from my own folly, and another's cruel ——But no; I will not apply harsh words towards one who is now no more.

Are you aware, madam, that your late husband, not two days before his death, when in all human probability he must have known himself to be ruined, accepted from me assistance in a matter of business, which the enclosed correspondence between my solicitor and yours will explain? This act of mine, done for the sake of an ancient friendship subsisting between my mother and Captain Rothesay, has rendered me liable for a debt so heavy, that in paying it my income is impoverished, and must continue to be so, for years.

Your husband gave me no security—I desired none. Therefore I have no legal claim of requital for this great and bitter sacrifice, which makes me daily curse my own folly in having trusted living man. But I ask of you, madam, who, secured from the effects of Captain Rothesay's insolvency, have, I understand, been left in comfort, if not affluence—I ask, is it right, in honour and in honesty, that I, a clergyman with a small stipend, should suffer the penalty of a deed wherein, with all charity to the dead, I cannot but think I was grievously injured?

Awaiting your answer, I remain, madam, your very obedient,

HAROLD GWYNNE.

'Harold Gwynne!'—Olive, repeating the name to herself, let the letter fall on the ground. Well was it that she stood hidden from sight by the 'great picture', so that her mother could not know the pang which came over her.

The mystery, then, was solved. Now she knew why in that last agony her dying father had written the name of 'Harold'—her poor father, who was here accused, by implication at least, of a wilful act of dishonesty! She regarded the letter with a sense of abhorrence—so coldly cruel it seemed to her, whose tenderness for a father's memory naturally a little belied her judgement. And the heartless charge was brought by the husband of Sara Derwent! There was bitterness in every association connected with the name of Harold Gwynne.

'Well, dear, who is the letter from? You were poring over it long enough,' said Mrs Rothesay, as they passed from the studio to their own apartment.

'It brings news that will grieve you. But never mind, mamma, darling— we will bear all our troubles together,' said Olive, as she prepared to read the letter aloud.

Well she knew the effect it would produce on her mother's feebler mind. Tears it brought, and angry exclamations, and bitter repinings; but the tender daughter soothed them all.

'Now, dear mamma,' she whispered, when Mrs Rothesay was a little composed, 'we must answer the letter at once. What shall we say?'

'Nothing! That cruel man deserves no reply at all.'

'Mamma!' cried Olive, somewhat reproachfully. 'Whatever he may be, the sum is evidently owed to him. Even Mr Wyld admits this, you see. We must not forget justice and honour—my poor father's honour.'

'No—no! You are right, my child. Let us do anything, if it is for the sake of his dear memory,' sobbed the widow, whose love death had sanctified, and endowed with an added tenderness. 'But, Olive, you must write—I cannot!'

Olive assented. She had long taken upon herself all similar duties. At once she sat down to pen this formidable letter. It took her some time; for there was a constant struggle between the necessary formality of a business letter, and the impulse of wounded feeling, natural to her dead father's child. The finished epistle was a curious mingling of both.

'Shall I read it aloud, mamma? and then the subject will be taken from your mind,' said Olive, as she came and stood by her mother's chair.

Mrs Rothesay assented.

'Well, then, here it begins—"Reverend Sir" (I ought to address him so, you know, because he is a clergyman, though he does seem so harsh, and so unlike what a Christian pastor ought to be).'

'He does, indeed, my child—but, go on.' And Olive read:

REVEREND SIR,

I address you by my mother's desire, to say that she was quite unaware of your claim upon my late dear father. She can only reply to it, by requesting your patience for a little time, until she is able to liquidate the debt—not out of the wealth you attribute to her, but out of her present restricted means. And I, my father's only child, wishing to preserve his memory from the imputations you have cast upon it, must tell you in his defence, that his last moments were spent in a speechless effort to explain a mystery which none could divine. It has been now revealed by your letter, stating his secret debt. Oh, sir! was it right or kind of you so harshly to judge the dead? My father *intended* to pay you. If you have suffered, it was through his misfortune—not his crime. Have a little patience with us, and your claim shall be wholly discharged.

OLIVE ROTHESAY

'You have said no word of Sara. I wonder if she knows all!' said the mother, as Olive folded up her letter.

'Hush, mamma! Let me forget everything that was once. Perhaps, too, she is not to blame. How, remembering the past, could Sara speak of *me* to her husband?'

Yet, with a look of bitter pain, Olive wrote the address of her letter— 'Harbury Parsonage'—Sara's home! She lingered, too, over the name of Sara's husband.

'*Harold Gwynne*! Oh, mamma! how different names look! I cannot bear the sight of this! It fills me with bitterness—even disgust.' So spoke the lofty, but rarely roused spirit of Angus Rothesay's daughter.

Years after, Olive remembered these words.

CHAPTER XX

If the old painter of Woodford Cottage was an ascetic and a misanthrope, never was the 'milk of human kindness'* so redundant in any human heart as in that of his excellent little sister, Miss Meliora Vanbrugh. From the day of her birth, when her indigent father's anticipation of a bequeathed fortune had caused her rather eccentric christian name, Miss Meliora began a chase after the wayward sprite Prosperity. She had hunted it during her whole lifetime, and never caught anything but its departing shadow. She had never grown rich, though she was always hoping to do so. She had never married, for no one had ever asked her. Whether she had loved—but that was another question. She had probably quite forgotten the days of her youth; at all events, she never talked about them now.

But though to herself her name had been a mockery, to others it was not so. Wherever she went, she always brought 'better things'—at least, in anticipation. She was the most hopeful little body in the world, and carried with her a score of consolatory proverbs, about 'long lanes' that had most fortunate 'turnings', and 'cloudy mornings' that were sure to change into 'very fine days'. She had always in her heart a garden full of small budding blessings; and though they never burst into flowers, she kept on ever expecting they would do so, and was therefore quite satisfied. Poor Miss Meliora! if her hopes never blossomed, she also never had the grief of watching them die.

Her whole life had been pervaded by one grand desire—to see her brother president of the Royal Academy. When she was a schoolgirl and he a student, she had secretly sketched his likeness—the only one extant of his ugly, yet soul-lighted face—and had prefixed thereto his name, with the magic letters, 'P.R.A.'. She felt sure the prophecy would be fulfilled one day, and then she would show him the portrait, and let her humble, sisterly love go down to posterity on the hem of his robe of fame.

Meliora told all this to her favourite, Olive Rothesay, one day when they were busying themselves in gardening—an occupation wherein their tastes met, and which contributed no little to the affection and confidence that was gradually springing up between them.

'It is a great thing to be an artist,' said Olive, musingly.

'Nothing like it in the world, my dear,' was the enthusiastic answer. 'Think of all the stories of little peasant-boys who have thus risen to be the companions of kings, whereby the kings ought to think themselves much honoured. Remember the stories of Francis I and Titian, of Henry VII and Hans Holbein, of Vandyck and Charles I!'*

'You seem quite learned in Art, Miss Vanbrugh. I wish you would impart to me a little of your knowledge.'

'To be sure I will, my dear,' said the proud, delighted little woman. 'You see, when I was a girl, I "read up" on Art, that I might be able to talk to Michael. Somehow, he never did care to talk with me; but perhaps he may yet.'

Olive's mind seemed wandering from the conversation, and from her employment, too; for the mignonette-bed she was weeding lost quite as many flowers as weeds. At last she said—

'Miss Meliora, do people ever grow *rich* as artists?'

'Michael has not done so,' answered her friend, a little confused (at which Olive began to blush for what seemed a thoughtless question). 'But Michael has peculiar notions. However, I feel sure he will be a rich man yet—like Sir Joshua Reynolds, and Sir Thomas Lawrence,* and many more.'

Olive began to muse again. Then she said, timidly, 'I wonder why, with all your love for Art, you yourself did not become an artist?'

'Bless you, my dear, I should never think of such a thing. I have no genius at all for anything—Michael always said so. I an artist!—a poor little woman like me!'

'Yet, some women have been painters.'

'Oh, yes, plenty. There was Angelica Kauffman, and Properzia Rossi, and Elizabetta Sirani.* In our day, there is Mrs A—— and Miss B——, and the two C——s. And if you read about the old Italian masters, you will find that many of them had wives, or daughters, or sisters, who helped them a great deal. I wish I had been such an one! Depend upon it, my dear girl,' said Meliora, waxing quite oracular in her enthusiasm, 'there is no profession in the world that brings fame, and riches, and happiness, like that of an artist.'

Olive only half believed in the innocent optimism of her companion. Still, Miss Vanbrugh's words impressed themselves strongly on her mind, wherein was now a chaos of anxious thought. From the day when Mr Gwynne's letter came, she had positively writhed under the burden of this heavy debt, which it would take years to discharge, unless a great deduction were made from their slender income. And how could she propose that—how bear to see her delicate and often-ailing mother deprived of the small luxuries which had become necessary comforts? To their letter no answer came—the creditor was then a patient one; but this thought the more stimulated Olive to defray the debt. Night and day it weighed her spirit down; plan after plan she formed, chiefly in secret, for the mention of this painful circumstance was more than her mother could bear. Among other schemes, she thought of entering on that last resource of helpless womanhood, the dreary life of a daily governess; but her desultory education, she well knew, unfitted her for the duty; and no sooner did she venture to propose the plan, than Mrs Rothesay's lamentations and entreaties rendered it impracticable.

But Miss Vanbrugh's conversation now awakened a new scheme, by which in time she might be able to redeem her father's memory, and to save her mother from any sacrifice entailed by this debt. And so—though this confession may somewhat lessen the romance of her character—it was from no yearning after fame, no genius-led ambition, but from the mere desire of earning money, that Olive Rothesay first conceived the thought of becoming an artist.

Very faint it was at first—so faint that she did not breathe it even to her mother. But it stimulated her to labour incessantly at her drawing; silently to try and acquire information from Miss Meliora; to haunt the painter's studio, until she had become familiar with many of its mysteries. She had crept into Vanbrugh's good graces, and he, with his customary, unconscious egotism, made her useful in a thousand ways.

But labouring secretly and without encouragement, Olive found her progress in drawing—she did not venture to call these humble efforts *Art*—very slow indeed. One day, when Mrs Rothesay was gone out, Meliora came in to have a chat with her young favourite, and found poor Olive sitting by herself, quietly crying. There was lying beside her an unfinished sketch, which she hastily hid, before Miss Vanbrugh could notice what had been her occupation.

'My dear, what is the matter with you—no serious trouble, I hope?' cried the painter's little sister, who always melted into anxious compassion at the sight of anybody's tears. But Olive's only flowed the faster—she being in truth extremely miserable. For this day her mother had sorrowfully alluded to Mr Gwynne's claim, and had begun to propose many little personal sacrifices on her own part, which grieved her affectionate daughter to the heart.

Meliora made vain efforts at womanly soothing, and then, as a last resource, she went and fetched two little kittens and laid them on Olive's lap by way of consolation; for her own delight and solace was in her household menagerie, from which she was ever evolving great future blessings. She had always either a cat so beautiful, that when sent to Edwin Landseer, it would certainly produce a revolution in the subjects of his animal pictures—or else a terrier so bewitching, that she intended to present it to her then girlish, dog-loving Majesty, thereby causing a shower of prosperity to fall upon the household of Vanbrugh.

Olive dried her tears, and stroked the kittens—her propensity for such pets was not her lightest merit in Meliora's eyes. Then she suffered herself to be tenderly soothed into acknowledging that she was very unhappy.

'I'll not ask you why, my dear, because Michael used to tell me I had far too much feminine curiosity,' said Miss Vanbrugh, humbly. 'I only meant, if I could comfort you in any way.'

There was something so unobtrusive in her sympathy, that Olive felt inclined to open her heart to the gentle Meliora. 'I can't tell you all,' she said, 'I think it would not be quite right'; and, trembling and hesitating, as if in the confession were something of shame, she whispered her longing for that great comfort, money of her own earning.

'You, my dear, you want money!' cried Miss Meliora, who had always looked upon her new inmate, Mrs Rothesay, as a sort of domestic gold-mine. But she had the delicacy not to press Olive farther.

'I do. I can't tell you why, but it is for a good purpose—a holy purpose! Oh, Miss Vanbrugh, if you could show me any way of earning money for myself! Think for me—you, who know so much more of the world than I.'

—Which truth did not at all ignore the fact, that innocent little Meliora was a very child in worldly knowledge. She proved it by her next sentence, delivered oracularly after some minutes of hard cogitation. 'My dear, there is but one way to gain wealth and prosperity. If you had but a taste for Art!'

Olive looked up eagerly. 'Ah, that is what I have been brooding over this long time; until I was ashamed of myself and my own presumption.'

'Your presumption?'

'Yes; because I have sometimes thought my drawings were not so very, very bad; and I love Art so dearly, I would give anything in the world to be an artist!'

'You draw! You long to be an artist!' It was the only thing wanted to make Olive quite perfect in Meliora's eyes. She jumped up, and embraced her young favourite with the greatest enthusiasm. 'I knew this was in you. All good people must have a love for Art. And you shall have your desire, for my brother shall teach you. I must go and tell him directly.'

But Olive resisted, for her poor little heart began to quake. What if her long-loved girlish dreams should be quenched at once—if Mr Vanbrugh's stern dictum should be that she had no talent, and never could become an artist at all!

'Well, then, don't be frightened, my dear girl. Let me see your sketches. I do know a little about such things, though Michael thinks I don't,' said Miss Meliora.

And Olive, her cheeks tingling with that sensitive emotion which makes many a young artist, or poet, shrink in positive agony, when the crude first-fruits of his genius are brought to light—Olive stood by, while the painter's kind little sister turned over a portfolio, filled with a most heterogeneous mass of productions.

Their very oddity showed the spirit of Art that dictated them. There were no pretty, well-finished, young-ladyish sketches of tumbledown cottages, and trees whose species no botanist could ever define;—no smooth chalk heads, with very tiny mouths, and very crooked noses. Olive's productions were all as rough as rough could be; few even attaining to the dignity of drawing-paper. They comprised numberless pen-and-ink portraits of the one beautiful face, dearest to the daughter's heart—rude studies, in charcoal, of natural objects—outlines, from memory, of pictures she had seen, among which Meliora's eye proudly discerned several of Mr Vanbrugh's; while, scattered on every scrap of paper, were original pencil designs, ludicrously voluminous, illustrating nearly every poet, living or dead.

Michael Vanbrugh's sister was not likely to be quite ignorant of Art. Indeed, she had quietly gathered up a tolerable critical knowledge of the same—love teaches women so much! She went through the portfolio, making remarks here and there. At last she closed it; but with a look so beaming and encouraging, that Olive trembled for very joy.

'Let us go to Michael, let us go to Michael,' was all the happy little woman said. So they went.

Unluckily, Michael was not himself; he had been 'pestered with a popinjay',* in the shape of a would-be connoisseur, and he was trying to smooth his ruffled feathers, and compose himself again to solitude and 'Alcestis'. His 'well, what d'ye want?' was a sort of suppressed bellow, softening down a little at sight of Olive.

'Brother,' cried Miss Meliora, trying to gather up her crumbling enthusiasm into one courageous point—'Michael, I have found out a new genius! Look here, and say if Olive Rothesay will not make an artist!'

'Pshaw—a woman make an artist! Ridiculous!' was the answer. 'Ha! take the rubbish away—don't come near my picture. The paint's wet. Get away!'

And he stood, flourishing his mahl-stick* and palette—looking very like a gigantic warrior, guarding the shrine of Art with shield and spear.

His poor little sister, quite confounded, tried to pick up the drawings which had fallen on the floor; but he thundered out 'Let them stay!' and then politely desired his sister to quit the room.

'Very well, brother—perhaps it will be better for you to look at the sketches another time. Come, my dear.'

'Stay, I want Miss Rothesay; no one else knows how to wear that purple chlamys properly, and I must work at the drapery today. I am fit for nothing else, thanks to that puppy who is just gone; confound him! I beg your pardon, Miss Rothesay,' muttered the old painter, in a slight tone of concession, which encouraged Meliora to another gentle attack.

'Then, brother, since your day is spoiled, don't you think if you were to look——'

'I'll look at nothing; get away with you, and leave Miss Rothesay here—the only one of you womenkind who is fit to enter an artist's studio.'

Here Meliora slyly looked at Olive with an encouraging smile, and then, by no means despairing of her kind-hearted mission, she made herself invisible.

Olive, very humbled and disconsolate, prepared for her voluntary duty as Vanbrugh's lay-figure. If she had not so reverenced his genius, she certainly would not have altogether liked the man. But her hero-worship was so intense, and her womanly patience so all-forgiving, that she bore his occasional strange humours almost as meekly as Meliora herself. Today, for the hundredth time, she watched the painter's brow smooth, and his voice soften, as upon him grew the influence of his beautiful creation. 'Alcestis', calmly smiling from the canvas, shed balm into his vexed soul.

But beneath the purple chlamys poor little Olive still trembled and grieved. Not until her hope was thus crushed, did she know how near her heart it had been. She thought of Michael Vanbrugh's scornful rebuke, and bitter shame possessed her. She stood—patient model!—her fingers stiffening over the rich drapery, her eyes wearily fixed on the one corner of the room, in the direction of which she was obliged to turn her head. The monotonous, silent attitude contributed to plunge her mind into that dull despair which produces immobility of frame;—Michael Vanbrugh had never had so excellent a model.

As Olive was placed, he could not see her face unless he moved. When he did so, he quite startled her out of a reverie by exclaiming—

'Exquisite! Stay just as you are. Don't change your expression. That's the very face I want for the Mother of Alcestis. A little older I must make it—but the look of passive misery, the depressed eyelids and mouth. Ah, beautiful—beautiful, Miss Rothesay—do, pray let me have that expression again, just for three minutes!' cried the eager painter.

He accomplished his end; for Olive's features, from long habit, had a great power of retaining immobility;—and she would willingly have acted all Le Brun's Passions,* if necessary, for artistic purposes. Delighted at his success, Mr Vanbrugh suddenly thought of his model, not *as* a model, but as a human being. He wondered what had produced the look which, now faithfully transferred to the canvas, completed 'a bit' that had troubled

him for weeks. He then thought of the drawings, and of his roughness
concerning them. Usually, he hated amateurs and their productions,
but perhaps these might not be so bad. He would not stoop to lift them,
but, fidgeting with his mahl-stick, he stirred them about once or twice—
accidentally as it seemed—until he had a very good notion of what
they were. Then, after half an hour's silent painting, he thus addressed
Olive.

'Miss Rothesay, what put it into your head that you wanted to be an
artist?'

Olive answered nothing. She was ashamed to speak of her girlish
aspirations, such as they had been; and she could not tell the other
motive—the secret about Mr Gwynne. Besides, Vanbrugh would have
scorned the bare idea of her entering on the great career of Art for money!
So she was silent.

He did not seem to mind it at all, but went on talking, as he sometimes
did, in a sort of declamatory monologue.

'I am not such a fool as to say that genius is of either sex, but it is an
acknowledged fact that no woman ever was a great painter, poet, or
musician. Genius, the mighty one, does not exist in weak female nature,
and even if it did, custom and education would certainly stunt its growth.
Look here, child,'—and, to Olive's astonishment, he snatched up one of
her drawings, and began lecturing thereupon—'here you have made a
design—of some original power, too. I hate your young lady copyists of
landscapes and flowers, and Jullien's paltry heads. Come, let us see this
epigraph, "Laon's Vision of Cythna",*

> Upon the mountain's dizzy brink she stood.

Good! Bold enough, too!'

And the painter settled himself into a long, silent examination of the
sketch. Then he said,

'Well, this is tolerable; a woman standing on a rock, a man a little
distance below looking at her—both drawn more correctly than most
amateurs could, only overlaid with drapery to hide ignorance of anatomy.
A very respectable design. But when one compares it with the poem!'
And, in his deep, sonorous voice, he repeated the stanzas from the
'Revolt of Islam'.

> She stood alone.
> Above, the heavens were spread; below, the flood
> Was murmuring in its caves; the wind had blown
> Her hair apart, through which her eyes and forehead shone.

A cloud was hanging o'er the western mountains;
Before its blue and moveless depth was flying,
Grey mists poured forth from the unresting fountains
Of darkness in the north—the day was dying.
Sudden the sun shone forth; its beams were lying
Like boiling gold on ocean, strange to see;
And on the shattered vapours, which defying
The power of light in vain, tossed restlessly
In the red heaven, like wrecks in a tempestuous sea.

It was a stream of living beams, whose bank
On either side by the cloud's cleft was made;
And where its chasms that flood of glory drank,
Its waves gushed forth like fire, and, as if swayed
By some mute tempest, rolled on *her*. The shade
Of her bright image floated on the river
Of liquid light, which then did end and fade.
Her radiant shape upon its verge did shiver
Aloft, her flowing hair like strings of flame did quiver.

'There!' cried Vanbrugh, his countenance glowing with a fierce inspiration that made it grand amidst its ugliness; 'there!—what woman could paint *that*? Or rather, what man? Alas! how feeble we are—we, boldest followers of an Art which is divine. Truly there was but one among us who was himself above humanity, Michael the Angel!'

And he went and gazed reverently at the majestic head of Buonarotti, which loomed out from the shadowy corner of the studio.

Olive experienced—as she often did, when brought into contact with this man's enthusiasm—a delight almost like terror; for it made her shudder and tremble as though within her own poor frame was that Pythian effluence, felt, not understood—the spirit of Genius.

Vanbrugh came back, and continued his painting, talking all the while.

'I said that it was impossible for a woman to become an artist—I mean, a *great* artist. Have you ever thought what that term implies? Not only a painter, but a poet; a man of learning, of reading, of observation. A gentleman—we artists have been the friends of kings. A man of high virtue, or how can he reach the pure ideal? A man of iron will, unconquered daring, and passions strong—yet stainless. Last and greatest, a man who, feeling within him the divine spirit, with his whole soul worships God!'

Vanbrugh lifted off his velvet cap and reverently bared his lofty crown; then he continued:

'This is what an artist must *be* by nature. I have not spoken of what he has to make himself. Years of study such as few can bear lie before him—

no life of a carpet-knight, no easy play-work of scraping colours on canvas. Why, these hands of mine have wielded not only the pencil, but the scalpel; these eyes have rested on scenes of horror, misery—even crime. I glory in it; for it was all for Art. At times I have almost felt like Parrhasius* of old, who exulted in his captive's dying throes, since upon them his hand of genius would confer immortality. But this is not meet for the ears of a woman—a girl,' added Vanbrugh, seeing Olive shudder at his words. Yet he had not been unmindful of the ardent enthusiasm which had dilated her whole frame while listening. It touched him like the memory of his own youth. Some likeness, too, there seemed between himself and this young girl to whom nature had been so niggardly. She might also be one of those who, shut out from human ties, are the more free to work the glorious work of genius.

After a few minutes of thought, Michael again burst forth.

'They who embrace Art, must embrace her with heart and soul, as their one only bride. And she will be a loving bride to them—she will stand in the place of all other joy. Is it not triumph for him to whom fate has denied personal beauty, that his hand—his flesh and blood hand—has power to create it? What cares he for worldly splendour, when in dreams he can summon up a fairyland so gorgeous that in limning it even his own rainbow-dyed pencil fails? What need has he for home, to whom the wide world is full of treasures of study—for which life itself is too short? And what to him are earthly and domestic ties? For friendship, he exchanges the world's worship, which *may* be his in life, *must* be, after death. For love——'

Here the old artist paused a moment, and there was something heavenly in the melody of his voice as he continued,

'For love—frail human love—the poison-flower of youth, which only lasts an hour—he has his own divine ideal. It flits continually before him, sometimes all but clasped; it inspires his manhood with purity, and pours celestial passion into his age. His heart, though dead to all human ties, is not cold, but burning. For he worships the ideal of beauty, he loves the ideal of love.'

Olive listened, her senses reeling before these impetuous words. One moment she looked at Vanbrugh where he stood, his age transfigured into youth, his ugliness into majesty, by the radiance of the immortal fire that dwelt within him. Then she sank at his feet, crying,

'I, too, am one of these outcasts; give me then this inner life which is beyond all! Friend, counsel me! master, teach me! Woman as I am, I will dare all things—endure all things. Let me be an artist!'

CHAPTER XXI

Olive Rothesay's desire,

> Like all strongest hopes,
> By its own energy fulfilled itself.

She became an artist—not in a week, a month, a year—Art exacts of its votaries no less service than a lifetime. But in her girl's soul the right chord had been touched, which began to vibrate unto noble music—the true seed had been sown, which day by day grew into a goodly plant.

Vanbrugh had said truly, that genius is of no sex; and he had said likewise truly, that no woman can be an artist—that is, a great artist. The hierarchies of the soul's dominion belong only to man, and it is right they should. He it was whom God created first, let him take the pre-eminence. But among those stars of lesser glory, which are given to lighten the nations, among sweet-voiced poets, earnest prose writers, who, by the lofty truth that lies hid beneath legend and parable, purify the world, graceful painters and beautiful musicians, each brightening their generation with serene and holy lustre—among these, let woman shine!

But her sphere is, and ever must be, bounded; because, however lofty her genius may be, it always dwells in a woman's breast. Nature, which gave to man the dominion of the intellect, gave to her that of the heart and affections. These bind her with everlasting links from which she cannot free herself—nay, she would not if she could. Herein man has the advantage. He, strong in his might of intellect, can make it his all in all, his life's sole aim and guerdon. A Brutus,* for that ambition which is misnamed patriotism, can trample on all human ties. A Michelangelo can stand alone with his genius, and so go sternly down unto a desolate old age. But there scarce ever lived the woman who would not rather sit meekly by her own hearth, with her husband at her side, and her children at her knee, than be the crowned Corinne of the Capitol.*

Thus woman, seeking to strive with man, is made feebler by the very spirit of love which in her own sphere is her chiefest strength. But sometimes chance or circumstance or wrong, sealing up her woman's nature, converts her into a self-dependent human soul. Instead of life's sweetnesses, she has before her life's greatnesses. The struggle passed, her genius may lift itself upward, expand and grow mighty; never so mighty as man's, but still great and glorious. Then, even while she walks with scarce-healed feet over the world's rough pathway, heaven's glory may rest upon her upturned brow, and she may become a light unto her generation.

Such a destiny lay open before Olive Rothesay.

She welcomed it as one who has girded himself with steadfast but mournful patience unto a long and dreary journey, welcomes the faint ray that promises to guide him through the desolation. No more she uttered, as was her custom in melancholy moods, the bitter complaint, 'Why was I born?' but she said to herself, 'I will live so as to leave the world better when I die. Then I shall not have lived in vain.'

It was long before Michael Vanbrugh could thoroughly reconcile himself to the idea of a girl's becoming a painter. But by degrees he learned to view his young pupil *as* a pupil, and never thought of her sex at all. Under his guidance, Olive passed from the mere prettinesses of most woman-painters to the grandeur of sublime Art. Strengthened by her almost masculine power of mind, she learned to comprehend and to reverence the mighty masters which Vanbrugh loved. He unveiled to her those heights and depths which are rarely opened to a woman's ken. And she, following as he led—following with a daring will, and a firm perseverance—applied herself to the most obstruse of Art-studies. Still, as he had said, there were bounds that she could not pass; but as far as in her lay, she sought to lift herself above her sex's weakness and want of perseverance; and by an arduous toil from which most women would have shrunk, to make herself worthy of being ranked among those painters who are not of the passing hour, but for all time.

That sense of personal imperfection which she deemed excluded her from a woman's natural destiny, gave her freedom in her own. Brought into contact with the world, she scarce felt like a young and timid girl, but as a being—isolated, yet strong in her isolation; who mingles, and must mingle, among men, not as a woman, but as one who, like themselves, pursues her own calling, has her own spirit's aim; and can therefore step aside for no vain fear, nor sink beneath any idle shame. And wherever she went, her own perfect womanliness wrapped her round as with a shield.

Still, Olive could do many things with an independence that would have been impossible to beautiful and unguarded youth. Oftentimes Mrs Rothesay trembled and murmured at the days of solitary study in the British Museum, and in various picture galleries; the long lonely walks, sometimes in wintertime extending far into the dusk of evening. But Olive always answered, with a pensive smile.

'Nay, mother; I am quite safe everywhere. Remember, I am not like other girls. Who would notice *me*?'

But she always accompanied any painful allusion of this kind by saying how happy she was in being so free, and how fortunate it seemed that there could be nothing to hinder her from following her heart's desire. She was growing as great an optimist as Miss Meliora herself, who— cheerful little soul—was in the seventh heaven of delight whenever she heard her brother acknowledge Olive's progress.

'And don't you see, my dear Miss Rothesay,' she said sometimes, 'that everything always turns out for the best; and that if you had not been so unhappy, and I had not come in and found you crying, you might have gone on pining in secret, instead of growing up to be an artist.'

Olive assented, and confessed it was rather strange that out of her chiefest trouble should have arisen her chiefest joy.

'It almost seems,' said she to her mother, laughing, 'as if that hard-hearted Mr Harold Gwynne had held the threads of my destiny, and helped to make me an artist.'

'Don't let us talk about Mr Gwynne; it is a disagreeble subject, my child,' was Mrs Rothesay's answer.

Olive did not talk about him, but she thought the more. And—though had he known it, the pelf-despising Mr Vanbrugh would never have forgiven such a desecration of Art—it was not Olive's lightest spur in the attainment of excellence, to feel that as soon as her pictures were good enough to sell, she might earn money enough to discharge the claim of this harsh creditor, whose very name sent a pang to her heart.

Day by day, as her spirit strengthened and her genius developed, Olive's existence seemed to brighten. Her domestic life was full of many dear ties, the chief of which was that wild devotion, less a senti-ment than a passion, which she felt for her mother. Her intellectual life grew more intense and all-vivifying; while she felt the stay and solace of having one pursuit to occupy the whole aims and desires of her future. Also, it was good for her to dwell with the enthusiastic painter and his meek contented little sister; for she learnt thereby that life might pass not merely in endurance, but in peace, without either of those blessings which in her early romance she deemed the chief of all—beauty and love. She felt that worth and genius were above them both.

The lesson was impressed more deeply by a little incident that chanced about this time.

Miss Vanbrugh sometimes took Olive with her on those little errands of charity which were not unfrequent with the gentle Meliora.

'I wish you would come with me today,' she said once, 'because, to tell the truth, I hardly like to go alone.'

'Indeed!' said Olive, smiling, for the little old maid was as brave as a lion among those gloomiest of all gloomy lanes. She would traverse them even in dark nights, and this was a sunny spring morning.

'I am not going to see an ordinary poor person, but that strange foreign-looking woman—Mrs Manners; who is one of my brother's models sometimes—you know her?'

'Scarcely; but I have seen her pass through the hall. Oh, she was a grand, beautiful woman, like an Eastern queen. You remember it was she from whom Mr Vanbrugh painted the 'Cleopatra'.* What an eye she had, and what a glorious mouth!' cried Olive, waxing enthusiastic.

'Poor thing! Her beauty is sadly wasting now,' said Meliora. 'She seems to be slowly dying, and I shouldn't wonder if it were of sheer starvation; those models earn so little. Yesterday she fainted as she stood—Michael is so thoughtless. He had to call me to give her some wine, and then we sent the maid home with her. She lives in a poor place, Jane says, but quite decent and respectable. I shall surely go and see the poor creature; but she looks such a desperate sort of woman, her eyes glare quite ferociously sometimes. She might be angry—so I had rather not be alone, if you will come, Miss Rothesay?'

Olive consented at once; there was in her a daring romance which, putting all sympathy aside, would have quite gloried in such an adventure.

They walked for a mile or two until they reached a miserable street by the riverside; but Miss Meliora had forgotten the number. They must have returned, their quest unsatisfied, had not Olive seen a little girl leaning out of an upper window—her ragged elbows on the sill, her wild elf-like black eyes watching the boats up and down the Thames.

'I know that child,' Olive said; 'it is the poor woman's. She left it in the hall one day at Woodford Cottage, and I noticed it from its black eyes and fair hair. I remember, too—for I asked—its singular and very pretty name, *Christal*.'

Talking thus, they mounted the rickety staircase, and inquired for Mrs Manners. The door of the room was flung open from without, with a noise that would have broken any torpor less deep than that into which its wretched occupant had fallen.

'*Ma mie** is asleep; don't wake her or she'll scold,' said Christal, jumping down from the window, and interposing between Miss Vanbrugh and the woman who was called Mrs Manners.

She was indeed a very beautiful woman, though her beauty was on a grand scale. She had flung herself, half-dressed, upon what seemed a heap of straw with a blanket thrown over. As she lay there, sleeping heavily, her arm tossed above her head, the large but perfect proportions of her form reminded Olive of the reclining figure in the group of the 'Three Fates'.*

But there was in the prematurely old and wasted face something that told of a wrecked life. Olive, prone to romance-weaving, wondered whether nature had in a mere freak invested an ordinary low-born woman with the form of the ancient queens of the world, or whether within that grand body lay ruined an equally grand soul.

Miss Meliora did not think about anything of the sort; but merely that her brother's dinner-hour was drawing near, and that if poor Mrs Manners did not wake, they must go back without speaking to her.

But she did wake soon—and the paroxysm of anger which seized her on discovering that she had intruding guests, caused Olive to shrink back almost to the staircase. But brave little Miss Vanbrugh did not so easily give up her charitable purpose.

'Indeed, my good woman, I only meant to offer you sympathy, or any help you might need in your illness.'

The woman refused both, in an accent that to Olive seemed rather Spanish—or perhaps she fancied so, because the dark face had a Spanish, or Creole* cast. 'I tell you, we want for nothing.'

'*Ma mie*! I am so hungry!' said little Christal, in a tone between complaint and effrontery. 'I will have something to eat.'

'You should not speak so rudely to your mother, little girl,' interposed Miss Meliora.

'My mother! No, indeed; she is only *ma mie*. My mother was a rich lady, and my father a noble gentleman.'

'Hear her, Heaven! oh, hear her!' groaned the woman on the floor.

'But I love *ma mie* very much—that's when she's kind to me,' said Christal; 'and as for my own father and mother, I don't remember them at all, for, as *ma mie* says, they were drowned together in the deep sea, years ago.'

'I would they had been—I would they had been,' was the muttered answer, as Mrs Manners clutched the child—a little, thin-limbed, cunning-eyed girl, of eight or ten years old—and pressed her to her breast, with a strain more like the gripe of a lioness than a tender woman's clasp.

Then she fell back quite exhausted, and took no more notice of anybody. Meliora's easily roused compassion forgot Mr Vanbrugh's dinner, and all things else, in making a few charitable arrangements, that resulted in a comfortable tea for little Christal and '*ma mie*'.

Sleep had again overpowered the sick woman, who appeared to be slowly dying of that anomalous disease called decline, in which the mind is the chief agent of the body's decay. Meanwhile, Miss Vanbrugh talked in an undertone to little Christal, who, her hunger satisfied, stood, her finger in her mouth, watching the two ladies with her fierce black eyes—the very image of a half-tamed gipsy. Indeed, Miss Meliora seemed rather uneasy, and desirous to learn more of her companions, for she questioned the child closely.

'And is the person you call *ma mie* any relation to you?'

'The neighbours say she must be my aunt, from the likeness. I don't know.'

'And her name is Mrs Manners—a widow, no doubt; for I remember she was in very respectable mourning when she first came to Woodford Cottage,' said Meliora, who, having thus far drawn on her lively imagination, deeply sympathized with the supposed heroine of her fanciful tale.

'Poor young creature!' she continued, sitting down beside the object of her compassion, who was, or seemed, asleep. 'How hard to lose her husband so soon! and I dare say she has gone through great poverty—sold one thing after another to keep her alive. Why, I declare,' added the simple and unworldly Meliora, who could make a story to fit anything, 'poor soul! she has even been forced to part with her wedding-ring.'

'I never had one—I scorned it!' cried the woman, leaping up with a violence that quite confounded the painter's sister. 'Do you come to insult me, you smooth-tongued English lady? Ah, you shrink away—I am too vile for your presence, am I?'

'I don't know anything about you, indeed,' said Meliora, creeping to the door; while Olive, who, as yet untouched by human passion, could not understand the mystery of half she witnessed, stood simply looking on in wonder—almost in admiration. To her there seemed a strange beauty, like that of a Pythoness, in the woman's attitude and mien.

'You know nothing of me? Then you shall know. I come from a country where are thousands of young maidens, whose blood, half-Southern, half-European, is too pure for slavery, too tainted for freedom. Lovely, and taught all accomplishments that can ennoble beauty, brought up delicately, in wealth and luxury, they yet have no higher future than to be the white man's passing toy—cherished, mocked, and spurned.'

She paused; and Miss Vanbrugh, astonished at this sudden outburst, in language so vehement, and above her apparent sphere, had not a word to say. The woman continued:

'I but fulfilled my destiny. How could such as I hope to bear an honest man's honest name? So, when my fate came upon me, I cast all shame to the winds, and lived out my life. I followed my lover across the seas; I clung to him, faithful in my degradation; and when his child slept on my bosom, I looked at it, and was almost happy. Now, what think you of me, virtuous English lady?' cried the outcast, as she tossed back her cloud of dark crisped hair, chief token of her Quadroon blood,* and fixed her eyes sternly, yet mockingly, upon her visitors.

Poor Miss Vanbrugh was conscious of but one thing, that this scene was most unmeet for a young girl; and that if once she could get Olive away, all future visits to the miserable woman should be paid by herself alone. Yet still she had the charity to say, in forbearing and half-disguised words,

'I will see you another day, Mrs Manners, but we cannot really stay now. Come away, my dear Miss Rothesay.'

And she and her charge quitted the room. Apparently, their precipitate departure still further irritated the poor creature they had come to succour; for as they descended the stairs, they heard her repeatedly shriek out Olive's surname, in tones so wild, that whether it was meant for rage or entreaty they could not tell.

Olive wanted to return.

'No, my dear; she would only insult you. Besides, I will go myself tomorrow. Poor wretch! she is plainly near her end. We must be merciful to the dying.'

Olive walked home thoughtfully, not speaking much. When they passed out of the squalid, noisy streets, into the quiet lane that led to Woodford Cottage, she had never felt with so keen a sense the blessing of a pure and peaceful home. She mounted to the pretty bedchamber which she and her mother occupied, and stood at the open window, drinking in the fresh, sweet odour of the bursting leaves. Scarce a breath stirred the soft spring evening—the sky was like one calm blue lake, and therein floated, close to the western verge, 'the new moon's silver boat'.

She remembered how it had been one of her childish superstitions always 'to wish at the new moon'. How often, her desire seeming perversely to lift itself towards things unattainable, had she framed one sole wish, that she might be beautiful and loved!

Beautiful and beloved! She thought of the poor erring creature whose fierce words yet rang in her shrinking ear. Beautiful and beloved? *She* had been both, and what was she now?

And Olive rejoiced that her own childish longings had passed into the wisdom of subdued and patient womanhood. Had she now to frame a wish; it would have been for that pure heart and lowly mind which are more precious than beauty; for that serene peace of virtue, which is more to be desired than love.

Now her fate seemed plain before her—within her home she saw the vista of a life of filial devotion, blest in

A constant stream of love that knew no fall.

As she looked forth into the world without, there rose the vision, dim, yet sweet, of the great aim, that might perhaps achieve a success under shadow of which the lonely woman might go down to the grave not unhonoured in her day. Remembering all this, Olive murmured no longer at her destiny. She thanked God, for she felt that she was not unhappy.

CHAPTER XXII

Perhaps, ere following Olive's fortunes, it would be as well to set the reader's mind at rest concerning the incident narrated in the preceding chapter. It turned out the olden tale of passion, misery, and death. No more could be made of it, even by the imaginative Miss Meliora.

A few words will comprise all that she discovered. Returning faithfully next day, the kind little woman found that the object of her charity needed it no more. In the night, suddenly it was thought, the spirit had departed. There was no friend to arrange anything for the living or the dead; so Miss Vanbrugh undertook it all. Her own unobtrusive benevolence prevented a pauper funeral.* But in examining the few relics of the deceased, she was surprised to find papers which clearly explained the fact, that some years before there had been placed in a London bank, to the credit of Celia Manners, a sum sufficient to produce a moderate annuity. The woman had rejected it, and starved.

But she had not died without leaving a written injunction, that it should be claimed by the child Christal, since it was 'her right'. This was accomplished, to the great satisfaction of Miss Vanbrugh and of the honest banker, who knew that the man—what sort of man he had quite forgotten—who deposited the money, had enjoined that it should be paid, whenever claimed by Celia or by Christal Manners.

Christal Manners was then the child's name. Miss Vanbrugh might have thought that this discovery implied the heritage of shame, but for the little girl's obstinate persistence in the tale respecting her unknown father and mother, who were 'a noble gentleman and grand lady', and had both been drowned at sea. The circumstance was by no means improbable, and it had evidently been strongly impressed on Christal by the woman she called *ma mie*. Whatever relationship there was between them, it could not be the maternal one. Miss Vanbrugh could not believe in the possibility of a mother's thus voluntarily renouncing her own child.

Miss Meliora put Christal to board with an old servant of hers, for a few weeks. But there came such reports of the child's daring and unruly temper, that, quaking under her responsibility, she decided to send her *protégée* away to school. The only place she could think of was an old-fashioned *pension** in Paris, where, during her brother's studies there, her own slender education had been acquired. Thither the little stranger was dispatched, by means of a succession of contrivances which almost drove the simple Meliora crazy. For—lest her little adventure of benevolence should come to Michael's ears—she dared to take no one into her confidence, not even the Rothesays. Madame Blandin, the mistress of the *pension*, was furnished with no explanations; indeed, there were none to give. The orphan appeared there under the character she so steadily sustained—as Miss Christal Manners, the child of illustrious parents lost at sea; and so she vanished altogether from the atmosphere of Woodford Cottage.

Olive Rothesay was now straining every nerve towards the completion of her first-exhibited picture—a momentous crisis in every young artist's life. It was March: always a pleasant month in this mild, sheltered neighbourhood where she had made her home. There, of all the regions about London, the leaves come earliest, the larks soonest begin to sing, and the first soft spring breezes blow. But nothing could allure Olive from that corner of their large drawing-room which she had made her studio, and where she sat painting from early morning until daylight was spent. The artist herself formed no unpleasing picture—at least, so her fond mother often thought; as Olive stood before her easel, the light from the half-closed-up window slanting downwards on her long curls, of that rare pale gold, the delight of the ancient painters, and now the especial admiration of Michael Vanbrugh. To please her master, Olive—though now a woman grown—wore her hair still in childish fashion, falling in most artistic confusion over her neck and shoulders. It seemed that nature had bestowed on her this great beauty, in order to veil that defect which, though made far less apparent by her maturer growth, and a certain art in dress, could never be entirely removed. Still there was an inexpressible charm in her purely outlined features, to which the complexion always accompanying pale-gold hair imparted such a delicate, spiritual colouring. Oftentimes her mother sat and looked at her, thinking she beheld the very likeness of the angel in her dream.

March was nearly passed—March, that month the most trying of the year to English artists and their 'forebears'. Olive's anxiety that the picture should be finished, and worthily finished, amounted almost to torture. At last, when there was but one week left—a week whose every hour of daylight must be spent in work, the hope and fear were at once terminated by her mother's sudden illness. Passing it was, and not dangerous; but to Olive's picture it brought a fatal interruption.

The tender mother more than once prayed her to neglect all a daughter's cares, rather than lose the year's exhibition; but Olive forsook not her duty. Yet it cost her somewhat—aye, more than Mrs Rothesay could understand, to give up a year's hopes. She felt this the more when came the Monday and Tuesday for sending in pictures to the Academy.

Heavily these days passed, for there was not now the attendance on the invalid to occupy Olive's mind. She was called hither and thither all over the house; since on these two days, for the only time in the year, there was at Woodford Cottage a positive *levée** of artists, patrons, and connoisseurs. Miss Rothesay was needed everywhere; first in the painting-room, to assist in arranging its various treasures, her taste and tact assisting Mr Vanbrugh's artistic skill. For the thousandth time, she helped to move the easel that sustained the small *purchasable* picture with which Michael this year condescended to favour the Academy; and admired, to the painter's heart's content, the beloved and long unsold 'Alcestis', which extended in desolate grandeur over one whole side of the studio. Then she flitted to Miss Vanbrugh's room, to help her to dress for this important occasion. Never was there such a proud, happy little woman as Meliora Vanbrugh on the first Monday and Tuesday in April, when at least a dozen carriages usually rolled down the muddy lane, and the great surly dog, kennelled under the mulberry-tree, was never silent 'from morn till dewy eve'; and all, thought the delighted Meliora, was an ovation to her brother's fame. Each year she fully expected that these visiting patrons would buy up every work of Art in the studio, to say nothing of those adorning the hall—the cartoons and frescoes of Michael's long-past youth. And each year, when the carriages rolled away, and the visitants' admiration remained nothing *but* admiration, she consoled herself with the thought that Michael Vanbrugh was 'a man before his age', but that his time for appreciation would surely come. So she hoped on till the next April: happy Meliora!

'Yes, you do seem happy, Miss Vanbrugh,' said Olive, when she had coaxed the stiff grizzled hair under a pretty cap of her own skilful manufacturing; and the painter's little sister was about to mount guard in the bay-window of the parlour, from whence she could see the guests walk down the garden, and be also ready to mark the expression of their faces as they came out of the studio.

'Happy!—to be sure I am! Everybody must confess that this last is the best picture Michael ever painted'—(his sister had made the same observation every April for twenty years). 'But, my dear Miss Rothesay, how wrong I am to talk so cheerfully to you, when *your* picture is not finished. But never mind, love! You have been a good, attentive daughter, and it will end all for the best.'

Olive smiled faintly, and said she knew it would. But she thought in her troubled heart how much seldomer were hopes fulfilled than disappointed.

'Perhaps,' continued Meliora, as a new and consolatory idea struck her, 'perhaps, even if you had sent in the picture, it might have been returned, or put in the octagon room, or among the miniatures, where nobody could see it; and that would have been much worse, would it not?'

'I suppose so; and, indeed, I will be quite patient and content.'

Patient she was, but not content. It was scarcely possible. Nevertheless, she quitted Miss Vanbrugh with smiles; and when she again sought her mother's chamber, it was with smiles too—or, at least, with that soft sweetness that ever dwelt in Olive's face. When she had left Mrs Rothesay to take her afternoon sleep, she thought what she was to do to pass away the hours that, in spite of herself, dragged very wearily. This day was so different to what she had hoped. No eager, delighted 'last touches' to her beloved picture; no exhibiting of it in its best light, in all the glory of the frame. It lay neglected below—she could not bear to look at it. The day was clear and bright—just the sort of day for painting; but Olive felt that the very sight of the poor picture would be more than she could bear. She did not go near it, but put on her bonnet and walked out.

'Courage! hope!' sang the larks to her, high up above the green lanes; but her heart was too sad to hear them. A year, a whole year, lost!—a whole year to wait for the next hope! And a year seems so long when one has scarce counted twenty. Afterwards, how fast it flies!

'Perhaps,' she said, her thoughts taking their colour from the general weariness of her spirits, 'perhaps Miss Vanbrugh was right, and I might have had the picture returned. It cannot be very good, or it would not have taken such long and constant labour. Genius, they say, never toils— all comes by inspiration. It may be that I have no genius; well then, where is the use of my labouring to excel?—indeed, where is the use of my living at all?'

Alas! how little is known of the struggles of young, half-formed genius!—struggles, not only with the world, but with itself; a hopeless, miserable bearing-down—a sense of utter unworthiness and self-contempt. At times, when the inner life—the soul's lamp—burns dimly, there rises the piteous moan—'Fool! fool! why strivest thou in vain? Thou hast deceived thyself; thou art no better than any brainless ass that plods through life.' And then the world grows so dull, and one's life seems so worthless, that one would fain blot it out at once.

Olive walked beneath this bitter cloud. She said to herself, that if her picture had been a work of genius, it would have been finished long ere the time; and that if she were destined to be an artist, there would not have come this cross. No! all fates were against her. She must be patient and submit, but she felt as if she should never have courage to paint again. And now, when her work had become the chief aim and joy of her life, how hard this seemed!

She came home, drearily enough; for the sunny day had changed to rain, and she was thoroughly wet. But even this was, as Meliora would have expressed it, 'for the best'; since it made her feel the sweetness of having a tender mother to take off her dripping garments, and smooth her hair, and make her sit down before the bright fire. And then Olive laid her head in her mother's lap, and thought how wrong—nay, wicked—she had been! She was thinking thus, even with a few quiet tears, when Miss Meliora burst, like a stream of sunshine, into the room.

'Good news—good news!'

'What? Mr Vanbrugh has sold his picture, as you hoped, to Mr——'

'No, not yet!' and the least possible shadow troubled the sister's face, 'but perhaps he will. And, meanwhile, what think you? Something has happened quite as good—at least, for somebody else. Guess!'

'Indeed, I cannot!'

'He has sold *yours*!'

Olive's face flushed, grew white, and then she welcomed this first success, as many another young aspirant to fame has done, by bursting into tears. So did the easily touched Mrs Rothesay, and so did the kind Miss Meliora, from pure sympathy. Never was good fortune hailed in a more lachrymose fashion.

But soon Miss Vanbrugh, resuming her smiles, explained how she had placed Olive's nearly finished picture in her brother's studio, where all the visitors had admired it, and one, a good friend to Art, and to young, struggling artists, had bought it.

'My brother managed all—even to the payment. The full price you will have when you have completed the picture. And, meanwhile, look here!'

She had filled one hand with golden guineas, and now poured a Danaë-stream into Olive's lap. Then, laughing and skipping about like a child, she vanished—the beneficent little fairy!—as swiftly as Cinderella's godmother.

Olive sat mute, her eyes fixed on the 'bits of shining gold',* which seemed to look different to all other pieces of gold that she had ever seen.

She touched them, as if half fearing they would melt away, or, like elfin coins, change into withered leaves. Then, brightly smiling, she took them up, one by one, and told them into her mother's lap.

'Take them, darling—my first earnings; and kiss me—kiss your happy little girl!'

How sweet was that moment—worth whole years of after fame! Olive Rothesay might live to bathe in the sunshine of renown—to hear behind her the murmur of a world's praise—but she never could know again the bliss of laying at her mother's feet the first-fruits of her genius, and winning, as its first guerdon, her mother's proud and happy kiss.

'You will be quite rich now, my child.'

'*We* will be,' said Olive, softly.

'And to think that such a great connoisseur as Mr—— should choose my Olive's picture. Ah! she will be a celebrated woman some time—I always thought she would.'

'*I will!*' said the firm voice in Olive's heart, as, roused to enthusiasm by this sweet first success, she felt stirring within her the spirit whose pulses she could not mistake—woman, nay, girl as she was—the spirit of Genius. Thinking on her future—the future that, with Heaven's blessing, she would nobly work out, her eye dilated and her breast heaved. And then on that wildly heaving bosom strayed a soft, warm hand—a tender voice whispered, 'My child.'

And Olive, flinging her arms round her mother's neck, hid her face there, and was a simple trembling child once more.

It was a very happy evening for them both—almost the happiest in their lives. The mother formed a score of plans for expending this newly won wealth, always to the winner's benefit solely; but Olive began to look grave, and at last said, timidly,

'Mamma, indeed I want for nothing; and for this money, let us spend it in a way that will make us both most content. Oh, mother! I can know no rest until we have paid Mr Gwynne.'

The mother sighed.

'Well, love, as you will. It is yours, you know; only, a little it pains me that my child's precious earnings should go to pay that cruel debt.'

'Not that they should go to redeem my father's honour?' said Olive, still gently. But she had her will.

When her picture was finished, and its price received, Olive, with a joyful heart, enclosed the sum to their long-silent creditor.

'His name does not look quite so fearful now,' she said, smiling, when she was addressing the letter. 'I can positively write it without trembling, and perhaps I may not have to write it many times. If I grow very rich, mamma, we shall soon pay off this debt, and then we shall never hear any more of Harold Gwynne. Oh! how happy that would be!'

The letter went, and an answer arrived in due form—not to Mrs, but to *Miss* Rothesay:

MADAM,

I thank you for your letter, and have pleasure in cancelling a portion of my claim. I would fain cancel the whole of it, but I must not sacrifice my own household to that of strangers.

Allow me to express my deep respect for a child so honourably jealous over a father's memory, and to subscribe myself,

Your very obedient,
HAROLD GWYNNE

'He is not so stony-hearted after all, mamma,' said Olive, smiling. 'Shall I put this letter with the other; we had better keep them both?'

'Certainly, my dear.'

'Look, the envelope is edged and sealed with black.'

'Is it? Oh, perhaps he has lost his mother. I think I once heard your poor papa say he knew her once. She must be now a very old woman; still her loss has probably been a grief to her son.'

'Most likely,' said Olive, hastily. She never could bear to hear of any one's mother dying; it made her feel compassionately even towards Mr Gwynne; and then she quickly changed the subject.

The two letters were put by in her desk, and thus—for a season at least—the Harbury correspondence closed.

CHAPTER XXIII

Seven summers more the grand old mulberry-tree at Woodford Cottage has borne leaf, flower, and fruit; the old dog that used to lie snarling under its branches, lies there still, but snarls no more. Between him and the upper air are two feet of earth, together with an elegant canine tomb-stone, on which Miss Rothesay, by the entreaty of the disconsolate Meliora, has modelled a very good head of the departed.

Snap is the only individual who has passed away at Woodford Cottage; in all things else there has been an increase, not a decrease. The peaches and nectarines cover two walls instead of one, and the clematis has mounted in white virgin beauty even to the roof. Altogether, the garden is changed for the better. Trim it is not, and never would be—thanks to

Olive, who, a true lover of the picturesque, hated trim gardens. But its wild luxuriance is that of flowers, not weeds; and luxuriant it is, so that every day you might pull for a friend that pleasantest of all pleasant gifts, a nosegay; yea, and afterwards find, that, like charity, the more you gave the richer was your store.

Enter from the garden into the drawing-room, and you will perceive a change, too. Its once gloomy barrenness has been softened by many a graceful adjunct of comfort and luxury. Half of it, by means of a crimson screen, is transformed into a painting-room. Olive would have it so, even when need no longer required. She did this for several reasons, the chief of which was, that whether the young paintress was working or not, Mrs Rothesay might never be out of the sound of her daughter's voice. For, alas! this same sweet, love-toned voice was all the mother now knew of Olive!

Gradually there had come over Mrs Rothesay the misfortune which she once feared. She was now quite blind. Relating this, it may seem though we were about to picture a scene of grief and desolation; but not so. A misfortune that steals on year by year—slowly—inevitably—often comes with so light a footstep that we scarcely hear it. In this manner had come Mrs Rothesay's blindness. Her sight faded so gradually, that its deprivation caused no despondency; and the more helpless she grew, the closer she was clasped by those supporting arms of filial love, which softened all pain, supplied all need, and were to her instead of strengh, youth, eyesight!

One only bitterness did she know—that she could not see Olive's pictures. Not that she understood Art at all; but everything that Olive did *must* be beautiful. She missed nought else—not even her daughter's face; for she saw it continually in her heart. Perhaps, in the grey shadow of a form, which she said her eyes could still trace in the dim haze, she pictured the likeness of an Olive ten times fairer than the real one—an Olive, whose cheek never grew pale with toil, whose brow was never crossed by that cloud of heart-weariness which all who labour in an intellectual pursuit must know at times. If so, the mother was saved from many of the pangs which visit those who see their beloved ones staggering under a burden which they themselves have no power either to take away or to bear.

And so, in spite of this affliction, the mother and daughter were happy—even quite cheerful, sometimes. For cheerfulness, originally foreign to Olive's nature, had sprung up there—one of those heart-flowers which Love, passing by, sows according as they are needed, until they bloom as though indigenous to the soil. To hear Miss Rothesay laugh, as she was laughing just now, you would have thought she was the merriest creature in the world, and had been so all her life. Moreover, from this blithe laugh, as well as from her happy face, you might have taken her for a young maiden of nineteen, instead of a woman of six-and-twenty—which she really was. But with some natures, after youth's first sufferings are passed, life's dial seems to run backward.

'My child, how very merry you are, you and Miss Vanbrugh!' said Mrs Rothesay, from her inner corner.

'Well, mamma, and how can we help it—talking of my "Charity", and the lady who bought it. Would you believe, darling, she told Miss Vanbrugh that she did so because the background was like a view in their park, and the two little children resembled the two young Masters Fludyer—a fortunate likeness for me!'

'Aye,' said Miss Meliora, 'only my brother would say you were very wrong to sell your picture to such stupid people, who know nothing about Art.'

'Perhaps I was; but,' she added, whisperingly, 'you know I have not sold my Academy picture yet, and mamma *must* go into the country this autumn.'

'Mrs Fludyer is a very nice ladylike woman,' observed the mother; 'and she talked of her beautiful country seat at Farnwood Hall. I think it would do me good to go there, Olive.'

'Well, you know she asked you, dear mamma.'

'Yes; but only for courtesy. She would scarce be troubled with a guest so helpless as I,' said Mrs Rothesay, half sighing.

In a moment Olive was by her side, talking away, at first softly, and then luring her on to smiles with a merry tale,—how Mr Fludyer, when the picture came home, wanted to have the three elder Fludyers painted in a row behind 'Charity', that thus the allegorical picture might make a complete family group. 'He also sent to know if I couldn't paint his horse "Beauty", and one or two greyhounds also, in the same picture. What a comical idea of Art this country squire must have!'

'My dear, every one is not so clever as you,' said the mother. 'I like Mrs Fludyer very much, because, whenever she came to Woodford Cottage about the picture, she used to talk to me so kindly.'

'And she has asked after you in all her letters since she went home. So she must be a good creature; and I too will like her very much indeed, because she likes my sweet mamma,' was Olive's caressing answer.

The determination was soon called into exercise; for the next half hour, to the surprise of all parties, Mrs Fludyer appeared.

She assigned no reason for her visit, except that being again in town, she had chosen to drive down to Woodford Cottage. She talked for half an hour in her mild, limpid way; and then, when the arrival of one of Olive's models broke the quiet leisure of the painting-room, she rose.

'Nay, Miss Rothesay, do not quit your easel; Miss Vanbrugh will accompany me through the garden, and besides, I wish to speak to her about her clematis. We cannot make them grow in S——shire; the Hall is perhaps too cold and bleak.'

'Ah, how I love a clear bracing air!' said Mrs Rothesay, with the restlessness peculiar to all invalids—and she had been a greater invalid than usual this summer.

'Then you must come down, as I said—you and Miss Rothesay—to S——shire; our part of the country is very beautiful. I should be most happy to see you at Farnwood.'

She urged the invitation with an easy grace, even cordiality, which charmed Mrs Rothesay, to whom it brought back the faint reflex of her olden life—the life at Merivale Hall.

'I should like to go, Olive,' she said, appealingly. 'I feel dull, and want a change.'

'You shall have a change, darling,' was the soothing but evasive answer. For Olive had a tincture of the old Rothesay pride, and had formed a somewhat disagreeable idea of the position the struggling artist and her blind mother would fill as charity guests at Farnwood Hall. So, after a little conversation with Mrs Fludyer, she contrived that the first plan should melt into one more feasible. There was a pretty cottage, the squire's lady said, on the Farnwood estate; Miss Fludyer's daily governess had lived there; it was all fitted up. What if Miss Rothesay would bring her mother there for the summer months? It would be pleasant for all parties.

And so, very quickly, the thing was decided—decided as suddenly and unexpectedly as things are, when it seems as though not human will, but destiny, held the balance.

Mrs Fludyer seemed really pleased and interested; she talked to Miss Meliora, less about her clematis than about her two inmates—a subject not less grateful to the painter's sister.

'There is something quite charming about Miss Rothesay—an air and manner of one who has always moved in good society. Do you know who she was? I should apologize for the question, but that a friend of mine, looking at her picture, was struck by the name, and desired me to enquire.'

Meliora explained that she believed Olive's family was Scottish, and that her father was a Captain Angus Rothesay.

'Captain Angus Rothesay! I think that was the name mentioned by my friend,' answered Mrs Fludyer, musing.

'Shall I call Miss Rothesay! Perhaps your friend is known to her,' observed Meliora.

'Oh no! Mrs—— that is, the lady I allude to, said it was needless to mention her name. And, by the by, there is no reason why you should trouble Miss Rothesay with my idle enquiry. Many thanks for the clematis, and good morning, my dear Miss Vanbrugh.'

She ascended her carriage with the easy, smiling grace of one born to fortune, marrying fortune, and dwelling hand-in-hand with fortune all her life. Miss Meliora gazed in intense admiration after her departing wheels, and forthwith retired to plan out of the few words she had let fall a glorious future for her dear Miss Rothesay. There was certainly some unknown wealthy relative who would probably appear next week, and carry off Olive and her mother to affluence—in a carriage as grand as Mrs Fludyer's.

She would have rushed at once to communicate the news to her friends, had it not been that she was stopped in the garden walk by the apparition of her brother escorting two gentlemen from his studio—a rare courtesy with him. Meliora accounted for it when, from behind a sheltering espalier, she heard him address one of them as 'my lord'.

But when she told this to Olive, the young paintress was of a different opinion. She had heard the name of Lord Arundale, and recognized it as that of a nobleman on whom his love of Art and science shed more honour than his title. That was why Mr Vanbrugh showed him respect, she knew.

'Certainly, certainly!' said Meliora, a little ashamed. 'But to think that such a clever man, and a nobleman, should be so ordinary in appearance. Why, he was not half so remarkable-looking as the gentleman who accompanied him.'

'What was *he* like?' said Olive, smiling.

'You would have admired him greatly. His was just the sort of head you painted for your "Aristides the Just"—your favourite style of beauty— dark, cold, proud, with such piercing, eagle eyes; they went right through me!'

Olive laughed merrily.

'Do you hear, mamma, how she runs on? What a bewitching young hero!'

'A hero perhaps, but not at all young; and as for bewitching, that he certainly might be, but it was in the fashion of a wizard or a magician. I never felt so nervous at the sight of any one in the whole course of my life,' continued Miss Meliora, chattering on, as she often did, just to amuse Mrs Rothesay, and make Olive smile. She would have gone on longer, but there was a knock at the drawing-room door.

'Come in,' said Olive, and Mr Vanbrugh entered.

For a moment he stood on the threshold without speaking; but there was a radiance in his face, a triumphant dignity in his whole carriage, which struck Olive and his sister with surprise.

'Brother—dear Michael, you are pleased with something; you have had good news.'

He passed Meliora by, and walked up to Miss Rothesay.

'My pupil, rejoice with me; I have found at length appreciation, my life's aim has won success—I have sold my "Alcestis".'

Miss Vanbrugh, in her frantic joy, rushed towards her brother to embrace him. Olive Rothesay, full of delight, would have clasped her master's hand, but there was something in his look that repelled them both. His was the stern solitary triumph of a man who exulted only in and for his art, neither asking nor needing any human sympathies. Such a look might have been on the face of the great Florentine, when he beheld the multitude bend half in rapture, half in awe, before his work in the Sistine chapel, and folding his coarse garments round him, walked through the streets of Rome to his hermit dwelling, and sat himself down in stern rejoicement and proud humility, under the shadow of his desolate renown.

Michael Vanbrugh continued,

'Yes, I have sold my grand picture, the dream—the joy of a lifetime. Sold it, too, to a man who is worthy to possess it. I shall see it in Lord Arundale's noble gallery; I shall know that it, at least, will remain where, after my death, it will keep from oblivion the name of Michael Vanbrugh. Glorious indeed is this my triumph—yet less mine, than the triumph of High Art. Do you not rejoice, my pupil?'

'I do, indeed, my dear and noble master,' said Olive, regarding him with reverent affection, for there had grown up a deep sympathy between her and the eccentric painter.

'And brother, brother—you will be very rich. The price you asked for the "Alcestis" was two thousand pounds,' said Meliora.

He smiled bitterly.

'You women always think of that—the paltry gold that rewarded genius brings.'

'But for you, only for you, dear Michael,' cried his sister; and her tearful eyes spoke the truth. Poor little soul! she could but go as far as her gifts went, and they extended no farther than to the thought of what comforts would this money procure for Michael—a richer velvet gown and cap, like one of the old Italian painters—perhaps a journey to refresh his wearied eyes among lovely scenes of nature. She explained this, looking, not angry, but just a little hurt.

'A journey! yes, I will take a journey—one which I have longed for these thirty years—I will go to Rome! Once again I will lie on the floor of the Sistine, and look up worshippingly to Michael the Angel.' (He always called him so.)

'And how long shall you stay, brother?'

'Stay? until my heart grows pulseless, and my brain dull. Why should I ever come back to this cold England? No; let me grow old, die, and be buried, under the shadow of the Eternal City.'

'He will never come back again—never,' said Miss Vanbrugh, looking at Olive with a vague bewilderment. 'He will leave this pretty cottage, and me, and everything.'

There was a dead silence, during which poor Meliora sat plaiting her white apron in fold after fold; as was her habit when in deep and perplexed thought. Then she went up to her brother.

'Michael, if you will take me, I should like to go with you.'

'What!' cried Mrs Rothesay, 'you, my dear Miss Vanbrugh, who are so thoroughly English—who always said you hated moving from place to place, and would live and die at Woodford Cottage!'

'Hush—hush! we'll not talk about that, lest he should hear,' said Meliora, glancing half frightened at her brother. But he stood absorbed by the window, looking out apparently on the sky, though his eyes saw nothing—nothing! 'Michael, do you quite understand—may I go with you to Rome?'

'Very well—very well, sister,' he answered, in the tone of a man who is indifferent to the subject, except that consent gives less trouble than refusal. Then he turned towards Olive, and asked her to go with him to his painting-room; he wanted to consult with her as to the sort of frame suited to the 'Alcestis'. Indeed, his pupil had now grown associated with all his pursuits, and had penetrated further in the depths of his inward life than any one else had been ever suffered to do. And Olive's ardent, almost masculine genius, sympathized deeply with the strange old artist; so that she became to him his cherished pupil—the child of his soul, to whom he would fain transmit the mantle of his fame. He had but one regret, sometimes touchingly expressed—that she was a woman—only a woman.

They went and stood before the picture, he and Olive, Meliora stealing after her brother's footsteps, noiseless but constant as his shadow. And this ever-following, faithful love clung so closely to its object, that, shadow-like, what all others beheld, by him was never seen. It is often so!

Michael Vanbrugh cast on his picture a look such as no living face ever had won, or ever would win, from his cold eyes. It was the gaze of a parent on his child, a lover on his mistress, an idolater on his self-created god. Then he took his palette, and began to paint, lingeringly and lovingly, on slight portions of background or drapery—less as though he thought this needed, than as if loath to give the last, the very last, touch to a work so precious. He talked all the while, seemingly to hide the emotion which he would not show.

'That Lord Arundale is an honour to his order, a *noble man* indeed. One does not often meet such, Miss Rothesay. It was a pleasure to receive him in my studio. It did me good to talk with him, and with his friend.'

Here Olive looked at Meliora and smiled. 'Was his friend, then, as pleasing as himself?'

'Not so brilliant in conversation, but far the higher nature of the two, or I have read the human countenance in vain. He said, boldly and frankly, that he was no artist, and no connoisseur, like Lord Arundale; but I saw from his eye, that, if he did not understand, he felt my picture.'

'How so?' said Olive, with growing interest.

'He looked at Alcestis,—the "Alcestis" I have painted,—sitting on her golden throne, her head on her husband's breast, waiting for death to call her from her kingdom and her lord: waiting solemnly, yet without fear. "See," said Lord Arundale to his friend, "how love makes this feeble woman stronger than a hero! See how fearlessly a noble wife can die!"— "A wife who loves her husband," was the answer, given so bitterly, that I turned to look at him. Oh, that I could have painted his head at that instant! It would have made a Heraclitus*—a Timon!'*

'And do you know who is this man?' asked Olive, unable to restrain her curiosity. 'Will he come here again?'

'No; for he was leaving London today. I wish it had not been so, for I would have asked him to sit to me. That grand, iron, rigid head of his, with the close curling hair, would be a treasure indeed!'

'But who is he, brother?' enquired Meliora.

'A man of science; well known in the world, too, Lord Arundale said. He told me his name, but I forget it. However, you may find a card somewhere about.'

Meliora ran to the mantelpiece, and brought one to her brother. 'Is this it?' He nodded. She went quickly to the light, and read aloud—

'*The Reverend Harold Gwynne.*'

CHAPTER XXIV

The subject of Harold Gwynne served Olive and her mother for a full half-hour's conversation during that idle twilight season which they always devoted to pleasant talk. It was a curious coincidence which thus revived in their memories a name now almost forgotten. For, the debt once paid, Mr Gwynne and all things connected with him had passed into complete oblivion, save that Olive carefully kept his letters.

These she had the curiosity to take from their hiding-place, and examine once more—partly for her mother's amusement, partly for her own; for it was a whim of hers to judge of character by handwriting,* and she really had been quite interested in the character which both Miss Vanbrugh and her brother unconsciously drew of this man.

'How strange that he should have been so near us, and we not know the fact! though he must have known it, of course. He seems quite to haunt us—to be positively our evil genius—our *Daimon*!'*

'Hush, my dear! It is wrong to talk so. Remember, too, that he is Sara's husband.'

Olive did remember it. Jestingly though she spoke, there was in her spirit a remembrance, as mournful as a thing so long ended could be, of that early friendship, whose falseness had been her loving heart's first blight. She had never formed another. There was a grand unity in her nature which made it impossible to build the shrine of a second affection on the ruins of the first. She found it so, even in life's ordinary ties. What would it have been with her had she ever known the great mystery of love.

She never had known it. She had lived all these years with a heart as virgin as mountain snows. When the one sweet dream which comes to all pure spirits in early maidenhood—the dream of loving and being loved—was crushed, her heart drew back within itself, and, after a time of suffering almost as deep as if for the loss of a real object instead of a mere ideal, she meekly prepared herself for her destiny. She went out into society, and there saw men, as they are *in society*—feeble, fluttering coxcombs, hard, grovelling men of business; some few men of pleasure, and of scarce-concealed vice; and, floating around all, the race of ordinary mankind, neither good nor bad. Out of these classes, the first she merely laughed at, the second she turned from with distaste, the third she abhorred and despised, the fourth she looked upon with a calm indifference. Some good and clever men she had met occasionally, towards whom she had felt herself drawn with a friendly inclination; but they had always been drifted from her by the ever-shifting currents of society.

And these, the exceptions, were chiefly old, or at least elderly persons; men of long-acknowledged talent, wise and respected heads of families. The 'new generation', the young men out of whose community her female acquaintances were continually choosing lovers and husbands, were positively disliked by Olive Rothesay. Gradually, when she saw how mean was the general standard of perfection, how ineffably beneath her own ideal—the man she could have worshipped—she ceased to regret that loneliness which on earth was, she deemed, her perpetual lot. She saw her companions wedded to men who from herself would never have won a single thought. So she gathered up all her passionate love-impulses into her virgin soul, and married herself unto her Art.

She indulged in some of her sage reflections on men and women, courtship and wedlock, in general, when she sat at her mother's feet talking of Harold Gwynne and of his wife.

'Sara, too, must have suffered—if Mr Gwynne be really the man that Miss Vanbrugh and her brother describe,' thought Miss Rothesay; and there recurred over and over again to her fancy the words, '*A wife who loved her husband.*' Olive at least knew too well that Sara Derwent, when she married, could not have loved hers. Wonderings as to what that marriage had been, and what was Sara's present fate, occupied her mind for a long, long time. She had full opportunity for thought; as her mother, oppressed by the sultry August evening, had fallen asleep with her hand on her daughter's neck, and Olive could not stir for fear of waking her.

Slowly she watched the twilight darken into a deeper shadow—that of a gathering thunderstorm. The trees beyond the garden began to sway restlessly about, and then, with a sudden flash and distant thunder growl, down came the rain in torrents. Mrs Rothesay started and woke; like most timid women, she had a great dread of thunder, and it took all Olive's powers of soothing to quiet her nervous alarms. These were increased by another sound that broke through the pouring rain—a violent ringing of the garden bell, which, in Mrs Rothesay's excited state, seemed a warning of all sorts of horrors.

'The house is on fire—the bolt has struck it. Oh, Olive, Olive, save me!' she cried.

'Hush, darling! You are quite safe with me.' And Olive rose up, folding her arms closely round her mother, who hid her head in her daughter's bosom. They stood—Mrs Rothesay trembling and cowering—Olive with her pale brow lifted fearlessly, as though she would face all terror, all danger, for her mother's sake. Thus they showed, in the faint glimmer of the lightning, a beautiful picture of filial love—to the eyes of a stranger, who that moment opened the door. She was a woman, whom the storm had apparently driven in for shelter.

'Is this Miss Vanbrugh's house?—is there any one here?' she asked; her accent was slightly foreign, as far as could be traced through the hurried manner.

Olive answered with a kindly civility, and invited her to enter.

'Thank you, forgive my intrusion, but I am frightened—half drowned. The thunder is awful; will you take me in till Miss Vanbrugh returns?'

'Certainly; go to her, Olive, Poor thing! How dreadful to be out in this storm!' said Mrs Rothesay, her alarm conquered by her quick sympathies.

A light was quickly procured, and Olive came to divest the stranger of her dripping garments.

'Thank you, no! I can assist myself—I always do.'

And she tried to unfasten her shawl—a rich heavy fabric, and of gaudy colours, when her trembling fingers failed; she knitted her brows, and muttered some sharp exclamation in French.

'You had better let me help you,' said Olive, gently, as, with a firm hand, she took hold of the shivering woman, or girl, for she did not look above seventeen, drew her to a seat, and there disrobed her of her drenched mantle.

Not until then did Miss Rothesay pause to consider further about this incognita, arrived in such a singular manner. But when, recovered from her alarm, the young stranger subsided into the very unromantic occupation of drying her wet frock by the kitchen fire, Olive regarded her with no small curiosity.

She stood, a picture less of girlish grace, than of such grace as French fashion dictates. Her tall, well-rounded form, struggled through a painful slimness; her whole attire had that peculiar *tournure** which we rude scornful islanders term Frenchified. Nay, there was something in the very tie of her neck-ribbon which showed it never could have been done by English fingers. She appeared, all over, 'a young lady from abroad'.

We have noticed her dress first, because that was itself most noticeable. The form it enveloped was that of a fine, tall, well-modelled girl, who would have been graceful had fashion allowed her. She had one beauty— a proud, arched, column-like neck, gliding into a well-set head, which she carried loftily. Her features were somewhat large, not pretty, and yet not plain. She had a good mouth and chin; her eyes were very dark and silken-fringed; and, what was rather singular, her hair was quite fair.*

This peculiarity caught Olive's eye at once; so much so, that she almost fancied she had seen the face before, but could not tell where. She puzzled about the matter, until the young guest, who seemed to make herself quite at home, had dried her garments, and voluntarily proposed that they should return to the drawing-room.

They did so; the stranger leading the way, and, much to Olive's surprise, seeming to thread with perfect ease the queer labyrinths of the house.

By this time the storm was over, and they found Mrs Rothesay sitting quietly waiting for tea. The young lady again apologized in her easy, foreign manner, and asked if she might stay with them until Miss Vanbrugh's return? Of course her hostess assented, and she talked for above an hour; chiefly of Paris, which she said she had just left; of French customs, music, and literature.

In the midst of this, Miss Vanbrugh's voice was heard in the hall. The girl started, as one does at the sound of some old tune, heard in youth, and forgotten for years; her gaiety ceased; she put her hand before her eyes; but when the door opened, she was her old self again.

No child 'frayed with a sprite'* could have looked more alarmed than Miss Meliora at the sudden vision of this elegant young damsel, who advanced towards her. The little old maid was quite overpowered with her stylish bend; her elegant salute, French fashion, cheek to cheek; and her anxious enquiries after Miss Vanbrugh's health.

'I am quite well, thank you, madam. A friend of Mrs Rothesay's, I suppose?' was poor Meliora's bewildered reply.

'No, indeed; I have not till now had the pleasure of hearing Mrs Rothesay's name. My visit was to you,' said the stranger, evidently enjoying the *incognito* she had kept, for her black eyes sparkled with most malicious fun.

'I am happy to see you, madam,' again stammered the troubled Meliora.

'I thought you would be so—I came to surprise you. My dear Miss Vanbrugh, have you really forgotten me? Then allow me to reintroduce myself. My name is Christal Manners.'

Miss Meliora looked as if she could have sunk into the earth! Year after year, from the sum left in the bank, she had paid the school bill of her self-assumed charge; but that was all. Afterthoughts, and a few prudish hints given by good-natured friends, had made her feel both ashamed and frightened at having taken such a doubtful *protégée*. Whenever she chanced to think of Christal's growing up, and coming back a woman, she drove the subject from her mind in positive alarm. Now the very thing she dreaded had come upon her. Here was the desolate child returned, a stylish young woman, with no home in the world but that of her sole friend and protectress.

Poor Miss Vanbrugh was quite overwhelmed. She sank on a chair, muttering, 'Christal Manners here! Dear me! I am so frightened—that is, so startled. Oh, Miss Rothesay, what shall I do?' And she looked appealingly to Olive.

But between her and Miss Rothesay glided the young stranger. The bright colour paled from Christal's face—her smile passed into a frown.

'Then you are not glad to see me—you, the sole friend I have in the world, whom I have travelled a thousand miles to meet—travelled alone and unprotected—you are not glad to see me? I will turn and go back again—I will leave the house—I will—I—'

Her rapid speech ended in a burst of tears. Poor Meliora felt like a guilty thing. 'Miss Manners—Christal—my poor child! I didn't mean that! Don't cry—don't cry! I am very glad to see you—so are we all—are we not, Olive?'

Olive was almost as much puzzled as herself. She had a passing recollection of the death of Mrs Manners, and of the child's being sent to school; but since then she had heard no more of her. She could hardly believe that the elegant creature before her was the little ragged imp of a child whom she had once seen staring idly down the river. However, she asked no questions, but helped to soothe the girl, and to restore, as far as possible, peace and composure to the household.

They all spent the evening together without any reference to the past. Only once, Christal—in relating how, as soon as ever her term of education expired, she had almost compelled her governess to let her come to England, and to Miss Vanbrugh,—said, in her proud way,

'It was not to ask a maintenance—for you know my parents left me independent; but I wanted to see you, because I believed that, besides taking charge of my fortune, you had been kind to me when a child. How, or in what way, I cannot clearly remember; for I think,' she added, laughing, 'that I must have been a very stupid little girl: all seems so dim to me until I went to school. Can you enlighten me, Miss Vanbrugh?'

'Another time, another time, my dear,' said the painter's sister, growing very much confused.

'Well! I thank you all the same, and you shall not find me ungrateful,' said the young lady, kissing Miss Meliora's hand, and speaking in a tone of real feeling, which would have moved any woman. It quite overpowered Miss Vanbrugh—the softest-hearted little woman in the world. She embraced her *protégée*, declaring that she would never part with her.

'But,' she added, with a sudden thought, a thought of intense alarm, 'What will Michael say?'

'Do not think of that tonight,' interposed Olive. 'Miss Manners is tired; let us get her to bed quickly, and we will see what morning brings.'

The advice was followed, and Christal disappeared; not, however, without lavishing on Mrs and Miss Rothesay a thousand gracious thanks and apologies, with an air and deportment that did infinite honour to the polite instruction of her *pension*.

Mrs Rothesay, confused with all that had happened, did not ask many questions, but only said, as she retired,

'I don't quite like her, Olive—I don't like the tone of her voice; and yet there was something that struck me in the touch of her hand—which is so different in different people.'

'Hers is a very pretty hand, mamma, It is quite classic in shape—like poor papa's!—which I remember so well!'

'There never was such a beautiful hand as your papa's. He said it descended in the Rothesay family. You have it, you know, my child,' observed Mrs Rothesay. She sighed, but softly; for, after all these years, the widow and the fatherless had learned to speak of their loss without pain, though with tender remembrance.

Thinking of him and of her mother, Olive thought, likewise, how much happier was her own lot than that of the orphan girl, who, by her own confession, had never known what it was to remember the love of the dead, or to rejoice in the love of the living. And her heart was moved with deep pity—nay, even tenderness, for Christal Manners.

When she had assisted her mother to bed—as she always did—Olive, in passing down stairs, moved by some feeling of interest, listened at the door of the young stranger. She was apparently walking up and down her room with a quick, hurried step. Olive knocked.

'Are you quite comfortable?—do you want anything?'

'Who's there? Oh! come in, Miss Rothesay.'

Olive entered, and found, to her surprise, that the candle was extinguished.

'I thought I heard you moving about, Miss Manners.'

'So I was. I felt restless and could not sleep. I am very tired with my journey, I suppose, and the room is strange to me. Come here—give me your hand.'

'You are not afraid, my dear child?' said Olive, remembering that she was, indeed, little more than a child, thought she looked so womanly. 'You are not frightening yourself in this gloomy old house, nor thinking of ghosts and goblins?'

'No—no! I was thinking, if I must tell the truth,' said the girl, with something very like a suppressed sob—'I was thinking of you and your mother, as I saw you standing when I first came in. No one ever clasped me so, or ever will! Not that I have any one to blame; my father and mother died; they could not help that. But if they had just brought me into the world and left me, as I have heard some parents have done, then I should cry out, "Wicked parents! if I grow up heartless, because I have no one to love me; and vile, because I have none to guide me—my sin be upon your head!" '

She said these words with vehement passion. But Olive answered, calmly, 'Hush, Christal!—let me call you Christal; for I am much older than you. Lie down and rest. Be loving, and you will never want for love; be humble, and you will never want for guiding. You have good friends here, who will care for you very much, I doubt not. Be content, my poor, tired child!'

She spoke very softly; for the darkness quite obliterated the vision of that stylish damsel who had put forth her airs and graces in the drawing-room. As she sat by Christal's bedside, Olive only felt the presence of a desolate orphan child. She said in her heart, 'Please God, I will do her all the good that lies in my feeble power. Who knows but that, in some way or other, I may comfort and help this child!'

So she stooped down and kissed Christal on the forehead, a tenderness that the girl passionately returned. Then Olive went and lay down by her blind mother's side, with a quiet and a happy heart.

CHAPTER XXV

In a week's time Christal Manners was fairly domiciled at Woodford Cottage. In what capacity it would be hard to say—certainly not as Miss Vanbrugh's *protégée*—for she assumed towards the little old maid a most benignant air of superiority. Mr Vanbrugh she privately christened 'the old Ogre', and kept as much out of his way as possible. This was not difficult, for the artist was too much wrapped up in his own peculiarities to meddle with any domestic affairs. He seemed to be under some mystification that the lively French girl was a guest of Miss Rothesay's, and his sister ventured not to break this delusion. Christal's surname created no suspicions; the very name of his former model, Celia Manners, had long since passed from his memory.

So the young visitor made herself quite at home—amused the whole household with her vivacity, clinging especially to the Rothesay portion of the establishment. She served Olive as general assistant in her studio, model included—or, at least, as lay figure; for she was too strictly fashionable to be graceful in form, and not quite beautiful enough in face to attract an artist's notice. But she did very well; and she amused Mrs Rothesay all the while with her gay French songs, so that Olive was glad to have her near.

The day after Christal's arrival, Miss Vanbrugh had summoned her chief state-councillor, Olive Rothesay, to talk over the matter. Then and there, Meliora unfolded all she knew and all she guessed of the girl's history. How much of this was to be communicated to Christal she wished Olive to decide; and Olive, remembering what had passed between them on the first night of her coming, advised that, unless Christal herself imperatively demanded to know, there should be maintained on the subject a kindly silence.

'Her parents are dead, that she is persuaded,' Olive urged. 'Whoever they were, they have carefully provided for her. If they erred or suffered, let neither their sin nor their sorrow go down to their child.'

'It shall be so,' said the good Meliora. And since Christal asked no further questions—and, indeed, her lively nature seemed unable to receive any impressions save of the present—the subject was not again referred to.

But the time came when the little household must be broken up. Mr Vanbrugh announced that in one fortnight he must leave Woodford Cottage, on his journey to Rome. He never thought of such mundane matters as letting the house, or disposing of the furniture; he left all those things to his active little sister, who was busy from morning till night— aye, often again from night till morning. When Michael commanded anything, it must be done, if within human possibility; and there never was any one to do it but Meliora. She did it, always;—how, he never asked or thought. He was so accustomed to her ministrations that he no more noticed them than he did the daylight. Had the light suddenly gone—then—Michael Vanbrugh would have known what it once had been!

Ere the prescribed time had quite expired, Miss Vanbrugh announced that all was arranged for their leaving Woodford Cottage. Her brother had nothing to do but to pack up his easels and his pictures; and this duty was quite absorbing enough to one who had no existence beyond his painting-room.

There was one insuperable difficulty, which perplexed Meliora. What was to be done with Christal Manners? She troubled herself about the matter night and day. At last she hinted something of it to the girl herself. And Miss Manners at once decided the question by saying, 'I will not go.'

She was of a strange disposition, was Christal, as they had already found out at Woodford Cottage. With all her volatile gaiety, when she chose to say 'I will!' she was as firm as a rock. No persuasions—no commands—could move her. In this case there were none tried. Her fortunes seemed to arrange themselves; for Mrs Fludyer, coming in one day to make the final arrangements for the Rothesays' arrival at Farnwood, took a vehement liking to the young French lady, as Miss Manners was generally considered, and requested that Mrs Rothesay would bring her down to Farnwood. Olive demurred a little, lest the intrusion of a constant inmate might burden her mother; but the plan was at last decided upon—Christal's own entreaties having no small influence in turning the scale.

Thus, all things settled, there came the final parting of the two little families who for so many years had lived together in peace and harmony. The Rothesays were to leave one day, the Vanbrughs the next. Olive and Meliora were both very busy—too busy to have time for regrets. They did not meet until evening, when Olive saw Miss Vanbrugh quietly and sorrowfully watering her flowers, with a sort of mechanical interest—the interest of a mother, who meekly goes on arranging all things for the comfort and adornment of the child from whom she is about to separate. It made Olive sad; she went into the garden, and joined Meliora.

'Let me help you, dear Miss Vanbrugh. Why should you tire yourself thus, after all the fatigues of the day?'

Meliora looked up.—'Ah! true, true! I shall never do this any more, I know. But the poor flowers should not suffer; I'll take care of them while I can. Those dahlias, that I have watched all the year, want watering every night, and will do for a month to come. A month! Oh! Miss Rothesay, I am very foolish, I know, but it almost breaks my heart to say goodbye to my poor little garden!'

Her voice faltered, and at last her tears began to fall—not bitterly, but in a quiet, gentle way, like the dropping of evening rain. However, she soon recovered herself, and began to talk of her brother and of Rome. She was quite sure that there his genius would find due recognition, and that he would rival the old masters in honour and prosperity. She was content to go with him, she said; perhaps the warm climate would suit her better than England, now that she was growing—not exactly old, for she was much younger than Michael, and he had half a lifetime of fame before him—but still, older than she had been. The language would be a trouble; but then she was already beginning to learn it, and she had always been used to accommodate herself to everything. She was quite certain that this plan of Michael's would turn out for the good of both.

'And as for the poor old cottage, when you return to London you will come and look at it sometimes, and write me word how it looks. You can send a bit of the clematis in a letter, too; and who knows, but if you get a very rich lady, you may take the whole cottage yourself some day, and come and live here again.'

'And you will come back from Rome, and visit me here?' said Olive, smiling; for she was glad to encourage any cheerful hope.

'No, no, I shall never leave Michael—I shall never leave Michael!' She said these words over to herself many times, and then took up her watering-pot and went on with her task.

Her affectionate companion followed her for some time; but Miss Vanbrugh did not seem disposed to talk, so Olive returned to the house.

She felt in that unquiet, dreary state of mind which precedes a great change, when all preparations are complete, and there is nothing left to be done but to ponder on the coming parting. She could not rest anywhere, or compose herself to anything; but wandered about the house, thinking of that last day at Oldchurch, and vaguely speculating when or what the next change would be. She passed into the drawing-room, where Christal was amusing Mrs Rothesay with her foreign ditties; and then she went to Mr Vanbrugh's studio to have a last talk about Art with her old master.

He was busily engaged in packing up his casts and remaining pictures. He just acknowledged his pupil's presence, and received her assistance, as he always did, with perfect indifference. Nay, he often suffered her, unaided, to do things which required the strength of a man; for, from mere carelessness, Vanbrugh had reduced the womankind about him to the condition of perfect slaves.

'There, that will do. Now bring me the great treasure of all—the bust of Michael the Angel.'

She climbed on a chair, and lifted it down, carefully and reverentially, so as greatly to please the artist.

'Thank you, my pupil; you are very useful; I cannot tell what I should do without you.'

'You will have to do without me very soon,' was Olive's gentle and somewhat sorrowful answer. 'This is my last evening in this dear old studio—my last talk with you, my good and kind master.'

He looked surprised and annoyed. 'Nonsense, child! If I am going to Rome, you are going too. I thought Meliora would arrange all that.'

Olive shook her head.

'No, Mr Vanbrugh; indeed, it is impossible.'

'What! not go with me to Rome!—you my pupil, unto whom I meant to unfold all the glorious secrets of my Art! Olive Rothesay, are you dreaming?' he cried, angrily.

She only answered him softly, that all her plans were settled, and that much as she should delight in seeing Rome, she could not think of leaving her mother.

'Your mother! What right have we artists to think of any ties of kindred, or to allow them for one moment to weigh in the balance with our noble calling?—I say *ours*, for I tell you now what I never told you before, that, though you are a woman, you have a man's soul—the soul of genius. I am proud of you; I design to make for you a glorious future. Even in this scheme I mingled you—how we should go together to the City of Art, dwell together, work together, master and pupil. **What great things we should execute! We should be like the brothers** Caracci—like Titian with his scholar and adopted son.* Would that you had not been a woman! that I could have made you my son in Art, and given you my name, and then died, bequeathing to you the mantle of my glory!'

His rapid and excited language softened into something very like emotion; he threw himself into his painting-chair, and waited for Olive's answer.

It came brokenly—almost with tears.

'My dear, my noble master, to whom I owe so much, what can I say to you?'

'That you will go with me—that when my failing age needs your young hand, it shall be ready; and that so the master's waning powers may be forgotten, in the scholar's rising fame.'

Olive answered nothing but, 'My mother, my mother—she would not quit England; I could not part from her.'

'Fool!' said Vanbrugh, roughly; 'does a child never leave a mother? It is a thing that happens every day; girls do it when they marry.' He stopped suddenly, and pondered; then he said, hastily, 'Child, go away; you have made me angry. I would be alone—I will call you when I want you.'

She disappeared, and for an hour she heard him walking up and down his studio with heavy strides. Soon after, there was a pause; Olive heard him call her name, and quickly answered the summons.

His anger had vanished; he stood calmly, leaning his arm on the mantelpiece, the lamp light falling on the long unbroken lines of his velvet gown, and casting a softened shadow over his rugged features. There was majesty, even grace, in his attitude; and his aspect bore a certain dignified serenity, that well became the man conscious of his genius.

He motioned his young pupil to sit down, and then said to her,

'Miss Rothesay, I wish to talk to you as to a sensible and noble woman (there are such I know, and such I believe you to be). I also speak as to one like myself—a true follower of our divine Art, who to that one great aim would bend all life's purposes, as I have done.'

He paused a moment, and seeing that no answer came, continued,

'All these years you have been my pupil, and have become necessary to me and to my Art. To part with you is impossible; it would change all my plans and hopes. There is but one way to prevent this. You are a woman; I cannot take you for my son, but I can take you for—my wife!'

Utterly astounded, Olive listened like one in a dream. 'Your wife—I—your wife!' was all she murmured.

'Yes,' he cried, still not changing the firm, grave, dignified tone in which he had spoken. 'I ask you—not for my own sake, but for that of our noble Art. I am a man long past my youth—perhaps even a stern, rude man. I cannot give you love, but I can give you glory. Living, I can make of you such an artist as no woman ever was before; dying, I can bequeath to you the immortality of my fame. Answer me—is this nothing?'

'I cannot answer—I am bewildered!'

'Then you will listen to me. You are not one of those foolish girls who would make sport of my grey hairs. I will be very tender over you, for you have been good to me. I will learn how to treat you with the mildness that women need. You shall be like a child to my old age. You will marry me, then, Olive Rothesay?'

He walked up to her, and took her hand, gravely, though not without gentleness; but she shrank away.

'I cannot, I cannot; it is impossible.'

He looked at her one moment, neither in angry reproach, nor in wounded tenderness, but with a stern, cold pride. 'I have been mistaken—pardon me.' Then he quitted her, walked back to his position near the hearth, and resumed his former attitude.

There was silence. Afterwards Michael Vanbrugh felt his robe touched, and saw beside him the small, delicate figure of his pupil.

'Mr Vanbrugh, my dear master and friend, look at me, and listen to what I have to say.'

He moved his head assentingly, without turning round.

'I have lived,' Olive continued, 'for six-and-twenty years, and no one has ever spoken to me of marriage. I did not dream that any one ever would—it is not my destiny. You have asked me to be your wife, and I have refused. This is not because of your age, or of my youth; but because you have, as you say, no love to give me, nor have I love to bring to you; therefore, for us to marry would be a heavy sin.'

'As you will, as you will. I thought you a great-souled, kindred genius—I find you a mere *woman*. Jest on at the old fool with his grey hairs—go and wed some young, gay——'

'Look upon me!' said Olive, with a mournful meaning in her tone; 'is such an one as I likely to marry?'

'I have spoken ill,' said Vanbrugh, in a touched and humbled voice. 'Nature has mocked us both; we ought to deal gently with one another. Forgive me, Olive.'

He offered her his hand; she took it, and pressed it to her heart. 'Oh! that I could be still your pupil—your daughter! My dear, dear master! I will never forget you while I live.'

'Be it so!' He moved away, and sat down, leaning his head upon his hand. Who knows what thoughts might have passed through his mind—regretful, almost remorseful thoughts of that bliss which he had lost or scorned—life's crowning sweetness, woman's love!

Olive went up to the old artist's side.

'I must go now. You will bid me goodbye—will you not, gently, kindly? You will not think the worse of me for what has passed this night?' And she knelt down beside him, pressing her lips to his hand.

He stooped and kissed her forehead. It was the first and last kiss that, since boyhood, Michael Vanbrugh ever gave to woman.

Then he stood up—the great artist only. In his eye was no softness, but the pride of genius—genius, the mighty, the daring, the eternally alone!

'Go, my pupil! and remember my parting words. Fame is sweeter than all pleasure, stronger than all pain. We give unto Art our life, and she gives us immortality.'

As Olive went out, she saw him still standing, stern, motionless, with folded arms and majestic eyes;—like a solitary rock, whereon no flowers grow, but on whose summit heaven's light continually shines.

CHAPTER XXVI

'Well, darling, how do you feel in our new home?' said Olive to her mother, when, after a long and weary journey, the night came down upon them at Farnwood—the dark, gusty, autumn night, made wildly musical by the neighbourhood of dense woods.

'I feel quite content, my child—I am always content everywhere, with you,' was Mrs Rothesay's affectionate reply. 'And I like the wind—it helps me to imagine the sort of country we are in.'

'A forest country, hilly and bleak. We drove through miles of forest-land, over roads carpeted with fallen leaves. The woods will look glorious this autumn time.'

'That will be very pleasant, my child,' said Mrs Rothesay, who was so accustomed to see with Olive's eyes, and to delight in the vivid pictures painted by Olive's eloquent tongue, that she never spoke like a person who is blind. Even the outward world was to her no blank of desolation. Wherever they went, every beautiful place, or thing, or person, that Olive saw, she treasured in memory.—'I must tell mamma of this,' or 'I must bring mamma here, and paint the view for her.' And so she did, in words so rich and clear, that the blind mother often said she enjoyed such scenes infinitely more than when the whole wide earth lay open to her unregardful eyes.

'I wonder,' said Olive, 'what part of S——shire we are in. We really might have been fairy-guided hither; we seem only aware that our journey began in London and ended at Farnwood. I don't know any-thing about the neighbourhood either.'

'Never mind the neighbourhood, dear, since we are settled, you say, in such a pretty house. Tell me, is it like Woodford Cottage?'

'Not at all! It is quite modern and comfortable. And they have made it all ready for us, just as if we were come to a friend's house on a visit. How kind of Mrs Fludyer!'

'Nay! I'm sure Mrs Fludyer never knew how to arrange a house in her life. She had no hand in the matter, trust me!' observed the sharply observant Christal.

'Well, then, it is certainly the same guiding fairy who has done this for us, too. And I am very thankful to have such a quiet, pleasant coming-home.'

'I, too, feel it like coming home,' said Mrs Rothesay, in a soft, weary voice. 'Olive, love, I am glad the journey is over; it has been almost too much for me. We will not go back to London yet awhile; we will stay here a long time.'

'As long as ever you like, darling. And now, shall I show you the house?'

'Showing' the house, implied a long description of it, in Olive's blithest language, as they passed from room to room. It was a pretty, commodious dwelling—perhaps the prettiest portion of which was the chamber which Miss Rothesay appropriated as her mother's and her own.

'It is a charming sleeping-room, with its white draperies, and its old oak furniture; and the quaint pier-glass, stuck round with peacocks' feathers, country fashion. And there, mamma, are some prints—a "Raising of Lazarus", though not quite so grand as my beloved "Sebastian del Piombo".* And here are views from my own beautiful Scotland—a "Highland Loch", and "Edinburgh Castle"; and oh, mamma! there is grand old "Stirling", the place where I was born! Our good fairy might have known the important fact; for, lo! she has adorned the mantelpiece with two great bunches of heather—in honour of me, I suppose. How pleasant!'

'Yes! But I am weary, love. I wish I were in bed and at rest.'

This was soon accomplished; and Olive sat down by her mother's side, as she often did, waiting until Mrs Rothesay fell asleep.

She sat, looking about her mechanically, as one does when taking possession of a strange room. Curiously her eye marked every quaint angle in the furniture, which would in time become so familiar. Then she thought, as one of dreamy mood is apt to do under such circumstances, of how many times she should lay her head down on the pillow in this same room, and when, and how would be the *last time*. For to all things on earth must come a last time.

But, waking herself out of such dreamy pondering, she turned to look at her mother. The delicate, placid face lay in the stillness of deep sleep—a stillness that sometimes startles one, from its resemblance to another and more solemn repose. While she looked, a pain entered the daughter's heart. To chase it thence, she stooped and softly kissed the face which to her was, and ever had been, the most beautiful in the world; and then, following the train of her former musings, came the thought that one day—it might be far distant, but still, in all human probability, it must come—she would kiss her mother's brow for the *last time*.

A moment's shiver, a faint prayer, and the thought passed. But long afterwards she remembered it, and marvelled that it should have first come to her then and there.

The morning that rose at Farnwood Dell—so the little house was called—was one of the brightest that ever shone from September skies. Olive felt cheerful as the day; and as for Christal, she was perpetually running in and out, making the wonderful discoveries of a young damsel who had never in all her life seen the real country. She longed for a ramble, and would not let Olive rest until the exploit was determined on. It was to be a long walk, the appointed goal being a beacon that could be seen for miles—a church on the top of a hill.

Olive quite longed to go thither, because it had been the first sight at Farnwood on which her eyes had rested. Looking out from her chamber-window, at the early morning, she had seen it gleaming goldenly in the sunrise. All was so new—so lovely! It had made her feel quite happy, just as though with that first sunrise at Farnwood had dawned a new era in her life. Many times during the day she looked at the hill-church; she would have asked about it, had there been any one to ask, so she determined that her first walk should be thither.

The graceful spire rose before them, guiding them all the way—which did not seem long to Olive, whose artist soul revelled in the beauties unfolded along their lonely walk—a winding road, bounding the forest, on whose verge the hill stood. But Christal's Parisian feet soon grew wearied, and when they came to the ascent of the hill, she fairly sat down by the roadside.

'I will go into this cottage, and rest until you come back, Miss Rothesay; and you need not hurry, for I shall not be able to walk home for an hour,' said the wilful young lady, as she quickly vanished, and left her companion to proceed to the church alone.

Slowly Olive wound up the hill, and through a green lane that led to the churchyard. There seemed a pretty little village close by, but she was too tired to proceed further. She entered the churchyard, intending to sit down and rest on one of the gravestones; but at the wicket gate she paused, to look around at the wide expanse of country that lay beneath the afternoon sunshine—a peaceful earth, smiling back the smile of heaven. The old grey church, with its girding wall of gigantic trees, shut out all signs of human habitation; and there was no sound, not even the singing of birds, to break the perfect quiet that brooded around.

Olive had scarce ever seen so sweet a spot. Its sweetness passed into her soul, moving her even to tears. From the hilltop she looked on the wide verdant plain—then up into the sky, and wished for doves' wings to sail out into the blue. Never had she so deeply felt how beautiful was earth, and how happy it might be made. And was Olive not happy? She thought of all those whose forms had moved through her life's picture; very beautiful to her heart they were—beautiful and dearly loved; but now it seemed as though there was one great want—one glorious image that should have risen above them all, melting them into a grand harmonious whole.

Half conscious of this want, Olive thought, 'I wonder how it would have been with me had I ever penetrated that great mystery which crowns all life—had I ever known Love!'

The thought glided into a solemn sadness, bringing with it the remembrance of Michael Vanbrugh's words about the eternal loneliness of genius.

'It may be true—perchance, all is well. Let me think so. If, on earth, I must ever feel this void, God grant that it may be filled at last, in that rich after-life to which all spirits tend!'

She pondered thus meekly, but the solitude oppressed her. She was rather glad to see it broken by the appearance of a little girl, who entered from a wicket gate at the other end of the churchyard, and walked, very slowly and quietly, to a gravestone, near where Miss Rothesay stood.

Olive approached, but the child, a thoughtful-looking little creature, of about eight years old, did not see her until she came quite close.

'Do not let me disturb you, my dear,' said she, gently, as the little girl seemed shy and frightened, and about to run away. But Miss Rothesay, who loved all children, began to talk to her, and very soon succeeded in conquering the timidity of the pretty little maiden. For she was a pretty creature, with a countenance full of the sweetness of childhood. Olive especially admired the eyes, which were large and dark, the sort of eyes she had always loved, for the sake of Sara Derwent. Looking into them now, she seemed carried back once more to the days of her early youth, and of that long-vanished dream.

'Are you fond of coming here, my child?'

'Yes; whenever I can steal quietly away, out of sight of papa and grandmamma. They do not forbid me; else, you know, I ought not to do it,' she added, with a certain sense of right; 'but they say it is not good for me to stay thinking here, and send me to go and play.'

'And why had you rather come and sit here than play?'

'Because there is a secret, and I want to try and find it out. I dare not tell you, for you might tell papa and grandmamma, and they would be angry.'

'But your mamma—you could surely tell mamma; I always tell everything to mine.'

'Do you? and have you got a mamma? Then, perhaps, you could help me in finding out all about mine. You must know,' added the child, lifting up her eager face with an air of mystery, 'when I was very little, I lived away from here—I never saw my mamma, and my nurse always told me that she had "gone away". A little while since, when I came home—my home is there,' and she pointed to what seemed the vicarage house, glimmering whitely through the trees—'they told me mamma was here, under this stone, but they would tell me nothing more. Now, what does it all mean?'

Olive discerned, through these words, that the child was playing upon her mother's grave. Only it seemed strange that she should have been left so entirely ignorant with regard to the great mysteries of death and immortality. Miss Rothesay was puzzled what to answer.

'My child, I can only tell you that if your mamma be here, it is her body only.' And Olive paused, startled at the difficulty she found in explaining in the simplest terms the doctrine of the soul's immortality. At last she continued, 'When you go to sleep do you not often dream of walking in beautiful places and seeing beautiful things, and the dreams are so happy that you would not mind whether you slept on your soft bed or on the hard ground? Well, so it is with your mamma; her body has been laid down to sleep, but her mind—her spirit, is flying far away in beautiful dreams. She never feels at all that she is lying in her grave under the ground.'

'But how long will her body lie there? and will it ever wake?'

'Yes, it will surely wake, though how soon we know not, and be taken up to heaven and to God.'

The child looked earnestly in Olive's face, and put the strange, startling question, 'What is heaven, and what is God?'

Miss Rothesay's amazement was not unmingled with a sense of horror. Her own religious faith had dawned so imperceptibly—at once an instinct and a lesson—that there seemed something awful in this question of an utterly untaught mind.

'My poor child,' she said, 'do you not know—has no one told you?'

'No one.'

'Then, I will.'

'Stay, madam,' said a man's voice behind, calm, cold, but not unmusical; 'it seems to me that a father is the best guide of his child's faith!'

'Papa—it is papa.' With a look of shyness almost amounting to fear, the child slid from the tombstone and ran away.

Olive stood face to face with the father.

He was a gentleman—a true *gentleman*; at the first glance any one would have given him that honourable and rarely earned name. His age might be about thirty-five, but his face was cast in the firm rigid mould over which years pass and leave no trace. He might have looked as old as now at twenty; at fifty he would probably look little older. Handsome he was, as Olive discerned at a glance, but there was something in him that controlled her much more than mere beauty would have done. It was a grave dignity of presence, which indicated that mental sway which some men are born to hold, first over themselves, and then over their kind. Wherever he came, he seemed to say, 'I rule—I am master here!'

Olive Rothesay, innocent as she was of any harm to this gentleman or to his child, felt as cowed and humbled as if she had done wrong. She wished she could have fled like the little girl—fled out of reach of his searching glance.

He waited for her to speak first, but she was silent; her colour rose to her very temples; she knew not whether she ought to apologize, or to summon her woman's dignity and meet the intruder with a pride equal to his own.

She was relieved when the sound of his voice broke the pause.

'I fear I startled you, madam; but I was not at first aware that it was a stranger talking to my little girl. Afterwards, the few words of yours which I overheard induced me to pause.'

'What words?'

'About sleep, and dreams, and immortality. Your way of putting the case was graceful—poetical. Whether a child would apprehend it or not, is another question.'

Olive was surprised at the half-sarcastic, half-earnest way in which he said this. She longed to ask what motive he could have had in bringing the child up in such perfect ignorance of the first principles of Christianity. The stranger seemed to divine her question, and answer it.

'No doubt you think it strange that my little daughter is so ill informed in some theological points, and still more that I should have stopped you when you were kind enough to instruct her thereon. But, being a father—to say nothing of a clergyman'—(now Olive looked at him in some surprise, and found that her interlocutor bore, in dress at least, a clerical appearance)—'I choose to judge for myself in some things; and I deem it very inexpedient that the feeble mind of a child should be led to dwell on subjects which are beyond the grasp of the profoundest philosopher.'

'But not beyond the reverent faith of a meek Christian,' Olive ventured to say.

He looked at her with his piercing eyes, and said eagerly, 'You think so, **you feel so?**' then recovering his old manner, 'Certainly—of course—I often find that the great beauty of a woman's religion. She pauses not to argue—she is always ready to believe; therefore you women are a great deal happier than the philosophers.'

It was doubtful, from his tone, whether he meant this in compliment or in sarcasm. But Olive replied as her own true and pious spirit prompted.

'It seems to me that while the intellect comprehends, the heart, or rather the instinct of the soul, is the only fountain of belief.* Without that, could a man dive into the infinite until he became as an angel in power?—could he "by searching find out God?"—still he could not believe.'

'Can *you* understand and believe in God?'

'I love God!' She said no more; but her countenance spoke faith, holiness, peace; and her companion saw it. He stood, as silently gazing as a man who in the desert comes face to fact with an angel.

Olive, recollecting herself, felt her shyness and humility rising up in blushes. 'I ought to apologize for speaking so freely of these things to a stranger and a clergyman—in this place too.'

'Can there be a fitter place, or one that so sanctifies, and at the same time accounts for this conversation?' was the answer, as the speaker glanced round the quiet domain of the dead. Then Olive remembered where they stood—that she was talking to the husband over his lost wife's tomb. The thought touched her with sympathy for this grave, reserved man, whose words, though so earnest, were yet so piercing. It seemed as though he would tear away every flimsy veil, to behold the shining image of Truth.

They were silent for a moment, and then he resumed, with a smile— the first that had yet lightened his face, and which now threw thereon an almost womanly sweetness—

'I ought to thank you for talking so kindly to my little daughter. I trust I have sufficiently explained why I interrupted your lessons.'

'Still, it seems strange,' said Olive. And her feeling of interest conquering that of diffidence, she asked how he, a clergyman, had possibly contrived to keep the child in such utter ignorance?

'She has not lived here with me,' he answered; 'my little Ailie has been brought up in complete solitude. It was best for a child, whose birth was soon followed by her mother's death.'

Olive trembled lest she had opened a wound; but his words and manner bore the grave composure of one who speaks of any ordinary event. Whatever grief he had felt, it had evidently long been healed. But there was an awkward pause, during which Miss Rothesay tried to think in what way she could best end the conversation. It was broken at last by little Ailie,* who crept timidly across the churchyard to her father.

'Please papa, grandmamma wants to see you before she goes out. She is going to John Dent's, and to Farnwood, and——'

'Hush, little chatterbox! this lady cannot be interested in our family revelations. Bid her "good-afternoon", and come!'

He tried to speak playfully, but it was a rigid playfulness. Though a father, it was evident he did not understand children. Bowing to Olive with a stately acknowledgement, he walked on alone towards the little wicket gate. She noticed that his eye never turned back, either to his dead wife's grave or to his living child. Ailie, while his shadow was upon her, had been very quiet; when he walked away, she sprang up, gave

Olive one of those rough, sudden, childish embraces, which are so sweet; and then bounded away after her father.

Miss Rothesay watched them both disappear, and then was seized with an eager impulse to know who were this strange father and daughter. She remembered the tombstone, the inscription of which she had not yet seen; for it was half-hidden by an overhanging cornice, and by the tall grass that grew close by. Olive had to kneel down in order to decipher it. She did so, and read—

SARA,
Wife of the Reverend Harold Gwynne,
Died——, Aged 21

Then, the turf she knelt on covered Sara!—the kiss, yet warm on her lips, was given by Sara's child! Olive bowed her face in the grass, trembling violently. Far—far, through long-divided years, her heart fled back to its olden tenderness. She saw again the thorn-tree and the garden walk, the beautiful girlish face, with its frank and constant smile. She sat down and wept over Sara's grave.

Then she thought of little Ailie. Oh! would that she had known this sooner! that she might have closer clasped the motherless child, and have seen poor Sara's likeness shining from her daughter's eyes! With a yearning impulse, Olive rose up to follow the little girl. But she remembered the father.

How strange—how passing strange, that he with whom she had been talking, towards whom she had felt such an awe, and yet a vague attraction, should have been Sara's husband, and the man whose influence had curiously threaded her own life for many years.

She felt glad that the mystery was now dissolved—that she had at last seen Harold Gwynne.

CHAPTER XXVII

Miss Rothesay was very silent during the walk home. She accounted for it to Christal by telling the simple truth—that in the churchyard she had found the grave of an early and dear friend. Her young companion looked serious, condoled in set fashion; and then became absorbed in the hateful labyrinths of the muddy road. Certainly, Miss Manners was never born for a simple rustic. Olive could not help remarking this.

'No; I was born for what I am,' answered the girl, proudly. 'My parents were high and noble—I am the same. Don't lecture me! Wrong or right, I always felt thus, and always shall. If I have neither friends nor relatives, I have at least this, my family and my name.'

She talked thus, as she did sometimes when she was in an earnest mood, until they came to the garden gate of Farnwood Dell. There stood an elegant carriage. Christal's eyes brightened at the sight, and she trod with a more patrician air.

The maid—a parting bequest of Miss Meliora's, and who had long and faithfully served at Woodford Cottage—came anxiously to communicate that there were two ladies waiting. One of them she did not know; the other was Mrs Fludyer. 'The latter would have disturbed Mrs Rothesay,' Hannah added, 'but the other lady said, "No; they would wait." ' Whereat Olive's heart inclined towards 'the other lady'.

She went in and found, with Mrs Fludyer, an ancient dame of large and goodly presence. Aged though she seemed, her tall figure was not bent; and dignity is to the old what grace is to the young. She stood a little aside, and did not speak, but Olive, labouring under the weight of Mrs Fludyer's gracious enquiries, felt that the old lady's eyes were carefully reading her face. At last Mrs Fludyer made a motion of introduction.

'No, I thank you,' said the stranger, in the clear, quick northern tongue, which, falling from poor Elspie's lips, had made the music of Olive's childhood, and to which her heart yearned evermore. 'Miss Rothesay, will you, for your father's sake, let me shake hands with his child? I am Mrs Gwynne.'

Thus it was that Olive received the first greeting of Harold's mother.

It startled—overpowered her; she had been so much agitated that day. She surprised the formal Mrs Fludyer with the childish weakness of a burst of tears. Mrs Gwynne came up to her, with a softness almost motherly.

'You are pained, Miss Rothesay; you remember the past. But I have now come to hope that everything may be forgotten, save that I was your father's old friend. For our Scottish friendship, like our pride, descends from generation to generation,' she added, with that cheerful smile that sometimes curiously mingled with her gravity. 'Fortune has made us neighbours, let us then be friends. It is my earnest wish, and that of my son Harold.'

'Your son!' echoed Olive; and then, half-bewildered by all these adventures, coincidences, and *éclaircissements*,* she told how she had already met him, and how that meeting had shown to her her old companion's grave.

'That is strange, too. Never while she lived did Mrs Harold Gwynne mention your name. And you loved her so! Well! 'twas like her—like her!' muttered Harold's mother; 'but peace be with the dead!'

She walked up, and laid her hand on Olive's shoulder.

'My dear, I am an old woman; excuse my speaking plainly. You know nothing of me and of my son, save what is harsh and painful. Forget all this, and remember only that I loved your father when he was quite a child, and that I am prepared to love his daughter, if she so choose. You must not think I am taking a hasty fancy—we Scottish folk never do that,' and she smiled again. 'But I have learnt much about you lately—more than you guess—and have recognized in the noble woman and duteous daughter that same "little Olive" of whose sweetness Angus Rothesay told me only a few days before his death.'

'Did you see my dear father then?—did he talk of me?' cried Olive, eagerly, as, forgetting all the painful remembrances attached to the Gwynne family, she began to look at Harold's mother almost with affection.

But Mrs Gwynne, who, probably moved by Olive's agitation, had unfolded herself in a way most unusual, now was relapsing into reserve. She said, rather coldly, 'We will talk of this another time, my dear. Now, I should desire much to see Mrs Rothesay.'

Olive went to fetch her. How she contrived to explain all that had transpired, she never clearly knew herself. However, she succeeded, and shortly reappeared, with her mother leaning on her arm.

And, beholding the pale, worn, but still graceful woman, who, with her sightless eyes cast down, clung tremblingly to her sole stay—her devoted child—Mrs Gwynne seemed deeply moved. There was even a sort of deprecatory hesitation in her manner, but it soon passed.—She clasped the widow's hands, and spoke to her in a voice so sweet, so winning, that all pain vanished from Mrs Rothesay's mind.

In a little while she was sitting calmly by Mrs Gwynne's side, listening to her speech. It went into the blind woman's heart. Soft the voice was, and kind; and, above all, there were in it the remembered accents of the northern tongue—the accents which had wooed her in her girlhood. In her advancing age, they were sacred still. She felt again like young Sybilla Hyde, creeping along in the moonlight by the side of her stalwart Highland lover, listening to his whispers, and thinking that there was in the wide world no one like her own Angus Rothesay—so beautiful and so brave!

When Mrs Gwynne quitted the Dell, she left on the hearts of both mother and daughter a pleasure which they sought not to repress. They were quite glad that the next day was Sunday, when they would go to Harbury, and hear Harold Gwynne preach. Olive told her mother all that had passed in the churchyard, and they agreed that he must be a very strange, though a very clever man. As for Christal, she had gone off with her friend Mrs Fludyer, and did not interfere in the conversation at all.

When Sunday morning came, Mrs Rothesay's feeble strength was found unequal to a walk of two miles. Christal, apparently not sorry for the excuse, volunteered to remain with her, and Olive went to church alone. She was loath to leave her mother; but then she did so long to hear Mr Gwynne preach! She thought, all the way, what kind of minister he would make. Not at all like any other, she was quite sure.

She entered the grey, still, village church, and knelt down to pray in a retired corner pew. There was a solemn quietness over her heart— a repose, soft and dewy as that of the morning before sunrise. She felt a meek happiness, a hopeful looking forth into life; and yet a touch would have awakened the fountains of tears.

She saw Mrs Gwynne walk up the aisle alone, with her firm, stately step, and then the service began. Olive glanced one instant at the officiating minister—it was the same stern face that she had seen by Sara's grave; nay, perhaps even more stern. She did not like Harold's reading either, for there was in it the same iron coldness. He repeated the touching liturgy of the English Church with the tone of a judge delivering sentence—an orator pronouncing his well-written, formal harangue. Olive had to shut her ears, else that day she could not have lifted her pious heart to prayer. It pained her too; there was something so noble in Mr Gwynne's face, so musical in his voice, that any shortcoming gave her a sense of disappointment. She felt troubled to think that this feeling would last; since he was the clergyman of the parish, and she must necessarily hear him every Sunday.

Harold Gwynne mounted his pulpit, and Olive listened intently. From what she had heard of him as a highly intellectual man, from the faint indications of character which she had herself noticed in their conversation, Miss Rothesay expected that he would have dived deeply into theological disquisition. She had too much penetration to look for the meek, beautiful Christianity of a St John—it was evident that such was not his nature; but she thought he would surely love to employ his powerful mind in wrestling with those knotty points of theology which might furnish arguments for a modern St Paul.*

But Harold Gwynne did neither. His sermon was a plain moral discourse—an essay such as Locke or Bacon might have written;* save that he took care to translate his high philosophy into language suitable to his hearers—the generality of whom were of the labouring class. Olive liked him for this, believing she recognized therein the strong sense of duty, the wish to do good, which overpowered all desire of intellectual display. And when she had once succeeded in ignoring the fact that his sermon was of a character more suited to the professor's chair than the pulpit, she listened with deep interest to his teaching of a lofty, but somewhat stern morality. Yet, despite his strong, clear arguments and his evident earnestness, there was about him a repellant atmosphere which prevented her inclining towards *the man*, even while she was constrained to respect the powerful and noble intellect of the preacher.

Nevertheless, when Mr Gwynne ended his brief discourse with the usual prayer, that it might be 'grafted inwardly'* in his hearers' minds, it sounded very like a mockery—at least, to Olive, who for the moment had almost forgotten that she was in a church. She could not kneel and say the prayer, and her pious spirit reproached her bitterly. During the silent pause of the congregation, she raised her eyes and looked at the minister. He, too, knelt like the rest, with covered face, but his hands were not folded in prayer—they were clenched like those of a man writhing under some strong and secret agony; and when he lifted his head, his rigid features were more rigid than ever. The organ awoke, pealing forth that jubilant orison of perfect faith—Handel's 'Hallelujah Chorus', and still the pastor sat motionless in his pulpit, his stern face showing white in the sunshine. The heavenly music rolled round him its angelic waves—they never touched his soul. Beneath, his simple congregation passed, exchanging with one another demure Sunday greetings, and kindly Sunday smiles: he saw them not. He sat alone, like one who shares no sympathy either with heaven or earth.

But there watched him from the hidden corner eyes he knew not of— the wondering, half-pitying eyes of Olive Rothesay. And while she gazed, there came into her heart—involuntarily, as if whispered by an unseen angel at her side—the words from the Litany—words which he himself had coldly read an hour before:

'*That it may please Thee to lead into the way of truth all such as have erred and are deceived. We beseech Thee to hear us, O Lord!*'

She knelt down and said them as her departing orison, ere she left the church.

Scarce conscious was she why she thus felt, or for whom she prayed; but, years after, it seemed to her that there had been a solemn import in these words.

Miss Rothesay was late in quitting her pew. As she did so, she felt her arm lightly touched, and saw beside her Mrs Gwynne.

'My dear, I am glad to meet you—we scarcely expected to have seen you at church today. Alone, too! then you must come with me to the Parsonage to lunch. You say nay? What! are we still so far enemies that you refuse our bread and salt?'

Olive coloured with sensitive fear lest she might have given pain. Besides, she felt a strong attraction towards Mrs Gwynne—a sense of looking-up, such as she had never before experienced towards any woman. For, it is needless to say, Olive's affection for her mother was the passionate, protecting tenderness of a nurse for a beloved charge—nay, even of a lover towards an idolized mistress; but there was nothing of reverential awe in it at all. Now Mrs Gwynne carried with her dignity, influence, command. Olive, almost against her will, found herself passing down the green alley that led to the Parsonage. As she walked along—her slight small figure pressed close to her companion, who had taken her 'under her arm',—she felt almost like a child beside Harold's mother.

At the door sat little Ailie, amusing herself with a great dog. She looked restless and wearied, as a child does, kept in the house under the restrictions of 'Sunday play'. At the sight of her grandmother, the little girl seemed half-pleased, half-frightened, and tried to calm Rover's frolics within the bounds of Sabbatic propriety. This being impossible, Mrs Gwynne's severe voice ordered both the offenders away in different directions. Then she apologized to Miss Rothesay.

'Perhaps,' she continued, 'you are surprised that Ailie was not with me this morning. But such is her father's will. My son Harold is peculiar in his opinions, and has a great hatred of cant, especially infantile cant.'

'And does Ailie never go to church?'

'No! but I take care that she keeps Sunday properly and reverently at home. I remove her playthings and her baby-books, and teach her a few of Dr Watt's moral hymns.'*

Olive sighed. She felt that this was not the way to teach the faith of Him who smiled with benign tenderness on the little child 'set in the midst'. And it grieved her to think what a wide gulf there was between the untaught Ailie, and that sincere, but stern piety over which had gathered the formality of advancing years.

Mrs Gwynne and her guest had sat talking for some minutes, when Harold was seen crossing the lawn. His mother called him, and he came to the window with the quick response of one who in all his life had never heard that summons unheeded. It was a slight thing, but Olive noticed it, and the loving daughter felt more kindly towards the duteous son.

'Harold, Miss Rothesay is here.'

He glanced in at the open window with a surprised, half-confused air, which was not remarkable, considering the awkwardness of this second meeting, after their first rencontre. Remembering it, Olive heard his steps down the long hall, with some trepidation. But entering, he walked up to her with the graceful ease of a true gentleman, took her hand, and expressed his pleasure in meeting her. He did not make the slightest allusion either to their former correspondence, or to their late conversation in the churchyard.

Olive's sudden colour paled beneath his serene, unconcerned air; her heart's faintly quickened pulses sank down into quietness; it seemed childish to have been so nervously sensitive in meeting Harold Gwynne. She felt thoroughly ashamed of herself, and was afraid lest her shyness might have conveyed to him and to his mother the impression, which she would not for worlds have given,—that she bore any painful or uncharitable remembrance of the past.

Soon the conversation glided naturally into ease and pleasantness. Mrs Gwynne had the gift of talking well—a rare quality among women, whose conversation mostly consists of disjointed chatter, long-winded repetitions, or a commonplace remark, and—silence. But Alison Gwynne had none of these feminine peculiarities. To listen to her was like reading a pleasant book. Her terse, well-chosen sentences had all the grace of easy chat, and yet were so unaffected that not until you paused to think them over, did you discover that you might have 'written them all down', and found there a style both elegant and pure.

Her son had not this gift; or, if he had, he left it unemployed. It was only a moment of great passion or earnestness that could draw more than ordinary words from the lips of Harold Gwynne; and such moments seemed to have been rare indeed with him. In most circumstances he appeared—as he did now to Olive Rothesay—the dignified, gentleman-like, but rather silent master of the household—in whose most winning grace there was reserve, and beneath whose very courtesy lurked an air that implied command.

He showed this when, after an hour's pleasant visit, Miss Rothesay moved to depart. Harold requested her to remain a few minutes longer.

'I have occasion to go to the Hall before evening service, and I shall be happy to accompany you on the way, if you do not object to my escort.'

If Olive had been quite free, probably she would have answered that she did; for her independent habits made her greatly enjoy a long quiet walk alone, especially through a beautiful country. She almost felt that the company of her redoubtable pastor would be a restraint. But in all that Harold Gwynne did or said there lurked an inexplicable sway: every one seemed to bend to this influence—even Olive. Almost against her will, she remained; and in a few minutes she was walking beside him to the little wicket gate.

Here he was interrupted by some one on clerical business. Mr Gwynne desired her to proceed, and he would overtake her ere she had descended the hill. Thither Olive went, half hoping that she might after all take her walk alone. But very soon she heard behind her footsteps, quick, firm, manly, less seeming to tread than to crush the ground. Such footsteps give one a feeling of being haunted—as they did to Olive. It was a relief when they came up with her, and she was once more joined by Harold Gwynne.

'You keep your word,' observed Miss Rothesay, by way of saying something.

'Yes, always; when I say *I will*, I do it,' was his characteristic answer.— 'The road is uneven and rough, will my arm aid you, Miss Rothesay?'

She accepted it, perhaps the more readily because it was offered less as a courtesy than a support, and one not unneeded, for Olive was rather tired with her morning's exertions, and with the excitement of talking to strangers. As she walked, there came across her mind the thought—what a new thing it was for her to have a strong, kindly arm to lean on! But it seemed rather pleasant than otherwise, and she felt gratefully towards Mr Gwynne.

They conversed on the ordinary topics, natural to such a recent acquaintance—the beauty of the country around, the chief peculiarities of forest scenery, &c. &c. Never once did the tenor of Harold's conversation assimilate to that which had so struck Olive when they stood beside poor Sara's grave. He seemed to have changed characters, as though the former Harold Gwynne—the object of her girlhood's dislike, her father's enemy, her friend's husband—had vanished for ever, and in his stead was a man whose deep thought and fine intellect already interested her. And over all this was cast a sense of mystery which roused up the lingering romance of Olive's nature, and made her observe his manner. and his words with a curious vigilance, as if to seek some new revelations of humanity in his character or his history. Therefore, every little incident of conversation in that first walk was carefully put by in her hidden nooks of memory, to amuse her mother with—and perhaps also to speculate thereupon herself.

They reached Farnwood Dell, and Olive's conscience began to accuse her of having left her mother for so many hours. Therefore her adieux and thanks to Mr Gwynne were somewhat abrupt. Mechanically she invited him to enter, and, to her surprise, he did so.

Mrs Rothesay was sitting out of doors, in her little garden chair. A beautiful picture she made, leaning back with a mild sweetness, scarce a smile, hovering on her lips. Her pale little hands were folded on her black dress; her soft braids of hair, already silver-grey, and her complexion, lovely as that of a young girl, showing delicately in contrast with her crimson garden-hood, the triumph of her daughter's skilful fingers.

Olive crossed the grass with a quick and noiseless step—Harold following. 'Mamma, darling!'

A light, bright as a sunburst, shone over Mrs Rothesay's face.—'My child! how long you have been away. Did Mrs Gwynne——'

'Hush, darling!'—in a whisper— 'I have been at the Parsonage, and Mr Gwynne has kindly brought me home. He is here now.'

Harold stood at a distance and bowed.

Olive came to him, saying, in a low tone, 'Take her hand, she cannot see you, she is blind.'

He started with surprise. 'I did not know—my mother told me nothing.'—And then, advancing to Mrs Rothesay, he pressed her hand in both his, with such an air of reverent tenderness and gentle compassion, that it made his face grow softened—beautiful, divine!

Olive Rothesay, turning towards him, beheld that look. It never afterwards faded from her memory.

Mrs Rothesay arose, and said in her own sweet manner, 'I am happy to meet Mr Gwynne, and to thank him for taking care of my child.' They talked for a few minutes, and then Olive persuaded her mother to return to the house.

'You will come, Mr Gwynne?' said Mrs Rothesay. He answered, hesitating, that the afternoon would close soon, and he must go to Farnwood Hall. Mrs. Rothesay rose up from her chair with the touching, helpless movement of one who is blind.

'Permit me,' said Harold Gwynne, as, stepping quickly forward, he drew her arm through his, arranging her shawl with a care equal to a woman's. And so he led her into the house, guiding her somewhat feeble steps with a tenderness beautiful to see.

Olive, as she followed silently after, felt her whole heart melted towards him. While she lived, she never forgot Harold's first meeting with her mother.

He went away, promising to pay another visit soon.

'I am quite charmed with Mr Gwynne,' said Mrs Rothesay. 'Tell me, Olive, what he is like.'

Olive described him, though not enthusiastically at all. Nevertheless, her mother answered, smiling, 'He must, indeed, be a remarkable person. He is such a perfect gentleman, and his voice is so kind and pleasant—

like his mother too, he has a little of the sweet Scottish tongue. Truly, I did not think there had been in the world such a man as Harold Gwynne.'

'Nor I!' answered Olive, in a soft, quiet, happy voice. She hung over her mother with a deeper tenderness—she looked out into the lovely autumn sunset with a keener sense of beauty and of joy. The sun was setting, the year was waning; but on Olive Rothesay's life had dawned a new season and a new day.

CHAPTER XXVIII

'Well, I never in my life knew such a change as Farnwood has made in Miss Manners!' observed old Hannah, the Woodford Cottage maid; who, though carefully kept in ignorance of any facts that could betray the secret of Christal's history, yet seemed at times to bear a secret grudge against her, as an interloper. 'There she comes, riding across the country like some wild thing—she who used to be so prim and precise!'

'Poor young creature, she is like a bird just let out of a cage,' said Mrs Rothesay, kindly. 'It is often so with girls brought up as she has been. Olive, I am glad you never went to school.'

Olive's answer was stopped by the appearance of Christal, followed by one of the young Fludyer boys, with whom she had become a first-rate favourite. Her fearless frankness, her exuberant spirits, tempered only by her anxiety to appear always 'the grand lady', made her a welcome guest at Farnwood Hall. Indeed, she was scarce ever at home, save when appearing, as she did now, on hasty visits, which quite disturbed Mrs Rothesay's placidity, and almost drove old Hannah crazy.

'He is not come yet, you see,' Christal said, with a mysterious nod to Charley Fludyer. 'I thought we should outride him—he can't manage a pony any more than a child. But he will surely be here soon?'

'*Who* will be here soon?' asked Olive, considerably surprised. 'Are you speaking of Mr Gwynne?'

'Mr Gwynne, no! Far better fun than that, isn't it, Charley? Shall we tell the secret or not? Or else shall we tell half of it, and let her puzzle it out till he comes?' The boy nodded assent. 'Well, then, there is coming to see you today Charley's tutor, who was away for the holidays. He only arrived at Farnwood last night, and since then he has been talking of nothing else but his old friend, Miss Olive Rothesay. So I told him to meet me here, and, lo! he comes.'

There was a hurried knock at the door, and immediately the little parlour was graced by the presence of an individual,—whom Olive did not recognize in the least. He seemed about twenty, slight and tall, of a complexion red and white; his features pretty, though rather girlish.

Olive bowed to him in undisguised surprise; but the moment he saw her his face became 'celestial rosy red',* apparently from a habit he had, in common with other bashful youths, of blushing on all ocasions.

'I see you do not remember me, Miss Rothesay. Of course, I could not expect it. But I have not forgotten you.'

Olive, though still doubtful, instinctively offered him her hand. The tall youth took it eagerly, and as he looked down upon her, something in his expression reminded her of a face she had herself once looked down upon,—her little knight of the garden at Oldchurch. In the impulse of the moment she called him again by his old name—'Lyle, dear Lyle!'

'Yes, it is indeed I!' cried the young man. 'Oh, Miss Rothesay, you can't tell how glad I am to meet you again.'

'I am glad, too,' said Olive, much moved; and she regarded him with that half-mournful curiosity with which we trace the lineaments of some long-forgotten face, belonging to that olden time, between which and now a whole lifetime seems to have intervened.

'Is that little Lyle Derwent?' cried Mrs Rothesay, catching the name. 'How very strange! Come hither, my dear boy! Alas, I cannot see you. Let me put my hand on your head.'

But she could not reach it, he was grown so tall. She seemed startled to think how time had flown.

'He is quite a man now, mamma,' said Olive; 'you know we have not seen him for many years——'

Lyle added, blushing deeper than before—'The last time—I remember it well—was in the garden, one Sunday in spring—nine years ago.'

'Nine years ago! Is it then nine years since my Angus died?' murmured the widow; and a grave sadness spread itself over all. In the midst of it Christal and Charley, seeing this meeting was not likely to produce the 'fun' they expected, took the opportunity of escaping.

Then came the questions, which after so long a period one shrinks from asking, lest the answer should be silence. Olive learnt that old Mr Derwent had ceased to scold, and wicked Bob played his mischievous pranks no more—the grave had closed over both. Worldly losses, too, had chanced, until the sole survivor of the family found himself condemned to the hard life of a tutor.

'I should not have had even that resource,' said Lyle, 'but for the kindness of my brother-in-law, Harold Gwynne.'

Olive started. 'Oh, true—I forgot all about that. How strangely every-thing seems mingled together! Then he has been a good brother to you!' added she, with a feeling of pleasure and interest.

'He has indeed. When my father died, I had not a relative in the world, save a rich old uncle who wanted to put me in his counting-house; but Harold stood between us, and saved me from a calling I hated. And when my uncle turned me off, he took me home. Yes! I am not ashamed to say that I owe everything in the world to my brother Harold. I feel this the more, because he was not quite happy in his marriage. She did not suit him—my sister Sara.'

'Hush!' said Olive, seeing that references to old times brought a cloud on her mother's face. She spoke on the subject no more, until, after tea, Lyle, who appeared rather a sentimental, poetical young gentleman, proposed a moonlight walk in the garden. Miss Christal, after eyeing Olive and her cavalier with a mixture of amusement and vexation, as if she did not like to miss so excellent a chance of fun and flirtation, consoled herself with ball-playing and Charley Fludyer.

As their conversation grew more familiar, Olive was rather disap-pointed in Lyle. In his boyhood, she had thought him quite a little genius; but the bud had given more promise than the flower was ever likely to fulfil. Now she saw in him one of those not uncommon charac-ters, who with sensitive feeling, and some graceful talent, yet never rise to the standard of genius. Strength, daring, and, above all, originality, were wanting in his mind. With all his dreamy sentiment—his lip-library of perpetually quoted poets—and his own numberless scribblings (of which he took care to inform Miss Rothesay)—Lyle Derwent would probably remain to his life's end a mere 'poetical gentleman'.

Olive's quick perception soon divined all this, and she began to weary a little of her companion and his vague sentimentalities, 'in linked sweet-ness long drawn out'.* Besides, thoughts much deeper had haunted her at times, during the evening—thoughts of the marriage which had been 'not quite happy'. This fact scarcely surprised her. The more she began to know of Mr Gwynne—and she had seen a good deal of him, considering the few weeks of their acquaintance—the more she marvelled that he had ever chosen Sara Derwent as his wife. Their union must have been like that of night and day, fierce fire and unstable water. Olive longed to fathom the mystery, and could not resist saying,

'You were talking of your sister a while ago. I stopped you, for I saw it pained mamma. But now I should so like to hear something about my poor Sara.'

'I can tell you little, for I was but a boy when she died. But things I then little noticed, I put together afterwards. It must have been quite a romance, I think. You know my sister had a former lover—Charles Geddes! Do you remember him?'

'Ah, I do!' and Olive sighed—perhaps over the remembrance of the dream born in that fairy time—her first girlish dream of ideal love.

'He was at sea when Sara married. On his return the news almost drove him wild. I remember his coming in the garden—our old garden, you know—where he and Sara used to walk. He seemed half mad, and I went to him, and comforted him, as well as I could, though little I understood his grief. Perhaps I should now!' said Lyle, lifting his eyes with rather a doleful, sentimental air; which, alas! was all lost upon his companion.

'Poor Charles!' she murmured, compassionately. 'But tell me more.'

'He persuaded me to take back all her letters, together with one from himself, and give them to my sister, the next time I went to Harbury. I did so. Well I remember that night! Harold came in, and found his wife crying over the letters. In a fit of jealousy he took them, and read them all through—together with that of Charles. He did not see me, or know the part I had in the matter, but I shall never forget *him*.'

'What did he do?' asked Olive, eagerly. Strange, that her question and her thoughts were not of Sara, but of Harold.

'Do? nothing! But his words—I remember them distinctly, they were so freezing, so stern. He grasped her arm, and said, "Sara, when you said you loved me, you uttered *a lie*! When you took your marriage oath, you vowed a lie! Every day since, that you have smiled in my face, you have looked a lie! Henceforth I will never trust you or any woman more."'

'And what followed?' cried Olive, now so strongly interested that she never paused to think if she had any right to ask these questions.

'Soon after, Sara came home to us. Her husband did not send her, but she came. She did not stay long, and then returned to Harbury. Harold was never unkind to her—that I know. But, somehow, she pined away; the more so after she heard of Charles Geddes' sudden death.

'Alas! he died too.'

'Yes; by an accident his own recklessness caused. But he was weary of his life, poor fellow! Well—Sara never quite recovered from that shock. After little Ailie was born, she lingered a few weeks, and then died. It was almost a relief to us all.'

'What! did you not love your sister?' cried Olive, reproachfully.

'Of course I did; but then she was older than I, and had never cared for me much. Now, as to Harold, I owe him everything. He has been to me less like a brother than a father; not in affection, perhaps that is scarcely in his nature, but in kindness and in counsel. There is not in the world a better man than Harold Gwynne.'

Olive unconsciously clasped Lyle's hand. 'I am sure of it, and I like you the more for saying so.' Then, in some confusion, she added, 'Pardon me for speaking so freely, but I had quite gone back to the old times, when you were my little pet. I really must learn to show more formality and respect to Mr Derwent.'

'Don't say *Mr Derwent*. Pray call me Lyle, as you used to do.'

'That I will, with pleasure. Only,' she continued, smiling, 'when I look up at you, I shall begin to feel quite an ancient dame, since I am so much older than you.'

'Not at all,' Lyle answered, with an eagerness, somewhat deeper than the mannish pride of youths who have just crossed the Rubicon* that divides them from their much-scorned '*teens*'. 'I have advanced, and you seem to have stood still; there is scarce any difference between us now.' And Olive, somewhat amused, let her old favourite have his way.

They spoke on trivial subjects, until it was time to return to the house. Just as they were entering, Lyle said,

'Look! there is my brother-in-law standing at the gate. Oh, Miss Rothesay, be sure you never tell him of the things we have been talking about.'

'It is not likely I shall ever have the opportunity. Mr Gwynne seems a very reserved man.'

'He is so; and of these matters he now never speaks at all.'

'Hush! he is here;' and with a feeling of unwonted agitation, as if she feared he had been aware of how much she had thought and conversed about him, Olive met Harold Gwynne.

'I am afraid I am an intruder, Miss Rothesay,' said the latter, with a half-suspicious glance at the tall, dark figure which stood near her in the moonlight.

'What! did you not know me, Harold,' cried the cheerful voice of Lyle. And he laughed—his laugh was something like Sara's.

It seemed to ring jarringly on Mr Gwynne's ear. 'I was not aware, Miss Rothesay, that I should find your house graced by the presence of my worshipful brother-in-law,' he said, with a rather forced attempt at jesting.

'Oh, Miss Rothesay and I were friends almost ten years ago. She was our neighbour at Oldchurch.'

'Indeed; I was not aware of that.' And Olive thought she discerned in his face—which she had already begun to read—some slight pain or annoyance. Perhaps it wounded him to know any one who had known

Sara. Perhaps—but conjectures were vain. She only saw that his face was darkening, and with a womanly kindness she tried to disperse the cloud.

'I am glad you are come,' she said to Harold. 'Mamma has been wishing for you all day. You know you are quite a favourite of hers. Lyle, will you go and tell her who is here. Nay, Mr Gwynne, surely you will come back with me to the house.'

He seemed half-inclined to resist, but at last yielded. So he made one of the little circle, and 'assisted' at this, the first of many social evenings, at Farnwood Dell. But at times, even when he seemed to unbend, and give out a little of his terse, keen, and though somewhat sarcastic conversation, Olive caught herself looking earnestly at him, and conjuring up in fancy the look and voice with which he had said the bitter words about 'never trusting woman more'.

He and Lyle went away together, and Christal, who had at last succeeded in apparently involving the light-hearted young tutor within the meshes of her smiles, took consolation in a little quiet drollery with Charlie Fludyer; but even this resource failed when Charlie spoke of returning home.

'I shall not go back with you tonight,' said Christal. 'I shall stay at the Dell. You may come and fetch me tomorrow, with the pony you lent me; and bring Mr Derwent too—to lead it. To see him so employed would be excellent fun.'

'You seem to have taken a sudden passion for riding, Christal,' said Olive, with a smile, when they were alone.

'Yes, it suits me. I like dashing along across the country—it is excitement; and I like, too, to have a horse obeying me—'tis so delicious to rule! To think that Madame Blandin should consider riding unfeminine! and that I should have missed that pleasure for so many years. But I am my own mistress now. By the way,' she added, carelessly, 'I wanted to have a few words with you, Miss Rothesay.' She had rarely called her *Olive* of late.

'Nay, my dears,' interposed Mrs Rothesay, 'do not begin to talk just yet—not until I am gone to bed—for I am very, very tired.' And so, until Olive came downstairs again, Christal sat in dignified solitude by the parlour fire.

'Well,' said Miss Rothesay, when she entered, 'what have you to say to me, my dear child!'

Christal drew back a little at the familiar word and manner, as though she did not quite like it. But she only said, 'Oh! it is a mere trifle; I am obliged to mention it, because I understand Miss Vanbrugh left my money matters under your care until I came of age.'

'Certainly—you know it was by your consent, Christal.'

'Oh yes! because it will save me trouble. Well! all I wanted to say was, that I wish to keep a horse.'

'To keep a horse!'

'Certainly—what harm can there be in that? I long to ride about at my own will—go to the meets in the forest—even to follow the hounds. I am my own mistress, and I choose to do it,' said Christal, in rather a high tone.

'You cannot, indeed, my dear,' answered Olive, mildly. 'Think of all the expenses it would entail—expenses far more than befit your income.'

'I myself am the best judge of that.'

'Not quite! Because, Christal, you are still very young, and have little knowledge of the world's ways; and to tell you the plain truth—must I?'

'If you will;—of all things I hate deceit and concealment.' Here Christal stopped; blushed a little; and, half-turning aside, hid further in her bosom a little ornament which occasionally peeped out—a silver cross and beads. Then she said in a somewhat less angry tone, 'You are right— tell me all your mind.'

'I think, then, that though your income is sufficient to afford you independence, it cannot provide luxuries; and besides,' she continued, speaking very gently, 'it seems to me scarcely right, that a young girl like you, without father or brother, should go riding and hunting in the way you propose.'

'That, still, is my own affair—no one has a right to control me.' Olive was silent. 'Do you mean to say *you* have? Because you are in some sort my guardian, are you to thwart me in this manner? I will not endure it,' cried Christal, vehemently.

And there rose in her the same fierce spirit which had startled Olive on the first night of the girl's arrival at Woodford Cottage, and which, something to her surprise, had lain dormant ever since, covered over with the light-hearted trifling which formed Christal's outward character.

'What am I to do?' thought Olive, much troubled. 'How am I to wrestle with this girl? But I will do it—if only for Meliora's sake. Christal,' she said, affectionately, 'we have never talked together seriously for a long time; not since the first night we met.'

'I remember, you were good to me then,' answered Christal, a little subdued.

'But I was grieved for you—I pitied you.'

'Pitied!' and the angry demon again rose. Olive saw she must not touch that chord again.

'My dear,' she said, still most kindly; 'indeed, I have neither the wish nor the right to rule you; I only advise.'

'And to advice I am ready to listen. Don't mistake me, Miss Rothesay,' said Christal, divided between her old affectionate ways and her newly assumed importance. 'I liked you—I do still—very much indeed; but you don't quite understand or sympathize with me now.'

'Why not, dear? Is it because I have little time to be with you, since I am so much occupied with my mother, and with my profession.'

'Ay, that is it,' said Christal, loftily. 'My dear Miss Rothesay, I am much obliged to you for all your kindness; but we do not suit one another. I have found that out since I visited at Farnwood Hall. There is a difference between an artist working for a livelihood, and an independent lady.'

Even Christal, abrupt as her anger had made her, blushed for the rudeness of this speech. But false shame kept her from offering any atonement.

Olive's slight figure expressed unwonted dignity. In her arose something of the old Rothesay pride, but still more of pride in her Art. 'There is a difference; but, to my way of thinking, it is on the side of those gifted by Heaven, not those enriched by man.'

Christal made no answer, and Olive continued, resuming her usual manner. 'But we will not discuss this matter. All that is to be decided now is, whether or not I shall aid you to draw the sum you will need, in order to carry out this wild scheme. I will, if you desire it; because, as you say, I have indeed no control over you. But, my dear Christal, I entreat you to pause and consider; at least till morning.'.

Olive rose, for she was unequal to further conversation. Deeply it pained her that this girl, whom she so wished to love, should evidently turn from her, not in dislike—that her meek spirit would have conquered—but in a sort of contemptuous indifference. Still she made one effort more. As she was retiring, she went up, bade her goodnight, and kissed her as usual.

'Do not let this conversation make any division between us, Christal.'

'Oh no,' said Christal, rather coldly. 'Only,' she added, in the passionate, yet mournful tone, which she had before used when at Woodford Cottage; 'only, you must not interfere with me, Olive. Remember, I was not brought up like you. I had no one to control me, no one to teach me to control myself. It could not be helped! and it is too late now.'

'It is never too late,' cried Olive, melting at once into tenderness. But Christal's emotion had passed, and she resumed her lofty manner.

'Excuse me, but I am a little too old to be lessoned; and, I have no

doubt, shall be able to guide my own conduct. For the future, we will not
have quite such serious conversations as this. Goodnight!'

Olive went away, heavy at heart. She had long been unaccustomed to
wrestle with an angry spirit. Indeed, she lived in an atmosphere so pure
and full of love, that on it never gloomed one domestic storm. She almost
wished that Christal had not come with them to Farnwood. But then it
seemed such an awful thing for this young and headstrong creature to be
adrift on the wide world. She determined that, whether Christal desired
it or no, she would never lose sight of her, but try to guide her with so
light a hand, that the girl might never even feel the sway.

Next morning Miss Manners abruptly communicated her determination not to have the horse, and the matter was never again referred to.
But it had placed a chasm between Olive and Christal, which the one
could not, the other would not pass. And as various other interests grew
up in Miss Rothesay's life, her anxiety over this wayward girl a little
ceased. Christal stayed almost wholly at Farnwood Hall; and in humble,
happy, Farnwood Dell, Olive abode, devoted to her Art and to her
mother.

CHAPTER XXIX

Weeks glided into months; and within the three-mile circle of the Hall,
the Parsonage, and the Dell, was as pleasant a little society as could be
found anywhere. Frequent meetings, usually confined to themselves
alone, produced the necessary intimacy of a country neighbourhood.

As it sometimes happens that persons, or families, taught to love each
other unknown, when well known, learn to hate; so, on the contrary, it is
no unfrequent circumstance for those who have lived for years in enmity,
when suddenly brought together, to become closer friends than if there
had been no former antipathy between them. So it was with the
Rothesays and the Gwynnes.

Once after Mrs Gwynne and her son had spent a long pleasant evening
at the Dell, Olive chanced to light upon the packet of Harold's letters,
which, years before, she had put by, with the sincere wish that she might
never hear anything of him more.

'You would not wish so now, Olive—nor would I,' said Mrs Rothesay,
when her daughter had smilingly referred to the fact. 'The society of the
Gwynnes has really proved a great addition to our happiness. How kind

and warm-hearted Mrs Gwynne is—so earnest in her friendship for us, too!'

'Yes, indeed, Do you know, it struck me that it must have been from her report of us, that Aunt Flora Rothesay sent the kind message which the Gwynnes brought today. I own, that did make me happy! To think that my long-past romantic dream should be likely to come true, and that next year we should go to Scotland and see papa's dear old aunt.'

'*You* will go, my child,' said Mrs Rothesay, in an undertone.

'And you too, darling. Think how much you would like it, when the summer comes. You will be quite strong, then; and how pleasant it will be to know that good aunt Flora, of whom the Gwynnes talk so much. She must be a very, very old lady now, though Mrs Gwynne says she is quite beautiful still. But she can't be so beautiful as my own mamma. Oh, darling, there never will be seen such a wondrous old lady as you, when you are seventy or eighty. Then, I shall be quite elderly myself too. We shall seem just like two sisters—growing old together.'

Olive never spoke, never dreamed of any other possibility than this.

Calmly, cheerfully, passed the winter, Miss Rothesay devoting herself, as heretofore, to the two great interests of her life; but she had other minor interests gathering up around her, which in some respects were of much service. They subdued her mind a little from that wild enthusiasm, which was sometimes more than her health would bear. Once when reading letters from Rome, from Mr Vanbrugh and Meliora, Olive said,

'Mamma, I think, on the whole, I am happier here than I was at Woodford Cottage. I feel less of an artist and more of a woman.'

'And Olive, I am happy too—happy to think that my child is safe with me, and not carried off to Rome.' For Olive had of course told her mother of that strange chance in her life, which might have changed its current so entirely. 'My daughter, I would not have you leave me to marry any man in the world!'

'I never shall, darling!' she answered. And she felt the promise to be no pain. Her heart was absorbed in her mother.

Nevertheless, the other interests, before mentioned, though quite external, filled up many little crevices in that loving heart which had room for so many affections. Among these was one which, in Olive's whole lifetime, had been an impulse, strong, but ever unfulfilled—love for a child. She took to her heart Harold's little daughter, less regarding it as his, than as poor Sara's. The more so, because, though a good and careful, he was not a very loving father. But he seemed gratified by the kindness that Miss Rothesay showed to little Ailie; and frequently suffered the child to stay with her, and be taught by her all things, save those in which it was his pleasure that his daughter should remain ignorant—the dogmas of the Church of England faith.

Sometimes in her Sunday-school teaching, and visiting of the poor, Olive saw the frightful profanities of that cant knowledge which young or ignorant minds acquire, and by which the solemn, almost fathomless mysteries of Christianity are lowered to a burlesque. Then she inclined to think that Harold Gwynne was right, and that in this prohibition he acted as became a wise father and 'a discreet and learned minister of God's word'. As such she ever considered him; though she sometimes thought he received and communicated that word less through his heart, than through his intellect. His moral character and doctrines were irreproachable, but it seemed to her as if the dew of Christian love had never fallen on his soul.

This feeling gave her, in spite of herself, a sort of shrinking awe of him, which she would not willingly have felt towards her pastor, and one whom she so much regarded and respected. Especially as on any other subject she ever held with him full and free communion, and he seemed gradually to unbend his somewhat hard nature unto that most gentle one of hers, as a man will do who inclines in friendship towards a mind that answers his, and finds added thereto the meekness of womanhood.

Perhaps here it would be as well to observe, that, close and intimate friends as they were, the tie was such that none of their two households, no, not even the most tattling gossips of Farnwood and Harbury, ever dreamed of saying that Harold Gwynne was in love with Olive Rothesay. The good folks did chatter now and then, as country gossips will, about him and Miss Christal Manners; and perhaps they would have chattered more, if the young lady had not been almost constantly at the Hall, whither Mr Gwynne rarely went. But they left the bond between him and Miss Rothesay untouched, untroubled by their idle jests. Perhaps those who remembered the beautiful Mrs Harold Gwynne, imagined the widower would never choose a second wife so different from his first; or perhaps there was cast about the daughter, so devotedly tending her blind mother, a sanctity which their unholy and foolish tongues dared not to violate.

Thus Olive went on her way, showing sweet tenderness to little Ailie, and, as it seemed, being gradually drawn by the child to the father. Besides, there was another sympathy between them, caused by the early associations of both, and by their common Scottish blood. For Harold had inherited from his father nothing but his name; from his mother everything. Born on northern soil, he was a Scotsman to the very depth of his nature. His influence awakened once more every feeling that bound Olive Rothesay to the land of her birth—her father's land. All things connected therewith, took, in her eyes, a new romance. She was happy, she knew not why—happy as she had been in her dreamy girlhood. It seemed as though in her life had dawned a second spring.

Perhaps there was but one thing which really troubled her; and that was the prohibition about little Ailie. She talked the matter over with her mother; that is, she uttered aloud her own thoughts, to which Mrs Rothesay meekly assented; saying, as usual, that Olive was quite right. And at last, after much hesitation, she made up her mind to speak openly on the subject with Mr Gwynne.

For this arduous undertaking, at which in spite of herself she trembled a little, she chose a time when he had met her in one of her forest walks, which she had undertaken, as she often did, to fulfil some charitable duty, usually that of the clergyman or the clergyman's family.

'How kind you are, Miss Rothesay; and to come all through the wintry forest, too! It was scarcely meet for you.'

'Then it certainly was not for Mrs Gwynne. I was quite glad to relieve her; and, then, it gives me real pleasure to do as I am now going to do— reading and talking with John Dent's sick mother. Much as she suffers, she is the happiest old woman I ever saw in my life.'

'What makes her happy, think you?' said Harold, continuing the conversation as if he wished it to be continued, and so falling naturally into a quiet arm-in-arm walk.

Olive answered, responding to his evident intention, and passing at once, as in their conversations they always did, to a subject of earnest interest, 'She is happy, because she has a meek and trusting faith in God; and though she knows little, she loves much.'

'Can one love Him, when one does not fully know?' It was one of the sharp searching questions that Mr Gwynne sometimes put, which never failed to startle Olive, and to which she could not always reply; but she made an effort to do so now.

'Yes, when what we do know of Him deserves our love. Does Ailie, even Ailie, thoroughly know her father? And yet she loves him.'

'That I cannot judge; but most true it is, we know as little of God as Ailie knows of her father—ay, and look up to Heaven with as blindfold ignorance as Ailie looks up to me,' said Harold, bitterly.

'Alas! Ailie's is indeed blindfold ignorance!' said Olive, not quite understanding his half-muttered words, but thinking they offered a good opportunity for fulfilling her purpose. 'Mr Gwynne, will you let me speak to you about something which has long troubled me.'

'Troubled you, Miss Rothesay? Surely I have no share in that; I would not for the world do aught that would give pain to one so good as you.'

He said this very kindly, pressing her arm with a brotherly gentleness, which passed into her heart; imparting to her not only a quick sense of pleasure, but likewise courage.

'Thank you, Mr Gwynne. But this does really pain me. It is the subject on which we talked the first time that ever you and I met, and of which we have never since spoken—your determination with respect to little Ailie.'

'Ah!' He gave a start, and a dark look crossed his face. 'Well, Miss Rothesay, what have you to say?'

'That I think you are not quite right—nay, quite wrong,' said Olive, gathering resolution. 'You are taking from your child her only strength in life—her only comfort in death. You hide from her the true faith; she will soon make to herself a false one.'

'Nay, what is more false than the idle traditions taught by ranting parents to their offspring—the Bible travestied into a nursery tale—heaven transformed into a pretty pleasure-house—and hell and its horrors brought to frighten children in the dark. Do you think I would have my child turned into a baby saint, to patter glibly over parrot-like prayers, to exchange pet sweetmeats for missionary pennies, and so learn to keep up a debtor and creditor account with Heaven? No, Miss Rothesay, I would rather see her grow up a heathen.'

Olive, awed by his language, which was bitter even to fierceness, at first made him no answer. At length, however, she ventured, not without trembling, to touch another chord.

'But—suppose that your child should be taken away, would you have her die as she is now, utterly ignorant of all holy things?'

'Would I have her die an infant bigot—prattling blindly of subjects which in the common course of nature no child can comprehend? Would I have her chronicled in some penny tract* as a "remarkable instance of infant piety", a small "vessel of mercy", to whom the Gospel was revealed at three years old?'

'Do not—oh! do not speak thus,' cried Olive, shrinking from him, for she saw in his face a look she had never seen before—an expression answering to the bitter, daring sarcasm of his tone.

'You think me a strange specimen of a Church of England clergyman. Well, perhaps you are right! I believe I am rather different to my class.' He said this with an irony impossible to describe. 'Nevertheless, if you will enquire concerning me in the neighbourhood, I think you will find that my moral conduct has never disgraced my cloth.'

'Never!' cried Olive, warmly. 'Mr Gwynne, pardon me if I have over-stepped the deference due to yourself and your opinions. In some things I cannot fathom them or you; but that you are a good, true, and pious man, I most earnestly believe.'

'*Do you?*'

Olive started. The two words were simple, but she thought they had an under-meaning, as though he were mocking either himself or her, or both. But she thought this could only be fancy; when, in a minute or two after, he said in his ordinary quiet, dignified manner,

'Miss Rothesay, we have been talking earnestly, and you have uncon-sciously betrayed me into speaking more warmly than I ought to speak. Do not misjudge me. All men's faith is free; and in some minor points of Christianity,' here he smiled, 'I perhaps think differently from my clerical brethren. As regards little Ailie, I thank you for your kind interest in this matter, which we will discuss again another time.'

They had now reached John Dent's cottage. Olive asked if he would not enter with her.

'No, no; you are a far better apostle than the clergyman. Besides, I have business at home, and must return. Good morning, Miss Rothesay.'

He lifted his hat with a courtly grace, but his eyes showed that rever-ence which no courts could command—the reverence of a sincere man for a noble-hearted woman. And so he walked back into the forest.

CHAPTER XXX

The dwelling which Miss Rothesay entered was one of the keeper's cottages, built within the forest. The door stood open, for the place was too lowly, even for robbers; and, besides, its inmates had nothing to lose. Still Olive thought it was wrong to leave a poor bedridden old woman in a state of such unprotected desolation. As her step was heard crossing the threshold, there was a shrill cry from the inner room.

'John, John—the lad!—hast thee found the lad?'

'It is not your son—'tis I. Why, what has happened, my good Margery?' But the poor old creature fell back and wrung her hands, sobbing bitterly.

'The lad!—dun ye know aught o' the lad? Poor Reuben!—he wunnot come back no more! Alack! alack!'

And with some difficulty Olive learnt that Margery's grandson, the keeper's only child, had gone into the forest some days before, and had never returned. It was no rare thing for even practised woodsmen to be lost in this wild, wide forest; and at night, in the winter time, there was no hope. John Dent had gone out with his fellows, less to find the living than to bring back the dead.

Filled with deep pity, Olive sat down by the miserable grandmother; but the poor soul refused to be comforted.

'John'll go mad—clean mad! There wasna in the world such a good lad as our Reuben; and to be clemmed to death,* and froze! O lord, tak' pity on us miserable sinners!'

For hours Olive sat in that desolate cottage by the old woman's bedside. The murky, winter day soon closed in, and the snow began to fall; but still there was nothing heard save the wind howling in the forest. Often Margery started up, crying out that there were footsteps at the door; and then sank back in dumb despair.

At last there was a tramp of many feet on the frozen ground, the latch was lifted, and John Dent burst in.

He was a sturdy woodsman, of a race that are often seen in this forest region, almost giant-like in height and bulk. The snow lay thick on his uncovered head and naked breast, for he had stripped off all his upper garments to wrap round something that was clasped tightly in his arms. He spoke to no one, looked at no one, but laid his burden before the hearth, supported on his knees. It was the corpse of a boy, blue and shrivelled, like that of one frozen to death. He tried to chafe and bend the fingers, but they were as stiff as iron; he wrung the melting snow out of the hair, and, as the locks became soft and supple under his hand, seemed to think there was yet a little life remaining.

'Why dunnot ye stir, ye fools! Get t' blanket—pull 't off th' ould woman. I tell'ee the lad's alive.'

No one moved, and then the frantic father began to curse and swear. He rushed into old Margery's room.

'Get up wi' thee. How darest thee lie hallooing there. Come and help t' lad!' And then he fled wildly back to where poor Reuben's body lay extended on the hearth, surrounded by the other woodsmen, most of whom were pale with awe, some even melting into tears. John Dent dashed them all aside, and took his son again in his arms. Olive, from the corner where she had crept, watched the writhings of his rugged features, but she ventured not to approach.

'Tak' heart, tak' heart, John!' said one of the men.

'He didna suffer much, I reckon,' said another. 'My owd mother was nigh froze to death in t' forest, and her said 'twas just like dropping to sleep. An' luck ye, the poor lad's face be as quiet as a child.'

'John Dent, mon!' whispered one old keeper; 'say thy prayers, thee doesna often do 't, and thee'll want it now.'

And then John Dent broke into such a paroxysm of despair, that one by one his comforters quitted the cottage. They, strong bold men, who feared none of the evils of life, became feeble as children before the awful power of Death. One only remained—the old huntsman who had given the last counsel to the wretched father. This man, whom Olive knew, was beckoned by her to Margery's room to see what could be done.

'I'll fetch Mr Gwynne to manage John, poor fellow! The devil's got un, sure enough; and it'll tak' a parson to drive 't away. But ourn be a queer gentleman. When I get to Harbury, what mun I say?' hesitated the man.

'Say that I am here, that I entreat him to come at once,' cried Olive, feeling her woman's strength sinking before this painful scene, from which in common charity she could not turn aside. She came once more to look at John Dent, who had crouched down before the hearth, with the stiff form of the poor dead boy extended on his knees, gazing at it with a sort of vacant, hopeless misery. Then she went back to the old woman, and tried to speak of comfort and of prayer.

It was not far to Harbury, but, in less time than Olive had expected, Harold Gwynne appeared.

'Miss Rothesay, you sent for me?'

'I did—I did. Oh, thank Heaven that you are come,' eagerly cried Olive, clasping his two hands. He regarded her with a surprised and troubled look, and took them away.

'What did you wish me to do?'

'What a minister of God is able—nay, bound to do—to speak comfort in this house of misery.'

And from the poor old woman's couch echoed the same entreaty—

'Oh, Mr Gwynne, you that be a parson, a man of God, come and help us.'

Harold looked round, and saw he had to face the woe that no worldly comfort or counsel can lighten;—that he had entered into the awful presence of the Power, which stripping man of all his earthly pomp, wisdom, and strength, leaves him poor, weak, and naked before his God.

The proud, the moral, the learned Harold Gwynne, stood dumb before the mystery of Death. It was too mighty for him. He looked on the dead boy, and on the living father; then cast his eyes down to the ground, and muttered within himself, 'What should *I* do here?'

'Read to him—pray with him,' whispered Olive. 'Speak to him of God—of heaven—of immortality.'

'God—heaven—immortality,' echoed Harold, vacantly, but he never stirred.

'They say that this man has been a great sinner, that he has done evil on earth, and scoffed at Heaven. Oh, tell him he cannot deceive himself now. Death knells into his ear that there is a God—there is a hereafter. Mr Gwynne, you, who are a minister, you can tell the poor wretch that at a time like this there is no comfort, no hope, save in God and in His word.'

Olive had spoken thus in the excitement of the moment; then recovering herself, she asked pardon for a speech so bold coming from her to him, as if she would fain teach the clergyman his duty.

'My duty—yes, I must do my duty,' muttered Harold Gwynne. And with his hard-set face—the face he wore in the pulpit—he went up to the father of the dead child, and said something about 'patience', 'submission to the decrees of Providence', and 'all trials being sent for good, and by the will of God'.

'Dun ye talk to me of God? I know nought about Him, parson—ye never larned me.'

Harold's rigid mouth quivered visibly, but he made no direct answer, only saying, in the same formal tone, 'You go to church—at least, you used to go—you have heard there about "God in his judgements remembering mercy."'

'Mercy! ye mun easy say that; why did He let the poor lad die i' the snow, then?'

And Harold's lips dared to profane those holy words, 'The Lord gave, and the Lord hath taken away.'

'He should ha' takken th' owd mother, then. She's none wanted; but the dear lad—the only one left out o' six—oh, Reuben, Reuben, wunna ye never speak to your poor father again?'

He looked on the corpse fixedly for some minutes, and then a new thought seemed to strike him.

'*That's* not my lad—my merry little lad!—I say,' he cried, starting up and catching Mr Gwynne's arm; 'I say, you parson that ought to know, where's my lad gone to?'

Harold Gwynne's head sank upon his breast: he made no answer. Perhaps—aye, and looking at him, the thought smote Olive with a great fear—perhaps to that awful question there was no answer in his soul.

John Dent passed him by, and came to the side of Olive Rothesay.

'Miss, folk say you're a good woman. Dun ye know aught o' these things—canna ye tell me if I shall meet my poor lad again?'

And then Olive, casting one glance at Mr Gwynne, who remained motionless, sat down beside the childless father, and talked to him of

God—not the Infinite Unknown, into whose mysteries the mightiest philosophers may pierce and find no end—but the God mercifully revealed,* 'Our Father which is in heaven'—He to whom the poor, the sorrowing, and the ignorant may look, and not be afraid.

Long she spoke; simple, meekly, and earnestly. Her words fell like balm; her looks lightened the gloomy house of woe. When, at length, she passed out of the threshold, John Dent's eyes followed her, as though she had been a visible angel of peace.

It was quite night when she and Harold went out of the cottage. The snow had ceased falling, but it lay on every tree of the forest like a white shroud. And high above, through the opening of the branches, was seen the blue-black frosty sky, with its innumerable stars. The keen, piercing cold, the utter stirlessness, the mysterious silence, threw a sense of death—white death—over all things. It was a night when one might faintly dream what the world would be, if the infidel's boast were true, and *there were no God*.

They walked for some time in perfect silence. Troubled thoughts were careering like storm-clouds over Olive's pure spirit. Wonder was there, and pity, and an undefined dread. As she leaned on Mr Gwynne's arm, she had a presentiment that in the heart whose strong beatings she could almost feel, was prisoned some great secret—some wild chaos of woe or wrong, before which her own meek nature would stand aghast. Yet such was the nameless attraction which drew her to this man, that the more she dreaded, the more she longed to unveil his mystery, whatsoever it might be. She determined to break the silence.

'Mr Gwynne, I trust you will not think it presumption in me to have spoken as I did; in your stead, as it seemed; but I saw how shocked and overpowered you were.'

He answered in the low tone of one struggling under great excitement. 'You would say, then, that I have mocked my calling—that I was summoned as a clergyman to give comfort in distress, and that I had none to offer.'

'Nay, you did attempt some consolation.'

'Ay, I tried to preach peace with my lips, and could not, because there was none in my heart. No, nor ever will be!'

Olive looked at him with amazement, but he seemed to shrink from her observation. 'I am indeed truly grieved,' she began to say, but he stopped her.

'Do not speak to me, I pray you. Let me have quiet—silence.'

She obeyed; but her woman's heart was yearning with tenderness and ruth over this man, whose spirit seemed at once so daring and so crushed.

Hitherto, in all their intercourse, whatever had been his kindness towards her, towards him she had continually felt a sense of restraint—even of fear. That controlling influence, that invisible rule, which he seemed to exercise over all with whom he deigned to associate, was heavy upon Olive Rothesay. Before him she felt more subdued than she had ever done before any one; in his presence she unconsciously measured her words and guarded her looks, as if meeting the eye of a master. And he was a master—a man born to rule over the wills of his brethren, swaying them at his lightest breath, as the wind bends the grass of the field.

But now the sceptre seemed torn from his hand—he was a king no more. He walked along—his head drooped, his eyes fixed heavily on the ground. And beholding him thus, there came to Olive, in the place of fear, a strong compassion, tender as strong, and pure as tender. Angel-like, it arose in her heart, ready to pierce his darkness with its shining eyes—to fold around him and all his misery its sheltering wings. He was a great and learned man, and she a lowly woman: in her knowledge not worthy to touch his garment's hem—in her faith able to watch him as from Heaven.

Olive was not deceiving herself in these emotions. With impassioned human love—the love of woman unto man—she did not love him. If she had, she could not have done as her heart now prompted—have summoned a strength proportioned to his weakness; resolving to wind her spirit around him—to soothe and comfort him; and so, with the devotion of a sister towards a brother, to force from him the secret of his woe.

She began very carefully. 'You are not well, I fear. This painful scene has been too much, even for you. It often seems to me that Death has more of horror to men than to feeble women.'

'Death!—do you think that I fear Death?' he broke out, fiercely; and he clenched his hand and shook it, as though he would battle with the great Destroyer. 'No!—I have stood as it were on life's verge, and gazed into the black abyss beyond, until my eyes were blinded, and my brain reeled. But what am I saying? Don't heed me, Miss Rothesay; I am troubled—bewildered—ill'; and, with a quick and alarmed air, he began to walk on hurriedly.

'You are ill, I am sure; and there is something that rests on your mind,' said Olive, in a quiet, soft tone.

'What!—have I betrayed anything? Nay, not that! I mean, have you aught to charge me with? Have I left any duty unfulfilled; said any words unbecoming a clergyman?' asked he, with a freezing haughtiness.

'No, no; forgive me, if I trespass beyond the bounds of our friendship. For we are friends—have you not often said so?'

'Yes, and with truth. I respect you, Miss Rothesay. You are no thought-less girl, but an earnest woman, whom the world has long tried. I have been tried, too; therefore it is no marvel we are friends. I am glad that it should be so.'

It was not often that he spoke so frankly, and never had he done what he now did—of his own accord, to take and clasp her hand with a friendly air of confidence. Long after the pressure passed from Olive's fingers, the strength and comfort it gave lingered in her heart. They walked on a little further; and then he said, not without some slight agitation,

'Miss Rothesay, if you are indeed my friend, listen to one request I make;—that you will not say anything, think anything, of whatever part of my conduct this day may have seemed strange to you. I know not what fate it is that has thus placed you, a year ago a perfect stranger, in a position which forces me to speak to you thus. Still less can I tell what there is in you which draws from me much that no human being has ever drawn before. Accept this acknowledgement, and pardon me.'

'Nay, what have I to pardon? Oh, Mr Gwynne, if I might be indeed your friend—if I could but do you any good!'

'You do good to *me*?' he muttered, bitterly. 'I tell you, we are as far apart as earth from heaven, nay, as heaven from hell; that is, if there be—— Mad fool that I am'; he broke off suddenly, with an alarmed look. 'Miss Rothesay, do not listen to me. Why do you lead me on, and make me speak thus?' he added, almost fiercely.

'I do not!—indeed I would not so beguile your confidence. Believe me, Mr Gwynne, I know very well the difference between us. I am a poor, weak, unlearned woman, and you——'

'Ay, tell me what I am—that is, what you think I am.'

'A wise, noble, and good man; but yet one in whom high and keen intellect may at times overpower that simple Faith, which is above all knowledge; that Love, which as saith the great apostle of our church——'

'Silence!' His deep voice rose and fell, like the sound of a breaking wave. Then he stopped, turned full upon her, and said, in a fierce, keen whisper, 'Would you learn the truth—the scathing truth? Know, then, that I believe in none of these things—I am an infidel!'

Olive's arm fell from him. She grew cold, pale, and mute as death.

'Do you shrink from me, then? Good and pious woman, do you think I am Satan standing by your side?'

'Oh, no, no!' she made an effort to restrain herself; then her courage failed, and she burst into tears.

Harold looked at her, and it seemed that his fierceness melted away.

'Thou meek and gentle soul!' he murmured. 'It would, perhaps, have been good for me had Olive Rothesay been born my sister.'

'I would I had—I would I had! But, oh! this is awful to hear. You, an unbeliever—you, who all these years have been a minister at the altar—what a fearful thing!'

'You say right—it is fearful! Think now what my life is, and has been! One long lie—a lie to man and to God! For I do believe in a God,' he added, solemnly; 'I believe in the one ruling Spirit of the universe—unknown, unapproachable. None but a madman would deny the existence of a God.'

He ceased, and looked upwards with his piercing eyes—piercing, yet full of restless sorrow. Then he moved a little towards his companion.

'Shall we walk on, or do you utterly renounce me?' said he, with a touching, sad humility.

'Renounce you!'

'Ah! you would not, could you know all I have endured. To me, earth has been a hell—not the place of flames and torments of which your divines prate, but the true hell—that of the conscience and the soul. I, too, a man whose whole nature was athirst for truth. I sought it first among its professors; there I found that they who, too idle or too weak to fathom their creed, took it upon trust, did what their fathers did, believed what their fathers believed—were accounted orthodox and pious men; while those who, in their earnest eager youth, dared—not yet to doubt, but meekly to ask a *reason* for their faith—*they* were at once condemned as impious. But I pain you: shall I go on, or cease?'

'Go on.'

'Truth, still truth, I yearned for in another form—in domestic peace—in the love of woman. My soul was famishing for any food; I snatched this—in my mouth it became ashes!' His voice seemed choking, but with an effort he continued. 'After this time I gave up earth's delights, and turned to interests beyond it. With straining eyes I gazed into the Infinite—and I was dazzled, blinded, whirled from darkness to light, and from light to darkness—no rest, no rest! This state lasted long, but its end came. Now I walk like a man in his sleep, without feeling or fearing,—no, thou mighty Unknown, I do *not* fear! But then I hope nothing: I believe nothing. Those pleasant dreams of yours—God, Heaven, Immortality—are to me meaningless words. At times I utter them, and they seem to shine down like pitiless stars upon the black boiling sea in which I am drowning.'

'Oh, God, have mercy!' moaned Olive Rothesay. 'Give me strength that my own faith fail not, and that I may bring Thy light unto this perishing soul!' And turning to Harold, she said aloud, as calmly as she could, 'Tell me—since you have told me thus far—how you came to take upon yourself the service of the Church; you who——'

'Aye, well may you pause and shudder! Hear, then, how the devil—if there be one—can mock men's souls in the form of an angel of light. But it is a long history—it may drive me to utter things that will make you tremble and shrink from me.'

'I *will* hear it.' There was in that soft, firm voice an influence which Harold perforce obeyed. She was stronger than he, even as light is stronger than darkness, heaven than hell.

Mr Gwynne began speaking quietly, even humbly. 'When I was a youth, studying for the Church, doubts came upon my mind, as they will upon most young minds whose strivings after truth are hedged in by a thorny rampart of old, worn-out forms. Then there came a sudden crisis in my life: I must either enter on a ministry in whose creed I only half believed, or let my mother—my noble, self-denying mother—starve. You know her, Miss Rothesay; but you know not half that she is, and ever was, to me.'

Olive clasped his hand. Infidel as he was, she could have clung to Harold Gwynne and called him brother.

'Well, after a time of great inward conflict, I decided—for my mother's sake. Though little more than a boy in years, struggling in a chaos of mingled doubt and faith, I bound myself to believe whatever the Church taught, to lead erring souls to Heaven in the Church's own way. These very bonds, this vow so blindly to be fulfilled, made me, in after years, an infidel.'

He paused to look at her.

'I listen—speak on,' said Olive Rothesay.

'As you say truly, I am one whose natural bent of mind is less to humble faith than to searching knowledge. Above all, I am one who hates all falsehood, all hypocritical show. Perchance in the desert I might have learned to serve God. Face to face with Him I might have worshipped His revealings. But when between me and the one great Truth came a thousand petty veils of cunning forms and blindly-taught precedents; when among my brethren I saw vile men preaching virtue—men with weak, uncomprehending brains set to expound the mighty mysteries of God—then I said to myself "The whole system is a lie!" So I cast it from me, and my soul stood forth in its naked strength before the Creator of all.'

'But why, oh why, did you still keep up this awful mockery?'

'Because,' and his voice sounded hoarse and hollow, 'just then, there was upon me a madness which all men have in youth—a human passion—a woman's love. For that I became a liar in the face of Heaven, of men, and of my own soul.'

'It was a sin, a heavy sin.'

'I know it; and, as such, it fell down upon my head in a curse. Since then I have been what you now see me—a very honest, painstaking clergyman; doing good, preaching, not doctrine, but decent moralities, carrying a civil face to the world, and a heart—Oh God! whosoever and whatsoever Thou art, Thou knowest what blackest darkness there is *there*!'

He leaned, almost staggering, against a tree. After awhile he murmured, 'You must forgive me, Miss Rothesay; I can speak no more.'

'You shall not. Rest, rest; and may God pity you, the merciful God whom you do not know, but whom you will know yet! I will pray for you—I will comfort you. Oh, friend, lean on me! Would that I were indeed your sister, that I might never leave you until I brought to you faith and peace.'

He smiled very faintly. 'Thank you; it is something to feel there is goodness in the world. I did not believe in any, except my mother's. Oh, if she had known all this—if I could have told her—perhaps I had not been the wretched man I am.'

'Hush; do not talk any more.' And then she stood beside him for some minutes quite silent, until he grew calm.

They were on the verge of the forest, close to Olive's home. It was about seven in the evening, but all things lay as in the stillness of midnight. They two might have been the only beings in the living world—all else dead and buried under the white snow. And then, lifting itself out of the horizon's black nothingness, arose the great red moon, like an immortal soul.

'Look!' said Olive. He looked once, and no more. Then, with a deep-heaved sigh, he placed her arm in his, and led her to her own door.

Arrived there, he bade her adieu, adding, 'I would bid God bless you; but in such words from me, you would not believe. How could you?'

He said this with a mournful emphasis, to which she could not reply.

'But,' he continued, in a tone of eager anxiety, 'remember that I have trusted you as I never trusted human being. My secret is in your hands. You will be silent, I know; silent as death, or eternity.—That is, as both are to me!'

Olive promised solemnly; and he left her. She stood listening, until the echo of his strong firm footfall ceased along the frosty road; then, clasping her hands, she lifted once more the petition 'for those who have erred and are deceived', the prayer which she had once uttered—unconscious how much and by whom it was needed. Now she said it with a yearning cry—a cry that would fain pierce heaven, and ringing above the loud choir of saints and angels, call down mercy on one perishing human soul.

CHAPTER XXXI

Never since her birth had Olive felt such a bewildering weight of pain, as when she awoke to the full sense of that terrible secret which she had learned from Harold Gwynne. This pain lasted, and would last, not alone for an hour or a day, but perpetually. It gathered round her like a mist, beyond which she saw nothing. She seemed to walk blindfold, and knew not whither. Never across her soul—in which the spiritual sense was ever so bright and undimmed—had come the image of such a mind as Harold's, a mind whose very eagerness for truth had led it into scepticism.* His doubts must be wrestled with, not with the religion of precedent—not even with the religion of feeling—but by means of that clear demonstration of reason which forces conviction.

In the dead of night, when all was still—when the frosty moon cast an unearthly light over her chamber, Olive lay and thought of these things. Ever and anon she heard the striking of the clock, and remembered with horror that it heralded the Sabbath morn, when she must go to Harbury church—and hear, oh, with what feelings! the holy service uttered by the lips of an infidel. Not until now had she so thoroughly realized the sacrilege of Harold's daily life. It rushed upon her mind; and she felt as though to think of him, to speak of his very name, were like associating herself with his sin.

But calmer thoughts enabled her to judge him more mercifully. She tried to view this awful position not as with her own eyes, but as it must appear in his. To him who believed nothing of the sanctity of the Christian faith, the repetitions of its forms could seem no sacrilege, but a mere idle mummery. He suffered, not for having outraged Heaven, but for having outraged his own conscience. So loving and desiring truth, this agony of self-humiliation must be to him a living death. Then, again, there awoke in Olive's heart a divine pity; and once more she dared to pray that this soul, in which was so much that was true and earnest, might not be cast out, but guided into the right way.

Yet, who should do it? He was, as he had said, drowning in a black abyss of despair, and there was no human hand to save him—none, save that feeble one of hers!

It were not meet here to dwell on the strivings of Olive's spirit; how she sought to strengthen her religion by arguments from the Holy Word; how she pondered and prayed, and then rose filled with a divine boldness to cope with the unbelief of this erring and most wretched soul. Aye, in its wretchedness lay the hope, her strength for herself, her trust for him. She, who had felt from her very childhood the joy and peace of believing—to whom her own holy faith had given light in darkness, strength in weakness, humility in success—whose love of God, transfused through all human channels, had filled her life with holiness and happiness—she *could not* be clinging to a broken reed. The creed, whose existence was thus proved, must be true. Can there be daylight without the sun?

Nevertheless, she suffered exceedingly. To bear the burden of this heavy secret; to keep it from her mother; to wear a feigned brow before Mrs Gwynne; above all, to go to church, and have the ministry of such an one as Harold between her and heaven—this last was the most awful point of all; but she could not escape it without betrayal of his trust. And it seemed to her that the sin—if sin it were—would be forgiven; nay, her voluntary presence might strike into the heart of the infidel like an accusing conscience.

It was so. When Harold beheld her, his cheeks grew ashen; but he controlled himself. Still, all through the service, his reading at times faltered, and his eyes were lowered. Once, too, during the epistle for the day, which chanced to be the sixth Sunday after Epiphany,* the simple words of St John seemed to attract his notice, and his voice took an accent of keen sorrow.

Yet, when Olive passed out of the church, she felt as though she had spent there years of torture—such torture as no earthly power should make her endure again. And it so chanced that she was not called upon to do so.

Within a week from that time Mrs Rothesay sank into a state of lingering feebleness, not indicating positive danger, but still so nearly resembling illness that Olive could never quit her, not even for an hour. This painful interest engrossing all her thoughts, shut out from them even Harold Gwynne. She saw little of him, though she heard that he came almost daily to enquire at the house. But for a long time he rarely crossed the threshold.

'Harold is like all men—he does not understand sickness,' said that most kind and constant friend, Mrs Gwynne. 'You must forgive him, both of you. I tell him often it would be an example for him, or for any clergyman in England, to see dear Olive here—the best and most pious daughter that ever lived. He thinks so too; for once, when I hoped that his own daughter might be like her, you should have heard the earnestness of his *"Amen!"* '

This circumstance touched Olive deeply, and strengthened her the more in that work to which she had determined to devote herself—to win him to the truth by patience and tenderness. And a secret hope told her that an erring soul is oftentimes reclaimed less by the zeal of a Christian's preaching, than by the silent voice of a Christian's life.

And so, though they never met again alone, and no words on the one awful subject passed between them, Harold gradually came to be often with the little circle at the Dell. Mrs Rothesay's lamp of life was paling so gradually, that not even her child knew how little space it would shine among those to whom its every ray was so precious and so beautiful—more beautiful as it drew nearer its close.

Yet there was no sorrow at the Dell, but great peace—a peace so holy that it seemed to rest upon all whose foot crossed the threshold. These were not few; never was there any one who gained so many kindly attentions as Mrs Rothesay. Even the wild young Fludyers came to enquire after her every day; and shot more game than ever, to ease their consciences by bringing it to Mrs Rothesay. Christal, who was almost domiciled at the Hall, and seemed by some invisible attraction most disinclined to leave it, was yet a daily visitor—her high spirit softened to a quiet gentleness whenever she came near the invalid.

As to Lyle Derwent, he positively haunted them. His affectations fell from him, he ceased his sentimentalities,.and never quoted a single line of poetry. To Olive he appeared in a more pleasing light, and she treated him with her old regard; and as for him, his glances seemed to adore the very ground she trod upon. A ministering angel could not have appeared more hallowed in his eyes. He often made Mrs Rothesay and Olive smile with his raptures; and the latter said sometimes that he was certainly the same enthusiastic little boy who had been her knight in the garden by the river. She never thought of him otherwise; and though he often tried, in half-jesting indignation, to assure her that he was quite a man now, he seemed still a child to her who had struggled so much in the wide arena of the world. There was the difference of a lifetime between his juvenile romance, and her calm reality of six-and-twenty years.

She did not always feel so old, though. When kneeling by her mother's side, amusing her with playful, almost childish caresses, Olive still felt a very child; and there were times when her spirit fell beneath the stern manhood of Harold Gwynne, and she grew once more a feeble, trembling, timid girl. But now that the secret bond between them was held in abeyance, their intercourse sank within its former boundary. Even his influence, and the awful interest attached to him, could not compete with that affection which had been the day-star of Olive's life. No other human tie could come between her and her mother.

Beautiful it was to see them, clinging together so closely that none of those who loved both, and regarded them with a mournful doubt, had the courage to tell them how soon they must part. Sometimes Mrs Gwynne would watch Olive with a look that seemed to ask, 'Child, hast thou strength to bear?' But she herself had not the strength to utter more. Besides, it seemed as though these close cords of love were knitted so tightly around the mother, and every breath of her fading life so fondly cherished, that she could not perforce depart. Months—nay, years might pass, ere that frail tabernacle was quite dissolved.

As the winter glided away, Mrs Rothesay seemed to grow much better. One evening in March, when Harold Gwynne came laden with a whole basket of violets, he said—and truly—that she was looking as blooming as the spring itself. Olive quite coincided in this opinion—nay, declared, in her cheerful happiness, that any one would fancy her mother was only making pretence of illness, to win more kindness and consideration.

'As if you had not enough of that from every one, mamma! I never knew such a spoiled darling in all my life; and yet see, Mr Gwynne, how meekly she bears it, and how beautiful and content she looks!'

It was true. Let us draw the picture which lived on Olive's memory evermore.

Mrs Rothesay sat in a little low chair, her own chair, which no one else ever claimed. She did not wear an invalid's shawl, but a graceful wrapping-gown of pale colours—such as she had always loved, and which suited well her delicate, fragile beauty. Closely tied over her silvery hair—the only sign of age—was a little cap, whose soft pink gauze lay against her cheek—that cheek which even now was all unwrinkled, and tinted with a lovely faint rose colour, like a young girl's. Her eyes were cast down; she had a habit of doing this, lest others might see there the painful expression of blindness; but her mouth smiled a serene, cheerful, holy smile, such as is rarely seen on human face, save when earth's dearest happiness is beginning to melt away, dimmed in the coming brightness of heaven. Her little thin hands lay meekly crossed on her knee, one finger playing, as she often did, with her wedding-ring, now worn to a mere thread of gold.

Her daughter looked at her with eyes of passionate yearning that threw into one minute's gaze the love of a whole lifetime. Harold Gwynne looked at her too, and then at Olive. He thought, 'Can she, if, knowing what I know—can she rest meekly, be resigned—nay, happy? Then, what a sublime faith hers must be!'

Olive seemed not to see *him*, but only her mother. She gazed and gazed, then she came and knelt before Mrs Rothesay, and wound her arms round her.

'Darling, kiss me! or I shall fear you are growing quite an angel—an angel with wings.'

There lurked a troubled tone beneath the playfulness; she rose up quickly, and began to talk to Mr Gwynne.

They had a pleasant evening, all three together; for Mrs Rothesay, knowing that Harold was lonely—since his mother and Ailie had gone away on a week's visit—prevailed upon him to stay. He read to them; Mrs Rothesay was fond of hearing him read; and to Olive the world's richest music was in his deep, pathetic voice, more especially when reading, as he did now, with great earnestness and emotion. The poem was not one of his own choosing, but of Mrs Rothesay's, whose interest was always most attracted by the simple tenderness of human feeling. She listened eagerly while he read from Tennyson's 'May Queen'.*

> Upon the chancel casement, and upon that grave of mine,
> In the early, early morning the summer sun will shine.
> I shall not forget you, mother; I shall hear you when you pass,
> With your feet above my head on the long and pleasant grass.
> Good night, good night! When I have said, good night, for evermore,
> And you see me carried out from the threshold of the door.
> Don't let Effie come to see me till my grave is growing green:
> She'll be a better child to you than I have ever been.

Here Harold paused, for, looking at Olive, he saw her tears falling fast; but Mrs Rothesay, generally so easily touched, was now quite unmoved. On her face was a soft calm. She said to herself, musingly,

'How terrible for one's child to go away thus! But I shall never know that grief, never! My Olive will not die first.' And then she bade Mr Gwynne go on.

He read—what words for him to read!—the concluding stanzas; and, as he did so, the movement of Mrs Rothesay's lips seemed silently to follow them.

> O sweet and strange it seems to me, that ere this day is done,
> The voice which now is speaking may be beyond the sun,
> For ever and for ever with those just souls and true,
> And what is life that we should moan? Why make we such ado?

For ever and for ever all in a blessed home,
And there to wait a little while till you and Effie come;
To lie within the light of God, as I lie upon your breast,
Where the wicked cease from troubling, and the weary are at rest.

As he concluded, they were all three very silent. What thoughts were in each heart? After a while, Mrs Rothesay said,

'Now, my child, it is growing late. Take and read to us yourself, out of the best Book of all.' And when Olive was gone to fetch it, she added, in her gentle, quiet way, 'Mr Gwynne will pardon my not asking him to read the Bible, but a child's voice sounds so sweet in a mother's ears, especially when——' She stopped, for Olive just then entered.

'Where shall I read, mamma?'

'Where I think we have come to—reading every night as we do—the last few chapters of the Revelations.'

Olive read them—the blessed words, the delight of her childhood—telling of the heavenly kingdom, and the after-life of the just. And *he* heard them: he who believed in neither. He sat in the shadow, covering his face with his hands, or lifting it at times with a blind, despairing look, like that of one who, staggering in darkness, sees afar a faint light, and yet cannot, dare not, believe in its reality.

When he bade Mrs Rothesay good night, she held his hand, and said, 'God bless you!' with more than her usual kindness. He shrank away, as if the words stung him. Then he wrung Olive's hand, looked at her a moment, as if to say something, but drew back and quitted the house.

The mother and daughter were alone. They clasped their arms round each other, and sat a little while listening to the wild March wind.

'It is just such a night as that on which we came to Farnwood, is it not, darling?'

'Yes, my child! And we have been very happy here; happier, I think, than I have ever been in my life. Remember that, love, always!'

She said these words with a beautiful, life-beaming smile. Then, leaning on Olive's shoulder, she lifted herself, rather feebly, from her little chair, and prepared to walk upstairs.

'Tired, are you? I wish I could carry you, darling; I almost think I could.'

'You carry me in your heart, evermore, Olive! You bear all my feebleness, troubles, and pains. God ever bless you, my daughter!'

When Olive came down once more to the little parlour, she thought it looked rather lonely. However, she stayed a minute or two, put her mother's little chair in the corner, and her mother's knitting basket beside it.

'It will be ready for her when she comes down again,' said the thoughtful Olive.

Then she went upstairs to bed; and mother and daughter fell asleep, as ever, closely clasped in each other's arms.

CHAPTER XXXII

'My child!'

The feeble call startled Olive out of a dream, wherein she walked through one of those lovely visionary landscapes—more glorious than any ever seen by day—with her mother and with Harold Gwynne.

'Yes, darling,' she answered, in a sleepy, happy voice, thinking it a continuation of the dream.

'Wake, Olive! I feel ill—very ill! I have a dull pain here, near my heart. I cannot breathe. It is so strange—so strange!'

Quickly the daughter rose, and groped through the faint dawn for a light; she was long accustomed to all offices of tender care by night and by day. This sudden illness gave her little alarm; her mother had so many slight ailments. But, nevertheless, she roused the little household, and applied herself to all the simple remedies which she so well knew how to use.

But there must come a time when all physicians' arts fail; it was coming now. Mrs Rothesay's illness increased, and the daylight broke upon a chamber where more than one anxious face bent over the poor blind sufferer who suffered so meekly. She did not speak much; she only held closely to Olive's hand or Olive's dress, murmuring now and then, with an accent of sorrow, 'My child—my child!' Once or twice she eagerly besought those around her to try all means for her restoration, and seemed anxiously to expect the coming of the physician. 'For Olive's sake—for Olive's sake!' was all the reason she gave.

And suddenly it entered into Olive's mind that her mother thought herself about to die.

Her mother about to die! She paused a moment, and then flung the horror from her as a thing utterly impossible—out of the bounds of human fear. So many illnesses as Mrs Rothesay had passed through—so many times as her daughter had clasped her close, and dared Death to come nigh one who was shielded by so much love? It could not be; there was no cause for dread. Yet Olive waited restlessly during the morning, which seemed of frightful length. She busied herself about the room, talking constantly to her mother; and by degrees, when the physician still delayed, her voice took a quick, sharp, anxious tone.

'Hush, love, hush!' was the soft reproof. 'Be content, Olive; he will come in time. I shall recover, if it so please God.'

'Of course—of course you will. Don't talk in that way, mamma!'—she dared not trust herself to say *darling*. She spoke even less caressingly than usual, lest her mother might think there was any dread upon her mind. But gradually, when she heard the strangely solemn patience of Mrs Rothesay's voice, and saw the changes in the beloved face, she began to tremble. Once her wild glance darted upward in an almost threatening despair. 'God! Thou wilt not—Thou canst not pour upon me this woe!' And when, at last, she heard the ringing of hoofs, and saw the physician's horse at the gate, she could not stay to speak with him, but fled out of the room in a passion of tears.

She composed herself in time to meet him when he came downstairs. She was glad that he was a stranger, so that she had to be restrained, and to ask him, in a calm, everyday voice, 'What he thought of her mother?'

'You are Miss Rothesay, I believe,' he answered, indirectly.

'I am.'

'Is there no one to aid you in nursing your mother—are you here quite alone?'

'Quite alone.' These dull, echoing answers, were freezing slowly at her heart.

Dr Witherington took her hand; kindly too. 'My dear Miss Rothesay, I would not deceive—I never do. If you have any relatives or friends to send for, any business to arrange——'

'Ah—I see, I know! Do not say any more!' She closed her eyes faintly, and leaned against the wall. Had she loved her mother with a love less intense, less self-devoted, less utterly absorbing in its passion, at that moment she would have gone mad, or died.

There was one little low sigh; and then upon her great height of woe she rose—rose to a superhuman calm.

'You mean to tell me, then, that there is no hope?'

He looked on the ground, and said nothing.

'And how long—how long?'

'It may be six hours—it may be twelve; I fear it cannot be more than twelve.' And then he began to give consolation in the only way that lay in his poor power, explaining that in a frame so shattered the spirit could not have lingered long, and might have lingered in much suffering. 'It was best as it was,' he said.

And Olive, knowing all, bowed her head, and answered, 'Yes.' She thought not of herself—she thought only of the enfeebled body about to be released from earthly pain, of the soul before whom heaven was even now opened. She caught the physician's arm.

'Does *she* know? Did you tell her?'

'I did. She asked me, and I thought it right.'

Thus, both knew, mother and child, that a few brief hours were all that lay between their love and eternity. And knowing this, they again met.

With a step so soft that it could have reached no ear but that of the dying woman, Olive re-entered the room.

'Is that my child!'

'My mother, my own mother!' Close, and wild, and strong—wild as love and strong as death—was the clasp that followed. No words passed between them, not one, until Mrs Rothesay said, faintly,

'My child, are you content—quite content?'

Olive answered, 'I am content!' And in her uplifted eyes was a silent voice that seemed to say, 'Take, O God, this treasure, which I give out of my arms unto Thine. Take and keep it for me, safe until the eternal meeting!'

Slowly the day sank, and the night came down. Very still and solemn was that chamber; but there was no sorrow there—no weeping, no struggle of life with death. After a few hours all suffering passed, and Mrs Rothesay lay quiet; sometimes in her daughter's arms, sometimes with Olive sitting by her side. Now and then they talked together, holding peaceful communion, like friends about to part for a long journey, in which neither wished to leave any words unsaid that spoke of love or counsel; but all was spoken calmly, hopefully, and without grief or fear.

As midnight approached, Olive's eyes grew heavy, and a strange drowsiness oppressed her. Many a watcher has doubtless felt this—the dull stupor which comes over heart and brain, sometimes even compelling sleep, though some beloved one lies dying. The old servant who sat up with Olive tried to persuade her to go down and take some coffee which she had prepared. Mrs Rothesay, overhearing, entreated the same. Most touching it was to see the mother just trembling on the verge of life, turn back to think of those little cares of love which had been shared between them for so many years.

Olive went down in the little parlour, and forced herself to take food and drink, for she knew how much her strength would be needed. As she sat there by herself, in the still night, with the wind howling round the cottage, she tried to realize the truth that her mother was then dying—that ere another day, in this world she would be alone, quite alone, for evermore. Yet there she sat, wrapped in that awful calm.

When Olive came back, Mrs Rothesay roused herself and asked for some wine. Her daughter gave it.

'It is very good—all things are very good—very sweet to me from Olive's hand. My only daughter—my life's comfort—I bless God for thee!'

After a while she said—passing her hand over her daughter's cheek—'Olive, little Olive, I wish I could see your face—just once, once more. It feels almost as small and soft as when you were a little babe at Stirling.'

And saying this, there came a cloud over Mrs Rothesay's face; but soon it changed into peace, as she continued, 'Child! listen to something I never told you—never could have told you, until now. Soon after you were born, I dreamt a strange dream—that I lost you, and there came to me in your stead an angel, who comforted me and guided me through a long weary way, until, in parting, I knew that it was indeed my Olive. All has come true, save that I did not *lose* you: I wickedly cast you from me. Ay, God forgive me! there was a time when I, a mother, had no love for the child I bore.'

She wept a little, and held Olive with a closer strain as she proceeded. 'I was punished, for in forsaking my child I lost my husband's love—at least not all, but for a time; and so for my suffering God pardoned me, and sent my child back to me as I saw her in my dream—an angel—to guard me through many troublous ways; to lead me safe to the eternal shore. And now, when I am going away, I say with my whole soul, God bless thee, thou most loving and duteous daughter that ever mother had; and God will bless thee evermore!'

One moment, with a passionate burst of anguish, Olive cried, 'O mother, mother, stay! Do not go and leave me in this bitter world alone.' It was the only moan she made. When she saw the suffering it brought to her so peacefully dying, she stilled it at once. And then God's comfort came down upon her; and that night of death was full of a peace so deep that it was most like happiness. In after years Olive thought of it as one thinks of a remembered dream of heaven.

Once, when Olive's voice sounded weak, Mrs Rothesay said, 'My child, you are tired. Lay your head down here beside me.'

And so, with her head on the same pillow, and her arm thrown round her mother's neck, Olive lay, as she had lain every night for so many years. Once or twice Mrs Rothesay spoke again, as passing thoughts seemed to arise; but her mind was perfectly composed and clear. She mentioned several that she regarded—among the rest, Mrs Gwynne, to whom she left 'her love'.

'And to Christal too, Olive. She has many faults; but, remember, she was good to me, and I loved her. Always take care of that child.'

'I will,' said Olive. Little she knew how solemnly would that promise be fulfilled. 'And is there none else?' she whispered, for to her thought, even then, there came another name.

'Yes—Harold Gwynne.' And, as if in that dying hour there came to the mother's heart a clear-sightedness of the present and the future, she said earnestly, 'I would he had been here, that I might have blessed him, and prayed him all his life long to show kindness and tenderness to my child.'

After this she spoke of earthly things no more, but her thoughts went, like heralds of her soul, far into the eternal land. Thither her daughter's followed likewise, until, like the martyr Stephen,* Olive almost seemed to see the heavens opened, and the angels of God standing around the throne. Her heart was filled, not with anguish, but with an awful joy. It passed not even when, lifting her head from the pillow, she saw that over her mother's face was coming a change—the change that comes but once.

'My child, are you still there?'

'Yes, darling.'

'Ah! that is well. All is well now. Little Olive, kiss me.'

Olive bent down and kissed her. With that last kiss she received her mother's soul.

Then she suffered the old servant to lead her from the room. She never wept; it would have appeared sacrilege to weep. She went to the open door, and stood, looking to the east, where the sun was rising gloriously. Through the golden clouds she almost seemed to behold, ascending, the freed spirit upon whom had just dawned the everlasting morning.

An hour after, when she was all alone in the little parlour, lying on the sofa with her eyes closed, she heard entering a well-known step. It was Harold Gwynne's. He looked much agitated; at first he drew back, as though fearing to approach; then he came up, and took her hand with a tender compassion.

'Alas, Miss Rothesay, what can I say to you?'

She shed a few tears, less for her own sorrow than because she was touched by his kindness.

'I would have been here yesterday,' continued he, 'but I was away from Harbury. Yet what help, what comfort could you have received from such as I?' he added, mournfully.

Olive turned to him her face, in whose pale serenity yet lingered the light which had guided her through the valley of the shadow of death.

'God,' she whispered, 'has taken from me the desire of my eyes, and yet I have peace—perfect peace!'

She ceased. Harold looked at her with astonishment.

'Tell me,' he muttered, involuntarily, 'whence comes this peace?'

'From God, and from the revelation of His word.'

He was silent. He sat, his head bent upon his hands; his aspect of hopeless misery went to Olive's heart. She came and stood beside him.

'Oh that I could give to you this peace—this faith!'

His keen, searching glance was tempered with deep sorrow, as he answered,

'Alas! if I knew what *reason* you have for yours.'

Olive paused. An awful thing it was, with the dead lying in the chamber above, to wrestle with the unbelief of the living. But it seemed as if the spirit of her mother had passed into her spirit, giving her strength to speak with words not her own; nay, constraining her, as by the influence of the faithful departed, to lift off the burden from Harold's tortured and despairing soul. What if, in the inscrutable purposes of Heaven, this hour of death was to be to him an hour of life—the moment when conviction would smite his stony heart, and bid faith's saving waters flow.

So, repressing all grief and weakness, Olive said, 'Let us speak of the things which in times like this come home to us as the only realities.'

'To you, not to me! You forget the gulf between us!'

'Nay,' Olive said, earnestly; 'you believe, as I do, in one God—the Creator and Ruler of this world?'

Harold made solemn assent.

'Of this world,' she continued, 'wherein is so much of beauty, happiness, and love. And can that exist in the created which is not in the Creator? Must not, therefore, the great Spirit of the Universe be a Spirit of Love?'

'Your argument contradicts itself,' was Harold's desponding answer. Can *you* speak thus—you, whose heart yet bleeds with recent suffering?'

'Suffering which my faith has overcome, and changed into joy. Never, until this hour, did I look so clearly from this world into the world of souls; never did I so strongly feel within me the presence of God's spirit, a pledge for the immortality of mine.'

'Immortality! Alas, that dream!' he sighed, in an incredulous, but still subdued tone. 'And yet,' he added, looking at her reverently, even with tenderness, 'I could half believe that a life like yours—so full of purity, goodness, and love—can never be destined to perish.'

'And can you believe in human love, yet doubt the love of Him who is its origin? Can you think that He would give the yearning for the hereafter, and yet deny its fulfilment? That what He made good He will not make happy, and what He makes happy He will not make immortal?'

Harold seemed struck. 'You speak plain, reasonable words—not like the vain babblers of perverted creeds. Yet you profess a creed—you join in the Church's service?'

'Because I think it pure—perhaps the purest of all human forms of worship. But I do not set up the Church and its ministrations between myself and God. I follow no ritual, and trust no creed, except so far as I find it in the Holy Word.'

'And how know you *that* is true?' cried Harold.

His look was eager; its dull misery seemed melting away. Olive thought of her beloved dead; she almost heard once more the faint words, 'I would Harold had been here, that I might bless him.' 'O mother!' she said in her heart, 'it may be so even now!'

Then she said, summoning all her faculties, and speaking as perchance she could not have spoken but for the awful inspiration of the time, 'My friend, think you that an all-wise God would leave His work so imperfect as to give to the creature He has made no revelation of Himself? Were the Bible not true, would He have suffered it to prevail from the earliest ages until now? Would He have caused all history to confirm its facts, and the purest codes of morality to be drawn from its fountains? Ask yourself, could the world exist without a Providence; and could this book, involving all that is precious to the soul, exist without the providence of God?'

As she spoke, her hand rested on the Bible out of which she had last read to her mother. It opened at the very place, and from it there dropped the little book-marker which Mrs Rothesay always used, one worked by Olive in her childish days. The sight drew her spirit down from the height of sublime faith to the helplessness of human woe.

'Oh, my mother!—my mother!' She bowed her head upon her knees, and for some minutes wept bitterly. Then she rose with a calm brow.

'I am going'—her voice failed.

'I know—I know,' said Harold.

'She spoke of you: they were almost her last words. You will come with me, friend?'

Harold was a man who never wept—never could weep—but his face grew pale, and there came over him a great awe. His step faltered, even more than her own, as he followed Olive upstairs.

Her hand paused a moment on the latch of the door. She stood still, and trembled. 'No,' she said, as if to herself—'no, it is not my mother; my mother is not here!'

Then she went in composedly, and looked on the face of the dead. Harold looked, too, standing beside her in silence.

Olive was the first to speak. 'See,' she whispered, 'how very placid and beautiful the image looks!—like her, and yet unlike. I never for a moment feel that it is *my mother*.'

Harold regarded with amazement the daughter newly orphaned, who stood serenely beholding her dead. Then he took Olive's hand, softly and with reverence, as if there were something sacred in her touch. *His* she scarcely seemed to feel, but continued, speaking in the same tranquil voice,

'An hour ago we were so happy, she and I, talking together of holy things—of the love we had borne each other on earth, and would still bear in heaven. And can such love end with death? Can I believe that one moment—the fleeting of a breath—has left *my mother* nought but this?'

She half turned from the frail clay, and met Harold's eye—intense—athirst—as if his soul's life were in her words.

'You are calm—very calm,' he murmured. 'You stand here, and have no dread.'

'No; for I have seen my mother die. Her last sigh was on my cheek. I *felt* her spirit pass, and I knew that it was passing unto God.'

'And you sorrow not, but rejoice?'

'Yes; since for all I lose on earth, heaven grows nearer to me. It will seem the more my home, now I have a mother there.'

Harold Gwynne fell on his knees beside the dead, crying out—

'Oh God—oh God—that I could believe!'

CHAPTER XXXIII

It was again the season of late summer; and Time's soothing shadow had risen up between the daughter and her grief. The grave in the beautiful churchyard of Harbury was bright with many months' growth of grass and flowers. It never looked dreary—nay, often seemed almost to smile. It was watered by no tears—it never had been. Those which Olive shed were only for her own loneliness, and at times she felt that even these were wrong. Many people, seeing how calm she was, and how, after a season, she fell into her old pursuits and her kindly duties to all around, used to say, 'Who would have thought that Miss Rothesay would have forgotten her mother so easily?'

But *she did not forget*. Selfish, worldly mourners are they, who think that the memory of the beloved lost can only be kept green by tears. Olive Rothesay was not of these. To her, her mother's departure appeared no more like death, than did one Divine parting—with reverence be it spoken!—appear to those who stood and looked heavenward from the hill of Bethany.* And thus should we think upon all happy and holy deaths—if we fully and truly believed the faith we aver.

Olive did not forget her mother—she could as soon have forgotten her own soul. In all her actions, words, and thoughts, this most sacred memory abided—a continual presence, silent as sweet, and sweet as holy. When her many and most affectionate friends had beguiled her into cheerfulness, so that they fancied she had lost thought of her sorrow, she used to say in her heart, 'See, mother, I can think of thee and not grieve. I would not, that, looking down from heaven, it should pain thee to know I suffer still!'

Yet human feelings could not utterly be suppressed; and there were many times, when at night-time she buried her face on the now lonely pillow, and blindly stretched out her arms into the empty darkness, crying, 'My mother, oh my mother!' But then strong love came between Olive and her agony, whispering, 'Child, wherever her spirit abides, thy mother forgets not thee!' And so the desolate one grew calm.

She looked very calm now, as she sat with Mrs Gwynne in the bay window of the little drawing-room at the Parsonage, engaged in some light work, with little Ailie reading a lesson at her knee. It was a lesson, too, taken from that lore—at once the most simple and most divine—the Gospels of the New Testament.

'I thought my son would prove himself right in all his opinions,' observed Mrs Gwynne, when the lesson was over and the child had run away. 'I knew he would allow Ailie to learn everything at the right time.'

Olive made no answer. Her thoughts turned to the day—now some months back—when, stung by the disobedience and falsehood that lay hid in a young mind which knew no higher law than a human parent's command, Harold had come to her for counsel. She remembered his almost despairing words, 'Teach the child as you will—true or false—I care not; so that she becomes like yourself, and is saved from those doubts which rack her father's soul.'

Harold Gwynne was not singular in this. Scarce ever was there an unbeliever who desired to see the image of his own scepticism reflected in his child.

Mrs Gwynne continued—'I don't think I can ever sufficiently thank you, my dear Miss Rothesay.'

'Say *Olive*, as you generally do,' was the affectionate whisper.

It seemed that her Christian name sounded so sweet and homelike from Harold's mother; especially now that, save from these kind lips, its sound had ceased on earth.

'*Olive*, then! My dear, how good you are to take Ailie so entirely under your care and teaching. But for that, we must have sent her to some school from home, and, I will not conceal from you, that would have been a great sacrifice, even in a worldly point of view, since our income is so diminished by my son's resigning his duties to his curate.' Mrs Gwynne had learned to talk to Olive with more unreserve that to any other human being. 'But tell me, do you think Harold looks any better? What an anxious summer this has been!'

And Olive, hearing the heavy sigh of the mother, whose whole existence was bound up in her son, felt that there was something holy even in that deceit, or rather concealment, wherein she herself was now a sorely tried sharer. 'You must not be anxious,' she said; 'you know that there is nothing dangerous in Mr Gwynne's state of health, only his mind has been overworked.'

'I suppose so; and perhaps it was the best plan for him to give up all clerical duties for a time. I think, too, that these short excursions of his do him good.'

'I hope so,' said Olive, observing that the anxious mother looked for an acquiescence.

'Besides, seeing that he is not positively disabled by illness, his parishioners might think it peculiar that he should continually remain among them, and yet discharge none of his duties. But my Harold is a strange being; he always was. Sometimes I think his heart is not in his calling—that he would have been more happy as a man of science than as a clergyman. Yet of late he has ceased even that favourite pursuit; and though he spends whole days in his study, I sometimes find he has not displaced one book, except the large Bible which I gave him when he went to college. God bless him—my dear Harold!'

Olive's inmost heart echoed the blessing, and in the same words. For of late—perhaps with more frequently hearing him called by the familiar home appellation, she had thought of him less as *Mr Gwynne* than as *Harold*. Alas! it is a serious thing for any woman, when, thinking of some friend, to her heart comes unconsciously not the name he bears in the world, but that which is uttered only by household affection or love.

'I wonder what makes your blithe Christal so late,' observed Mrs Gwynne, abruptly, as if, disliking to betray further emotion, she wished to change the conversation. 'Lyle Derwent promised to bring her him-self—much against his will, though,' she added, smiling. 'He seems quite afraid of Miss Manners; he says she teases him so!'

'But she suffers no one else to do it. If I say a word against Lyle's little peculiarities, she is quite indignant. I rather think she likes him—that is, as much as she likes any of her friends.'

'There is little depth of affection in Christal's nature. She is too proud. She feels no need of love, and therefore cares not to win it. Do you know, Olive,' continued Mrs Gwynne, 'if I must unveil all my weaknesses, there was a time when I watched Miss Manners more closely than any one guesses. It was from a mother's jealousy over her son's happiness, for I heard her name coupled with Harold's.'

'So have I, more than once,' said Olive. 'But I thought at the time how idle was the rumour.'

'It was idle, my dear; but I did not quite think so then.'

'Indeed!' There was a little quick gesture of surprise; and Olive, ceas-ing her work, looked enquiringly at Mrs Gwynne.

'I knew that a man must love; that, having once been wedded, Harold's necessity for a wife's sympathy and affection would be the greater. I always expected that my son would marry again, and therefore I eagerly watched every young woman whom he might meet in society, and be disposed to choose. All men, especially clergymen, are better married—at least in my opinion. Even you yourself, as Harold's friend, his most valued friend, must acknowledge that he would be happier with a wife.'

What was there in this frank speech that smote Olive with a secret pain? Was it the unconscious distinction drawn between her and all other women on whom Harold might look with admiring eyes, so that his mother, while calling her his *friend*, never dreamed of her being anything more?

Olive knew not whence came the pain, yet still she felt it was there. 'Certainly he would,' she answered, speaking in a slow, quiet tone. 'Nevertheless, I should scarcely think Christal a girl whom Mr Gwynne would be likely to select.'

'Nor I. At first, deeming her something like the first Mrs Harold, I had my doubts; but they quickly vanished. My son will never marry Christal Manners.'

Olive, sitting at the window, looked up. It seemed to her as if over the room had come a lightness like the passing away of a cloud.

'Nor, as I believe now,' pursued Mrs Gwynne, 'does it appear to me likely that he will marry at all. I fear that domestic love—the strong, yet quiet tenderness of a husband to a wife, is not in his nature. Passion is, or was, in his youth; but he is not young now. In his first hasty marriage I knew that the fire would soon burn itself out—it has left nothing but ashes. Once he deceived himself with a mistaken passion, and sorely he has reaped the fruits of his folly. The result is, that he will live to old age without ever having known the blessing of true love.'

'Is that so mournful, then?' said Olive, more as if thinking aloud than speaking.

Mrs Gwynne did not hear the words, for she had started up at the sound of a horse's hoofs at the gate. 'If that should be Harold! He said he would be at home this week or next. It is—it is he! How glad I am—that is, I am glad that he should be in time to see the Fludyers and Miss Manners before their journey tomorrow.'

Thus, from long habit, trying to make excuses for her overflowing tenderness, she hurried out. Olive heard Mr Gwynne's voice in the hall— his anxious, tender enquiry for his mother; even the quick, flying step of little Ailie bounding to meet 'papa'.

She paused: her work fell, and a mist came before her eyes. She felt then, as she had sometimes done before, though never so strongly, that it was hard to be in the world alone.

This thought haunted her a while; until at last it was banished by the influence of one of those pleasant social evenings, such as were often spent at the Parsonage. The whole party, including Christal and Lyle, were assembled in the twilight, the two latter keeping up a sort of Benedick and Beatrice* warfare; Harold and his mother seemed both very quiet—they sat close together, her hand sometimes resting caressingly on his shoulder or his knee. It was a new thing, this outward show of affection; but of late, since his health had declined (and, in truth, he had often looked and been very ill), there had come a touching softness between the mother and son.

Olive Rothesay sat a little apart, a single lamp lighting her at her work; for she was not idle. Following her old master's example, she was continually making studies from life for the picture on which she was engaged. She took a pleasure in filling it with idealized heads, of which the originals had place in her own warm affections. Christal was there, with her gracefully turned throat, and the singular charm of her black eyes and fair hair. Lyle, too, with his delicate, womanish, but yet handsome face. Nor was Mrs Gwynne forgotten—Olive made great use of her well-outlined form, and her majestic sweep of drapery. There was one only of the group who had not been limned by Miss Rothesay.

'If I were my brother-in-law I should take it quite as an ill compliment that you had never asked him to sit,' observed Lyle. 'But,' he added in a whisper, 'I don't suppose any artist would care to paint such a hard, rugged-looking fellow as Gwynne.'

Olive looked on the pretty red and white face of the boyish dabbler in Art—for Lyle had lately taken a fancy that way too—and then at the noble countenance he maligned. She did not say a word on the subject; but Lyle, hovering round her, found his interference somewhat sharply set aside during the whole evening.

When assembled round the supper-table they talked of Christal's journey. It was undertaken by invitation of Mrs Fludyer, to whom the young damsel had made herself quite indispensable. Her liveliness charmed away the idle lady's *ennui*, while her pride and love of aristocratic exclusiveness equally gratified the same feelings in her patroness. And from the mist that enwrapped her origin, the ingenious and perhaps self-beguiled young creature had contrived to evolve such a grand fable of 'ancient descent', and 'noble but reduced family', that everybody regarded her in the light that she regarded herself. And surely, as the quick-sighted Mrs Gwynne often said, no daughter of a long illustrious line was ever prouder than Christal Manners.

She indulged the party with a brilliant account of Mrs Fludyer's anticipations of pleasure at the gay seaside watering-place whither the whole family at the Hall were bound.

'Really, we shall be quite desolate without a single soul left at Farnwood, shall we not, Olive?' observed Mrs Gwynne.

Olive answered, 'Yes—very,' without much considering of the matter. Her thoughts were with Harold, who was leaning back in his chair absorbed in one of those fits of musing, which with him were not unfrequent, and which no one ever regarded, save herself. How deeply solemn it was to her at such times to feel that she alone held the key to this great soul—that it lay open, with all its secrets, to her, and to her alone. What marvel was it if this knowledge sometimes moved her with strange sensations; most of all, while, beholding the reserved exterior which he bore in society, she remembered the times when she had seen this cold, quiet man goaded into terrible emotion, or softened to the weakness of a child.

At Olive's mechanical answer, 'Yes,' Lyle Derwent brightened up amazingly. 'Miss Rothesay, I—I don't intend going to Brighton, believe me!'

Christal turned quickly round. 'What are you saying, Mr Derwent?'

He hung his head and looked foolish. 'I mean, that Brighton is too gay, and thoughtless, and noisy a place for me—I would rather stay at Harbury.'

'You fickle, changeable, idle creature! 'Tis only an excuse to get out of your pupils' way'; and reckless Christal burst into a fit of laughter much louder than seemed warranted by the occasion.

'I assure you, Miss Manners, this is to be instead of my regular yearly holiday. I arranged it all with Mrs Fludyer a week ago.'

'A week ago! Mr Derwent turned a schemer! How could he keep the mighty secret in his innocent breast for seven long days!'

'I can, and more secrets too,' muttered Lyle, in a tone varying between anger and sentimentality, as he looked alternately from Christal to Miss Rothesay. Whereupon the latter considerately interposed, and passed with a smile to some other subject, which lasted until the hour of departure.

The three walked to the Dell together, Christal jesting merrily, either with or at Lyle Derwent, compelling him, perforce, to laugh and be amused. Olive walked beside them, rather silent than otherwise. She had been so used to walk home with Harold Gwynne, that any other companionship along the old familiar road seemed unwelcome. Remembering how they two had talked together, the light laughter beside her was even painful to her ear. As she passed along, from every bush, every tree, every winding of the lane, seemed to start some ghostlike memory; until there came over her a feeling almost of fear, to see how full her thoughts were of this one friend, how to pass from his presence was like passing into gloom, and the sense of his absence seemed a heavy void.

'It was not so while my mother lived,' Olive murmured, sorrowfully. 'I never needed any friend save her. What am I doing! Whither is my mind whirling?'

She trembled, and dared not answer the question.

At the Dell they parted from Lyle. 'I shall see you once again before you leave, I hope,' he said to his blithe companion, Christal.

'Oh, yes; you will not get rid of your tormentor so easily, Sir Minstrel.'

'Get rid of you, fair Cruelty! Would a man wish to put out the sun because it scorches him sometimes?' cried Lyle, lifted to the seventh heaven of poetic fervour by the influence of a balmy night and a glorious harvest moon. Which said luminary shining on Christal's face, saw there—she only, pale Lady Moon—an expression fine and rare—quivering lips, eyes not merely bright, but flaming as such dark eyes only can.

As Miss Rothesay was passing up the steps to the hall door, Christal, a little in the rear, fell, crying out as with pain. She was quickly assisted into the house, where, recovering, she complained of having sprained her ankle. Olive, full of compassion, laid her on the sofa, and hurried away for some simple medicaments, leaving Christal alone.

That young lady, as soon as she heard Miss Rothesay's steps overhead, bounded to the half-open window, moving quite as easily on the injured foot as on the other. Eagerly she listened; and soon was rewarded by hearing Lyle's voice carolling down the road, in most sentimental fashion, the ditty,

> Io ti voglio ben assai,
> Ma tu non pensi a me!*

' 'Tis my song, mine! I taught him!' said Christal, laughing to herself. 'He thought to stay behind and escape me and my "cruelty". But we shall see—we shall see!'

Though in her air was a triumphant, girlish coquetry, yet something there was of a woman's passion, too. But she heard a descending step, and had only just time to regain her invalid attitude and her doleful countenance, when Olive entered.

'This accident is really unfortunate,' said Miss Rothesay. 'How will you manage your journey tomorrow?'

'I shall not be able to go,' said Christal, in a piteous voice, though over her averted face broke a comical smile.

'Are you really so much hurt, my dear?'

'Do you doubt it? I am sorry to have to trouble you; but I really cannot leave the Dell,' was the girl's half-indignant speech.

Very often did she try Olive's patience thus; but the faithful daughter always remembered those feeble, dying words, 'Take care of Christal.'

So, her gentle nature excusing all, she tended the young sufferer carefully until midnight, and then went down stairs secretly to perform a little act of self-denial, by giving up an engagement she had made for the morrow. While writing to renounce it, she felt, with the former sense of vague apprehension, how keen a pleasure it was she thus resigned—a whole long day in the forest with her pet Ailie, Ailie's grandmamma, and—Harold Gwynne.

CHAPTER XXXIV

Midnight was long passed, and yet Olive sat at her desk; she had finished her note to Mrs Gwynne, and was poring over a small packet of letters carefully separated from the remainder of her correspondence. If she had been asked the reason of this, perhaps she would have made answer that they were unlike the rest—solemn in character, and secret withal. She never looked at them, but the expression of her face changed; when she touched them, she did it softly and tremulously, as one would touch a living sacred thing.

They were letters which at intervals, during his various absences, she had received from Harold Gwynne.

Often had she read them over—so often, that, many a time waking in the night, whole sentences came distinctly on her memory, vivid almost as a spoken voice. And yet, scarce a day passed that she did not read them still. Perhaps this was from their tenor, for they were letters such as man rarely writes to woman, or even friend to friend.

Let us judge, extracting portions from them at will.

*   *   *

The first, dated months back, began thus:

You will perhaps marvel, my dear Miss Rothesay, that I should write to you, when for some time we have met so rarely, and then apparently like ordinary acquaintance. Yet, who should have a better right than we to call each other *friends*? And like a friend you acted, when you consented that there should be between us for a time this total silence on the subject which first bound us together by a tie which we can neither of us break if we would. Alas! sometimes I could almost curse the weakness which had given you—a woman—to hold my secret in your hands. And yet so gently, so nobly have you held it, that I could kneel and bless you. You see I can write earnestly, though I cannot speak. . . .

I told you, after that day when we two were alone with death (the words are harsh, I know, but I have no smooth tongue), I told you that I desired silence for weeks, perhaps months! I must 'commune with my own heart, and be still'.* I must wrestle with this darkness alone. You assented; you forced on me no long argumentative homilies—you preached to me with your life, the pure, beautiful life of a Christian woman. Sometimes I tried to read, with open eyes and keenly searching heart, the morality of Jesus, which I, and sceptics worse than I, must perforce allow to be perfect of its kind, and it struck me how nearly you approached to that divine life which I had thought impossible to be realized.

*   *   *

I have advanced thus far in my solemn seeking. I have learned to see the revelation—imputedly divine—as clear and distinct from the mass of modern creeds with which it has been overladen. I have begun to read the book on which—as you truly say—every form of religion is founded. I try to read with my own eyes, putting aside all human interpretations, earnestly desiring to cast from my soul all long-gathered prejudices, and

to bring it, naked and clear, to meet the souls of those who are said to
have written by divine inspiration. . . .

The book is a marvellous book. The history of all ages can scarcely
show its parallel. What diversity, yet what unity! The stream seems to
flow through all ages, catching the lights and shadows of different peri-
ods, and of various human minds. Yet it is one and the same stream—pure
and shining as truth. Is it truth?—is it divine?

*   *   *

I will confess, candidly, that if the scheme of a world's history—with
reference to its Creator, as set forth in the Bible—were true, it would be
a scheme in many things worthy of a divine benevolence: such as that in
which you believe. But can I imagine Infinity setting itself to work out
such trivialities? What is even a world? A mere grain of dust in endless
space? It cannot be. A God who could take interest in man, in such an
atom as I, would be no God at all. What avails me to have risen unto more
knowledge, more clearness in the sense of the divine, if it is to plunge me
into such an abyss as this? Would I had never been awakened from my
sleep—the dull stupor of materialism* into which I was fast sinking. Then
I might, in the end, have conquered even the last fear, that of 'something
after death', and have perished like a soulless thing, satisfied that there
was no hereafter. Now, if there should be? I whirl and whirl; I can find no
rest. I would I knew for certain that I was mad. But it is not so.

*   *   *

You answer, my kind friend, like a woman—like the sort of woman that
I believed in in my boyhood—when I longed for a sister, such an one as
you. It is very strange, even to myself, that I should write so freely as I do
to you. I know that I could never speak thus. Therefore, when I return
home, you must not marvel to find me just the same reserved being as
ever—less to you, perhaps, than most people, but still reserved. Yet,
never believe but that I thank you for all your goodness most deeply. . . .

You say that, like most women, you have no power of keen philosophical argument. Perhaps not; but there is in you a spiritual sense that may
even transcend knowledge. I once heard—was it not you who said so?—
that the poet who 'reads God's secrets in the stars', soars nearer Him than
the astronomer who calculates by figures and by line. As, even in the
material universe, there are planets and systems, which mock all human
ken; so in the immaterial world there must be a boundary where all
human reasoning fails, and we can trust to nothing but that inward
inexplicable sense which we call faith. This seems to me the great
argument which inclines us to receive that supernatural manifestation of

the all-pervading spirit which is termed revelation. And there we go back again to the relation between the finite—humanity, and the infinite—Deity. . . .

One of my speculations you answer by an allegory—Does not the sun's light make instinct with life not only man, but the meanest insect, the lowest form of vegetable existence? But is it therefore needful that every ray should pierce, impelled by the force of individual will, to an individual object? The sun shines. His light at once revivifies a blade of grass, and illumines a world. If thus it is with the created, must it not be also with the Creator? There is something within me that answers to this reasoning. . . .

If I have power to conceive the existence of God, to look up from my lowly nothingness unto His great height, to meditate, to argue, to desire nearer insight into His being, there must be in my soul something not unworthy of Him—something that, partaking His divinity, instinctively turns to the source whence it was derived. Shall I suffer myself to be guided by this power? Shall I seek less to doubt than to believe? . . .

My whole education has been contrary to this. I remember my first mathematical tutor once said to me, 'If you would know anything, begin by doubting everything.'* I did begin, but I have never yet found an end.

*   *   *

I will take your advice, my dear friend; advice given so humbly, so womanly, that it touches me more than ever did that of any living being. Yet I think you deal with me wisely. I am a man who never could be preached or argued into belief. I must find out the truth for myself. And so, according to your counsel, I will again carefully study the Holy Bible, trying to look upon it—not as an ingenious work of man, but as the clearest revelation which God has allowed of Himself on earth. Finding any contradictions or obscurities, I will remember, as you say, that it was not, and does not pretend to be, written visibly and actually by the finger of God, but by His inspiration conveyed through many human minds, and of course always bearing to a certain extent the impress of the mind through which it passes. Therefore, you say, of all its prophet histories, none convey the sense of all-perfect righteousness save that of Him who came in latter days to crown what was before holy with the example of the Divine.

You see how my mind echoes your words, my friend! I am becoming, I think, more worthy to call you by this name. There is a child-like peace creeping into my heart. All human affections are growing closer and dearer unto me. I can look at my good and pious mother without feeling, as I did at times, that she is either a self-deceiver or deceived. I do not now shrink from my little daughter, nor think with horror that she owes to me that as yet undefiled being which may lead her one day to 'curse God and die'. Still, I cannot rest at Harbury. All things there torture me, while my mind is in this chaos. As for resuming my duties as a minister, that seems all but impossible. What an accursed hypocrite I have been! If this search after truth should end in a belief anything like that of the Church of England, I shall marvel that Heaven's lightning has not struck me dead.

*   *   *

. . . You speak joyfully and hopefully of the time when we shall be one in faith, and both give thanks together unto the merciful God who has lightened my darkness. I cannot say this *yet*; but the time may come. And if it does, what shall I not owe to you, who first revived my faith in humanity? Many other things you have taught me—less in words than by your holy life. It has solved to me many of those enigmas of Providence which in my blindness I thought impugned the justice of God. Now I see how goodness is sufficient to itself, and how the trials which seem the wrongs of fortune are but tests ordained by Heaven to elicit the strength and devotion of its creatures. All circumstances reflect the nature of the soul. Hardship becomes sweet unto patience; content creates abundance out of poverty; faith translates death into immortality. My friend, is not this a creed something approaching yours? It ought to be, since it is drawn from the silent teaching of your own life. If ever I lift up a prayer worthy to reach the ear of God, it is that He may bless you, my comforter.

*   *   *

Olive refolded the letters, and sat long in mute thought. Then broken words came from her of thanksgiving and joy. Amidst them she often uttered the name which on her lips was now silent evermore, save at solemn seasons like this, when, clear above all earthly strife and turmoil, rose the unforgotten memory of the departed.

'Oh, mother, mother!' she murmured, 'surely it would rejoice thee in thy heaven to know that even thy death left a blessing behind, and that I, out of my bitter grief, have been able, God helping me, to bring faith and peace unto this erring soul.'

And here, reader, for a moment, we pause. Following whither our subject led, we have gone far beyond the bounds usually prescribed to a book like this. After perusing the present chapter, you may turn to the title-page, and read thereon, 'Olive, a *Novel*.' 'Most incongruous—most strange!' you may exclaim. Nay, some may even accuse us of irreverence in thus bringing into a fictitious story those subjects which are acknowledged as most vital to every human soul, but yet which most people are content, save at set times and places, tacitly to ignore. There are those who sincerely believe that in such works as this there should never once be named the Holy Name. Yet what is a novel, or, rather, what is it that a novel ought to be? The attempt of one earnest mind to show unto many what humanity is—ay, and more, what humanity might become; to depict what is true in essence through imaginary forms; to teach, counsel, and warn, by means of the silent transcript of human life. Human life without God! Who will dare to tell us we should paint *that*?

Authors, who feel the solemnity of their calling, cannot suppress the truth that is within them. Having put their hands to the plough, they may not turn aside, nor look either to the right or the left. They must go straight on, as the inward voice impels; and He who seeth their hearts will guide them aright.

CHAPTER XXXV

Some days passed in quiet uniformity, broken only by the visits of good-natured Lyle, who came, as he said, to amuse the invalid. Whether that were the truth or no, he was always a frequent and a welcome guest at the Dell. Only he made the proviso, that in all the amusements which he and Christal shared, Miss Rothesay should be in some way united. So, morning after morning, the sofa whereon the invalid gracefully reclined was brought into the painting-room, and there, while Olive worked, she listened, sometimes almost in envy, to the gay young voices that mingled in song, or contended in the light battle of wits. How much older, and graver, and sadder, she seemed than they!

Harold Gwynne did not come. This circumstance troubled Olive. Not that he was in the habit of paying long morning visits, like young Derwent; but still, when he was at Harbury, it usually chanced that every few days they met somewhere, or on some excuse; and so habitual had this intercouse become, that a week's complete cessation of it seemed a positive pain.

Ever, when Olive rose, the morning-gilded spire of Harbury Church brought the thought, 'I wonder, will he come today!' And at night, when he did not come, she could not conceal from herself, that looking back on the past day, over all duties done therein, all little pleasures planned, there rose a pale mist. She seemed to have only half lived. Alas! it is an awful thing when one's own life becomes insufficient—when all in the world grows dull, save where one other life interpenetrates—all dark, save where one other presence shines!

Olive knew, though she scarce would acknowledge it to herself, that for many months this interest in Harold Gwynne had been the one great interest of her existence. At first it came in the form of a duty, and as such she had entered upon it. She was one of those women who seem born ever to devote themselves to some one. When her mother died, it had comforted Olive to think there was one other human being who stretched out to her entreating hands, saying, 'I need thee! I need thee!' Nay, it even seemed as if the voice of the saint departed called upon her to perform this sacred task. Thereto tended her thoughts and prayers. And thus there came upon her the fate which has come upon many another woman—while thus devoting herself she learned to love. But so gradual had been the change that she yet knew it not.

'Why am I restless?' she thought. 'One is too exacting in friendship: one should give all and ask nothing back. Still, it is not quite kind of him to stay away thus. But a man is not like a woman. He must have so many conflicting and engrossing interests, whilst I——' Here her thought broke and dissolved like a rock-riven wave. She dared not yet confess that she had no interest in the world save what was linked with him.

'If he comes not so often,' she recommenced her musings, 'even then I ought to be quite content. I know he respects and esteems me; nay, that he has for me a warm regard. I have done him good, too; he tells me so. How fervently ought I to thank God if any feeble words of mine may so influence this noble soul, as in time to lead it from error into truth. My friend, my dear friend! I could not die, knowing or fearing that the abyss of eternity would lie between my spirit and his. Now, whatever may part us during life——'

Here again she paused, for there came upon her a consciousness of pain. If there was gloom in the silence of a week, what would a whole life's silence be? Something whispered, that even in this world it would be bitterness to part with Harold Gwynne.

'You are not painting, Miss Rothesay; you are thinking. What about?' suddenly cried Lyle Derwent.

Olive started almost with a sense of shame. 'Has not an artist a right to dream a little?' she said. Yet she blushed deeply. Were her thoughts wrong, that they needed to be thus glossed over? Was there stealing into her heart a secret that taught her to feign?

'What! are you, always the idlest of the idle, reproving Miss Rothesay for being idle too?' said Christal, somewhat sharply. 'No wonder she is dull, and I likewise. You have not half amused us today. You are getting as solemn as Mr Gwynne himself. I almost wish he would come in your place.'

'Do you? Then "reap the misery of a granted prayer", for there is a knock. It may be my worthy brother-in-law himself.'

'If so, for charity's sake, give me your arm, and help me into the next room. I cannot abide his gloomy face.'

'O woman!—changeful—fickle—vain!' laughed the young man, as he performed the duty of supporting the not very fragile form of the fair Christal.

Olive stood alone. Why did she tremble? Why did her pulse sink, slower and slower? She asked herself this question, even in self-disdain. But there was no answer.

Harold entered.

'I am come with a message from my mother,' said he, in a rather formal apology; but added, anxiously, 'How is this, Miss Rothesay? You look as if you had been ill?'

'Oh, no; only weary with a long morning's work. But will you sit?'

He received, as usual the quiet smile—the greeting gentle and friendly. He was deceived by them as heretofore.

'Are you better than when last I was at the Parsonage? I have seen nothing of you for a week, you know.'

'Is it so long? I did not note the time.' These words of his fell carelessly, as it seemed; but they wounded Olive's heart. He 'did not note the time'. And she had told every day by hours—every hour by minutes!

'I should have come before,' he continued, 'but I have had so many things to occupy me. Besides, I am so dreary and dull. I should only trouble you.'

'You never trouble me.'

'It is kind of you to say so. Well, let that pass. Will you now return with me and spend the day. My mother is longing to see you.'

'I will come,' said Olive; and a brightness shone over her face. There was a little demur about Christal's being left, but it was soon terminated by the incursion of a tribe of the young lady's 'friends' whom she had made at Farnwood Hall.

Soon Olive was walking with Mr Gwynne along the well-known road. The sunshine of the morning seemed to gather and float around her heart. She remembered no more the pain—the doubt—the weary waiting. All was happiness now!

Gradually they fell into their old way of conversing. 'How beautiful all seems,' said Harold, as he stood still, bared his head, and drank in, with a long sighing breath, the sunshine and the soft air. 'I would that I could be happy in this happy world.'

'You feel it is so, then; that it is God's world, and as He made it—good,' answered Olive, softly.

'Much that you say I see like a vision afar off. I cannot realize it. But I pray you, do not speak to me of these things. My soul is in a wild labyrinth, from which it must work its way out alone. Nevertheless, my friend, keep near me!' Unconsciously, she clung closer to his arm. He started, and turned his head away. The next moment he added, in a somewhat constrained voice, 'I mean—let me have your friend-ship—your silent comforting—your prayers. Yes! thus far I believe. I can say, "Pray God for me", doubting not that He will hear—you, at least, if not me. Therefore, let me go on and struggle through this darkness.'

'Until comes the light! It will come—I know it will!' Olive looked up at him, and their eyes met. In hers was the fullness of joy, in his a doubt—a contest. He removed them, and walked on in silence, pride sitting on his brow. The very arm on which Olive leaned seemed to grow coldly rigid—like a bar of severance between them.

'I would to Heaven!' Harold suddenly exclaimed, as they approached Harbury—'I would to Heaven I could get away from this place altogether. I think I shall do so. My knowledge and reputation in science is not small. I might begin a new life—a life of active exertion. In fact, I have nearly decided it all.'

'Decided what? It is so sudden. I do not quite understand,' said Olive, faintly.

'To leave England—to enter as tutor in some academy of science abroad. What think you of the plan?'

What thought she? Nothing. There was a dull sound in her ears as of a myriad waters—the ground whereon she stood seemed reeling to and fro—yet she did not fall. One minute, and she answered him.

'You know best. If good for you, it is a good plan.'

He seemed relieved, and yet disappointed. 'I am glad you say so. I imagined, perhaps, you might have thought it wrong.'

'Why wrong?'

'Women have peculiar feelings about home, and country, and friends. I shall leave all these; perhaps for ever. I would not care ever to see England more. I would put off this black gown, and with it every remem-brance of the life of vile hypocrisy which I have led here. I would drown the past in new plans—new energies—new hopes. And, to do this, I must break all ties, and go alone. My poor mother! I have not dared yet to tell her this. To her, the thought of parting would be like death, so dearly does she love me.'

He spoke all this rapidly, never looking towards his silent companion. When he ceased, Olive feebly stretched out her hand, as if to grasp something for support, then drew it back again, and, hid under her mantle, pressed it tightly against her heart. On that heart Harold's words fell, rending away all its disguises, laying it naked and bare to the cold, bitter truth. 'To me,' she thought—'to me, also, this parting is like death. And why? Because I, too, love him—dearer than ever mother loved son, or sister brother; ay, dearer than my own soul. O miserable me!'

'You are silent,' said Harold. 'You think I am acting cruelly towards one who loves me so well. Men often act so. Human affections are to us secondary things. We scarce need them; or, when our will demands, we can crush them from our hearts—thus.'

He stamped fiercely on the ground, not heeding that there had fluttered to his feet from the hedge a young, tender-winged autumn butterfly. As he passed on before her to open the churchyard-gate, Olive saw the poor crushed insect lying dead. She took it up tenderly, and sighed. She might even have wept, but that her tears seemed all scorched up.

'Poor thing, poor thing! But he has done no wrong. He knew it not: he never shall know it. It is best so!'

She laid the dead butterfly on a mound of grass, followed Harold, and, at his silent gesture, again linked her arm in his.

'I think,' she said—when, without talking any more, they had nearly reached the Parsonage—'I think, that wherever you go, you ought to take your mother with you; and little Ailie, too! With them your home will be complete.'

'Yet I have friends to leave—one friend at least—*yourself*,' he said, abruptly.

'I, as others, shall miss you; but all true friends should desire, above all things, each other's welfare. I shall be satisfied if I hear at times of yours.'

He made no answer, and they went in at the hall door.

There was much to be done and talked of that afternoon at the Parsonage. First, there was a long lesson to be given to little Ailie; then, at least an hour was spent in following Mrs Gwynne round the garden, and hearing her dilate on the beauty of her hollyhocks and dahlias.

'I shall have the finest dahlias in the country next year,' said the delighted old lady.

Next year! next year! It seemed to Olive as if she were talking of the next world!

In some way or other the hours went by; how, Olive could not tell. She did not see, hear, or feel anything, save that she had to make an effort to appear in the eyes of Harold, and of Harold's mother, just as usual—the same quiet little creature—gently smiling, gently speaking—who had already begun to be called 'an old maid'—whom no one in the world suspected of any human passion—least of all, the passion of *love*.

After their early dinner Harold went out. He did not return even when the misty autumn night had began to fall. As the daylight waned and the firelight brightened, Olive felt terrified at herself. One hour of that quiet evening commune, so sweet of old, and her strength and self-control would have failed. Making some excuse about Christal, she asked Mrs Gwynne to let her go home.

'But not alone, my dear; you will surely wait until Harold comes in?'

'No, no! It will be late, and the mist is rising. Do not fear for me; the road is quite safe; and, you know, I am used to being alone,' said Olive, feebly smiling.

'You are a brave little creature, my dear. Well, do as you will.'

So, ere long, Olive found herself on her solitary homeward road. It lay through the churchyard. Closing the Parsonage gate, the first thing she did was to creep across the long grass to her mother's grave.

'Oh! mother, mother, why did you go and leave me? Else this misery had not befallen me. I should never have loved any one if my mother had not died!'

And burning tears fell, and burning blushes came. With these came also the sense of self-degradation which smites a woman when she knows, that, unwooed, unrequited, she has dared to love.

'What have I done?' she cried. 'O earth, take me in and cover me! Hide me from myself—from my misery—my shame.' Suddenly she started up. 'What if he should pass and find me here! I must go. I must go home.'

She fled out of the churchyard and down the road. For a little way she walked rapidly, then gradually slower and slower. A white mist arose from the meadows; it folded round her like a shroud; it seemed to creep even into her heart, and make its beatings grow still. Down the long road, where she and Harold had so often passed together, she walked alone. Alone—as once had seemed her doom through life—and must now be so unto the end.

It might be the *certainty* of this which calmed her. She had no maiden doubts or hopes; not one! The possibility of Harold's loving her, or choosing her as his wife, never entered her mind.

Since the days of her early girlhood, when she wove such a bright romance around Sara and Charles, and created for herself a beautiful ideal for future worship, Olive had ceased to dream about love at all. Feeling that its happiness was for ever denied her, she had bravely relinquished all those airy imaginings in which young maidens indulge. In their place had come the intense devotion to her Art, which, together with her passionate love for her mother, had absorbed all the interests of her secluded life. Scarcely was she even conscious of the happiness that she lost; for she had read few of those books which foster sentiment or passion; and in the wooings and weddings she heard of, were none that aroused either sympathy or her envy. Coldly and purely she had moved in her sphere, superior to both love's joy and love's pain.

Reaching home, Olive sought not to enter the house, where she knew there could be no solitude. She went into the little arbour—her mother's favourite spot—and there, hidden in the shadows of the mild autumn night, she sat down, to gather up her strength, and calmly to think over her mournful lot.

She said to herself, 'There has come upon me that which I have heard is, soon or late, every woman's destiny. I cannot beguile myself any longer. It is not friendship I feel; it is love. My whole life is threaded by one thought—the thought of him. It comes between me and everything else on earth—almost between me and Heaven. I never wake at morning but his name rises to my heart—the first hope of the day; I never kneel down at night but in my prayer, whether in thought or speech, that name is mingled too. If I have sinned, oh God! forgive me! Thou knowest how lonely and desolate I was—how, when that one best love was taken away, my heart ached and yearned for some other human love. And this has come to fill it. Alas for me!

'Let me think—will it ever pass away? There are feelings which come and go—light girlish fancies. But I am six-and-twenty years old. All this while I have lived without loving any man. And none has ever wooed me by word or look, except my master, Vanbrugh, whose feeling for me was not love at all. No! no! I am, as they call me, "an old maid", destined to pass through life alone and unloved.

'Perhaps, though I have long ceased to think on the subject—perhaps my first girlish misery was true, and there is in me something repulsive— something that would prevent any man's seeking me as a wife. Therefore, even if my own feelings could change, there will never come any soothing after-tie to fill up my heart's affection, and chase away the memory of this utterly hopeless love.

'Hopeless I know it is. He admires beauty and grace—I have neither. Yet I will not do him the injustice to believe he would contemn me for this. Even once I overheard him say, there was such sweetness in my face, that he had never noticed my being "slightly deformed". Therefore, did he but love me, perhaps—O fool!—dreaming fool that I am! It is impossible!

'Let me think calmly once more. He has given me all he could—kindness, friendship, brotherly regard; and I have given him love—a woman's whole and entire love, such as she can give but once, and be beggared all her life after. I to him am like any other friend—he to me is all my world. Oh! but it is a fearful difference!

'I will look my doom in the face—I will consider how I am to bear it. No hope is there for me of being loved as I love. I shall never be his wife—never be more to him than I am now; in time, perhaps, even less. He will go out into the world, and leave me, as brothers leave sisters (even supposing he regards me as such). He will form new ties; perhaps he will marry; and then this silent, secret love of mine would be—sin!'

Olive pressed her hands tightly together, and crushed her hot brow upon them, bending it even to her knees. Thus bowed, she lay until the fierce struggle passed.

'I do not think that misery will come. His mother, who knows him best, was surely right when she said he would never take a second wife. Therefore I may be his sister still. Neither he nor any living soul will ever know that I loved him otherwise than as a sister might love a brother. Who would dream there could be any other passion in me—a pale, unlovely thing—a woman past her youth (for I seem very old now)?—It ought not to be so; many women are counted young at six-and-twenty; but they are those who have been nurtured tenderly in joyous homes, while I have been struggling with the hard world these many years. No wonder I am not as they—that I am quiet and silent, without mirth or winning grace—a creature worn out before her time—pale, joyless, *deformed*. Yes! let me teach myself that word, with all other truths that can quench this mad dream. Then, perhaps, knowing all hope vain, I may be able to endure.

'What am I to do? Am I to try and cleanse my heart of this love, as if it were some pollution? Not so. Sorrow it is—deep, abiding sorrow; but it is not sin. If I thought it so, I would crush it out, though I crushed my life out with it. But I need not. My heart is pure—O God, Thou knowest!

'Another comfort I have. He has not deceived me, as men sometimes deceive, with wooing that seems like love, and yet is only idle, cruel sport. He has ever treated me as a friend—a sister—nothing more! Therefore, no bitterness is there in my sorrow, since he has done no wrong.

'I will not cease from loving—I would not if I could. Better this suffering than the utter void which must otherwise be in my heart eternally, seeing I have neither father, mother, brother, nor sister, and shall never know any nearer tie than the chance friendships which spring up on the world's wayside, and wither where they spring. I know there are those who would bid me cast off this love as it were a serpent from my bosom. No! Rather let it creep in there, and fold itself close and secret. What matter, even if its sweet sting be death?

'But I shall not die. How could I, while my heart's beloved lived, and might need aught that I could give? Did he not say, "Keep near me!" Ay, I will! Though a world lay between us, my spirit shall follow him all his life long. Distance shall be nothing—years nothing! Whenever he calls "Friend, I need thee", I will answer, "I am here!" If I could condense my whole life's current of joy into one drop of peace for him, I would pour it out at his feet, smile content, and die.

'And then, after death, I shall await him in the land of souls. Oh, Harold! whom in this world I never may call *my* Harold, with full and perfect love my spirit shall meet thee *there*.'

Thrice, with an accent of most divine tenderness, she sighed his name; and then rose up and went forth, her step wavering not, her countenance serene and clear.

The mist had all passed away, and over her shone the dark night-blue heaven, with its eternal stars.

CHAPTER XXXVI

I know that I am promulgating a new theory of love; I know that in Olive Rothesay I dare to paint a woman full of all high, pure, maidenly virtues, who has yet given her heart away unrequited—cast it down irretrievably and hopelessly at the feet of a man who knows not of the gift he has never sought to win. The case, I grant, is rare. I believe that a woman seldom bestows her love save in response to other love—silent or spoken—real or imaginary. Should this prove false, either she has deceived herself, or has been deceived.

But the thing is quite possible—aye, and chances sometimes—that a woman unselfish in her nature, in all her affections more prone to give than to receive, free from idle notions of lovers and weddings, may be unconsciously attracted by some image of perfection in the other sex, and be thus led on through the worship of abstract goodness until she wakes to find that she has learned to love *the man*. For what is love, in its purest and divinest sense, but that innate yearning after the ideal which we vainly dream is realized in some other human soul? Why should not this be felt by woman as by man? Ay, and by hearts most pure from every thought of unfeminine boldness, vanity, or wrong.

I know, too, that from many a sage and worthy matron my Olive has for ever earned her condemnation, because at last discovering her mournful secret, she did not strive in horror and shame to root out this misplaced love. Then, after years of cruel self-martyrdom, she might at last have pointed to her heart's trampled garden, and said, 'Look what I have had strength to do!' But from such a wrecked and blasted soil what aftergrowth could ever spring?

Better, a thousand times, that a woman to whom this doom has come, should lift her brow and gaze upon it without fear. It is vain to wrestle with it—she cannot! Let her meet it as she would meet death—solemnly, calmly, patiently. Then let her draw nigh and look upon the bier of her life's dead hope, until the pale image grows beautiful as sleep; or, per-chance, at last rises from the clay, transfigured into a likeness no longer human, but divine.

It is time that we women should begin to teach and to think thus. It is meet that we—maidens, wives, mothers, to whom the lines have fallen in more pleasant places—should turn and look on that pale sisterhood—some carrying meekly to the grave their heavy unuttered secret, some living unto old age, to bear the world's smile of pity, even of derision, over an 'unfortunate attachment'. Others, perhaps, furnishing a text where-upon prudent mothers may lesson romantic daughters, saying, 'See that you be not like these "foolish virgins"; give not *your* heart away in requital of fancied love; or, madder still, in worship of ideal goodness—give it for nothing but the safe barter of a speedy settlement, a comfort-able income, a husband, and a ring.'

Olive Rothesay, pale virgin martyr! hide the arrow close in thy soul—lay over it thy folded hands and look upwards. Far purer art thou than many a young creature, married without love, living on in decent dignity as the mother of her lord's children, the convenient mistress of his household, and so sinking down into the grave, a pattern of all matronly virtue. But thou, unwedded and childless woman, envy her not! A thou-sand times holier and happier than such a destiny is that silent lonely lot of thine.

With meekness, yet with courage, Olive Rothesay prepared to live her appointed life. At first it seemed very bitter, as must needs be. Youth, while it is still youth, cannot at once and altogether be content to resign love. It will yearn for that tie which Heaven ordained to make its nature's completeness; it will shrink and quail before the long dull vista of a solitary, aimless existence. Sometimes, wildly as she struggled against such thoughts, there would come to Olive's fancy dreams of what her life might have been. The joys of lovers' love, of wedded love, of mother-love, would at times flit before her imagination; and her heart, still warm, still young, trembled to picture the lonely old age, the hearth blank and silent, the utter isolation from all those natural ties whose place not even the dearest bonds of adopted affection can ever entirely fill. But, when-ever these murmurings arose, Olive checked them; sometimes almost with a feeling of shame.

She devoted herself more than ever to her Art, trying to make it as once before the chief interest and enjoyment of her life. It would become the same again, she hoped. Often and often in the world's history had been noted that of brave men who rose from the wreck of some bitter love, and found happiness in their genius and their fame. But Olive had yet to learn that, with women, it is rarely so.

She felt more than ever the mournful change which had come over her, when it happened that great success was won by one of her later pic-tures—a picture unconsciously created from the inspiration of that sweet love-dream. When the news came—tidings which a year ago would have thrilled her with pleasure—Olive only smiled faintly, and a few minutes after went into her chamber, hid her face, and wept.

There was not, and there could not be, any difference made in her ordinary way of life. She still went to the Parsonage, and walked and talked with Harold, as he seemed always to expect. She listened to all his projects for the future—a future wherein she, alas! had no part. Eagerly she strove to impress this fact upon her mind—to forget herself entirely, to think only of him, and what would be best for his happiness. Knowing him so well as she did, and having over him an influence in which he seemed rather to rejoice, and which, at least, he never repelled, she was able continually to reason, encourage, and sympathize with him. He often thanked her for this, little knowing how every quiet word of hers was torn from a bleeding heart. Walking home with her at nights, as usual, he never saw the white face turned upwards to the stars—the eyes wherein tears burned, but would not fall; the lips compressed in a choking agony, or opened to utter calm ordinary speech, in which his ear detected not one tremulous or discordant tone. When he sat in the house, absorbed in anxious thought, little he knew what mournful looks were fastened on his face, as if secretly to learn by heart every beloved lineament, against the time which his visible likeness would be beheld no more.

Thus miserably did Olive struggle. The record of that time, its every day, its every hour, was seared on her heart as with a burning brand. Afterwards, she never thought of it but with a shudder, marvelling how she had ever been able to endure all and live.

At last the inward suffering began to be outwardly written on her face. Some people said—Lyle Derwent first—that Miss Rothesay did not look so well as she used to do. But indeed it was no wonder, she was so engrossed in her painting, and worked far too much for her strength. Olive neither dissented nor denied; but she never complained, and still went painting on. Harold himself saw she was ill, and sometimes treated her with almost brotherly tenderness. Often he noticed her pale face, paler than ever beneath his eye, or in wrapping her from the cold observed how she shivered and trembled. And then Olive would go home and cry out in her misery.

'How long, how long? Oh, that this struggle might cease, or else I die!'

She was quite alone at the Dell now, for Mrs Fludyer had paid a flying visit home, and had taken back with her both Christal and the somewhat unwilling Lyle. Solitude, once sweet and profitable, now grew fearful unto Olive's tortured mind. And to escape it she had no resource, but that which she knew was to her like a poison-draught, and for which she yet thirsted evermore—the daily welcome at the Parsonage. But the web of circumstance, which she herself seemed to have no power to break, was at length apparently broken for her. One day she received a letter from her father's aunt. Mrs Flora Rothesay, inviting, nay entreating her to visit Edinburgh, that the old lady might look upon the last of her race.

For a moment Olive blessed this chance of quitting the scenes now become so painful. But then, Harold might need her. In his present conflict of feeling and of purpose he had no confidant save herself. She would have braved years of suffering, if her presence could have yielded him one hour's relief from care. But of this she must judge, so she set off at once to the Parsonage.

'Well, my dear,' said Mrs Gwynne, with a smiling and mysterious face, 'of course you will go at once! It will do your health a world of good. Harold said so only this morning.'

'Then he knew?'

'Yes, your aunt wrote and told him. In fact, I half suspect him of originating the plan. So kind and thoughtful as he is, and such a regard as he has for you! You must certainly go, Olive.'

Then *he* had done it all. He could let her part from him, easily, as friend from friend. Yet, what marvel! They were nothing more. She never thought of opposing anything he seemed to wish, so she answered, quietly, 'I will go.'

She told him so when he came in; he appeared much pleased; and said, with more than his usual frankness,

'I should like you to know aunt Flora. You see, I call her *my* aunt Flora, too, for she is of some distant kin, and I have dearly loved her ever since I was a boy.'

It was something to be going to one whom Harold 'dearly loved'. Olive felt a little comfort in her proposed journey.

'Besides, she knows you quite well already, my dear,' observed Mrs Gwynne. 'She tells me Harold used often to talk about you during his visit with her this summer.'

'I had a reason,' said Harold, his dark cheek changing a little. 'I wished her to know and love her niece, and I was sure her niece would soon learn to love *her*.'

'Why, that is kind, and like yourself, my son. How thoughtfully you have been planning everything for Olive.'

'She will not be angry with me for that, will you, Olive?' he said, and stopped. It was the first time she had ever heard him utter her christian name. At the sound her heart leaped wildly, but only for an instant. The next, Harold had corrected himself, and said, '*Miss Rothesay*', in a distinct, cold, and formal tone. Very soon afterwards he went away.

Mrs Gwynne persuaded Olive to spend the day at the Parsonage. They two were alone together, for Harold did not return. But in the afternoon their quietness was broken by the sudden appearance of Lyle Derwent.

'So soon back from Brighton! Who would have thought it?' said Mrs Gwynne, smiling.

Lyle put on his favourite sentimental air, and muttered something about 'not liking gaiety, and never being happy away from Farnwood'.

'Miss Rothesay is scarcely of your opinion, at all events she is going to try the experiment of leaving us for a while.'

'Miss Rothesay leaving us?' And Lyle, looking troubled and alarmed, came hastily to Olive's side.

'It is indeed, true,' she said, with an effort. 'You see I have not been well of late, and my kind friends are so anxious for me; and I want to see my aunt in Scotland.'

'Then it is to Scotland you are going—all that long dreary way! You may stay there weeks, months! and that while what will become of me— I mean, of us all at Farnwood?'

His evident regret touched Olive deeply. It was something to be missed, even by this boy—he always seemed a boy to her, partly because of old times, partly because he was so unsophisticated in mind and manner.

'My dear Lyle, how good of you to think of me in this manner! But indeed I will not forget you when I am away.'

'Oh no; I hope not! And you will not go and make other friends, and never come back to Farnwood? You promise that?' cried Lyle, eagerly.

Olive promised—with a sorrowful thought, that none asked this pledge, none needed it, save the affectionate Lyle!

He was still inconsolable, poor youth! He looked so drearily pathetic, and quoted such doleful poetry, that Mrs Gwynne, who in her matter-of-fact plainness had no patience with any of Lyle's 'romantic vagaries', as she called them, began to exert the dormant humour by which she always quenched his little ebullitions. Olive at last considerately came to the rescue, and proposed an evening stroll about the garden, to which Lyle eagerly assented.

There he still talked of her departure, but his affections were now tempered by real feeling.

'I shall miss you bitterly,' he said, in a low tone, 'but if your health needs change, and this journey is for your good, of course I would not think of myself at all.'

—The very expressions she had herself used to Harold! This coincidence touched her, and she half reproached herself for feeling so coldly to all her kind friends, and chiefly to Lyle Derwent, who evidently regarded her with such affection. But all other affections grew pale before the one great love. Every lesser tie that would fain come in the place of that which was unattainable, smote her with only a keener pain.

Still, half remorsefully, she looked on her old favourite, and wished that she could care for him more. So thinking, her manner became gentler than usual, while that of Lyle grew more earnest and less dreamy.

'I wish you would write to me while you are away, Miss Rothesay; or, at all events, let me write to you.'

'That you may; and I shall be so glad to hear all about Harbury and Farnwood.' Here she paused, half-shaming to confess to herself that for this reason chiefly would she welcome the letters of poor Lyle.

'Is that all? Will you not care to hear about *me*? Oh, Miss Rothesay,' cried Lyle, 'I often wish I was again a little boy in the dear old garden at Oldchurch.'

'Why so?'

'Because, because'—and some inexplicable feeling brought the quick blood, crimsoning his boyish cheek. 'No, no, I cannot tell you now; but perhaps I may, sometime,' he murmured.

'Just as you like,' answered Olive, absently. Her thoughts, wakened by the long-silent name, were travelling over many years; back to her old home, her happy girlhood. She almost wished she had died then, and never known this bitter love. But her mother!

'No, I am glad I lived to comfort *her*,' she mused. 'Perhaps it may be true that none ever pass from earth until their ministry here is no longer needed. So I will even patiently live on.'

Unable to talk more with Lyle, Olive re-entered the Parsonage. Harold sat there reading.

'Have you long come in?' she asked in a somewhat trembling voice.

He answered, 'About an hour.'

'I did not see you enter.'

'Of course not, you were too much engaged in conversation. Therefore I would not disturb you, but took my book.'

He spoke in the abrupt, cold manner he sometimes used. Olive thought something had happened to annoy him and in her gentle, womanly fashion, she sat down and talked with him until the cloud passed away.

Many times during the evening Lyle renewed his lamentations over Miss Rothesay's journey; but Harold never uttered one word of regret. Bitter, bitter was the contrast to Olive's heart. When she departed, however, Mr Gwynne offered to accompany her home.

'You need not. It is a cold night, and I have Lyle's kindness to depend upon.'

'Very well, since you choose it so,' and he sat down again. But Olive saw she had wounded his pride—*only* his pride;—she said this to her heart, to keep down its unconscious thrill. Yet never for a moment would she grieve him in anything; so she went up to him with a sweet, contrite look,

'You know I am always glad to talk to you, and be with you, my dear friend. We shall not have many more walks home together, therefore will you come?'

And he came. Moreover, he contrived to keep her beside him. Lyle, poor fellow, went whistling in solitude down the other side of the road, until at the Dell he said goodnight, and vanished.

Harold had talked all the way on indifferent subjects, never once alluding to Olive's departure. He did so now, however, but carelessly, as if with an accidental thought.

'I wonder whether you will return to Harbury before I start for

Heidelberg*—that is, if I should really go. I should like to see you once again. Well, chance must decide.'

Chance! when she would have controlled all accidents, provided against all hindrances, woven together all purposes, to be with him for one single day!

At once the thought broke through the happy spell which, for the time, his kindness had laid upon her. She felt that it was *only* kindness; and as such, he meant it, no more! In his breast was not the faintest echo of the devotion which filled her own. A sense of womanly pride arose, and with it a pang of womanly shame. These lasted while she bade him goodnight, somewhat coldly; then both sank at once, and there remained to her nothing but helpless sorrow.

She listened, as she ever did, for the last sound of his footsteps down the road. But she heard them not; and thought, half-sighing, how quickly he must have walked away! What if an hour hence she had seen or known—but how could she, with her poor heart crushed beneath the weight of a love so great, yet so humble—her eyes blinded with the mist of perpetual tears?

A very few days intervened between Miss Rothesay's final decision and her departure. During this time, she only once saw Harold Gwynne. She thought he might have met her a little oftener, seeing they were so soon to part. But he did not; and the pain she suffered from this warned her that all was chancing for the best. Her health failing—her cheerful spirit broken—even her meek temper growing embittered with this mournful struggle, she saw that in some way or other it must be ended. She was thankful that all things had arranged themselves so plainly before her feet. There was a Father's care over her still. Though, remembering her own unworthiness, and feeling that this intense human love had been nigh unto idolatry,—often when she knelt down at night she could offer unto Heaven nothing but speechless tears.

There was planned no farewell meeting at the Parsonage; but Mrs Gwynne spent at the Dell the evening before Olive's departure. Harold would have come, his mother said, but he had some important matters to arrange; he would, however, appear some time that evening. However, it grew late, and still his welcome knock was not heard. At last there sounded one; it was only Lyle, who came to bid Miss Rothesay goodbye. He did so, dolorously enough, but Olive scarce felt any pain. The one pang absorbed all the rest.

'It is of no use waiting,' said Mrs Gwynne. 'I think I will go home with Lyle—that is, if he will take my son's place for the occasion. It is not quite right of Harold; he does not usually forget his mother.'

Olive unconsciously urged some excuse. She was ever prone to do so, when any shadow of blame fell on Harold.

'You are always good, my dear. But still he might have come, even for the sake of proper courtesy to you.'

Courtesy! Alas! a poor balm for the breaking heart!

Mrs Gwynne entreated Olive to call at the Parsonage on her journey next morning. It would not hinder her a minute. Little Ailie was longing for one goodbye, and perhaps she might likewise see Harold. Miss Rothesay assented. It would have been so hard to go away without one more look at the beloved face—one more clasp of the beloved hand.

Yet both seemed denied her. Trembling with the excitement of parting from home, and of taking that long journey—her first journey alone—Olive reached the Parsonage. But Harold was not there. He had gone out riding, little Ailie thought; no one else knew anything about him.

'It was very wrong and unkind,' said Mrs Gwynne, in real annoyance.

'Oh no, not at all,' was all that Olive murmured. She took Ailie on her knee, and hid her face upon the child's curls.

'Ah, dear Miss Rothesay, you must come back soon,' whispered the little girl. 'We can't do without you. We have all been much happier since you came to Harbury; papa said so, last night.'

'Did he?'

'Yes; when I was crying at the thought of your going away, and he came to my little bed, and comforted me, and kissed me. Oh, you don't know how sweet papa's kisses are! Now, I get so many of them. Before he rode out this morning he gave me half-a-dozen here, upon my eyes, and said I must learn all you taught me, and grow up a good woman, just like you. What, are you crying? Then I will cry too.'

Olive laid her thin cheek to the rosy one of Harold's daughter; she wept, but could not speak.

'What kisses you are giving me, dear Miss Rothesay, and just where papa gives me them, too. How kind! Ah, I love you—I love you dearly,' murmured the little affectionate voice, haunting Olive long after she had torn herself away.

'God bless and take care of you, my dear child—almost as dear as though you had been born my own,' was Mrs Gwynne's farewell, as she bestowed on Olive one of her rare embraces. And then the parting was over.

Closing her eyes—her heart—striving to make her thoughts a blank, and to shut out everything save the welcome sense of blind exhaustion that was creeping over her; Olive lay back in the carriage, and was whirled from Harbury.

She had a long way to journey across the forest-country until she reached the nearest railway station. When she arrived, it was already late, and she had barely time to take her seat ere the carriages started. That moment her quick ear caught the ringing of a horse's hoofs, and as the rider leaped on the platform she saw it was Harold Gwynne. He looked round eagerly—more eagerly than she had ever seen him look before. The train was already moving, but they momently recognized each other, and Harold smiled—his own frank affectionate smile. It fell like a sunburst upon poor lonely Olive Rothesay.

Her last sight of him was as he stood with folded arms, intently watching the winding northward line. Fervently she blessed him in her faithful heart, that, giving so much, was content with so little; and then, feeling that this one passing sight of him had taken away half her pain, she was borne upon her solitary journey.

CHAPTER XXXVII

There is not in this world a more exquisite sight than a beautiful old age. It is almost better than a beautiful youth. Early loveliness passes away with its generation, and becomes at best only a melancholy tradition recounted by younger lips with a half-incredulous smile. But if one must live to be the last relic of a past race, one would desire in departing to leave behind the memory of a graceful old age. And since there is only one kind of beauty which so endures, it ought to be a consolation to those whom fate has denied the personal loveliness which charms at eighteen, to know that we all have it in our power to be beautiful at eighty.

Miss, or rather Mrs Flora Rothesay—for so she was always called— appeared to Olive the most beautiful old lady she had ever beheld. It was a little after dusk on a dull wet day, when she reached her journey's end. Entering, she saw around her the dazzle of a rich warm firelight, her cloak was removed by light hands, and she felt on both cheeks the kiss of peace and salutation.

'Is that Olive Rothesay, Angus Rothesay's only child? Welcome to bonnie Scotland—welcome, my dear lassie!'

The voice lost none of its sweetness for bearing, strongly and unmistakably, the 'accents of the mountain tongue', such as still lingers with ancient Scottish ladies. Mrs Flora used, without a trace of vulgarity, the tones and some of the phrases of her native Doric,* as spoken a century ago.

Surely the mountain breezes that rocked Olive's cradle had sung in her memory for twenty years, for she felt like coming home the moment she set foot in her father's land. She expressed this to Mrs Flora, and then, quite overpowered, she knelt and hid her face in the old lady's lap, and her excitement melted away in a soft dew—too sweet to seem like tears.

'The poor lassie! she's just wearied out!' said Mrs Flora, laying her hands on Olive's hair. 'Jean, rin awa' and get her some tea. Now, my bairn, lift up your face, and let me see ye. Ay, there it is—a Rothesay's, every line! and with the golden hair, too. Ye have heard tell o' the weird saying, about the Rothesays with yellow hair? No? Ah well, we'll no talk of it now.' And the old lady suddenly looked thoughtful—even somewhat grave. When Olive rose up, she made her bring a seat opposite to her own armchair, and there watched her very intently.

Olive herself noticed with curious eyes the outward likeness of her aunt. Mrs Flora's attire was quite a picture, with the ruffled elbow-sleeves and the long, square bodice, above which a close white kerchief hid the once lovely neck and throat of her whom old Elspie had chronicled—and truly—as 'the Flower of Perth'. The face, Olive thought, was as she could have imagined that of Mary Queen of Scots when grown old. But age could never obliterate the charm of the soft languishing eyes, the almost infantile sweetness of the mouth. Therein sat a spirit, ever young and lovely, because ever loving; smiling away all natural wrinkles—softening down all harsh lines. You regarded them no more than the faint shadows in a twilight landscape, over which the soul of peace is everywhere serenely diffused. There was peace, too, in the very attitude—leaning back, the head a little raised, the hands crossed, each folded round the other's wrist. Olive particularly noticed these little hands, shrunk but not withered. On the right was a marriage-ring, which had outlasted two lives, mother and daughter; on the left, at the wedding-finger, was another, a hoop of gold with a single diamond. Both seemed less ornaments than tokens—gazed on, perhaps, as the faint landmarks of a long past journey, which now, with its joys and pains alike, was all fading into shadow before the dawn of another world.

'So they called you "Olive", my dear,' said Mrs Flora. 'A strange name! the like of it is not in our family.'

'My mother gave it to me from a dream she had.'

'Ay, I mind it weel; Harold Gwynne told me, saying that Mrs Rothesay had told *him*. Was she, then, so sweet and dainty a creature—your mother? Once Angus spoke to me of her—little Sybilla Hyde. She was his wife then, though we did not know it. That was no richt. Poor Angus, we loved him very much—better than he thought. Tears again, my dearie? Then we'll speak nae mair o' the like o' that.

'And so you know my dear Alison Balfour. She was a deal younger than I, and yet you see we are both grown auld wives thegither. Little Olive— I think I will call you so, such a wee bit thing as you are—little Olive! know you that you have come to me on my birth day. The ae day I have lived just eighty years in a dark, dowie* world, as they ca' it. And yet 'tis no sae dark nor dowie while there's aye light in the life aboon.'*

The old lady reverently raised her pale blue eyes—true Scottish eyes—limpid and clear as the dew on Scottish heather. Cheerful they were withal, for they soon began to flit hither and thither, following the motions of Jean's 'eident hand' with most housewifely care. And Jean herself, a handmaid, prim and ancient indeed, but youthful compared to her mistress, seemed to watch the latter's faintest gesture with most affectionate observance. Of all the light traits which reveal character, none is more suggestive than the sight of a mistress whom her servants love.

After tea, Mrs Flora insisted on Olive's retiring for the night. 'I hae gi'en ye a room wi' a bonnie prospect owerlooking the Braid Hills.* They ca' them hills here; but oh! for the broad blue mountains sweeping in waves from the old castle in Perth. Night and day I was wearying to see them, for years after I came to live at Morningside. But ane must e'en dree one's weird!* My puir brother was dead and gane, and I had tint a' the rest of my kin, save some young folk in Edinburgh, that were sib to my mother—she was a Lowland woman, ye see. Thae puir bairns were wanting me sair, so I left the dear auld hame, for gude and a'!'

She always spoke in this rambling way, wandering from the subject, after the fashion of old age. Olive could have listened long to the pleasant stream of talk, which seemed murmuring round her, wrapping her in a soft dream of peace. She laid down her tired head on the pillow, with an unwonted feeling of calmness and rest. Even the one weary pain that ever pursued her sank into momentary repose. Her last waking thought was still of Harold; but it was more like the yearning of a spirit from another world than the passionate longing of one who struggles with the misery of a hopeless love.

Just between waking and sleeping Olive was roused by what seemed an almost spirit-like strain of music. Her door had been left ajar, and the sound she heard was the voices of the household, engaged in their evening devotion. The tune was that sweetest of all Presbyterian psalmody, 'plaintive Martyrs'. Olive caught some words of the hymn—it was one with which she had often been lulled to sleep in poor old Elspie's arms. Distinct and clear its quaint rhymes came back upon her memory now:

> The Lord's my shepherd, I'll not want,
>   He makes me down to lie
> In pastures green, and leadeth me
>   The quiet waters by.
>
> .   .   .   .   .   .
>
> Yea, though I walk in death's dark vale,
>   Yet will I fear none ill;
> For Thou art with me, and Thy rod
>   And staff me comfort still.

Poor lonely Olive lay and listened. Then rest, deep and placid, came over her, as over one who, escaped from a stormy wrack and tempest, falls asleep amid the murmur of 'quiet waters', in a pleasant land.

She awoke at morning, as if waking in another world. The clear cold air, threaded with sunshine, filled her room. It was the 'best room', furnished with a curious mingling of the ancient and the modern. The pretty chintz couch laughed at the oaken, high-backed chair, stiff with its century of worm-eaten state. On either side the fireplace hung two ancient engravings, of Mary Stuart and 'bonnie Prince Charlie', both garnished with verses, at once remarkable for devoted loyalty and eccentric rhythm. Between the two was Sir William Ross's sweet, maidenly portrait of our own Victoria.* Opposite, on a shadowy wall, with one sunbeam glinting on the face, was a large, well-painted likeness, which Olive at once recognized. It was Mrs Flora, then young Flora Rothesay, at eighteen. No wonder, Olive thought, that she was called 'the flower of Perth'. But strange it was, that the fair flower had been planted in no good man's bosom; that this lovely and winning creature had lived, bloomed, withered—'an old maid'. Olive, looking into the sweet eyes that followed her everywhere—as those of some portraits do—tried to read therein the foreshadowing of a life-history of eighty years. It made her dreamy and sad, so she arose and looked out upon the sunny slopes of the Braid Hills until her cheerfulness returned. Then she descended to the breakfast-table.

It was too early for the old lady to appear, but there were waiting three of four young damsels—invited, they said, to welcome Miss Rothesay, and show her the beauties of Edinburgh. They talked continually of 'dear Auntie Flora', and were most anxious to 'call cousins' with Olive herself, who, though she could not at all make out the relationship, was quite ready to take it upon faith. She tried very hard properly to inform herself concerning the three Miss M'Gillivrays, daughters of Sir Andrew Rothesay's half-sister's niece, and Miss Flora Anstruther, the old lady's third cousin and name-child, and especially little twelve-year-old Maggie Oliphant, whose grandfather was Mrs Flora's nephew on the mother's side, and first cousin to Alison Balfour.

All these conflicting relationships wrapped Olive in an inexplicable net; but it was woven of such friendly arms that she had no wish to get free. Her heart opened to the loving welcome; and when she took her first walk on Scottish ground, it was with a sensation more akin to happiness than she had felt for many a long month.

'And so you have never before seen your aunt,' said one of the M'Gillivrays;—for her life, Olive could not tell whether it was Miss Jane, Miss Janet, or Miss Marion, though she had tried for half-an-hour to learn the difference. 'You like her of course—our dear old Auntie Flora?'

'Aunt to which of you,' said Olive, smiling.

'Oh, she is everybody's Auntie Flora; no one ever calls her anything else,' observed little Maggie Oliphant, who, during all their walk, clung tenaciously to Miss Rothesay's hand, as most children were prone to do.

'I think,' said the quiet Miss Anstruther, lifting up her dreamy brown eyes, 'that in all *our* lives put together, we will never do half the good that Aunt Flora has done in hers. Papa says, every one of her friends ought to be thankful that she has lived an old maid!'

'Yes, indeed, for who else would have taken care of her cross old brother, Sir Andrew, until he died?' said Janet M'Gillivray.

'And who,' added her sister, 'would have come and been a mother to us when we lost our own, living with us, and taking care of us for seven long years?'

'I am sure,' cried blithe Maggie, 'my brothers and I used often to say, that if Auntie Flora had been young, and any disagreeable husband had come to steal her from us, we would have hooted him away down the street, and pelted him with stones.'

Olive laughed; and afterwards said, thoughtfully, 'She has then lived a happy life—has this good Aunt Flora!'

'Not always happy,' answered the eldest and gravest of the M'Gillivrays. 'My mother once heard that she had some great sorrow in her youth. But she has outlived it, and conquered it in time. People say such things are possible—I cannot tell,' added the girl, with a faint sigh—that of unbelieving youth just beginning to find out the difference between romance and reality. Olive thought how some other time she would have a little quiet talk with Marion M'Gillivray.

There was no more said of Mrs Flora, but oftentimes during the day, when some passing memory stung poor Olive, causing her to turn wearily from the mirth of her young companions, there came before her in gentle reproof the likeness of the aged woman who had lived down her one great woe—lived, not only to feel, but to impart cheerfulness.

A few hours after, Olive saw her aunt sitting smiling amidst a little party which she had gathered together, playing with the children, sympathizing with those of elder growth, and looked up to by old and young with an affection passing that of mere kindred. And then there came a balm of hope to the wounded spirit that had felt life's burden too heavy to be borne.

'How happy you are, and how much every one loves you!' said Olive, when Mrs Flora and herself were left alone, and their hearts inclined each to each with a vague sympathy. 'Yours must have been a noble woman's life.'

'I hae tried to mak it sae, as far as I could, my dear bairn,' answered the old lady. 'And a' the little good I hae dune has come back upon me fourfold. It is always so.'

'And you have been content—nay, happy?'

'Ay, I have! God quenched the fire on my own hearth, that I might learn to make that of others bright. My dear lassie, one's life never need be empty of love, even though, after seeing all near kindred drop away, one lingers to be an old maid of eighty years.'

CHAPTER XXXVIII

'No letters today from Harbury!' observed Mrs Flora to her niece, as, some weeks after Olive's arrival, they were taking their usual morning airing along the Queen's Drive. 'My dear, are you not wearying for news from home?'

'Aunt Flora's house has grown quite home-like to me,' said Olive, affectionately. It was true. She had sunk down, nestling into its peace like a tired, broken-winged dove. As she sat beside the old lady, and drank in the delicious breezes that swept across from the Lothians,* she was quite another creature from the pale drooping Olive Rothesay who had crept wearily up Harbury Hill. Still, the mention of the place even now took a little of the faint roses from her cheek.

'I am weel pleased that you are sae happy, my dear niece,' answered Mrs Flora; 'yet I wadna like that they should forget you at hame.'

'They do not. Christal writes now and then from Brighton, and Lyle Derwent indulges me with a long letter every week,' said Olive, trying to smile. She did not mention Harold; she would fain have hidden how much his silence grieved her. It felt like a mist of cold estrangement rising up between them. Yet—as sometimes she tried to think—perhaps it was best so! She would thus earlier learn to bear meekly the burden which must last through life.

'Alison Gwynne was aye the worst of all correspondents,' pursued the old lady, 'but Harold might write to you; I think he did so once or twice when he was living with me here, this summer.'

'Yes!' said Olive, 'we have always been good friends.'

'I ken that, my dearie. It wasna little that we talked about you. He told me all that chanced long ago atween your father and himsel. Ah, that was a strange, strange thing!'

'It was so. But we have never once spoken of it—neither I, nor Mr Gwynne.'

'Harold could not. He was sair grieved, and bitterly he repented having "robbed" you, as he ca'd it. But he was no the same man then that he is noo. She cost him muckle dule,* that gay young wife of his—fair and fause, fair and fause. It's ill for a man wha in his young days comes to love sic a woman. I would like unco weel to see my dear Harold wed to some leal-hearted lassie—winsome and winning. But I fear me it will never be.'

Thus the old lady's talk gently wandered on. Olive listened in silence, her eyes vacantly turned towards the wide open country that sweeps down from Duddingston Loch.* The yellow, harvest-clad valley smiled; but beneath the same bright sky the loch lay quiet, dark, and still. The sunshine passed over it, and entered it not. Olive wistfully regarded the scene which seemed a symbol of her own fate. She did not murmur at it, for day by day a solemn peace was gathering over her spirit. She tried to respond with cheerfulness to the new affections that greeted her on every side; to fill each day with those duties, that by the alchemy of a meek nature are so often transmuted into pleasures. Still, at her heart's core, lay ever one long sighing thought of Harold Gwynne.

The rest of the drive was rather dull, for Mrs Flora, usually the most talkative, cheerful old lady in the world, seemed disposed to be silent and thoughtful. Not sad—sadness rarely comes over the face of old age. All strong feelings, whether of joy or pain, belong to youth alone.

'Noo, my bairn, ye maun bide wi' Marion M'Gillivray the day,' said Mrs Flora, after a somewhat protracted silence. 'Twa young things thegither will be aye happier alane, than wi' an auld wifie like me.'

Olive disclaimed this, affirming, and with her whole heart, that she was never so happy as when with her good Aunt Flora.

''Tis pleasant to hear ye say the like o' that. Ye are a sweet, sweet lassie, Olive! But it must be even as I say—I hae kept this 20th of September in my ain house alane for five-and-forty year,' said the old lady, unconsciously gliding more than usual into the speech of her youth. And then she was silent until the carriage stopped at the house of the M'Gillivrays.

'I will see ye again the morn,' she once more observed, as her niece descended. And then, after looking up pleasantly to the window that was filled with a whole host of juvenile M'Gillivrays vehemently nodding and smiling, Aunt Flora pulled down her veil and drove away.

'I thought you would be given up to us for today,' said Marion, as she and Olive, now grown almost into friends, strolled out arm-in-arm along the shady walks of Morningside.

'Indeed! Did Aunt Flora say——'

'She said nothing—she never does. But for years I have noticed this 20th of September; because, when she lived with us, on this day, after teaching us in the morning, she used to go to her own room, or take a long, lonely walk, come back very pale and quiet, and we never saw her again that night. It was the only day in the year that she seemed to keep away from us. Afterwards, when I grew a woman, I found out why this was.'

'Did she tell you?'

'No; Aunt Flora never talks about herself. But from her maid and foster-sister, an old woman who died awhile ago, I heard a little of the story, and guessed the rest—we women easily can,' added quiet Marion, whose grave young brow already 'told a tale'.

'I think I guess, too. But let me hear,' said Olive Rothesay; 'that is, if I *may* hear.'

'Oh yes. 'Tis many, many years ago. Aunt Flora was quite a girl then, and lived with Sir Andrew, her elder brother. She had "braw wooers", in plenty, according to Isbel Graeme (you should have seen old Isbel, cousin Olive). However, she cared for nobody; and some said it was for the sake of a far-away cousin of her own, one of the "gay Gordons". But he was anything but "gay"—delicate in health, plain to look at, and poor besides. While he lived he never said to her a word of love; but after he died—and that was not until both were past their youth—there came to Aunt Flora a letter and a ring. She wears it on her wedding-finger to this day!'

'And this 20th of September must have been the day he died,' said Olive.

'I think so. But she never says a word, and never did.'

And the two walked on silently. Olive was thinking of the long woe-wasted youth—the knowledge of love requited come too late—and then of the noble spirit which after this great blow could gird up its strength and endure, for nearly fifty years. Ay, so as to find in life not merely peace, but sweetness. Her own path looked less gloomy to the view. From the depths of her forlorn heart uprose a feeble-winged hope; it came and fluttered about her pale lips, bringing to them

> The smile of one,
> God-satisfied; and earth-undone.*

Marion turned round and saw it. 'Cousin Olive! how very mild, and calm, and beautiful you look! Before you came, Aunt Flora told us she had heard you were "like a dove". I can understand that now. I think, if I were a man, I should fall in love with you.'

'With me; surely you forget! Oh no, Marion, not with me; that would be impossible!'

Marion coloured a little, but then earnestly continued, 'I don't mean any one who was young and thoughtless, but some grave, wise man, who saw your beautiful soul shining in your face, and learned, slowly and quietly, to love you for your goodness. Ay, in spite of—of—' (here the frank, plain-speaking Marion again hesitated a little, but continued boldly) 'any little imperfection which may make you fancy yourself different to other people. If that is your sole reason for saying, as you did the other day, that——'

'Nay, Marion, you have talked quite enough of me,' interrupted Miss Rothesay.

'But you will forgive me! I could hate myself if I have pained you, seeing how much I love you, how much every one learns to love you.'

'Is it so? Then I am very happy!' And the smile sat long on her face, until some chance word, or thought, awoke as ever the olden sting. Poor Olive! her spirit changed within her every hour. Yet how brave and meek a spirit it was, Heaven only knew!

'Can you guess whither I am taking you?' said Marion, as they paused before a large and handsome gateway. 'Here is the Roman Catholic convent—beautiful St Margaret's, the sweetest spot at Morningside. Shall we enter?'

Olive assented. Of late she had often thought of those old tales of forlorn women, sorrow-stricken or wronged, who, sick of life, had hidden themselves from the world in solitudes like this. Sometimes she had almost wished she could do the same. A feeling deeper than curiosity attracted her to the convent of St Margaret's.

It was indeed a sweet place; one that a weary heart might well long after. The whole atmosphere was filled with a soft calm—a silence like death, and yet a freshness as of new-born life. When the heavy door closed it seemed to shut out the world; and, without any sense of regret or loss, you passed, like a passing soul, into another existence.

They entered the little convent-parlour. There, from the plain, ungarnished walls, looked the two favourite pictures of Catholic worship; one, thorn-crowned, ensanguined, but still Divine; the other, bearing the pale endurance of womanhood, the Mother lifted above all mothers in blessedness and suffering. Olive gazed long upon both. They seemed meet for the place. Looking at them one felt as if all trivial earthly sorrows must crumble into dust before these two grand images of sublimated woe.

'I think,' said Miss Rothesay, 'if I were a nun, and had known ever so great misery, I should grow calm by looking at these pictures.'

'The nuns don't pass their time in that way I assure you,' answered Marion M'Gillivray. 'They spend it in making such things as these.' And she pointed to a case of quaint baby-like ornaments, pincushions, and artificial flowers.

'How very strange,' said Olive, 'to think that the interests and duties of a woman's life should sink down into such trifles as these. I wonder if the nuns are happy?'

'Stay and judge, for here comes one, my chief friend here, Sister Ignatia.' And Sister Ignatia—who was, despite her quaint dress, the most bright-eyed, cheerful-looking little Scotswoman imaginable—flitted in, kissed Marion on both cheeks, smiled a pleasant welcome on the stranger, and began talking in a manner so simple and hearty, that Olive's received notions of a 'nun' were quite cast to the winds. But after a while, there seemed to her something painfully solemn in looking upon the serene face, where not one outward line marked the inward current which had run on for forty years—how, none could tell. All was silence now.

They went all over the convent. There was a still pureness pervading every room. Now and then a black-stoled figure crossed their way, and vanished like a ghost. Sister Ignatia chattered merrily of their work, their beautiful flowers, and the pupils of the convent school. Happy, very happy, she said they all were at St Margaret's; but it seemed to Olive like the aimless, thoughtless happiness of a child. Still, when there came across her mind the remembrance of herself—a woman, all alone, struggling with the world, and with her own heart; looking forward to a life's toil for bread and for fame, with which she must try to quench one undying thirst—when she thus thought, she almost longed for such an existence as this quiet monotony, without pleasure and without pain.

'You must come and see our chapel, our beautiful chapel,' said sister Ignatia. 'We have got pictures of our St Margaret* and all her children.' And when they reached the spot—a gilded, fairy-like, flower-strewn, garden temple, she pointed out with great interest the various memorials of the sainted Scottish Queen.

Olive thought, though she did not then say, that good St Margaret, the mother of her people, the softener of her half-savage lord, the teacher and guide of her children, was more near the ideal of womanhood than the simple, kind-hearted, but childish worshippers, who spent their lives in the harmless baby-play of decking her shrine with flowers.

'Yet these are excellent women,' said Marion M'Gillivray, when, on their departure, Olive pursued her thoughts aloud. 'You cannot imagine the good they do in their restricted way. But still, if one must lead a solitary maiden life, I would rather be Aunt Flora!'

'Yes, a thousand, thousand times! There is something far greater and holier in a woman who goes about the world, keeping ever her pure nun's heart sacred to Heaven, and to some human memories; not shrinking from her appointed work, but doing it meekly and diligently, hour by hour, through life's long day; waiting until at eve God lifts the burden off, saying, "Faithful handmaid, sleep!"'

Olive spoke softly, but earnestly. Marion did not quite understand her. But she thought everything Miss Rothesay said must be true and good, and was always pleased to watch her the while, declaring that whenever she talked thus her face became 'like an angel's'.

Miss Rothesay spent the evening very happily, though in the noisy household of the M'Gillivrays. She listened to the elder girl's music, and let the younger tribe of 'wee toddling bairnies' climb on her knee and pull her long gold curls. Finally, she began to think that some of these days there would be a sweetness in becoming an universal 'Aunt Olive' to the rising generation.

She walked home, escorted valiantly by three stout boys, who guided her by a most circuitous route across Bruntsfield Links,* that she might gain a moonlight view of the couchant lion of Arthur's Seat.* They amused her the whole way home with tales of high school warfare. On reaching the garden-gate she was half surprised, yet glad, to hear the unwonted cheerfulness of her own laugh. The sunshine she daily strove to cast around her was falling faintly back upon her own heart.

'Goodnight, goodnight! Allan, and Charlie, and James. We must have another merry walk soon!' was her gay adieu as the boys departed, leaving her in the garden walk, where Mrs Flora's tall hollyhocks cast a heavy shadow up to the hall door.

'You seem very happy, Miss Rothesay,' said a voice. It came from some one standing close by. The next instant her hand was taken in that of Harold Gwynne.

But the pressure was very cold—scarcely that even of a friend. Olive's heart, which had leaped up within her, sank down heavily, so heavily, that her greeting was only the chilling words,

'I did not expect to see you here!'

'Possibly not; but I—I had business in Edinburgh. However it will not, I think, detain me long.' He said this sharply, even bitterly.

Olive, startled and overwhelmed by the suddenness of this meeting, could make no answer, but as they stood beneath the lamp she glanced at the face, whose every change she knew so well. She saw that something troubled him. Forgetful of all else, her heart fled to him in sympathy and tenderness.

'There is nothing wrong, surely! Tell me, are you quite well, quite happy? You do not know how glad I am to see you, my dear friend?'

And her little gentle hand alighted on his arm like a bird of peace. Harold pressed it and kept it there, as he often did; they were used to that kind of friendly familiarity.

'You are very good, Miss Rothesay. Yes, all is well at Harbury. Pray, be quite easy on that account. But I thought, hearing how merry you were at the garden gate, that amidst your pleasures here you scarcely remembered us at all.'

His somewhat vexed tone went to Olive's heart. Alas! and upon that wildly swelling heart was a mournful seal. She could not say anything more than the quiet words,

'You were not quite right there. I never forget my friends.'

'No, no! I ought to have known that. Forgive me; I speak rudely, unkindly; but I have so many things to embitter me just now. Let us go in, and you shall talk my ill humour away, as you have done many a time.'

There was a repentant accent in his voice as he drew Olive's arm in his. And she—she looked, and spoke, and smiled, as she had long learned to do. In the little quiet face, the soft, subdued manner, was no trace of any passion or emotion.

'Have you seen Aunt Flora,' said Olive, as they stood together in the house.

'No! When I came she had already retired. I have only been here an hour. I passed that in walking about the garden. Jean told me you would come in soon.'

'I would have come sooner had I known. How weary you must be after your journey! Come, take Aunt Flora's chair here, and rest!'

He did indeed seem to need rest. As he leaned back with closed eyes on the cushions she had placed, Olive stood and looked at him a moment. She thought, 'Oh, that I were dead, and become an invisible spirit, that I might lean over him and kiss his poor worn brow into peace. But I shall never do it. Never in this world!'

She pressed back two burning tears, and then began to move about the room, arranging little household matters for his comfort. She had never done so before, and now the duties seemed sweet and homelike, like those of a sister, or—a wife. Once she thought thus—but she dared not think again, or she could not have remained unmoved. And Harold was watching her, too; following her—as she deemed—with the vacant listless gaze of weariness. But soon he turned his face from her, and whatever was written thereon Olive read no more.

He was to stay that night, for Mrs Flora's house was always his home in Edinburgh. But he seemed disinclined to talk. One or two questions Olive put about himself and his journey to Heidelberg, but they seemed to increase his restlessness.

'I cannot tell; perhaps I shall go; perhaps not at all. We will talk the matter over tomorrow—that is, if you are still kind enough to listen.'

She smiled faintly. 'Little doubt of that, I think.'

'Thank you! And now I will say good night,' observed Harold, rising.

Ere he went, however, he looked down curiously into Olive's face.

'You seem quite strong and well now, Miss Rothesay. You have been happy here?'

'Happy—oh, yes! quite happy.' Poor heart! that was forced to coin the mournful falsehood.

'I thought it would be so—I was right! Though still—but I am glad, very glad to hear it. Goodnight.'

He shook her hand—an easy, careless shake; not the close, lingering clasp—how different they were! Then he went quickly upstairs to his chamber.

But hour after hour sped; the darkness changed to dawn, the dawn to light, and still Olive lay sleepless. Her heart, stirred from its serenity, again swayed miserably to and fro. Vainly she argued with herself on her folly in giving way to these emotions; counting over, even in pitiful scorn, the years that she had past her youth.

—'Three more, and I shall be a woman of thirty. Yet here I lie, drowning my pillow with tears, like a lovesick girl. Oh that this madness had visited me long ago, that I might have risen up from it like the young grass after rain! But now it falls on me like an autumn storm—it tears me, it crushes me; I shall never, never rise.'

When it was broad daylight, she roused herself, bathed her brow in water, shut out the sunbeams from her hot, aching eyes, and then laid down again and slept.

Sleeping, she dreamed that she was walking with Harold Gwynne, hand in hand, as if they were little children. Suddenly he took her in his arms, clasping her close as a lover his betrothed; and in so doing pressed a bright steel into her heart. Yet it was such sweet death, given lovingly amidst kisses and passionate tears, that, waking, she would fain have wished it true.

But she lifted her head, saw the sunlight dancing on the floor, and knew that morning was come—that she must rise once more to renew her life's bitter strife.

CHAPTER XXXIX

Olive dressed herself carefully in her delicate-coloured morning robe. She was one of those women who take pains to appear freshest and fairest in the early hours of the day; to greet the sun as the flowers greet him, rich 'in the dew of youth'. Despite her weary vigil, the balmy morning brought colour to her cheek and a faint sweetness to her heart. It was a new and pleasant thing to wake beneath the same roof as Harold Gwynne; to know that his face would meet her when she descended, that she would walk and talk with him the whole day long.

Never did any woman think less of herself than Olive Rothesay. Yet as she stood twisting up her beautiful hair, she felt glad that it *was* beautiful. Once she thought of what Marion had told her about some one saying she was 'like a dove'. Who said it? Not Harold—that was impossible. Arranging her dress, she looked a moment, with half-mournful curiosity, at the pale, small face reflected in the mirror.

'Ah, no! There is no beauty in me. Even did he care for me, I could give him nothing but my poor, lowly woman's heart. I can give him that still. There is something sweet and holy in pouring round him this invisible flood of love. It must bring some blessing on him yet; and, despite all I suffer, the very act of loving is blessedness to me!'

So thinking, she left her chamber.

It was long before the old lady's time for rising. There was no one in the breakfast-room, but she saw Harold walking on the garden terrace. Very soon he came in with some heliotrope in his hand. He did not give it to Olive, but laid it by her plate, observing, half-carelessly,

'You were always fond of my mother's heliotropes, Miss Rothesay.'

'Thank you for remembering my likings'; and Olive put the flowers in her bosom. She fancied he looked pleased; and suddenly she remembered the meaning given to the flower, 'I love you!' At the thought, she began to tremble all over; though contemning her own folly the while. Even had the words been true, she and Harold were both too old for such sentimentalities.

They breakfasted alone. Harold still looked pale and weary, nor did he deny the fact that he had scarce slept. He told her all the Harbury news, but spoke little of himself or of his plans. 'They were yet uncertain,' he said, 'but a few more days would decide all.' And then he remained silent until, a little time after, they were standing together at the window. From thence it was a pleasant view. Close beneath, a little fountain rose in slender diamond threads, and fell again with a soft trickling, like a Naiad's* sigh. Bees were humming over the richest of autumn flower gardens, which sloped down, terrace after terrace, until its boundary was hid in the little valley below. Beyond—looking in the pure September air so close that you almost see the purple of the heather—lay the Braid Hills, a horizon-line soft as that which enclosed the Happy Valley of Prince Rasselas.*

There came a trembling over Harold's features.

'How beautiful and calm this is! It looks like a little quiet nest—a *home* to comfort a man's tired heart and brain. Tell me, friend, do you think one could ever find such in this world?' said he, turning suddenly round upon Olive Rothesay.

'A home!' she repeated, somewhat confusedly; for his voice had startled her from a long, silent, secret gaze upon his face. 'You have often said that man needed none; that his life was in himself—in his intellect and his power. It is only we women who have a longing after rest and home.'

Harold made no immediate reply; but after a while he said,

'I want to have a quiet talk with you about—yes, about Heidelberg. And I long to see once more my favourite haunt, the Hermitage of Braid.* 'Tis a sweet place, and we can walk and converse there at our leisure. You will come?'

She never said him nay in anything, and he somehow unconsciously used a tone of command, like an elder brother—but there was such sweetness in being ruled by him! Olive obeyed at once; and soon, for the thousandth time, she and Harold were walking out together arm in arm.

If ever there was a 'lover's walk', it is that which winds along the burn-side in the Hermitage of Braid. On either side

The braes ascend like lofty wa's,*

shutting out all but the small blue rift of sky above. Even the sun seems slow to peep in, as if his brightness were not needed by those who walk in the light of their own hearts. And the little birds warble, and the little burnie* runs, as if neither knew there was a weary world outside, where many a heart, pure as either, grows dumb amidst its singing, and freezes slowly as it flows.

Olive walked along by Harold's side, like one in a happy dream. He looked so cheerful, so 'good',—a word she had often used, and he had smiled at—meaning those times when, beneath her influence, the bitter-ness melted from his proud and somewhat sarcastic spirit. Such times there were—else she could never have learned to love him as she did. Then, as now, his eyes were wont to lighten, and his lips to smile, and there came an almost angelic beauty over his face.

'I think,' he said, apparently forgetting Heidelberg and all pertaining thereto, 'I think my spirit is changing within me. I feel as if I had never known life until now. In vain I say unto myself, that this must be a mere fantasy of mine; I, who am marked with the "frost of eild", who will soon be—let me see—seven-and-thirty years old. What think you of that?'

His eyes, bent on her, spoke more than mere curiosity; but Olive, unaware, looked up and smiled.

'Why, I am getting an elderly dame myself; but I heed it not. One need mind nothing if one's heart does not grow old.'

'Does yours?'

'I hope not. I would like to lead a life like Aunt Flora's—a quiet stream, that goes on singing to the end.'

'Look me in the face, Olive Rothesay,' said Harold, abruptly. 'Nay—pardon me, but I speak like one athirst, who would fain know if any other human lips are ever satisfied. Tell me, do you look back on your life with content, and forward with hope? Are you happy?'

Olive's eyes sank on the ground.

'Do not question, me so,' she said, tremblingly. 'In life there is nothing perfect; but I have peace, great peace. And for you there might be not only peace, but happiness.'

Again there fell between them one of those pauses which rarely come save between two friends or lovers, who know thoroughly—in words or in silence—the speech of each other's hearts. Then Harold, guiding the conversation as he always did, changed it suddenly.

'I am thinking of the last time I walked here—when I came to Edinburgh this summer. There was with me one whom I regarded highly, and we talked—as gravely as you and I do now, though on a far different theme.'

'What was it?'

'One suited to the season and the place, and my friend's ardent youth. He was in love, poor fellow, and he asked me about his wooing. Perhaps you may think he chose an adviser ill fitted to the task.'

Harold spoke carelessly as it seemed; and waiting Olive's reply, he pulled a handful of red-brown leaves from a tree that overhung the path, and began playing with them.

'You do not answer, Miss Rothesay. Come, there is scarce a subject we have not discussed some time or other, save this. Let us, just for amusement, take my friend's melancholy case as a text, and argue concerning what young people call "love".'

'As you will.'

'A cold acquiescence! You think, perhaps, the matter is either above or beneath *me*—that I can have no interest therein?' And his eyes, bright, piercing, commanding, seemed to force an answer.

It came, very quietly and coldly.

'I have heard you say that love was the brief madness of a man's life; if fulfilled, a burden; if unfulfilled or deceived, a curse.'

'I said so, did I! Well, you give my opinions—what think you of *me*? Answer truly—like a friend.'

She did so! She never could look in Harold's eyes and tell him what was not true.

'I think you are one of those men in whom strong intellect prevents the need of love. Youthful passion you may have felt; but true, deep, earnest love you never did know, and, as I believe, never will! Nay, forgive me if I err; I only take you on your own showing.'

'Thank you, thank you! You speak honestly and frankly—that is something for a woman,' muttered Harold; and then there was a long, awkward pause. Oh, how one poor heart ached the while!

At last, fearing lest her silence annoyed him, Olive took courage to say, 'You were going to talk to me about Heidelberg. Do so now; that is, if you are not angry with me,' she added, with a little deprecatory soothing in her manner.

It seemed to touch him. 'Angry! how could you think so? I am never angry with you. But what do you desire to hear about Heidelberg—whether I am going, and when? Do you then wish—I mean, advise me to go?'

'Yes, if it is for your good! If leaving Harbury would give you rest on that one subject of which we never speak.'

'But of which I, at least, think night and day, and never without a prayer—(I can pray now)—for the good angel who brought light into my darkness,' said Harold, solemnly. 'That comfort is with me, whatever else may—— But you wanted to hear about Heidelberg?'

'Yes; tell me all. You know I like to hear.'

'Well, then, I have only to decide, and I might depart immediately. Mine would be a safe, sure course; but, at the beginning, I might have a hard struggle. I do not like to take any one to share it.'

'Not your mother, who loves you so?'

'No, because her love would be sorely tried. We should be strangers in a strange land; perhaps poverty would be added to our endurance; I should have to labour unceasingly, and my temper might fail. These are hard things for a woman to bear.'

'Oh, you do not know what a woman's affection is!' said Olive, earnestly. 'How could she be desolate when she had you with her! Little would she care for being poor! And if, when sorely tried, you were bitter at times, the more need for her to soothe you. We women can bear all things for those we love.'

'Is it so?' Harold said, thoughtfully, his countenance changing, and his voice becoming soft as he looked upon her. 'Do you think that any woman—I mean my mother, of course—would love *me* with this love?'

And once more, Olive, sealing up her bursting heart, answered calmly, 'I do think so.'

Again there was a silence. Harold broke it by saying, 'You would smile to know how childishly my last walk here haunts me; I really must go and see that love-stricken friend of mine. But you, I suppose, take no interest in his wooing?'

'Oh yes! I like to hear of young people's happiness,' said Olive, trying to wear an indifferent smile.

'But he was not quite happy. He did not know whether the woman he loved loved him. He had never asked her.'

'Wherefore not?'

'There were several reasons. First, because he was a proud man, and, like many others, had been deceived *once*. He would not again let a woman mock his peace. And he was right! Do you not think so?'

'Yes, if she were one who would do this. But no true woman ever mocked true love. Rarely, *knowingly*, would she give cause for it to be cast before her in vain. If your friend be worthy, how knows he but that she may love him all the while?'

'Well, well, let that pass. He has other reasons.' He paused and looked towards her, but Olive's face was drooped out of sight. He continued—'Reasons such as men only feel. Women know not what an awful thing it is to cast one's pride, one's hope—perhaps the weal or woe of one's whole life—upon a light "Yes" or "No" from the lips of a thoughtless girl. I speak,' he added, abruptly, 'as my friend, the youth in love, would speak.'

'Yes, I know—I understand. But tell me more,' said Olive, drawn with trembling interest to the subject.

'His other reasons were—that he was poor; that, if betrothed, he might have to wait years before they could marry; or perhaps, as his health was feeble, he might die, and never call her wife at all. Therefore, though he loved her as dearly as ever man loved woman, he deemed it right, and good, and just, to keep silence evermore.'

'Did he deem, even in his lightest thought, that she loved him?'

'He could not tell. Sometimes it almost seemed so.'

'Then he was wrong—cruelly wrong! He thought of his own pride, not of *her*. Little he knew the long, silent agony that she must bear—the doubt of being loved bringing even the shame of loving. Little he saw of the daily struggle: the poor heart sometimes frozen into dull endurance, and then wakened into miserable throbbing life by the shining of some hope, which passes and leaves it darker and colder than before. Poor thing—poor thing!'

And utterly forgetting herself, forgetting all but the compassion learnt from sorrow, Olive spoke with strong agitation.

Harold watched her intently. 'Your words are sympathizing and kind. Say on! What should he, this lover, do?'

'Let him tell her that he loves her—let him save her from the mournful struggle that wears away youth, and strength, and hope.'

'What! and bind her by a promise which may take years to fulfil?'

'If he has won her heart, she is already bound. It is mockery to talk, as the world talks, of the sense of honour that leaves a woman "free". Tell him so! Bid him take her to his heart, that, come what will, she may feel she has a place there. Let him not shame her by the doubt that she dreads poverty or long delay. If she loves him truly, she will wait years, a whole lifetime, until he claim her. If he labour, she will strengthen him; if he suffer, she will comfort him; in the world's fierce battle, her faithfulness will be to him rest, and help, and balm.'

'But,' said Harold, his voice hoarse and trembling, 'what if they should live on thus for years, and never marry? What if he should die?'

'Die!'

'Yes. If so, far better that he should never have spoken—that his secret should go down with him to the grave.'

'What, you mean that he should die, and she never know that he loved her! O Heaven! what misery could equal that!'

As Olive spoke, the tears sprang into her eyes, and, utterly subdued, she stood still and let them flow.

Harold, too, seemed strangely moved, but only for a moment. Then he said, very softly and quietly, 'Miss Rothesay, you speak like one who feels every word. These are things we learn in but one school. Tell me—as a friend, who night and day prays for your happiness—are you not speaking from your own heart? You love, or you have loved?'

For a moment Olive's senses seemed to reel. But his eyes were upon her—those truthful, truth-searching eyes. 'Must I look in his face and tell him a lie,' was her half-frenzied thought. 'I cannot, I cannot! And he will never, never know.'

She bowed her head, and answered, in a low, heart-broken murmur, one word—'Yes!'

'And, with a woman like you, to love once is to love for evermore?'

Again Olive bent her head, speechlessly—and that was all. There was a sound as of crushed leaves, and those with which Harold had been playing fell scattered on the ground. He gave no other sign of emotion or sympathy.

For many minutes they walked on slowly, the little laughing brook beside them seeming to rise like a thunder-voice upon the dead silence. Olive listened to every ripple, that fell as it were like the boom of an engulfing wave. Nothing else she heard, or felt, or thought, until Harold spoke.

His tone was soft and very kind, and he took her hand the while. 'I thank you for this confidence. You must forgive me if I did wrong in asking it. Henceforth I shall ask no more. If your life be happy, as I pray God it may, you will have no need of me. If not, hold me ever to your service as a true friend and brother.'

She stooped, she leaned her brow upon the two clasped hands—her own and his—and wept as if her heart were breaking.

But very soon all this ceased, and she felt a calmness like death. Upon it broke Harold's cold, clear voice—as cold and clear as ever.

'Once more, let me tell you all I owe you—friendship, counsel, patience—for I have tried your patience much. I pray you pardon me! From you I have learned to have faith in Heaven, peace towards men, reverence for woman. Your friendship has blessed me—may God bless you!'

His words ceased, somewhat tremulously; and she felt, for the first time, Harold's lips touch her hand. If she could have snatched his, buried it in her bosom, and poured out upon it her whole soul's love in one long kiss, she would have sunk down, and let life and being part from her as easily as from a sun-exhaled cloud.

Quietly and mutely they walked home; quietly and mutely, nay, even coldly, they parted. The time had come and passed; and between their two hearts now rose the silence of an existence.

CHAPTER XL

Olive and Harold parted at Mrs Flora's gate. He had business in town, he said, but would return to dinner. So he walked quickly away, and Olive went in and crept upstairs. There, she bolted her door, groped her way to the bed, and lay down. Life and strength, hope and love, seemed to have ebbed from her at once. She felt no power or desire to weep. Once or twice, she caught herself murmuring, half aloud,

'It is all over—quite over. There can be no doubt now.'

And then she knew, by this utter death of hope, that it must have lived *once*—a feeble, half-unconscious life, but life it was. Despite her reason, and the settled conviction to which she had tutored herself, she must have had some faint thought that Harold loved her, or would love her in time. Now, this dream gone, she might perhaps rise, as a soul rises from the death of the body, into a new existence. But of that she could not yet think. She only lay, motionless as a corse,* with pale hands folded, and eyes heavily closed. Sometimes, with a strange wandering of fancy, she seemed to see herself thus, looking down, as a spirit might do upon its own olden self, with a vague compassion. Once she even muttered, in a sort of childish way,

'Poor little Olive! Poor, crushed, broken thing!'

Thus she lay for many hours, sometimes passing into what was either a swoon or a sleep. At last, she roused herself, lifted her head, and saw by the shadows that it was quite late in the day. There is great mournfulness in waking thus of one's own accord, and alone; hearing the various noises of the busy midday household, and feeling as if all would go on just the same without thought of us, even if we had died in that weary sleep.

Olive wished she had!—that is, had Heaven willed it. She could so easily have crept out of the bitter world, and no one have missed her! Still, if it must be, she would try once more to lift her burden, and pursue her way.

There was a little comfort for her the minute she went downstairs. Entering the drawing-room, she met Mrs Flora's brightest smile.

'My dear lassie, welcome! I thocht the day unco lang without ye. But ye're douf and dowie like. Hae ye no slept after your weary walk this morning?'

'This morning!' echoed poor Olive. She had half forgotten what had happened then, there had come such a death-like cloud between.

'Ye were baith away at the Hermitage, Harold tauld me. Ah! puir Harold, I am sair grieved for him.'

'Wherefore?' asked Olive, awaiting to hear some horrible thing. All misfortunes seemed to come so naturally now, she felt as though she would scarce have marvelled had they told her Harold was dead.

'Because I hae scarce seen aught o' my dear Harold, and he has gane awa'.'

'He is gone away,' repeated Olive, slowly, as her cold hands fell heavily on her lap. She gave no other sign.

'I am sair fashed aboot it,' continued the unconscious old lady. 'All is no richt wi' that laddie. He cam ben frae the toun, unco wearied like, and said he must gang awa' hame at once.'

'He was here then?'

'Only for a wee while. I would hae sent till ye, my dearie, but Jean thocht you were sleeping, and Harold said we had best not waken ye, for ye had seemed sair wearied. He couldna bide longer, so he bade me say fareweel to ye. Lassie—lassie, whar are ye gaun?' But Olive had already crept out of the room.

He was gone then. That last clasp of his hand was indeed the last. Oh, miserable parting! Not as between two who love, and, loving, can murmur the farewell, heart to heart, until its sweetness lingers there long after its sound has ceased; but a parting that has no voice—no hope—wherein one soul follows the other in a wild despair, crying—'Give me back my life that is gone after thee!' and from the void silence there comes no answer, until the whole earth grows blank and dark, like an universal grave.

For many days after *that* day, one of those which form the solemn epochs of life, Olive scarce lifted her head. There came to her some friendly physical ailment, cold or fever, so that she had an excuse to comply with Mrs Flora's affectionate orders, and take refuge in the quietness of a sick chamber. There, such showers of love poured down upon her, that she arose refreshed and calmed. After a few weeks, her spirit came to her again like a little child's, and she was once more the quiet Olive Rothesay, rich in all social affections, and even content, save for the one undying thirst which on earth could never be satisfied.

After a season of rest, she began earnestly to consider her future, especially with respect to her Art. She longed to go back to it, and drink again at its wells of peace. For dearly, dearly she loved it still. Half-smiling, she began to call her pictures her children, and to think of the time when they, a goodly race, would live, and tell no tale of their creator's woe. This Art-life—all the life she had, and all she would leave behind—must not be sacrificed by any miserable contest with an utterly hopeless human love. Therefore she determined to quit Harbury—and at once, before she began to paint her next picture. Her first plan had been to go and live in London, but this was overruled by Mrs Flora Rothesay.

'Bide ye here wi' me, my dear niece. Come and dwell amang your ain folk, your father's kin. Ye'll be aye happy, for ye are dearly loved.'

And so it was at last fixed to be. But first Olive must go back to Farnwood, to wind up the affairs of her little household, and to arrange about Christal. She had lately thought a good deal of this young girl; chiefly, perhaps, because she was now so eagerly clinging to every interest that could occupy her future life. She remembered, with a little compunction, how her heart had sprung to Christal on her first coming, and how that sympathy had slowly died away, possibly from its being so lightly reciprocated. Though nominally one of the household at the Dell, Miss Manners had gradually receded from it; so that by degrees the interest with which Olive had once regarded her, melted down into the quiet, duty-bound liking of an ordinary domestic tie. Whether this should be continued became now a matter of question. Olive felt almost indifferent on the subject, but determined that Christal herself should decide. She never would give up the girl, not even to go and live in the dear quiet household of Aunt Flora. Having thus far made up her mind, Miss Rothesay fixed the day for her return to Farnwood—a return looked forward to with a mixture of fear and yearning. But the trial must be borne. It could not be for long.

Ever since his departure Olive had never heard the sound of Harold's name. Mrs Flora did not talk of him at all. This, her niece thought, sprang from the natural forgetfulness of old age, which, even when least selfish, seems unconsciously to narrow its interests to the small circle of its own simple daily life. But perhaps the old lady was more quick-sighted than Olive dreamed; for such a true and tried woman's heart could hardly be quite frozen, even with the apathy of eighty years.

A few days before Olive's journey Mrs Flora called her into her own room.

'I've got ae thing or anither to say to ye, lassie; ye'll listen till 't, if sae be ye're no weary o' the clavers* of an auld, auld wife.'

'Aunt Flora!' said Olive, in affectionate reproach, and, sitting down at her feet, she took the withered hand and laid it on her neck.

'My sweet, wee lassie—my bonnie, bonnie birdie!' said the tender-hearted old lady, who often treated her grand-niece as if she were a child. 'And to think that for sae mony a year I should live here, and no ken that puir Angus had left a daughter. My bairnie, ye maun come back soon.'

'In a month, dear Auntie Flora.'

'A month seems unco lang. At eighty years one shouldna boast o' the morrow. That is why I ettle to tell ye now what rests on my mind. But dinna look sae feared—it's just naething ava.'

'Well, dear aunt, let me hear it now.'

' 'Tis anent the warldly gear that I will leave ahint me—ower muckle as some folk say. Maybe so—maybe not. I hae been aye careful o' the gude things Heaven lent.'

—She paused; but Olive, not quite knowing what to say, said nothing at all. Mrs Flora continued:

'God has gi'en me length o' days—I hae seen the young grow auld, and the auld perish. Some I wad fain hae chosen to come after me on earth hae gane awa' to heaven before me; some hae wealth eneuch, and need nae mair. Of all my kith and kin there is nane to whom the bit siller can do gude, but my niece Olive, and Harold Gwynne. Ye turn frae me—does that grieve ye, lassie? Nay, his right is no like your ain. But he comes of blood that was ance sib to ours. Alison was a Gordon by the mother's side.'

As Mrs Flora uttered the name, Olive felt a movement in the left hand that lay on her neck; the aged fingers were fluttering to and fro over the diamond ring. She looked up, but there was perfect serenity on the face. And, turning back, she prayed that the like peace might come to *her* in time.

'Afore ye came hither,' continued Mrs Flora, 'I thocht to mak Harold my heir, and that he should take the name of Gordon—for dearly I loed that name, in auld lang syne. But nae mair o' that. Ah, lassie! even in this warld God can wipe away all tears from our eyes, so that we may look clearly forth unto the eternal land.'

'Amen, amen!' murmured Olive Rothesay—aye, though while she uttered the prayer, her own tears blindingly rose. But her aunt's soft cold hand glided silently on her drooped head, pressing its throbbings into peace.

'I am wae to think,' continued the old lady, 'that ye are the last o' the Rothesay line. The *name* maun end, even should Olive marry.'

'I shall never marry, Aunt Flora! I shall live as you have done—God make my life equally worthy!'

And her eyes, full of solemn patience, met the penetrating gaze of her aunt.

'Is it e'en sae? Then, Olive, my child! God comfort thee with His peace.'

Mrs Flora said this, kissed her on the forehead, and asked no more. It might be that she divined all. Shortly afterwards, she again began to speak about her will. She wished to be just, she said, and to leave her property where it would be most required. Her heart inclined chiefly to her niece, as being a woman, struggling alone through the world; whereas Harold, firmly settled in his curacy, would not need additional fortune.

'Oh, but he does need it; you little know how sorely!' cried Olive.

'Eh, my dear? He, a minister—sae weel to do i' the warld! What mean ye?'

Olive drew back, afraid lest she had betrayed too much of the secret so painfully shared between her and Harold Gwynne. She trembled and blushed beneath the old lady's keen eyes. At last she said, beseechingly,

'Aunt Flora, do not question me—I cannot, ought not, to tell you any more than this—that there may come a time when this money might save him from great misery.'

'Misery aye follows sin,' said Mrs Flora, almost sternly. 'Has he dune wickedly in the sight o' God or man? Am I deceived in him, my dear Harold—poor Alison's Harold?'

'No, no, no! He is noble, just, and true. There is no one like him in the whole world,' cried Olive, passionately; and then stopped, covered with blushes. But soon the weakness passed, and she said, quietly though very earnestly, 'Listen to me, Aunt Flora, for this once. Harold Gwynne'—she faltered not over the name—'Harold Gwynne is, and will be always, my dear friend and brother. I know more of his affairs than any one else; and I know, too, that he may be in great poverty one day. For me, I have only my poor self to work for; and work I must, since it is the comfort of my life. As to this fortune, I need it not—how should I? I pray you leave all to him.'

Mrs Flora wrapped her arms round her niece without speaking—nor did she again refer to the subject, either then, or at any other time.

But the night before Olive left Edinburgh she bade her farewell with a solemn blessing—the more solemn, as it was given in words taken out of the Holy Book which she had just closed—words never used lightly by the aged and strict Presbyterian.

'The Lord bless thee and keep thee! The Lord cause His face to shine upon thee! *The Lord give thee thy heart's desire, and fulfil all thy mind.*'

Olive rose with an indescribable sense of hope and peace. As she left the room she looked once more at her aunt. Mrs Flora sat in her crimson chair, her hands laid on her knee, her face grave, but serene, and half lifted, as that of one who hearkens to some unseen call. A secret consciousness struck Olive that in this world she should never more hear the voice, or see the face, of one who had been truly a saint on earth.

It was indeed so.

CHAPTER XLI

Coming home!—coming home! In different hearts how differently sound the words! They who in all their wanderings have still the little, well-filled, love-expectant nest whereto they may wing their way, should think sometimes of the many there are to whom the whole wide world is all alike; whose sole rest must be in themselves; who never can truly say, 'I am going home', until they say it with eyes turned longingly towards a Home unseen.

Something of this mournfulness felt Olive Rothesay. It was dreary enough to reach her journey's end alone, and have to wait some hours at the small railway station; and then, tired and worn, to be driven for miles across the country through the gloomiest of all gloomy November days. Still, the dreariness passed, when she saw, shining from afar, the light from the windows of Farnwood Dell. As the chaise stopped, out came running old Hannah, the maid, with little Ailie too; while, awaiting her in the parlour, were Christal and Mrs Gwynne. *No one else!* Olive saw that in one moment, and blamed herself for having wished—what she had no right to hope—what had best not be.

Mrs Gwynne embraced her warmly—Christal with dignified grace. The young lady looked gay and pleased, and there was a subdued light in her black eyes which almost softened them into sweetness. The quick, restless manner in which she had indulged at times since she came to Farnwood seemed melting into a becoming womanliness. Altogether, Christal was improved.

'Well, now I suppose you will be wanting to hear the news of all your friends,' said Miss Manners, with smiles bubbling round her pretty mouth. 'We are not all quite the same as you left us. To begin with—let me see—Mr Harold Gwynne—'

'Of that, Miss Christal, I will beg you not to speak. It is a painful subject to me,' observed Mrs Gwynne, with a vexed air. 'You need not look at me so earnestly, dear, kind Olive! All is well with me and with my son; but he has done what I think is not exactly good for him, and it somewhat troubles me. However, we will talk of this another time.'

'More news do you want, Olive?' (Christal now sometimes called her so.) 'Well, then, Dame Fortune is in the giving mood. She has given your favourite Mr Lyle Derwent a fortune of £1,000 a year, and a little estate to match!'

'I am so glad! for his sake, good dear Lyle!'

'*Dear* Lyle!' repeated Christal, turning round with a sparkle either of pleasure or anger in her glittering eyes; but it was quenched before it met those of Olive. 'Well, winning is one thing, deserving is another!' she continued, merrily. 'I could have picked out a dozen worthy, excellent young men, who would have better merited the blessing of a rich uncle, ay, and made a better use of his money, too.'

'Lyle would thank you if he knew,' said Mrs Gwynne.

'That he ought, and that he does, and that he shall do, every day of his life!' cried Christal, lifting up her tall figure with a sudden haughtiness, not the less real because she laughed the while; and then making one light bound, she vanished from the room.

Olive, left alone with Mrs Gwynne, would fain have taken her hands, and said, as she had oft done before, 'Friend, tell me all that troubles you—all that concerns you and *him*.' But now a faint fear repelled her. However, Harold's mother, understanding her looks, observed,

'You are anxious, my dear. Never was there such a faithful friend to me and to my son! I wish you had been here a week ago, and then you might have helped me to persuade him not to go away.'

'He is gone, then, to Heidelberg?'

'Heidelberg!—who mentioned Heidelberg?' said Mrs Gwynne, sharply. 'Has he told you more than he told me?'

Olive, sorely repentant for the words that had burst from her unwittingly, began to soothe the natural jealousy which she had aroused. 'You know well, Mr Gwynne has no nearer friend than his mother; only I have heard him talk of having friends at Heidelberg—of wishing to go thither.'

'He has not gone, then. He has started with his friend, Lord Arundale, to travel all through Europe. It is scarce meet, I think, for one of his cloth, and it shows a wandering and restless mind. I know not what has come over my dear Harold.'

'Was it a sudden journey?—is it long since he went,' said Olive, shading her eyes from the firelight.

'Only yesterday. I told him you were coming today; and he desired me to say how grieved he was that he thus missed you, but it was unavoidable. He had kept Lord Arundale waiting already, and it would not be courteous to delay another day. You will not mind?'

'Oh no! oh no!' The hand was pressed down closer over the eyes. No other word or gesture betrayed the cold sharp pain, not stilled even yet. Poor Olive!

Mrs Gwynne pursued. 'Though I have all confidence in my son, yet I own this sudden scheme has troubled me. His health is better—why could he not stay at Harbury?'

Olive, wishing to discover if she knew aught, or how much, of her son's sad secret, observed, 'It is a monotonous life that Mr Gwynne leads here—one hardly suited for him.'

'Ah, I know,' said the mother, sighing. 'His heart is little in his calling. I feared so long ago. But it is not that which drives him abroad; for I told him if he still wished to resign his duties to his curate, we would give up the Parsonage, and he should take pupils. There is a charming little house in the village that would suit us. But no, he seemed to shrink from this plan too; he said he must go away from Harbury.'

'And for how long?'

'I cannot tell—he did not say. I should think, not above a year—his mother may not have many more years to spend with him'; and there was a little trembling of Mrs Gwynne's mouth; but she continued with dignity: 'Do not imagine, Olive, that I mean to blame my son. He has done what he thought right. Against my wish, or my happiness, he would not have done it at all. So I did not let him see any little pain it might have given me. 'Twas best not. Now we will let the subject rest.'

But though they spoke no more, Olive speculated vainly on what had induced Harold to take this precipitate journey. She thought she had known him so thoroughly—better than any one else could. But in him lay mysteries beyond her ken. She could only rest on that sense, which had comforted her as she suffered—an entire faith in him and in all his goodness. While a woman has that, even the most hopeless or sorrow-tried love cannot be altogether bitterness.

Mrs Gwynne sat an hour or two, and then rose to return to the Parsonage. 'We must be home before it is dark, little Ailie and I. We have no one to take care of us now.'

There was a light trace of pain visible as she said this. When she took her grandchild by the hand, and walked down the garden, it seemed to

Olive that her step was less firm than usual. The heart so true to Harold sprang tenderly to Harold's mother.

'Let me walk with you a little way, Mrs Gwynne. I am thoroughly rested now; and as for coming back alone, I shall not mind it.'

'What a little trembling arm it is for me to lean on!' said Mrs Gwynne, smiling, when, after some faint resistance, she had taken Olive for a companion. ''Tis nothing like my Harold's, and yet I am glad to have it. I am afraid I shall often have to look to it now Harold is away. Are you willing, Olive?'

'Quite, quite willing!' And, oh! how glad, how thankful she felt, that her passionate devotion could expend itself upon one who was dear unto him!

Olive went nearly all the way to Harbury. She was almost happy, walking between Harold's mother and Harold's child. But when she parted from them she felt alone, quite alone. Then first she began to realize the truth, that the dream of so many months was now altogether ended! It had been something, even after her sorrow began, to feel that Harold was near; that, although days might pass without her seeing him, still he *was* there—within a few miles. Any time, sitting wearily in her painting-room, she might hear his knock at the door; or in any walk, however lonely and sad, there was at least the possibility of his face crossing her path, and, despite herself, causing her heart to bound with joy. Now, all these things could not be again. She went homeward along the dear old Harbury road, knowing that no possible chance could make his well-beloved image appear to brighten its loneliness; that where they had so often walked, taking sweet counsel together as familiar friends, she must learn to walk alone. Perhaps, neither there nor elsewhere would she ever walk with Harold more!

In her first suffering, in her brave resolve to quit Harbury, she had not thought how she should feel when all was indeed over. She had not pictured the utter blankness of a world wherein Harold was not. The snare broken and her soul escaped, she knew not how it would beat its broken wings in the dun air, meeting nothing but the black, silent waste, ready once more to flutter helplessly down into the alluring death.

Olive walked along with feet heavy and slow. In her eyes were no tears—she had wept them all away long since. She did not look up much; but still she saw, as one sees in a dream, all that was around her—the white, glittering grass, the spectral hedges, the trees laden with a light snow, silent, motionless, stretching their bare arms up to the dull sky. No, not the sky, that seemed far, far off; between it and earth interposed a mist, so thick and cold that it blinded sight and stifled breath. She could not look up at God's dear heaven—she almost felt that through the gloom the pitying Heaven could not look at her. But after a while the mist changed a little, and then Olive drew her breath, and her thoughts began to form themselves as she went along.

'I am now alone, quite alone. I must shut my life up in myself—look to no one's help, yearn for no one's love. What I receive I will take thankfully; but I have no claim upon any one in this wide world. Many pleasant friendships I have, many tender ties, but none close enough to fill the void in a soul that was ever thrilling with its store of passionate love. Once it spent them wildly, till Heaven said, "It is enough!" and took my idol. It has been the same once more. Now I must sweep out my heart's silent chamber, and keep it pure and empty for the Divine Guest.'

Over and over again she said to herself, 'I am alone—quite alone in the world'; and at last the words seemed to strike the echo of some old remembrance. But it was one so very dim, that for a long time Olive could not give it any distinct form. At last she recollected the letter which, ten years ago, she had put away in the secret drawer of her father's desk. Strange to say, she had never thought of it since. Perhaps this was because, at the time, she had instinctively shuddered at the suggestions it gave, and so determined to banish them. And then the quick-changing scenes of life had prevented her ever recurring to the subject. Now, when all had come true, when on that desert land which, still distant, had seemed so fearful to the girl's eyes, the woman's feet already stood, she turned with an eager desire to the words which her father had written— '*To his daughter Olive, when she was quite alone in the world.*'

Reaching home, and hearing Christal's light voice warbling some Italian song, Olive stayed not, but went at once to her own apartment, half parlour, half studio. There was a fire lit, and candles. She fastened the door that she might not be interrupted, and sat down before her desk.

She found some difficulty in opening the secret drawer, for the spring was rusty from long disuse, and her own fingers trembled much. When at last she held the letter in her hand, its yellow paper and faded ink struck her painfully. It seemed like suddenly coming face to face with the dead.

A solemn, anxious feeling stole over her. Ere breaking the seal, she lingered long; she tried to call up all she remembered of her father—his face—his voice—his manners. Very dim everything was! She had been such a mere child until he died, and the ten following years were so full of the action, passion, and endurance of much-tired womanhood, that they made the old time look pale and distant. She could hardly remember how she used to feel then, least of all how she used to feel towards her father. She had loved him, she knew, and her mother had loved him, ay, long after love became only memory. He had loved them, too, in his quiet way. Olive thought, with tender remembrance, of his kiss on that early morning when, for the last time, he had left his home. And for her mother! Often, during Mrs Rothesay's declining days, had she delighted to talk of the time when she was a young, happy wife, and of the dear love that Angus bore her. Something, too, she hinted of her own faults, which had once shadowed that love, and something Olive's own childish memory told her that this was true. But she repelled the thought, remembering that her father and mother were now together before God.

At length, with an effort, she opened the letter. She started to see its date—the last night Captain Rothesay ever spent at home—the night, which of all others, she had striven to remember clearly, because they were all three so happy together, and he had been so kind, so loving, to her mother and to her. Thinking of him on this wise, with a most tender sadness, she began to read:

OLIVE ROTHESAY—MY DEAR CHILD!

It may be many—many years—(I pray so, God knows!) before you open this letter. If so, think of me as I sit writing it—or rather as I sat an hour ago—by your mother's side, with your arms round my neck. And, so thinking of me, consider what a fierce struggle I must have had to write as I am going to do—to confess what I never would have confessed while I lived, or while your mother lived. I do it, because remorse is strong upon me; because I would fain that my Olive—the daughter who may comfort me, if I live—should, if I die, make atonement for her father's sins. Ay, sins. Think how I must be driven, thus to humble myself before my own child—to unfold to my pure daughter that—— But I will tell the tale plainly, without any exculpation or reserve.

I was very young when I married Sybilla Hyde. God be my witness! I loved her then, and in my inmost heart I have loved her evermore. Remember, I say this—hear it, as if I were speaking from my grave— Olive, *I did love your mother.* Would to Heaven she had loved me, or shown her love, only a little more!

Soon after our marriage I was parted from my wife for some years. You, a girl, ought not to know—and I pray may never know—the temptations of the world and of man's own nature. I knew both, and I withstood both. I came back, and clasped my wife to see the most loving and faithful heart that ever beat in a husband's breast. I write this even with tears—I, who have been so cold. But in this letter—which no eye will ever see until I and your mother have lain together long years in our grave—I write as if I were speaking, not in my own worldly self, but as I should speak then.

Well, between my wife and me there came a cloud. I know not whose was the fault—perhaps mine, perhaps hers; or, it might be, both. But there the cloud was—it hung over my home, so that I could find therein no peace, no refuge. It drove me to money-getting excitement, to amusement—at last to crime!

In the West Indies there was one who had loved me, in vain,—mark you, I said *in vain*—but with the vehemence of her southern blood. She was a Quadroon lady—one of that miserable race, the children of planters and slaves,* whose beauty is their curse, whose passion knows no law except a blind fidelity. And, God forgive me! That poor wretch was faithful unto me.

She followed me to England without my knowledge. Little she had ever heard of marriage; she cared nothing for mine. I did not love her—not with a pure heart as I loved Sybilla. But I pitied her. Sometimes I turned from my dreary home—where no eye brightened at mine, where myself and my interests were nothing—and I thought of this woman, to whom I was all the world. My daughter Olive, if ever you be a wife, and would keep your husband's love, never let these thoughts darken his spirit! Give him your whole heart, and he will ask no other. Make his home sweet and pleasant to him, and he will not stray from it. Bind him round with cords of love—fast—fast. Oh, that my wife had had strength so to encircle me!

But she had not; and so the end came! Olive, you are not my *only* child.

I have no desire to palliate my sin. Sin, I know it was, heavy and deadly; against God's law, against my trusting wife, and against that hapless creature on whom I brought a whole lifetime of misery. Ay, not on her alone, but on that innocent being who has received from me nothing but the heritage of shame, and to whom in this world I can never make atonement. No man can! I felt this when she was born. It was a girl, too—a helpless girl. I looked on the little face, sleeping so purely, and remembered that on her brow would rest through life a perpetual stain; and that I, her father, had fixed it there! Then there awoke in me a remorse which can never die. For, alas, Olive, I have more to unfold! My remorse, like my crimes, was selfish at the root, and I wreaked it on her, who, if guilty, was less guilty than I.

One day I came to her, restless, bitter in spirit, unable to hide the worm that was continually gnawing at my heart. She saw it there, and her proud spirit rose up in anger; she poured on me a torrent of reproachful words.

I answered them as one who had erred like me was sure to answer. Poor wretch! I reviled her as having been the cause of my misery. When I saw her in her fury, I contrasted her image with that of the pale, patient, trusting creature I had left that morning—my wife, my poor Sybilla—until, hating myself, I absolutely loathed *her*—the enchantress who had been my undoing. With her shrill voice yet pursuing me, I precipitately left the house. Next day mother and child had disappeared! Whither, I knew not; and I never have known, though I left no effort untried to solve a mystery which made me feel like a *murderer*.

Nevertheless, a feeling rests with me that they are still alive—these wretched two. If I thought not so, I should almost go mad at times.

Olive, have pity on your father, and hearken to what I implore. Whilst I live, I shall continue this search—but I may die without having had the chance of making atonement. In that case I entreat of my daughter Olive, who will, I foresee, grow up noble and virtuous among women, to stand between her father and his sin. If you have no other ties—if you never marry, but live alone in the world—seek out and protect that child! Remember, she is of your own blood—*she*, at least, never wronged you. In showing mercy to her, you do so to me, your father; who, when you read this, will have been for years among the dead, though the evil that he caused may still remain unexpiated. Oh! think that this is his voice crying out from the dust, beseeching you to absolve his memory from guilt. Save me from the horrible thought, now haunting me evermore, that the being who owes me life may one day heap curses on her father's name!

Herewith enclosed you will find instructions respecting an annuity I wish paid to—to the woman. It was placed in ——'s bank by Mr Wyld, whom, however, I deceived concerning it—I am now old enough in the school of hypocrisy. Hitherto the amount has never been claimed.

Olive, my daughter, forgive me! Judge me not harshly. I never would have asked this of you while your mother lived—your mother, whom *I loved*, though I wronged her so grievously. In some things, perhaps, she erred towards me; but I ought to have shown her more sympathy, and have dealt gently with her tender nature, so unlike my own. May God forgive us both!—God, in whose presence we shall both be, when you, our daughter, read this record. And may He bless you evermore, prays your loving father,

ANGUS ROTHESAY

In my shame, I have not yet written the name of that hapless woman. It was Celia Manners. To the child, I remember, she gave a remarkable name—I think, that of *Christal*.

It ceased—this voice from the ten-years'-silent grave of Angus Rothesay. His daughter sat motionless, her fixed eyes blindly out-gazing, her whole frame cold and rigid, frozen into the likeness of a statue of stone.

CHAPTER XLII

Riveted by an inexplicable influence, Olive had read the letter through, without once pausing or blenching—read it as though it had been some strange romance of misery, not relating to herself at all. She felt unable to comprehend or realize it, until she came to the name—'Christal'. Then the whole truth burst upon her, wrapping her round with a cold horror, and, for the time, paralysing all her faculties. When she awoke, the letter was still in her hand, and from it still there stood out clear the name, which had long been a familiar word. Therefore, all this while, destiny had been leading her to work out her father's desire. The girl who had dwelt in her household for months, whom she had tried to love, and generously sought to guide, was—*her sister*.

But what a chaos of horror was revealed by this discovery! Olive's first thought was of her mother, who had showered kindness on this child of shame; who, dying, had unconsciously charged her to 'take care of Christal'.

With a natural revulsion of feeling, Olive thrust the letter from her. Its touch seemed to pollute her fingers.

'Oh, my mother—my poor wronged mother!—well for you that you never lived to see this day. You—so good, so loving, so faithfully remembering him even to the last. But I—I have lived to shrink with abhorrence from the memory of my own father.'

Suddenly she stopped, aghast at thinking that she was thus speaking of the dead—the dead from whom her own life had sprung

'I am bewildered,' she murmured. 'Heaven help me! I know not what I say or do.' And Olive fell on her knees.

She had no words to pray with; but, in such time of agony, all her thoughts were prayers. After a while, these calmed her, and made her strong to endure one more trial—different from, perhaps even more awful than, all the rest.

Much sorrow had been her life's portion; but never until this hour had Olive Rothesay stood face to face with crime. She had now to learn the crowning lesson of virtue—how to deal with vice. Not by turning away in saintly pride, but by boldly confronting it, with an eye stern in purity, yet melting in compassion; remembering ever—

> How all the souls that were, were forfeit once;
> And He who might the vantage best have took
> Found out the remedy.*

Angus Rothesay's daughter read over once more the record of his sin. In so doing, she was struck with the depth of that remorse which, to secure a future expiation, threw aside pride, reserve, and shame. How awful must have been the repentance which had impelled such a confession, and driven a father to humble himself in the dust before his own child! She seemed to hear, rising from the long-closed grave, that mournful, beseeching cry, 'Atone my sin!' It silenced even the voice of her mother's wrongs.

This duty then remained, to fulfil which—as it would appear—Olive had been left alone on earth. The call seemed like that of fate; nay, she half-shuddered to think of the almost supernatural chance, which had arranged everything before her, and made her course so plain. But it had often happened so. Her life appeared, as some lives do, all woven about with mysteries; threads of guidance, first unseen, and then distinctly traced, forcing on the mind that sweet sense of invisible ministry which soothes all suffering, and causes a childlike rest on the Omnipotence which out of all evil continually evolves good.

With this thought there dawned upon Olive a solemn sense of calm. To lay down this world's crown of joys, and to take up its cross—no longer to be ministered unto, but to minister—this was to be her portion henceforth, and with this holy work was her lonely life to be filled.

'I will do it,' she cried. 'O, my poor father, may God have forgiven you, as my mother would, and as I now do! It is not mine to judge your sin; enough for me is the duty to atone it. How can this be best fulfilled?'

She sat long in silence, mournfully pondering. She tried to collect every scattered link of memory respecting what she had heard of Christal's mother. For such, she now knew, was the woman who, for the time, had once strongly excited her girlish imagination. That visit, and its incidents, now came vividly back upon her memory. Much there was which made her naturally revolt from the thought of this unhappy creature. How could it be otherwise with her mother's child? Still, amidst all, she was touched by the love of this other most wretched mother, who—living and dying—had renounced her maternal claim; and impressed upon her daughter's mind a feigned story, rather than let the brand of illegitimate birth rest upon the poor innocent.

Suddenly she heard from the next room Christal's happy, unconscious voice, singing merrily.

'My sister!' Olive gasped. 'She is my sister—my father's child!'

And there came upon her, in a flood of mingled compassion and fear, all that Christal would feel when she came to know the truth! Christal—so proud of her birth—her position—whose haughty nature, inherited from both father and mother, had once struggled wrathfully against Olive's mild control. Such a blow as this would either crush her to the earth, or, rousing up the demon in her nature, drive her to desperation. Thinking thus, Olive forgot everything in pity for the hapless girl—everything, save an awestruck sense of the crime which, as its necessary consequence, entailed such misery from generation to generation.

It seemed most strange that Christal had lived for so many years, cherishing her blind belief, nay, not even seeking to investigate it when it lay in her power. For since the day she returned from France, she had never questioned Miss Vanbrugh, nor alluded to the subject of her parentage. Such indifference seemed incredible, and could only be accounted for by Christal's light, careless nature, her haughtiness, or her utter ignorance of the world.

What was Olive to do? Was she to reveal the truth, and thus blast for ever this dawning life, so full of hope? Was her hand to place the stigma of shame on the brow of this young creature?—a girl too! There might come a time when some proud, honourable man, however loving, would scruple to take to his bosom as a wife one whose erring mother had never known that name. But then—was Olive to fix on her own soul the perpetual burden of this secret—the continual dread of its betrayal—the doubt, lest one day, chance might bring it to Christal's knowledge, perhaps when the girl would no longer be shielded by a sister's protection, or comforted by a sister's love?

While she struggled in this conflict, she heard a voice at the door.

'Olive—Olive!'—the tone was more affectionate than usual. 'Are you never coming? I am quite tired of being alone. Do let me into the studio?'

With a mazed, terrified look, Olive sprang to her desk and hid the letter therein. Then, without speaking—she had no power to speak—she mechanically unlocked the door.

'Well, I am glad to get at you at last,' cried Christal, merrily. 'I thought you were going to spend the night here. But what is the matter? You are as white as a ghost. You can't look me in the face. Why, one would almost imagine you had been planning a murder, and I was the "innocent, unconscious victim", as the novels have it.'

'You—a victim—alas! alas!' cried Olive, in fearful agitation. But by an almost superhuman effort, she repressed it, and added, quietly, 'Christal, my dear, don't mind me. It is nothing—only I feel ill—excited.'

'Why, what have you been doing?'

Well for Olive she could answer as she did, with truth, 'I have been sitting here alone—thinking of old times—reading old letters.'

'Whose? nay, but I will know,' answered Christal, half playfully, half in earnest, as though there were some distrust in her mind.

Again Olive murmured the truth: 'It was my father's—my poor lost father's.'

'Is that all? Oh, then don't vex yourself about any old father dead and gone. I wouldn't! Though, to be sure, I never had the chance. Little I ever knew or cared about mine,' added the girl, lightly.

Olive turned away, and was silent; but Christal, who seemed, for some reason best known to herself, to be in a particularly unreserved and benignant humour, said kindly, 'You poor little trembling thing, how ill you have made yourself! You can scarcely stand alone; give me your hand, and I'll help you to the sofa.'

But Olive shrank from the touch as if there had been a sting in the slender fingers which lay on her arm. She looked at them, and a circumstance, long forgotten, rushed back upon her memory—something she had noticed to her mother the first night that the girl came home. Tracing the beautiful hereditary mould of the Rothesay line, she now knew why Christal's hand was like her own father's.

A shiver of instinctive repugnance came over her, and then the mysterious voice of kindred blood awoke in her heart. She, the poor lonely one, took and passionately clasped that hand—the hand of *her sister*.

'O Christal! let us love one another—we two, who have no other tie left to us on earth,' she cried, weeping.

But Christal was rarely in a pathetic mood. She only shrugged her shoulders, and then stroked Olive's arm with a patronizing air. 'Come, your journey has been too much for you, and you had no business to wander off in that way with Mrs Gwynne; you shall lie down and rest a little, and then go to bed.'

But Olive shrank from night and its solitude. She knew there was no slumber for her. When she was a little recovered, feeling unable to talk, she asked Christal to read aloud.

The young lady looked annoyed. 'Pleasant! to be made a mere lady's companion! Miss Rothesay forgets who I am, I think,' muttered she, though apparently not meaning Olive to hear her proud speech.

But Olive did hear, and shuddered at the hearing.

Miss Manners carelessly took up the newspaper, and read the first paragraph which caught her eye. It was one of those mournful episodes which are sometimes revealed at the London police courts. A young girl—a lady swindler—had been brought up for trial there. In her defence came out the story of a life, cradled in shame, nurtured in vice, and only working out its helpless destiny—that of a rich man's deserted illegitimate child. The report added, that 'The convict was led from the dock in a state of violent excitement, calling down curses on her parents, but especially on her father, who, she said, had cruelly forsaken her mother. She ended by exclaiming that it was to him she herself owed all her life of misery, and that her blood was upon his head.'

'It *was* upon his head,' burst forth Christal, whose sympathies, as by some fatal instinct, seemed ever attracted by a case like this. 'If I had been that girl, I would have hunted my vile father through the world. While he lived, I would have heaped my miseries in his path, that everywhere they might torture and shame him. When he died, I would have trampled on his grave, and cursed him!'

She stood up, her eyes flashing, her hands clenched in one of those paroxysms of fierce emotion, which to her came so rarely, but, when roused, were terrible to witness. Her mother's soul was in the girl. Olive saw it, and from that hour knew that, whatever it cost her, the secret of Christal's birth must be buried in her own breast for evermore.

Most faithfully Miss Rothesay kept her inward vow, to watch over her sister evermore. But it entailed upon her the necessity of changing her whole plans for the future. For some inexplicable reason, Christal refused to go and live with her in Edinburgh, or, in fact, to leave Farnwood at all. Therefore Olive's despairing wish to escape from Harbury, and all its bitter associations, was entirely frustrated. It would be hard to say whether she lamented or rejoiced at this. The brave resolve had cost her much, yet she scarcely regretted that it would not be fulfilled. There was a secret sweetness in living near Harbury—in stealing, as it were, into a daughter's place beside the mother of him she still so fervently loved. But, thinking of him, she did not suffer now. For all great trials there is an unseen compensation; and this last shock, with the change it had wrought, made her past sorrows grow dim. Life became sweeter to her, for it was filled with a new and holy interest. It could be so filled, she found, even when love had come and vanished, and only duty remained.

She turned from all repining thoughts, and tried to make for herself a peaceful nest in her little home. And thither, above all, she desired to allure and to keep, with all gentle wiles of love, her sister. *Her sister!* Often, yearning for kindred ties, she longed to fall on Christal's neck, and call her by that tender name! But she knew it could never be, and her heart had been too long schooled in the patience of silent, self-denying, unrequited love, to murmur because in every human tie this seemed to be perpetually her doom. Her *doom*? Say, rather, her glory!

Harold Gwynne wrote frequently from Rome, but only to his mother. However, he always mentioned Miss Rothesay, and kindly. Once, when Mrs Gwynne was unable to write herself, she asked Olive to take her place, and indulge Harold with a letter.

'He will be so glad, you know. I think of all his friends there is none whom my son regards more warmly than you,' said the mother. And Olive could not refuse. Why, indeed, should she feel reluctance? He had never been her lover; she had no right to feel wounded, or angry at his silence. Certainly, she would write.

She did so. It was a quiet, friendly letter, making no reference to the past—expressing no regret, no pain. It was scarce like the earnest letters which she had once written to him—that time was past. She struggled to make it an epistle as from any ordinary acquaintance—easy and pleasant, full of everything likely to amuse him. She knew he would never dream how it was written—with a cold, trembling hand and throbbing heart, its smooth sentences broken by pauses of burning, blinding tears.

She said little about herself or her own affairs, save to ask that, being in Rome, he would contrive to find out the Vanbrughs, of whom she had heard nothing for a long time. Writing, she paused a moment to think whether she should not apologize for giving him this trouble. But then she remembered his words—almost the last she had heard him utter—that she must always consider him 'as a friend and brother'.

'I will do so,' she murmured; and despite all her pain at his silence, there was great sweetness in the thought. 'I will not doubt him, or his true regard for me. It is all he can give; and while he gives me that, I shall endure life contentedly, even unto the end.'

CHAPTER XLIII

It was mid-winter before the inhabitants of the Dell were visited by their friend, Lyle Derwent, now grown a rich and important personage. Olive rather regretted his apparent neglect, for it grieved her gentle spirit to suspect a change in any one whom she regarded. Christal only mocked the while, at least in outside show. Miss Rothesay did not see with what wild eagerness the girl listened to every sound, nor how every morning, fair and foul, she would restlessly start to walk up the Harbury road and meet the daily post.

It was during one of these absences of hers that Lyle made his appearance. Olive was sitting in her painting-room, arranging the contents of her desk. She was just musing, for the hundredth time, over her father's letter, considering whether or not she should destroy it, lest any unforeseen chance—her own death, for instance—might bring the awful secret to Christal's knowledge. Lyle's entrance startled her, and she hastily thrust the letter within the desk. From this cause in meeting him her manner was rather flustered, and her greeting scarce so cordial as she would have wished it to be. The infection apparently communicated itself to her visitor, for he sat down, looking decidedly agitated and uncomfortable.

'You are not angry with me for staying so long away, are you, Miss Rothesay?' said Lyle, when he had received her congratulations on his recent acquisitions. 'You don't think this change in fortune will make any change in my heart towards you?'

Olive half-smiled at his sentimental way of putting the matter, but it was the young man's peculiarity. So she frankly assured him that she had never doubted his regard towards her. At which poor Lyle fell into ecstasies of delight.

They had a long talk together about his dawning prospects, in all of which Olive took a warm and lively interest. He told her of his new house and grounds; of his plan of life, which seemed very Arcadian and poetical indeed. But he was a simple-minded, warm-hearted youth, and Miss Rothesay listened with pleasure to all he said. It did her good to see that there was a little happiness to be found in the world.

'You have drawn the sweetest possible picture of rural felicity,' she said, smiling; 'I earnestly hope you may realize it, my dear Lyle—— But I suppose one must not call you so any more, since you are now Mr Derwent, the young squire of Holly-wood.'

'Oh, no; call me Lyle, nothing but Lyle. It sounds so sweet from your lips—it always did, even when I was a little boy.'

'I am afraid I have treated you quite like a boy until now. But you must not mind it, for the sake of old times.'

'Do you remember them still?' asked Lyle, a tone of deeper earnestness stealing through his affectations of sentiment. 'Do you remember how I was your little knight, and used to say I loved you better than all the world?'

'I do, indeed. It was an amusing rehearsal of what you will begin to enact in reality some of these days. You, with your poetic vein, would make the beau ideal of a lover.'

'Do you think I should? Oh, Miss Rothesay, do you really think I should?' And then the poor youth's eagerness subsided into most girlish blushes, which positively caused Olive pain. She began to fear that, unwittingly, she had been playing on some tender string, and that there was more earnest feeling in Lyle than she had ever dreamed of. She would not for the world have jested thus, had she thought there was any real attachment in the case. So, a good deal touched and interested, she began to talk to him in her own quiet, affectionate way.

'You must not mistake me, Lyle; you must not think I am laughing at you. Nothing would make me happier than to see you a *true* lover, worthily loving and loved. But I did not know that you had ever considered these things. Tell me candidly—you know you may—do you think you were ever seriously in love with any one?'

Lyle drooped his head in almost painful confusion. 'It is very strange for you to ask me these questions.'

'Then do not answer them. Forgive me, I only spoke from the desire I have to see you happy; you, who are so mingled with many recollections; you, poor Sara's brother, and my own little favourite in olden time.' And speaking in a subdued and tender voice, Olive held out her hand to Lyle.

He snatched it eagerly. 'How I love to hear you speak thus! Oh, if I could but tell you all.'

'You may, indeed,' said Olive, gently. 'I am sure, my dear Lyle, you can trust me. Tell me the whole story.'

'—The story of a dream I had, all my boyhood through, of a beautiful, noble, winning creature, whom I reverenced, admired, and at last have dared to love,' Lyle answered, in much agitation.

Olive felt quite sorry for him. 'I did not expect this,' she said. 'You poetic dreamers have so many light fancies. My poor Lyle, is it indeed so? You, whom I should have thought would choose a new idol every month, have you all this while been seriously and heartily in love, and with one girl only? Are you quite sure it was but one?' And Olive, though her sympathies were warmly excited, was unable to reconcile this new revelation of Lyle with her old belief in his easy, thoughtless temperament.

He seemed now more confused than ever. 'Nobody can speak anything but truth to you,' he murmured. 'You make me tell you everything, whether I will or no. And if I did not, you might hear it from some one else, and that would make me very miserable.'

'Well, what was it?'

'That though I never loved but this my beautiful lady, once—only once, for a very little while, I assure you—I was half disposed to like some one else you know.'

Olive thought a minute, and then said, very seriously, 'Was it Christal Manners?'

'It was. She led me into it, and then she teased me out of it. But indeed it was not love—only a mere passing fancy.'

'Did you tell her of your feelings?'

'Only in some foolish verses, which she laughed at.'

'You should not have done that. It is very wicked to make any pretence about love.'

'Oh! dearest Miss Rothesay, you are not angry with me?' cried Lyle, bending over her in real emotion. 'Whatever my folly, you must know well that there is but one woman in the world whom I ever truly loved—whom I do love, most passionately! It is *yourself.*'

Olive looked up in blank astonishment. She almost thought that idle sentiment had driven him into some mad vagary. But he went on with an earnestness that could not be mistaken, though it was mingled with the extravagance of a boyish lover.

'All the good that is in me I learned from you when I was a little boy. I thought you an angel even then, and used to lie dreaming about you for hours. When I grew older, I made you into an idol. All the poetry I ever wrote was about you—your golden hair, and your sweet eyes. You seemed to me then, and you seem now, the most beautiful creature in the whole world.'

'Lyle, you are mocking me,' said Olive, in slow, sad speech.

'Mocking you! Oh, it is very cruel to tell me so,' and he turned away with an expression of deep pain.

Olive began to wake from the bewilderment into which his words had thrown her. But she could not realize the possibility of a young man like Lyle Derwent loving *her*, his senior by some years, many years older than he in heart; pale, worn, *deformed*. For the sense of personal defect which had so haunted her throughout her life, was present still, even against much evidence that might well have removed it from her mind. But when she looked again at Lyle, she regretted having spoken to him so harshly.

'Forgive me,' she said. 'All this is so strange; you cannot really mean it. It is utterly impossible that you can love me. I am old, compared with you; I have no beauty, nay, even more than that—' here she paused, and her colour sensitively rose.

'I know what you would say,' quickly added the young man. 'But I think nothing of it—nothing! To me you are, as I said, like an angel. I have come here today on purpose to tell you so; to ask you to share my riches, and teach me to deserve them. Dearest Miss Rothesay, listen to me, and be my wife?'

There was no doubting him now. The strong passion within him gave him dignity and manhood. Olive scarcely recognized in the earnest wooer before her, the poesy-raving, blushing, sentimental Lyle. A sense of pity, sorrow, pain, came over her. She had never dreamed of one trial—that of being loved by another as hopelessly as she herself loved.

'You do not answer, Miss Rothesay? What does your silence mean? That I have presumed too much! You think me a boy; a foolish, romantic boy; but I can love you, for all that, with my whole heart and soul.'

'Alas! alas! that it should be so. Oh, Lyle, would that you had never talked to me in this way; you do not know how deeply it grieves me.'

'It grieves you—you do not love me, then? Well,' he added, sighing, 'I could hardly expect it at once; but you will grant me time, you will let me try to prove myself worthy of you—you will give me hope to win you one day?'

Olive shook her head mournfully. 'It can never, never be! Lyle, dear Lyle, forget all. It is a wild, youthful dream; it will pass, I know it will. You will choose some young girl who is suited for you, and to whom you will make a good and happy husband.'

Lyle turned very pale. 'That means to say, that you think me unworthy to be yours.'

'No—no—I did not say you were unworthy; you are dear to me, you always were, though I never dreamed of this. It goes to my very heart to inflict even a momentary pain; but I cannot, cannot marry you!'

And then Olive, deeply agitated, hid her face and wept. Lyle moved away to the other end of the room. Perhaps, with manhood's love was also dawning manhood's pride.

'There must be some reason for this,' he said at last. 'If I am dear to you, though ever so little, a stronger love for me might come in time. Will it be so?'

'No, never, never!'

'Perhaps I am too late,' he continued, bitterly. 'You may have already promised your love. Tell me, I have a right to know.'

She blushed crimson, and then arose, a pale, sorrowful dignity resting on her brow. 'I think, Lyle, you go too far; I have given you no cause to pain me thus.'

'Forgive me, forgive me!' cried Lyle, melted at once, and humbled too. 'I will ask no more—I do not wish to hear. It is misery enough for me to know that you can never be mine, that I must not love you any more!'

'But you may regard me tenderly still. You may learn to feel for me as a sister—an elder sister, as I am most meet to be to you. You yourself will think so, in time.' And Olive truly believed what she said. Perhaps she judged him rightly: that this passion was indeed only a boyish romance, such as most men have in their youth, which fades painlessly in the realities of after years. But now, at least, it was most deep and sincere.

As Miss Rothesay spoke, once more as in his childish days Lyle threw himself at her feet, taking both her hands, and looking up in her face with the wildest adoration.

'I must—must worship you still; I always shall! You are so good—so pure; I look up to you as to some saint. I was mad to think of you in any other way. But you will not forget me; you will guide and counsel me, and be my life's angel. Only, if you should be taken away from me—if you should marry——'

'I shall never marry,' said Olive, uttering the words she had uttered many a time, but never more solemnly than now: 'Heaven made my life lonely. It must be so. I am content.' And her eyes—so mournful, yet so full of calm, passing Lyle, looked out beyond into the winter sky, where, dimly, Harbury church spire rose.

Lyle regarded her for a long and breathless space, and then, laying his head on her knees, he wept like a little child.

That moment, at the suddenly opened door there stood Christal Manners! Like a vision, she came—and passed. Lyle never saw her at all. But Olive did; and when the young man had departed, amidst all her own agitation, there flashed before her, as it were an omen of some woe to come—that livid face, lit with its eyes of fire.

Not long had Olive to ponder, for the door once more opened, and Christal came in. Her hair had all fallen down, her eyes had the same intense glare, her bonnet and shawl were still hanging on her arm. She flung them aside, and stood in the doorway.

'Miss Rothesay, I wish to speak with you; and that no one may interrupt us, I will do this.' She bolted and locked the door, and then clenched her fingers over the key, as if it had been a living thing for her to crush.

Olive sat utterly confounded. For in her sister's look she saw two likenesses; one, of the woman who had once shrieked after her the name of 'Rothesay',—the other, that of her own father, in his rare moments of passion, as she had seen him the night he had called her by that opprobrious word which had planted the sense of personal humiliation in her heart for life.

Christal walked up to her. 'Now tell me—for I *will* know—what has passed between you and—him who just now went hence.'

'Lyle Derwent?'

'Yes. Repeat every word—every word!'

'I cannot—I ought not. You are not acting kindly towards me,' said Olive, trying to resume her wonted dignity, but still speaking in a placable, quiet tone. 'My dear Christal, you are younger than I, and have scarcely a right to question me thus.'

'Right! When it comes to that, where is yours? How dare you suffer Lyle Derwent to kneel at your feet? How dare you, I say!'

'Christal—Christal! Hush!'

'I will not! I will speak. I wish every word were a dagger to stab you— wicked, wicked woman! who have come between me and my lover—for he is my lover, and I love him."

'Alas! alas! I feared it—I knew it,' murmured Olive.

'You knew it, and yet you stole him from me—you bewitched him with your vile flatteries. How else could he have turned from *me* to *you*?'

And lifting her graceful, majestic height, she looked contemptuously on poor shrinking Olive—ay, as her father—the father of both—had done before. Olive remembered the time well. For a moment a sense of wrong pressed down her compassion, but it rose again. Who was most injured, most unhappy—she, or the young creature who stood before her, shaken by this storm of rage?

She stretched her hands imploringly—'Christal, listen to me. Indeed, indeed, I am innocent of this wickedness. It is not my fault that Lyle Derwent sought me. I shall never marry him—never! I have just told him so.'

'He has asked you, then?'—and the girl almost gnashed her teeth— 'Then he has deceived me. No, I will not believe that. It is you who are deceiving me now. Could Lyle Derwent woo any one, and woo in vain?'

'What am I to do—how am I to convince you! Ah, me! how bitter this is!'

'Bitter! What, then, must it be to me? You did not think this passion was in me, did you? You judged me by that meek, cold-blooded heart of yours. But mine is all burning—burning! Woe be to those who kindled the fire.'

She began to walk to and fro, sweeping past Olive with angry strides. She looked, from head to foot, her mother's child. Hate and love, melting and mingling together, flashed from her black, southern eyes. But in the close mouth there was an iron will, inherited with her northern blood. Suddenly she stopped, and confronted Olive.

'You consider me a mere girl—you would mock me with my eighteen years. But I learned to be a woman early. I had need.'

'Poor child!—poor child!'

'How dare you pity me? You think I am dying for love, do you? But no! It is pride—only pride! Why did I not always scorn that pitiful boy? I did once, and he knows it. And afterwards, because there was no one else to care for, and I was lonely, and wanted a home—haughty, and wanted a position—I have humbled myself thus.'

'Then, Christal, if you never did really love him——'

'Who told you that? Not I!' she cried, her broken and contradictory speech revealing the chaos of her mind. 'I say, I did love him—more than you, with your cold prudence, could ever dream of! What could such an one as you know about love? Yet you have beguiled him, and allured him from me.'

'I tell you, no! Never till this day did he breathe one word of love to me. I can show you his letters.'

'Letters! He wrote to you, then, and I never knew it. Oh! how I hate you! I could kill you where you stand!'

She went to the open desk, and began searching there with her trembling hands.

'What—what are you going to do?' cried Olive, with sudden terror.

'To take those letters, and read them. I do it in your presence, for I am no dishonourable thief. But I will know everything. You are in my power—you need not stir or shriek.'

But Olive did shriek, for she saw that Christal's hand already touched the one fatal letter. A hope there was that she might pass it by, unconscious that it contained her doom! But no! her eye had been attracted by her own name, mentioned in the postscript.

'More wicked devices against me!' cried the girl, passionately. 'But I will find out this plot too,' and she began to unfold the paper.

'The letter—give me that letter. Oh Christal! for the happiness of your whole life, I charge you—I implore you not to read it!' cried Olive, springing forward, and catching her arm.

But Christal thrust her back with violence. ' 'Tis something you wish to hide from me; but I defy you! I *will* read!'

Nevertheless, in the confusion of her mind, she could not at once find the passage where she had seen her own name. She began, and read the letter all through, though without a change of countenance until she reached the end. Then the change was so awful, none could be like it, save that left by death on the human face. Her arms fell paralysed, and she staggered dizzily against the wall.

Trembling, Olive crept up and touched her; Christal recoiled and stamped on the ground, crying,

'It is all a lie, a hideous lie! *You* have done it—to shame me in the eyes of my lover.'

'Not so,' said Olive, most tenderly; 'no one in the wide world knows this, but we two. No one ever shall know it! Oh would that you had listened to me, then I should still have kept the secret, even from you! My sister—my poor sister!'

'*Sister*! And you are his child, his lawful child, while I—— But you shall not live to taunt me. I will kill you, that you may go to your father, and mine, and tell him that I cursed him in his grave!'

As she spoke, she wreathed her arms round Olive's slight frame, but the deadly embrace was such as never sister gave. With the marvellous strength of fury, she lifted her from the floor, and dashed her down again. In falling, Olive's forehead struck against the marble chimney-piece, and she lay stunned and insensible on the hearth.

Christal looked at her sister for a moment—without pity or remorse, but in a sort of motionless horror. Then she unlocked the door and fled.

CHAPTER XLIV

When Olive returned to consciousness she was lying on her own bed, the same whereon her mother had died. Olive almost thought that she herself had died too, so still lay the shadows of the white curtains, cast by the one faint night-lamp that was hidden on the floor. She breathed heavily in a kind of sigh, and then she was aware of some watcher close beside, who said, softly, 'Are you sleeping, my dear Olive?'

In her confused fancy, the voice seemed to her like Harold's. She imagined that she was dead, and that he was sitting beside her bier— sorrowfully—perhaps even in tenderness, as he might look on her, *then*. So strong was the delusion that she feebly uttered his name.

'It is Harold's mother, my dear,' said Mrs Gwynne, rather surprised. 'Were you dreaming of him?'

Olive was far too ill to have any feeling of self-betrayal or shame; nor was there any consecutive memory in her exhausted mind. She only stretched out her hands to Harold's mother with a sense of refuge and peace.

'Take care of me! Oh, take care of me!' she murmured; and as she felt herself drawn lovingly to that warm breast—the breast where Harold had once lain—she could there have slept herself into painless death, wherein the only consciousness was this one thought of him.

But, after an hour or two, the life within her grew stronger, and she began to consider what had happened. A horrible doubt came, of something she had to hide.

'Tell me, do tell me, Mrs Gwynne, have I said anything in my sleep? Don't mind it, whatever it be. I am ill, you know.'

'Yes, you have been ill for some days. I have been nursing you.'

'And what has happened in this house the while! Oh, where is Christal—poor Christal?'

There was a frown on Mrs Gwynne's countenance—a frown so stern that it brought back to Olive's memory all that had befallen. Earnestly regarding her, she said, 'Something has happened—something awful. How much of it do you know?'

'Everything! But, Olive, we must not talk.'

'*I* must not be left to think, or I should lose my senses again. Therefore, let me hear all that you have found out, I entreat you!'

Mrs Gwynne saw she had best comply, for there was still a piteous bewilderment in Olive's look. 'Lie still,' she said, 'and I will tell you. I came to this house when that miserable girl was rushing from it. I brought her back—I controlled her, as I have ere now controlled passions as wild as hers, though she is almost a demon.'

'Hush, hush!' murmured Olive. 'My sister, my poor wronged sister!'

'Ay, I learnt that too when I entered the room. But all is safe, for I have possession of the letter; and I have nursed you myself, alone.'

'Oh, how good, how wise, how faithful you have been!'

'I would have done all and more for your sake, Olive, and for the sake of your unhappy father. But, oh! that ever I should hear this of Angus Rothesay. Alas! it is a sinful, sinful world. Never knew I one truly good man, save my son, Harold.'

The mention of this beloved name fell on Olive's wandering thoughts like balm, turning her mind from the horror she had passed through. Besides, from her state of exhaustion, everything was growing dim and indistinct to her mind.

'You shall tell me more another time,' she said; and then sinking back on her pillow, still holding fast the hand of Harold's mother, she lay and slept till morning.

When, in the daylight, she recovered a little more, Mrs Gwynne told her all that had happened. From the moment that Christal saw her sister carried upstairs, dead, as it were—her passion ceased. But she exhibited neither contrition nor alarm. She went and locked herself up in her chamber, from whence she had never stirred. She let no one enter except Mrs Gwynne, who seemed to have over her that strong rule which was instinctive in a woman like Harold's mother. She it was who brought Christal her meals, and compelled her to take them; or else, in her sullen misery, the girl would, as she threatened, have starved herself to death. And though many a stormy contest arose between the two when Mrs Gwynne, stern in her justice, began to reprove and condemn, still she ever conquered so far as to leave Christal silent, if not subdued.

Subdued she was not. Night after night, when Olive was recovering, they heard her pacing up and down her chamber, sometimes even until dawn. A little her spirit had been crushed, Mrs Gwynne thought, when there was hanging over her what might become the guilt of murder; but as soon as Olive's danger passed, it again rose. No commands, no persuasions, could induce Christal to visit her sister, though the latter entreated it daily, longing for the meeting and reconciliation.

But for this sorrow there was great peace in Olive's illness, as there is in illness sometimes, especially after a long mental struggle. In the dreamy quiet of her sick-room, all things belonging to the world without, all cares, all sufferings, grew dim. Ay, even her mournful, hopeless love. It became sanctified, as though it had been an affection beyond the grave. She lay for hours together, thinking of Harold; of all that had passed between them—of his goodness, his tender friendship; of hers to him, more faithful than he would ever know; and sometimes there came to her an inward consciousness of the sacred self-devotion of a love like this, so that her heart was healed of the oftrecurring pang of shame.

It was very sweet, too, to be nursed so tenderly by Harold's mother— to feel that there was growing between them a bond like that of parent and child. Often Mrs Gwynne even said so, wishing that in her old age she could have a daughter like Olive; and now and then, when Olive did not see, she stole a penetrating glance, as if to observe how her words were received. Perhaps she too had gained some womanly quickness of perception, or at all events was indulging in some desire for the future of one she had learned to love so well.

One day when Olive was just able to sit up, and looked, in her white drapery and close cap, so like her lost mother—Mrs Gwynne entered with letters. Olive grew pale. To her fancy every letter that came to Harbury could only be from Rome.

'Good tidings, my dear; tidings from my Harold. But you are trembling.'

'Everything sudden startles me now. I am very weak, I fear,' murmured Olive. 'But you look so pleased!—All is well with him?' added she, trying to talk.

'All is quite well. He has written me a long letter, and here is one for you!'

'For me!' The poor pale face lighted up, and the hand was eagerly stretched out. But when she held the letter, she could not open it for trembling. In her feebleness, all power of self-control vanished. She looked wistfully at Harold's writing, and burst into tears.

In Mrs Gwynne's eyes there rose a troubled enquiry, not unmingled with pity. Her vague suspicion gained completeness every hour. She regarded Olive for a moment, as *his* mother would, jealous over her own claim, yet not blaming the one whose sorrow was 'loving where *she* did'. But she said nothing, or in any way betrayed the secret thus learnt. Perhaps, after all, she was proud that her son should be so truly loved, and by such a woman.

Leaning over Olive, she soothed her with beautiful tenderness. 'You are indeed too weak to hear anything of the world without. I ought to have taken better care of you, my dear child. Nay, never mind, because you gave way a little,' she said, seeing the burning blushes that rose one after the other in Olive's face. 'It was quite natural. The most trifling thing must agitate one who has been so very—very ill. Come, will you read your letter, or shall I put it by till you are stronger?'

'No, no, I should like to read it. He is very good to write to me,—very good indeed. I felt it the more from being ill; that is why it made me weep,' said Olive, faintly.

'Certainly, my dear; but I will leave you now, for I have not yet read mine. I am sure Harold would be pleased to know how glad *we both* are to hear from him,' said Mrs Gwynne, with a light but kindly emphasis. And then Olive was left alone.

Oh that Harold had seen her as she sat, her love-beaming eyes drinking in every written line! Oh that he had heard her broken words of thankful joy, when she read of his welfare! Then he might at last have felt what blessedness it was to be so loved; to reign like a throned king in a pure woman's heart, where no man had ever reigned before, and none ever would, until that heart was dust!

Harold wrote much as he had always done, perhaps a little more reservedly, and with a greater degree of measured kindliness. He took care to answer every portion of Olive's letter, but wrote little about himself, or his own feelings. He had not been able to find out the Vanbrughs, he said, though he would try every possible means of so doing before he left Rome for Paris. Miss Rothesay must always use his services in everything, when needed, he said, nor forget how much he was 'her sincere and faithful friend'.

'He is so, and will be always to me! I am content, quite content'; and she gazed down, calmly smiling at the letter on her knee. Fain would she have laid her cheek on the paper where Harold's hand had lain—a girlish impulse—but it passed. Her love was far too deep, too solemn, for any passionate outward show.

Yet this news from Rome seemed to have given her new life. Hour by hour she grew rapidly better, and the peace in her own heart made it the more to yearn over her unhappy sister, who, if sinning, had been sinned against, and who, if she erred much, must bitterly suffer too.

'Tell Christal I long to see her,' she said. 'Tomorrow I shall be quite strong, I think, and then I will go to her room myself, and never quit her until we are at peace.'

But Christal was deaf to all these her beseechings; no power, she declared, would induce her to meet Olive more.

'Alas! what are we to do?' cried Olive, sorrowfully; and the whole night, during which she was disturbed by the restless sounds in Christal's room, she lay awake, planning numberless compassionate devices to soothe and win over this obdurate heart. Something told her they would not be in vain; love rarely is! When it was almost morning, she peacefully fell asleep.

It was late when she awoke, and then the house, usually so quiet, seemed all astir. Hasty feet were passing in all directions, and Mrs Gwynne's voice, sharpened and agitated, was heard in the next room. Very soon she stood by Olive's bed, and told her troubled tale.

Christal had fled! Ere any one had risen, whilst the whole household must have been asleep, she had effected her escape. It was evidently done with the greatest ingenuity and forethought. Her door was still bolted, and she had apparently descended from the window, which was very low, and made accessible by an espalier. But the flight, thus secretly accomplished, had doubtless been long arranged and provided for, since all her money and ornaments, together with most of her attire, had likewise disappeared. In whatever way the mystery had been planned and executed, the fact was plain that it had thoroughly succeeded. Christal was gone; whither, there was at first not a single clue to tell.

But when afterwards her room was searched, they found a letter addressed to Miss Rothesay. It ran thus:

I would have killed myself, days since, but that I know, so doing, I should release you from a burden and a pang which I wish to last your life, as it must mine. Also, had I died, I might have gone to hell, and there met him whom I hate—my wicked, wicked father. Therefore I would not die.

But I will not stay to be tyrannized over, or insulted by hypocritical pity. I will neither eat your bread, nor live upon the cowardly charity of ——the man who is dead. I intend to work for my own maintenance; most likely, to offer myself as a teacher in the school where I was brought up. I tell you this, plainly; though I tell you, at the same time, that if you dare to seek me there, or drag me thence——. But no! you will be glad to be freed from me for ever.

One thing only I regret; that in justice to my own mother, I must no longer think tenderly of *yours*. For yourself, all is ended between us. Pardon I neither ask nor grant; I only say, Farewell.

CHRISTAL MANNERS

The letter was afterwards apparently reopened, and a hasty postscript added:

Tell Lyle Derwent that I have gone for ever; or, still better, that I am dead. But if you dare to tell him anything more, I will hunt you through the world but I will be revenged.

Mrs Gwynne read this letter aloud. It awoke in the stern, upright, God-fearing Scotswoman, less of pity, than a solemn sense of retributive justice, which she scarce could repress, even though it involved the condemnation of him whose memory was mingled with the memories of her youth.

But Olive, more gentle, tried to wash away her dead father's guilt with tears; and for her living sister, she offered unto Heaven that beseeching never offered in vain, a pure heart's humble prayers.

CHAPTER XLV

Many a consultation was held between Mrs Gwynne and Olive, as to what must be done concerning that hapless child: for little more than child she was in years, though her miserable destiny had nurtured in her so much of woman's suffering, and more than woman's sin. Yet still, when Olive read the reference to Mrs Rothesay, she thought there yet might be a lingering angel sitting in poor Christal's heart.

'Oh that some one could seek her out and save her, some one who would rule and yet soothe her; who, coming from us, should not be mingled with us in her fancy, so that no good influence might be lost.'

'I have thought of this,' answered Mrs Gwynne. 'But, Olive, it is a solemn secret—your father's, too. You ought never to reveal it, except to one bound to you by closest ties. If you married, your husband would have a right to know it, or you might tell your brother.'

'I do not quite understand,' said Olive; yet she changed colour a little.

Mrs Gwynne kindly dropped her eyes, and avoided looking at her companion as she said, 'You, my dear, are my adopted daughter; therefore, my son should be to you as a brother. Will you trust Harold?'

'Trust him? There is nothing with which I could not trust him,' said Olive, earnestly. She had long found out that praise of Harold was as sweet to his mother's heart as to her own.

'Then trust him in this. I think he has almost a right—or one day he may have.'

Mrs Gwynne's latter words sank indistinctly, and scarce reached Olive. Perhaps it was well; such light falling on her darkness might have blinded her.

Ere long the decision was made. Mrs Gwynne wrote to her son, and told him all. He was in Paris then, as she knew. So she charged him to seek out the school where Christal was. Sustained by his position as a clergyman, his grave dignity, and his mature years, he might well and ably exercise an unseen guardianship over the girl. His mother earnestly desired him to do this, from his natural benevolence, and for *Olive's sake*.

'I said that, my dear,' observed Mrs Gwynne, 'because I know his regard for you, and his anxiety for your happiness.'

These words thrilling in her ear, made broken and trembling the few lines which Olive wrote to Harold, saying how entirely she trusted him, and how she implored him to save her sister.

And now came back tenfold into Olive's bosom the measure she had meted unto Harold Gwynne. Her influence passing into his heart, had shaken it from its proud coldness, and disposed it to charity for all men. Her faith penetrating his soul, had purified and strengthened it into all goodness. Now, reclaimed himself, he was able to reclaim another.

'I am ready to do all you wish,' wrote Harold, in reply. 'O, my dear friend, to whom I owe so much, most happy should I be if in any way I could do good to you and yours!'

From that time, his letters came frequently and regularly. Passages from them will best show how his work of mercy sped.

PARIS, JAN.—I have had no difficulty in gaining admittance to the *pension*, for I chanced to go in Lord Arundale's carriage, and Madame Blandin would receive any one who came under the shadow of an English *milord.* Christal is there, in the situation she planned. I found out speedily—as she, poor girl, will find—how different is the position of a poor teacher from that of a rich pupil. I could not speak with her at all. Madame Blandin said she refused to see any English friends; and besides, she could not be spared from the schoolroom. I must try some other plan. . . . Do not speak again of this matter being 'burdensome' to me. How could it be so, when it is for you and your sister? Believe me, though the duty is somewhat new, it is most grateful to me for your sake, my dear friend.

. . . I have seen Christal. It was at mass. She goes there with some Catholic pupils, I suppose. I watched her closely, but secretly. Poor girl! a life's anguish is written in her face. How changed since I last saw it! Even knowing all, I could not choose but pity her. When she was bending before a crucifix, I saw how her whole frame trembled with sobs. It seemed not like devotion—it must be heartbroken misery. I came closer, to meet her when she rose. The moment she saw me her whole face blazed. But for the sanctity of the place, I think she could not have controlled herself. I never before saw at once such anger, such defiance, and yet such bitter shame. She turned away, took her little pupils by the hand, and walked out of the chapel. I dared not follow her; but many times since then I have watched her from the same spot, taking care that she should not see me. Who would think that haggard woman, sharp in manner, careless in dress—you see how closely I observe her—was the blithe Christal of old! But I sometimes fancied, even from her sporting, that there was the tigress nature in that girl. Poor thing! And she had the power of passionately loving, too. Ah! we should all be slow to judge. We never can look into the depths of one another's hearts.

*   *   *

. . . Christal saw me today. Her eye was almost demoniacal in its threatening. Perhaps the pity she must have read in mine only kindled her wrath the more. I do not think she will come to the chapel again.

*   *   *

. . . My dear Miss Rothesay, I do not like playing this underhand game—it almost makes me despise myself. Yet it is with a good intent; and I would do anything from my friendship for you.

I have heard much about your sister today from a little girl who is a *pensionnaire** at Madame Blandin's. But fear not, I did the questioning skilfully, nor betrayed anything. My friend, you know me well, as you say; but even you know not how wisely I can acquire one secret and hold fast another. An honourable school of hypocrisy I learnt this in, truly! But to my subject—Little Clotilde does not love her instructress. Poor Christal seems to be at war with the whole household. The richly paying pupil and the poor teacher must be very different in Madame Blandin's eyes. No wonder the girl is embittered—no marvel are those storms of passion, in which, according to Clotilde, she indulges, 'just as if she were a great English *miladi*, when she is nobody at all, as I told her once', said the triumphant little French girl.

'And what did she answer?' asked I.

'She went into a great fury, and shook me till I trembled all over; then she threw herself on her own bed, at one end of the dormitory, and all that night, whenever I woke, I heard her crying and moaning. I would have been very sorry for her, except that she was *only* the teacher—a poor, penniless *Anglaise*.'

This, my friend, is the lesson that Christal must soon have to learn. It will wring her heart, and either break it or soften it. But trust me, I will watch over her continually. Ill fitted I may be, for the duty is more that of a woman—such a woman as you are. But you have put something of your own nature into mine. I will silently guard Christal as if I had been her own brother—and yours.

* * *

... The crisis must be coming, from what the little girl tells me. Miss Manners and Madame Blandin have been at open war for days. Clotilde is in great glee since the English teacher is going away. Poor forlorn Christal, whither can she go? I must try and save her, before it is too late.

... I sit down at midnight to inform you of all that has happened this day, that you may at once answer and tell me what further I am to do. I went once more to visit Madame Blandin, who poured out upon me a whole stream of reproaches against Christal.

—'She was *un petit diable* always; and now, though she has been my own pupil for years, I would rather turn her out to starve than keep her in my house for another day.'

'But,' said I, 'you might at least find her some other situation.'

'I offered, if she would only tell me who she is, and what are her connections. I cannot recommend as governess a girl without friends—a *nobody*.'

'Yet you took her as a pupil.'

'Oh, Monsieur, that was a different matter; and then I was so liberally paid. Now, if you should be a relative——'

'I am not, as I told you,' said I, indignant at the woman's meanness. 'But I will see this poor girl, nevertheless, if she will permit me.'

'Her permission is no matter. No one cares for Miss Manners's whims now,' was the careless reply, as Madame ushered me into the deserted schoolroom, and then quickly vanished. She evidently dreaded a meeting with her refractory teacher. Well she might, for there sat Christal—but I will tell you all minutely. You see how I try to note down every trifle, knowing your anxiety.

Christal was sitting at the window, gazing at the high, blank, convent-like walls. Dull, helpless misery was in every line of her face and attitude. But the moment she saw me she rose up, her eyes darting fire.

'Have you come to insult me, Mr Gwynne? Did I not send you word I would see no one? What do you mean by haunting me in this way?'

I spoke to her very quietly, and begged her to remember I was a friend, and had parted from her as such only three months before.

'But you know what has happened since? Attempt not to deceive me—you do! I read it in your eyes long ago, at the chapel. You are come to pity the poor nameless wretch—the—— Ah! you know the horrible word. Well, do I look like that? Can you read in my face my mother's shame?'

She was half beside herself, I saw. It was an awful thing to hear her, a young girl, talk thus to me, ay, and without one natural blush. I said to her, gently, 'that I knew the unhappy truth; but, as regarded herself, it could make no difference of feeling in any right-judging mind, nor would with those who had loved her, and who now anxiously wished to hear from me of her welfare.'

'You mean your mother, who hates me as I hate her; and Olive Rothesay, whom I tried to murder!' (Friend, you did not tell me that.)

I drew back the hand I had offered. Forgive me, Olive!—let me this once call you so!—forgive me that I felt a momentary abhorrence for the miserable creature who might have taken your precious life away. My heart melts when I think of it. And you would not reveal the secret—even to me! Remembering this, I turned again to your sister; who cannot be altogether evil since she is dear to you. I said, and solemnly, I know, for I was greatly moved,

'Christal, from your own lips have I first heard of this wickedness, Your sister's were sealed, as they would have been on that other bitter secret. Are you not softened by all this goodness?'

'No! She thinks to crush me down with it, does she? But she shall not do so. If I grow wicked, ay, worse than you ever dream of, I shall be glad. It will punish her for the wrong her father did, and so I shall be revenged upon his child. Remember, it is all because of him! As to his daughter, I could have loved her once, until she came between me and——'

'I know all that,' said I, heedlessly enough; but I was not thinking of

Christal just then. She rose up in a fury, and demanded what *right* I had to know? I answered her as, after a struggle with myself, I thought best—*how*, I will tell you one day; but I must hasten on now. She was calmed a little, I saw; but her passion rose again when I mentioned Lyle.

'Speak of that no more,' she cried. 'It is all past and gone. There is no feeling in my heart but hatred and burning shame. Oh, that I had never been born!'

I pitied her from my soul, as she crouched down, not merely weeping, but groaning out her misery. Strange, that she should have let me see it; but she was so humbled now; and perceiving that I trusted her, perhaps she was the more won to trust me—I had considered this when I spoke to her as I did. My dear friend Olive, I myself am learning what I fain would teach this poor girl—that there is sometimes great evil done by that selfishness which we call a just pride.

While we were talking, I very earnestly, and she listening much subdued, there entered Madame Blandin. At sight of her the evil spirit awoke again in unhappy Christal. She did not speak, but I saw the flaming of her eyes—the haughtiness of her gesture. It was not tempered by the woman's half-insulting manner.

'I am come to make one last offer to Mademoiselle—who will do well to accept it, always with the advice of her English friend, or—whatever he may be,' she added, smirking.

'I have already told you, Madame, that I am a clergyman, and that this young lady is my mother's friend,' said I, striving hard to restrain my anger, by thinking of one meek spirit, for whom I ought and would endure all things.

'Then Monsieur can easily explain the mystery about Mademoiselle Christal; and she can accept this situation. For her talents I myself will answer. It is merely requisite that she should be of Protestant principles and of good parentage. Now, of course, the latter is no difficulty with a young lady who was once so enthusiastic about her family.'

Christal looked as if she could have sprung at her tormentor, and torn her limb from limb. Then turning deadly white, she gasped out, 'Take me away; let me hide my head anywhere from the scoffing world.'

Madame Blandin began to make bitter guesses at the truth. I feared lest she would drive the girl mad, or goad her on to the perpetration of some horrible crime. I dared not leave her in the house another hour. A thought struck me. 'Come, Christal!' I said, 'I will take you home with me.'

'Home with you! What then would they say of me—the cruel, malicious world? I am beginning to be very wise in crime, you see!' and she laughed frightfully. 'But it matters not what is done by my mother's child. I will go.'

'You shall,' I said, gravely; 'to the care of my friend, the wife of Lord Arundale. It will be enough for her to hear that you come from Harbury, and are known to Harold Gwynne.'

Christal resisted no more. There seemed a numbing stupor coming over her, which was not removed even when I brought her to share the kindness of good Lady Arundale, who needed no other guarantee than that it was a kindness asked by me. Olive (may I begin to call you so? Acting as your brother, I feel to have almost a right)—Olive, be at rest. Tonight, ere I sat down to write, I heard that your sister was quietly sleeping beneath this hospitable roof. It will shelter her safely until some other plan can be formed. I also feel at peace, since I have given peace to you. Peace, too, I see in both our futures, when this trouble is overpast. God grant it!—He to whom, as I stand at this window, and look up at the stars shining down into the midnight river, I cry, 'Thou art my God!'

*　　*　　*

I have an awful tale to tell—one that I should fear to inform you, save that I can say, 'Thank God with me that the misery has passed—that He has overruled it into good.' So, reading this, do not tremble—do not let it startle you—feeble, as my mother tells me, you still are. *'Poor little Olive.'* She calls you so—may not I?

Last night, after I closed my letter, I went out to take my usual quiet ramble before going to rest. I went to the Pont Neuilly,* near which Lord Arundale resides. I walked slowly, for I was thinking deeply—of what, it matters not now. On the whole, my thoughts were happy—so happy that I did not see how close to me was standing Misery—misery in the shape of a poor wretch, a woman! When I did see her, it was with that pang, half shame, half pity, which must smite an honest man, to think how vile and cruel are some among his brethren. I went away to the other wall of the bridge—I could not bear that the unhappy creature should think I watched her crouching there. I was just departing without again looking round, when my eye was unconsciously caught by the glitter of white garments in the moonlight.

She was climbing the parapet to leap into the arms of Death!

I know not how that awful moment passed—what I said—or did, for there was no time for words. But I saved her. I held her fast, though she struggled with miraculous strength. Once she had nearly perilled both our lives, for we stood on the very edge of the bridge. But I saved her.— Olive, cry with me, 'Thank God, thank God!'

At last, half-fainting, she sank on the ground, and I saw her features bare in the moonlight. It was Christal's face! Olive, if I had not been kept wandering here, filled with these blessed thoughts (which, please Heaven! I will tell you one day), your sister might have perished! Say again with me—thank God! His mercy is about us continually.

I cannot clearly tell what I did in that first instant of horror. I only remember that Christal, recognizing me, cried out in piteous reproach, 'You should have let me die! you should have let me die!' But she is saved—Olive, be sure that she is saved. Her right spirit will come into her again, it is dawning even now, for she is with kind Lady Arundale, a woman almost like yourself. To her, when I carried Christal home, I was obliged to reveal something of the truth, though not much. How the miserable girl contrived to escape, we cannot tell; but it will not happen again. Do not be unhappy about your sister; take care of your own health. Think how precious you are to my mother and to—all your friends. This letter is abrupt, for my thoughts are still bewildered, but I will write again soon. Only let me hear that you are well, and that in this matter you trust to me.

*   *   *

. . . 'I have not seen Christal for many days until yesterday. She has had a severe illness; during which Lady Arundale has been almost like a mother to her. We thought it best that she should see no one else; but yesterday she sent for me, and I went. She was lying on a sofa, her high spirit utterly broken down and crushed into pale humility. She faintly smiled when I came in, but her mouth had a patient sunken look, such as I have seen you wear when you were ill last year. She reminded me of you much—I could almost have wept over her. Olive, my friend—do you not think my nature is strangely changed?—I do sometimes—but no more of this now.

Christal made no allusion to the past. She said, 'She desired to speak to me about her future—to consult me about a plan she had.' It was one at which I did not marvel. She wished to hide herself from the world altogether, in some life which in its eternal quiet might be likest death.

I said to her, 'I will see what can be done, but it is not easy. There are no convents or monasteries open to us Protestants.'

Christal looked for a moment like her own scornful self. '*Us Protestants*,' she echoed; and then she said, humbly; 'One more confession can be nothing to me now. I have deceived you all—I am—and I have ever been, a Roman Catholic.'

She thought, perhaps, I should have blamed her for this long course of religious falsehood. I blame *her*! (Olive, for God's sake do not let my mother read all I write to you. She shall know everything soon, but not now.)

'But you will not thwart me,' Christal said; 'though you are an English clergyman, you will find me some resting-place, some convent where I can hide, and no one ever hear of me any more.'

I found that to oppose her was useless; little religion she ever seemed to have had, so that no devoteeism urged her to this scheme, she only wanted rest. Olive, you will agree with me that it is best she should have her will, for the time at least.

*   *   *

... I have just received your letter. Yes! yours is a wise and kindly plan; I will write at once to Aunt Flora about it. Poor Christal! perhaps she may find peace as a novice at St Margaret's. Some little fear I had in communicating the scheme to her; for she still shudders at the very mention of her father's name, and she might refuse to go to her father's land. But she is so helpless in body and mind, that in everything she has at last implicitly trusted to my guidance.

*   *   *

... I suppose you, too, have heard from Edinburgh? Dear Aunt Flora! despite her growing feebleness, her mind is continually seeking to do good. I, like you, judged it better not to tell her the whole story; but only that Christal was an orphan who had suffered much. At St Margaret's she will see no one but the good nuns, until, as your aunt proposes, you yourself go to Edinburgh. You may be your sister's saving angel still.

*   *   *

Christal is gone. Lady Arundale herself will take her safe to St Margaret's, where your aunt has arranged all. Olive, we must not fail both to go to Edinburgh soon. Something tells me this will be the last good deed done on earth by our noble Aunt Flora.—For what you say in your last letter, thank you! But why do you talk of gratitude? All I ever did was not half worthy of you. You ask of myself, and my plans? I have thought little of either lately, but I shall now. Tell my mother that all her letters came safe, and welcome—especially *the first* she wrote.

*   *   *

Lord Arundale stays abroad until the year's close. For me, in the early spring, when I have finished my duties with him, I shall come home. *Home*! Thank God!

CHAPTER XLVI

Night and day, there rang in Olive's heart the last words of Harold's letter: 'I shall come home!' Simple they were; but they seemed so strangely joyful—so full of hope. She could not tell why, but thinking of him now, her whole world seemed to change and sublimate into content. He was coming back! With him came spring and sunshine, youth and hope!

It was yet early in the year. The little crocuses peeped out—the violets purpled the banks. Now and then came soft west winds, sighing sweetness over the earth. Not a breeze passed her by—not a flower sprang in her sight—not one sunny day dawned to ripen the growing year, but Olive's heart leaped within her; for she said, 'He will come with the spring—he will come with the spring!'

How and with what mind he would come—whether he would tell her he loved her, or ask her to be his wife—she counted none of these things. Her love was too unselfish, too utterly bound up in him. She only thought that she would see his face, clasp his hand, and walk with him—the same as in the dear old time. Not quite, perhaps, for she was conscious that in the bond between them had come a change, a growth. How, she knew not, but it had come. Sometimes she sat thinking—would he tell her all those things which he had promised, and what could they be? And, above all, would he call her, as in his letters, *Olive*? Written, it looked most beautiful in her sight; but when spoken, it must be a music of which the world could hold no parallel.

A little she strove to temper her happiness, for she was no lovesick girl, but a woman, who, giving her heart—how wholly none but herself could tell—had given it in the fear of God, and in all simplicity. Having known the sorrow of love, she was not ashamed to rejoice in love's joy. But she did so meekly and half-tremblingly, scarce believing that it was such, lest it should overpower her. She set herself to all her duties, and, above all, worked sedulously at a picture which she had begun.

'It must be finished before Harold comes home,' said Harold's mother. 'I told him of it in my letters, you know.'

'Indeed. I do not remember that. And yet for this long while you have let me see all your letters, I think.'

'All—except one I wrote when you were ill. But never mind it, my dear. I can tell you what I said—or, perhaps, Harold will,' answered Mrs Gwynne, her face brightening in its own peculiar smile of heartfelt benevolence and lurking humour. And then the brief conversation ceased.

For a while longer, these two loving hearts waited anxiously for Harold's coming. At last he came.

It was in that sweetest month, the opening gate of the summer year—April. Mrs Gwynne and Olive—only they two—had spent the day together at Harbury; for little Ailie, a child too restless to be ruled by quiet age, was now sent away to school. Mrs Gwynne sat in her armchair, knitting. Olive stood at the window, thinking how beautiful the garden looked, just freshened with an April shower; and how the same passing rain-cloud, melting in the west, had burst into a most gorgeous sunset. Her happiness even took a light tone of girlish romance. Looking at the thorn-tree, now covered with pale green leaves, she thought with a pleasant fancy, that when it was white with blossoms Harold would be here. And her full heart, scarce conscious why, ran over with a trembling joy.

Nevertheless, amidst all her own hope, she remembered tenderly her poor sister far away. And also Lyle, whom since that day he parted from her she had never seen. Thinking, 'How sweet it is to feel happy!' she thought likewise—as those who have suffered ever must—'Heaven make all the world happy too!'

It was just after this silent aspiration, which of all others must bring an answering blessing down, that the long-desired one came home. His mother heard him first.

'Hark—there's some one in the hall. Listen, Olive! It is his voice—I know it is! He is come home—my son!—my dear son Harold.' And with eager, trembling steps; she hurried out.

Olive stayed behind. She had no right to go and meet him, as his mother did. And after one wild throb, her heart sank, so faintly that she could hardly stand.

His voice—his long-silent voice! Hearing it, the old, passionate love came over her. She felt, now, that she must have *his* too, or die. The whole pent-up tide of nature was breaking loose at last. She shuddered, even with a sort of fear. 'Heaven save me from myself! Heaven keep my heart at peace and pure! Perhaps he will not suffer himself to love me, or does not wish me to love him. I have thought so sometimes. Then, rather than pain him, I will hide it eternally. Yes! I am quite calm—quite ready to meet him now.' And she felt herself growing all white and cold as she stood.

The door opened, and Harold came in alone. Not one step could she advance to meet him, not one word of welcome fell from her lips—nor from his, which were pale as her own. But as he clasped her hands and held them fast, she felt him gazing down upon her—now, for the first time, beginning to read her long-tried, long-patient heart. Something in that look was drawing her closer to him—something that bade her lean forward to his breast and call him 'Harold!' It might have happened so—that moment might have proved the crowning moment of life, which blends two hearts of man and woman into one love, making their being complete and all perfect, as God meant it should be.

But at the same instant Mrs Gwynne came in. Their hands fell from one another; Harold quitted Olive's side, and began talking to his mother.

Olive stood by herself in the window. She felt as if her whole destiny was changing—melting from cloud to glory—like the sunset she had watched an hour before. Whatever was the mystery that had kept him silent, whether he would ever ask her to be his wife or no—she believed that in the secret depth of his heart Harold loved her. Once she had thought, that were this knowledge true, the joy would surely overpower her reason. Now, it came with such a solemnity, that all agitation ceased. Her hands were folded on her heart, her eyes looked heavenwards. Her prayer was—'O God, if this should be, even on earth, make me worthy of my happiness—worthy of him!—If not, keep us both safe until the eternal meeting!'

Then, all emotion having passed away, she went back quietly to Harold and his mother.

They were sitting together on the sofa, Harold holding his mother's hand in one of his. When Olive approached, he stretched out the other, with a smile of beautiful home-affection, saying, 'Come to us, little Olive—come! Shall she, my mother?'

'Yes,' was Mrs Gwynne's low answer. But Olive heard it. It was the lonely heart's first welcome home.

For an hour afterwards she sat by Harold's side in the gathering darkness, feeling her hand safe clasped in his. Never was there any clasp like Harold's—so firm, yet soft—so gentle, yet so close and warm. It filled her with a sense of rest and protection—she, long tossed about in the weary world. Once or twice she moved her hand, but only to lay it again in his, and feel his welcoming fingers close over it, as if to say, 'Mine—mine—always mine!'

So they sat and talked together—she, and Harold, and Harold's mother—talked as if they were one loving household, whose every interest was united. Though, nevertheless, not one word was spoken that might break the seal upon any of their hearts.

'How happy it is to come home!' said Harold. 'How blessed to feel that one has a home! I thought so more strongly than ever. I had done before, one day, at Rome, when I was with Olive's old friend, Michael Vanbrugh.'

'Oh, tell me of the Vanbrughs,' cried Olive eagerly. 'Then you did see them at last, though you never said anything about it in your letters?'

'No; for it was a long story, and both our thoughts were too full. Shall I tell it now? Yet it is sad, it will pain you, Olive.' And he pressed her hand closer while he spoke.

She answered, 'Still, tell me all!' And she felt that, so listening, the deepest worldly sorrow would have fallen light.

'I was long before I could discover Mr Vanbrugh, and still longer before I found out his abode. Day after day I met him, and talked with him at the Sistine, but he never spoke of his home, or asked me thither. He had good reason.'

'Were they so poor, then? I feared this,' said Olive, compassionately.

'Yes, it was the old story of a shattered hope. As I think, Vanbrugh was a man to whom Fortune could never come. He must have hunted her from him all his life, with his pride, his waywardness, his fitful, morose ambition. I soon read his nature—for I had read another very like it, once. But that is changed now, thank God,' said Harold, softly. 'Well, so it was; the painter dreamed his dream, the little sister stayed at home and starved.'

'Oh, no! you cannot mean it!' cried Olive.

'It would have been so, save for Lord Arundale's goodness, when we found them out at last. They lived in a miserable house, which had but one decent room—the studio. "Michael's room must always be comfortable", said Miss Meliora—I knew her at once, Olive, after all you had told me of her. The poor little woman! she almost wept to hear the sound of my English voice, and to talk with me about you. She said, "she was very lonely among strangers, but she would get used to it in time. She was not well too, but it would never do to give way—it might trouble Michael. She would get better in the spring." '

'Poor Meliora! But you were very kind to her—you went to see her often?—I knew you would,' said Olive.

'There was no time,' Harold answered, sadly. 'The day after this we sought out Michael Vanbrugh, in his old haunt up the Sistine. He was somewhat discomposed, because his sister had not risen in time to set his palette, and get all things ready in his painting-room at home. I went thither, and found her—dying.'

Harold paused—but Olive was too much moved to speak. He went on—

'So sudden was the call that she would not believe it herself. She kept saying continually, that she must contrive to rise before Michael came back at night. Even when she knew she was dying, she seemed to think only of him; but always in her simple, humble way. I remember how she talked, brokenly, of some white draperies she had to make for his model that day—asking me to get some one else to do it, or the picture would be delayed. Once she wept, saying who would take care of Michael when she was gone! She would not have him sent for—he never liked to be disturbed when he was at the Sistine. Towards evening she seemed to lie eagerly listening, but he did not come home. At last she bade me give her love to Michael: she wished he had come, if only to kiss her before she died—he had not kissed her for thirty years. Once more, just when she seemed passing into a deathlike sleep, she half-roused herself, to beg some one would take care that Michael's tea was all ready for him against he came home. After this she never spoke again.'

'Poor Meliora; poor simple, loving soul!' And Olive melted into quiet tears. After a while she enquired in what way this blow had fallen upon Michael Vanbrugh.

'Strangely, indeed,' said Harold. 'It was I who told him first of his sister's death. He received the news quite coldly—as a thing impossible to realize! He even sat down to the table, as if he expected her to come in and pour out his tea; but afterwards, leaving the meal untouched, he went and shut himself up in his painting-room, without speaking a word. And then I quitted the house.'

'But you saw him again?'

'No; for I left Rome immediately. However, I had a friend who watched over him and constantly sent me news. So I learnt that after his sister's death a great change came over him. His one household stay gone, he seemed to sink down helpless as a child. He would wander about the house, as though he missed something—he knew not what; his painting was neglected, he became slovenly in his dress, restless in his look. No one could say he grieved for his sister, but he missed her—as one misses the habit of a lifetime. So he gradually changed, and grew speedily to be a worn-out, miserable, old man. A week since I heard that his last picture had been bought by the Cardinal F——, and that Michael Vanbrugh slept eternally beneath the blue sky of Rome.'

'He had his wish—he had his wish!' said Olive, gently. 'And his faithful little sister had hers; for nothing ever parted them. We women are content when we can thus give up our lives to some one beloved. The happiness is far beyond the pain.'

'You told me so once before,' answered Harold, in a low tone. 'Do you remember? It was at the Hermitage of Braid.'

He stopped, thinking she would have replied; but she was silent, so heavy still was the remembrance of that bitter, bitter hour! Her silence seemed to grow over him like a cloud. When the lights came in, he looked the same proud, impassive Harold Gwynne, such as he used to look in the old time. Already his clasp had melted from Olive's hand. Before she could guess the reason why, she found him speaking, and she answering coldly, indifferently. All the sweetness of that sweet hour had with it passed away.

This sudden change so pained her, that very soon she began to talk of returning home. Harold rose to accompany her, but he did so with the formal speech of necessary courtesy—'Allow me the pleasure, Miss Rothesay.' It stung her to the heart.

'Indeed, you need not, when you are already tired. It is still early. I had much rather go home alone.'

Harold sat down again at once.

She prepared to depart. She shook hands with his mother, and then with himself, saying, in a voice that, lest it should tremble, she made very low, quiet, and cold, how glad she was that he had come home safe. However, before she reached the garden gate, Harold followed her.

'Excuse me, but my mother is not content for you to set off thus; and we may as well return to our old custom of walking home together—just once more.'

What could he mean? Olive would have asked him, but she dared not. Even yet there was a veil between their hearts. Would it ever be drawn aside?

There were few words spoken on the way to Farnwood, and those few were of ordinary things. Once Olive talked of Michael Vanbrugh and his misfortunes.

'You call him unfortunate; how know you that?' said Harold, quickly. 'He needed no human affection, and so, on its loss, suffered no pain; he had no desire save that of fame; his pride was never humbled to find himself dependent on earthly love. The old painter was a great and a happy man.'

'Great he was, but not happy. There can be little happiness in a heart barren of love. I think I had rather be the poor little sister who spent her life for him.'

'Ay, in a foolish affection, that was all in vain.'

'Affection is never in vain. I have thought sometimes that as to give is better than to receive, they who love are happier than they who are loved.'

Harold was silent. He remained so until they stood at Miss Rothesay's door. Then, bidding her goodbye, he took her two hands, saying, as if enquiringly, 'Olive?'

'Yes!' she answered, trembling a little—but not much—for her dream of happiness was fading slowly away, and she was sinking back into her old patient, hopeless self. That olden self alone spoke as she added, 'is there anything you would say to me?'

'No, no—nothing—only goodnight.' And he hastily walked away.

An hour after, Olive closed her heavy eyes, that burned with long weeping, and lay down to sleep, thinking there was no blessing like the oblivion of night, after every weary day! She lay down, little knowing what mystery of fate that quiet night was bearing in its bosom.

From her first sleep she started, filled with the vague terror of one who has been suddenly awakened. There was a great noise—knocking—crashing—a sound of mingled voices—and, above all, her name called. Anywhere, waking or sleeping, she would have known *that* voice, for it was Harold Gwynne's. At first, she thought she must still be dreaming some horrible dream; but consciousness came quick, as it often does at such a time. Before the next outcry was raised, she had guessed its meaning. Upon her had come that most awful waking—the waking in a house on fire.

There are some women who in moments of danger gain an almost miraculous composure and presence of mind. Olive was one of these. Calmly she answered Harold's half-frenzied call from without her door.

'I am awake and safe; the fire is not in my room. Tell me, what must I do?'

'Dress quickly—there is time. Think of all you can save, and come,' she heard Harold reply. His passionate cry of 'Olive!' had ceased; he was now as self-possessed as she.

Her room was light as day, with the reflection of the flames that were consuming the other end of the long, straggling house. She dressed herself, her hands never trembling—her thoughts quick, vivid, and painfully minute. There came into her mind everything she would lose—her household mementos—the unfinished picture—her well-beloved books. She saw herself penniless—homeless—escaping only with life. But that life she owed to Harold Gwynne. How everything had chanced she never paused to consider. There was a sweetness, even a wild gladness, in the thought of peril from which Harold had come to save her.

She heard his voice, eager with anxiety. 'Olive—Olive! hasten. The fire is gaining on us fast!' And added to his was the cry of her faithful old servant, Hannah, whom he had rescued too. He seemed to stand firm amidst the confusion and terror, ruling every one with the very sound of his voice—that knew no fear, except when it trembled with Olive's name.

'Quick—quick! I cannot rest till I have you safe. Olive! for God's sake, come! Bring with you anything you value, only come!'

She had but two chief treasures, always kept near her—her mother's portrait, and Harold's letters; the letters she hid in her bosom, the picture she carried in her arms. Thus laden, she quitted the burning house.

It was an awful scene. The utter loneliness of the place precluded any hope of battling with the fire; but, the night being still and windless, it advanced slowly. Sometimes, mockingly, it almost seemed to die away, and then rose up again in a hurricane of flame.

Olive and Harold stood on the lawn, she clinging to his hand like a child. 'Is there no hope of saving it—my pretty cottage—my dear home, where my mother died!'

'Since you are safe, let the house burn—I care not,' muttered Harold. He seemed strangely jealous even of her thoughts—her tears. 'Be content,' he said—'you see, much has been done.' He pointed to the lawn strewn with furniture. 'All is there—your picture—your mother's little chair—everything I thought you cared for I have saved.'

'And my life, too. Oh! it is so sweet to owe you all!'

He quitted her for a moment to speak to some of the men whom he had brought with him from Harbury, then he came back, and stood beside Olive on the lawn—she watching the doomed house—he only watching her.

'The night is cold—you shiver. I am glad I thought to bring this.' He took off his plaid and wrapped her in it, holding his arm round her the while. But she scarce felt it then. Through the yawning, blazing windows, she saw the fire within, lighting up in its laughing destruction her beloved studio and the little parlour where her mother used to sit, twining round the white-curtained bed, whereon her mother's last breath had been sighed away peacefully in her arms. She stood all speechless, gazing upon this piteous household ruin, wherein were engulfed so many memories. But very soon there came the crash of the sinking roof, and then a cloud of dense smoke and flame arose, sweeping over where she and Harold stood, falling in showers of sparks around their feet.

Instinctively, Olive clung to Harold, hiding her blinded eyes upon his arm. She felt him press her to him, for an instant only, but with the strong true impulse, taught by one only feeling. Yet he struggled against it still.

'You must not stay here,' he said, 'Come with me home!'

'Home!' and she looked wistfully at the ruins of her own.

'Yes—to my home—my mother's. You know for the present it must indeed be yours. Come!'

He gave her his arm to lean on. She tried to walk, but, quite overpowered, she staggered, fainted, and fell. When she awoke, she felt herself borne like a child in Harold's arms, her head lying on his breast. No power had she to move or speak—all was a dizzy dream. Through it, she faintly heard him whisper as though to himself, 'I have saved her—I hold her fast—little Olive—little Olive!'

When they reached the Parsonage door, he stood still a moment, passionately looking down upon her face. One minute he strained her closer to his heart, and then placed her quietly and tenderly in his mother's arms.

'She is safe—oh thank God!' cried Mrs Gwynne, joyfully. 'And you, too, my dear son—my brave Harold!' And she turned to him as he stood, leaning breathless against the wall.

He tried to speak, but in vain. There was one gasp; the blood poured in a torrent from his mouth, and he fell down at his mother's feet.

CHAPTER XLVII

'He has given his life in saving mine. Oh, would that I had died for thee—my Harold—my Harold!'

This was evermore Olive's cry during the days of awful suspense, when they knew not but that every hour might be Harold's last. He had broken a blood-vessel in the lungs; through some violent and secret emotion, the physician said. Nothing else could have produced such results in his usually strong and manly frame.

'And it was for me—for me!' moaned Olive. 'Yet I doubted him—I almost called him cruel. Oh, Harold, that I should never have known thy heart until now!'

Every feeling of womanly shame vanished before the threatening shadow of death. Night and day, Olive hovered about the door of Harold's room, listening for any sound. But there was always silence. No one passed in and out except his mother—his mother, on whom Olive scarce dared to look, lest—innocent though she was—she might read reproach in Mrs Gwynne's sorrowful eye. Once, she even ventured to hint this.

'I angry, because it was in saving you that this came upon my son? No Olive, no! Whatever God sends, we will bear together.'

Mrs Gwynne said this kindly, but her heart seemed frozen to every thought except one. She rarely quitted Harold's chamber, and scarcely noticed any person—not even Olive.

One night, or rather early morning, during a time of great crisis, she came out, and saw Olive standing in the passage, with a face whereon was written such utter woe, that before it even the mother's sorrow paled. It seemed to move Mrs Gwynne deeply.

'Olive, how long have you been here?'

'All night.'

'Poor child—poor child!'

'It is all I can do, for him and you. If I could only——'

'I guess what you would say. No, no! He must be perfectly quiet; he must not see or hear *you*.' And the mother turned away, as though she had said too much. But what to Olive was it now to know that Harold loved her? She would have resigned all the blessing of his love to bring to him health and life. So crushed, so hopeless was her look, that Harold's mother pitied her. Thinking a moment, she said,

'He is fast asleep now. If it would comfort you, poor child, to look at him for one moment—but it must be only one——'

Olive bowed her head—she was past speaking—and followed Mrs Gwynne. With a step as silent and solemn as though she were going to look on death, she went and looked on the beloved of her heart.

Harold lay in the dim light; his face perfectly blanched, his dark hair falling heavily on the pillow, as if never to be stirred by life or motion more. They stood by his bed—the mother that bore him, and the woman who loved him dearer than her own soul. These two—the strongest of all earthly loves—so blended in one object, constrained them each to each. They turned from gazing on Harold, and—all silently still—sank into one another's arms.

For a few more days continued this agonized wrestling with death, during which they who would have given their life for Harold's could only look on and pray. During this time there came news to Olive from the world without—news that otherwise would have moved her, but which was now idly received, as of no moment at all. Lyle Derwent had married; as, from his variable nature he was sure to do, when his dreamy passion came to an end. And Mrs Flora Rothesay had passed away; dying in the quiet night-time, peacefully, and without pain, for they found her hands folded as if she slept.

But even for her Olive had no tears. She only shuddered over the letter, because it spoke of death. All the world seemed full of death. She walked in its shadow night and day. Her only thought and prayer was, 'Give him life—give him life, O God!'

And Harold's life was given him. But the hope came very faintly at first, or it might have been too much joy for Olive to bear. Day by day it grew stronger, until all present danger was gone. But there were many chances to be guarded against; and so, as soon as this change for the better arrived, Olive came to look at him in his sleep no more. His mother was very cautious over his every look and word, so that Olive could not even learn whether he had ever given any sign that he thought of her. And now that his health was returning, her womanly reserve came back; she no longer lingered at his door; even her joy was restrained and mingled with a trembling doubt.

At length, Harold was allowed to be moved to his mother's dressing-room. Very eager and joyful Mrs Gwynne was, ransacking the house for pillows to make him lie easy on the sofa; and plaids to wrap him in;—full of that glad, even childish excitement with which we delight to hail the recovery of one beloved, who has been nearly lost. The pleasure extended itself over the whole household, to whom their master was very dear. Olive only, not daring to mingle in anything, sat in her own room, listening to every footstep.

Mrs Gwynne came to her at last. 'It is all done, my dear, and he is not so weak as we feared. But he is very much exhausted still. We must take great care even now.'

'Certainly,' answered Olive. She knew what the anxious mother meant, and dared not utter the longing at her heart.

'I scarce know what to do,' said Mrs Gwynne, restlessly. 'He has been asking for you.'

'For me—for me! Oh, let me see him,' cried Olive, imploringly.

'I told him not today, and I was right. Child, look at your own face now! Until you can calm yourself, you shall not see Harold,' was the mother's firm, almost angry speech. Without offering any answer, Olive sat down sorrowfully. Mrs Gwynne was melted. 'Nay,' she said, 'you shall do as you will, little patient one! I left him asleep now; you shall stay by him until he wakes. Come.'

She took her to the door, but quitted her there, perhaps remembering the days when she too was young.

Olive entered noiselessly, and took her place by Harold's side. He was sleeping; though it was not the deathlike sleep in which she had beheld him, that mournful night; but a quiet healthful slumber. His whole face seemed softened and spiritualized, as is often the case with strong men, whom a long illness has brought low. With childlike helplessness there seems to come a childlike peace. Olive knew now why Mrs

Gwynne had said, a few days since, that Harold looked as he had done when he was a little boy, whose only shelter in the wide world was in his mother's arms.

For a few minutes Olive sat silently watching. She felt how utterly she loved him—how, had he died, the whole world would have faded from her like a blank dream. And even now, should she have to part from him in any way—

'I cannot—I cannot. It would be more than I could bear.' And from the depth of her heart rose a heavy sigh.

Harold seemed to hear it. He moved a little, and said, faintly, 'Who is there?'

'It is I.'

'Olive—little Olive.' His white cheek flushed, and he held out his hand to her.

She could have sunk beside him, weeping for joy, but remembering his mother's caution, she only whispered, 'I am so glad—so glad!' clasping tenderly his feeble hand.

'It is a long time since I saw you,' he said, brokenly. 'Stand so that I can look at you, Olive!' She came and stood in front of him. He looked long at her face, 'You have been weeping, I see. Wherefore?'

'Because I am so happy to know you are better—to see you once again!'

'Is that true? Do you think so much of me?' And a pale but most joyful smile broke over his face; though, leaving it, the features trembled with emotion. Olive was alarmed.

'You must not talk now—not one word. Remember how very, very ill you have been. I will sit by you here. Nay, let me keep your hand! Oh! what can I ever do or say in gratitude for all you have done for me?'

'Gratitude!' Harold echoed the word, as if with pain, and then lay still, looking up at her no more. Gradually there came a change over his countenance, as if some bitter thought were slowly softening into calmness. 'Olive,' he said, 'you speak of gratitude, then what must be mine to you? In those long hours when I lay conscious, but silent, knowing that there might be but a breath between me and eternity, how should I have felt had I not learnt from you that holy faith which conquers death?'

'Thank God! thank God! But you are weak, and must not speak.'

'I must, for I am stronger now; I draw strength from your very presence—you, who have been my life's good angel. Oh! let me tell you so while I can.'

'While you can!'

'Yes; for I sometimes think that, though I am thus far better, I shall never be like my own self again; but slowly, perhaps without suffering, pass away from this world.'

'Oh, no!—oh, no!' And Olive clasped his hand tighter, looking up with a terrified air. 'You cannot—shall not die! I will not let you part from me.' And then her face was dyed with a crimson blush—soon washed away by a torrent of tears.

Harold turned feebly round, and laid his right hand on her head. 'Little Olive! To think that you should weep thus, and I should be so calm!' He waited a while, until her passionate emotion had ceased. Then he said, 'Lift up your face; let me look at you. Nay, tremble not, for I am going to speak very solemnly—of things that I might never have uttered, save for such an hour as this. You will listen, my own dear friend, my sister, as you said you would be?'

'Yes—yes, always!'

'Ah! Olive, you thought not that you were more to me than any friend—any sister—that I loved you—not calmly, brotherly—but with all the strength and passion of my heart, as a man loves the woman he would choose out of all the world to be his wife.'

These words trembled on lips white as though they had been the lips of death. Olive heard; but so solemnly had the love-confession been breathed, that it awoke in her no passionate response: she only pressed his hand without speaking.

Harold went on. 'I tell you this, because now, when I feel so changed that all earthly things grown dim, I am not too proud to say I love you. Once I was. You stole into my heart before I was aware. Oh! how I wrestled against this love—I, who had been once deceived, until I believed in no woman's truth. At last, I resolved to trust in yours; but I would try to find out your heart first. I did so; you remember how I talked to you, and how you answered, in the Hermitage of Braid? Then I knew you loved, but I thought you loved not me.'

'I loved not you? Oh! Harold—Harold!'

As she uttered his name, tremulously, as a woman breathes for the first time the beloved name in the beloved ear, Harold started. But still he answered calmly.

'Whether that thought was true or not, would not change what I am about to say now. All my pride is gone—I only desire that you should know how deeply I loved you; and that, living or dying, I shall love you evermore.'

There was a brief silence, and then Olive, gliding from her seat, knelt beside the couch where Harold lay. She tried to speak—she tried to tell him the story of her one great love—so hopeless, yet so faithful—so passionate, yet so dumb. But she could utter nothing save the heart-bursting cry—'Harold! Harold!' And therein he learnt all.

Looking upon her, there came into his face an expression of unutterable joy. He made an effort to raise himself, but in vain. 'Come,' he murmured, 'come near me, Olive—my little Olive that loves me!—is it not so?'

'Ever—from the first; you only—none but you!'

'Kiss me, then, my own faithful one,' he said, faintly.

Olive leaned over him, and kissed him on the eyes and mouth. He tried to fold his arms round her, but his powers failed.

'I have no strength at all,' he said, sorrowfully. 'I cannot take her to my heart—my darling—my wife! So worn-out am I—so weak.'

'But I am strong,' Olive answered. She put her arm under his head, and drew him close to her, until he leaned upon her breast. He looked up to her, helplessly, yet peacefully as a child—so solemn, so calm, and yet so infinite was her tenderness.

'Oh, this is sweet, very sweet!' Harold murmured, closing his eyes with a look of exhaustion. 'I could sleep—I could almost die—thus——'

'No, God will not let you die, my Harold,' whispered Olive; and then neither of them spoke more.

Overpowered by an emotion which was too much for his feeble strength, Harold lay quiet. By degrees, when the shadows of the room darkened—for it was evening time—his breathing grew deeper, and he fell asleep, his head still resting on Olive's shoulder.

She looked down upon him—his thin, wasted face—his pale hand, that, even in slumber, still clung helplessly to hers. What a tide of emotion swept through her heart! It seemed that therein was gathered up for him every tenderness that woman's soul could know. She loved him at once with the love of mother, sister, friend, and wife—loved him as those only can who have no other kindred tie—nothing in the whole wide world to love beside. She laid her cheek upon his brow—but softly, lest she should waken him.

'I thought to have led a whole long life of silent love for thee, my Harold! And I would have led it, without murmuring, either against Heaven's will or thine, knowing my own unworthiness. But since it is not to be so, I will give thee a whole life of faithful love—a wife's love—such as never was wife's before.'

And then, over a long course of past time, her fancy went back, discerning how all things had worked together to this end. She saw how patience had ripened into hope, and suffering into joy. Not one step of the whole weary way had been trodden in vain—not one thorn had pierced her feet, that had not while entering there distilled a saving balm.

Travelling over many scenes, her memory beheld Harold, as in those early days when her influence and her prayers had, as it were, brought down a merciful angel to change his heart, and lead him from darkness to light. Again, as in the first bitterness of her hopeless love; when continually his words and actions wrung her heart—he never dreaming of the wounds he gave. And once more, as in the time, when knowing her fate, she had calmly prepared to meet it, and tried to make herself a humble, patient sister unto him—he so unresponsive, cold, and stern. Remembering him thus, she looked at him as he lay, turning for rest and comfort to her loving breast. Once more she kissed his forehead as he slept, and then her lips uttered the words with which Mrs Flora had blessed her.

'O God, I thank Thee, for Thou hast given me my heart's desire!'

Soon after, Mrs Gwynne entered the room, and beheld her thus. But no blush came to Olive's cheek—too solemn was her joy.

'Hush!' she whispered; 'do not wake him. He loves me—I know it now. He is mine, and I am his, evermore!'

Harold's mother stood a long time in silence. Heaven only knows what struggle there might have been in her heart—so bound up as it was in him—her only child. Ere it ended—he awoke.

'Mother!—is not that my mother?'

'Yes!' Mrs Gwynne answered. she went up and kissed them both, first her son, and afterwards Olive. Then, without speaking, she quitted the room, leaving them alone together.

CHAPTER XLVIII

It was a Sunday afternoon, not bright, but dull. All the long day the low clouds had been dropping freshness down;—the soft May rain, which falls warm and silent, as if the spring were weeping itself away for very gladness. Through the open window came the faint odour which the earth gives forth during rain—an odour of bursting leaves and dew-covered flowers. On the lawn you could almost 'have seen the grass grow'. And though the sky was dull and grey, still the whole air was so full of summer, so rich in the promise of what the next day would be, that you did not marvel to hear the birds singing as merrily as if it had been sunshine. There was one thrush to which Olive had stood listening for half an hour.

He sat sheltered in the heart of the great syringa bush. Though the rain kept dropping continually from its flowers, he poured out a song so loud and full of joyance, that he even disturbed his friends in the parlour—the happy silent three—mother, son, and the son's betrothed.

Mrs Gwynne, who sat in the far corner, put down her book—the best Book, for Sunday and all other days—the only one she ever read now. Harold, still feeble, lying back in his armchair by the window, turned his face and listened to the happy bird.

'Do you like to hear it, or shall I close the window?' said Olive, coming towards him.

'Nay, it does me good; everything does me good now,' he answered, smiling. And then he lay a long time, quietly looking out on the garden and the misty view beyond. Olive sat, looking alone at him; watching him in that deep peace, that satisfied content with which our eyes drink in every lineament beloved, when, all sorrow past, the fulness of love has come. No need had she to seek his glance, as though saying restlessly, 'Harold, love me!' In her own love's completeness she desired no outward show of his. To her it was perfect joy only to sit near him and to look at his face; the face which, whether seen or remembered, shone distinct from every other face in the wide world; and had done so from the first moment when it met her sight. Very calm and beautiful it was now; so beautiful, that even his mother turned round and looked at him for a moment with dimmed eyes.

'You are sure you feel quite well today? I mean, as well as usual. You are not sitting up too long, or wearying yourself too much?'

'Oh, no, mother! I think I could even exert myself more; but there is such sweetness in this dreamy life. I am so happy! It will be almost a pain to go back to the troublous world again.'

'Do not say so, my son,' answered Mrs Gwynne, with a quick anxiety; the cause of which she did not name. 'Indeed, we must have you quite well soon—the sooner the better—and then you will return to all your old duties, you know. When I sat in church this morning, I was counting how many Sundays it would possibly be before I heard my son Harold's voice there again.'

Harold moved restlessly.

'What say you, Olive, my dear?' continued Mrs Gwynne. 'Will it not be a pleasure to hear him in his own pulpit again? How soon, think you, will he be able to preach?'

'I cannot tell,' answered Olive, in a low voice; and she looked anxiously at her betrothed. For well she knew his heart, and well she guessed that though that heart was pure and open in the sight of God and in *her* sight, it might not be so in that of every man. And although his faith was now the Christian faith—even, in most points, that of the Church—still, there was in his nature a stern simplicity which somewhat cast aside forms. Added to this, came the remembrance of that old bitter life which he had led at Harbury, and which, did he remain there, must for ever haunt him. Though he nothing said, still Olive had lately begun to doubt whether he would ever be a Church of England minister again. No wonder that she watched his face in anxious love, and then looked from him to his mother, who, all unconscious, continued to speak.

'In truth, all your parishioners will be glad to have you back again. Even Mrs Fludyer was saying so yesterday; and noticing that it was a whole year since you had preached in your own church. A long absence! Of course, it could not be helped; still, it was rather a pity. Please God, it shall not happen again—shall it, Harold?'

'Mother—mother!' His hands were pressed together, and on his face was a look of pain. Olive stole to his side.

'He looks ill! Perhaps we are talking too much for him. Shall we go away, Harold, and leave you to sleep?'

'Hush, Olive! hush!' he whispered. 'I have thought of this before. I knew I must tell it to her—all the truth.'

'But not now—not now. Wait till you are stronger; wait a week—a day.'

'No, not an hour. It is right!'

'What are you talking to my son about?' said Mrs Gwynne, with a quick jealousy, which even yet was not altogether stilled.

Neither of the betrothed spoke.

'You are not hiding anything from me, Harold; from me, your mother!'

'My mother—my noble, self-denying mother!' murmured Harold, as if thinking aloud. 'Surely, if I sinned for her, God will forgive me!'

'Sinned for me! What are you talking of, Harold? Is there anything in your thought—anything I do not know?' And her look—still tender, yet becoming cold with a half-formed suspicion—was fixed, searchingly, on her son. And when, as if to shield him even from his mother, Olive leaned over him, Mrs Gwynne's voice grew stern with reproof.

'Stand aside, Olive. Let me see his face. Not even you have a right to interpose between me and my son.'

Olive moved a little aside. Very meek was her spirit—meek as had need to be that of one whom Mrs Gwynne would call daughter, and Harold wife. Yet by her meekness she had oftentimes controlled them both. She did so now.

'Olive—darling,' whispered Harold, his eyes full of love; 'my mother says right. Let her come and sit by me a little. Nay, stay near, though. I must have your face in my sight—it will strengthen me.'

She pressed his hand, and went away to the other end of the room.

Then Harold said, tenderly, 'Mother, come and talk to me—I want to tell you something.'

'It is no misfortune—no sin? Oh, my son, I am too old to bear either!' she answered, as she sat down, trembling a little. But she let him take her hands, and her face softened as he continued,

'My own mother—my mother that I love, dearer now than ever in my life before—listen to me, and then judge me. Twelve or fourteen years ago, there was a son—an only son—who had a noble mother. She had sacrificed everything for him—the time came when he had to sacrifice something for her. It was a point of conscience; light, perhaps, *then*—but still, it caused him a struggle. He must conquer it, and he did so. He stifled all scruples, pressed down all doubts, and became minister of a Church in whose faith he only half believed.'

'Go on,' said Mrs Gwynne, hurriedly, 'I had a fear once—a bitter fear. But no matter! Go on!'

'Well, he did this sin, for sin it was, though done for his mother's sake. He had better have supported her by the labour of his hands, than have darkened his soul by a lie. But he did not think of that, then. All the fault was his—not his mother's; mind—I say *not his mother's.*'

She looked at him, and then looked away again, with a bewildered sorrow in her eyes.

'He could blame no one but himself—he never did—though his doubts grew, until they prisoned him like a black mist, through which he could see neither earth nor heaven. God makes men's natures different; his was not meant for that of a quiet village priest. Circumstances, associations, habits of mind—all were against him. And so his scepticism and his misery increased, until in despair of heaven, he plunged into the oblivion of an earthly passion. He went mad for a woman's beauty,—for her beauty only!'

Harold pressed his hand upon his brow, as if old memories stung him still. His betrothed saw it, but she felt no pain. She knew that her own strong, pure, infinite love had shone down into his heart's dark depths, removing every stain, binding up every wound. By that love's great might she had controlled his. She had saved him, and won him, and would have power to keep him evermore.

'Mother,' Harold pursued, 'I must pass on quickly to the end. This man's one error seemed to cause all fate to rise against him that he might become an infidel to God and to man. At last he had faith in no living soul except his mother. This alone saved him from being the vilest wretch that ever crawled, as he was already the most miserable.'

A faint groan—only one—broke from the depth of the mother's heart, but she never spoke.

'There was no escape—his pride shut out that. So, year after year, he fulfilled his calling, and lived his life honestly, morally—in some things towards man, at least; but towards Heaven it was one long, awful lie. For he—a minister in God's temple—was in his heart an atheist.'

Harold stopped. In his strong excitement he had forgotten his mother. She, letting go his hand, glided to her knees; there she knelt for a long time, her lips moving silently. At last she rose, her grand figure lifted to its utmost height, her face very stern, her voice without one tone of tremulous age, or mother's anguish.

'And this hypocrite in man's sight—this blasphemer in the face of God—is my son Harold!'

'Was, but is not—never will be more. Oh, mother, have mercy! for Heaven has had mercy too.—Now, at last, I believe!'

Mrs Gwynne uttered a great cry, and fell on his neck. Never since the time when he was a child in her arms had he received such a passionate clasp—an embrace mingled with weeping that shook the whole frame of the aged mother. For a moment she lifted her head, murmured a thanksgiving for the son who 'was dead, and alive again—was lost, and found',* and then she clung to him once more.

Olive stayed aloof, until, seeing what a ghastly paleness was coming over the face of her betrothed, she came and stood beside him, saying,

'Do not talk more, you are too weak. Let me tell the rest.'

'You there, Olive? Go! Leave my son to me; you have no part here,' said Mrs Gwynne, putting her aside.

But Harold held his betrothed fast— 'Nay, mother, I beseech you, no harsh words to her. Take her and bless her, for it was she who saved your son.'

And then, in a few broken words, he told the rest of the tale; told it so that not even his mother's passionate affection could be wounded by the thought of a secret known to Olive and concealed from her—of an influence that over her son's spirit was more powerful than her own. Afterwards, when Olive's arms were round her neck, and Olive's voice was heard imploring pardon for both, her whole heart melted within her. Solemnly she blessed her son's betrothed, and called her 'daughter'. And then she sank again into the calm, reserved Alison Gwynne, whose vehement passions had been once frost-bound by circumstance, and, save at rare intervals such as this, would remain so until unsealed by life-renewing death.

'Now, my Harold!' she said, when, all trace of emotion passed from either, she sat by her son's side. 'Now I understand all. Olive is right; with your love of action, and a spirit that would perhaps find a limitation in the best forms of belief, you never can be again a minister of the English Church. We must not think of it any more.'

'But, mother, how shall we live? That is what tortures me! Whither shall we turn if we go from Harbury? Alone, I could bear anything, but you——'

'No matter for me! My Harold,' she added, a little moved, 'if you had trusted me, and told me your sufferings at any time all these years—I would have given up everything here, and lived, as I once did, when you were a youth at college. It was not hard then, nor would it have been now. O my son, you did not know your mother!'

He looked at her, and slowly, slowly there rose in his eyes—those clear, proud, manly eyes!—two great crystal tears. He was not ashamed of them; he let them gather and fall. And Olive loved him dearer, ay, ten thousand times, even though these tears—the first and last she ever beheld him shed—were given, not to her, but to his mother.

Mrs Gwynne resumed.

'Let us think, my son, what we must do; this day—this hour, for we have no time to lose. As soon as you are quite strong, you must give up the curacy, and we will leave Harbury.'

'Leave Harbury! your dear old home, from which you have often said you could never part? Oh, mother, mother!'

'It is nothing—do not think of it, my son! Afterwards, what must you do?'

'I cannot tell—I am faint, bewildered. Olive, my faithful one, think for me!' said Harold, looking helplessly towards her.

Olive advised—timidly at first, but growing firmer as she proceeded—that he should carry out his old plan of trying to be a scientific professor in some university abroad. They talked over the project for a long time, until it grew matured. Ere the afternoon closed, it was finally decided on—at least, so far as Harold's yet doubtful health permitted.

'But I shall grow strong now, I know. Oh mother—Oh, Olive! my heart is lightened of the load of years!'

And truly there was great peace and serenity in his face—nay, when tea-time came, he even rose and walked across the room with something of his old firm step, as if the spirit of returning health were rising strong within him.

After tea, Harbury bells broke out in their evening chime. Mrs Gwynne arose; Olive asked if she were thinking of going to church?

'Yes—to thank God!' she answered, speaking tremulously, as if her heart were full.

'Go with her, Olive,' said Harold, as he watched his mother pass from the room. Olive followed, but Mrs Gwynne said she would rather go to church alone, and Harold must not be left. For a while Olive stayed, rendering all those little services which youth can so sweetly pay towards age. And sweet, too, was the reward when Harold's mother kissed her, and once more called her 'daughter'. So, full of content, she went down-stairs to her betrothed.

Harold was again sitting in his favourite armchair by the window. The rain had lately ceased, and just at the horizon there had come to the heavy grey sky a golden fringe—a line of watery light, so dazzling that the eye could scarce bear to gaze. It filled the whole room, and fell like a glory on Harold's head, so that for a moment Olive stood still to look at him. Coming closer, she saw that he was not asleep, though his eyes were cast down in painful thought. Something in his expression re-minded her of that which he had worn on the night when he first came to Edinburgh, and she had leaned over him, longing to comfort him—as she had now a right to do. She did so! He felt the kiss on his brow, and smiled.

'Little Olive—good little Olive, she always comes when I most need her,' he said, fondly.

'Little Olive is very happy in so doing. And now, Harold, tell me what you were thinking of, that you pressed your lips together, and knotted your forehead—the broad, beautiful forehead that I love? It was not good of you, my Harold.'

'Do not jest, Olive; I cannot! There is a thought rankling in my heart so bitterly. If I go abroad, I must go alone. What will become of my mother and Ailie?'

'They shall stay and comfort me. Nay,' she said, trying to veil half her loving intents, 'you will not forbid it. How could I go on with my painting, living all alone?'

'Ay, there is another sting,' he answered. 'Not one word say you—but I feel it. How many years you may have still to work on alone!'

'Do you think I fear that? Nay—I did not give my heart like some women I have known—from a dread of living to be an old maid, or from a wish to gain a house, a name, and a husband—I gave it for love, pure love! If I were to wait for years—if I were never your wife at all, but died only your betrothed, still I should die satisfied. Oh, Harold, you know not how sweet it is to love you, and be loved by you—to share all your cares, and rejoice in all your joys! Indeed—indeed I am content.'

'You might, my gentle one, but not I. Little you think how strong is man's pride—how stronger still is man's love. We will not look to such a future—I could not bear it. If I go, you shall go with me, my wife! Poor or not, what care I, so you are mine?'

He spoke hurriedly, and in his countenance rose the proud Harold of old—ay, the pride mingled with a stronger passion still. But in Olive's eyes was such sweet calmness that she gazed both into peace.

'Harold,' she said, parting his hair with her cool soft hands, 'do not be angry with me! You know I love you dearly—but how dearly none knows, save Heaven. Sometimes I think I must have loved you before you loved me, long. Yet I am not ashamed of this, my Harold.'

'Ah!' he muttered, 'how often I must have made you suffer, when I knew it not—how often, blindly struggling with my own pride, have I tortured you. But still—still I loved you. Forgive me, dear!'

'Nay, there is nothing to forgive. The joy has blotted out all the pain.'

'It shall do so, when you are once mine. That must be soon, Olive—soon.'

She answered firmly, though a little blushing the while: 'I would it were this week, this day; if for your good. But it would not be. You must not be troubled with bitter worldly cares. To see you so would break my heart. No—your spirit must be free to work its way, and gain fame and success. My love shall never fetter it down to anxious poverty. I regard your glory even dearer than yourself, you see!'

Thus said she, striving to be to him a faithful betrothed, and true unselfish wife, such as a man of learning or of genius needs. And gradually she led him in the way she wished—even to consent to her entreaty that they should both work together for their dearest ones; and that in the home which she with her slender means could win, there should ever be a resting-place for Mrs Gwynne and for little Ailie.

Then they put aside all anxious talk, and sat in the pale twilight, with clasped hands, speaking softly and brokenly; or else never speaking at all; only feeling that they were together—they two, whose being was all in all to each other, while the whole world of life went whirling outside, never touching that sweet centre of complete repose. At last, Olive's full heart ran over.

'Oh, Harold!' she cried, 'this happiness is almost more than I can bear. To think that you should love me thus—me, poor little Olive! Sometimes I feel—as I once bitterly felt—how unworthy I am of you.'

'Darling! why?'

'Because I have no beauty; and, besides—I cannot speak it, but you know—you know!'

She hid her face, burning with blushes The words and act revealed how deeply in her heart lay the sting which had at times tortured her her whole life through—shame for that personal imperfection with which Nature had marked her from her birth, and which, though now so slight as to be forgotten in an hour* by those who learned to love her, still seemed to herself a perpetual humiliation. The pang came, but only for the last time, ere it quitted her heart for ever.

For, dispelling all doubts, healing all wounds, fell the words of her betrothed husband—tender, though grave: 'Olive, if you love me, and believe that I love you, never grieve me by such thoughts again. To me you are all beautiful—in heart and mind, in form and soul.'

Then, as if silently to count up her beauties, he kissed her little hands, her soft-smiling mouth, her long gold curls. And Olive hid her face in his breast, murmuring,

'I am content, since I am fair in your sight, my Harold—my only love!'

CHAPTER XLIX

Late autumn, that season so beautiful in Scotland, was shining with a flood of pale sunshine into the house at Morningside. She, its mistress, who had there lived from middle life to far-extended years, and then glided from the weakness of age to the fresh youth of immortality, was seen no more within its walls. But her spirit seemed to live there still; in the flowers which at early spring she had planted for other hands to gather at summer time; in the fountain she had placed, which sang its song of murmuring freshness to soothe many an ear and heart, when *she*, walking by the streams of living waters, needed those of earth no more.

Mrs Flora Rothesay was dead; but she had lived one of those holy lives whose influence never wholly dies, but is fruitful throughout generations. So, though now for months past her name had gradually ceased from familiar lips, and from her house and garden walks, her image faded slowly in the thoughts of those who best loved her; still she lived, even on earth, in the good deeds she had left behind—in the happiness she had created wherever her own sore-wounded footsteps trod.

In the dwelling from which she had departed there seemed little change. Everything looked as it had done more than a year before, when one poor bruised heart had come thither, and found rest and peace. There were fewer flowers in the autumnal garden, and the Hermitage woods beyond were all brown and gold; but there was the same clear line of the Braid Hills, their purple slopes lying in the early morning sun. No one looked at them, though, for the breakfast-room was empty. But very soon there stole into it, with the soft footstep of old, with the same quiet smile—Olive Rothesay.

No, reader! Neither you nor any one else will ever see Olive *Rothesay* more. She wears on her finger a golden ring, she bears the well-beloved name—her husband's name. She is Harold Gwynne's wife now.

To their fortunes Heaven allowed, as Heaven sometimes does, the sweetness of a brave resolve, the joy of finding that the trial is not needed. Scarcely had Olive and her betrothed prepared to meet their future, and go on, faithfully loving, though perhaps unwedded for years, when a change came which made everything plain before them. They learned that Mrs Flora Rothesay, by a will made a little before her death, had devised her whole fortune to Harold, on condition that he should take the name of his ancestors on the mother's side, and be henceforth Harold Gordon Gwynne. She made no reservations, save that she wished her house and personal property at Morningside to go to her grand-niece Olive, adding in the will the following sentence:

'I leave her this, and *no more*, that she may understand how deeply I reverenced her true woman's nature, and how dearly I loved herself.'

And Olive did understand all; but she hid the knowledge in her rejoicing heart, both then and always. It was the only secret she ever kept from her husband.

She had been married some weeks only; yet she felt as if the old life had been years gone by, so faint and dreamlike did it seem. No wild raptures had she known—no thrilling honeymoon bliss; such were not likely to mark the crowning of a love which had been so solemn, almost sad, from its beginning to its end. Its *end*?—say, rather, its new dawn— its fulfilment in a deeper, holier bond than is ever dreamed of by girlish sentiment or boyish passion—the still, sacred love of marriage. And, however your modern heart-infidels may doubt, and your free-thinking heart-desecrators scoff, *that* is the true love—the tie which God created from the beginning, making man and woman to be one flesh, and pronouncing it 'good'.

It is good! None can question it who sees the look of peace and full contentment—a look whose like one never beholds in the wide world save then, as it sits smiling on the face of a bride who has married for true love. Very rare it is, indeed—rare as such marriages ever are; but one sees it sometimes;—*we* saw it, reader, a while since, on a young wife's face, and it made us think of little Olive in her happy home at Morningside.

She stood by the window for a minute or two, her artist-soul drinking in all that was beautiful in the scene; then she went about her little household duties, already grown so sweet. She took care that Mrs Gwynne's easy chair was placed in its proper angle by the fire, and that Harold had beside his plate the great ugly scientific book which he always liked to read at breakfast. Indeed, it was a saying of Marion M'Gillivray's—from whose bonnie face the cloud had altogether passed, leaving only a thoughtful gravity meet for a girl who would shortly leave her maiden home for one far dearer—Marion often said that Mr Gwynne was trying to make his wife as learned as himself, and that his influence was robbing their Scottish Academy of no one knew how many grand pictures. Perhaps it might be—it was a natural and a womanly thing that in her husband's fame Olive should almost forget her own.

When she had seen all things meet for the morning welcome, Olive went away upstairs, and stood by a child's bed—little Ailie's. Not the least sweet of all her new ties was it, that Harold's daughter was now her own. And tender, like a mother's, was the kiss with which she wakened the child. There was in her hand a book—a birthday gift; for Ailie was nine years old that day.

'Oh, how good you are to me, my sweet, dear, new mamma!' cried the happy little one, clinging round Olive's neck. 'What a pretty, pretty book! And you have written in it my name—"Ailie". But,' she added, after a shy pause, 'I wish, if you do not mind, that you would put there my whole long name, which I am just learning to write.'

'That I will, my pet. Come, tell me what shall I say—word for word, "Alison——".'

'Yes, that is it—my beautiful long name, which I like so much, though no one ever calls me by it—*Alison Sara Gwynne*.'

'Sara! did they call you Sara?' said Olive, letting her pen fall. She took the little girl in her arms, and looked long and wistfully into the large oriental eyes—so like those which death had long sealed. And her tears rose, remembering the days of her youth. How strange—how very strange, had been her whole life's current, even until now! She thought of her who was no more—whose place she filled, whose slighted happiness was to herself the crowning of all joy. But Heaven had so willed it, and to that end had made all things tend. It was best for all. One moment her heart melted, thinking of the garden at Oldchurch, the thorn-tree at the riverside, and afterwards of the long-closed grave at Harbury, over which the grass waved in forgotten silence. Then, pressing Ailie to her bosom, she resolved that while her own life lasted, she would be a faithful and most loving mother unto poor Sara's child.

A *Mother*!—The word brought back—as it often did when Harold's daughter called her by that name—another memory, never forgotten, though sealed among the holy records of the past. Even on her marriage day the thought had come—'Oh thou, to whom in life I gave all love, all duty—now needed by thee no more, both pass unto *him*. If souls can behold and rejoice in the happiness of those beloved on earth—mother, look down from heaven and bless my husband!'

Nor did it wrong the dead, if this marriage bond involved another, which awakened in Olive feelings that seemed almost a renewal of the love once buried in Mrs Rothesay's grave. And Harold's wife inly vowed that while she lived his mother should never want the devotion and affection of a daughter.

In the past fading memories of Olive's former life was one more, which now grew into a duty, over whose fulfilment, even amidst her bridal happiness, she pondered continually; and talked thereof to her husband, to whom it was scarcely less absorbing.

Since they came home to Morningside, they had constantly sought at St Margaret's for news of Christal Manners. Many times Olive had written to her in her own beautiful and tender way, but no answer came. The silence of the convent walls seemed to fold itself over all revelations of the tortured spirit which had found refuge there. However, Christal had taken no vows. Mrs Flora and Harold had both been rigid on that point, and the good nuns reverenced their order too much to admit any one who might have sought it from the impulse of despair, rather than from any pious 'vocation'.

Olive's heart yearned over her sister. On this day she resolved to make one more effort to break the silence between them. So, in the afternoon, she went to the convent, quite alone, walking through the pleasant lanes where she had formerly walked with Marion M'Gillivray. Strange contrast between the present and the past! When she stood in the little convent parlour, and remembered how she had stood there with a bursting heart, that longed for any rest—any oblivion, to deaden the pang of its hopeless love—Olive's spirit trembled with the happiness that filled it now. And she felt how solemn is the portion of those whose cup God has crowned with blessing, in order that they may pour it out before Him continually, in offerings of thanksgiving and of fruitful deeds.

Sister Ignatia entered—the same bright-eyed, benevolent, simple soul. 'Ah, you are come again this week, too, my dear Mrs Harold

Gwynne—(I can hardly remember your new name even yet)—but I fear
your coming is vain; though, day after day, I beseech your sister to see
you.'

'She will not, then. Alas! how sad this is,' said Olive, sighing.

'Yet she says she has no bitterness against you. How could she? However, I ask no questions, for the past is all kept in silence here. And I love
the poor young creature. Oh, if you knew her fasts and her vigils and her
prayers! God and the Virgin pity her, poor broken-hearted thing!' said the
compassionate nun.

'Speak to her once more. Do not tell her I am here; only speak of me
to her,' said Olive. And she waited anxiously until Sister Ignatia came
back.

'She says, she is glad you are happy, and married to that good friend of
hers, to whom she owes so much; but she is dead to the world, and wishes
to hear of no one any more. Still, when I told her you lived at
Morningside, she began to tremble. I think—I hope, if she were to see
you suddenly, before she had time to reflect—only not now—you look so
agitated yourself.'

'No, no; I can always be calm at will—I have learned that long,' said
Olive. 'Your plan is kind; let it be today. It may end in good, please God.
Where is my dear sister?'

'She is sitting in the dormitory of the convent school. She stays a great
deal with our little girls, and takes much care of them, especially some
orphans that we have.'

Olive sighed. Well she read unhappy Christal's thought. But the way in
which it was betrayed showed some softening of the stony heart. Almost
hopeful, she followed Sister Ignatia to the dormitory.

It was a long, narrow room, lined with tiny white beds. Over its pure
neatness good fairies might have continually presided. Through it swept
the fresh air coming from the open window which overlooked the garden.
And there, darkening it with her tall black shadow, stood the only present
occupant of the room, Christal Manners.

She wore a garb half-secular, half-nun-like. Her black serge dress
betrayed no attention to fashion, scarcely even to neatness; her beautiful
hair was all put back under a white linen veil, and her whole appearance
showed that last bitter change in a woman's nature, when she ceases to
have a woman's instinctive personal pride. Olive saw not her face, except
the cheek's outline, almost worn to the straightness of age. Nor did
Christal observe her sister until Olive had approached quite close.

Then she gave a wild start, the old angry flush mounted to her temples,
and sank.

'Why did you come here?' she said hoarsely; 'I sent you word I wished to see no one—that I was utterly dead to the world.'

'But not to me—oh, not to me, my sister!'

'Sister!' she repeated, with flashing eyes, and then crossed herself humbly, muttering, 'The evil spirit must not rise again. Help me, Blessed Mother—good saints, help me!'

She told her rosary over once, twice, and then turned to Olive with a subdued, composed look.

'Now say what you have to say to me. I told you I had no anger in my heart—I even asked your forgiveness. I only desire to be left alone—to spend the rest of my bitter life in penance and prayer.'

'But I cannot leave you, my sister.'

'I wish you would not call me so, nor take my hand, nor look at me as you do now—as you did the first night I saw you, and again on that awful, awful day!' And Christal sank back on one of the little beds—the pure, thornless pillow where some happy child slept—and there gushed out her soul in many a bitter sob.

More than once she motioned Olive away, but Olive would not go. 'Do not send me away! If you knew how I suffer daily from the thought of you!'

'You suffer? happy as they tell me you are—you, with your home and your husband!'

'Ah, Christal, even my husband grieves—my husband, who would do anything in the whole world for your peace. You have forgotten Harold.'

A softness came over Christal's face. 'No, I have not forgotten him. Day and night I pray for him who saved more than my life—my soul. For that deed God bless him!—and God pardon me.'

She said this in a low voice, shuddering, too, as though at some awful memory. So deeply it moved her that, after a while, she spoke to Olive in a gentler tone, for the first time lifting her eyes to her sister's face.

'You seem well in health, and you have a peaceful look. I am glad of it—I am glad you are happy, and married to Harold Gwynne. He told me of this love between you.'

'But he could not tell you all. If I am happy, I have suffered too. We must all suffer, some time; but patience works out joy,' said Olive, soothingly.

'Not with me—not with me,' Christal answered in sorrow, though without bitterness. 'But I desire not to think of myself.'

'Shall I talk then about your friend Harold—your *brother*. He told me to say he would ever hold you as his dear sister,' said Olive, striving in her own winning way to awaken Christal's sympathies by what seemed the strongest emotion on the girl's heart. And something she succeeded; for, during a long space, her sister listened quietly, and with some show of interest, while she spoke of Harold and of their dear home.

'It is so near you, too; we can hear the convent bells when we walk in our pretty garden. You must come and see it, Christal.'

'No, no; I have rest here; I will never go beyond these walls. As soon as I am of age, I shall become a nun, and then I, with all my sorrows, will be buried out of sight for evermore.'

So said she; and Olive did not contradict her at the time. But she thought that if there was any strength in faithful affection and earnest prayers, the peace of a useful life, spent, not in barren solitude, but in the fruitful garden of God's world, should be Christal's portion yet.

One only doubt troubled her, for which she longed to see deeper into the girl's wounded heart. After considering for a long time, she ventured to say:

'I have told you now nearly all that has happened among us this year. You have spoken of all your friends, save one.' She hesitated, and at last uttered the name of Lyle.

'Hush!' said Christal. But her cheek's paleness changed not; her heavy eye neither kindled nor drooped. 'Hush! I do not wish to hear that name. It has passed out of my world for ever—blotted out by the horrors that followed.'

'Then you have forgotten——'

'Forgotten all. It was but a dream of my old vain life—it troubles me no more.'

'Thank God!' murmured Olive, though in her heart she marvelled to think how many false reflections there were of the one true love—the only love that can endure—such as had been hers.

She bade an affectionate farewell to her sister, who went with her to the outer court of the convent. Christal did not ask her to come again, but she kissed her when they parted, and once looked back ere she again passed into the quiet silent home which she had chosen as her spirit's grave.

Olive walked on quickly, for the afternoon was closing. Very soon she heard overtaking her a footstep, whose sound quickened her pulse even now. 'How good and thoughtful of him, my dear Harold—my husband!'

My husband! Never did she say or think the words, but her heart swelled with inexpressible emotion, remembering the old time of hopeless suffering, the long, silent struggle, the wasting care. Yet she would have borne it all a thousand times—ay, even had the end come never in her life on earth—rather than not have known the sweetness of loving—the glory of loving such a one as he!

Harold met her with a smile. 'I have been waiting long—I could not let my little Olive walk home alone.'

She, who had walked through the world alone for so many weary years! But she would never do so any more. She clung to her husband's arm, clasping over it both her little hands in a sweet, caressing way; and so they went on together.

Olive told him all the good news she had to tell, and he rejoiced with her for Christal's sake. He agreed that there was hope and comfort for their sister still; for he could not believe there was in the whole world a heart so hard and cold, that it could not be melted by Olive's gentle influence, and warmed by the shining of Olive's spirit of love.

They were going home, when she saw that her husband looked tired and dull—he had been poring over his books all day. For though now independent of the world, as regarded fortune, he could not relinquish his scientific pursuits; but was every day adding to his acquirements, and to the fame which had been his when only a poor clergyman at Harbury. So, without saying anything Olive led him down the winding road that leads from Edinburgh towards the Braid Hills, laughing and talking with him the while, 'to send the cobwebs out of his brain,' as she often told him. Though at the time she never let him see how skilfully she did this, lest his man's dignity should revolt at being so lovingly beguiled. For he was still as ever the very quintessence of pride. Well for him his wife had not that quality—yet perhaps she loved him all the better for that he possessed it.

At the gate of the Hermitage Harold paused. Neither of them had seen the spot since they last stood there—she weeping, leaning her forehead against his hands in the speechless woe whose mystery he could not, would not read. At the remembrance, he seemed greatly moved.

His wife looked lovingly up to him. 'Harold, are you content? You would not send me from you?—you would not wish to live your whole life without me now?'

'No—no!' he cried, pressing her hand close to his heart. The mute gesture said enough—Olive desired no more.

They walked on a long way, even climbing to the summit of the Braid Hills. The night was coming on fast—the stormy night of early winter—for the wind had risen, and swept howling over the heathery ridge.

'But I have my plaid here, and you will not mind the cold, my lassie—Scottish born,' said Harold to his wife. And in his own cheek, now brown with health, rose the fresh mountain-blood, while the bold mountain-spirit shone in his fearless eyes. No marvel that Olive, stealing beside him, looked with pride to her noble husband, and thought that not in the whole world was there such another man!

'I glory in the wind,' cried Harold, tossing back his head, and shaking his wavy hair, something lion-like. 'It makes me strong and bold. I love to meet it, to wrestle with it; to feel myself in spirit and in frame, stern to resist, daring to achieve, as a man should feel!'

And on her part, Olive, with her clinging sweetness, her upward gaze, was a type of true woman. But Harold did not bend his look upon her; he was just then in the mood when a great man needs no human intervention—not even a wife's—between him and the aspirations which fill his soul.

'I think,' he cried, 'that there is a full, rich life before me yet. I will go forth and rejoice therein; and if misfortune come, I will meet it—thus!'—

He planted his foot firmly on the ground, lifted his proud head, and looked out fearlessly with his majestic eyes.

'And I,' said Olive, 'thus.'

She stole her two little cold hands under his plaid, laid her head upon them, close to his heart, and, smiling, nestled there.

And the loud, fierce wind swept by, but it harmed not them, thus warm and safe in love. So they stood, true man and woman, husband and wife, ready to go through the world without fear, trusting in each other, and looking up to Heaven to guide their way.

The Half-Caste*

An Old Governess's Tale

FOUNDED ON FACT

'We know what we are, but we know not what we may be', as my quaintly clever niece and namechild, Cassia, would say. And truly who could have thought that I, a plain governess, should in my old age have become writer. Yet, for the life of me, I cannot invent a plot—I must write nothing but truth.* Here I pause, recollecting painfully that in my first sentence I have sinned against truth by entitling Cassia 'my niece and namechild', when, strictly speaking, she is neither the one nor the other. She is no blood relation at all, and my own name happens to be Cassandra. I always disliked it heartily until Mr Sutherland called me—— But I forget that I must explain a little.—Mr Sutherland was—no, thank Heaven!—*is*, a very good man; a friend of my late father, and of the same business—an Indian merchant.* When in my twenty-fifth year, my dear father died, and we were ruined—a quiet way of expressing this, but in time one learns to speak so quietly of every pang: Mr Sutherland was very kind to my mother and to me. I remember, as though it were yesterday, one day when he sat with us in our little parlour, and, hearing my mother calling me 'Cassie', said laughingly that I always put him in mind of a certain Indian spice. 'In fact,' he added, looking affectionately at my dear, gentle, little mother, and approvingly—yes, it was approvingly, at me— 'in fact, I think we three sitting thus, with myself in the centre, might be likened to myrrh, aloes, and cassia.' One similitude was untrue; for he was not bitter, but 'sweet as summer'.* However, from that time he always called me Cassia. I rather like the name; and latterly it was very kind of him to—— There, I am forestalling my history again!

When I was twenty-five, as I said, I first went out as a governess. This plan was the result of many consultations between my mother and myself. A hard thing was my leaving home; but I found I could thereby earn a larger and more regular salary, part of which being put by, would some time enable me to live altogether with my mother. Such were her plannings and hopes for the future. As for my own—— But it is idle to dwell upon things so long past. God knew best, and it all comes to the same at the end of life. It was through Mr Sutherland that I got my first situation. He wrote my mother a hurried letter, saying he had arranged for me to enter a family, concerning whom he would explain before my departure. But something hindered his coming: it was a public meeting, I remember; for though still a young man, he was held in much honour among the city merchants, and knew the affairs of India well from early residence there. Of course, having these duties to fulfil, it was natural he should not recollect my departure; so I started without seeing him, and without knowing more of my future abode than its name, and that of my employer. It was a Yorkshire village, and the gentleman whose family I was going to was a Mr Le Poer. My long journey was dreary—God knows how dreary! in youth one suffers so much; and parting from my mother was any time a sufficient grief. In those days railways were not numerous, and I had to journey a good way by coach. About eleven at night I found myself at my destination. At the door a maid-servant appeared; no one else: it was scarcely to be expected by 'the governess'. This was a new and sad 'coming home' to me. I was shewn to my bedroom, hearing, as I passed the landing, much rustling of dresses and 'squittling' away of little feet. (I ought to apologize for that odd expression, which, I think, I learned when I was quite a child, and used to go angling with my father and Mr Sutherland. It means a scampering off in all directions, as a shoal of minnows do when you throw a pebble among them.)—I asked if the family were gone to bed, and was informed, 'No'; so I arranged my dress and went downstairs, unconsciously reassured by the fact, that the house was neither so large nor so aristocratic as my very liberal salary had at first inclined me to expect.

'Who shall I say, miss?' asked the rather untidy servant, meeting me in the lobby, and staring with open eyes, as if a stranger were some rare sight. 'Miss Pryor,' I said, thinking regretfully that I should be henceforth that, and not 'Cassia'; and seeing the maid still stared, I added with an effort: 'I am the new governess.' So under that double announcement I appeared at the parlour door. The room was rather dark: there were two candles; but one had been extinguished, and was being hurriedly relighted as I entered. At first I saw nothing clearly; then I perceived a little pale lady sitting at one end of the table, and two half-grown-up girls, dressed in 'going-out-to-tea' costume, seated primly together on the sofa. There was a third; but she vanished out of the door as I entered it.

'Miss Pryor, I believe?' said a timid voice—so timid that I could hardly believe that it was a lady addressing her governess. I glanced at her: she was a little woman, with pale hair, and light eyes—frightened-looking eyes—that just rose, and fell in a minute. I said 'I was Miss Pryor, and concluded I addressed Mrs Le Poer.' She answered: 'Yes, yes'; and held out hesitatingly a thin, cold, birdlike hand, which I took rather warmly than otherwise; for I felt really sorry for her evident nervousness. It seemed so strange for anybody to be afraid of *me*. 'My daughters, Miss Pryor,' she then said in a louder tone. Whereupon the two girls rose, curtseyed, blushed—seemingly more from awkwardness than modesty— and sat down again. I shook hands with both, trying to take the initiative, and make myself sociable and at home—a difficult matter, my position feeling much like that of a fly in an ice-house.

'These are my pupils then?' said I cheerfully. 'Which is Miss Zillah?'— for I remembered Mr Sutherland had mentioned that name in his letter, and its peculiarity naturally struck me.

The mother and daughters looked rather blankly at each other, and the former said: 'This is Miss Le Poer and Miss Matilda: Zillah is not in the room at present.'

'Oh, a third sister?' I observed.

'No, ma'am,' rather pertly answered Miss Le Poer; 'Zill is not our sister at all, but only a sort of a distant relation of Pa's, whom he is very kind to and keeps at his expense, and who mends our stockings and brushes our hair of nights, and whom we are very kind to also.'

'Oh, indeed!' was all I said in reply to this running stream of very provincially spoken and unpunctuated English. I was rather puzzled too; for if my memory was correct—and I generally remembered Mr Sutherland's letters very clearly, probably because they were themselves so clear—he had particularly mentioned my future pupil Zillah Le Poer, and no Miss Le Poer besides. I waited with some curiosity for the girl's reappearance; at last I ventured to say: 'I should like to see Miss Zillah. I understood'—here I hesitated, but thought afterwards that plain speech was best—'I understood from Mr Sutherland that she was to be my pupil.'

'Of course, of course,' hastily said the lady, and I fancied she coloured slightly. 'Caroline, fetch your cousin.'

Caroline sulkily went out, and shortly returned followed by a girl older than herself, though clad in childish, or rather servant fashion, with short petticoats, short sleeves, and a big brown-holland pinafore. 'Zill wouldn't stay to be dressed,' explained Caroline in a loud whisper to her mother; at which Mrs Le Poer looked more nervous and uncomfortable than ever. Meanwhile I observed my pupil. I had fancied the Zillah so carefully entrusted to my care by Mr Sutherland to be a grown young lady, who only wanted 'finishing'. I even thought she might be a beauty. With some surprise I found her a half-caste girl—with an olive complexion, full Hindoo lips, and eyes very black and bright. She was untidily dressed; which looked the worse, since she was almost a woman; though her dull, heavy face had the stupidity of an ultra-stupid child. I saw all this; for somehow—probably because I had heard of her before—I examined the girl more than I did the two other Misses Le Poer. Zillah herself stared at me much as if I had been a wild animal, and then put her finger in her mouth with a babyish air. 'How do you do, my dear?' said I desperately, feeling that all four pair of family eyes were upon me. 'I hope we shall be good friends soon.' And I put out my hand. At first the girl seemed not to understand that I meant to shake hands with her. Then she irresolutely poked out her brown fingers, having first taken the precaution to wipe them on her pinafore. I made another remark or two about my being her governess, and her studying with her cousins; at which she opened her large eyes with a dull amaze, but I never heard the sound of her voice.

It must have been now near twelve o'clock. I thought it odd the girls should be kept up so late; and began at last to speculate whether I was to see Mr Le Poer. My conjectures were soon set at rest by a loud pull at the doorbell, which made Mrs Le Poer spring up from her chair, and Zillah vanish like lightning. The two others sat cowed, with their hands before them; and I myself felt none of the bravest. So upon this frightened group the master of the house walked in.

'Hollo, Mrs Le Poer! Cary! Zill, you fool! Confound it, where's the supper?' (*I* might have asked that too, being very hungry.) 'What the deuce are you all about?'

'My dear!' whispered the wife beseechingly, as she met him at the door, and seemed pointing to me.

Certainly I could not have believed that the voice just heard belonged to the gentleman who now entered. The *gentleman*, I repeat; for I never saw one who more thoroughly looked the character. He was about fifty, very handsome, very well dressed—his whole mien bespeaking that stately, gracious courtliness which now, except in rare instances, belongs to a past age. Bowing, he examined me curiously, with a look that somehow or other made me uncomfortable. He seemed viewing over my feminine attractions as a horse-dealer does the points of a new bargain. But soon the interest of the look died away. I knew he considered me as all others did—a very plain and shy young woman, perhaps ladylike (I believe I was that, for I heard of some one saying so), but nothing more. 'I have the pleasure of meeting Miss Pryor?' said he in an ultra-bland tone, which after his first coarse manner would have positively startled me, had I not always noticed that the two are often combined in the same individual. (I always distrust a man who speaks in a very mild, measured, womanish voice.) I mentioned the name of his friend Mr Sutherland. 'Oh, I recollect,' said he stiffly: 'Mr Sutherland informed you that—that'——He evidently wished to find out exactly what I knew of himself and his family. Now, it being always my habit to speak the plain truth, I saw no reason why I should not gratify him; so I stated the simple facts of our friend's letter to my mother—that he had found for me a situation in the family of a Mr Le Poer, and had particularly charged me with completing the education of Miss Zillah Le Poer. 'Oh!' said Mr Le Poer abruptly; 'were those all your instructions, my dear Miss Pryor?' he added insinu-atingly. I answered that I knew no more, having missed seeing Mr Sutherland before I came away. 'Then you come quite a stranger into my family? I hope you have received the hearty welcome a stranger should receive, and I trust you will soon cease to merit that name.' So saying, he graciously touched the tips of my fingers, and in mellifluous tones or-dered supper, gently reproaching his wife for having delayed that meal. 'You know, my dear, it was needless to wait for me; and Miss Pryor must be needing refreshment.'

Indeed I was so, being literally famished. The meal was ordinary enough—mere bread, butter, and cheese; but Mr Le Poer did the honours with most gentlemanly courtesy. I thought, never did a poor governess meet with such attention. The girls did not sup with us: they had taken the earliest opportunity of disappearing; nor was the half-caste cousin again visible. We had soon done eating—that is, Mrs Le Poer and I; for the gentleman seemed so indifferent to the very moderate attrac-tions of his table, that from this fact, and from a certain redness of his eyes, I could not help suspecting he had well supped before. Still, that did not prevent his asking for wine; and having politely drunk with me, he composed himself to have a little confidential talk while he finished the decanter.

'Miss Pryor, do you correspond with Mr Sutherland?'

The abruptness of his question startled me. I felt my cheeks tingling, as I answered most truthfully: 'No.'

'Still you are a dear and valued friend of his, he tells me.'

I felt glad, so glad that I forgot to make the due answer about Mr Sutherland's being 'very kind'.

My host had probably gained the information he wanted, and became communicative on his part. 'I ought, my dear young lady, to explain a few things concerning your pupils, which have been thus accidentally omit-ted by my friend Mr Sutherland, who could not better have acceded to my request than by sending a lady like yourself to instruct my family.' Here he bowed and I bowed. We did a great deal in that way of dumb civility, as it saved him trouble and me words. 'My daughters you have seen. They are, I believe, tolerably well informed for such mere chil-dren.' I wondered if I had rightly judged them at thirteen and fourteen. 'My only trouble, Miss Pryor, is concerning my niece.' Here I looked surprised, not suspecting Zillah to be so near a relative. 'I call her niece through habit, and for the sake of her father, my poor deceased brother,' continued Mr Le Poer, with a lengthened and martyr-like visage; 'but in

truth she has no real claim to belong to my family. My brother—sad
fellow always—Indian life not overscrupulous—ties between natives and
Europeans: in fact my dear Miss Pryor, Zillah's mother—— You understand?' Ignorant as I was, I did dimly understand, coloured deeply, and
was silent. In the unpleasant pause which ensued I noticed that Mrs Le
Poer had let her knitting fall, and sat gazing on her husband with a blank,
horrified look, until he called her to order by an impressive 'A little more
wine, my dear?' Her head sunk with an alarmed gesture, and her lord and
master continued addressing me. 'Of course this explanation is in strict
confidence. Regard for my brother's memory induces me to keep the
secret, and to bring up this girl exactly as my own—except,' he added,
recollecting himself, 'with a slight, indeed a necessary difference. Therefore you will educate them all alike; at least so far as Zillah's small
capacity allows I believe'—and he smiled sarcastically—'her modicum of
intellect is not greater than generally belongs to her mother's race. She
would make an excellent *ayah*,* and that is all.'

'Poor thing!' I thought, not inclined to despise her even after this
information; how could I, when—— Now that fairly nonplussed me: what
made the girl an object of interest to Mr Sutherland? and why did he
mention her as Miss Zillah Le Poer when she could legally have no right
to the name? I should, in my straightforward way, have asked the question, but Mr Le Poer's manner shewed that he wished no more conversation. He hinted something about my fatigue, and the advisability of
retiring; nay, even lighted my candle for me, and dismissed his wife and
myself with an air so pleasant and gracious, that I thought I had scarcely
ever seen such a perfect gentleman.

Mrs Le Poer preceded me upstairs to my room, bade me goodnight,
asked timidly, but kindly, if all was to my liking, and if I would take
anything more—seemed half-inclined to say something else, and then,
hearing her husband's voice, instantaneously disappeared.

I was at last alone. I sat thinking over this strange evening—so strange,
that it kept my thoughts from immediately flying where I had supposed
they were sure to fly. During my cogitations there came a knock to the
door, and on my answering it, a voice spoke without, in a dull, sullen tone,
and an accent slightly foreign and broken: 'Please, do you want to be
called tomorrow, and will you have any hot water?' I opened the door at
once to Zillah. 'Is it you, my dear? Come in and say goodnight to me.'
The girl entered with the air and manner of a servant, except for a certain
desperate sullenness. I took her hand, and thanked her for coming to see
after my comforts. She looked thoroughly astonished; but still, as I went
on talking, began to watch me with more interest. Once she even smiled,
which threw a soft expression over her mouth. I cannot tell what reason

I had—whether from a mere impulse of kindness, with which my own state of desolation had something to do, or whether I compelled myself from a sense of duty to take all means of making a good first impression on the girl's feelings—but when I bade Zillah goodnight, I leaned forward and just touched her brown cheek with mine—French fashion; for I could not really *kiss* anybody except for love. I never saw a creature so utterly amazed! She might have never received that token of affection since her birth. She muttered a few unintelligible words—I fancy they were in Hindostanee*—flung herself before me, Eastern fashion, and my poor hand was kissed passionately, weepingly, as the beloved ladies' hands are in novels and romances.—But mine was never kissed save by this poor child! All passed in a moment, and I had hardly recovered my first surprise when Zillah was gone. I sat a little while, feeling as strange as if I had suddenly become the heroine of a fairy tale; then caught a vision of my own known self, with my pale, tired face, and sad-coloured gown. It soon brought me back to the realities of life, and to the fact that I was now 200 miles away from my mother and from—London.

I had not been three weeks resident in the Le Poer family, before I discovered that if out of the domestic mysteries into which I became gradually initiated I could create any fairy tale, it would certainly be that of 'Cinderella'; but my poor Cinderella had all the troubles of her prototype without any of the graces either of mind or person. It is a great mistake to suppose that every victim of tyranny must of necessity be an angel. On most qualities of mind oppression has exactly the opposite effect. It dulls the faculties, stupefies the instinctive sense of right, and makes the most awful havoc among the natural affections. I was often forced to doubt whether Mr Le Poer was very far wrong when he called Zillah by his favourite name of the 'ugly little devil'. There was something quite demoniac in her black eyes at times. She was lazy too—full of the languor of her native clime. Neither threats nor punishments could rouse her into the slightest activity. The only person to whom she paid the least attention was Mrs Le Poer, who alone never ill-used her. Poor lady! she was too broken-spirited to ill-use anybody; but she never praised. I do not think Zillah had heard the common civility, 'Thank you,' until I came into the house; since, when I uttered it, she seemed scarcely to believe her ears. When she first joined us in the schoolroom I found the girl was very ignorant. Her youngest cousin was far before her even in the commonest knowledge; and, as in all cases of deadened intellect, it cost her incalculable trouble to learn the simplest things. I took infinite pains with her, ay, and felt in her a strong interest too—ten times stronger than in the other two; yet for weeks she seemed scarcely to have advanced at all. To be sure it must be taken into account that she was rarely suffered to remain with me half the school hours without being summoned to some menial duty or other; and the one maid-servant bestowed on me many black looks, as being the cause why she herself had sometimes to do a morning's household work alone. Often I puzzled myself in seeing how strangely incompatible was Zillah's position with Mr Sutherland's expressed desire concerning her. Sometimes I thought I would write and explain all to him; but I did not like. Nor did I tell my mother half the *désagréments* and odd things belonging to this family—considering that such reticence even towards her nearest kindred is every governess's duty. In all domestic circles there must be a little Eleusinia, the secrets of which chance observers should strictly keep.

More than once I determined to take advantage of the very polite and sociable terms which Mr Le Poer and myself were on, to speak to him on the subject, and argue that his benevolence in adopting his brother's unfortunate child might not suffer by being testified in a more complete and gracious form. But he was so little at home—and no wonder; for the miserably dull, secluded, and painfully economical way in which they lived could have little charms for a man of fashion and talent, or at least the relics of such, which he evidently was. And so agreeable as he could be! His conversation at meals—the only time I ever saw him—was a positive relief from the dull blank, broken only by the girls' squabbles and their mother's faint remonstrances and complaints. But whenever, by dint of great courage, I contrived to bring Zillah's name on the tapis,* he always so adroitly crept out of the subject, without pointedly changing it, that afterwards I used to wonder how I had contrived to forget my purpose, and leave matters as they were. The next scheme I tried was one which, in many family jars and family bitternesses among which my calling has placed me, I have found to answer amazingly well. It is my maxim that 'a wrong is seldom a one-sided wrong'; and when you cannot amend one party, the next best thing is to try the other. I always had a doctrine likewise, that it is only those who have the instinct and the sins of servitude who will hopelessly remain oppressed. I determined to try if there was anything in Zillah's mind or disposition that could be awakened, so as to render her worthy of a higher position than that she held. And as my firm belief is, that everything and everybody in time rise or sink to their own proper level, so I felt convinced that if there were any superiority in Zillah's character all the tyranny in the world would not keep her the pitiable Cinderella of such ordinary people as the Le Poers. I began my system by teaching her, not in public, where she was exposed to the silent but not less apparent contempt of her cousins, but at night in my own room after all the house had retired. I made this hour as little like lessons as possible, by letting her sit and work with me, or brush my hair, teaching her orally the while. As much as her reserve permitted, I lured her into conversation on every indifferent subject. All I wanted was to get at the girl's heart. One day I was lecturing her in a quiet way on the subject concerning which she was the first young woman I ever knew that needed lecturing—care over her personal appearance. She certainly was the most slovenly girl I ever saw. Poor thing! she had many excuses; for though the whole family dressed shabbily, and, worse—tawdrily, her clothes were the worst of all. Still, nothing but positive rags can excuse a woman for neglecting womanly neatness. I often urged despairingly upon poor Zillah that the meanest frock was no apology for untidy hair; that the most unpleasant work did not exclude the possibility of making face and hands clean after it was over. 'Look at yours, my dear,' said I once, taking the reluctant fingers and spreading them out on mine. Then I saw what I have often noticed in the Hindoo race,* how delicate her hands were naturally, even despite her hard servant's work. I told her so; for in a creature so crushed there was little fear of vanity, and I made it a point to praise her every good quality, personal and mental.

Zillah looked pleased. 'My hands are like my mother's, who was very handsome, and a Parsee.'

'Do you remember her?'

'A little, not much; and chiefly her hands, which were covered with rings. One, a great diamond, was worth ever so many hundred rupees. It was lost once, and my mother cried. I saw it, a good while after, on my father's finger when he was dying,' continued she carelessly; and afterwards added mysteriously: 'I think he stole it.'

'Hush, child! hush! It is wrong to speak so of a dead father,' cried I, much shocked.

'Is it? Well, I'll not do it if it vexes you, Miss Pryor.'

This seemed her only consciousness of right and wrong—pleasing or displeasing me. At all events it argued well for my influence over her and her power of being guided by the affections. I asked again about her father; somehow, with a feminine prejudice, natural though scarcely right, I felt a delicacy in mentioning the mother. But she was the only parent of whom Zillah would speak. 'I hardly know', 'I can't remember', 'I don't care', were all the answers my questions won. 'You saw your father when he was dying?' I persisted: 'an awful sight it must have been.' Zillah shuddered at the recollection. 'What did he say to you?'

'I don't remember, except that I was like my mother. All the rest was swearing, as uncle swears at me. But uncle did not do it then.'

'So Mr Le Poer was present?'

'Yes; and the ugly, horrible-looking man they said was my father talked to him in whispers, and uncle took me on his knee, and called me "My dear". He never did it afterwards.'

I asked her one question more—'How long was this ago?' and she said, 'Several years; she did not recollect how many.'

I talked to her no more that night, but bade her go to rest. In fact my mind was so full of her that I was glad to get her visible self out of the way. She went, lazily and stupidly as ever. Only at the door she paused. 'You won't tell what I have been saying, Miss Pryor?—You'll not mention my mother before them? I did once, and they laughed and made game of her, uncle and all. They did—they'——She stopped, literally foaming at the mouth with rage.*

'Come in again; do, my poor child,' said I, gently approaching. But she shut the door hurriedly, and ran downstairs to the kitchen, where she slept with her dire enemy, yet sole companion, the servant-maid.

Six months after my coming to the Le Poers I began heartily to wish for some of my salary; not that I had any doubt of it—Mr Sutherland had said it was sure—but I wanted some replenishment of my wardrobe, and besides it was near my mother's birthday, when I always took care she had some nice useful gift. It quite puzzled me to think what little luxury she wanted, for she wrote me word Mr Sutherland brought her so many.—'He was just like a son to her,' she said.—Ah me!—One day, when disconsolately examining my last pair of boots—the 'wee boots', that for a foolish reason I had, were one of my few feminine vanities—I took courage to go downstairs and ask Mr Le Poer 'if he could make it convenient', &c. &c. 'My dear Miss Pryor,' said he with most gentle-manly *empressement*,* 'if I had thought—indeed you should have asked me before. Let me see, you have been here six months, and our stipulated sum was——' I thought he hesitated on account of the delicacy some gentlemen feel in business-dealings with a lady; indeed I supposed it was from that cause he had never spoken to me about money matters. How-ever, I felt no such delicacy, but answered plainly: 'My salary, Mr Sutherland said, was to be 100 guineas a year.' 'Exactly so; and payable yearly, I believe?' Mr Le Poer added carelessly. Now, I had not remem-bered that, but of course he knew. However, I looked and felt disap-pointed. At last, as Mr Le Poer spoke with the kindest politeness, I confessed the fact that I wanted the money for habiliments. 'Oh, is that all? Then pray, my excellent young lady, go with Caroline to H—— at once. Order anything you like of my tradespeople. Bid them put all to my account: we can settle afterwards. No excuses; indeed you must.' He bowed me away with the air of a benefactor disdaining gratitude, and set off immediately on one of his frequent jaunts. There was no help for it; so I accepted his plan, and went to H—— with Caroline and Matilda.

It seemed a long time since I had been in any town, and the girls might never have been there in their lives, so eagerly did they linger at shop windows, admiring and longing after finery. The younger consoled the elder, saying that they would have all these sort of grand things some time. 'It's only four years,' whispered she—'just four years, and then that stupid Zill——' Here Caroline pushed her back with an angry 'hush!' and walked up to my side with a prim smile. I thought it strange, but took no notice, always disliking to play the governess out of school hours.

Another odd thing happened the same week. There came a letter to Mr Le Poer from Mr Sutherland. I could not help noticing this, as it lay on the mantel-shelf two days before the former returned, and I used to see it always when I sat at meals. His—Mr Sutherland's I mean—was a fair large hand, too, which would have caught anyone's eye: it was like old times to see it again. I happened to be by when Mr Le Poer opened the letter. He was so anxious over it that he did not notice my presence. Perhaps it was wrong of me to glance toward him, but yet natural, considering it was a friend's letter. I saw a little note enclosed, the address of which, I was almost sure, bore my own name. I waited, thinking he would give it me. I even made some slight movement to attract his attention. He looked up—he actually started—but next moment smiled as only Mr Le Poer could smile. 'News from our friend, you see!' said he, showing me the outside envelope. 'He is quite well, and—let me consider'—glancing over his own letter—'he sends his kindest remembrances to you. A most worthy man is Mr Sutherland.' So saying he folded the epistle, and placed it in his desk. The little note, which he had turned seal uppermost, he quietly put, unopened, into his pocket. It must have been my own delusion then.—Not the first, nor yet the last!

At the expiration of my first year as a governess, just as I was looking with untold eagerness to my midsummer holidays, when I was at length to go home to my mother—for the journey to London was too expensive to admit of that happiness more than once a year—there happened a great disaster to the Le Poer family: no less than that terrible scourge, typhus fever. Matilda took it first, then Caroline, then the mother. These three were scarcely convalescent when Zillah caught the fever in her turn, and had it more dangerously than any of the rest. Her life was in danger for many days, during which I had the sole anxiety and responsibility; for Mr Le Poer, on the first tidings of the fever, had taken flight, and been visible at home no more. True, he wrote every other day most touching letters, and I in return kept him constantly informed as to the progress of his wife and children. When Zillah was taken ill, however, I did not think it necessary to send him word concerning her, feeling that the poor orphan's life was precious to no one. I never was more surprised than when on Mr Le Poer's venturing back and finding Zillah in the crisis of her disease, his terror and anxiety appeared uncontrollable. 'Good God!' he cried, 'Zillah ill? Zillah going to die? Impossible! Why was I not informed before? Confound you, madam'—and he turned furiously to his still ailing wife—'did you not think?—Are you mad—quite mad?'

I declare I thought *he* was. Mrs Le Poer only sobbed in silence. Meanwhile the outcries of the delirious girl were heard in the very parlour. I had given her my room; I thought, poor soul, she should not die in her damp kitchen closet.

Mr Le Poer turned absolutely white with terror—he, who had expressed only mild concern when his wife and daughters were in peril. 'Miss Pryor,' said he hoarsely, 'something must be done. That girl *must* be saved; I'd snatch her from the very fiend himself! Send for advice, physicians, nurses; send to Leeds, Liverpool—to London even. Only, by ——, she must not die!'

Poor Zillah did not die. She was saved for Heaven's strange purposes; though I, in my then blindness, often and often, while sitting by her bedside, thought it would be better did she slip quietly out of the bitter world in which she seemed to be only an unsightly and trampled weed. Mr Le Poer's unwonted anxiety did not end with her convalescence, which was very slow. 'She may die yet!' I heard him muttering to himself the first day after he saw his niece. 'Miss Pryor, my wife is a foo—— I mean, a rather undecided person. Tell me what *you* think ought to be done for Zillah's recovery?' I prescribed, but with little hope that my advice would be followed—immediate change to sea air. 'It shall be done!' at once said he. 'Mrs Le Poer and the girls can take care of her; or stay—she likes you best. Miss Pryor, are you willing to go?'

This question perfectly confounded me. I had been so longingly anticipating my going home—delayed, as in common charity I could not but delay it, on account of the fever. Now this trouble was over I had quite counted on my departure. That very week I had been preparing my small wardrobe, so as to look as nice as possible in my mother's eyes. She had given me a hint to do so, since she and I were to spend the vacation together at Mr Sutherland's country house, and old Mrs Sutherland was so very particular.—'Why do you hesitate?' said Mr Le Poer rather sharply. 'Are you thinking of the money? You shall have any additional salary—£50 more if you choose. Upon my soul, madam, you shall! only I entreat you to go.' I would not have minded his entreaties, but I was touched by those of Zillah, who seemed terrified at the idea of going to a strange place without me. Then, too, the additional money, not unneeded; for Mr Sutherland, so kindly generous in other things, had the still rarer generosity never to offer us *that*. I determined to write and tell my mother the position of affairs. Her good judgement would decide, or if hers failed, she would be sure to appeal to her trusty and only adviser since my father died; and I was content to abide by *his* decision. He did decide. He told my mother that it was his earnest wish I should stay a little longer with Zillah Le Poer, whom he called 'his ward'. Her history, he said, he would inform me of when we met, which must be ere long, as he was contemplating returning to India for some years.

Mr Sutherland returning to India! And before his departure he must see me—*me*! It was a very simple and natural thing, as I felt afterwards, but not then. I did what he desired—as indeed I had long been in the habit of doing—and accompanied Zillah.

I had supposed that we should go to some near watering-place, or at all events to the Liverpool shore. Indeed I had pointedly recommended Tranmere,* where, as I stated to Mr Le Poer, there was living an aunt of Mr Sutherland's, who would have taken lodgings or done anything in her power for her nephew's ward. To my surprise he gently objected to this plan. After staying a night in Liverpool, instead of crossing to the opposite shore, as I expected, he put us all—that is, Zillah, the two other girls, and myself—on board the Belfast boat, and there we found ourselves floating across the Irish Channel! The two Misses Le Poer were considerably frightened; Zillah looked most happy. She said it reminded her of her voyage to England when she was a little child. She had never seen the sea since. Long after we got out of sight of land she and I sat together on the deck in the calm summer evening, talking of this Indian voyage, and what it was like, and what people did during the long four months from land to land. She gave me much information, to which I listened with strange interest. I well remember, fool that I was! sitting on the deck of that Belfast boat, with the sun dipping into the sea before us, and the moon rising on the other side—sitting and thinking what it would be to feel one's self on the deck of some India-bound ship, alone, or else in companionship that might make the word still correct, according to its original reading—*all one*: an etymological notion worthy of a governess!

The only remarkable event of our voyage was my sudden introduction by Mr Le Poer to a personage whom I had not thought existed. 'My son, Miss Pryor; my eldest and only son, Lieutenant Augustus Le Poer.' I was very considerably surprised, as I had never heard of the young gentleman.

I could only hurriedly conjecture, what I afterwards found to be the truth, that this was the son of a former marriage, and that there had been some family quarrel, lately healed. The lieutenant bowed to me, and I to him. Zillah, who sat by me, had no share in the introduction, until the young man, sticking his glass into his eye, stared at her energetically, muttering to his father some question, in which I just detected the words, 'odd fish'. 'Only Zillah,' answered Mr Le Poer carelessly. 'Child, this is your cousin Augustus, lately returned from foreign service. Shake hands with him.' Zillah listlessly obeyed; but her 'cousin' seemed not at all to relish the title. He cast his eyes superciliously over her. I must confess my poor child's appearance was not very attractive. I did not wonder that Lieutenant Augustus merely nodded his head, twirled his moustache, and walked away. Zillah just looked lazily after him, and then her eyes declined upon the beautiful expanse of sea.

For my part I watched our new friend with some curiosity and amusement, especially when Caroline and Matilda appeared, trying to do the agreeable. The lieutenant was to them evidently the beau ideal of a brother. For myself, I did not admire him at all. Unluckily, if I have three positive aversions in the world, it is for dandies, men with moustaches, and soldiers—and he was a compound of all three. Also, he was a small man; and I, like most little women, have a great reverence for height in the other sex—not universally, for some of my truest friends have been diminutive men—excellent, worthy, admirable Zaccheuses. Still, from an ancient prejudice, acquired—no matter how—my first impression, of any man is usually in proportion to his inches: therefore Lieutenant Le Poer did not stand very high in my estimation.

Little notice did he condescend to take of us, which was rather a satisfaction than otherwise; but he soon became very fraternal and confidential with his two sisters. I saw them all chattering together until it grew dusk; and long after that, the night being fine, I watched their dark figures walking up and down the other side of the deck. More than once I heard their laughter, and detected in their talk the name of Zillah; so I supposed the girls were ridiculing her to their brother. Poor child! she was fast asleep, with her head on my shoulder, wrapped closely up, so that the mild night could do her no harm. She looked almost pretty—the light of the August moon so spiritualized her face. I felt thankful she had not died, but that, under Heaven, my care had saved her—for what? Ay, for what? If, as I kissed the child, I had then known—— But no, I should have kissed her still!

Our brief voyage ended, we reached Belfast and proceeded to Holywood*—a small sea-bathing village a few miles down the coast. To this day I have never found out why Mr Le Poer took the trouble to bring us all over the water and settle us there; where, to all intents and purposes, we might as well have been buried in the solitudes of the Desert of Sahara. But perhaps that was exactly what he wanted.

I think that never in her life, at least since childhood, could Zillah have been so happy as she was during the first week or two of our sojourn at Holywood. To me, who in my youth, when we were rich and could travel, had seen much beautiful scenery, the place was rather uninteresting; to her it was perfection! As she grew stronger life seemed to return to her again under quite a new aspect. To be sure, it was a great change in her existence to have no one over her but me—for her uncle and cousin Augustus had of course speedily vanished from this quiet spot—to be able to do just what she liked, which was usually nothing at all. She certainly was not made for activity; she would lie whole days on the beach, or on the grassy walk which came down to the very edge of highwater mark—covering her eyes with her poke bonnet, or gazing sleepily from under her black lashes at the smooth Lough,* and the wavy line of hills on the opposite shore. Matilda and Caroline ran very wild too: since we had no lessons I found it hard work to make them obey me at all; indeed it was always a great pain for a quiet soul like me to have to assume authority. I should have got on better even with Mrs Le Poer to assist me; but she, poor little woman, terrified at change, had preferred staying quietly at home in Yorkshire. I was not quite sure but that she had the best of it after all.

In the course of a week, my cares were somewhat lightened. The lieutenant reappeared, and from that time forward I had very little of the girls' company. He was certainly a kind brother; I could not but acknowledge that. He took them about a great deal, or else stayed at Holywood, leaving us by the late evening train, as he said, to go to his lodgings at Belfast. I, the temporary mistress of the establishment, was of course quite polite to my pupils' brother, and he was really very civil to me, though he treated me with the distance due to an ancient duenna. This amused me sometimes, seeing I was only twenty-six—probably his own age; but I was always used to be regarded as an old maid. Of Zillah the lieutenant hardly ever took any notice at all, and she seemed to keep out of his way as much as possible. When he left us in the evening—and there was always a tolerable confusion at that time, his two sisters wanting to see him off by the train, which he never by any chance allowed—then came the quietest and pleasantest half-hour of the day. The Misses Le Poer disliked twilight rambles, so Zillah and I always set off together. Though oftentimes we parted company, and I was left sitting on the beach, while she strolled on to a pleasant walk she said she had found—a deserted house, whose grounds sloped down to the very shore. But I, not very strong then, and weighed down by many anxious thoughts, loved better to sit and stupefy myself with the murmur of the sea—a habit not good for me, but pleasant. No fear had I of Zillah's losing herself, or coming to any harm; and the girl seemed so happy in her solitary rambles that I had not the desire to stop them, knowing how a habit of self-dependence is the greatest comfort to a woman, especially to one in her desolate position. But though, as her nature woke up, and her dullness was melting away, Zillah seemed more *self-contained*, so to speak; more reserved, and relying on her own thoughts for occupation and amuse-ment, still she had never been so attentive or affectionate to me. It was a curious and interesting study—this young mind's unfolding, though I shame to say that just then I did not think about Zillah as much as I ought to have done. Often I reproached myself for this afterwards; but, as things turned out, I now feel, with a quiet self-compassion, that my error was pardonable.

I mind one evening—now *I mind* is not quite English, but I learned it, with other Scottish phrases, in my young days, so let it stand!—I mind one evening, that, being not quite in a mood to keep my own company, I went out walking with Zillah; somehow the noise of the sea wearied me, and unconsciously I turned through the village and along the high road—almost like an English road, so beautiful with overhanging trees. I did not talk much, and Zillah walked quite silently, which indeed was nothing new. I think I see her now, floating along with her thin but lithe figure, and limp, clinging dress—the very antipodes of fashion—nothing about her that would really be called beautiful except her great eyes, that were perfect oceans of light. When we came to a gateway—which, like most things in poor Ireland, seemed either broken down or left half-finished—she looked round rather anxiously.

'Do you know this, my dear?'

'It is an old mansion—a place I often like to stroll in.'

'What! have you been there alone?'

'Of course I have,' said she quickly, and slightly colouring. 'You knew it: or I thought you did.'

She appeared apprehensive of reproof, which struck me as odd in so inoffensive a matter, especially as I was anything but a cross governess. To please and reassure her I said: 'Well, never mind, my dear; you shall show me your pet paradise. It will be quite a treat.'

'I don't think so, Miss Pryor. It's all weeds and disorder, and you can't endure that. And the ground is very wet here and there. I am sure you'll not like it at all.'

'Oh, but I will, if only to please you, Zillah,' said I, determined to be at once firm and pacific—for I saw a trace of her old sullen look troubling my pupil's face, as if she did not like her haunts to be intruded upon even by me. However she made no more open opposition, and we entered the grounds, which were almost English in their aspect, except in one thing—their entire desolation. The house might not have been inhabited, or the grounds cultivated, for twenty years. The rose-beds grew wild—great patches of white clover overspread the lawn and flower-garden, and all the underwood was one mass of tall fern.

I had not gone far in and out of the tangled walks of the shrubbery when I found that Zillah had slipped away. I saw her at a distance standing under a tall Portugal laurel seemingly doing nothing but meditate—a new occupation for her; so I left her to it, and penetrated deeper in what my old French governess would have called the *bocage*.* My feet sunk deep in fern, amidst which I plunged, trying to gather a great armful of that and of wild flowers; for I had, and have still, the babyish propensity of wishing to pluck everything I see, and never can conquer the delight I feel in losing myself in a wilderness of vegetation. In that oblivion of childlike content I was happy—happier than I had been for a long time. The ferns nearly hid me, when I heard a stirring in the bushes behind, which I took for some harmless animal that I had disturbed. However, hares, foxes, or even squirrels, do not usually give a loud 'Ahem!' in the perfectly human tone which followed. At first I had terrors of some stray keeper, who might possibly shoot me for a rabbit or a poacher, till I recollected that I was not in England but in Ireland, where unjust landlords are regarded as the more convenient game.

'Ahem!' reiterated the mysterious voice—'ahem! Is it you, my angel?' Never could any poor governess be more thoroughly dumbfounded. Of course the adjective was not meant for me. Impossible! Still it was unpleasant to come into such near contact with a case of philandering. Mere philandering it must be, for this was no village tryst, the man's accent being refined and quite English. Besides, little as I knew of love-making, it struck me that in any serious attachment people would never address one another by the silly title of 'my angel'. It must be some idle flirtation going on among the strolling visitants whom we occasionally met on the beach, and who had probably wandered up through the gate which led to these grounds. To put an end to any more confidential disclosures from this unseen gentleman, I likewise said 'Ahem!' as loud as I could, and immediately called out for Zillah. Whereupon there was a hasty rustling in the bushes, which, however, soon subsided, and the place became quite still again, without my ever having caught sight of the very complimentary individual who had in this extempore manner addressed me as his 'angel'. 'Certainly,' I thought, 'I must have been as invisible to him as he to me, or he never would have done it.'

Zillah joined me quickly. She looked half frightened, and said she feared something was the matter: had I seen anything?' At first I was on the point of telling her all, but somehow it now appeared a rather ridiculous position for a governess to be placed in—to have shouted for assistance on being addressed by mistake by an unknown admirer, and besides I did not wish to put any love notions into the girl's head: they come quite soon enough of their own accord. So I merely said I had been startled by hearing voices in the bushes—that perhaps we were intruders on the domain, and had better not stay longer. 'Yet the place seems quite retired and desolate,' said I to Zillah as we walked down the tangled walk that led to the beach, she evidently rather unwilling to go home. 'Do you ever meet any strangers about here?'

She answered briefly: 'No.'

'Did you see any one tonight?'

'Yes'—given with a slight hesitation.

'Who was it?'

'A man, I think—at a distance.'

'Did he speak to you?'

'No.'

I give these questions and answers verbatim, to show—what I believed then, and believe now—that, so far as I questioned, Zillah answered truthfully. I should be very sorry to think that either at that time or any other she had told me a wilful lie. But this adventure left an uncomfortable sensation on my mind—not from any doubt of Zillah herself, for I thought her still too much of a child, and, in plain words, too awkward and unattractive to fear her engaging in love affairs, clandestine or otherwise, for some time to come. Nevertheless, after this evening, I always contrived that we should take our twilight strolls in company, and that I should never lose sight of her for more than a few minutes together. Yet even with this precaution I proved to be a very simple and short-sighted governess after all.

We had been at Holywood a whole month, and I began to wonder when we should return home, as Zillah was quite well, indeed more blooming than I had ever seen her. Mr Le Poer made himself visible once or twice, at rare intervals: he had always 'business in Dublin', or 'country visits to pay'. His son acted as regent in his absence—I always supposed by his desire; nevertheless I often noticed that these two lights of the family never shone together, and the father's expected arrival was the signal of Mr Augustus's non-appearance for some days. Nor did the girls ever allude to their brother. I thought family quarrels might perhaps have lessoned them in this, and so was not surprised. It was certainly a relief to all when the head of the family again departed. We usually kept his letters for him, he not being very anxious about them, for which indifference, as I afterwards comprehended, he might have good reasons. Once there came a letter—I knew from whom—marked in the corner, '*If absent, to be opened by Miss Pryor.*' Greatly surprised was I to find it contained a banknote, apparently hurriedly enclosed, with this brief line: 'If Zillah requires more, let me know at once. She must have every luxury needful for her health.—A.S.' The initials meant certainly his name—Andrew Sutherland—nor could I be mistaken in the hand. Yet it seemed very odd, as I had no idea that he held over her more than a nominal guardianship, just undertaken out of charity to the orphan, and from his having slightly known her father. At least so Mr Le Poer told me. The only solution I could find was the simple one of this being a gift springing from the generosity of a heart whose goodness I knew but too well. However, to be quite sure, I called Caroline into counsel, thinking, silly as she was, she might know something of the matter. But she only tittered, looked mysteriously important, and would speak clearly on nothing, except that we had a perfect right to use the money—Pa always did; and that she wanted a new bonnet very badly indeed. A day or two after, Mr Le Poer, returning unexpectedly, took the note into his own possession, saying smilingly, 'That it was all right;' and I heard no more. But if I had not been the very simplest woman in the world I should have certainly suspected that things were not 'all right'. Nevertheless, I do not now wonder at my blindness. How could I think otherwise than well of a man whom I innocently supposed to be a friend of Mr Sutherland?

'Zillah, my dear, do not look so disappointed. There is no help for it. Your uncle told me before he left us that we must go home next week.' So said I, trying to say it gently, and not marvelling that the girl was unhappy at the near prospect of returning to her old miserable life. It was a future so bitter that I almost blamed myself for not having urged our longer stay. Still, human nature is weak, and I did so thirst for home—my own home. But it was hard that my pleasure should be the poor child's pain. 'Don't cry, my love,' I went on, seeing her eyes brimming, and the colour coming and going in her face—strange changes which latterly, on the most trifling occasions, had disturbed the apparent stolidity of her manner. 'Don't be unhappy: things may be smoother now; and I am sure your cousins behave better and kinder to you than they did; even the lieutenant is very civil to you.' A sparkle, which was either pleasure or pride, flashed from the girl's eyes, and then they drooped, unable to meet mine. 'Be content, dear child; all may be happier than you expect. You must write to me regularly—you can write pretty well now, you know: you must tell me all that happens to you, and remember that in everything you can trust me entirely.' Here I was astonished by Zillah's casting herself at my knees as I sat, and bursting into a storm of tears. Anxiously I asked her what was the matter.

'Nothing—everything! I am so happy—so wretched! Ah! what must I do?'

These words bubbled up brokenly from her lips, but just at that unlucky moment her three cousins came in. She sprang up like a frightened deer, and was off to her own room. I did not see her again all the afternoon, for Lieutenant Augustus kept me in the parlour on one excuse or another until I was heartily vexed at him and myself. When I went upstairs to put on my bonnet—we were all going to walk that evening—Zillah slipped away almost as soon as I appeared. I noticed that she was quite composed now, and had resumed her usual manner. I called after her to tell the two other girls to get ready, thinking it wisest to make no remarks concerning her excitement of the morning.

I never take long in dressing, and soon went down, rather quietly perhaps; for I was meditating with pain on how much this passionate child might yet have to suffer in the world. I believe I have rather a light step; at all events I was once told so. Certainly I did not intend to come into the parlour stealthily or pryingly; in fact, I never thought of its occupants at all. On entering, what was my amazement to see standing at the window—Lieutenant Augustus and—my Zillah! He was embracing—in plain English, kissing her. Now, I am no prude; I have sometimes known a harmless fatherlike or brotherlike embrace pass between two, who, quite certain of each other's feelings, gave and received the same in all frankness and simplicity. But generally I am very particular, more so than most women. I often used to think that, were I a man, I would wish, in the sweet day of my betrothal, to know for certain that mine was the first *lover's* kiss ever pressed on the dear lips which I then sealed as wholly my own. But in this case, at one glance, even if I had not caught the silly phrase, 'My angel!'—the same I heard in the wood (ah, that wood!)—I or any one would have detected the truth. It came upon me like a thunderbolt; but knowing Zillah's disposition, I had just wit enough to glide back unseen, and re-enter, talking loudly at the door. Upon which I found the lieutenant tapping his boots carelessly, and Zillah shrinking into a corner like a frightened hare. He went off very soon—he said, to an engagement at Belfast; and we started for our ramble. I noticed that Zillah walked alongside of Caroline, as if she could not approach or look at me.

I know not whether I was most shocked at her, or puzzled to think what possible attraction this young man could find in such a mere child—so plain and awkward-looking too. That he could be 'in love' with her, even in the lowest sense of that phrase, seemed all but an impossibility; and if not in love, what possible purpose could he have in wooing or wanting to marry her?—for I was simple enough to suppose that all wooing must necessarily be in earnest.

Half-bewildered with conjectures, fears, and doubts as to what course I must pursue, did I walk on beside Matilda, who, having quarrelled with her sister, kept close to me. She went chattering on about some misdoings of Caroline. At last my attention was caught by Zillah's name.

'I won't bear it always,' said the angry child: 'I'll only bear it till Zillah comes of age.'

'Bear what?'

'Why, that Carry should always have two new frocks to my one. It's a shame!'

'But what has that to say to Zillah's coming of age?'

'Don't you know, Miss Pryor?—oh, of course you don't, for Carry wouldn't let me tell you: but I will!' she added maliciously.

I hardly knew whether I was right or wrong in not stopping the girl's tongue, but I could not do it.

'Do you know,' she added in a sly whisper, 'Carry says we shall all be very rich when Zillah comes of age. Pa and ma kept it very secret; but Carry found it out, and told it to brother Augustus and to me.'

'Told what?' said I, forgetful that I was prying into a family secret, and stung into curiosity by the mention of Augustus.

'That Zillah will then be very rich, as her father left her all he had; and Uncle Henry was a great nabob,* because he married an Indian princess, and got all her money. Now, you see,' she continued with a cunning smile, shocking on that young face, 'we must be very civil to Zillah, and of course she will give us all her money. Eh, you understand?'

I stood aghast. In a moment all came clear upon me: the secret of Mr Sutherland's guardianship—of his letter to me intercepted—of the money lately sent—of Mr Le Poer's anxiety concerning his niece's life—of his desire to keep her hidden from the world, lest she might wake to a knowledge of her position. The whole was a tissue of crimes. And, deepest crime of all! I now guessed why Lieutenant Augustus wished, unknown to his father, to entrap her still childish affections, marry her, and secure all to himself. I never knew much of the world and its wickedness: I believed all men were like my father or Mr Sutherland. This discovery for the time quite dizzied my faculties. I have not the slightest recollection of anything more that passed on that seaside walk, except that, coming in at the door of the cottage, I heard Zillah say in anxious tones: 'What ails Miss Pryor, I wonder?' I had wisdom enough to answer: 'Nothing, my dears!' and send them all to bed.

'Shall, you be long after us?' asked Zillah, who, as I said, was my chamber companion. 'An hour or two,' I replied, turning away. I went and sat alone in the little parlour, trying to collect my thoughts. To any governess the discovery of a clandestine and unworthy love affair among her pupils would be most painful, but my discoveries were all horror together. The more I thought it over, the more my agonized pity for Zillah overcame my grief at her deceitfulness. Love is always so weak, and girlish love at fifteen such a fascinating dream. Whatever I thought of the young lieutenant, he was very attractive to most people. He was, besides, the first man Zillah had ever known, and the first human being except myself who had treated her with kindness. He had done that from the first; but what other opportunities could they have had to become lovers? I recollected Zillah's wanderings, evening after evening, in the grounds of the deserted estate. She must have met him there. Poor girl! I could well imagine what it must be to be wooed under the glamour of summer twilight and beautiful solitude. No wonder Zillah's heart was stolen away! Thinking of this now, I feel I am wrong in saying 'heart' of what at best could have been mere 'fancy'. Women's natures are different; but some natures I have known were gravely, mournfully, fatally in earnest, even at sixteen.

However, in earnest or not, she must be snatched from this marriage at all risks. There could be no doubt of that. But to whom should I apply for aid? Not to Mr Le Poer certainly. The poor orphan seemed trembling between the grasp of either villain, father and son. Whatever must be done for her I must do myself, of my own judgement, and on my own responsibility. It was a very hard strait for me. In my necessity I instinctively turned to my best friend in the world, and, as I suddenly remembered, Zillah's too: I determined to write and explain all to Mr Sutherland. How well I remember that time! The little parlour quite still and quiet, except for the faint sound of the waves rolling in; for it was rather a wild night, and our small one-storeyed cottage stood by itself in a solitary part of the beach. How well I remember myself! sitting with the pen in my hand, uncertain how to begin; for I felt awkward, never having written to him since I was a child. At first I almost forgot what I had to write about. While musing, I was startled by a noise like the opening of a window. Now, as I explained, our house was all on one flat, and we could easily step from any window to the beach. Shuddering with alarm, I hurried into Zillah's room. There, by the dim night-light, I saw her bed was empty. She had apparently dressed herself—for I saw none of her clothes—and crept out at the window. Terrified inexpressibly, I was about to follow her, when I saw the flutter of a shawl outside, and heard her speaking.

'No, cousin—no, dear cousin! Don't ask me. I can't go away with you tonight. It would be very wrong when Miss Pryor knows nothing about it. If she had found us out, or threatened, and we were obliged to go——' (Immediately I saw that with a girl of Zillah's fierce obstinacy discovery would be most dangerous. I put out the light and kept quite still.)

'I can't, indeed I can't,' pursued Zillah's voice, in answer to some urging which was inaudible; adding with a childish laugh: 'You know, Cousin Augustus, it would never do for me to go and be married in a cotton dressing gown; and Miss Pryor keeps all my best clothes. Dear Miss Pryor! I would much rather have told her, only you say she would be so much the more surprised and pleased when I came back married. And you are quite sure that she shall always live with us, and never return to Yorkshire again!'

Her words, so childish, so unconscious of the wrong she was doing, perfectly startled me. All my notions of girlish devotion following its own wild will were put to flight. Here was a mere child led away by the dazzle of a new toy to the brink of a precipice. She evidently knew no more of love and marriage than a baby. For a little time longer, the wicked—lover I cannot call him—suitor urged his suit, playing with her simplicity in a manner that he must have inwardly laughed at all the time. He lured her to matrimony by puerile pet names, such as 'My angel'—by idle rhapsodies, and pictures of fine houses and clothes. 'I don't mind these things at all,' said poor Zillah innocently; 'only you say that when I am married I shall have nothing to do, and you will never scold me, and I shall have Miss Pryor always with me. Promise!' Here was a pause, until the child's simple voice was heard again: 'I don't like that, cousin. I won't kiss you. Miss Pryor once said we ought never to kiss anybody unless we love them very much.'

'And don't you love me, my adorable creature?'

'I—I'm not quite sure: sometimes I love you, and sometimes not; but I suppose I shall always when we are married.'

'That must be very soon,' said the lieutenant, and I thought I heard him trying to suppress a yawn. 'Let us settle it at once, my dear, for it is late. If you will not come tonight, let me have the happiness, the entire felicity, of fetching you tomorrow.'

'No, no,' Zillah answered; 'Miss Pryor will want me to help her to pack. We leave this day week: let me stay till the night before that; then come for me, and I'll have my best frock on, and we can be married in time to meet them all before the boat sails next day.'

In any other circumstances I should have smiled at this child's idea of marriage: but now the crisis was far too real and awful; and the more her ignorance lightened her own error, the more it increased the crime of that bad man who was about to ruin her peace for ever. A little he tried to reverse her plan and make the marriage earlier; but Zillah was too steady. In the obstinacy of her character—in the little influence which, lover as he was, he seemed to have over her—I read her safeguard, past and present. It would just allow me time to save her in the only way she could be saved. I listened till I heard her say goodbye to her cousin, creep back into the dark room through the open window, and fasten it securely as before. Then I stole away to the parlour, and, supported by the strong excitement of the moment, wrote my letter to Mr Sutherland. There would be in the six days just time for the arrival of an answer, or— himself. I left everything to him, merely stating the facts, knowing he would do right. At midnight I went to bed. Zillah was fast asleep. As I lay awake, hour after hour, I thanked Heaven that the poor child, deluded as she had been, knew nothing of what love was in its reality. She was at least spared that sorrow.

During all the week I contrived to keep Zillah as near me as was possible consistent with the necessity of not awaking her suspicions. This was the more practicable, as she seemed to cling to me with an unwonted and even painful tenderness. The other girls grumbled sadly at our departure; but luckily all had been definitively arranged by their father, who had even, strange to say, given me money for the journey. He had likewise gracefully apologized for being obliged to let us travel alone, as he had himself some business engagements, while his son had lately rejoined his regiment. I really think the deceiving and deceived father fully credited the latter fact. Certainly they were a pretty pair! I made all my plans secure, and screwed up my courage as well as I could; but I own on the evening previous to our journey—the evening which, from several attesting proofs, I knew was still fixed for the elopement—I began to feel a good deal alarmed. Of Mr Sutherland was no tidings. At twilight I saw plainly that the sole hope must lie in my own presence of mind, my influence over Zillah, and my appeal to her sense of honour and affection. I sent the children early to bed, saying I had letters to write, and prepared myself for whatever was to happen. Now many may think me foolish, and at times I thought myself so likewise, for not going at once to Zillah and telling her all I had discovered; but I knew her character better than that. The idea of being betrayed, waylaid, controlled, would drive her fierce Eastern nature into the very commission of the madness she contemplated. In everything I must trust to the impulse of the moment, and to the result of her suddenly discovering her own position and the villainous plans laid against her.

Never in my life do I remember a more anxious hour than that I spent sitting in the dark by the parlour window, whence, myself unseen, I could see all that passed without the house; for it was a lovely night: the moon high up over the Lough and making visible the Antrim hills. I think in all moments of great peril one grows quiet: so did I. At eleven there was a sound of wheels on the beach, and the shadow of a man passed the window. I looked out. It was the most unromantic and commonplace elopement with an heiress: he was merely going to take her away on an outside car. There was no one with him but the carman, who was left whistling contentedly on the shore. The moment had come; with the energy of desperation, I put off the shawl in which I had wrapped myself in case I had to follow the child; for follow her I had determined to do were it necessary. Quietly, and with as ordinary a manner as I could assume, I walked into Zillah's room. She was just stepping from the window. She had on her best frock and shawl, poor innocent! with her favourite white bonnet, that I had lately trimmed for her, carefully tied up in a kerchief. I touched her shoulder. 'Zillah, where are you going?' She started and screamed. 'Tell me: I must know,' I repeated, holding her fast by the arm, while Augustus rather roughly pulled her by the other.

'Cousin, you hurt me!' she cried, and instinctively drew back. Then for the first time the lieutenant saw me.

I have often noticed that cunning and deceitful people—small villains, not great ones—are always cowards. Mr Augustus drew back as if he had been shot. I took no notice of him, but still appealed to Zillah.

'Tell me, my child, the plain truth, as you always do: where were you going?'

She stammered out: 'I was going to—to Belfast—to be married.'

'To your cousin?'

She hung her head and murmured: 'Yes.'

At this frank confession the bridegroom interposed. He perhaps was the braver for reflecting that he had only women to deal with. He leaped in at the chamber window, and angrily asked me by what right I interfered. 'I will tell you,' said I, 'If you have enough gentlemanly feeling to leave my apartment, and will speak with me in the open air.' He retreated, I bolted the window, and still keeping a firm hold on the trembling girl, met him outside the front door. It certainly was the oddest place for such a scene; but I did not wish to let him inside the house.

'Now, Miss Pryor,' said he imperatively, but still politely—a Le Poer could not be otherwise—'will you be so kind as to let go that young lady, who has put herself under my protection, and intends honouring me with her hand?'

'Is that true, Zillah? Do you love this man, and voluntarily intend to marry him?'

'Yes, if you will let me, Miss Pryor. He told me you would be so pleased. He promises always to be kind to me, and never let me work. Please don't be angry with me, dear Miss Pryor: O do let me marry my cousin!'

'Listen to me a few minutes, Zillah,' said I, 'and you shall choose.' And then I told her, in as few words as I could, what her position was—how that it had been concealed from her that she was an heiress, and how, by marrying her, her cousin Augustus would be master over all her wealth. So unworldly was she, that I think the girl herself hardly understood me; but the lieutenant was furious.

'It is all a lie—an infamous cheat!' he cried. 'Don't believe it, Zillah. Don't be frightened, little fool! I promised to marry you, and, by Heaven! marry you I will!'

'Lieutenant Le Poer,' said I very quietly, 'that may not be quite so easy as you think. However, *I* do not prevent you, as indeed I have no right; I only ask my dear child Zillah here to grant me one favour, as for the sake of my love for her'—(here Zillah sobbed)—'I doubt not she will: that she should do as every other young woman of common-sense and delicacy would do, and wait until tomorrow, to ask the consent of one who will then probably be here, if he is not already arrived—her guardian, Mr Andrew Sutherland.'

Lieutenant Augustus burst out with an oath, probably mild in the mess room, but very shocking here to two women's ears. Zillah crept farther from him and nearer to me.

'I'll not be cheated so!' stormed he. 'Come, child, you'll trust your cousin? you'll come away tonight?'—and he tried to lift her on the car, which had approached—the Irish driver evidently much enjoying the scene.

'No, cousin; not tonight,' said the girl resisting. 'I'd rather wait and have Miss Pryor with me, and proper bridesmaids, and all that—that is, if I marry you at all, which I won't unless Miss Pryor thinks you will be kind to me. So goodbye till tomorrow, cousin.' He was so enraged by this time that he tried forcibly to drag her on the car. But I wound my arms round my dear child's waist, and shrieked for help.

'Faith, sir,' said the sturdy Irishman, interfering half in amusement, half in indignation, 'ye'd bether lave the women alone. I'd rayther not meddle with an abduction.'

So Zillah was set free from the lieutenant's grasp, for, as I said before, a scoundrel is often a great coward. I drew the trembling and terrified girl into the house—he following with a storm of oaths and threatenings. At last I forcibly shut the door upon him, and bolted him out. Whether this indignity was too much for the valorous soldier, or whether he felt sure that all chance was over, I know not; but when I looked out ten minutes after, the coast was clear. I took my erring, wronged, yet still more wronged than erring, child into my bosom, and thanked Heaven that she was saved. The next morning Mr Sutherland arrived.

After this night's events I have little to say, or else had rather say but little of what passed during the remainder of that summer. We all travelled to England together, going round by Yorkshire to leave Mr Le Poer's daughters at their own home. This was Mr Sutherland's plan, in order that the two girls should be kept in ignorance of the whole affair, and especially of their father's ill deeds. What they suspected I know not: they were merely told that it was the desire of Zillah's guardian to take her and her governess home with him. So we parted at Halifax, and I never saw any of the family again. I had no scruples about thus quitting them, as I found out from Mr Sutherland that I had been engaged solely as governess to his ward, and that he had himself paid my salary in advance, the whole of which, in some way or other, had been intercepted by Mr Le Poer. The money of course was gone; but he had written to me with each remittance, and thus I had lost his letters. That was hard! I also found out, with great joy and comfort, that my Zillah was truly Zillah Le Poer—her father's legitimate heiress. All I had been led to believe was a cruel and wicked lie. The whole history of her father and mother was one of those family tragedies, only too frequent, which, the actors in them being dead, are best forgotten. I shall not revive the tale.

In late autumn Mr Sutherland sailed for India. Before he quitted England, he made me sole guardian in his stead over Zillah Le Poer, assigning for her a handsome maintenance. He said he hoped we should all live happily together—she, my mother, and I—until he came back. He spent a short time with us all at his country seat—a time which, looking back upon, seems in its eight days like eight separate years.

I ought to speak of Zillah, the unmoved centre of so many convolving fates. She remained still and silent as ever—dull, grieved, humiliated. I told her gradually and gently the whole truth, and explained from how much she had been saved. She seemed grateful and penitent: her heart had never been touched by love; she was yet a mere child. The only evidence of womanly shame she gave was in keeping entirely out of her guardian's way: nor did he take much notice of her except in reproaching himself to me with being neglectful of his charge; but he had so thoroughly trusted in the girl's uncle as being her best protector. The only remark he ever made on Zillah's personal self was that she had beautiful eyes, adding, with a half-sigh, 'that he liked dark Oriental eyes'. One day his mother told me something which explained this. She said he had been engaged to a young lady in India, who on the eve of their marriage had died. He had never cared much for women's society since, and his mother thought he would probably never marry. After his departure she told me the whole story. My heart bled over every pang that he had suffered: he was so good and noble a man. And when I knew about his indifference to all women, I felt the more gratefully what trust he showed in me by making me Zillah's guardian in his absence, and wishing me to write to him regularly of her welfare. The last words he said were to ask me to go and see his mother often; and then he bade God bless me, and called me 'his dear friend'. He was very kind always!

We had a quiet winter, for my health was not good—I being often delicate in wintertime. My mother and Zillah took care of me, and I was very grateful for their love. I got well at last, as the springtime began, and went on in my old ways.

There are sometimes long pauses in one's life—deep rests or sleeps of years—in which month after month, and season after season, float on each the same; during which the soul lies either quiet or torpid, as may be. Thus, without any trouble, joy, or change, we lived for several years—my mother, Zillah Le Poer, and I. One morning I found with a curious surprise, but without any of the horror which most women are supposed to feel at that fact, that I was thirty years old! We discovered by the same reckoning that Zillah was just nineteen. I remember she put her laughing face beside mine in the glass. There was a great difference truly. I do not mean the difference in her from me, for I never compared that, but in her from her former self. She had grown up into a woman, and, as that glass told her, and my own eyes told me, a very striking woman too. I was little of a judge in beauty myself; still, I knew well that everybody we met thought her handsome. Likewise, she had grown up beautiful in mind as well as in body. I was very proud of my dear child. I well remember this day, when she was nineteen and I thirty. I remember it, I say, because our kind friend in India had remembered it likewise, and sent us each a magnificent shawl; far too magnificent it was for a little body like me, but it became Zillah splendidly. She tucked me under her arm as if I had been a little girl, and walked me up and down the room; for she was of a cheerful, gay temper now—just the one to make an old heart young again, to flash upon a worn spirit with the brightness of its own long-past morning. I recollect thinking this at the time—I wish I had thought so oftener! But it matters little: I only chronicle this day, as being the first when Zillah unconsciously put herself on a level with me, becoming thenceforward my equal—no longer a mere pet and a child.

About this time—I may as well just state the fact to comfort other maidens of thirty years' standing—I received an offer of marriage, the first I ever had. He who asked me was a gentleman of my own age, an old acquaintance, though never a very intimate friend. I examined myself well, with great humility and regret, for he was an excellent man; but I found I could not marry him. It was very strange that he should ask me, I thought. My mother, proud and pleased—first, because I had had the honour of a proposal; secondly, that it was refused, and she kept her child still—would have it that the circumstance was not strange at all. She said many women were handsomer and more attractive at thirty than they had ever been in their lives. My poor, fond, deluded and deluding mother, in whose sight even I was fair! That night I was foolish enough to look long into the glass, at my quiet little face, and my pale, grey-blue eyes—not dark, like Zillah's—foolish enough to count narrowly the white threads that were coming one by one into my hair. This trouble—I mean the offer of marriage—I did not quite get over for many weeks, even months.

The following year of my life there befell me a great pang. Of this—a grief never to be forgotten, a loss never to be restored—I cannot even now say more than is implied in three words—*my mother died*! After that Zillah and I lived together alone for twelve months or more.

There are some scenes in our life—landscape scenes, I mean—that we remember very clearly: one strikes me now. A quiet, soft May-day; the hedges just in their first green, the horse-chestnuts white with flowers: the long, silent country lanes swept through by a travelling-carriage, in the which two women, equally silent, sat—Zillah Le Poer and I. It was the month before her coming of age, and she was going to meet her guardian, who had just returned from India. Mrs Sutherland had received a letter from Southampton, and immediately sent for us into the country to meet her son, her 'beloved Andrew'. I merely repeat the words as I remember Zillah's doing so, and laughing at the ugly name. I never thought it ugly. When we had really started, however, Zillah ceased laughing, and became grave, probably at the recollection of that humiliating circumstance which first brought her acquainted with her guardian. But despite this ill-omened beginning, her youth had blossomed into great perfection. As she sat there before me, fair in person, well cultured in mind, and pure and virgin in heart—for I had so kept her out of harm's way that, though nearly twenty-one, I knew she had never been 'in love' with any man—as she sat thus, I felt proud and glad in her, feeling sure that Mr Sutherland would say I had well fulfilled the charge he gave.

We drove to the lodge-gates. An English country-house is always fair to see: this was very beautiful—I remembered it seven years ago, only then it was autumn, and now spring. Zillah remembered it likewise: she drew back, and I heard her whisper uneasily: 'Now we shall soon see Mr Sutherland.' I did not answer her a word. We rolled up the avenue under the large chestnut-trees. I saw some one standing at the portico; then I think the motion of the carriage must have made me dizzy, for all grew indistinct, except a firm, kind hand holding me as I stepped down, and the words, 'Take care, my dear Cassia!' It was Mr Sutherland! He scarcely observed Zillah, till in the hall I introduced her to him. He seemed surprised, startled, pleased. Talking of her to me that evening he said he had not thought she would have grown up thus; and I noticed him look at her at times with a pensive kindness. Mrs Sutherland whispered me that the lady he had been engaged to was a half-caste like Zillah, which accounted for it. His mother had been right: he had come back as he went out—unmarried.

When Zillah went to bed she was full of admiration for her guardian. He was so tall, so stately. Then his thick, curling, fair hair—just like a young man's, with scarcely a shadow of grey. She would not believe that he was over forty—ten years older than myself—until by some pertinacity I had impressed this fact upon her. And then she said it did not signify, as she liked such 'dear old souls' as him and me much better than any young people. Her fervour of admiration made me smile; but after this night I observed that the expression of it gradually ceased. Though I was not so demonstrative as Zillah, it will not be supposed but that I was truly glad to see my old friend Mr Sutherland. He was very kind, talked to me long of past things, and as he cast a glance on my black dress, I saw his lips quiver: he took my hand and pressed it like a brother. God bless him for that! But one thing struck me—a thing I had not calculated on—the alteration seven years had made in us both. When he took me down to dinner, I accidentally caught sight of our two figures in the large pier-glass. Age tells so differently on man and woman: I remembered the time when he was a grown man and I a mere girl; now he looked a stately gentleman in the prime of life; and I a middle-aged, old-maidish woman. Perhaps something more than years had done this; yet it was quite natural, only I had never thought of it before. So, when that first meeting was over, with the excitement, pleasurable or otherwise, that it brought as a matter of course to us all—when we had severally bade each other goodnight, and Mr Sutherland had said smiling that he was glad it was only goodnight, not goodbye—when the whole house was quiet and asleep, to use the psalmist's solemn words: '*At night on my bed I communed with my own heart in my chamber, and was still.*'

'Cassia, I want to speak to you particularly,' said Mr Sutherland to me one morning as after breakfast he was about to go into his study. Zillah placed herself in the doorway with the pretty obstinacy, half-womanish, half-girlish, that she sometimes used with her guardian—much to my surprise. Zillah was on excellent terms with him, considering their brief acquaintance of three weeks. In that time she had treated him as I in my whole lifetime had never ventured to do—wilfully, jestingly, even crossly, yet he seemed to like it. They were very social and merry, for his disposition had apparently grown more cheerful as he advanced in life. Their relation was scarcely like guardian and ward, but that of perfect equality—pleasant and confidential, which somewhat surprised me, until I recollected what opportunities they had of intercourse, and what strong friendships are sometimes formed even in a single week or fortnight when people are shut up together, in a rather lonely country house. This was the state of things among us all on the morning when Mr Sutherland called me to his study. Zillah wanted to go likewise. 'Not today,' he answered her, very gently and smilingly. 'I have business to talk over with Miss Pryor.' (I knew he said 'Miss Pryor' out of respect, yet it hurt me—I had been 'Cassia' with him so many years. Perhaps he thought I was outgrowing my baby name now.)

The business he wished to speak of was about Zillah's coming of age next week, and what was to be done on the occasion. 'Should he, ought he, to give a ball, a dinner, anything of that sort? Would Zillah like it?'

This was a great concession, for in old times he always disliked society. I answered that I did not think such display necessary, but I would try to find out Zillah's mind. I did so. It was an innocent, girlish mind, keenly alive to pleasure, and new to everything. The consequences were natural—the ball must be. A little she hesitated when I hinted at her guardian's peculiarities, and offered cheerfully to renounce her delight. But he, his eyes beaming with a deeper delight still, would not consent. So the thing was settled. It was a very brilliant affair, for Mr Sutherland spared no expense. He seemed to take a restless eagerness in providing for his young favourite everything she could desire. Nay, in answer to her wayward entreaties, he even consented to open the ball with her, though saying, 'he was sure he should make an old idiot of himself'. That was not likely! I watched them walk down the room together, and heard many people say with a smile what a handsome pair they were, notwithstanding the considerable difference of age. It was a very quiet evening to me. Being strange to almost every one there, I sat near old Mrs Sutherland in a corner. Mr Sutherland asked me to dance once, but I did not feel strong, and indeed for the last few years I had almost given up dancing. He laughed, and said merrily: 'It was not fair for him to be beginning life just when I ended it.'—A true word spoken in jest. But I only smiled.

The ball produced results not unlikely, when it was meant for the introduction into society of a young woman, handsome, attractive, and an heiress. A week or two after Zillah's birthday Mr Sutherland called me once more into his study. I noticed he looked rather paler and less composed than usual. He forgot even to ask me to sit down, and we stood together by the fireplace, which I remember was filled with a great vase of lilacs that Zillah had insisted on placing there. It filled the room with a strong, rich scent which now I never perceive without its calling back to mind that room and that day. He said: 'I have had a letter today on which I wish to consult with you before showing it to Miss Le Poer.' I was rather startled by the formal word, since he usually said 'Zillah', as was natural. 'It is a letter—scarcely surprising—in fact to be expected after what I noticed at the dinner-party yesterday; in fact—— But you had better read it yourself.' He took the letter from his desk, and gave it to me. It was an earnest and apparently sincere application for the hand of his ward. The suitor was of good family and moderate prospects. I had noticed he was very attentive to Zillah at the ball, and on some occasions since; still I was a good deal surprised, more so even than Mr Sutherland, who had evidently watched her closer than I. I gave him back the letter in silence, and avoided looking at his face.

'Well, Cassia,' he said after a pause, and with an appearance of gaiety, 'what is to be done? You women are the best counsellors in these matters.' I smiled, but both he and I very soon became grave once more. 'It is a thing to be expected,' continued he in a voice rather formal and hard. 'With Zillah's personal attractions and large fortune she was sure to receive many offers. Still it is early to begin these affairs.' I reminded him that she was twenty-one. 'True, true. She might, under other circumstances, have been married long before this. Do you think that she;——' I suppose he was going to ask me whether she was likely to accept Mr French, or whether she had hitherto formed any attachment. But probably delicacy withheld him, for he suddenly stopped and omitted the question. Soon he went on in the same steady tone: 'I think Zillah ought to be made acquainted with this circumstance. Mr French states that this letter to me is the first confession of his feelings. That was honourable on his part. He is a gentleman of good standing, though far her inferior in fortune. People might say that he wanted her property to patch up the decayed estate at Weston Brook.' This was spoken bitterly, very bitterly for a man of such kind nature as Andrew Sutherland. He seemed conscious of it, and added: 'I may wrong him, and if so I regret it. But do you not think, Cassia, that of all things it must be most despicable, most mean, most galling to a man of any pride or honest feeling, the thought of the world's saying that he married his wife for money, as a prop to his falling fortunes, or a shield to his crumbling honour? I would die a thousand deaths first!'

In the passion of the moment the red colour rushed violently to his cheek, and then he became more pallid than ever. I beheld him: my eyes were opened now. I held fast by the marble chimney-piece, so that I could stand quite upright, firm, and quiet. He walked hurriedly to the window, and flung it open, saying the scent of the lilacs was too strong. When he came back, we were both ready to talk again. I believe I spoke first—to save him the pain of doing so. 'I have no idea,' said I, and I said truly, 'what answer Zillah will give to this letter. Hitherto I have known all her feelings, and am confident that while she stayed with me her heart was untouched.' Here I waited for him to speak, but he did not. I went on: 'Mr French is very agreeable, and she seems to like him; but a girl's heart, if of any value at all, is rarely won in three meetings. I think, however, that Zillah ought to be made acquainted with this letter. Will you tell her, or shall I?'

'Go you and do it—a woman can best deal with a woman in these cases. And,' he added, rising slowly and looking down upon me from his majestic height with that grave and self-possessed smile which was likewise as sweet as any woman's, 'tell Zillah from me, that though I wish her to marry in her own rank and with near equality of fortune, to save her from all those dangers of mercenary offers to which an heiress is so cruelly exposed; still, both now and at all times, I leave her to the dictates of her own affections, and her happiness will ever be my chief consideration in life.' He spoke with formal serenity until the latter words, when his voice sank a little. Then he led me to the door, and I went out.—Zillah lay on a sofa reading a love story. Her crisped black hair was tossed about the crimson cushions, and her whole figure was that of rich Eastern luxuriance. She had always rather a fantastic way of dress, and now she looked almost like a princess out of the Arabian Nights. Even though her skin was that of a half-caste, and her little hands were not white, but brown, there was no denying that she was a very beautiful woman.* I felt it—saw it—knew it! After a minute's pause I went to her side; she jumped up and kissed me, as she was rather fond of doing. Her kisses were very strange to me just then. I came as quickly as possible to my errand, and gave her the letter to read. As she glanced through it her cheeks flushed, and her lips began to curl. She threw the letter on my lap, and said abruptly: 'Well, and what of that?' I began a few necessary explanations. Zillah stopped me.

'Oh, I heard something of the sort from Mr French last night. I did not believe him, nor do I now. He is only making a jest of me.'

I answered that this was impossible. In my own mind I was surprised at Zillah's having known the matter before, and having kept it so quietly. Mr French's statement about his honourable reticence towards the lady of his devotions must have been untrue. Still this was not so remarkable as Zillah's own secrecy on the subject. 'Why did you not tell me, my dear?' said I: 'you know your happiness is of the first importance to me as well as to your guardian.' And, rather hesitating, I repeated word by word, as near as I could, Mr Sutherland's message. Zillah half-hid her face within the cushions, and then drew it out burning red.

'He thinks I am going to accept the creature then? He would have me marry a conceited, chattering, mean-looking, foolish boy!' (Now Mr French was certainly twenty-five.) 'One, too, that only wants me for my fortune, and nothing else. It is very wrong and cruel and unkind of him, and you may go and tell him so.'

'Tell who?' said I, bewildered by this outburst of indignation, and great confusion of personal pronouns.

'Mr Sutherland, of course! Who else would I tell? Whose opinion else do I care for? Go and say to him—— No,' she added abruptly: 'no, you needn't trouble him with anything about such a foolish girl as I. Just say, I shall not marry Mr French, and will he be so kind as to give him his answer, and bid him let me alone?' Here, quite exhausted with her wrath, Zillah sank back and took to her book, turning her head from me. But I saw that she did not read one line, that her motionless eyes were fixed and full of a strange deep expression. I began to cease wondering what the future would bring. Very soon afterwards I went back to Mr Sutherland, and told him all that had passed: just the plain facts without any comments of my own. He apparently required none. I found him sitting composedly with some papers before him—he had for the last few days been immersed in business which seemed rather to trouble him: he started a little as I entered, but immediately came forward and listened with a quiet aspect to the message I had to bring. I could not tell whether it made him happy or the contrary: his countenance could be at times so totally impassive that no friend, dearest or nearest, could ever find out from it anything he did not wish to betray.

'The matter is settled then,' said he gravely: 'I will write to Mr French today, and perhaps it would be as well if we never alluded to what has passed. I, at least, shall not do it: tell Zillah so. But, in the future, say that I entreat she keeps no secret back from you. Remember this, my dear Cassia: watch over her as you love her—and you do love her?' continued he, grasping my hand. I answered that I did, and, God knows, even then I told no lie. She was a very dear child to me always! Mr Sutherland seemed quite satisfied and at rest. He bade me a cheerful goodbye, which I knew meant that I should go away, so accordingly I went. Passing the drawing-room door I saw Zillah lying in her old position on the sofa; so I would not disturb her, but went and walked for an hour under a clump of fir-trees in the garden. They made a shadow dark and grave and still; it was pleasanter than being on the lawn, among the flowers, the sunshine, and the bees. I did not come in until dinner-time. There were only ourselves, just a family party—Mr Sutherland did not join us until we reached the dining-room door. I noticed that Zillah's colour changed as he approached, and that all dinner-time she hardly spoke to him; but he behaved to her as usual. He was rather thoughtful, for, as he told me privately, he had some trifling business anxieties burdening him just then; otherwise he seemed the same. Nevertheless, whether it was his fault or Zillah's, in a few days the fact grew apparent to me that they were not quite such good friends as heretofore. A restraint, a discomfort, a shadow scarcely tangible, yet still there, was felt between them. Such a cloud often rises—a mist that comes just before the day dawn; or, as happens sometimes, before the night.

For many days—how many I do not recollect, since about this time all in the house and in the world without seemed to go on so strangely—for many days afterwards nothing happened of any consequence, except that one Sunday afternoon I made a faint struggle of politeness in some remark about 'going home' and 'encroaching on their hospitality', which was met with such evident pain and alarm by all parties, that I was silent; so we stayed yet longer. One morning—it was high summer now—we were sitting at breakfast: we three only, as Mrs Sutherland never rose early. I was making tea, Zillah near me, and Mr Sutherland at the foot of the table. He looked anxious, and did not talk much, though I remember he rose up once to throw a handful of crumbs to a half-tame thrush who had built on the lawn—he was always so kind to every living thing. 'There, my fine bird, take some home to your wife and weans!' said he pleasantly; but at the words became grave, even sad, once more. He had his letters beside him, and opened them successively until he came to *one*—a momentous one, I knew; for though he never moved, but read quietly on, every ray of colour went out of his face. He dropped his head upon his hand, and sat so long in that attitude that we were both frightened.

'Is anything the matter?' I said gently, for Zillah was dumb.

'Did you speak?' he answered with a bewildered stare. 'Forgive me; I—I have had bad news'—and he tried to resume the duties of the meal; but it was impossible: he was evidently crushed, as even the strongest and bravest men will be, for the moment, under some great and unexpected shock. We said to him—I repeat *we*, because, though Zillah spoke not, her look was enough, had he seen it—we said to him those few soothing things that women can, and ought to say, in such a time. 'Ay,' he answered, quite unmanned—'ay, you are very kind. I think—if I could speak to some one—Cassia, will you come?' He rose slowly, and held out his hand to me. *To me*! That proof of his confidence, his tenderness, his friendship, I have always remembered, and thought, with thankful heart, that, though not made to give him happiness, I have sometimes done him a little good when he was in trouble.

We walked together from the room. I heard a low sob behind us, but had no power to stay; besides, a momentary pang mattered little; the sobs would be hushed ere long.—Standing behind the chair where he sat, I heard the story of Mr Sutherland's misfortunes—misfortunes neither strange nor rare in the mercantile world. In one brief word, he was ruined; that is, so far as a man can be considered ruined who has enough left to pay all his creditors, and start in the world afresh as a penniless honest man. He told me this—an everyday story; nay, it had been my own father's—told it me with great composure, and I listened with the same. I was acquainted with all these kind of business matters of old. It was very strange, but I felt no grief, no pity for his losses; I only felt, on my own account, a burning, avaricious thirst for gold; a frantic envy—a mad longing to have for a single day, a single hour, wealth in millions.

'Yes, it must be so,' said he, when, after talking to me a little more, I saw the hard muscles of his face relax, and he grew patient, ready to bear his troubles like a man—like Andrew Sutherland. 'Yes, I must give up this house, and all my pleasant life here; but I can do it, since I shall be alone.' And then he added in a low tone: 'I am glad, Cassia, very glad of two things: my mother's safe settlement, and the winding-up last month of all my affairs with—Miss Le Poer.'

'When,' said I, after a pause—'when do you intend to tell Zillah what has happened?' I felt feverishly anxious that she should know all, and that I should learn how she would act.

'Tell Zillah? Ay,' he repeated, 'tell her at once—tell her at once.' And then he sunk back into his chair, muttering something about 'its signifying little now.'

I left him, and with my heart nerved as it were to anything, went back to the room where Zillah was. Her eyes met me with a bitter, fierce, jealous look—jealous of me, the foolish child!—until I told her what had happened to our friend. Then she wept, but only for a moment, until a light broke upon her. 'What does it signify?' cried she, echoing, curiously enough, his own words. 'I am of age—I can do just what I like: so I will give my guardian all my money. Go back and tell him so!' I hesitated. 'I tell you I will: all I have in the world is not too good for him. Everything belonging to me is his, and——' Here she stopped, and catching my fixed look, became covered with confusion. Still the generous heart did not waver. 'And—when he has my fortune, you and I will go and live together, and be governesses.' I felt the girl was in earnest, nor wished to deceive me; and though I let her deceive herself a little longer, it was with joy—ay, with joy, that in the heart I clasped to mine was such unselfishness, such true nobility, not unworthy even of what it was about to win. I went once more through the hall—the long, cool, silent hall, which I trod so dizzily, daring not to pause—into Mr Sutherland's presence. 'Well!' he said, looking up.

I told—in what words I cannot remember now; but solemnly, faithfully, as if I were answering my account before Heaven—the truth, and the whole truth. He listened, pressing his hands on his eyes, and then gave vent to one heavy sigh like a woman's sob. At last he rose and walked feebly to the door. There he paused, as though to account for his going. 'I ought to thank her, you know. It must not be—not by any means: still I ought to go and thank her—the—dear—child!' His voice ceased, broken by emotion. Once more he held out his hand: I grasped it, and said: 'Go!' At the parlour door he stopped, apparently for me to precede him in entering there; but, as if accidentally, I passed on and let him enter alone. Whether he knew it or not, I knew clear as light what would happen then and there. The door shut—they two being within, and I, without. In an hour I came back towards the house. I had been wandering somewhere I think under the fir-wood. It was broad noon, but I felt very cold; it was always cold under those trees. I had no way to pass but near the parlour window; and some insane attraction made me look up as I went by. They were standing—they two—close together, as lovers stand. His arm folded her close; his face, all radiant, yet trembling with tenderness, was pressed upon hers—O my God!

I am half-inclined to blot out the last sentence, as it seems so foolish to dilate on the love-makings of people now twelve years married; and besides, growing older, one feels the more how rarely and how solemnly the Holy Name ought to be mingled with any mere burst of human emotion. But I think the All-Merciful One would pardon it then. Of course no reader will marvel at my showing emotion over the union of these my two dearest objects on earth.

From that union I can now truly say I have derived the greatest comforts of my life. They were married quickly, as I urged, Mr Sutherland settling his wife's whole property upon herself. This was the only balm his manly pride could know; and no greater proof could he give of his passionate love for her, than that he humbled himself to marry an heiress. As to what the world thought, no one could ever suspect the shadow of mercenary feeling in Andrew Sutherland. All was as it should be—and so best.

After Zillah's marriage, I took a situation abroad. Mr Sutherland was very angry when he knew; but I told them I longed for the soft Italian air, and could not live an idle life on any account. So they let me go, knowing, as he smiling said, 'That Cassia could be obstinate when she had a mind—that her will, like her heart, was as firm as a rock.' Ah me!

When I came back, it was to a calm, contented, and cheerful middle age; to the home of a dear brother and sister; to the love of a new generation; to a life filled with peace of heart and thankfulness towards God; to——

Hey-day! writing is this moment become quite impossible; for there peeps a face in at my bedroom door, and, while I live, not for worlds shall my young folk know that Aunt Cassia is an authoress. Therefore good-bye, pen!—And now come in, my namesake, my darling, my fair-haired Cassia,* with her mother's smile, and her father's eyes and brow—I may kiss both now. Ah, God in heaven bless thee, my dear, dear child!

EXPLANATORY NOTES

A number of Craik's references to poetry remain unidentified.

3 *waesome*: woeful, sorrowful.

4 *'boatie'*: a little boat.

Murrays o' Perth: the Murray line goes back to Freskin in the twelfth century who owned extensive lands in Moray, as well as Strathbrock in Linlithgow. Lord George Murray (b. 1694) joined Prince Charles Edward in 1745 and was a crucial figure in the Jacobite uprising. Elspeth's pride in her lineage introduces the theme of Scottish singularity in the novel.

no canny: unlucky.

Stirling: a royal burgh, seaport, and parish on the south bank of the river Forth. While Craik emphasizes Stirling's natural beauty and its royal associations (which dated back to 1124 with the death of Alexander I, when the settlement was granted royal status), by the mid-nineteenth century, with a population of about 9,000, it had seen the growth of textiles, coal-mining, and agricultural engineering. The woollen industry was Stirling's principal branch of trade at the time *Olive* was written.

5 *Ben Ledi*: a mountain near Callander in Perthshire, with fine views of the Forth on the east and of the vale of Clyde on the south.

extirpated at Flodden-field and again at Pinkie: two famous battles in which the Scottish armies were disastrously defeated, the first on 9 September 1513 in which Henry VIII's forces killed James IV, his son, many of the nobility, and several thousand soldiers, and the second in 1547, instigated by the English Regent, Somerset, in which casualties were again in the thousands and the remnants of the Scottish army were chased to the gates of Edinburgh. Craik is making gentle fun here of the gory legends of Scottish nationalism, with their emphasis on battlefield martyrdom.

6 *lamiter*: a lame or crippled person.

7 *siller*: silver (hence money in general).

9 *Venus de Medici*: *The Birth of Venus* (1485) by Sandro Botticelli (1446–1510), commissioned by Lorenzo di Pierfrancesco de' Medici, now in the Uffizi, Florence.

Brussels veil: veil made of fine Brussels lace.

braw: handsome, of fine physique.

10 *and of his people, and of all of his race*: 'people' and 'race' here embrace the categories of family, nation, and ethnicity. By the 1840s, what the Scottish ethnologist, Robert Knox, called the 'new sense of race', those profound categories of difference within mankind, were challenging older meanings of 'race' as lineage, although most writers (see Charlotte Brontë, *Jane Eyre*, 1847) use race in both senses.

11 *James the Fifth's reckless court*: James V (1512–42) the only surviving son of James IV and Mary Tudor. He left seven known illegitimate children.

Mistress Katherine Rothesay: Elspie's catalogue of the 'remarkable' bold, beautiful and often transgressive women of the Rothesay line emphasizes Scottish female 'difference' from Sybilla's more conventional English femininity. Olive's royal Scottish lineage accentuates her deformity but also foreshadows the development of her own heroic stature, which combines the traits and temperament of her English and Scottish inheritance.

Culloden: the battle of Culloden on 16 April 1746. Culloden became the symbol of the death of the old order as well as the emblem of the brutality of the Duke of Cumberland.

13 *Sassenach*: English, or English-speaking.

16 *not the festal ceremony . . . Elspie's own church*: the differences between a Church of England baptism and a Scottish Presbyterian one, marked less by doctrine than by the more ornate ritual and the 'christening robes' in the former.

19 *Bridge of Allan*: a village four miles north of Stirling, close to the mineral spring of Airthrie, and the Well of Dunblane, both known for their healing properties.

20 *havers*: nonsense, foolishness

21 *mutch*: a head-dress, especially a close fitting day cap of white linen or muslin with a goffered, gathered or trimmed border.

gang your gate: be off.

23 *the last daughter of the ever-beautiful Rothesay line*: last, meaning most recent, but also carrying the suggestion that Olive will have no children of her own. The subsequent infant deaths of Olive's younger brothers reinforce the meaning of 'last' as 'final', a concern which anticipates late-nineteenth-century biologization of, and preoccupation with, degeneration.

27 *the debatable ground between Highlands and Lowlands*: the Highlands, generally regarded as the real Scotland, refers to the land that lies North West of the Great Fault that runs from Dumbarton to Stonehaven. Stirling is known as the gateway to the Highlands. The arbitrary line dividing the Highlands and Lowlands is really a myth said to have been drawn by Queen Victoria's tailor from Aberdeen to Glasgow.

33 *Oldchurch*: in part, a fictionalized version of Newcastle under Lyme where Craik grew up.

35 *'we saw men as trees walking'*: Mark 8: 24: 'I see men as trees, walking.'

36 *Those strange furnace-fires*: fires from the potteries in the district.

John of Gaunt had built a castle there: almost nothing remains of John of Gaunt's castle in Newcastle under Lyme, which was said to have been originally built in a pool.

37 *the Old Church, gloomy and Norman*: the Norman church is a fictional addition. Neither Newcastle under Lyme nor Stoke-on-Trent had a standing Norman church; indeed it is characteristic of the area that there are few medieval survivals.

Coronation day: the Coronation of George IV in 1820.

Mrs Hofland: (1770–1844), Barbara, née Wreaks, wrote children's tales with a didactic Christian message.

Sandford and Merton: the schoolboy protagonists of Thomas Day's (1748–89) children's tale of the same name, published in three parts between 1783–89. Selfish, rich Master Tommy Merton is reformed through the guidance of the Revd Barlow and by association with Harry Sandford the virtuous farmer's son.

41 *Dante's terrors in the haunted wood*: Dante Alighieri (1265–1321), *The Divine Comedy* (?1309–21) 'Inferno', i. 1–4: 'In the middle of the journey of our life, I came to myself within a dark wood, where the straight way was lost. Ah, how hard a thing it is to tell of that wood, savage and hard and dense, the thought of which renews my fear!' (Trans. John D. Sinclair, OUP, 1961).

48 *'Smith's Wealth of Nations'*: Adam Smith's treatise, *An Inquiry into the Nature and Causes of the Wealth of Nations* (1776). There is an intended irony in Angus Rothesay's armchair dip into the founding text of classical economic theory, which soberly championed free trade and the market economy, and Craik's description of him in the previous chapter as a 'rash and daring speculator, who was continually doubling and trebling his fortune by all the thousand ways of legal gambling in which men of capital and merchandise can indulge.' (p. 48) Craik may be contrasting the practice with the theory.

49 *'Comus'*: a masque by John Milton first performed at Ludlow Castle, 29 September 1634. 'Sabrina' is a song within the masque. The story of 'Sabrina' was a legend of the Severn River which Milton borrowed from Spenser's 'Faerie Queene'. There is heavy pathos in this vignette of the deformed child sketching a woman who was seen to represent Divine Grace. Both Angus and Olive are marked as serious and intellectual through their choice of reading in this passage, in contrast to Sybilla whose more limited interests and intelligence are indicated through her traditionally feminine occupation of embroidery.

53 *where lingers 'the curfew's solemn sound'*: the ringing of the curfew bell, a practice originating in medieval Europe, survived long after its original purpose was obsolete.

54 *'The Queen of the May', and 'The Miller's Daughter'*: both published in Alfred Lord Tennyson's *Poems* (1833). 'The Miller's Daughter' is about a happy marriage remembered in old age.

57 *My pensive Sara! thy soft cheek reclined, &c.*: Samuel Taylor Coleridge, 'The Eolian Harp', first published as 'Effusion Thirty-five' in *Poems on Various Subjects*, 1795.

positive love letters, full of 'dearest's and 'beloved's, and sealing-wax kisses: for an account of the shifting definitions of love between women in the nineteenth century, see Lillian Faderman, *Surpassing the Love of Men: Romantic Friendship and Love Between Women from the Renaissance to the Present* (New York: William Morrow, 1981).

58 *We also have been in Arcadia*: et in Arcadia Ego (and I too in Arcadia) was a tomb inscription of disputed meaning often depicted in classical painting.

64 *cadet*: younger brother.

65 *Too early seen unknown, and known too late*: Shakespeare, *Romeo and Juliet*, I. v. 138.

70 *'coming home' of a bride*: general reference to the bride entering her husband's home after the marriage ceremony.

74 *'puts an enemy into his mouth to steal away his brains'*: Shakespeare, *Othello*, II. iii. 281–3: 'O God that men should put an enemy in their mouths to steal away their brains

79 *that affair of poor Huskisson!*: William Huskisson MP (1770–1830) was the victim of the first railway accident in England, on the occasion of the opening of the Manchester and Liverpool railway. He lost his balance getting into a carriage, and fell in front of the advancing engine.

81 *'perpetual curate'*: a curate appointed and licensed to be in charge of the chapel or church of an ecclesiastical district, although he may be deputy to an incumbent clergyman who is non-resident or unable to fulfil his duties due to age or illness.

    Harbury: possibly Harbury, otherwise known as Harberbury, in Warwickshire; population 1,045 in 1831. However reference to the 'D——shire hills, might also place it near Milwich in Staffordshire.

82 *Where grew the turf, in many a mouldering heap*: misquotation from Thomas Gray (1716–71) 'Elegy written in a Country Churchyard' (1751): 'Beneath those rugged elms, that yew tree's shade. | Where heaves the turn in many a mould'ring heap, | Each in his narrow cell for ever laid, | The rude forefathers of the hamlet sleep.'

85 *'church-going bell'*: probably a quotation from William Cowper (1731–1800), 'Verses, Supposed to be written by Alexander Selkirk, during his solitary abode in the Island of Juan Fernandez', 29: 'But the sound of the church-going bell | These valleys and rocks never heard.'

88 *he sides with no party, high church or evangelical*: tolerance of the spectrum of theological opinion was characteristic of a Broad Church position, which believed in the comprehensiveness of the Protestant faith; however, the Broad Church commitment to religious experience, feeling, and intuition would be distinctly at odds with Harold's scientific leanings, and is perhaps more characteristic of Mrs Gwynne's holistic version of liberal belief.

89 *more that of a man of science and learning*: the strikingly eclectic mix of theology, science, and philosophy in Harold's study suggests not only his move away from belief and orthodoxy, but the wider struggle between science and religion at the opening of the decade which would see the publication of Darwin's *Origin of Species*. Robert Leighton (1611–84) and John Flavel (1630–91) were popular seventeenth-century Presbyterian divines. Harold's bias towards science and his exploration of other religions is suggested by the dust on the pious John Newton's *Sermons*, beside the 'well-thumbed' volume of Isaac Newton, the telescope balancing on the unread 'Religious Society's Tracts' (produced by the Religious Tract Society) and the equal space given to Mahomet, Swedenborg, Calvin, and the Talmud; Craik's own preference is clearly the volume 'on the farthest shelf . . . the great original of all creeds—the Book of Books'.

90 *the holy Hebrew mothers—of Rebecca or of Hannah*: Rebecca was the wife of Isaac, who transferred some of her love from her husband to her son (Genesis 24, 27). Hannah was the favourite of the two wives of Elkanah. She vowed if she gave birth to a son she would devote him to God (1 Samuel 1). With this biblical reference, Craik underlines Mrs Gwynne's wholehearted love of her son, in contrast to the imperfect parental affection that the Rothesays had for Olive.

95 *'Boast not thyself of tomorrow'*: Proverbs 27: 1.

96 *all the mystic horrors of Calvinistic predestination*: the doctrine that God's decision about who is to be saved or condemned is predetermined, and not purchased through virtue in this world. This doctrine declined in the nineteenth century; Craik's point is that, its crueller implications aside, it allowed Olive to believe that everything was in God's hands.

'shallow river' . . . 'sang madrigals': quotations from Christopher Marlowe (1564–93), 'The Passionate Shepherd to his Love': 'And we will sit upon the rocks | And see the shepherds feed their flocks | By shallow rivers to whose falls | The birds sing madrigals.'

106 *'one flesh'*: John Milton, *Paradise Lost* (1667), ix. 1957.

109 *'Child, thou art bone of my bone, and flesh of my flesh, as when I brought thee into the world!'*: Luke 2: 19. An echo of the final chapter of Charlotte Brontë's *Jane Eyre* (1847): 'ever more absolutely bone of his bone and flesh of his flesh.' In *Jane Eyre* the reference is used to convey both the sexuality and cross-gendered identification of married love. In *Olive* it is transposed into the generational bond between mother and daughter.

112 *the Rhodian sculptor*: an inaccurate allusion to the myth of Pygmalion, king of Cyprus, who in Ovid's *Metamorphoses* made a statue of an ideal woman and fell in love with it. Aphrodite took pity on him and brought it to life.

the great Florentine master: Michelangelo Buonarroti (1475–1564).

"Alcestis": daughter of Pelias and Anaxibia, whose heroic self-sacrifice to save her husband, Admetus, from death is the subject of Euripides' play, *Alcestis*. In myth, Alcestis is saved by Persephone who admires her devotion to her husband, but in the play, by Heracles, who wrestles death for Alcestis, and wins her back.

113 *'Cassandra raving'*: daughter of Priam, king of Troy, and Hecabe, Cassandra was known for her prophesies. Before she spoke these, Cassandra would go into an ecstatic trance, and her family believed her to be mad.

116 *'milk of human kindness'*: Shakespeare, *Macbeth* (1606), I. v. 17.

117 *the stories of Francis I and Titian, of Henry VII and Hans Holbein, of Vandyck and Charles I!*: Henry VII is an error or misprint for Henry VIII. Francis I, king of France (1494–1547), Henry VIII (1491–1547), and Charles I (1600–49) were all patrons of the arts. Titian (*c.*1487–1576) never met Francis I, but on commission from his friend, the art critic Pietro Aretino, painted two portraits of him, working from a portrait medal by Benvenuto Cellini. Holbein (1497/8–1543) was court painter to Henry VIII; Vandyck (1599–1641) was knighted at St James Palace in 1632 and painted a series of portraits of the royal family in 1633.

118 *Sir Joshua Reynolds, and Sir Thomas Lawrence*: Reynolds (1723–92), specialist in portraiture and historical painting and first president of the Royal Academy; Lawrence (1769–1830), after Reynolds the pre-eminent portrait painter, was much employed by British and Continental Royalty.

Angelica Kauffman, Properzia Rossi, and Elizabetta Sirani: Angelica Kauffman (1741–1807), Swiss neo-classical painter, who moved to England in 1766. She began as a popular portraitist, but branched out to produce pioneering pictures, illustrating Homer, Shakespeare, and English history. Properzia Rossi (*c*.1490–1530), of Bologna, a notable Renaissance woman sculptor, whose two reliefs for the exterior of S. Petronio in Bologna, Joseph and Potiphar's Wife, and Solomon and the Queen of Sheba are both resonant subjects for a woman artist. She is memorialized by the widely read woman poet Felicia Hemans in 'Properzia Rossi', *Records of Woman* (1828). Elisabetta Sirani (1638–65) of Bologna, one of the most prolific and renowned painters of her day. She trained other women, and painted several sacred and secular heroines. Her two sisters were also artists.

121 *'pestered with a popinjay'*: Shakespeare, *1 Henry IV* (1597) I. iii. 50.

mahl-stick: a long stick used to steady the hand holding the paintbrush.

122 *Le Brun's Passions*: Charles Le Brun (1619–90), French historical painter. A court painter to Louis XIV, he executed much of the decoration of the palace of Versailles. In 1698 he published a treatise *Méthode pour apprendre a dessiner les passions proposée dans un conférence sur l'expression générale et particulière*, in which he codified the visual expression of the emotions in painting.

"Laon's Vision of Cythna": the longest poem of Percy Bysshe Shelley (1792–1822), a symbolic epic of twelve cantos in Spenserian stanzas, was published in 1817 as 'Laon and Cythna' but instantly recalled and reissued in January 1818 as *The Revolt of Islam*. 'Upon the mountain's dizzy brink she stood' and the stanzas quoted by Vanbrugh below and on p. 124 are all from canto XI, stanzas I-III.

125 *Parrhasius*: Athenian painter of the late fifth and early fourth centuries BC. More interested in linear rather than modelled forms.

126 *Brutus*: Julius Caesar's friend, who played a leading part in his assassination, supposedly for the good of the country.

Corinne of the Capitol: the heroine of Mme De Staël's novel, *Corinne, or Italy* (1807), was a Roman poet and improvisatrice, and a great beauty. She follows her English aristocratic lover to England, but loses him and dies tragically. *Corinne* was a favourite of generations of English women readers and writers. Mention of Corinne at the opening of this chapter foreshadows the introduction of Celia Manners whose story follows some of the contours of *Corinne*.

129 *'Cleopatra'*: Cleopatra, queen of Egypt, (69–30 BC) was not a common subject for painting in the early nineteenth century, nor was it usual to paint her with dark skin; few Victorians continued to believe that the early Egyptians were black. However, both Craik and Charlotte Brontë, in *Villette* (1853), describe contemporary portraits of Cleopatra as depicting a very large, dark-skinned woman— *Villette's* 'Dr John' sneeringly calls her 'a mulatto'. Gustave Charlier (*Passages: Essais*, Brussels, 1947) has traced Brontë's model to a picture by De Biefve, titled

'Une Almée' (A Dancing Girl) which Brontë saw at the Salon de Bruxelles in 1842; in *Villette* she alters and exaggerates some of its details and promotes the dancing girl to queen. A lithograph copy of the painting confirms the Egyptian theme, but not the dark skin or the bulk which Brontë ascribes to her 'Cleopatra', characteristics which are, however, present in Craik's 'Cleopatra'. Vanbrugh's model, the 'quadroon' Celia Manners, was 'a very beautiful woman, though her beauty was on a grand scale' with 'large but perfect proportions . . . with the form of the ancient queens of the world' (pp. 129–30). It seems possible that Brontë borrowed elements from *Olive*'s 'Cleopatra' in fashioning her own much longer and more unsympathetic vignette. Lucy Snowe, Brontë's heroine, dismisses the picture she sees in the fictionalized Brussels, of 'this huge, dark-complexioned gipsy queen' with contempt and distaste as an 'enormous piece of claptrap' (*Villette*, ch. 19, 'The Cleopatra').

Ma mie: French: my pet, my darling.

130 *'Three Fates'*: in Greek mythology, Lachesis, Clotho, and Atropos. The three Fates become a relatively popular subject for painting in the seventeenth and eighteenth centuries.

Creole: originally a person of European descent, usually Spanish or French but born in the West Indies, but also someone of African descent born there, as against first generation immigrants or aborigines. In Louisiana, Creoles were French-speaking; in Mexico, whites of Spanish blood. Creole was often carelessly used to denote those of mixed blood, and in Mrs Manners's case, as in Bertha Mason's in Brontë's *Jane Eyre*, this ambiguity is played upon.

132 *Quadroon blood*: one who has a quarter of Negro blood, often someone descended from a white person and a mulatto. Craik keeps the reader in suspense about Celia's racial origin. Miss Meliora calls her initially the 'strange, foreign-looking woman' (p. 129). Celia describes her 'blood' in more guarded terms as 'half-Southern, half-European' (p. 131).

133 *a pauper funeral*: where the deceased and the family were so destitute that the parish must pay for burial. A pauper funeral was a great social stigma in Victorian times.

134 *pension*: boarding school.

135 *levée*: public reception.

137 *Danaë-stream . . . 'bits of shining gold'*: Zeus visited Danaë as a shower of gold; she bore a son, Perseus, from that union.

146 *Heraclitus*: philosopher, *fl.* 500 BC, who emphasized the processes of change.

Timon: Athenian misanthrope of the late fifth century BC; the protagonist of Shakespeare's *Timon of Athens* (1607).

147 *to judge of character by handwriting*: the pseudo-science of graphology, used as a method of reading character, which gained full currency later in the century.

Daimon: operator of more or less unexpected and intrusive events in human life; in Homer and other early authors, the gods and Olympians; later, Fate or other supernatural power.

149 *tournure*: French: appearance.

what was rather singular, her hair was quite fair: Craik uses this dissonance between dark eyes and fair hair as a clue to Christal's mixed racial origins, a visible symptom of what may be unnatural and unassimilable in such unions and their issue.

150 *'frayed with a sprite'*: frightened by a spirit. Shakespeare, *Troilus and Cressida*, III. ii. 32: 'she does so blush, and fetches her wind so short, as if she were frayed with a spirit.'

157 *the brothers Caracci—like Titian with his scholar and adopted son*: the Carracci were an Italian family of artists; Agostino (1557–1602) and Annibale (*c.*1560–1609) were brothers. The Italian painter Titian had a son who was also a painter, Orazio Vecellio.

161 *"Raising of Lazarus" ... "Sebastian del Piombo"*: Sebastiano del Piombo (*c.*1485–1547), Venetian painter who worked in Rome in contact with the Raphael circle. His gigantic *Raising of Lazarus* (1517–19) showed the influence of Michelangelo at its height.

165 *while the intellect comprehends, the heart ... is the only fountain of belief*: Olive's steadfast Christian faith is here set up against Harold's doubt and rationalism, in part the effect of his scientific interests.

166 *Ailie*: Scottish: pet form of Aileen.

168 *éclaircissements*: solutions, explanations.

170 *meek, beautiful Christianity of a St John ... a modern St Paul*: St John, Apostle of Christ, became associated with suffering. The contrast is with St Paul (d. *c.*65) as a powerful thinker whose Epistles were important to the development of Christian theology.

plain moral discourse—an essay such as Locke or Bacon might have written: Harold translates his preferred philosophical and scientific thinkers into everyday ethics for his 'labouring class' congregation. Olive is relieved that he doesn't bore them with obscure theological issues, and admires his intellectual powers but is repelled by his coldness.

171 *'grafted inwardly'*: Book of Common Prayer: 'Grant ... that the words ... may through thy grace, be so grafted inwardly in our hearts.'

172 *Dr Watts's moral hymns*: Isaac Watts (1674–1748), Calvinist turned Unitarian in his last years, writer of hymns, who infused emotion into hymn, and was instrumental in its revival.

177 *'celestial rosy red'*: Anna Seward (1742–1809), 'Knowledge, a Poem in the manner of Spencer', l. 15. The phrase is taken out of the context of the poem, but is relevant in other ways to the themes of *Olive*: 'While yet unknown the principles of art, | Impervious veils must shroud its radiance clear; | When sluggish ignorance surrounds the heart | No lustres can pervade the darkness drear, | But as all colours to the blind appear; | Where Pleasure's tint, celestial, rosy red, | Majestic purple, scarlet, hue of war, | The undulating mantle of the mead, | And Heaven's gay robe, a dark, unmingled mass is spread.'

178 *'in linked sweetness long drawn out'*: a common phrase in Romantic and Victorian verse, to be found in poems by Thomas Cooper, Aubrey Thomas de Vere, and Thomas Hood.

180 *crossed the Rubicon*: take a decisive, even final, step. The ancient name of a small stream on the east coast of northern Italy, the Rubicon was crossed by Caesar in 49 BC, thus starting the war with Pompey.

188 *in some penny tract*: Harold is parodying the vulgar piety of contemporary popular religious instruction for (and about) children.

190 *to be clemmed to death*: to starve to death.

193 *not the Infinite Unknown . . . but the God mercifully revealed*: Harold's philosophical search for the existence of God is set against Olive's practical, everyday faith.

199 *a mind whose very eagerness for truth had led it into scepticism*: Craik constructs Harold's atheism, not as wickedness, but as driven by his own thirst for knowledge and truth.

200 *the sixth Sunday after Epiphany*: Epiphany is 6 January. The epistle for this day, given in the Book of Common Prayer, is 1 John 3: 1.

203 *Tennyson's 'May Queen'*: 'The May Queen' (1832). A poem in three sections. Craik quotes verses 6 and 11 from part 2, 'New Year's Eve' and verses 14 and 15 of the 'Conclusion', added in 1842. The poem tells the story of 'Alice', an arrogant beauty whose pride leads her astray, and brings on her death. Dying she turns to her beloved mother and sister, and eventually to God. Quoted at length here, the poem draws out the theme of mother–daughter love in *Olive*. It also foreshadows Mrs Rothesay's own death in the next chapter, suggesting how much parent–child roles have been reversed in the novel, with the vain and erring mother, now blind and feeble, dependent on the ever virtuous daughter.

209 *like the martyr Stephen*: (d. *c*.35), deacon and protomartyr of the Christian Church, probably a Hellenistic Jew, who defended Christianity against those who resisted the spirit and killed Christ. When he was stoned for blasphemy he saw a vision of Christ on God's right hand (Acts of the Apostles 7: 56), hence Olive's allusion to the 'heavens' opening.

213 *those who stood and looked heavenward from the hill of Bethany*: widely visited by Christian pilgrims, Bethany is a biblical site on the eastern slopes of the Mount of Olives, just outside Jerusalem. The home of Mary, Martha, and their brother Lazarus; the miracle of Lazarus' resurrection took place there (John 11).

216 *Benedick and Beatrice*: the skirmishing would-be lovers in Shakespeare's *Much Ado About Nothing*.

219 *Io ti voglio . . . a me!*: popular Italian folk song: 'I truly love you | But you never think of me.'

220 *'commune with my own heart, and be still'*: Psalms 4: 4, in the 1662 Prayer Book version: 'Stand in awe, and sin not: commune with your own heart, and in your chamber, and be still.'

221 *the dull stupor of materialism*: the theory that matter alone exists, implying the non-existence of minds, spirits, and divine beings.

222 *'If you would know anything, begin by doubting everything'*: paraphrase of René Descartes (1596–1650), *Discourse on the Method of Rightly Conducting Reason and reaching the Truth in the Sciences* (1637). Descartes's 'method of doubt' is grounded in the laws of God, and offers a view of science as a unified system, with metaphysical foundations.

239 *Heidelberg*: the University of Heidelberg, founded in 1386, declined in the seventeenth and eighteenth centuries but in the nineteenth became a centre for excellence in the sciences and philosophy.

241 *Doric*: 'broad' or rustic English dialect either from the North of England or Scotland.

243 *dowie*: sad, melancholy, dreary.

aboon: above, figuratively, in heaven.

Braid Hills: On the south side of Edinburgh.

dree one's weird: put up with one's fate.

244 *Sir William Ross's ... our own Victoria*: Sir William Ross (1794–1860), miniature painter, descended from a Scottish family, painted Queen Victoria in 1837.

246 *Lothians*: district on the south side of the Firth of Forth; rich agricultural land.

247 *muckle dule*: much sorrow.

Duddingston Loch: bird sanctuary at the base of Arthur's Seat, a conspicuous hill in Queen's Park southeast Edinburgh.

249 *The smile of one ... earth-undone*: Elizabeth Barrett Browning (1806–61), *'Isobel's Child'*, ll. 517–18: 'Like pathos o'er her face, as one | God-satisfied and earth-undone; | The babe upon her arm was dead: | And the nurse could utter forth no cry,— | She was awed by the calm in the mother's eye.'

251 *St Margaret*: Queen Margaret of Scotland (1046–93), named patron saint of Scotland in 1673. One of the last members of the Anglo-Saxon royal family, known for her beauty, intelligence, and devout Christianity, she civilized the Scottish court, and helped reform the Church. Craik emphasizes her maternal role as monarch and mother.

Bruntsfield Links: in southwest central Edinburgh.

couchant lion of Arthur's Seat: the hill is outlined by a lion couchant and has a remarkable view.

255 *Naiad*: a river nymph.

Happy Valley of Prince Rasselas: Rasselas, Prince of Abyssinia, in Samuel Johnson's philosophical romance *Rasselas* (1759). He leaves a remote and protected 'Happy Valley' where no evil exists for the world outside, only to discover that virtue may not be rewarded with happiness.

Hermitage of Braid: mansion on Braid Burn, Edinburgh, with a public park.

256 *The braes ascend like lofty wa's*: Robert Burns (1759–96), 'The Birks of Aberfeldie': 'The braes ascend like lofty wa's, | The foaming stream, deep-roaring fa's | O'er hung with fragrant-spreading shaws, | The birks of Aberfeldie.'

burnie: small stream or brook.

261 *corse*: dead body.

264 *clavers*: idle talk, gossip.

272 *one of that miserable race, the children of planters and slaves*: see Celia's own more melodramatic description of her origins on p. 131.

275 *'How all the souls that were . . . the remedy'*: Shakespeare, *Measure for Measure*, II. ii, Isabella's plea to Angelo.

294 *pensionnaire*: French: boarder.

298 *Pont Neuilly*: second oldest bridge across the Seine in Paris.

319 *lost, and found*: Luke 15: 24. The reference is to the story of the Prodigal Son.

323 *personal imperfection . . . now so slight as to be forgotten in an hour*: in the first part of the novel 'cripple' and 'deformity' are used freely to refer to Olive and her physical defect; in the conclusion it is only spoken of euphemistically and represented as barely noticeable. For similar magical recoveries related to romantic resolutions, compare the return of Rochester's sight in *Jane Eyre* (1847) and of Esther Summerson's beauty, after smallpox, in Dickens's *Bleak House* (1853).

333 *HALF-CASTE*: someone of mixed race, a half-breed; in India, often someone descended from a European father and an Indian mother.

335 *I must write nothing but truth*: since the narrator is called Cassandra, it is implied that she will speak truth, but not be believed. See note to p. 113.

Indian merchant: an Englishman trading in Indian goods. India came under British supremacy in 1763.

'sweet as summer': Shakespeare, *Henry VIII*, IV. ii. 54.

340 *ayah*: in the East, in Africa, and in other parts of the British Empire, a maid-servant, nursemaid, or governess, especially one of Indian or Malay origin.

341 *Hindostanee*: the dialect of Hindi spoken in Delhi and used as a common language throughout India.

342 *on the tapis*: into the conversation.

343 *Hindoo race*: inhabitants of Hindustan or the general area around the Ganges where Hindi is the predominant language, and Hinduism the religion. Craik implies that it is a biologically separate racial type.

344 *foaming at the mouth with rage*: compare Christal's rage in *Olive*, pp. 285–7, attributed to her 'southern' (i.e. African) blood, or the bestial imagery associated with Bertha Mason's madness in *Jane Eyre*.

empressement: attentiveness

347 *Tranmere*: perhaps Tranmore, a town on the Mersey.

348 *Holywood*: perhaps Hollywood, a parish in the barony of Balrothery, 4 miles from Balbriggan, County Dublin.

349 *Lough*: from the Irish loch, meaning lake or long, narrow bay.

351 *bocage*: the wooded countryside characteristic of northern France, with small irregular-shaped fields and many hedges and copses.

355 *nabob*: someone of great wealth, especially one who returned to England from India with a large fortune acquired there.

367 *there was no denying that she was a very beautiful woman*: Zillah's beauty is always negatively acknowledged, *in spite* of being a 'half-caste'.

372 *my fair-haired Cassia*: nature and culture combine in rendering Zillah and Andrew Sutherland's daughter more and more English, suggesting that the family line is losing the tint and taint of colour. Contemporary racial thinking argues that no new mixed race will emerge from miscegenation, but that the stronger race will predominate.